THE UNTAMEABLE

GUILLERMO ARRIAGA

THE UNTAMEABLE

Translated from the Spanish by
Frank Wynne & Jessie Mendez Sayer

MACLEHOSE PRESS
QUERCUS · LONDON

First published in the Spanish language as *El salvaje*
by Editorial Alfuguara, Madrid, in 2016.
First published in Great Britain in 2021 by

MacLehose Press
An imprint of Quercus Editions Ltd
Carmelite House
50 Victoria Embankment
London EC4Y 0DZ

An Hachette UK company

A CIP catalogue record for this book is available from the British Library.

ISBN (HB) 978 0 85705 819 5
ISBN (TPB) 978 0 85705 820 1
ISBN (Ebook) 978 0 85705 821 8

10 9 8 7 6 5 4 3 2 1

Designed and typeset in Minion by Libanus Press, Marlborough
Printed and bound in Great Britain by Clays Ltd, Elcograf S.p.A.

For Mariana and Santiago, my mentors

Blood

I woke at seven after a long siesta. It was hot. The summer was far too hot for a city that was almost always cold. My room was on the ground floor. My father had cobbled it together next to the guest bathroom from sheets of chipboard. No windows, lit only by a bare bulb dangling from a length of wire. A camp bed, a small desk.

Everybody else slept upstairs. Through the paper-thin walls I could hear their daily comings and goings. Their voices, their footsteps, their silences.

I got up dripping with sweat. I opened the bedroom door and stepped into the living room. The whole family was home. My grandmother, sitting on the brown sofa, was watching a quiz show on television – an enormous contraption that took up half the room. My mother, in the kitchen, was making dinner. My father, at the dining table, was leafing through travel brochures for their trip to Europe. It would be the first time anyone in our family had taken a transatlantic flight. My parents were leaving for Madrid the following morning to spend two months travelling through various countries. Hunkered on the floor, my brother Carlos, six years my senior, was stroking our dog King, a brindle boxer with an ugly scar on the left side of his lip, the result of a stab wound from a drunkard he had playfully jumped up on as a pup. The Australian parakeets, Whisky and Vodka, hopped nervously from perch to perch, waiting for my grandmother to throw a blanket over their cage so they could sleep.

This is the image of my family that most often comes to me when I wake. It was the last time I saw them all together. Within four years, they would be dead. My brother, my parents, my grandmother, the parakeets, King.

The first death – that of my brother, Carlos – came twenty-one days after that evening. This was the moment when my family began to be buried by an avalanche of death. Death upon death upon death.

I had two brothers. Both died because of me. Even if I wasn't entirely to blame, I was certainly responsible.

I shared that dark cavern they call the womb. For eight months, an identical twin grew alongside me. We both listened to our mother's heartbeat, suckled on the same blood, floated in the same amniotic fluid, our hands, our feet, our heads touching. These days, it's possible for scans to show twins fighting for space in their mother's belly. Fierce, remorseless territorial struggles in which one twin eventually dominates.

My mother clearly did not think of the spasms inside her as part of a brutal battle. In her mind the twins (she was convinced they were girls) lived in harmony. But she was wrong. In one of these uterine brawls I cornered my brother against the wall of the womb until he became tangled in the umbilical cord. The trap was set: with every movement the cord tightened around his throat, strangling him.

The battle ended four weeks before the pregnancy reached full term. Unbeknownst to her, my mother became a coffin for one of her twins. For eight days she carried the corpse deep inside her. Death's fatal fluids leached into the amniotic sac, tainting the blood that fed me.

The brother I defeated in this foetal battle would have his revenge. He all but killed me. When the gynaecologist examined my mother – who had shown up at his surgery complaining of indigestion – he could hear only one heartbeat, and that was growing fainter by the second. The doctor put down his stethoscope and turned to her.

"We need to perform a caesarean."

"When, doctor?"

"Right now."

At the hospital, they took her straight into surgery and quickly made the caesarean incision. They removed my brother's bloated body before delivering me, gasping like a tadpole pulled out of the mud.

I needed several transfusions. Poisoned by my brother, it took time to filter my blood and eliminate the toxins. I spent eighteen days in hospital.

In the six years between my brother Carlos's birth and mine, my mother had miscarried three times. Two girls and a boy. None survived beyond five months. Desperate to conceive a child who could come through these fatal first five months and survive, they consulted one doctor after another and subjected themselves to various treatments. From herbal remedies to pelvic exercises, from hormone injections to alternating hot and cold showers, from charting basal temperature to trying different sexual positions. Something must have worked, because then I came along.

My parents came home devastated. My mother slipped into depression. She did not want to hold or feed me. My father rejected me. Present at the surgical procedure during which I was born, dragged into the room by the chaos and speed of events, he was sickened by the death stench that clung to the skin of his newborn child.

For years I slept in a room with two cots. My parents kept the neutral yellow outfit that had been intended for my brother or sister to wear once home from hospital. They laid it over what would have been his cot. Sometimes, at night, they would set spinning the mobile that hung from the ceiling, with its little giraffes and elephants. The mobile would whirl in the darkness, its lights like stars, to amuse an empty cot and a captivated mother.

My paternal grandmother came to my rescue. She moved in when she realised how much I repulsed my parents, and devoted herself to feeding me, changing me and dressing me until my mother finally stirred from her prolonged stupor and her maternal instinct resurfaced, just as I was about to turn one.

Some children grow up with imaginary friends; I grew up with an invisible brother. My parents were determined that I should know the details of the tragic stillbirth and, as a result, I felt responsible for his death. To compensate for my guilt, for years I played with my twin's ghost, shared my toys with him, told him about my fears, my dreams. In bed I always left space for him to lie next to me in bed. And I could feel his breath, his warmth. When I looked in the mirror, I knew that he would have had the same face as I did, the same eyes, the same hair, the same height, the same hands. The same hands? If a gypsy were to read his palm, would it say the same as mine?

My parents named my twin Juan José, and me Juan Guillermo. On the stone marking his tiny grave, his date of death was the same as his date of birth. This was a lie: Juan José had died a week earlier. He had never been born. He never evolved beyond the life aquatic, beyond a fish-like existence.

I grew up obsessed by my blood. Many times, my grandmother told me I had survived only thanks to the generous donations from anonymous people who had infused my bloodstream with their red blood cells, their platelets, their leucocytes, their D.N.A., their preoccupations, their pasts, their vitality, their nightmares. For years I lived with the knowledge that within me lived others whose blood was commingled with mine.

Once, as a teenager, I considered tracking down the list of donors to thank them for saving my life. An uncle told me a truth I would have preferred not to know: "Thank them for what? The fuckers were paid dearly for every drop of that blood." (Only years later was the blood market outlawed.) There had been no altruistic donors, only people desperate to sell their blood. Syringes extracting the crude oil of life from withered, wizened bodies. I was disappointed to discover I had been nourished by a gang of mercenaries.

I was nine years old when I saw my own blood flow for the first time. I was playing football with my friends out in the street when our ball landed in the garden of a divorced, alcoholic lawyer who, whenever he got out of his car, always flashed the semi-automatic strapped to his waist. The walls surrounding the house were covered in creepers and topped with broken glass to discourage trespassers. The lawyer was never home, so it was easy to climb the creepers, avoid the shards of glass and jump down to get the ball. Getting in was simple. On my way out, I shinned up the wall again, but, as I jumped down, I felt my trousers rip. I fell to the ground and scrabbled to my feet. My friends stared at me, rooted to the spot. Blood was streaming through the tear in my trousers. I looked down at my leg and saw a deep wound gushing blood. I prised open the wound with my fingers and saw something off-white. I assumed that a piece of glass or something had been buried inside me. It was my femur. The world began to turn black. Luckily a neighbour arrived just in time to see me slump to the ground, dizzy and pale, a crimson puddle spreading at my feet. She picked me up, bundled me into the back seat of her Ford 200 and drove me to a squalid medical clinic about ten minutes away on Avenida Ermita Ixtapalapa.

*

Another blood transfusion. More strangers' blood. A new army of mercenaries pumping through the chambers of my heart: whores, drunks, single mothers, horny teens in need of cash for an afternoon in a motel, unemployed office workers, builders desperate to put food on the table for their children, labourers trying to make ends meet, addicts desperate for their next fix. People on the margins coursing through my veins.

The surgeon who operated told me it was a bullfighter's wound, a deep stab wound perforating the femoral artery, like when a bull's horn penetrates the matador's thigh. The doctor had worked as a surgical assistant in the bullring on Plaza México. In the bleak operating theatre of the filthy clinic I was taken to, he knew exactly how to suture my torn femoral artery. It was his skill, and the prompt action of the woman who rescued me, that ensured I didn't bleed out that day.

I was kept in hospital for two weeks. The clinic had only four beds. My grandmother, my mother and my brother took turns sleeping in one of them. From time to time, chronic drunks or someone injured in a road accident would turn up. A man showed up with stab wounds to the chest one afternoon; he too was saved by the young doctor's surgical skill.

It was on the nights when Carlos stayed to watch over me that we really got to know each other. The six-and-a-half-year gap between us had made spending time together difficult. But as we whispered in the dead of night, as Carlos checked that my wound was draining properly, made sure the nurses did not forget my antibiotics, helped me to the toilet, used a sponge to dab the long gash across my leg, this vast age difference no longer mattered. He monitored my recovery with genuine devotion. It occurred to me that he too had shared our mother's dark womb, that we were of the same bloodstock. I moved from my invisible brother, Juan José, to Carlos, the visible one. I understood that my true twin had been born six and a half years before me, and we became inseparable.

For two months I was forbidden from carrying heavy objects, crouching, and walking – even with crutches. Since my parents could not afford to pay for a wheelchair, they ferried me to school in a wheelbarrow.

On the first day I was allowed out on my own, I set off to find the bloodstain I had left on the pavement. I gazed at the black butterfly traced by the many bloods that made up my own, this small reminder of the life that had almost drained away there on the street.

My mother found me, spellbound, staring at the smear. She brought out a bucket, soap and a scrubbing brush, and made me scour until every last trace was gone. The stain faded away, but on the glass that had slashed my leg from thigh to calf there remained a scab of dried blood that even countless downpours could not wash away.

One year later, I scaled the wall carrying a hammer, broke off the glass shard that had cut me and put it a box. I expect this is what bullfighters do with the bull's horn that impaled them.

I was left with a long scar on my leg that spanned about forty centimetres. I lost most of the feeling at the back of my knee, around my ankle and on my instep. Numbness is somehow less bearable than pain. With pain, at least it feels as though that part of the body is still alive. Numbness is a near certainty that something in you has died.

The woman who saved my life that afternoon was the mother of the guy who five years later would become my sworn enemy, my brother's killer. To some degree I was complicit in this murder, the one that unleashed the chain of deaths that would destroy my family.

There exists an African tribe that believes that human beings have two souls: one light, the other heavy. When we dream, it is the lighter soul that leaves our body and roams the borderlands of reality; when we faint, it is because the light soul has suddenly disappeared; when it leaves never to return, we become insane.

The light soul comes and goes. Not so the heavy soul. It leaves the body only at the moment of death. Since the heavy soul has never ventured into the outside world, it does not know the path that leads to the land of the dead, the place where it will live forever. And so, three years before we die, the light soul makes a voyage of discovery. Not knowing which way to go, it seeks out a baobab, the first tree of creation, and from its topmost branches scans the horizon to determine the route. It then visits menstruating women. For a few days, those who menstruate hover on the border between life and death. Amid the blood and pain, they lose the being that might have been but will not be. During the days of their period, women gain wisdom. They skirt the border between existence and non-existence and thus can direct the light soul towards death's chasm.

The light soul sets out on its journey. It traverses valleys, crosses deserts, climbs mountains. After many months, it reaches its destination and pauses at the edge of the misty precipice. Transfixed by awe it gazes into the abyss. The great mystery appears before its eyes. It returns to tell the heavy soul all that it has seen and steadily shepherds it towards death.

Moon

"You can't be fucking serious, Cinco," Pato said, when I told them about the African legend. I had memorised it for my World History class at school. The teacher had said that if we told a story he didn't already know or if he couldn't guess the ending, he would give us full marks. I found the book among the dozens that lay scattered across Carlos's bedroom floor, and sat down and read it. Carlos had stolen most of the books from libraries and bookshops. Never from a friend's house, he told me, because their parents had terrible taste and their shelves were lined with nothing but tacky bestsellers.

At the age of eighteen, my brother dropped out of school. My father was furious when he found out. For him, education was the key to a life he had not been able to attain. He had worked hard to give us the best he could. He and my mother worked double shifts to put us through private school. Carlos and I were the only kids on the block who didn't go to the local state schools: Centenario, Secundaria 74 and Preparatoria 6. Bitterly disappointed, my father threatened to cut him off without a cent if he refused to go back to school. Carlos didn't care. By the time he was nineteen, he was earning much more money than our father.

"I'm telling you, man, that story is seriously cheesy," Jaibo said.

Jaibo, Pato, Agüitas and I liked to spend our nights hanging out and talking on the roof terrace where Mrs Carbajal would hang her washing. At thirteen, Jaibo was already getting through two packs of Delicados a day. He looked like an idiot when he smoked because he didn't know how to inhale. Agüitas (as in "Drippy" – so named for his

15

soppy nature and his tendency to tear up) would bring beers and share them with Pato. I didn't smoke or drink. I had decided to do sober what others only dared to do when drunk.

Most of the kids in the neighbourhood found refuge on the rooftops. No-one bothered us up there. Ever since the '68 riots, the Tlatelolco student massacre and the government's paranoia about Commies, we would see *julias* roaming through the neighbourhood every day – those armoured police vans fitted with two wooden benches into which they would toss prisoners. The policemen would stand on the rear running-board, keeping watch, clinging to the bars that ran along the sides. If you were spotted hanging around on the street, they would leap down and arrest you on charges of vagrancy and sedition (although they had no idea what the word meant) and drag you off to the cells in handcuffs so tight they cut off your circulation. While you were banged up, they would beat you, kick you and administer electric shocks to your testicles until someone arrived with enough money to bribe them to release you. If you were lucky, they would only chase you down the street and hit you a couple of times with their batons – "maybe that'll teach you to cut your hair short, not wear it like a little lady". They would let you go after threatening: "If we catch you on the street with long hair again we'll chop your balls off, you little fuck, that way you really will be a girl."

The only ones who remained unscathed by these police assaults were the so-called Good Boys who belonged to the Young Catholics Movement. The Good Boys had close-cropped hair, long-sleeved shirts buttoned to the top and a crucifix around their necks. They never used swear words, they went to Mass every day, helped old ladies carry their shopping home from the supermarket and delivered food to orphanages. They were every mother's, every mother-in-law's dream: dutiful sons, diligent students, fine young men. Clean, decent, tidy, hard-working and honest.

It was a muggy night. The tiled roof radiated heat, and there was

16

not a breath of air to keep us cool. Jaibo was chain-smoking. He would light each cigarette with the butt of his last.

"How is it fake?" I asked Jaibo.

"It just is."

"What the fuck do you know, *cabrón*?" I laughed. "It wasn't long ago you thought women didn't get their period until they lost their virginity."

Jaibo was from Tampico. His father had been a sailor who died after a drunken fall from the prow of his merchant ship. His widow, just as much of a drunk, set off for Mexico City with her five children in tow and turned up on her brother's doorstep. The poor guy had just got married, and had no choice but to support the six of them on his paltry salary as a surveyor.

"I know a lot about women," he declared.

"Oh yeah? Tell me, what's a hymen?" I challenged him.

Jaibo kept quiet. Of course he didn't know what a hymen was. Pato took a gulp of his beer and turned to look at me.

"You're saying a woman on her period knows where to find death?" he said scornfully.

"When a woman gets her period, she loses what could have been a baby," I said.

"So when I jerk off, do I suddenly gain in wisdom too?" Agüitas interrupted. "I mean a fuckload of sperms come out that could have been babies."

The three of them were still laughing when we heard a voice behind us.

"Don't be retards."

We turned round. It was Carlos. Who knew how long he had been listening. He walked towards us and my friends stopped laughing. Carlos was respected on the block. He stood in front of Agüitas.

"Women only have between four and six hundred ova. And when they have their period, the egg comes out in bloody pieces and they

17

feel terrible pain. Their hormones change their mood, their bodies swell up. Your sperm comes out even when you're asleep, and when you jerk off all you feel is pleasure. Women know shit we haven't got a clue about."

My friends said nothing. They knew better than to argue with him: Carlos read voraciously, devouring books of philosophy, history, biology and literature. He had left school because he was bored, sick of reading what he considered to be second-rate texts. Carlos had a vast knowledge and spoke like no-one else in the neighbourhood. He used language with precision and he knew the meanings of high-flown and arcane words. Even if my friends had known as much as he did, they would never have dared challenge him. They were scared of him. Everyone was scared of him.

Carlos pointed to the box of Delicados poking out from Jaibo's shirt pocket.

"Can I bum a cigarette?" he asked.

Jaibo sat up and handed him the packet. Carlos took out a cigarette and Jaibo passed him a lighter. Carlos lit the cigarette, studied the box as if it were some strange object, crumpled it up until it fell to pieces and tossed it into the street below. Jaibo looked at him indignantly.

"What did you do that for?"

"So you won't die of cancer," Carlos answered quickly as he stubbed his cigarette out on the wire fence. I smiled, and so did Carlos when he caught my eye. He turned to gaze up at the moon.

"In forty-six days, Apollo XI will land on the Sea of Tranquillity," he said, pointing up to some unidentified location.

The four of us stared at the moon. The impossible journey dreamt up by humankind was about to be fulfilled.

"Gravity on the moon is one sixth of what we experience on Earth," he said, without turning away.

"What?" Agüitas said.

Carlos smiled.

"I'll explain: if your fat lump of a mother weighs a hundred kilos here, up there she'd only weigh sixteen."

Carlos was aware of Agüitas's sentimental temperament and knew that such a joke might make him well up, but Agüitas was too busy trying to figure out the maths to cry. In fact, Carlos was being pretty generous; Agüitas's mother weighed a hundred and forty kilos at least.

"To return to Earth, the space capsule needs to use the gravitational force of the moon. If Apollo XI doesn't succeed in entering lunar orbit, it will just keep drifting into space and there will be no way to bring it back."

My brother had already explained this hypothesis to me. I had been horrified. Three men in a spaceship missing their one opportunity to return to Earth and floating off into the infinite. Three men peering through the hatchway, watching as their planet got further and further away. What would they discover on their journey into nothingness? How would they feel up there, adrift in boundless space? Would they die slowly or did they have cyanide pills they could take to end it sooner? How long would the oxygen last before they slipped into the irrevocable stupor of death? Would they fight over food in order to stay alive, if only for a few days? Far from feeling excited about the moon landing, I felt apprehensive. Triplets in a metal uterus, floating in the artificial liquid of zero gravity, fighting for survival. The metaphor was all too familiar and painful.

Carlos kicked the sole of my plimsoll.

"Let's go have dinner."

He held out a hand to help me up.

"See you tomorrow," I said to my friends.

Carlos and I left, dodging wires, cables, clothes lines and water tanks as we went. We came to the edge of the Ávalos' rooftop. To get home, we had to leap across the metre-and-a-half gap separating the houses of the Ávalos and the Prietos. Generally we made the jump without even thinking. It was part of our daily routine. But the risk was real. Four months earlier, a skinny, pretty, blue-eyed seventeen year old called Chelo and her boyfriend "Canicas" had been having sex on the roof of the Martínez house, between the clothes lines – we knew this because of the dried-out condoms we found there the next day – and, heading home in the dark, she had jumped first, but misjudged the distance and tumbled into the void. She landed on her knees on the roof of Mr Prieto's Coronet. Her life was saved because the shock absorbers took some of the impact. Both of her legs were shattered, but her spine and her skull remained intact. Even then, she was lucky that Colmillo, the Prietos' huge wolf-dog (a cross between an Alaskan Malamute and a Canadian wolf, they'd named him Colmillo, "Fang", in honour of Jack London's White Fang) was chained up. Otherwise he would have ripped her limb from limb. Alerted by the crash and Colmillo's barking, Fernando Prieto came out into the backyard. He found Chelo on the ground with splintered bones sticking through her thighs.

It would take Chelo a year and a half of painful rehabilitation to recover from the fractures. After countless operations, her legs were left zigzagged with scars. In the afternoons, she would emerge and hobble down the street on her crutches, barely able to keep her balance, then go back home to do her intensive physical therapy routine. The physiotherapist's instructions and Chelo's whimpers of pain could be heard through the hedge. Despite the pain, she always had a smile. Happy, cheerful, always in a good mood. Years later, Chelo made love to me so sweetly that she saved me from going mad.

Carlos jumped first, then stopped to wait for me. I made it across with ease. I found leaping the void exhilarating. Sometimes I would deliberately make it more difficult for myself, just to experience that sense of danger: taking off with little momentum, eyes closed, hands behind my back. Carlos once caught me doing this. Furious, he started shouting at me, but I paid no heed and jumped again. Carlos caught up with me and grabbed me by the shoulders. He lifted me into the air (I was eleven at the time) and stood on the edge of the roof, threatening to throw me off.

"You like danger, motherfucker?"

I looked down. Six metres. Far from being scared, I found it funny and burst out laughing.

"What's the matter with you?" Carlos said, taken aback.

He had done his best to teach me a lesson, but there I was in his arms, so close to slipping over the edge, and I couldn't stop laughing.

Carlos turned and threw me down onto the Ávalos' rooftop.

"If you ever do that again," he said, "I'll beat the shit out of you."

I smiled and nonchalantly jumped back and forth across the gap before sprinting off across the rooftops.

We walked back towards our flat roof. As we got closer we could hear the cries of the chinchillas in the darkness. Carlos bred hundreds, he had set up a farm that spanned our roof and those of the Prietos and Martínez. Dozens of small cages stacked on top of each other, a block of flats for furry rodents. On hot days the reek of urine would invade the nearby houses. To avoid complaints, Carlos paid Gumaro, a young, slightly simple black guy, to scrub the area with bleach and disinfectant three times a day.

Carlos fished a torch from his pocket and shone it around. The bright beam set some of the chinchillas racing around in circles, bumping into the bars of their hutches. Others rose up on their hind legs to see what was going on. Carlos always carried the torch with him so he could check for feral cats, the chief enemy of his thriving business. The cats would stick their paws through the bars, grab a chinchilla's head, clamp the muzzle to suffocate it, then rip it to shreds.

My brother kept a rusty .22 hidden in a kennel. If he saw a cat nearby, he would grab the rifle, aim for the head and shoot. The rifle's sight was not very accurate and he often hit them in the belly. It wasn't unusual to come across half-dead cats cowering under cars, whimpering in pain, trailing their guts behind them.

The whole chinchilla business started when one of our uncles gave Carlos a doe for his sixteenth birthday. A couple of weeks later, Carlos bought a buck. They mated, and in less than two months they produced a litter of ten kits. Carlos had read in a magazine that chinchilla was valuable. He went into the city and tracked down a Jewish furrier who bought chinchilla pelts wholesale. Carlos asked our parents if he could build hutches on the flat roof, then bought twenty more chinchillas. A year and half later, he was selling close to four hundred pelts a month. He staggered the breeding, so that the females gave birth according to the level of demand.

Although Carlos made a killing with his chinchillas, it wasn't his most profitable business.

Wetness

My life was divided between two different worlds. One was the barrio, where I felt I belonged, a landscape of streets and rooftops. The other was a private school my parents struggled to pay for. A school where my classmates went on holiday to New York and Europe. A school where the teachers were addressed as "Miss", made us speak English during break time, and boasted of their iron discipline. A school that felt like a prison to me, and where they refused us scholarships. "A good education costs money, señora," the headmistress told my mother when she asked if she could pay in instalments. The humiliation of having to go to her cap in hand must have been excruciating. "Just give us until the end of the year to pay, that's when my husband gets his bonus," my mother said. "I'm sorry," said the proprietor-principal-profiteer-prig, "I have teachers to pay."

That night, over dinner, I watched my father brooding when my mother told him the headmistress planned to expel us if the school fees were a month late.

"I'll find the money somewhere," he said quietly.

"Where?" asked my mother.

My father said nothing for a moment. He wiped his forehead.

"I can ask the company for a loan."

"Really? And how will we pay them back?"

My father turned his head to ease the crick in his neck.

"We should move them to a state school," my mother said.

My father whipped round and stared at her as if she had insulted him.

"Their education is the only thing we can give them," he snapped.

They fell silent again. My father took a deep breath and reached for my mother's hand.

"We'll find a way, don't worry."

Since I seemed to be concentrating very hard on my plate, they assumed I wasn't listening to what they were saying. I was nine years old, and my leg was still healing. My parents had spent all their savings on my surgery and my medical bills. Mistrustful of government, they refused to send us to the public clinics. No social security, nothing that reeked of state bureaucracy, be it schools, hospitals or jobs. And now they could find no way to pay for our school fees.

Carlos helped me back to my room. My father had built it on the ground floor so I didn't have to climb stairs while I was recuperating (I never moved back upstairs). He sat on the end of my bed, looking thoughtful.

"You think they'll make us change schools?" I asked.

Carlos began to mutter, irritated.

"I'll beat that old bitch's brains out. She's got no right to treat my mother that way."

His jaw tensed and he stood up and pulled back the sheets.

"Get into bed."

I got in, and Carlos covered me with the blanket.

"Night," he said, and gently patted my forehead before he left.

My parents managed to pay the school on time. They paid off this and other debts by selling my father's beloved Mercury. He was proud to have bought it with years of backbreaking work. Now the Mercury was gone, and with it his pride. With no car, my father had no choice but to take public transport. I remember him waking up at 4.30 a.m. so he could shower, have breakfast and head for the Popo-Sur 73 bus stop on the far side of Río Churubusco. I remember him coming home at ten o'clock, shattered after a double shift.

There was nobody now to take us to school. At 6 a.m. Carlos

and I would walk to the bus station in San Andrés Tetepilco, crossing stretches of waste ground with uneven football pitches that were crudely sketched in chalk, which flooded when it rained and quickly turned to swamp. We would hop from stone to stone so as not to get mud on our uniforms, but would inevitably slip and get splashed. At the school entrance there was a porter whose job was to check that uniforms were spotless, boys' hair was short, girls' skirts were long, and details of personal hygiene were satisfactory (nails trimmed, ears washed). I was sent home several times for having mud stains on my trousers. Since there was no-one to collect me, Carlos was forced to take me home. It wasn't a complete disaster. We would go to the Natural Science Museum to see dissected animals or sneak into the stables next to the racetrack to watch them groom and train the thoroughbreds.

Four months after my parents managed to pay the school fees, which amounted to seventy-five per cent of my father's salary, they had an urgent phone call from the headmistress insisting that they both come to the school immediately.

My parents showed up, nervous and apprehensive. The school had never summoned them so urgently. On the long bus journey to the school, they imagined the worst: an accident, a punch-up, a robbery.

Giving no thought to the fact that both my parents had had to leave work early, that bitch of a headmistress made them wait for two hours. Two hours that could have spared them rushing to get there and missing out on a day's pay.

Walking into the headmistress's office and seeing me sitting there, my parents looked at me in alarm. They'd assumed they had been called because of Carlos, who was being increasingly rebellious at that time; they'd never imagined it might be about me.

The headmistress gestured for them to sit and they sat down on the leather chairs. She nodded towards me.

"We have decided to expel Juan Guillermo. The decision is final and cannot be appealed."

My parents glanced at each other, then my mother looked at me.

"What did he do?" she asked, almost in a whisper.

The principal's lips curled into an expression of disgust.

"This school will not tolerate pupils like your son."

"But what did he do?" insisted my mother.

The director, who liked to be called "Miss" Ramírez, turned to me and raised her chin.

"He can tell you himself."

My parents waited for me to speak but I didn't dare open my mouth. The headmistress came and stood next to me, oozing menace.

"Go on, tell your parents what you did."

I looked at her out of the corner of my eye. My mother turned to face me.

"Tell us what you did."

Still I said nothing.

"Come on, tell them," Miss Ramírez said in English, knowing my parents would not understand. "Don't be a coward."

I kept my mouth shut. Far from intimidating me, the headmistress's attitude made me more and more angry.

"You can't expel him in the middle of the school year," my mother argued.

"I can expel who I want when I want, señora. And if this young man refuses to tell you what he did, I suppose I shall have to tell you myself . . ."

Just as she was about to launch into her sermon, I interrupted.

"I kissed a girl, Mamá."

My father, who had kept quiet so far, challenged the headmistress.

"You're going to expel my son because he kissed a girl?"

"Of course not, señor, I am going to expel him because we found him half-naked, sexually assaulting a half-naked girl. Your son committed an act of gross indecency that will not be tolerated at this school."

"My son is a child."

"No, señor, your son is a pervert."

Class. Recess. Silence. Glances. Breaths. Heartbeats. Hands. Skirt. Knees. Thighs. Skin. Caresses. Glances. Knickers. Breaths. Heartbeats. Strokes. Crotch. Silence. Knickers. Finger. Crotch. Wetness. Moans. Gasps. Trousers. Zip. Hands. Breaths. Glances. Tremors. Buttons. Hands. Prick. Hard-on. Touches. Pussy. Strokes. Fear. Excitement. Glances. Friction. Prick. Pussy. Inside. Wetness. Sweat. Skin. Heartbeats. Breaths. Bell. Glances. Separation. Silence. Goodbye. Classroom. Door. Silence. Heartbeats. Voices. Classmates. Teacher. Classroom. Glances. Secret.

Carlos turned off the flashlight, grabbed the rifle from the kennel and loaded the chamber.

"Let's see if a cat turns up," he said, leaning back against the wall.

We kept quiet. The chinchillas squealed in the darkness. In the sky hung the moon that was about to be conquered. Is it possible to conquer the unconquerable? The stain of a spaceship sullying the Sea of Tranquillity. Mankind and his obsession with trampling over everything.

In the distance, you could hear cars driving along Río Churubusco. What had once been a river of crystalline water, home to fish, frogs, axolotls and turtles, which my father and his friends used to swim in on hot afternoons, was now a motorway. Río Piedad, Río Mixcoac, Río de los Remedios. Rivers filled in and turned into streets. Rivers levelled by tonnes of bitumen. My city's riverine massacre.

"What was the name of that girl you fucked in primary school?" asked Carlos.

"I never fucked anyone."

Carlos smiled, silhouetted against the darkness. The barrel of the gun gleamed in the light of the moon, about to be trampled.

"That girl, come on, you know who I mean."

27

"Fuensanta."

"That's it, her. I forgot. Fuensanta. Shit! You couldn't have chosen a girl with another name? *Fue santa* – she was a saint. Don't hold back, come on."

Carlos switched on the torch and checked the cages. The chinchillas' eyes glowed red. He turned it off again.

"Did you suck your finger after you put it in her pussy?"

Of course I sucked it, smelled it, sucked it again. Savoured the taste of her on my tongue. Savoured it. Fuensanta. *Fuente santa.* Sacred fountain, fountain of secrets, fountain of wetness.

"I already told you, no," I snapped.

Carlos smiled. He'd asked me the question a hundred times, and a hundred times I'd said no. I'd lied to him a hundred times, and each of those hundred times he expected me to finally tell him the truth.

"I bet your finger still stinks of Fuensanta."

Yes, my finger still smelled of Fuensanta, it would never stop smelling of her.

"My finger doesn't smell of anything," I told him.

"Remember how you made Mamá cry because you were so horny for that little saint?"

We listened to the chinchillas stir agitatedly. Carlos flicked on the torch. Between the cages, a pair of yellow eyes glittered. Carlos shouldered the rifle, then shifted the torch so that he could look through the sight. Seeing the light, the cat jumped onto the parapet and was about to escape when the shot rang out. The cat hissed and tumbled into the street. We ran and peered over the edge. The cat lay for a moment with its paws in the air, then shakily stood up and crawled under a car.

"That cat won't be eating chinchilla again," Carlos said.

Some psychologists argue that when one twin loses the other – to death, separation, or for any other reason – they forever feel a deep-rooted sense of abandonment. The solitary twin lives with the scar of this amputation, a permanent wound. The solitary twin seeks out companionship to compensate for this emotional void. In my case, this did not mean friends or playmates, but women. Ever since I was a boy of four or five, all I had thought about was women, I felt a desperate need for their presence, their gaze, their nakedness. Stroking a woman's skin relieved that itch of absence. At first, it was simply the brush of an arm, a glimpse of thigh. And then Fuensanta came along.

Standing in the middle of her office, the headmistress glared at me reproachfully. My mother hung her head in shame.

My father straightened in his chair.

"Who saw it?"

"Half the school, Mr Valdés. His teacher, a number of pupils. Juan Guillermo had his trousers around his knees, he had pulled down the girl's underwear and was touching her."

My mother quietly began to sob. My rage grew and grew. My father, confused, tried to fit the pieces together.

"And the girl?"

"What about the girl?"

"Did she consent or did Juan Guillermo force her?"

"It's obvious that he forced her, Mr Valdés."

I stood up and confronted the headmistress.

"That's not true. She wanted to."

"Shut up and sit down," the headmistress barked.

"It's not true," I said again, indignant. "I didn't force her."

"Sit down, now."

I remained standing. My father faced the headmistress.

"What does the girl say?"

"What could she possibly say? For goodness' sake . . ."

"What did she say? Did he force her or did she consent?"

"Of course she didn't consent."

"I want to hear it from her own lips," my father said angrily.

"Her dignity has been sufficiently tarnished without putting her through any more," the headmistress said with an air of melodrama worthy of a *telenovela*.

My father began to get worked up.

"I assume she will also be expelled."

"You assume incorrectly. There is only one person to blame here and that is Juan Guillermo. He is permanently expelled. We do not want him in this school."

"She wanted to as well," I insisted.

"Don't lie!" the headmistress said.

Fury.

"I'm not lying. We both wanted to."

The headmistress turned and went to sit at her desk.

"I will not say another word on the matter. The boy is expelled, as is Juan Carlos. I will not have them here. Now, if you would be so kind . . . I have work to do."

My father leaned towards her, now livid.

"What has this got to do with Juan Carlos?"

"I disapprove of the way you have raised your children, Mr Valdés, and now I am asking you to leave."

"What?" my father said, incredulous.

As if we were not even there, she picked up a sheaf of papers and began to read. Her attitude incensed me. I stalked over to the desk, snatched the papers from her hands and tossed them to the ground.

"What are you doing, you stupid bitch?"

I swept everything off her desk. The headmistress scrabbled to her feet and retreated to the window.

"Your son is a demon!" she shouted at my parents. "Get out, or I will call the police!"

My mother took me by the hand and led me towards the door. My father, still furious, was about to say something but my mother stopped him, tugging on his arm.

"Don't humiliate yourself," she said, then turned to me.

"Go to the classroom and get your things," she ordered.

"She wanted it too, honest," I said.

"Go get your things," my mother repeated.

I went to get my belongings. They were in the middle of a lesson. The teacher allowed me in on condition that I only take a minute. I grabbed my pens, my exercise books and my schoolbooks and stuffed them into my rucksack. My classmates stared, whispering among themselves. I made ready to leave. I exchanged a look with Fuensanta and walked out. It was the last time I ever saw her.

Rain

"What did you say?" We were playing football on the street when I heard a voice behind me. I couldn't afford to be distracted, Chato "the Flea" Tena was about to score against us.

"What did you say?" the voice said again. I kicked the ball and turned. Antonio, one of the Good Boys and a member of the neighbourhood's venerated Young Catholics Movement, was peering at me, his eyes narrowed.

"What did I say about what?"

Antonio was three years older than Carlos, his parents owned a stationery shop on the next street. He was tall and fat, with short, curly hair, and, like the rest of the Good Boys, he wore a long-sleeved shirt, a white vest underneath and a crucifix around his neck.

"What did you say to your friend?"

"I don't remember."

"You'd better remember."

I started laughing. I had no idea what the fat guy wanted.

"Well, I can't remember."

He took a step towards me.

"What did you shout at him?"

He pointed to Papita, who, like everyone else, had stopped playing to listen.

"Oh, to Papita? I do remember! I said, 'Don't be a fucking idiot, just kick the ball.'"

Antonio's eyes bored into me.

"That's the last time you or any of your friends say bad words on the street."

I didn't understand what he meant.

"What?"

"I don't want to hear you swearing again. The women on this street deserve respect."

I looked around; there were no women.

I laughed. "What women?"

"I'm warning you," he said, and turned to the others. "I am warning all of you."

He turned on his heel and left. He had not gone ten metres when I shouted at the top of my lungs:

"Go fuck your mother, you fucking motherfuckers!"

Everyone laughed. Enraged, Antonio stormed back and threw a punch that floored me. Chato Tena jumped on him, but Antonio – nine years older, and taller and stronger than the rest of us – grasped Chato by the shoulders and, using a judo move, picked him up and slammed him onto the ground (Good Boys learned judo and karate). I got to my feet and punched him in the ear, but he managed to grab my shirt and in one movement he smashed my face into the tarmac.

The others did not dare intervene. Antonio jabbed a finger at me.

"I'm warning you: I don't want to hear another swear word come out of your mouth."

He turned to my friends.

"Like it or not, we'll teach you to be respectful. If not me, one of us will come and sort you out. So be careful."

He stared defiantly at the group, then turned and left without a backward glance. Blood again, a lot of blood, gushing from my nose.

The afternoon that I first made love with Chelo, it rained constantly. It had been raining solidly since the morning of the previous day, when we buried my parents, just as it had been raining when we buried Carlos. My parents died three years after him. Their car skidded on the motorway and went over the edge of a cliff. Try as they might, my mother and father never came to terms with Carlos's death. Ghost parents walking through the house, weighed down with the guilt that they had been on holiday in Europe when their son was murdered on a nearby rooftop. Ghost parents who would suddenly burst into tears in the middle of dinner. Ghost parents I would stumble upon at dawn, staring at the empty chair where my brother used to sit at dinner. Ghost parents.

They worked harder than ever. My father managed to buy another car, but this time he felt no pride or satisfaction. He bought it while in a place of terrible grief, of tears and brutal depression. So brutal that my father did not even notice the death of my grandmother, who was also depressed, inconsolable because she had not been able to prevent the death of her much-loved grandson. My grandmother died sitting in front of the T.V., watching one of her quiz shows. Frail and anorexic, she closed her eyes and passed away without a sound. Sitting at the dining room table reading the nutritional information on a cereal box for the hundredth time, my father did not realise that the life that had given him life had perished. My father was so ghostly that he switched off the light in the dining room, said goodnight to my already dead grandmother, kissed her on the forehead and went up to his room. I was the one who knocked on the door at dawn to tell him Grandmother had left the T.V. on, that she wasn't moving. My father was orphaned by his mother, orphaned by his son.

My parents bought the car as a warhead to bring about their own deaths. A missile on four wheels they used to end it all. My father, considered by his friends to be an excellent driver and a master on the motorway, lost control on an easy bend. He and my mother fell forty metres into an abyss. They had been on their way to my grandmother's village to deposit her ashes in a family vault in the middle of the Tamaulipas jungle.

The ten of us who braved the rain at their funeral were drenched and muddy by the end ("unkempt", the porter at my school would have said). My friends stood by my side; Agüitas could not stop crying.

The storm did not let up during the burial. Rain filling the graves where my parents were to be buried. Rain beating down as the gravediggers shovelled dirt onto the coffins. Rain and more rain. Experts decided that the wet road had caused the car to skid. But I knew otherwise. My father had probably looked at my mother, she had looked back at him, and they'd both realised that they had neither the will nor the strength to resist anymore. My father probably took his hands off the steering wheel, allowing the car to veer out of control, towards the cliff. That is what I believe.

No-one spoke as we drove back from the funeral. Everyone was shivering and lost in thought. My uncles dropped me at the house and my friends went home, feeling sad. I was alone. I went into the house where the two parakeets and the brindle boxer were waiting. This vast house inhabited by my invisible brothers, parents and grandmother.

The following afternoon, I went out and walked in circles in the rain. I couldn't bear to be in the house any longer. Seeing me from her window, Chelo hobbled out into the storm on crutches and hugged me. No condolences, no "I'm so sorry for your loss", she simply hugged me.

We made love that afternoon on the cot bed in the lair of a wounded animal that was my room. Chelo asked me to switch off the light. She was worried that I would be repulsed by the ugly scars from the ten operations needed to piece her bones together.

I didn't switch off the light. I dropped my trousers and showed her the long scar running down my leg. She knew nothing of the incident with the broken glass. I kissed her as I unbuttoned her skirt, my scar to hers, my wound against hers. After she had fallen six metres, her parents treated her with scorn. "That's what you get for acting like a little slut up on that roof," her father had sneered. Her boyfriend Canicas had pledged undying love, but he never called to ask how she was doing. Carlos and Fernando Prieto were the only ones to go to the hospital. Carlos visited every morning without fail.

We made love as grief welled up in my throat. I didn't use a condom. She didn't care if she got pregnant. She wrapped herself around my body and there I stayed, seeking refuge from so much death.

At the school gates, the boys would sit on long benches waiting to be collected. The girls would sit on a bench opposite. My parents had given permission for Juan Carlos to take me home. But although I didn't need to wait for anyone, I liked to sit for a while with my class-mates because Fuensanta was on the opposite bench.

Anyone misbehaving was made to sit on the opposite bench. For a boy to have to sit with the girls was considered humiliating. This was not how I saw it. I did whatever it took to be punished so I could sit next to Fuensanta, something that became a regular event.

Fuensanta was blonde, with light brown eyes and freckles. There is a Mexican saying that a woman with no freckles is like a taco with no salt. Well, Fuensanta had plenty of salt. She had freckles on her turned-up nose, at the top of her breasts, on her arms. Long hair, slim, serious, gentle. Her mother was an American from Kansas, her father a biochemist from Coahuila who ended up in politics. I fancied her from the moment I first saw her. More than any girl I had fancied in my nine years on the planet.

Our relationship – if you can call it that – began with a piece of chewing gum. I asked her for a piece. She said she only had the one she was chewing. "If I gave it to you, would you put it in your mouth?" she asked. I nodded. She spat it out and gave it to me. I put it in my mouth, excited to have her saliva on my tongue. After a while, I worked up the courage to say, "If I give it back, would you put it in your mouth too?" For ten seconds that felt like an eternity, she said nothing. Then she nodded, took the gum and delicately popped it into her mouth.

Swapping chewing gum became a daily routine at break time, it was our way of kissing.

During break time we were only allowed to speak English. "Pass me the ball." "Do you want a piece of my sandwich?" "It's awesome." Iowa in the heart of Mexico. To ensure we were speaking English (and to control and monitor us) the school set up a perverse spy network they called "Safety Patrols". Those with the best grades were the elite members of this mini-Gestapo. They policed the halls during recess. An accusation from a safety monitor (patrol) – even if made up or unjust – earned a pupil five demerits. Two fives meant a suspension for three days, three warranted a two-week suspension, and four guaranteed immediate expulsion. The safety monitors had an ample arsenal with which to threaten and blackmail. Mindless fascism in the hands of nine or ten year olds.

Being an outstanding pupil, Fuensanta was a safety monitor. At ten years and five months, she was the eldest in the class; I was the youngest at nine and two months. She had been kept back because of the year she had spent in Buenos Aires, where her father had worked at the embassy. She was different from the rest of us. She knew more than anyone else and she spoke both English and French fluently.

Over time, our chewing-gum game became more sophisticated as we passed the gum not only from hand to hand but from mouth to mouth. For a few seconds I would feel her warm lips, her tongue placing the chewing gum on mine.

At break time we would meet up in one of the deserted corners of the playground. We had only a few minutes, since she had to get back to her work as a spy. We talked very little, and never about ourselves. I was afraid that if I told her about my world of rooftops and parents who had sold their car to pay the fees she would dump me. I later found out that she was ashamed of her family: her father was a corrupt politician and a vicious drunk who would beat her beautiful but emotionally stunted mother. We kept our private lives to ourselves, limiting our conversation to gossiping about our classmates, talking about teachers we liked and disliked, and complaining about homework.

One day I saw Carlos playing a game he called *arañitas* with a girl. The game was simple: you placed a closed fist on a girl's knee and opened it slowly, your fingers gently stroking her as if they were *arañitas* – little spiders. When Carlos did it, the girl blushed and her skin broke out in goose bumps. I decided it would be a great idea to play it with Fuensanta.

During break time, in our distant corner, I suggested we play *arañitas*.

"What's that?" she asked.

"Give me your knee."

She brought her left leg closer. I placed my right hand gently on her knee and slowly spread my fingers. She shuddered and instantly got goose bumps. I looked up and saw that her legs were parted. I could just make out the white of her underwear. She saw me looking, but did not close her legs.

"Do you want to keep playing?" I asked.

She thought for a second and nodded. I placed my fist on the inside of her right thigh and slowly moved my fingers over her skin. She wriggled and her skin prickled again.

"Did you like it?"

Fuensanta breathed deeply. Her neck began to flush red. We looked at each other for a moment, both of us panting for breath. My heart was hammering in my chest.

"One more time?" I said, my voice quavering.

She nodded. "Uh huh."

I inched the "little spiders" to the very top of her thigh, splaying my fingers until I touched her knickers. Fuensanta flinched and looked around, breathing heavily, then she relaxed as I continued to stroke her crotch. She gazed at me, but did not try to push my hand away.

Suddenly, she closed her legs and moved away. She jerked her chin: two of her friends were coming up behind me. I stood up, tugging at my trousers to hide my erection.

"See you," I said.

She forced a smile and tried to say something but choked up. I could not say a word. I walked past her friends and melted into a crowd of boys playing basketball.

It is said that Viking men would not marry virgins. They found the idea that a woman had not been desired by other men suspicious. To them, virginity was not a virtue but a flaw. While in Middle Eastern countries a woman may be stoned for bringing dishonour on her family by losing her virginity, among Vikings a woman was thought to bring dishonour on herself if she did not arouse men's passions. Surely a virgin hid insufferable vices: surliness, bad breath, gracelessness, idiocy. For some perverse reason her hymen was still intact. Who could love a woman who had been scorned by others?

Smoke

Carlos, Sean and Diego ran down the street. They vaulted the gate of the Montes' house and raced up the spiral staircase to the roof. Eight police officers brandishing guns were hot on their heels. Four followed them over the gate, while the others continued down the street. Pato and I saw them in the distance as we fed the chinchillas. Carlos and his friends zigzagged deftly between the lines of laundry, moving ahead of their pursuers.

Unfamiliar with the labyrinthine rooftops, the cops almost plunged into the gap between the Rodríguez and Padilla houses. They hesitated for a minute, unsure whether to jump or find another route – long enough for Carlos and the others to disappear across the rooftops.

Furious at losing sight of them, the officers decided to conduct a house-to-house search. They did not ask permission, they simply forced their way in. The neighbours did not protest. In neighbourhoods like ours, police did not need arrest warrants or judicial sanctions: their power and authority were enough. Laws and human rights might prevail in those parts of the city where my classmates lived, but not here. The police spent hours searching for my brother and his friends, ransacking wardrobes, looking under beds, forcing locks, scouring rooms, threatening neighbours. But they found nothing. Not a trace. My brother and his friends had vanished in a puff of smoke.

Sometimes Chelo would stay the night with me. She invented university field trips to reassure her parents (she was studying medicine, which required her to do social work in rural areas). Chelo would

41

pack her bags, pile them into a classmate's car and say goodbye to her parents, only to stop a little further down the street and sneak into my house under the knowing gaze of her accomplice.

Chelo was loving and she looked after me. I barely had the strength to eat, to bathe or make the bed. She would bring me food, shower with me, help me cook, wash up and clean. She helped prevent me being crushed by my sudden status as an orphan.

We had an unspoken agreement: our relationship was temporary, there was no future for us. Chelo told me that one night she would simply stop coming around and made me promise I wouldn't go looking for her. I was faced with being an orphan, with losing Chelo. This time, at least, the loss would not be sudden and brutal. There would be no invisible Chelo, just a woman in a parallel existence, who might reappear later in my life.

I had no reason to fall in love, but I fell in love. With her blue eyes, her slender body, her downy skin. With her unceasing touch, her gentleness, her joy. I kissed her legs, the barbed wire of her scars. I kissed her lips, her eyes, her neck, her back, her buttocks, her clitoris, her anus. I drank her sweat, her vaginal fluids and sometimes her tears. She was not sentimental like Agüitas, quite the opposite, her joy was almost unshakable. But when we made love, she would cry and hold me tight and kiss me over and over.

We slept in each other's arms. There was barely room in my narrow camp bed. Sometimes I would be woken by the heat of her body, by the humid sweat of our closeness. I would lift the sheet and shake it to cool us down and then wrap myself around her again.

Chelo was promiscuous. She had slept with a lot of guys in the neighbourhood. She liked to think of herself as a hippie, a free spirit unconstrained by bourgeois hang-ups. If it pained me to imagine her so much as kissing someone else, picturing her naked, being fucked by other men, drove me mad with grief. And so, when we made love, I turned my face away and stared at the floor, at a corner of the room, at nothing. I did not look into her eyes so I did not have to picture other men screwing her or her screwing them.

I didn't want her to know about my jealousy. Why? She wasn't mine. No matter how much I loved her, she would never be mine. She cared for me, she loved me, kissed me gently. She had numerous orgasms, often multiple ones. She told me I was the only man who could do this, and that none of her previous lovers could. Opening up the Pandora's box of jealousy would only make her leave sooner. The death of my family was enough for me to deal with. Why poison a relationship that already had an expiry date?

Chelo promised not to get involved with anyone else while she was with me. But I couldn't believe her. Her promiscuousness seemed more like addiction than freedom. Every day, she kissed me goodbye and I lived in permanent fear that this kiss might be the last. Chelo never knew how fearful I felt every time she left.

I had not been raised Catholic, or with any religion. The words god, sin and penitence were not mentioned at home or at school. My father was an atheist and my mother had increasingly drifted from Catholicism. They raised me to believe that poverty and social injustice, not sexuality, were the true sins. Why then did I feel so hurt by the idea that the woman I loved had a past?

I thought about the Vikings. Carlos had told me the legend. Even with her obvious scars, Chelo was a woman desired by men. I should have been happy that she made love to me, took care of me, slept beside me. Flatteringly, she said that I was the best lover on her extensive list. What comfort was that? Touched, manhandled, screwed, slavered over, licked, sullied by others. My mind was a clash of civilisations: the host of Christ and his sexless morality versus the heathen hordes of Thor and Odin joyously, lovingly accepting a woman possessed by others.

My parents had been dead barely a month and I was weathering the storm of jealousy.

*

"Which way did they go?"

Pato pointed across the rooftops.

"That way."

"Which way exactly?"

Pato gulped nervously. The captain clearly did not have much patience.

"That direction."

"Which direction?"

Pato swallowed hard.

"It was pretty dark, I couldn't really see."

The captain turned to me.

"O.K. You. Which way did they go?"

I hadn't seen which way my brother and his friends had gone. I lost sight of them when they passed the water tanks on the Padillas' roof.

"Dunno."

"You don't know?"

"No, I don't know."

The captain summoned another officer.

"Juárez, over here!"

A fat guy came over, his upper lip glistening with beads of sweat.

"Yes, sir?"

"Grab this little faggot's balls."

The fat cop reached for my testicles, but I took a couple of steps back. The fat cop smiled.

"You'll enjoy it, girlie. Come on, come closer."

Pato was ashen, he didn't dare move. The fat cop suddenly turned and grabbed him by the neck. Pato tried to wriggle free.

"Let go of me."

The fat cop squeezed his fingers tighter, paralysing him. The *comandante* pushed his face towards Pato's.

"Where are they hiding?"

"I don't know, I swear."

44

The fat cop squeezed harder. Pato writhed in pain.

"Leave him alone!" I shouted.

Another policeman stood behind me.

"Shut up, bitch."

The *comandante* persisted.

"Where the fuck did they go?"

"On my mother's life, I swear, I don't know."

The *comandante* sneered.

"Fucking runt."

He turned to the fat cop.

"Let him go."

After one last squeeze, the fat cop let him go and he instantly took off across the rooftops. The *comandante* stepped towards me.

"When they eventually poke their snouts out of their hole, you tell those little rats that Captain Adrián Zurita is going to fuck them over."

With a wave he rounded up his men and they headed back across the Martínez family's roof.

Owing to her excellent grades Fuensanta always had a senior position among the safety monitors. The deputy headmistress, Mademoiselle Duvalier, a wrinkled redheaded French woman, was the one who awarded the positions of power within the spy squadrons. Fuensanta had a ninety-eight per cent average and impeccable manners, so was promoted by Miss Duvalier to second floor monitor, responsible for keeping third and fourth years under surveillance, ensuring they did not go into the classrooms during break, and patrolling the school bathrooms for any girls smoking or using make-up. Fuensanta only had to accuse someone to get them suspended for two weeks. She swore she had never snitched on anyone and never would.

To prevent students entering classrooms during break, the safety monitors hung a yellow chain across the doorways. Any student who was found crossing it was given five demerits for misconduct. Even after the bell rang, students could only go into their classrooms when the chain had been removed by a Category A safety monitor, of whom there were only three. Fuensanta, of course, was one.

One day at break time she asked me to join her on patrol. We toured the second floor and she explained her duties and responsibilities. When we came to our own classroom – Year 4, Class B – we crept inside and she shut the door. By now, we had played *arañitas* several times and knew it would be more exciting to play in private. It had been her idea to exploit her authority to use the classroom.

Fuensanta had been babbling non-stop, but as soon as the door was closed, we both fell silent. She sat down on the bench, I sat down next to her. We glanced at one another.

"Give me your knee," I said.

She twisted her knee closer. She looked up towards me and for a moment we stared into each other's eyes. I placed my closed fist on her knee and slowly splayed my fingers. She quivered more intensely than usual. A second spider inched further up her thigh, a third one found her crotch. Her breath was faster now. Again and again I let my fingers wander across her mound. She was panting now. We glanced at one another again. I pushed her legs a little wider and this time the little spider invaded her knickers. She tried to push my hand away, but I tensed my arm. I went on stroking her. I felt wetness, as though she were sweating. I didn't want to look her in the eyes in case she told me to stop. I stroked the lips of her vagina. They were wet, really wet. Surreptitiously, I slipped a finger into her slit. She squirmed but did not try to push my hand away. I slipped my finger a little further in. I looked up, but she had closed her eyes. She moaned softly and licked her lips. With my left hand, I grabbed the waistband of her knickers and began to pull. She squeezed her legs shut, but I gently prised them open and she shyly allowed me to carry on. I pulled her knickers down to her ankles. For the first time, I was looking at a woman's vagina. A thin slit that, when touched, opened like an anemone. I went on stroking, slowly fingering her. Fuensanta threw her head back. I unzipped my trousers and took out my dick. She didn't notice, she was still whimpering softly. I tugged my trousers down to my knees. Keeping my finger inside her, I edged closer. When she sensed this, her eyes flew open and, seeing me with my trousers down, she pushed me away.

"What are you doing?"

My heart was beating fit to burst. My throat was dry. She edged away and started to pull up her knickers. I stopped her.

"Just let me touch my pee-pee to your pee-pee," I said.

"No," she said, her eyes wide. "Are you crazy? We could have a baby."

Her chest and her throat were red and blotchy, her breathing ragged. She kept tugging at her knickers. With my left hand, I stopped her.

"Just one little touch, that's all."

"No, I don't want to."

"Just one."

"No," she said, flatly.

I knew the only way to convince her was to keep stroking her with my right hand. I went on tracing the lips of her vagina with my finger. She began to moan again and closed her eyes.

Her knickers were halfway up her thighs and it was difficult to manoeuvre. I tried to push them down, but though she kept her eyes closed, she would not let me. I moved closer and climbed on top of her. She opened her eyes.

"I said no!"

This time she did not push me away. My dick was only inches from her pubis.

"Let's just touch pee-pees and that's it."

She didn't say another word and she stopped resisting. I kept moving my body closer to hers until my penis was touching her. I rubbed it against her. The contact with her wetness excited me even more. She hugged me and pulled me towards her. She began to shudder. Our

47

breathing became faster and more ragged. Suddenly she jumped back and away from me.

"That's enough. Get away."

"Just a little bit more," I begged.

"No," she said, decisively. She got to her feet, pulled up her underwear and smoothed her skirt. "Zip up your pants," she ordered.

I did as I was told. Soon afterwards the bell rang.

"Can anyone come into the classroom?"

"No, not until I move the yellow chain."

"So no-one could have seen us?"

"No."

She glanced at the clock on the classroom wall.

"I need to go move the cord," she said.

"Should I come with you?"

"No, go to the bathroom at the end of the hall and wait until everyone else is in class."

This strategy seemed carefully planned, though it can only have occurred to her then. Carlos was right: women knew things men had no idea about.

Fuensanta got up to go, and as she opened the door she turned back to me.

"If I end up having a baby because of you, I'll kill you."

John Hunter was an eighteenth-century Scottish surgeon. Years spent dissecting cadavers had made him an expert anatomist. A connoisseur of the body's labyrinthine passageways, he began to suggest innovative operations.

His scientific curiosity pushed him to extremes. He convinced friends and family to donate their bodies after death so he could perform autopsies. He had no qualms about cutting open his nearest and dearest. Whenever he heard of a death resulting from deformity or some strange illness, he would steal the body or bribe the grave-diggers to get his hands on it. This is how he came into possession of the corpse of Charles Byrne, the "Irish Giant". More than seven and a half feet tall, Byrne had drunk himself to death with the money he earned as a circus freak.

As he lay dying, Byrne asked that he be buried at sea so that he would not suffer the slash of the scientist's scalpel. John Hunter bribed the undertakers and removed the body under cover of darkness. On the very afternoon that Byrne's relatives sent a coffin weighted with stones to the bottom of the sea, John Hunter was dissecting the giant's body.

John Hunter assembled a vast collection of medical and scientific curiosities: skeletons, embryos, deformed creatures, tumours, brains, fossils, albinos. Much of the Hunterian Museum survived the Nazi bombing raids on London, and Charles Byrne's towering skeleton can still be seen by visitors.

Hunter died on October 16, 1793 during a public argument with the board of St George's Hospital, where he worked. So obsessed was he by science that his final wish was for his body to be dissected to determine the cause of death. His students found advanced arteriosclerosis of the brain and heart.

To this day, John Hunter is considered one of the most influential scientists in the history of medicine and the study of the human body.

Formaldehyde

In a glass cabinet in the biology lab of my new secondary school, there were several glass jars containing human foetuses suspended in formaldehyde. I don't know how the school managed to get hold of so many embryos at so many different stages of development. They must have had some kind of shady deal with an obstetrics clinic. They also had embryos of dogs, rabbits, cats, even one of a snake. I would stare at them transfixed, fascinated by their shape, their texture, their size.

It was while studying Darwin that I had a revelation: as it develops, an embryo goes through every stage of the evolution of its species. It begins when two cells fuse to become one, which immediately divides into two, then four, then eight, creating new cells, and later tiny creatures that begin to evolve. Closely observed, embryos move from being larvae, to fish, to reptiles, to birds. There is even a point at which a human foetus has a tail. Using a microscope, our biology teacher, a pathologist by profession, showed us the red blood cells of a human foetus ten days after conception, and then the red blood cells of a reptile. They were almost identical in structure: a red ring with a dark centre.

I had a nagging doubt: if a human being evolves after nine months' gestation, what of those of us who are born premature? I came to the conclusion that, in such cases, evolution is interrupted. Those born prematurely hover somewhere between the human and the animal. And while socialisation and education can compensate for this lack of development within the womb, those of us who are premature forever bear the mark of the animal.

I grew up with the notion that I would forever be half-savage, half-animal. When we were young, my brother wanted to be "Carlos the Courageous"; I wanted to be "Juan Guillermo the Untameable".

"Faggot!" shouted Carlos. Antonio, who was carrying his mother's shopping from the supermarket, turned.

"Have some respect for my mother."

Carlos smiled sarcastically.

"Ma'am, did you know that your son is a little fag?"

Antonio set the bags down on the ground and marched over to my brother.

"Shut your mouth or I'll shut it for you!"

"I'll break your jaw, you little queer."

I had said nothing to my brother about the incident with Antonio, but Jaibo had. "Antonio, you know, the fat kid from the Young Catholics Movement, he punched your brother and broke his nose." Obviously, Carlos had no intention of letting Antonio go unpunished.

There, in the middle of the street, Antonio adopted a karate pose.

"Don't be so fucking ridiculous, lardass," Carlos taunted. "Fight like a man, none of this faggot Japanese bullshit."

Antonio's mother tugged at his arm, pleading with him not to fight.

"The boy's a thug. Come on."

Carlos turned his anger on the woman.

"A thug? Your son here is a coward who only picks fights with little kids. He punched my brother, who's only fourteen. Congratulations on raising a faggot coward."

"Please, Antonio," the mother urged her son again, "come on. You don't want to get involved with these people."

Antonio pushed her away.

"Let me put this troglodyte in his place."

Good Boys never used bad language. Instead, they spoke in a stilted, absurd language, with insults that sounded as though they came from Spanish Golden Age novels.

"Egad, you scurvy varlet," my brother scoffed, "come belabour me."

If anyone knew Spanish Golden Age literature, it was my brother. Antonio held his karate pose, his lip trembling.

"Not scared, are you, little piggy?"

Carlos's smile vanished, his jaw tightened, he glanced at me, then turned and lunged at Antonio. Two full metres before he reached the young man, he hurled himself with all his might and punched him square in the nose. The fat fucker toppled backwards and, when he tried to struggle to his feet, Carlos leaped on him and pummelled his head. Blood streamed down Antonio's face.

"Leave him alone, you brute," his mother shouted.

Nothing was going to stop my brother. The fat guy lashed out with his foot, but my brother dodged the kick. Carlos did not kick back – the code of the barrio dictated that men did not kick; such tactics were for cowards and girls. No kicking, no scratching, no hair-pulling, no hitting a man when he was on the ground or from behind.

"Big man, aren't you, picking on little kids? Come on then."

The fat fucker snorted to get rid of the blood streaming from his nose, then lashed out with another kick, which Carlos deftly eluded.

"I could fuck you up with my hands behind my back."

Antonio bounded towards Carlos, trying for a judo hold, grabbing at his shirt, but Carlos slipped away. The fat guy staggered back, and as he lurched forwards Carlos followed with a right hook to his mouth. Dazed and in pain, Antonio stumbled. Carlos jabbed again, a straight punch to the head, and finished with a left uppercut. Antonio flew backwards and cowered against a wall, trying to shield himself. Carlos could smell Antonio's fear, and in a blind fury he started to pummel him again.

Terrified, Antonio's mother rang the nearest doorbell. One of our neighbours appeared, a retired pilot called Rodolfo Cervantes, and she begged him to intervene. Captain Cervantes got between Antonio and my brother.

"Stop it," he declared.

Carlos stopped, but stood a few paces away, ready to attack if necessary. The captain reached out an arm to ward him off.

"Carlos, that's enough. Get out of here."

Carlos stared down at the fat boy, now bleeding heavily from his forehead, nose and mouth.

"Touch my brother again and I'll kill you."

"You're a brute," shouted the mother.

Carlos shot her a scornful look.

"I told you, Carlos, get out of here."

The pilot had known us since we were little kids. He was a good man, someone we admired and respected.

"Yes, sir, captain, sir," Carlos said, turning on his heel. "Let's go."

We headed home. After half a block I looked back at them. Antonio was still cringing against the wall, his mother dabbing the blood from his face with a handkerchief. We did not know it then, but the countdown to my brother's death had begun.

I spent weeks planning the robbery. I decided I could get to the jar by using a scalpel to cut away the back panel of the display cabinet between classes. Like a prisoner slowly and painstakingly digging an escape tunnel in his cell to escape. The biology lab was guarded by Manuel, who was zealous about his responsibilities. He only ever left his post to answer the phone or go to the toilet. During these rare absences, I had to act quickly and precisely. One neat groove a day, no rash hacking that might reveal my intentions.

Of all the foetuses in the cabinet, I chose the one at eight months' gestation. I would hide the heavy jar containing the almost-child – stillborn at the same moment I was born – under my bed. I would shake it at night, hold it up to the light of my bedside lamp to bring some life to its world of formaldehyde, like shaking a snow globe to bring a Christmas scene to life. I wanted to see Juan José and myself as I watched it float in formalin. To see my being reflected in that pale, crumpled thing.

After twenty-five days of cutting, the hole in the wooden panel was almost finished. All I had to do was think of a way to get the foetus out of the school. The jar was sixty centimetres high and thirty-five centimetres in diameter and weighed at least five kilos – difficult for a twelve year old to conceal. My plan was to wrap it in a lab coat, stick it in my locker – I had already emptied out my books and school supplies – and take it home one Saturday, after my technical classes in shorthand and typing. (Being a technical school, we were awarded both a secondary-school diploma and a "technical certificate". "Bilingual secretary", in my case. Aware that I struggled with maths, my mother had signed me up for the secretarial rather than the accountancy course. It was an astute decision: with six boys in the class and thirty girls, I learned to type without ever looking at the keys.) Few students bothered to come to class on Saturdays, supervision was more relaxed, and if I was the last person to leave I could easily sneak out the jar.

The day arrived. Through the classroom window, I spotted Manuel heading towards the school office. He would be back within ten minutes, just enough time to finish cutting away the panel and remove the jar. I asked for permission to go to the toilet and, wearing my lab coat, walked to the biology lab, took out the scalpel, and turned the cabinet around to find a thick sheet of plywood screwed over the panel I had carefully cut. Two more centimetres and I could have removed the panel and taken the specimen jar. Just two. Manuel had obviously worked out what I was up to. I accepted defeat. Weeks of painstaking work, all for nothing, thanks to Manuel's astuteness. I turned the glass cabinet back and gazed forlornly at the eight-month-old unborn child I had come so close to possessing.

Days went by. Neither Manuel nor the biology teacher commented on the mysterious hole in the glass cabinet. School continued as always. One morning, I was sitting alone, having lunch in the cafeteria – a few rickety tables under a plastic roof that had been a handball court. The bell for class had not yet rung, but most of the pupils were already heading back in. Busy with the plantain my mother had packed in my lunchbox, I didn't notice Manuel approaching my table.

"Mind if I sit with you?" he asked, holding a coffee.

"Yeah, sure, of course," I said, surprised. It was unusual for teachers or technicians to spend time with students in the cafeteria.

Manuel sat, took a sip of coffee and then stared at the crumbling back wall.

"When I first started working here, this place was still a house. This is where the owner and his kids played pelota."

I looked at the wall. At some point it had probably been painted green, with neat yellow borders. Now it was cracked and covered in graffiti.

He took another sip of coffee. Something about Manuel seemed off.

"How long have you worked here?" I asked.

"Twenty-two years," he replied.

We both stared at the wall. Tufts of grass grew in the cracks. Manuel turned back to me.

"You still want the foetus?"

I didn't know what to say. I swallowed hard.

"What foetus?"

"The one you tried to steal."

"I didn't try to . . ."

"I can get you one for a couple hundred pesos," he said, and looked me in the eye. Two hundred pesos was a fortune back then, especially for a twelve year old.

"Why would I want one?"

"I don't know, you tell me. You think I didn't notice that you were trying to cut open the cabinet to steal it?"

Either I denied everything, or I could actually get my hands on one.

"Where would you get one from?"

"A cousin of mine works in a neonatal department."

"I don't have two hundred pesos," I told him.

"What's the most you think you can come up with?"

"About fifteen."

"Fifteen? No way, *hombre*. Find a way to get more, then let me know."

I managed to borrow twenty-four pesos and arranged to meet Manuel. I showed him the money. He considered me gravely.

"It's really not much, but I think I can find you something."

I handed it over. Three days later, he came back with a mayonnaise jar with a tiny human embryo floating inside. I felt disappointed.

"I wanted one as big as the one in the lab."

"Hold up, Juan Guillermo! You can't find those anywhere anymore. Parents are sentimental, they want to bury them. Besides, the law is pretty strict, you can't get foetuses that size anymore."

I took the jar and peered at the little larva bobbing in formaldehyde.

"But I really want a big one."

"No can do," Manuel snapped. "You want this one or not?"

"O.K. Give it here."

I took it. When I got home my mother noticed the jar and I quickly tried to hide it.

"What's that?"

"Nothing."

"What do you mean 'nothing'? What are you hiding? Is it booze?"

I showed her the jar.

"It's a dog foetus," I lied.

"Why on earth would you want such a thing? Throw it away."

"I can't, Mamá, it's for a school project."

"Well, do your project and then throw it away."

"Yes, Mamá."

I hid it in the chest of drawers.

Where did my brother hide when the police were chasing him? They never did find him. He would climb up onto the rooftops and disappear without trace. They searched and they interrogated the neighbours, but came up with nothing. Not Carlos, not Sean, not Diego. For a long time, I didn't know, until one night he told me his secret. And confiding in me cost him his life.

Music

"Come Together." "Octopus's Garden." "Yesterday." my classmates sang in unison, conducted by the teacher, Kurt Holland, a short guy with delusions of grandeur. "Again, kids, let's try 'Obladi, Oblada' . . ." Holland would say, and all the kids would enthusiastically wail the words to some Beatles song. They loved the Beatles. They knew every last detail about John, Paul, George and Ringo. They pasted photographs on their exercise books, on their rucksacks, even on their desks. Traumatised by rumours that Paul McCartney was dead, no-one talked about anything else for days. Delirious with rapture, they looked forward to music lessons – three times a week – when they could perform their infantile karaoke. For homework, we had to listen to Beatles singles, and learn the English lyrics by heart, so we could "learn through fun".

I loathed the Beatles. Coming out of school, boarding an over-crowded bus where I was crushed to death for an hour, taking a tram for another half an hour, getting off, picking my way across muddy football fields and coming home to my barrio – to a world of chinchilla pelts, sanctimonious Catholic judo freaks, girls who plummeted from six-metre roofs and wolf-dogs and dog fights – simply did not square with listening to "She Loves You."

Nothing in the Beatles mirrored anything in my life, absolutely nothing, not the sickly-sweet lyrics, not the catchy tunes, not their clichéd movies. I found our music lessons a grotesque experience. Dozens of boys and girls singing some hackneyed song like it was the anthem of their generation. At a school where god was never even mentioned, criticising the Beatles was blasphemy.

One of the many demerits I copped was for an anti-Beatles outburst. In English, the teacher asked me to name my favourite Beatles song. I told her that I didn't have one. "So you love all of them, like me?" she said with an asinine smile. "No, Miss Carmelita, I don't like any of their songs." Still smiling, she scanned the rest of the class, as if to say "Have you ever heard anything so outrageous?", then turned back to me. "And why not, pray tell?" I could have given a hundred different answers – "They're just not my thing" or "I don't really like the tunes" – but instead I blurted out something Carlos had once said about the Beatles: "It's music for prissy, pretentious pansies."

At our school, serious misdemeanours warranted serious punishments: you were forced to stay behind after school for three hours. They used the English word "detention", which basically meant being locked in a classroom and forced to write out "I have to behave well in school. I have to behave well in school . . ." two thousand times. But it didn't end there. The punishment continued the following day in P.E., when, instead of playing football or basketball, you were forced to march up and down for an hour and a half. Left, Right, Left, Right, Halt, Quick March. The P.E. teacher, a fuckwit called Toral, must have seriously hated me, because even after I had served my sentence he forced me to march with no pauses, no water, no toilet breaks during every lesson (I did so much marching in primary school, they should have awarded me a Military Service medal).

My classmates were deeply offended at being called "prissy, pretentious pansies". Some of them didn't even know what "pansy" meant, but Miss Carmelita's fury convinced them it was more insulting than it really was.

Hiding in the empty classroom, Fuensanta and I played *arañitas* nine more times. We both enjoyed the game. We would emerge from the classroom breathless, panting, unable to speak, incredibly excited though we had no idea what we were doing, but eager to do it again as soon as the opportunity presented itself. As Carlos would say, we were just a couple of horny kids.

We would never have been caught if it had not rained that day. In order not to undermine the authority of their juvenile spies, even teachers did not cross the line or move the cord which was the sole responsibility of the safety monitors. Fuensanta and I counted on this inviolable rule: no-one would enter the classroom until she gave permission.

We had just started rubbing our pee-pees together when the rain started. A sudden downpour, with fierce winds gusting from every direction. Pupils sought shelter in the stairwells, but the wind whipped the sheets of rain, drenching them completely. To prevent the pupils from getting any more soaked, the teachers defied the rule of the yellow cord and set a pack of children racing down the corridor to the classrooms, where they burst through the door and discovered us half-naked, performing our caricature of copulation.

Juan Carlos and I were expelled from Miss Ramírez's authoritarian school with its paramilitary platoons of student spies. Her decision – as she said until she was blue in the face – was irrevocable. She did not bargain with my parents' stubborn defiance.

Being expelled in the middle of the school year would make it extremely difficult to enrol elsewhere. It would mean losing all academic credits, not to mention the money spent attaining them. No school would accept credits for uncompleted coursework. My parents were aware of this and camped outside Miss Ramírez's office in an attempt to come to some kind of agreement. The headmistress refused to see them.

I did not hear from Fuensanta. After I was expelled, I had no way of communicating with her. I had never asked for her number or her address. The few classmates I had been friendly with either didn't know or refused to tell me.

61

I had no idea whether she had been punished too, whether they had stripped her of the title of safety monitor. I thought about her every morning when I woke up. Not just our sexy games, but our silent walk to the classroom, those times I had misbehaved during home time so I would be made to sit next to her on the girls' bench, and our conspiratorial glances when the break-time bell rang. In other words, I missed her.

Miss Ramírez was of the opinion that Fuensanta had been a victim. A girl with such excellent grades and exemplary manners would never have consented to the lewd act that had been witnessed by dozens of our classmates. She was convinced that I had coerced or tricked her. Only one of us could be guilty, the other was innocent. It was Fuensanta the saint pitted against a debauched Dionysus. Beauty and the Beast. Red Riding Hood and the Wolf.

My parents refused to accept this simplistic version of events. They assumed that the headmistress had expelled me – and Carlos – because she was terrified of Fuensanta's powerful father, now undersecretary to the Treasury after a dazzling political career as a senator, deputy and house majority whip. Eager to avoid a scandal, Miss Ramírez had decided the best solution was to expel us. There was also an element of class prejudice. Why allow two scruffy students to remain, when their parents could barely manage to pay the fees?

My parents turned to friends, acquaintances, even to lawyers in search of help. Nothing. Everyone recommended they drop the matter. The undersecretary was famously corrupt and ruthless. A powerful and belligerent man. There was nothing to be done. Still my parents refused to give up.

The solution came from the most unexpected of places. My father had spent almost three years studying Chemical Engineering, only to drop out of university when my grandfather died and he found himself having to support my grandmother and my two aunts (his younger sisters) and forced to work as a chauffeur, a salesman and a waiter, until he eventually became supervisor in a dairy company – the closest thing to being a chemical engineer he could find. He enjoyed the job, though it was badly paid. He got a part-time evening job in a water treatment plant. He worked in the dairy from 9.00 a.m. to 5.00 p.m., and at the plant from 5.30 to 10 p.m. Given his comprehensive knowledge of chemistry, he was also employed to teach science at a preparatory school. He loved teaching; to him, education was the best way of changing the world.

My father mentioned my expulsion to the headmaster of the school where he taught, and asked his advice. The headmaster was not encouraging. "There's nothing to be done, you would be taking on one of the most prestigious schools in the country, and the daughter of a government minister. Just let it drop." He slapped him on the back – he considered my father one of his best teachers – and retreated to his office. Dismayed, my father headed to class, when a student came up to him.

"Excuse me, Profesor Valdés, I couldn't help overhearing what you said and I think my father might be able to help you."

"How?"

Jaime Molina was a cheerful, curly-haired boy who had been expelled from countless schools for poor grades, and – though nobody knew it – was the son of Senator Ignacio Molina, former governor of Veracruz and former Minister for Agriculture. And Senator Molina was a bitter enemy of the undersecretary to the Treasury.

The following day, my father visited the home of Senator Molina, who thanked him for the patience and attention he had lavished on his son. Although my father did not feel he had given the boy any special attention, Jaime Molina thought otherwise: he had raved about my father's classes and was considering studying Chemical Engineering at the Universidad Nacional Autónoma de México.

The senator listened, amused, to the detailed account of my sexual misadventures with Fuensanta and the ensuing audience with Miss

Ramírez. What the headmistress regarded as an outrage, Molina saw as "just kids playing 'Doctor'".

"I think you should sue the school," the senator said.

"I don't have money to hire a lawyer," my father replied.

"That's not a problem," insisted the senator. "I'll take care of everything."

"The thing is . . ." my father protested.

The senator set down his glass of cognac and leaned towards my father.

"Look, Ramos is a son of a bitch. Everyone knows that. But he doesn't know that his daughter is a little slut, and that's something I want him and the whole world to know. Ramos is a closet prude, Profesor Valdés, so nothing could hurt him more than finding out that his pampered princess is a slutty little whore. I'll pay for the lawyer, just for the pleasure of fucking him over."

My father knew that he should reject the senator's offer. Fuensanta was not a slut and it was not right to make this little girl a pawn in this sleazy political game. On the other hand, he had no alternative. My parents had spent all their savings on our education, only to have a snobbish, sanctimonious headmistress unfairly expel us.

My father agreed.

Rifle in hand, Carlos lay in wait for the cat so that when it crept out from under the car, he could kill it. The chinchillas, still traumatised by the cat's smell, were scrabbling in their cages, their coats glinting silver in the moonlight.

A chinchilla's natural habitat is among the mountains of Peru, the rocky cliffs of the Andes, where it escapes its prey by scaling steep rock faces. It is quick and cunning, and fiendishly difficult to catch. Who the hell thought it was a good idea to domesticate it, breed it, lock it in tiny cages, feed it dog food, slaughter it and skin it to make fashionable coats to be sold in New York, Paris and London? Unable to slink through chinks in the cliffs, the chinchillas found themselves at the mercy of a terrifying enemy: stray cats. Seven or eight died every week, torn to pieces, while the others panicked and scurried around in their cages, desperately seeking a cleft, a rock.

The cat crept further under the car and leaned against the tyre; all that was visible was its tail, twitching every now and then. Carlos bided his time, peering into the gunsight, waiting to take the shot, but after a while the tail stopped twitching and we saw a single paw appear next to the wheel.

"It's a goner," Carlos said.

He lowered the rifle and stowed it back in the kennel.

"Right, let's go have dinner," he said as he walked towards the spiral staircase that led down to our roof.

Chateaux

By the time my parents got back from Europe, Carlos was no more than a mass of rotting flesh and gas buried six feet deep in mud. It had not stopped raining for days. Water trickling through the earth and into the coffin of my brother. My rain-soaked corpse-brother, my corpse-brother belching putrid gases, my corpse-brother buried next to my other corpse-brother. The family of the dead. My drowned brothers being drowned again in a never-ending torrent. Rain, rain and more rain. Gas, decomposition and rain. At what point does the brother you eat breakfast with, chat with, play with, hang out with, tell secrets to, ask for advice, give advice to, care about, the brother you love, become a haze of noxious gas, an unbearable absence, an irreversible death, a desperate guilt, a premeditated murder, an uncontrollable rage, a thirst for revenge, a nightmare, a punch in the gut, an urge to vomit, an excruciating pain, a toxic miasma?

My parents found out about my brother's death six days after it happened. We had agreed that they would phone once a week to make sure we were alright. Transatlantic phone calls were expensive, so they had to be brief. They had not left the phone numbers of their hotels where they would be staying and it proved impossible to track them down. Where could we call to tell them their eldest son had drowned, that my grandmother could not stop crying, that I was partly to blame for his death and that sooner or later I would try to murder those who had murdered him?

Itinerary of a day in Europe (from my mother's travel diary):

    8.15 a.m.: My parents wake up.

8.45 a.m.: They arrive in the hotel dining room for coffee, croissants and jam. Breakfast is included.

9.18 a.m.: They join eighteen people for a "Europe within Reach" tour, boarding the coach heading for the chateaux of the Loire.

Travelling through the French countryside, my father says that he thinks France is the most beautiful country in the world.

11.23 a.m.: They arrive at Chambord. The guide told them that the chateau was once used as a royal hunting lodge.

12.08 p.m.: They visit the royal bedchambers of Francis I and Louis XIV.

12.40 p.m.: They leave for Chenonceau. Through the window of the coach they spot a red deer running through the forest.

5.40 a.m. (Mexico): I am running across the rooftops, trying to save my brother.

1.37 p.m. (France): They arrive at Château de Chenonceau. The guide explains that it is known as "The Ladies' Castle" because Diana de Poitiers and Catherine of Medici used to live there.

My mother writes: "It is the most beautiful castle I've ever seen, it seems to float on the water."

6.37 a.m. (Mexico): My brother is floating inside a water tank. He has been there for hours.

3.02 p.m. (France): The tour ends. The guide jokes: "You guys must be hungry enough to eat each other alive."

3.27 p.m.: The coach pulls into the car park of a nearby restaurant. The tour group are seated on long refectory benches as the guide announces that they are to eat like the lords and ladies of the past. The menu includes pheasant with grapes, duck à l'orange, fillet of venison au poivre, honey-glazed wild boar ribs and, for those with a less adventurous palate, chicken chasseur or steak frites. The meal is accompanied by magnificent regional wines and still mineral water.

While my parents are feasting on game, Carlos my brother is gasping for breath. It is 3.36 p.m. French time.

3.42 p.m.: Dessert: tarte aux fraises, crème brûlée, white chocolate mousse or traditional Normandy cheeses with forest fruits.

3.45 p.m. (France) / 8.45 a.m. (Mexico): Carlos is pounding on the sides of the cistern in a last desperate effort to escape. His murderers hear him pounding and they laugh.

3.48 p.m. (France): My father extols the virtues of the Brie he chose: "I've never tasted anything like it in my life." My mother refuses to try it, just the smell of the cheese is too much for her.

3.59 p.m. (France) / 8.59 a.m. (Mexico): My brother is beginning to swallow water. He calls out, but his cries go unheard, and those who do hear – his killers – do nothing to save him.

4.02 p.m.: My parents board the coach heading for Amboise. My father says this is the finest meal he has ever tasted, that he now understands why hunters hunt.

4.03 p.m. (France) / 9.03 a.m. (Mexico): My brother's kicks are weaker now. His lungs are filling with water.

4.05 p.m.: The coach pulls away. A tourist races to catch up. He had been in the toilet and the guide had not realised. They very nearly leave him marooned at a chateau two hours' drive from Paris. "Stranded," says the guide, who does not know the Spanish word *varado*.

4.05 p.m. (France) / 9.05 a.m. (Mexico): My brother Carlos finally drowns, having survived for twenty-one hours in the water tank.

5.00 p.m.: The coach arrives in Amboise. My father is delighted to find out that Leonardo da Vinci is buried in the chapel.

5.01 p.m. (France) / 10.01 a.m. (Mexico): My brother's body is floating, lifeless.

5.29 p.m.: My parents climb the highest turret of the castle and marvel at the stunning countryside and the river Loire snaking beneath the castle.

6.02 p.m.: The coach leaves Amboise and heads back to Paris.

6.14 p.m. (France) / 11.14 a.m. (Mexico): The killers check that my brother is dead and they leave his body floating in the cistern.

On the drive back, my parents sleep in each other's arms. My brother sleeps in his watery bier.

8.30 p.m. precisely (the time stated in the brochure): The coach arrives back in Paris. Happy and tired my parents go up to their hotel room without dinner: they are still full from their banquet in Chenonceau.

My brother is bloated with water. His corpse is increasingly swollen, painfully heavy.

10.17 p.m.: My mother's last note in her travel diary, written in code: "W.M.L. – it was so romantic".

Later I found out that W.M.L. meant We Made Love.

Y.E.S.D.: Your Eldest Son Drowned.

Chelo would hum when we made love. A soft, sweet song. She would cry quietly while we did it. Her tears wetting my cheeks, trickling into my neck. She would hum and smile and sob and cling to me. Then she would quicken her thrusts and come, arching her belly against my pelvis. She would moan for a few seconds and then her breathing would slow, she would cradle my head in her hands, look into my eyes and smile. Even when she sobbed, Chelo always smiled. Again she would hum, embrace me, smile and sob, shuddering through orgasm after orgasm. Nobody had ever made her come the way I did, she said, with other men she had two orgasms, max, but with me it was something else. Far from being happy, I was hurt. Why would she tell me about the orgasms she had with other men? What was the point? I was eaten up with jealousy. Jealousy, damn jealousy.

Sometimes I would watch her at the stove while she made dinner. She would stare at the frying pan as she fried eggs or cured meat. I found her beautiful, her blue eyes, her permanent limp, her indestructible joy. She hummed while she cooked too. So much peace for a woman who suffered from chronic pain. Whenever she caught me looking, she would smile and gesture to the napkins and the cutlery.

"Come on, help me out here. Go set the table."

Dutifully, I would lay the table, she would serve the meal, sit next to me and kiss me.

"Go on, eat up! I don't want you wasting away."

When we finished, we would wash the dishes and then go back to my camp bed to make love again. She would coil her legs around me as I slipped inside her. When I came inside her, she never washed away the semen. She called it "my little potion", she said it turned her on when she wore a skirt in class and felt my cum running down her thigh, her calf. "I want my little potion," she would say whenever she wanted to fuck, and she insisted on doing it everywhere: the kitchen, the living room, the bathroom, my parents' bedroom. Jealousy. How many other men had heard the words "I want my little potion", and did she fuck them wherever and whenever?

Every night, after we made love, she would dress in silence and kiss me goodbye. I would lie there naked, alone in the house of my dead, struggling between grief and jealousy.

I never left the house. Chelo would do the shopping. I gave her money to do it. When I emptied my father's drawers, I found wads of banknotes stuffed inside his socks. A small fortune, enough to live comfortably for a year, maybe a year and a half. Chelo was a born manager. She made sure that the money lasted. Without her, I would have squandered it within a month.

In the mornings, when she wasn't there, I would go up to my brother's room and rummage through his books. His library of stolen books was vast, ranging from Rulfo to Einstein, Faulkner to Nietzsche, biographies of Mozart and Marx, atlases, old maps, philosophical treatises, dictionaries. I would lie on his bed and read. (Do the drowned have beds, sheets, clothes? To whom do the objects of the dead belong? To the dead or those who survive them?) On every page of every book I discovered a note, an underlined word, a comment. In some places, he had crossed out a sentence he thought was badly written. Reading his books was a way of sustaining a silent conversation with him.

With King lying at my feet, I would read for hours until I heard Chelo's key in the door and then I would go down to greet her. If it was not cold, Chelo and I would wander around the house naked. At first she was timid, she was still ashamed of her scars. But eventually she grew more comfortable and we would both walk around naked and uninhibited. Sometimes "I want my little potion" would surprise us in the living room. We would throw ourselves down onto the carpet to make love. King thought our sexual tussles were a game. He would bark or jump on top of us, licking our asses or our legs. Chelo would laugh as he covered us in drool.

It was she who introduced me to Deep Purple and John Mayall, to La Revolución de Emiliano Zapata. She would talk excitedly about Antonioni, Truffaut, Godard, Buñuel, De Sica, "El Indio" Fernández, and her favourite Mexican film, "Viento Negro". She would lend me books by her favourite authors: Pío Baroja, Dostoevsky. Everything about her was passionate, vital, joyous, curious.

Chelo's real name was María Consuelo Reyes López. Consuelo, consolation. Given the circumstances I couldn't have fallen for someone with a more appropriate name. "Soy tu Consuelo," she would say, and she was right, she was my consolation, my earth, my heaven, my dream, my country, my home. In all the ways it is possible for a woman to be a man's homeland, Chelo was mine.

I can imagine Miss Ramírez's face as she received a series of summons from Court 13 to respond to a lawsuit charging her with defamation, child cruelty and fraud . . . In total, eighteen suits were filed by Ortiz, Arellano, Portillo & Associates, the most powerful practice in the country, whose managing partner, Alberto Ortiz, had never lost a case. Well connected within the political establishment, intimately familiar with the corridors of judicial power, mindful of the bribes necessary

71

to win over judges, lawyers and witnesses, Ortiz, Arellano, Portillo & Associates were the apex predators of the legal food chain.

If Miss Ramírez had assumed that the matter of our expulsions was settled, she had not reckoned on the avalanche of audits, court proceedings, expenses and threats now raining down on her. Senator Molina's approach quickly bore fruit: Undersecretary Ramos and his family found themselves the subject of a tangled web of gossip, rumours and lies, Fuensanta was called to testify and Senator Molina's people ensured this made the news. Although it was illegal to publish the name of a minor involved in legal proceedings, the mere mention that it was "one of Undersecretary Ramos's daughters" was enough to fuel chatter.

Ramos did not expose his daughter any further. He sent her to stay with some of his wife's cousins in Kansas, and pressured Miss Ramírez into negotiating with my parents to avoid exacerbating the scandal.

Carlos and I were re-admitted with a full scholarship, not just for the rest of the year, but for the following two, which didn't exactly fill me with joy. I detested that school. Much to her chagrin, Miss Ramírez apologised to my family and me. Accustomed to her imperious position at the school and ordering around the employees, teachers and parents, she suddenly found herself face to face with a major adversary who had gone undercover and revealed the scale of her business: only twenty per cent of fees was spent on running the school, the rest was profit. The fine for tax evasion – she declared only ten per cent of her income – was so severe that she was nearly bankrupted. Beaten into submission by the lawsuits, she was left with no option other than to agree to my parents' demands.

Just like Senator Molina had planned, the episode affected the undersecretary's family life as much as it did his professional one. His clumsy attempts to alleviate the situation had the opposite effect. Every statement he made to try and make the scandal disappear got him into deeper water. The journalists paid by Molina portrayed Fuensanta as a sex-crazed Lolita. They accused him of being a bad father. His bouts of drunkenness and the beatings suffered by his wife came to light. In the corridors of power rumours began to fly around about him and Fuensanta. The corrupt moralist, deceitful in his business dealings, and his filthy eleven-year-old daughter.

Two months later Undersecretary Ramos resigned. Senator Molina was then able to go ahead with the property development projects that Ramos had been obstructing in order to benefit his own people. He bought land at giveaway prices to then build houses and sell them at hyperbolic prices.

Carlos and I returned to school, where we were seen in a whole new light. Two pupils who had never travelled to Europe, who came to school by public transport, who lived in a neighbourhood nobody had heard of, two "problem" children who had been definitively expelled, were welcomed back – with full scholarships – and were now treated with deference and respect by the headmistress while Fuensanta Ramos, the perfect girl, the exemplary student who had visited Europe, Japan, Australia and South America, the girl who had been "molested" by the precocious and degenerate boy, disappeared from school without explanation.

Fuensanta vanished. Even her closest friends never heard from her again. Did she think about me? Did she miss me as I missed her? Had I hurt her? Fuensanta faded into a distant Kansas prairie while I went back to that horrible school, to that concrete quadrangle with no grass, no trees, from which I was expelled for good after finishing Year 6 of primary school thanks to my anti-Beatles diatribes.

"Hello."

"Hi."

"Juan Guillermo?"

". . ."

"Can you hear me, son?"

"…"

"Juan Guillermo, it's Papá. Can you hear me?"

"Yes, I hear you."

"We're calling from Florence, in Italy. You can't imagine how beautiful the city is. Your mother and I are having a wonderful time."

"…"

"Can you hear me?"

"Yes."

"How are things?"

"Papá …"

"Your mother wants to know if you've paid the electricity and gas bills, she left money on the kitchen counter."

"Papá, we have been trying to get hold of you."

"What for?"

"Something bad has happened."

"What? What's happened?"

"You need to come home."

"Is your grandmother alright?"

"Yes, she's fine … You need to come home."

"I don't understand … What's happened?"

"It's Carlos."

"What about Carlos?"

"…"

"Is your brother alright?"

"No, he's not alright."

"Where is he?"

"…"

"Answer me, son. Your mother is here, she's worried."

"…"

"Juan Guillermo. Can you hear me?"

"Come home, I'll explain everything when you get back."

"Tell me now, what's happened to your brother?"

"..."

"Tell me."

"They killed him."

"What?"

"They killed him. Carlos."

"..."

"Papá, you have to come home."

"Is this some kind of joke?"

"No, Papá, Carlos is dead."

"No, I don't believe it."

"They murdered him six days ago. We had to bury him."

"I don't believe it. Who murdered him?"

"Just come home, please."

"What happened? Tell me."

"I'll explain when you get here. Just come home. Grandma isn't doing so good."

"We'll try and get home as soon as possible."

"..."

"This isn't a prank?"

"No, Papá."

"Your mother is crying her eyes out here. Are you sure?"

"Yes, Papá. Carlos is dead. Come back now."

An aboriginal tribe in Australia believes that when a person dies they journey west, towards the sun dropping over the horizon. Along the last rays of sunset towards ultimate darkness, across a bridge between light and shadow. Excepting children. Children who pass away, who are taken before their time, do not deserve to end up in the murky province of the dead. Hence, they remain forever in the golden twilight limbo.

When someone dies who should not have died, a child comes from the dusk and guides the dead soul back to its cast-off body. The corpse draws in the soul, shuddering as it returns, a shudder is proof that it has been reborn. The child looks upon the corpse returned to life and, gratified, returns home to its twilight limbo.

Chords

Felipe jemmies the window. Opens it. We creep into the house. Humberto guides us through the darkness. Faces covered by our hoods. God is with us, Humberto says. We come to the stairs. We climb them in single file. Silently. Clutching baseball bats. Hammers. Screwdrivers. Humberto jerks his chin towards a door. The master bedroom. Antonio advances two steps. Steels himself. I take a deep breath. Antonio bursts through the door. The elderly couple are in bed. The woman screams. The old man gets up. He does not know what is happening. Strike one from Felipe's baseball bat fells him. The woman lets out a wail. Antonio drags her into the bathroom. Gags her. Felipe brings down the bat again: strike two. A strangled cry. Strike. Strike. We are god's right arm. Another strike. For rejecting Christ. Heretic Jews. Enemies of god. The old man whimpers. I look down at him. Humberto says: Your turn. I hesitate. Humberto gestures to my bat. Do it, he orders. I raise it high. Please no, the old man moans. I lash out. The old man curls into a ball. Again, Humberto growls. I hit him again. He writhes in pain. I hit him a few more times. God is with us. I have no fear. No pity. Adrenaline. A rush of adrenaline. God's right arm. God's fist. God's army here on Earth. The woman passes out. Her legs white against the tiled floor. The bluish tracery of veins. Heathen Jews. Perfidious Jews. Enemies of god. The old Kike lies on the floor. Sobs. "Don't kill him," Humberto orders. "This is a lesson. Nothing more." The old man stops moving. The senseless woman sprawled on the bathroom floor. Her hair white against the blue tiles. Her pale legs, her pale arms, her grubby nightdress, her livid cheeks, her open mouth, her people, her god. God is with us. The old man. Is he dead? Felipe asks. He's breathing, Antonio says. The old man groans. Take stuff. Make it look like a robbery, Humberto orders. We ransack drawers. Jewellery. Money. All to be donated to the Church. Nothing for ourselves. We creep out. Close the window on the old man. On the woman. Their pale legs. Their hatred of god. I take a deep breath. I am shaking. We run three blocks. We take off our balaclavas. We walk faster. God's army.

We take the spiral staircase from the rooftop down to the yard. King scampers to meet us, wagging his stubby tail. He licks my hand, covers my clothes in drool. Carlos grabs a carton of eggs. Grandmother is on the living room sofa watching television. From the kitchen you can hear the nasal twang of the game show host. "You want eggs?" Carlos asks me. I say yes. He makes me the same dinner as always: three fried eggs, six pieces of bread and a litre of chocolate milk. Next week, he says, we have an order for a hundred chinchilla pelts. We need to groom the chinchillas, get them ready for sacrifice.

We finish dinner. Go up to his room. Carlos closes the door and locks it. When he does this, I know he wants to talk about his "other business" and he doesn't want our parents to overhear.

"I need someone to collect a package. Who do you know who's trustworthy?"

Carlos refuses to involve me in his "other business", but sometimes he asks me to recommend a friend to pick up the merchandise or store it for a few days.

"I would send Jaibo again."

Carlos thinks for a moment.

"Do you think he knows what's inside?"

"No, I don't think so. Both times we sent him, the parcel came back wrapped and sealed."

My brother seems dubious. Jaibo is not the most intelligent of my friends, but he is the most discreet.

"I don't think it's a good idea to get anyone else involved."

78

Carlos takes off his shirt. A small knife in a sheath is strapped to his right forearm. Carlos has learned to whip it out in a single, fluid movement. He cut himself several times while practising, but has now mastered the knack of sliding it into the palm of his hand. In his left trouser pocket, he has a knuckleduster; in his right, a flick-knife. He has honed his belt buckle with a whetstone until it is razor sharp. He could slit someone's throat with it if he wanted. In his shirt pocket, there is a pack of cigarettes in which he hides four straws of different sizes. He never goes anywhere without them. Of all his work tools (his term for the arsenal of knives, blades and knuckledusters), the straws are the most important; no-one can know what they are for.

"O.K., ask Jaibo."

"How much do I offer him?"

"A hundred."

A hundred pesos was a small fortune.

"Why can't you just give me the money?" I protest.

Carlos laughs.

"You'll get much more than that one of these days, you'll see."

Almost no-one in our neighbourhood goes out without a weapon. Sometimes even I wear a small knife strapped to my forearm. Carlos needs to be extra careful because of his business. The Policía Judicial are always hanging around, using threats of prison to blackmail him. Sometimes a dispute with a client can turn violent. Or guys who try to steal his merchandise.

"Go to sleep," he orders.

"Night."

I go out of his room and down the stairs. My grandmother has fallen asleep in front of the television again. I put a blanket over her and kiss her forehead.

"Night," I whisper.

I step behind her chair, noiselessly open the door to my room, go in and lie on my bed. On the ceiling I have a poster of Raquel Welch dressed as a cavewoman. I say goodnight to her, close my eyes and fall asleep.

At night he howled. His was a deep, piercing howl. If I had an invisible brother, Colmillo had an invisible wolf pack he summoned by his howling. His howls were answered by far-off dogs. A chorus of disparate yowls. Colmillo howled with the strength of the forest, of the tundra. His D.N.A. hungered for snow, for winter cold, for the wolf pack. Colmillo needed frozen steppes, blood, needed to run, to fight, to control, to hunt. Much wolf still lurked within him.

He was ferocious. He would attack someone simply because they were not part of the Prieto family. He couldn't be let out without a muzzle. One afternoon Colmillo got loose and mauled the arm of a mechanic, a strapping giant of a man who was fixing the Tena family's car. No sooner had he slipped out of the house than Colmillo launched himself at him, catching him unawares as he was peering under the bonnet. The man had no time to react. Colmillo sprang at his neck but managed only to sink his teeth into his arm, then landed heavily, without letting go, ripping a large chunk of muscle with him.

Fernando Prieto rushed over to grab him, but Colmillo pulled free and attacked again. The terrified mechanic leaped onto the roof of the car. Colmillo bounded onto the boot, trying to reach him. The man shouted frantically for the Prietos to restrain the dog. Eventually, Fernando, his father and his brother managed to subdue the wolf-dog. Once they had dragged Colmillo some distance away, the mechanic scrambled into the car and locked all the doors. His blood spattered the seats, the steering wheel, the floor. A bloodbath. A deep gouge ringed by teeth marks marked the place where his bicep should have been: Colmillo had ripped away the whole muscle.

The Prietos paid for surgery and medical bills, but the man could no longer work as a mechanic. How could he regulate a differential gear, tighten a wheel nut, change a tyre or replace a fuel pump with a useless arm? His demand for damages was so high that the Prietos refused to pay. The medical bills had exhausted their savings, they did not have the funds to offer him even three months' salary. They were sorry, but there was nothing they could do to help.

The mechanic swore he would kill Colmillo, even if he had to burn the house down to do it.

I first heard this music when I went round there with Pato. One of his cousins had brought him back a record from Chicago. Hearing the first jangling guitar chords, I realised that *this* was music that spoke to me, understood me, thrilled me. If the Beatles were the antithesis of my neighbourhood, Hendrix epitomised it in three seconds flat. Jimi Hendrix. I didn't understand a word of his lyrics. Hendrix could have been singing nonsense, saying la-la-la or reading out his shopping list. It didn't matter. His intricate musical notes seduced me instantly.

I told Carlos about my discovery. He hadn't heard of Hendrix either. Together we made a pilgrimage from one shop to the next in search of his record, until we found it in one in the Zona Rosa. It was incredibly expensive. Carlos bought it and gave it to me.

As soon as we got home we placed it on the record player. The moment Carlos heard it he turned to me. "What is this mad genius?" Mozart and Nietzsche and the torture of African slaves and the smell of the street and wisdom and nature and life and death and love and power and fire and air and storms and Faulkner and Kant. If Colmillo was a wolf-dog, Hendrix was a wolf-musician. His music was pure ferocity. Hendrix understood the street, the rooftops, wounds, scars. He must have known about fights, knives, about coats trimmed with chinchilla fur. Hendrix knew. The Beatles wrote catchy tunes that were easy to hum. It was impossible to hum along to Hendrix.

My father grumbled about how his sons didn't listen to Mexican music or at least music with Spanish lyrics. My parents' generation grew up with the voices of Pedro Infante, Jorge Negrete, Pedro Vargas,

María Victoria. I tried listening to it all and Mexican music of other genres: ballads, polkas, boleros, even César Costa and Angélica María's innocent rock. Nothing sounded like Hendrix. There was nothing like that discordant guitar, those unexpected harmonies, those frenzied chords.

In less than a week the cult of Hendrix had spread through the barrio. We knew he was black, that he had Mexican blood in his veins, that he was born in Seattle, that he wore leather coats, that he took as many drugs as possible, that he turned up to his shows intoxicated, that he was left-handed but played the guitar right-handed. I would go to sleep listening to Hendrix, wake up listening to Hendrix.

I took my Hendrix record to tedious Kurt Holland's class, my only intention being to provoke him. He picked it up and scrutinised it thoroughly, as if he could read the music in the grooves of the vinyl. The Beatles incident had just happened and my leaving at the end of the school year was a given. I was sure Holland would hate Hendrix and that's why I wanted him to play it in class.

He stood in front of the group and showed them the record.

"Valdés brought this and wants to share it with us."

He looked at me and sneered.

"I imagine this is much better than the Beatles."

He laughed and several of my classmates laughed along with him.

He placed it on the record player and lowered the needle. As soon as Hendrix's rasping guitar played the first notes of "Voodoo Child", Holland's expression hardened.

"This is a joke, right?" he said, and after thirty seconds he lifted the stylus from the record.

"No, it's not a joke. I like it."

"This crap?"

I didn't respond. I had told him I liked it and that was enough. Holland turned to the rest of the class.

"Does anyone here appreciate this crap?"

Nobody raised their hand. There were only giggles and murmurs. Holland removed the record from the player and put it back in its sleeve.

"You don't belong in this school, you never have. It's the best thing for you and for us that you're leaving."

He handed me the record.

"I hope one day you can change, or at least that your taste in music improves," he said with a disdainful look.

Immediately afterwards the class sang "Yellow Submarine" all together. As we were leaving the class, Jaime, a fat guy I played football with, came up to me.

"I liked it," he said. "What's it called?"

"It's Hendrix, Jimi Hendrix."

The fat guy's eyes lit up.

"Jimi? He's got the same name as me! Jaime."

He smiled happily at the coincidence and walked away down the hall.

Memento Mori

Memento mori the Romans called it. *Remember thou must die.* Anyone who has seen a creature die knows that death is not a final, definitive event. Death is a series of little deaths. We are not individuals but a collection of cells that together form the shape of what we believe to be an individual. Death is the death of a mass of multiple living beings. Body tissues don't suddenly perish, but gradually expire, one after the other.

I learned this slaughtering the chinchillas. Carlos paid my friends and me three pesos to kill them, clean them, skin them and prepare the pelts for tanning. We would grab them by the scruff of the neck with one hand, tilt their heads slightly, and then jerk the tail downwards with the other hand. The jerk snapped the chinchillas' necks without causing pain and without damaging their fur. The disconnection between their brain and their bodies meant instant death, but for some minutes they would continue to move. Their legs would spasm, their ears twitch, their backs shudder.

Agüitas, sentimental as always, cried the first few times he had to snap their necks, but quickly grew accustomed to the dry crack of dislocating vertebrae.

The afternoons I spent killing them were lessons in biology, anatomy, nature and philosophy. I learned what fasciae are, how tendons work, where fat accumulates, what colour muscles are, the name of the membrane that surrounds the heart, and the fine line between life and death.

Skinning the chinchillas was a laborious process. We would cut open the skin from the crotch to the base of the jaw, careful not to nick

84

internal organs. Blood, urine and faeces would damage the fur and render it worthless. Once the incision was made, we would ease our fingers under the skin and, using gentle pressure, separate it from the muscle, careful not to tear it. Furriers only bought whole pelts. Once finished, we would sprinkle the pelt with unslaked lime and stretch them out on a clothes line to dry.

It took ten minutes to skin a chinchilla: we could skin six an hour, thirty in an afternoon. At first Carlos only sold the furs, and we would boil the meat for King or one of the neighbours' dogs to eat. After a while, he found a cat-food factory to buy the meat. This doubled our work: now we had to skin and gut. By the end of the afternoon we were exhausted, with skins pegged on the wires and gutted bodies drying on wooden crates. It was ironic that we were working to feed the enemy: cats.

Carlos sold the pelts for thirty pesos apiece. Sometimes there might be a thousand orders for pelts a month. Carlos streamlined the breeding and sales process according to mathematical variables. Four to six kits per litter; fifteen per cent stillborn on average; six to eight months to reach ideal size; two pesos per animal per month for food; three pesos for labour; five per cent of net profits to the neighbours for the use of their rooftop; one hundred pesos a month to Gumaro for cleaning and disinfecting; fifteen pesos per kilo of meat – approximately six chinchillas; fifty chinchillas a month sold to pet shops at forty pesos apiece (and sold on for seventy). In total, Carlos made between twenty and twenty-five thousand pesos a month. From this he took five hundred to buy does for breeding, a hundred and fifty pesos for personal expenses, and the rest he invested in buying merchandise for his other business.

According to some psychoanalysts, living beings are inclined to return to the pure and tranquil state of the inorganic. Existence is a constant tension and effort, an agonised daily battle for food, territory, reproduction and water; only by returning to nothing can living things finally be at rest. The Dutch philosopher Spinoza believed the opposite. He thought that living beings strive to preserve their immanence. *Unaquaeque res, quantum in se est, in suo esse perseverare conatur.* "Each thing, as far as it can by its own power, strives to persevere in its being." Paraphrasing Spinoza, Borges wrote: "The stone wants to be a stone and the tiger a tiger, forever."

Having snapped the necks of hundreds of chinchillas, I decided Spinoza was right. The tiger wants to remain a tiger, the stone a stone, the chinchilla a chinchilla, the man a man. It is the survival instinct that prevails, not the death drive. Hence terror in its purest form: fear of death.

One afternoon there was a knock on the door. My grandmother opened it. She came back and told me "some neighbours" were looking for me. I went out. Ten of the Good Boys were waiting, among them, Humberto – a tall scrawny guy – who was their leader. Antonio was there, with a bandage tied round his head; he had trouble speaking, after Carlos's punch to the jaw.

"Hello," Humberto greeted me.

They seemed to be wearing uniforms. Formal trousers in beige or brown, impeccably ironed white shirts with white vests underneath, crucifixes around their necks, close-cropped hair, polished black lace-up shoes, fake gold watches on their left wrists. No trainers, no boots, no garish shirts, no jeans, no bracelets, no rings, long hair. Spotless, clean, dapper.

"What's up?" I asked.

"We heard about the altercation you and your brother had with Antonio."

"And?"

"Antonio wants to apologise to you both, but especially to you. He shouldn't have hit you."

Antonio stepped forward and we exchanged a glance.

"I'm sorry. I was riled by your insolence, but, nonetheless, my behaviour was improper."

Francisco de Quevedo would have loved the way they talked.

"It's fine, don't worry."

"Do you forgive him?" Humberto said eagerly.

It seemed I had no choice. In front of me stood ten crazy karate freaks.

"Sure."

Jerking his chin, Humberto summoned Antonio closer.

"Could you confirm your forgiveness by offering him your hand?"

I suspected a trick. Antonio came forward and obediently held out his hand. I thought that as soon as I took it he would pull it to immobilise me, and the others would beat me senseless. I shook his hand.

"Well done," Humberto said.

The fat guy's hand was sweaty and chubby. I discreetly wiped my hand on my trousers.

"I wanted to ask, and I say this respectfully, whether you and your friends would please stop swearing in the street. It isn't right. There are girls, mothers, grandmothers who might hear you," Humberto said. If only he knew that my grandmother said "You drive me up the fucking wall, you son of a bitch" whenever she was angry.

"We'll do our best," I told him.

"We would also like you, Carlos and your friends to come around to our place. We meet on Mondays and Wednesdays at seven at my house. We have soft drinks, watch films, listen to music, discuss various subjects and we have interesting people who come to give us lectures. I'm sure you would enjoy it."

"O.K.," I said.

Humberto gave me the beatific look of a good man.

"I hope you enjoy the rest of your day. We hope to see you next Monday. God bless you."

They turned and left, and I waited, watching them walk away. Humberto was the son of the woman who had saved my life years earlier.

Who would his parents have been? Where would he have been born? What would they have called him? Would he have been a Pisces or Cancer or Taurus or Scorpio? Would he have been an alcoholic? Would he have grown up to be a footballer, a builder, a beggar, a murderer? Would he have believed in god? Would he have had children? Would he have been handsome or ugly? Tall or short? So many ruined possibilities floating in a mayonnaise jar. I held the foetus up to my bedroom lamp. It bobbed in the cloudy formaldehyde, bumping against the glass. The organs were visible through the translucent skin. The eyes were two black dots in a shapeless face. The legs, two stubby tails. A big pinkish head. Hands that looked like fins. Fish-man, reptilian-man, man who was not man.

The foetus in the mayonnaise jar was a metaphor for the death of my brothers. This must be how Carlos had floated the morning he drowned, while his killers celebrated. This was how Juan José's body must have bobbed in my mother's womb as she pushed the trolley around in the supermarket deciding whether to buy beetroot or carrots.

I slept with the light on and the jar resting on my chest. In the early hours, I felt a hand trying to take it from me. Instinctively I clutched it tightly and opened my eyes. Chelo was sitting on my bed. I had not heard her come in.

"What time is it?" I said. It was still dark.

"Six fifteen."

She stared at the jar.

"What is that?"

"It's a dog foetus," I lied.

"Let me see."

I gripped the jar, but she easily took it from me. She held it up to the light from the doorway, studied it from every angle, then turned to me.

"This is not a dog foetus, it's human," she said. I had no idea how she could make out any human features.

She stepped forward and held up the jar. The embryo jolted against the lid.

"What exactly are you doing with this thing?"

I had never seen her so serious and so upset.

"I bought it."

"You bought it?" she said, incredulous.

"Yeah, I bought it in first year in secondary school from the guy who ran the biology lab."

"What for?"

"So I could have it."

"So you could have it," she echoed.

She gazed at the floor as though to find the words she was searching for.

"Why don't you take it out of the jar, clean it, wrap it in a new hand-kerchief, put it in a wooden box and bury it in a place with lots of trees?"

Being a medical student, Chelo must have examined hundreds of foetuses, autopsied dead bodies and practised surgery on dead animals. Why was she so worried about an embryo floating in formaldehyde?

"I want to keep it. I look at it every day."

Chelo thought for a moment and then looked me in the eye.

"Haven't you had enough of death by now?"

Her question chilled me. What did a foetus in a mayonnaise jar have to do with the deaths of my family? I started to sob and couldn't stop. I had not cried when Carlos died, or my parents, or my grand-mother. I never cried. Ever. My father used to tell his friends that he had never seen me cry. And it was true, I couldn't remember having cried since I was four. I never cried and now I couldn't stop.

Chelo hugged me.

"I'm sorry, I didn't mean to hurt you."

It was not that she had hurt me. It was all the death that surrounded me.

"Forgive me," she whispered. She covered my face with kisses. Still I could not stop sobbing. They were tears of grief, of rage, of helplessness, of a desire for revenge. Revenge. I felt ashamed. Nobody had seen me cry since I was a child and now the woman I loved saw. I wanted to choke back the tears, to hide them, destroy them. I never cried.

Chelo undressed as she kissed my tears away. I clung to her. Feeling her nakedness, I felt myself calm down. I laid my head on her shoulder and fell asleep.

Definition of death: the total and permanent cessation of all the vital functions of an organism.

Definition of death: the total and permanent cessation of all the vital functions of an organism.

Definition of death: the total and permanent cessation of   the vital functions of an organism.

Definition of death: the total and permanent cessation of   the functions of an organism.

Definition of death: the total and permanent cessation of
        an organism.

Definition of death: cessation of
        an organism.

Definition of death: cessation of
        organism.

Definition of death: cessation
        organism.

Definition   death: cessation

death: cessation

death:

d ath:

d th:

d   h:

d   :

        :

        .

Prairies

Amaruq had seen him once or twice. He was huge, his coat a deep charcoal grey. A growl was enough to make the other wolves obey him. The huge grey wolf had appeared out of nowhere and deposed Tulugak in a vicious fight. Tulugak had been leader of the pack for two winters. Amaruq had named him Tulugak because he was black as a raven.

Mortally wounded by the deep bites, Tulugak roamed the snowy prairies leaving a trail of blood behind him. Amaruq followed the tracks and finally came across the wolf's black body in a deep hollow. The pelt was worthless. Ragged and tattered from the wounds. Large chunks of flesh had been ripped away.

Amaruq had been hunting Tulugak for months, but the wolf had never come near his traps or offered a clean target. He was a wary, cunning animal. Amaruq squatted down to inspect the body. It was a magnificent beast. Amaruq ran his hand through the dark fur. He could feel warmth still radiating from the lifeless body. He cut off the tail and hung it from his belt.

In the days that followed, Amaruq kept a close watch on the prairie through his binoculars. He wanted to find the pack now led by the big grey wolf. He could see nothing, not even tracks in the snow, and could only hear their deep howls at night. Every day when he woke up, he packed up his tent, rolled up the furs on which he slept, placed them on the sled, put on his snowshoes and set off through the remote wilderness in the direction from which the howls had come.

After two weeks, he finally found a trail in the snow. Fifteen wolves. From the size of the paw prints, Amaruq judged there were nine bitches, three young males, two adults and the big grey wolf, the alpha male.

For five days Amaruq followed, as the large grey wolf led them towards a dense forest. Only once did Amaruq see them in the distance. The wolf stopped, sniffed the crystal-clear morning air and glanced back towards Amaruq. Through the binoculars, Amaruq could just make out the yellow eyes, the breath hanging in the air. Then the wolf turned and trotted on, followed by the pack.

Amaruq had realised right away that this was the wolf that his grandfather had warned him about: "Of all the wolves you see in your life, one alone will be your master. You will belong to him. You will hunt him and he will elude you again and again. You will see him vanish in an instant. He will become your obsession. You will devote your life to hunting him. That wolf will be your god. You will hear his howls at night and know that he is calling not to other wolves but to you. One day you will look into his eyes and see who you are. The wolf is you. Every day, you will go in search of the voice that calls to you, the voice of your unfathomable god. And if, in this life, you cannot snare him, you must hunt him through your other lives until you finally can."

From a mountain peak, Amaruq watched as the big grey wolf and his pack disappeared into the trees. He decided to name him Nujuaqtutuq: "The Untameable".

He put the spoon down in the bowl of cereal and looked at me.

"When did he say this?"

"Yesterday afternoon. He made Antonio apologise to me."

"Apologise?"

"Yes, apologise."

Carlos was thoughtful for a moment.

"What are they up to?"

"It's what Christ says, isn't it? That you must forgive people."

"Christ? Turn the other cheek and all that shit?"

"Yes."

"What else did they say?"

"He invited us to join them for their meetings at Humberto's house on Mondays and Wednesdays at seven."

Carlos toyed with his Corn Flakes.

"Are you thinking of going?"

"No. It'll be boring."

"I'd like to go," he said.

I looked at him in disbelief.

"Why?"

"So I can find out what they want."

"To teach us about Christ, I guess. Thou shalt not kill, Thou shalt not steal, Thou shalt not covet thy neighbour's wife, all that shit."

"I don't think so. I figure those bastards have something else up their sleeves."

Carlos stared thoughtfully into his cereal.

"Why don't you go for a couple of months and let me know what they're up to."

"No way! What a pain in the ass!"

"I need to know what they're up to."

"We can go together."

"I'll go later. But you go first. Make them think you're into all that shit."

"Why would I do that?"

"Because they're not going to tell you what they're *really* up to unless they think they've converted you. And I need to know."

Eventually, I gave in. The following Monday, at 7 p.m., I knocked on Humberto's door.

My mother took a shirt from Carlos's wardrobe and held it up.

"What about this one?"

It was a lumberjack shirt, red and black checked flannel. My father had brought it back from Wisconsin where he had been sent by the dairy company to study quality control. For almost two years, Carlos

95

had hardly taken it off. When I close my eyes and picture my brother, he's wearing that shirt.

"I don't know if I'll wear it, but I'll keep it."

"I asked whether you'll wear it, not whether you'll keep it."

"Yes, yes I'll wear it."

She put it on the pile of shirts to which I had said "yes". It felt strange, having to decide whether I planned to wear my dead brother's clothes.

My parents had not been able to come back from Europe immediately. They did not have the money to pay for new flights. They had to wait six days until the tour bus brought them back to Madrid before they could fly back to Mexico. When they arrived, my parents looked gaunt and exhausted. That night in Florence, after the phone call telling them their elder son had been murdered, they had hugged each other and cried (just as, three years later, I hugged Chelo and sobbed when they were dead). Now that they were home, they had no tears left.

For a week they visited the cemetery every day to sit by their son's grave. Just like my mother had once stared at the empty cot of the twin she had lost, now she stared at the grave of her son who had been drowned by murderers devoted to Christ. Like a blind woman reading braille, my mother traced the inscription on the headstone over and over, tracing the name of the son who lay beneath the earth, to be sure that he was really dead. The constant chafing of the rough stone made her fingers bleed. My father tried to stop her, but she refused.

Some days later, they opened the heavy suitcases filled with gifts from Europe. For my grandmother, a miniature Eiffel Tower, a tablecloth from Bruges and an embossed golden letter-opener from Toledo. For Carlos, a white linen shirt, a book about Leonardo da Vinci and a figurine of a wild boar, a replica of a fountain in Florence. And for me, a woolly jumper from Berlin, a hunting knife from San Sebastián and Italian shoes that didn't fit.

My mother laid the linen shirt, the boar and the book on Carlos's bed and left them there, as though waiting for the spirit of her son to come and claim them. The next day, without her knowing, I took them. I read the book about Da Vinci, placed the wild boar so it was visible when you entered my room. I hung the linen shirt in my wardrobe, promising myself that on the day I avenged him I would wear it with pride.

My father swore he would devote his life to getting justice. He had managed to get the school to concede defeat and readmit us; he would make sure that his son's killers went to prison. He did not reckon on the corruption of the Mexican judicial system, or the collusion between the murderers and those expected to punish them. The moral purity of young Catholics conniving with the efficient cruelty of the police.

A doctored autopsy declared my brother's death an accident. My father insisted it was murder. He had irrefutable proof, witness statements, evidence. Determined, he dragged me from one government department to another to bear witness to what had happened. Nobody took any interest. Nobody would listen to my terrible story. Delinquents like my brother were responsible for the depravity of today's youth. The bottom line was that the Good Boys had not murdered a son, a brother, a friend, a grandson, but a thug intent on destroying the social fabric of the community. Besides, the autopsy had concluded that death was accidental, that my brother had drowned while trying to escape. Case closed.

My father loitered in the waiting rooms of public prosecutors' offices, waiting to be heard. To no avail. Once the cogs in the machine begin to grind, you can expect only to be crushed. The furthest my father got was a glimpse of my brother's case file. His death was summed up in a single word: accidental. On the other hand, the list of his crimes was long: drug trafficking, possession with intent to supply, illegally breeding animals, possession of firearms, organised crime, on it went. Nowhere did it say that he was an intelligent young man who knew about Aristotle and Kant, Zola and Stendhal, Dr Atl and Diego Rivera – names that were unfamiliar to those who killed him.

My father set the file down on the grey steel desk and said to the court secretary that these were lies, that his son had not deserved to die, that justice must be done. The secretary – in a clumsy attempt at comforting him – told him to be patient and trust in god's law. Trust in god? Trust in the serene being that had inspired his murderers?

In vain my father tried to contact Senator Molina, who would not return his calls. He contacted the lawyers of Ortiz, Arellano, Portillo & Associates who had helped in our case against the school. He met them, they listened attentively and asked him to phone the following day. They never answered. A secretary came up with dozens of excuses to avoid putting him through: they were at lunch, in a meeting, in court. After he had called a dozen times, the secretary took pity on him. "Please, Señor Valdés, don't keep calling, they wouldn't accept this case if you paid them triple their fee. It's a waste of time." A waste of time? His dead son, brutally, callously drowned by a group of religious fanatics, a waste of time?

I told my father that the only option left to us was revenge. Humberto, Josué and Antonio had been sent away to Lagos de Moreno until the situation calmed down. There, in the heartland of the Cristero Rebellion, the clandestine ultra-Catholic organisations would protect them. "But some day they will come back," I said to my father, "and then we'll kill them."

He was horrified to hear his fourteen-year-old son talk of death and revenge. "We're not like that," he declared. "We don't do such things." "So, what do we do?" I asked. (Don't you think your son would want us to punish his killers? Should we whisper over his grave: "Your murderers are walking free, searching for their next victim?") "Sooner or later I will get justice," he said. "No," I said, "sooner or later I will get my revenge." My father lifted my chin and looked me in the eye.

"Your humanity should never depend on that of others. If they are murderers, that does not mean you should be one."

We chose a spot on the edge of Avenida Churubusco for the burial, in the long grass beneath the trees. It was the first time I had left the house in the two months since my parents' death. It had rained that morning, but by the afternoon the sky was a clear, intense blue. We went there on foot. A few metres away, cars hurtled past at eighty kilometres an hour. It was a curious place for a cemetery, but Chelo wanted somewhere nearby that she could visit.

I wanted to bury it inside the jar. To know it was there, still preserved, in case I wanted to dig it up and take it home to watch it bob against the glass. Chelo refused. Any possibility of bringing it back from under the ground needed to be eradicated.

We removed the foetus from the jar. The rancid smell of formaldehyde nearly made me retch. We poured the liquid down the sink and Chelo delicately cradled the embryo in her hands. She rinsed it under cold water, washing it as though it were a baby. She turned to me.

"What should we call it?" she asked me.

"I don't even know if it's a boy or a girl," I said.

Chelo peered between the tiny webbed legs. There was no way to determine its sex, but Chelo said confidently: "It's a boy." She named him Luis. I could not understand her need to give the little amphibian a name. Chelo finished washing the body, looked at it for a moment and offered it to me.

"Wrap him up."

The feel of the skin against my fingers was strange. The viscid skin glistened in the lamplight. I looked into the tiny black dots of the eyes. I had often tried to see them as it floated in the jar. Now, for the first time, we came face to face.

I unfolded the red silk kerchief Chelo had bought for the occasion, ceremonially wrapped the body and placed it in a small wooden box that had once contained hazelnut nougat. Once it was closed, Chelo tied it with a red ribbon.

We arrived at the chosen place. King trailed behind, panting from the effort. He was old and fat and it was hard for him to scrabble up the embankment. I kneeled down next to one of the trees and used a trowel to dig a hole. It smelled of damp soil. A couple of earthworms wriggled away through the roots. Unintentionally, I cut one in half with the trowel. One half continued to wriggle while the other slithered into a hole.

King was curious, and poked his nose into the crack. I had to push him away so I could keep digging. Every time I pushed him aside, he clambered up on me to see what was going on. My trousers were covered with muddy paw prints. When I finished digging, Chelo handed me the box.

"Goodbye, Luis," she said and then walked away along a path. I wanted to call her back. She was the one who had persuaded me to arrange this burial, and now she was walking away. I watched her go. A truck passed, belching a black cloud of smoke. It distracted me just long enough to tear my eyes from Chelo and concentrate on the minuscule funeral instead.

I dug to a depth of sixty centimetres. I did not want some dog to dig Luis up and devour him. I placed the box at the bottom, covered it with a heavy stone and filled the grave with muddy soil. When I was done, I flattened the ground and covered it with grass. King sniffed the grave, scratched at it with his paw. I pushed him away and he stood, staring fixedly at the dirt and grass covering the grave.

I got to my feet and looked around. Chelo was sitting at the foot of one of the pylons along the main road. I walked over to her, King sticking close to me. When she saw me, she smiled sadly, held out her hand and then gently pulled me down to sit by her side.

"All done?"

I nodded. From the foot of the pylon, we had a view of the rooftops, including Barrera's roof, where Carlos had died. I stared at it for a second then turned to Chelo.

"I'll never cry again," I said.

"Don't be ridiculous, crying is good."

"Never again, really. I'll never cry again. I promise you."

Chelo looked at me and stroked my cheek.

"I believe you," she said.

The wapiti emerged from the pine forest and stopped. He sniffed the air and exhaled a plume of mist. For a moment, he stood motionless, mistrustful, then loped to join the herd of females grazing on a patch of grass in the snow. He began to graze. A shot rang out. The stag recoiled and stumbled a few paces. Frightened, the does scattered, then stopped to see what was happening. The stag stumbled and fell, his legs flailing.

Amaruq lowered the rifle. It had taken him the best part of the day to get close enough to shoot. There were fewer wapiti these days. Three brutal winters had decimated the numbers of wapiti, deer and buffalo. And the population of wolves had also decreased. The days of plenty were long gone. But with this one stag, Amaruq would have food for fifteen days and bait for the traps.

He made his living selling wolf pelts. His grandfather had taught him to hunt. "To hunt a wolf, you must be a wolf." And so, he was called Amaruq: "Wolf". His grandfather had insisted on the name, so that he would never forget the maxim. Amaruq was not pureblood Inuit. His father had been a furrier, a white Canadian of Scottish ancestry who bought pelts from his grandfather. This was how his father had met his mother, a shy Inuit.

His grandfather was estranged from his tribe. A feud with his brothers had become a brutal war. One day, his grandfather had beaten one of his brothers, leaving him badly wounded. The defeated brother had sworn revenge. His grandfather decided he should leave and, his wife and daughter sitting on a dog sled, they headed south-east, far from the caribou, the seals and the polar bears. Far from the unending ice. His tribe had traded seal fat, bear meat and caribou hides for flour, matches and lanterns. But in the south, people did not buy meat or fat. It was here that he learned the value of wolf pelts, for making coats for rich people. He could sell a pelt for ten, twenty dollars. A small fortune for a man like him.

Amaruq saw little of his father, a tall, stocky man with blue eyes and red hair. His father would arrive by train, stay a few nights in their house near the station and then leave until the following month. When Amaruq was ten years old, his father said that next time he would bring some children he wanted Amaruq to meet. Some weeks later he appeared with two boys and a girl. All three were blonde. The girl's eyes were blue, the boys' brown. Amaruq and the children greeted each other. At first they did not know what to do or say, but by the afternoon they were playing with the sled dogs' puppies. The following day they left again. Just before he set off, his father told Amaruq they were his brothers and sister. Amaruq never saw them again.

To hunt wolves, Amaruq had given up his sled. With the shortage of game, it was difficult to feed sled dogs. He had to kill at least one wapiti or deer every five days for their food. Instead, he himself pulled the sled that carried his supplies, his ammunition and his clothes. He became a solitary, nomadic hunter.

He would sit for hours on a mountain crag surveying the land through his binoculars. "Think like a wolf," he would say to himself. And he did think like a wolf. Often, he would manage to kill most of a pack, though he always left three bitches and one male so that they could reproduce.

But although Amaruq could think like a wolf, Nujuaqtutuq was different. The great grey wolf did not follow the usual patterns of his species, it was impossible to predict his movements. He led his pack to places that were increasingly remote and inaccessible.

For days, Amaruq followed them without a sighting. One morning he woke to find that they had circled his tent. Nujuaqtutuq's pack were what the Inuit call *nujuisiriartutuq*: animals that come close to a hunter and then vanish. A reckless wolf, a ghost wolf, Nujuaqtutuq was almost impossible to hunt.

Ghosts

Four times, Zurita and his officers raided the neighbourhood attempting to arrest my brother and his friends, and four times they left empty-handed. Carlos had become an obsession. The *comandante* did not know what he looked like; he had only a vague description provided by informants. He was not hunting Carlos because of his criminal activities, but because Carlos did not observe the tacit understanding between cops and criminals, according to which the *comandante* should receive a percentage of all earnings. Captain Zurita did not need to meet my brother, or make a deal. An envelope stuffed with cash would have sufficed. When one of the informants suggested that Carlos send the chief a bribe, my brother's response was clear: "Tell him to go fuck his mother." The informant delivered the message; war had been declared. Carlos would not fall into line and Zurita was not about to let some two-bit dealer challenge his authority and set a bad example to others.

He tried different methods to catch Carlos. He stationed officers outside our house waiting for Carlos to show up, but of course they never saw him. It was easy for my brother, he would simply walk along the rooftops and, rather than climbing down onto our street, Retorno 201, he would emerge on Río Churubusco or Retorno 207. Besides, La Modelito, where we lived, was a warren of lanes too narrow for cars. Only those who knew the area well could get in and out. If we were being chased by police, it was easy to lose them. We had only to weave through the lanes, hop over a wall and climb a flight of steps to the roof, and we were free. We learned to make fools of the uniformed cops who would leap out of the *julias* clutching their truncheons and chase us. Eventually the *julias* stopped their patrols. What was the point of driving in circles through empty streets? The uniformed officers disappeared, and Zurita's undercover cops arrived.

They thought they were invisible when they dressed as street sweepers or pushed carts selling sweet potatoes or tamales. But we spotted them immediately. One of them tried making a living from a sweet cart, but he was so clueless that he did not know the local tradition of "double or nothing", where a *merenguero* tossed a coin: heads, the meringue was free; tails, the customer paid double. When we suggested a coin toss, the idiot didn't know what we were talking about. He was obviously from some other city, and knew nothing of our ways or customs.

Sometimes plain clothes officers would turn up asking for "gear". They would pull up in a battered Volkswagen, roll down the window and ask if there was somewhere they could buy "gear". "Of course," we would say, and send them to the inscrutable Modelito, or to Pedro Jara, the leader of the "Nazis" – the largest and most violent gang in the area. An undercover cop dressed as a hippie was beaten half to death.

We only ever came down from the rooftops to kick a football, to buy snow cones from El Güero or live fish from Don Román, who always carried plastic bags filled with fish, frogs and turtles. We could recognise those who belonged in the barrio.

The Policía Judicial never managed to catch my brother. They could have tortured every one of our neighbours, but no-one knew how Carlos was able to disappear without a trace. He and his friends would simply climb up to the rooftops and vanish.

To be honest, Carlos's businesses hardly constituted serious criminal activity. He was not involved in theft, murder, kidnapping, grievous bodily harm or blackmail. He dealt in what he called "doors of perception", quoting William Blake, and, obviously, The Doors. A generation was struggling to distance itself from the preceding one, challenging a rigid status quo that reacted with brutality and repression. Not content with mass killings, incarceration and fierce political persecution, the regime sought to control every aspect of an individual's social life. A regime that understood that authoritarianism works better on a micro-level, where a citizen fears being arrested simply for stepping out into the street, sometimes simply because of how they look. Hence the armoured cars, the constant patrols, the officers harassing young men with long hair, the arbitrary reprisals, the undercover spies, the constant veiled threats. And therefore someone like Carlos had to be taught a lesson, punished, controlled; Captain Zurita intended to do just that.

That afternoon, Chelo did not go to her university lectures. After we buried Luis, we took a shower together in my parents' bathroom. She got out first, wrapped herself in a towel and went down to my bedroom. When I got there, I found her lying naked on the bed, curled into a foetal position. I lay down and curled myself around her. Feeling my presence, she shifted closer.

We slept until dark. When I woke, Chelo was no longer lying next to me. I got up and I found her in the living room, in the dark, sitting naked on the sofa where my grandmother always sat to watch television. Her body was lit by the glow of the upstairs bathroom light we had forgotten to switch off. She was crying. I sat next to her.

"Are you O.K.?"

She did not answer. I gently took her chin and turned her face towards me.

"What is it?"

She took a deep breath, then stared into my eyes.

"Didn't Carlos tell you?"

"Tell me what?"

Chelo took another deep breath and sighed.

"Forget it."

"What was Carlos supposed to tell me?"

She was clearly very hurt, because she bowed her head and began to sob bitterly. Her smooth back glistened in the light from the stairwell.

I stroked her, running my hands lightly down her back. She wept for some time. Then she lifted her face and looked at me. She tried to say something, failed, tried again and faltered until finally she managed to summon her courage.

"Carlos and I were sleeping together. I thought you knew."

No, no I didn't know. I closed my eyes. I felt sick. Confused.

"I was sleeping with him for three years."

A torrent of confessions followed. Carlos had been the second man Chelo had ever slept with, and they were still sleeping together the day before he died. One weekend, while I was with my parents in Oaxtepec, Carlos locked himself in the house with Chelo and they had sex in his bedroom, my grandmother's room, my parents' room, in the kitchen, on the stairs, in the living room, in the bathrooms, on the sofa, on my camp bed. It wasn't Canicas she had been fucking the night she fell from the Prietos' rooftop, but Carlos. After they had finished she pulled on her clothes – Carlos had completely undressed her – and, in a rush to get home, since Canicas was picking her up to take her to the cinema, she had thoughtlessly jumped and fallen between the rooftops. As she fell, she hit a ledge and rebounded towards the Coronet. This was what had saved her life.

Canicas had found out his girlfriend had had sex with someone on the rooftops and that was why he refused to visit her in the hospital. He never spoke to her again. Carlos did not find out about the accident until the following day and, feeling guilty, he visited her every morning while she recovered. He did not care if she slept with other people, something that bothered Chelo. She was in love with him. She wanted them to be together, to love each other, be faithful, maybe get married. But although Carlos was fond of Chelo and found her attractive, he did not want a relationship. This had been the beginning of Chelo's serial promiscuity. She'd fucked one guy after another. Whether or not she had a boyfriend, Chelo would sleep with whomever she felt like, and always with Carlos.

Then came what, for me, was the most difficult confession: Carlos had got Chelo pregnant. She knew that the baby had to be his because, at the point when she had conceived, he was the only guy she was sleeping with, and the only one she had ever allowed not to use a condom. Although he was aware of Chelo's sexual encounters, Carlos assumed that the baby was his. They agreed that she would have an abortion. They ended up in a backstreet clinic in San Rafael, the walls hung with images of the Virgin of Guadalupe, of saints and Christ crucified. The abortionist spoke in a slow, soothing voice, like a patronising, good-natured grandfather who had no qualms about charging them five hundred pesos.

After the abortion they trudged away, depressed, from that place that stank of chloroform and religion. Weeks went by, but the symptoms of Chelo's pregnancy persisted, she suffered from morning sickness, and her belly was swelling by the day. One month later, they went back to ask the doctor what was going on. He explained that the "product" could not always be removed, that some embryos are more resistant than others and that was not his problem. Now that the pregnancy was much further advanced, he said, the rate would be much higher. Carlos protested that they had already paid for the abortion, and that it was because of his incompetence that it had not worked. The doctor refused to back down: "Either you pay me what I charge or the young lady stays pregnant." They negotiated a price that Carlos paid through gritted teeth.

Chelo was taken into a room and twenty minutes later a secretary called my brother. "The doctor is asking you to come in," she said. Carlos found Chelo anaesthetised, with her feet in stirrups, lying on a makeshift table. Her thighs were drenched in blood. A nurse was using forceps to keep her tongue out of her mouth. Sitting in a swivel chair, the doctor – if he was a doctor – was scraping the wall of her uterus with a spoon. Blood was gushing out. Carlos paused to catch his breath. He was shocked to see Chelo like that. The doctor asked him to come closer: "I want you to see how nothing comes out when I scrape." Again and again the doctor inserted the spoon. "See? Nothing." He kept going until tiny fleshy pieces began to appear. "There it is," the doctor said. "It was hiding right at the back." The nurse noticed that my brother looked faint and, still holding the forceps restraining Chelo's tongue, gestured for him to leave.

Carlos went into the waiting room and sat on an orange plastic chair. An hour later, Chelo staggered out, clearly in pain. The doctor ushered them into his office. He gave Chelo a course of antibiotics to take, and advised her not to walk in high heels, not to leave the house for three days, to spend the rest of the afternoon in bed, to wear pads rather than tampons for the next five months and to come back and see him if she felt ill or bled excessively.

When he had finished, he swivelled in his chair and produced a plastic bag filled with red liquid. "I'm giving you this so you know that all of it came out," he said, laying the bag on the desk. It was the "product". Chelo looked. It was just possible to make out the small, dismembered foetus, the large head, the two black spots for eyes, the developing arms, the webbed legs. It was exactly the same age as the foetus I had kept in that jar.

Carlos and Chelo did not take the aborted embryo with them when they left – they assumed the doctor would dispose of it or burn it – but the bloody image of what might have been her child kept Chelo awake for months. In her mind, she had given him a name: Luis. In burying the embalmed foetus with me, Chelo was also burying the other Luis.

That night when I found her naked and sobbing in the dark living room, Chelo confessed her deepest regret: Carlos was dead, she would never have the chance to have a child with the man she loved. A child by Carlos, my brother.

Carlos my brother, Carlos my rival, Carlos inside her, touching her, Carlos everywhere, Carlos dead, Carlos alive, Carlos kissing the breasts

I had kissed, Carlos spilling his semen where I had spilled mine, Carlos sharing a womb with me again, Carlos in Chelo's saliva, in her sweat, in her juices, in her eyes, in her clitoris, in her heart, Carlos stroking her ass, licking her neck, Carlos the father of the aborted child of the woman I love, Carlos defeated, Carlos hounded, Carlos drowned, Carlos fucking her on my camp bed, on the rooftop between the clothes lines, Carlos stealing her from me even in death, Carlos in her tears, Carlos in our grief, Carlos spilled over the woman I love, Carlos impregnating the woman I love, Carlos absent, Carlos present, Carlos distant, Carlos near, Carlos saving me, Carlos burying me, Carlos help me, tell me what to do, Carlos take away this jealousy, Carlos, make her love me, Carlos please, Carlos help me.

I live in a world filled with ghosts, Chelo. Please don't summon any more. I cannot take it anymore.

Jungle

The jungle, the mosquitoes, the heat, the humidity. They move along the riverbank. A burst of gunfire. Bullets whistle over their heads. They throw themselves on the ground. Bradley falls, a bullet in his neck. Sean crawls towards him. The enemy fires. Sean calls his name. Bradley. Bradley. He turns, bleeding. Can you hear me? Bradley nods. Pressed to the ground, Sean reaches him; pulls him into the undergrowth. Blood is pumping from Bradley's neck. Bullets shriek. Two more men fall. The platoon retreats. An ambush. The shots are coming from several directions. Sean manages to get Bradley into a hollow, rips off a piece of his own shirt and ties it around his neck to stanch the blood. Sean hears someone whimper. He finds Paul. He has been shot in the belly. His intestines are a bubbling mess. Sean inches towards him. Bullets hit all around. The enemy fire intensifies. There are hundreds of them. There are only fifteen in the platoon. Four already dead. Sean reaches Paul, who screams in pain. The enemy trains its fire on the sound. Sean covers Paul's mouth as he writhes. Sean turns him onto his back and drags him away. The bullets keep coming. Paul is still whimpering. Sean tells him to shut up. Sean stumbles and Paul falls face down, his intestines are now caked with mud, with leaves and insects. You're gonna be fine, you're gonna be fine, Sean says over and over. They reach the hollow. Sean pushes Paul; he slithers to the bottom. Screams. Pain. Guts. Bradley looks at him in silence. Sean glances around. There are now seven dead. His friends. His comrades. He swallows hard. A bullet hits him in the shoulder, another in the stomach, another one in the calf. He falls and lies there. He hears the enemy's voices. The shouted orders of the platoon leader to

111

retreat. Still the bullets keep coming. He stares at the grass. At the sky. At the dead men around him. He closes his eyes and he slips into unconsciousness.

Three times, the mechanic tried to kill Colmillo, and each time the wolf-dog survived. First he tried to poison him, taking advantage of the fact that the Prietos kept him chained up. They could not risk him sticking his head through the railings and biting a passer-by. The mechanic tossed him balls of meat laced with rat poison. Colmillo gobbled them down. That night Fernando found the great wolf-dog laid out on the ground, eyes glassy, a pool of spittle at his mouth. They rushed him to the vet who pumped his stomach and saved him.

Frustrated, the mechanic got hold of a .32-20 revolver and shot Colmillo through the railings. He emptied the cylinder, all six bullets. Three shots hit the wall, one shattered a bucket. Two hit their target: one in the chest and another in his haunch. Colmillo was badly injured, but not fatally. The bullets missed every vital organ. Another trip to the vet. Two separate operations to remove the bullets and patch up the wounds.

The mechanic decided to go all out. For his final attempt, he tossed a Molotov cocktail made from a beer bottle that exploded in front of Colmillo. Burning petrol spread through the garage. The kennel was burnt to ashes, but the wolf-dog's coat was only singed. It took the Prietos more than an hour to douse the flames.

Tired of his attacks, Fernando and his father paid a visit to Pedro Jara, the leader of the "Nazis", and asked for help. The following day, eight men on motorbikes showed up at the mechanic's workshop. As soon as he saw them, the man tried to hide. The "Nazis" came in, dragged him by his hair onto the street, beat him to a bloody pulp and left the mechanic sprawled on the pavement with four broken ribs, concussion, a bloody nose and a gash on his forehead. His thirst for revenge vanished, never to return.

Sean Jordan Page. Born: Denver, Colorado. Age: 26. Height: 6'1".
Weight: 168 lb. Drafted into U.S. Army in 1963. Served multiple tours
in Vietnam. Honourable discharge due to injuries sustained in combat.
Medals: Bronze Star, Purple Heart. Multiple surgical procedures. Six
months in psychiatric hospital. Morphine addict. Multiple changes
of address. Last known U.S. address: Las Cruces, New Mexico. Crossed
the border at Del Rio, Texas in a 1958 Ford pickup truck with Montana
plates 15-1813. Current address: Retorno 207 #63, Colonia Unidad
Modelo, Delegación Ixtapalapa, México D.F., Zona Postal 13. Frequently
crosses the border and registers with military hospitals to keep up
his treatments. Suspected of trafficking and distributing narcotics.
Known as "El Loco".

In the barrio, there were regular dog fights. They had previously been
staged in garages or in the narrow alleys of La Modelito, but as a result
of police harassment the fights – like everything else – moved up onto
the rooftops.

The dog fights were not between pit bulls, but between ordinary
breeds. Barrera's Doberman against Veracruz's Alsatian, Tamal's
Dalmatian against the Aldamas' mongrel. They were vicious, bloody
fights. Ears torn, lips split, eyes gouged out, tongues ripped out. The
guys who laid bets regularly encouraged Fernando to put Colmillo up
against another dog, a mastiff–Great Dane cross they called "Sonny" in
honour of the American heavyweight boxer Sonny Liston, a huge,
fierce dog. Fernando refused. Like the rest of us, he hated the dog
fights. Our local football team in the barrio was called Canines, because
we loved dogs, and we hated the idea of making them try to kill one
another. But the gamblers pressed him, promised him double or
nothing: if Colmillo won, Fernando would take home five thousand
pesos. The offer was too tempting.

The fight took place on the flat roof over the Belmonts' place. Nearly a hundred and fifty people turned out to watch. "Sonny" was unbeaten – he had killed all fifteen dogs he had fought and the punters felt certain he would beat Colmillo. The bets were three to one in his favour.

Fernando and his brother appeared with Colmillo, muzzled and restrained by two chains to prevent him from attacking people. Even wearing a muzzle, Colmillo could still knock someone down or give them a brutal blow to the stomach.

The rooftop offered the perfect arena for the dog fights ever since Mr Belmont had tried to build the perfect pigeon loft – a waist-high concrete wall enclosing a space of eight metres by five. Mr Belmont had been obsessed with carrier pigeons since he'd seen a documentary about them carrying messages during World War I. Determined to become a breeder and to sell the birds to armies around the world, he had squandered all his savings on thirty pedigree pigeons. They survived for exactly a week before the local cats found a hole in their netting and devoured them all. Devastated, Mr Belmont tore down the cages, but the quadrangle remained. After a while, the local dog fighters began to hire the space. Two hundred pesos for a fight was easy money.

The Prietos stood with Colmillo in one corner of the pit, facing Sonny and his owners. The moment he saw Sonny, Colmillo's hackles rose and his whole body tensed. Fernando took off his muzzle. Colmillo did not move; he glowered at his rival.

The excited spectators spread out along the enclosing wall, whooping and whistling. Sonny glanced around, panicked by the noise. Colmillo did not seem to notice it.

What happened next was a catastrophe. When Fernando released Colmillo, the dog did not attack Sonny but the people sitting against the opposite wall, dodging past the other dog and hurling himself at a fat man drinking beer, sending him sprawling and sinking his teeth into the man's chest. Those around him tried to kick Colmillo off the

114

man, but the dog turned and savaged them. Body count: six people bitten, three of them seriously. More threats to kill the Prietos' dog.

Sean Jordan Page. Born: Denver, Colorado (*only child, parents divorced when the boy was four. Father remarried. Mother never remarried*). Age: 26 (*living in Mexico for the past three years*). Height: 6'1". Weight: 168 lb (*at one point during his convalescence he weighed only fifty kilos*). Drafted into U.S. Army in 1963 (*he had been planning to go to university when he was called up. The order was clear: you sign up or you go to jail*). Served multiple tours in Vietnam (*infantry soldier: cannon fodder*). Honourable discharge due to injuries sustained in combat (*small intestine ruptured by bullets leading to septicaemia that left him delirious for days, one shoulder shattered by a dumdum bullet, a suppurating wound in his right calf*). Medals: Bronze Star (*for extraordinary valour during acts of war*), Purple Heart (*awarded to those wounded or killed while serving*). Multiple surgical procedures (*reconstruction of the shoulder, surgery to save the leg from amputation, resection of the bowel*). Six months in psychiatric hospital (*as if a year and a half in operating theatres and shitting into a colostomy bag weren't enough, Sean received electric shocks every week to control his fits of rage*). Morphine addict (*clinging to the one substance that made it possible for him to walk, to sleep, to eat. Clinging to the one possibility of respite from his convulsions of pain. Is that addiction?*). Multiple changes of address. Last known U.S. address: Las Cruces, New Mexico (*gradually creeping closer to the Mexicans, growing more comfortable around los Pérez and los López than the Browns and the Jacksons*). Crossed the border at Del Rio, Texas in a 1958 Ford pickup truck with Montana plates 15-1813 (*after the divorce, his father had gone to live on a ranch near Helena, Montana. Sean saw little of him as a child but stayed on the ranch when he came back from 'Nam. They didn't understand one another. Sean was a stranger in his own country and a stranger in his father's house. When he left, his father gave him the pickup*). Current address: Retorno 207 #63, Colonia Unidad Modelo, Delegación Ixtapalapa, México D.F., Zona Postal 13. Frequently crosses the border and registers with military hospitals to keep up his treatments (*is it possible to get rid of chronic pain? Is there some way to switch it off, even for a couple of hours?*). Suspected of trafficking and distributing narcotics. Known as "El Loco" (*I was the one who gave him the nickname. El Loco is my brother Carlos's business partner and one of his best friends*).

Agüitas, Pato and Jaibo half-heartedly tagged along with me to the meeting with the Good Boys at Humberto's house. "Why the fuck are we even going? This is going to be so boring," Pato protested. I told him Carlos and I were curious to find out what they were like. This explanation did not satisfy them, and they had a point – why the fuck *were* we going?

We rang the doorbell and heard a loud buzzer inside. So loud that the neighbours' dogs barked. Josué opened the door and looked surprised to see us.

"Hello, we didn't think you'd show up. Please come in."

We followed him down a long hall lined with half-dead plants in grimy, broken pots, through a spartan living room with few pieces of furniture, and down the stairs to a basement. A basement was a novelty in the barrio. It was like a metaphor for everything that divided us. They hung out under their houses, we hung out on the roofs. We were closer to heaven, they to hell.

We were led into a room where twenty folding chairs were set up in a circle, there were tables piled with soft drinks, crisps, peanuts and paper cups and plates, and on the walls hung religious paintings, posters of biblical quotations and two large crucifixes. All the Good Boys were there. The minute Humberto saw us, he came over and shook hands.

"Welcome, I'm so glad you came!"

He seemed genuinely happy to see us. He offered us drinks. Jaibo poured himself three cups of Coke and drank them all in a row, then filled a paper plate with crisps and sat in a corner, eating them.

"Today we will be talking about a very interesting subject," Humberto said, "and Father Chava will be joining us."

Humberto would not let us sit together. We were to split up so we could get to know the rest of the group. I sat next to him and we chatted for a few minutes with whoever was next to us. Then Humberto got to his feet and gestured for us all to do the same. Everyone stood, serious and silent. Eduardo, a short boy with a shrill voice, welcomed us to the meeting of Young People Committed to Christ, the south-east chapter of the Young Catholics Movement.

"Join us in the love of Christ, seek within you for his kindness, his love and his forgiveness," he said.

Pato and I exchanged a look. If this was just the beginning, what should we expect at the end? Antonio started to speak. "Let us pray." The Good Boys lowered their heads and started to mumble the Lord's Prayer. Neither Pato, Agüitas nor I knew the words. Only Jaibo seemed to follow, though afterwards he admitted he had been muttering meaningless gibberish.

After they had finished, the Young People Committed to Christ crossed themselves several times. With a priestly air, Humberto extended his arms and gestured for us to sit, then pointed at Saúl, a dark-skinned guy with black hair.

"Saúl, what is the topic for today?"

"Today I will be talking about sex," he said without batting an eyelid, as though he was talking about shampoo or trigonometry. Pato sat up in his chair. At least the subject sounded interesting.

"What have you prepared for us on the subject of sex?" Humberto asked.

Saúl opened a briefcase, took out a folder containing eight typed pages and started to read. "Sex is one of the purest of all human

117

activities if it occurs in the context of love, and of the Christian doctrine of marriage. The sexual relations between a man and a woman should at all times express their love for Christ our Lord . . ."

The sermon went on for another twenty minutes. The more he read, the more disturbing I found it. Unsurprisingly, the words "sin", "penance", "virginity", "chastity" and "purity" came up regularly, and Christ was mentioned at least fifty times. Pato and Agüitas could not believe what they were hearing. Jaibo was not listening; he was munching his crisps.

When Saúl's sermon was over, Humberto turned to Jaibo.

"What did you think of Saúl's presentation?"

Jaibo stared at him, then looked to me for help.

"I thought it was cool," he said, spluttering crumbs.

"Why did you think it was 'cool'?" Humberto inquired solemnly.

"Well, it's just . . . what he said was, like, dope, it was fly, it was badass."

"I would ask that you use words that we understand, Javier." It felt strange, hearing Humberto refer to Jaibo by his real name.

"You don't know the word 'fly'?"

"No," Humberto said. "Now please give us your opinion on what Saúl just said."

Jaibo thought about his answer.

"I think the stuff he said about sex with love and Christ is fantastic."

"Why is it fantastic?"

My friendship with Jaibo was not based on his intellectual abilities but his loyalty and his sense of humour. Nobody could make us laugh the way he could. Now Humberto was cornering him because he knew Jaibo was the weak link in the group.

"Why?"

"Because screwing is nicer when you're in love," Jaibo said, intimidated. The word "screwing" immediately made the Good Boys anxious. Antonio was the first to speak up.

"We asked you to not swear on the street, and now you come and do it here, with Christ as our witness."

Jaibo turned and looked at us, confused.

"'Screwing' is a swear word?" he said.

"Of course it is," replied Humberto, irritated.

"What do you call it, then?"

"Having sexual relations."

"Ah! O.K. then, I think it's good to have sexual relations if baby Jesus is looking out for us," Jaibo said.

"Well done, Javier," Humberto said, "but that is not enough. We need to look out for ourselves to make sure we do not give in to temptation."

Humberto had not been conceived in holy wedlock. His mother became pregnant with him at sixteen, after a one-night stand in Acapulco with a guy she never heard from again. She was the black sheep of a thoroughly conservative family; she had wanted to get a termination but could not find the money. When the baby was born, her father threw her and her son out onto the street. Over the years, she had a lot of different boyfriends. Every week, Humberto would find a different guy at the breakfast table. Some stank of sweat, some of booze, some beat his mother and some beat him. A fractured jaw, bloody noses, bruises. His mother wasn't always able to leave work early enough to pick him up from school on time, and although her parents never forgave her, they looked after their grandchild for the eight hours she was at work, and the many hours she spent with whoever was her current lover. Humberto grew up in the shadow of a strict, religious grandfather who never missed an opportunity to disapprove of his daughter's behaviour. Humberto gradually absorbed his grandfather's distorted view of religion and began to judge his mother and everything she represented: adolescent sex, abortion, multiple partners, neglectful mothers, abuse; it warped his mind. Even as Humberto reinvented himself as a young man who was moral, chaste, upstanding and religious, deep down he never stopped being the vulnerable, intolerant, unstable boy he had been as a child. For years his nickname in the barrio had been "basta", short for "bastard", but he soon got them to stop calling him that, through threats and violence.

"We should respect our bodies and above all respect the bodies of women," Humberto said. "That is why it is important for men to remain unpolluted and for women to remain virgins until they are joined in holy marriage."

The Good Boys all nodded. Pato and I exchanged another look. What Humberto was saying sounded absurd, even funny, but it wasn't. The moment had come to show them that we were different.

"Do you know what Viking men thought about virgins?" I said.

The Good Boys turned to me, attentive. And I launched into my story.

I go into my dead parents' bedroom
                the curtains closed the dust
                                floating
the bed still unmade
                        where they slept the night
                        before the accident
hurtling towards the cliff screams the shriek of metal the broken glass the
fall tumbling in space the first crash
                                the second crash
                                        the certainty
                                                of the end
                                                        the
last thoughts the door ripped off the windscreen shattered the
smell of petrol the car rolling over and over
                                        cactus sky rocks
sky cactus sky shouts
and
                                        then the silence
                                        the wind
                                                the wardrobe
door open my dead parents' clothes the photos on the dresser
the suspended time of
                        their suspended smiles
                                        the photo of my father
wearing his best suit on the day of
                his fifth birthday my mother sitting on a bench

in a park when she was fifteen
                              their coffins side by side in the
funeral home
at home the unwashed clothes that still smell of them
                    the sweet smell of my mother
                    the sweet smell of my father
the dresser drawers
          my father's neat and orderly
                         my mother's a
little disorganised
the wedding dress hanging at the back of the wardrobe
                         my father's suits
his ties his five pairs of shoes
                         my mother's tights
the underwear
                    that she would never let me see that she
          would wash
                    secretly
their bodies at the bottom of a ravine a car
two lives destroyed
destroyed
a stash of love letters in a chocolate box
some condoms hidden among my father's socks
the books they were reading on their bedside tables
their medicines in their amber phials
the shape of their heads on each of their pillows
the alarm clock set for five thirty a.m.
my mother's hairs on the brush
                         my father's razor
with the last traces of his stubble
          their wedding photographs
a baby picture of Carlos

122

                    a baby picture of me
the pyjamas we wore as children sealed in plastic bags with locks of
our hair stuck to a card
                              an upturned car wheels spinning in the air
                              and two dead people face down
a funeral in the rain
a wedding under the moon
                    the cufflinks that belonged to my father to my
grandfather to my great-grandfather
                    a medal that belonged to my mother a coin that
belonged to her mother that belonged to her mother's mother
                    documents neatly ordered in box files
taxes electricity bills telephone bills
                              my dead mother
leaning against the passenger door
                              my dead father
crushed against the steering wheel
                    the roof of the car pressed against their heads
my father's slippers
his grey dressing gown
my mother's sandals
her pink dressing gown her razor her lipsticks her earrings her
                                        toothbrush
the half-used tube of toothpaste
the soaps they used to wash their skin, the soap I will never touch
again
          the chinchilla stole that Carlos gave my mother
              the rabbit fur coat he gave my father
the nights
          in this bed where they made love where they slept
              where they woke before going to work where they woke
before taking the motorway to their deaths.

                                                                    my
mother's hairspray
my father's cheap aftershave the stick deodorant that
smells of him
his smell mingled with
the smell of petrol mingled with
the smell of his blood mingled with
the smell of death mingled with
the smell of the bisnaga that stuck to their bodies
                                        tumbling in the air
slamming against rocks
            the jewellery the baubles
the foreign coins collected on their trip to Europe
which they hid, ashamed
                        their son dying while they were on holiday while
they are in a car whirling and spinning
while I am sitting on the edge of their bed staring at the room
they left empty
                        and in the mirror I see the son they left an

o r p h a   n.

Rivers

Amaruq wondered whether he should cross the frozen river. Nujuaqtutuq had led the pack across two days earlier. His grandfather had been right: this wolf was his master. In order to follow him, he had had to ignore his better judgement and now found himself in unknown territory. He did not recognise these mountains, these snowy plains that stretched out into the distance. He had never encountered a pack this nomadic. When prey is scarce, wolves will travel up to twenty kilometres a day, but nothing like these distances. Still Nujuaqtutuq kept leading the pack further northward.

Amaruq had not seen a wapiti or a deer for a long time. They seemed to have vanished from the forests. There were no tracks, nothing to suggest their presence. The winter was bitter, the coldest in a century. For the past four years they had experienced the harshest winters. But that alone did not explain their total disappearance.

Amaruq only had two bullets left. He had used the others to kill two wapiti, a red deer, two lynxes and a lone wolf. Now, far from home, he would need to use his last two bullets wisely. He had meat enough to last twenty days, but he had been tracking Nujuaqtutuq and the pack for more than two months. He reckoned that his house by the train station was at least a hundred and fifty kilometres due south, and he had seen no signs of civilisation since: no towns, no cabins, not a single human being.

He stared at the icy river. He had to decide whether to cross or turn back home. To carry on could mean death. The temperature was still plummeting and his caribou coat was torn. He had patched it with a piece of wapiti pelt, but he still felt the wind on his chest. He had

125

suffered hypothermia more than once. He knew the drowsiness that lulled you first to sleep and then towards death, the brutal headaches that could last for weeks afterwards, the toes turning black with frost-bite in his boots, the gangrene that could set in and the possibility of losing your toes. No, Amaruq did not want to die. If he crossed the river he risked never coming back; if he did not, he would never again have the chance to hunt Nujuaqtutuq. The big grey wolf would disappear into the mountains to the north, and Amaruq would be condemned to hunt him through many more lives before finally managing to catch him. No, this was the moment to follow him. He would not give up.

Dragging the sled behind him, Amaruq crossed the river.

After confessing about her relationship with Carlos, Chelo told me she needed time to think. "Think about what?" I asked. "To think, just think," she said. Of all my rivals, my beloved brother was the one rising from his grave to come between me and the woman I loved. To think about what? About the afternoons she had spent making love with my brother? About their aborted son? Would I have to console her for her lost loves, Carlo and Luis? What the fuck did Chelo need to think about? I loved her, I wanted her here with me. Sooner or later she would walk out of my life – I had known that from the start – but after such a brutal confession? She couldn't leave me now, having just ripped the ground from under my feet, leaving me fighting an avalanche of doubts and fears.

Chelo disappeared. I promised not to call, not to look for her. Not that this stopped me calling her house in the early hours of the morning. Sometimes she would answer. I wanted to say: "I love you, I need you, please come back." But I would simply listen to her voice and then hang up. Chelo was my country; the only land where I belonged. Now she had gone away to "think". Think about what?

My friends knew that, to all intents and purposes, Chelo lived with me, so they rarely visited. They wanted to give us privacy, but when they found out that she had left me they came to see me. They brought bread, a mayonnaise jar (without foetus), some ham, a tin of jalapeños, two family-sized bottles of Coca-Cola and a handful of Gansito chocolate bars. With Chelo gone, they assumed there would be no food in the house, so they brought enough to have a picnic on the back terrace.

Pato prepared sandwiches while Jaibo and Agüitas dragged the chairs and the dining table out into the yard. It was a warm, sunny day, with cloudless skies after weeks of thunderstorms.

We sat down to eat. King lay by the table, gobbling up pieces of leftover bread. My friends tried to console me the only way they knew how. They told stupid jokes and gossiped about the neighbours from the barrio: the Richards were going on holiday to Disneyland; Jorge Padilla was about to finish his veterinary degree; Chato Tena was about to play his first match for Club Necaxa; the Rovelos' car had been stolen; Ernesto Martínez had gone to live in Costa Rica. Such titbits would have interested me once, but right now I couldn't bring myself to care. But there was one piece of news that got my attention.

"The Prietos are moving to a more upmarket neighbourhood, and their dad decided to have Colmillo put down," Agüitas told me.

"Put down?" I asked. This was the phrase we'd used to describe snapping the chinchillas' necks, a nice way of avoiding the word "slaughter".

"Yes," replied Agüitas. "They're thinking of having him put to sleep next week."

Putting him to sleep – another euphemism for "kill" – meant injecting the dog with a powerful anaesthetic that would render him unconscious and then stop his heart.

"Why don't they take him with them to their new house?" I asked.

"The parents are sick and tired of that dog. They don't want any trouble in their new neighbourhood, it's very posh," Pato said.

"But Colmillo isn't a dog, he's a wolf-dog," I said.

"Whatever, Cinco, they're still going to put him down," Pato said.

We finished the picnic as night drew in. My friends made me laugh, entertained me, helped me get through at least one day. When they left, they all hugged me. Agüitas and Jaibo headed off and Pato stayed behind for a second.

"Cinco, do you want me to track down Chelo and tell her to come?"

"No, let her be."

"Do you want me to stay and keep you company?"

"No thanks, I'd rather be alone."

"That's cool. If you need anything, just call."

He smiled and raced to catch up with the others. I went back into the house. King was lying outside my bedroom, snoring. When he sensed me, he pricked up his ears and got up to lick my hand. I gave him a few firm pats and he lay down again. I never let him sleep with me. His snoring kept me awake.

I stretched out on the camp bed, eyes open, staring into the darkness. I heard Colmillo howl. A deep, piercing howl that could probably be heard streets away. Soon he would be silenced forever. They would muzzle him and bind his legs. The vet would fill a syringe with Pentobarbital and ask Fernando and his brothers to hold him still, then find a vein in his hind leg and slowly inject the lethal drug. Colmillo would go to sleep and never wake up. Colmillo dead, with no offspring. Colmillo dead, and with him the invisible pack he howled to every night; gone forever the spirit of the wild within him, the icy plains, the prey he had never hunted, gone forever the snowy nights of his ancestors.

I closed my eyes and drifted to sleep, listening to his howls.

Carlos introduced me to the guy one night. He was of above average height and spoke very good Spanish. I asked how he had learned it. "Listening to Mexican radio," he said. There were two metal tags around his neck. He caught me looking. "Dog tags," Sean explained, showing them to me. "If you get killed in battle, these have your details so that they can work out who you are. Often as not, they are the only way to identify a soldier." He knew what he was talking about. He had seen G.I.s blown to bits by landmines, seen black, smouldering heaps of bodies inside shelled vehicles, bodies half buried in mud, their guts spilling out, their faces obliterated by bullets.

That night Sean told me why he had settled in the barrio. One day while he was in military hospital, trying to ease his pain with morphine, he had decided to leave the U.S. and move to Mexico. He had fought a war for his country, but his country had not fought for him. When he came back from 'Nam they had locked him in a psychiatric clinic, pumped 460 volts through his brain, stupefied him. By the time he was finally released, he felt adrift. Three of his army buddies had killed themselves. Two more were in prison for armed robbery. He couldn't get a job. Women were afraid of him, they found his tattoos hideous. No decent woman would date a man with tattoos. No-one except whores or old, fat chicks. "A Purple Heart is only good for stirring coffee," a sergeant had once told him. He was right. The heroes of this war waged in a strange Asian country were pariahs. Infected with syphilis or gonorrhoea, reeking of napalm and blood, physically and emotionally stunted, thousands of Vietnam vets came home to a country that turned its back on them. Sean had decided to go in search of a new homeland in Mexico, somewhere he could rebuild himself.

He had crossed the border at Del Río. Exactly halfway across the International Bridge, he stopped the Ford pickup, got out and looked at the wide river snaking between the two countries. Americans called it the Río Grande, Mexicans, Río Bravo. He placed one foot on the American side, the other on the Mexican, and stood for a few seconds, divided. Then he took a step towards the Mexican bank, raised a hand and called out, "Goodbye, U.S.A.!", climbed back into his pickup and drove across the bridge into his new country.

He pulled up at the customs post to register the pickup. Any car with American plates required a permit once outside the 25-mile buffer zone. He walked into an office with a single desk, and a tall, thin customs official wearing sunglasses. The ceiling fan didn't work and the air in the office was stale and muggy. "Even the walls reeked of sweat," Sean said.

The process required filling in some forms on an ancient typewriter. Sean asked the official if he could do it by hand. Impossible, the documents were valid only if typed. There were so many forms that it took Sean an hour to do it. When he had finished, the customs official came out to check his luggage, made him open the suitcases and inspected every item, then asked whether he was carrying any electronic equipment.

Sean showed him an old battery-operated radio. The customs official told him it was a prohibited item in Mexico, but for twenty dollars he might make an exception. Sean handed over the money without protest. Although the transistor was barely worth three bucks, it had belonged to his grandfather, who had used it to listen to night-time talk shows, country music and the news bulletin announcing the end of World War II. He was not about to hand it over to a corrupt customs officer. He was asked whether he had anything to declare. "Nothing," Sean said. The customs officer walked listlessly around the pickup, opened the door and checked under the seats, then went back into the office and reappeared with some stamped documents. "All done, you can go," he told him.

Sean got back into the pickup and drove off. Luckily the customs officer had not thought to check the icebox. Hidden inside bottles of milk was enough morphine to last him three months. He had legally bought five ampoules, to which he was entitled as a wounded veteran. The other fifty he'd bought from a hospital clerk who'd pilfered them from the pharmacy, one by one.

He wandered the streets of Ciudad Acuña, passing the restaurants and bars for gringos on the main avenue. The blistering heat was suffocating. How could people go outside, when it was more than forty degrees in the shade? The heat was so intense it felt almost solid.

He asked a man for the best hotel and followed the directions to a few scattered rooms in the desert, off the motorway towards Piedras Negras. He took room 13F. The owner's birthday was March 13, and he'd decided that all the rooms should begin with 13, thereby defying superstition.

He entered the room and switched on the fan, peeled off his shirt, picked up a tourist brochure lying on the ramshackle built-in desk and threw himself down onto the bed to read it. Ciudad Acuña was named after a poet who had killed himself at the age of twenty-four after being spurned by a girl called Rosario, he read. This was the moment he began to love Mexico; he had just crossed the border and already the country was surprising him: a sweltering city that owed its name to a suicidal poet.

"Seriously?"

"Yes, honestly, that's what they were saying."

Carlos couldn't believe what I told him about the meeting with the Good Boys.

"They're really stuck in the Middle Ages?"

"Worse."

After I had told them about the Vikings and their ideas about virginity, the Good Boys had launched into a tirade about "women of easy virtue". "You're talking about a barbarous people. Their view of things is wrong," Humberto spluttered angrily. "It is insulting to our mothers, our sisters. Who could love a sinful woman who luxuriates in the miasma of sex . . ." (I was surprised by his poetic streak) ". . . a woman who does not even respect herself?" He could barely contain his fury. He enumerated the virtues that any decent woman should possess. She should be demure, faithful, discreet, attentive, obedient,

131

home-loving, maternal (virtues his mother singularly lacked).

"Well," I said, "I've gone once, and I don't want to go back."

"You have to go back."

"What for?"

"So that you don't fall into sin."

"No, seriously, what for?"

"Because I've heard rumours about those fucking goody-goodies."

"Like what?"

"Like that they want to destroy my business."

"Those guys?"

"Yeah. A week ago, a couple of guys in hoods beat up four of my clients. Fucked them over really badly and told them that it was in their interest to stop taking dope because they were planning to finish off all the junkies."

"I don't think they'd dare do something like that."

"I think it's for the best if you learn your onions."

Know your onions, keep an eye out, eyeball, rubberneck, get the gen, know your two-by-twos – in other words, keep shtum and get as much information as possible.

"Go with the flow. Tell them stories from the Bible, not stuff about Vikings and their horny women."

We laughed. I decided to stop taunting them. My goal was to blend in, not antagonise.

"The 'Europe within Reach' itinerary includes visits to the most important places of the Old World: Madrid, Barcelona, Paris, the chateaux of the Loire valley, Rome, Florence, Milan, Bruges, London, San Sebastián, Brussels. We will visit palaces, castles, museums, restaurants, magnificent avenues, winding backstreets and beautiful landscapes."

My father read the itinerary again and again. As newlyweds my parents had not had the money to take a real honeymoon, they could barely afford three days in Veracruz. Their dream had always been to cross the Atlantic and see Europe. They were able to pay for the trip in instalments after the school gave us scholarships. They spent their nights before the trip researching the places they were going to visit, poring over the *Encyclopaedia Britannica* or the *Illustrated Larousse*, comparing notes about the places that most appealed to them. They almost always agreed. My parents genuinely got along.

Carlos had offered to pay for the trip. My father had been offended. He had never accepted a peso from anybody, and he was not about to let his son give him money. My parents were blissfully ignorant of Carlos's alternative business, until after his death, when Captain Zurita made sure they heard every last detail about their son's illegal activities.

Two months after Carlos's death, the postcards my parents had sent from Europe began to arrive. One after the other. Some were for my grandmother, others for Carlos or me. The antiquated Mexican postal service slowly delivered every chapter of the trip my parents ended up cursing.

Every postcard was suffused with their love for us. They told us about the galleries, the churches, the restaurants, told us to look after each other, to take care of our grandmother, to remember how much they loved us. Worried about our ability to deal with everyday tasks, my mother scrawled instructions in the margins: the electricity bill, the water and gas bills, how to do a weekly supermarket shop. They were so excited about their trip, they sent postcards almost every day, cards that, when they arrived, brought only grief. Six months later, they were still arriving. My parents didn't throw away any of the cards they had sent to Carlos or my grandmother. When I was clearing out my room after their death, I found them in a folder, neatly catalogued by date and location. One by one, I read them all. My dead writing to my dead. And yet life still pulsed and throbbed, diaphanous. The beating heart of life captured in my parents' handwriting.

The ancient Greeks spoke of a remote land beyond the North Wind: Hyperborea. Here, they said, for half the year the sun did not set, for half it did not rise.

Travelling by sea at night was inadvisable. Tall cliffs, shaped like the bodies of women, claimed lives and wrecked any boat that came near.

It was believed that those who lived in Hyperborea did not know sadness. They were always happy. The land was fruitful and the four rivers that crossed it teemed with fish and frogs. Possessed of a natural immortality, its inhabitants were able to choose the moment of their death. This was not suicide, but a joyful way to bid farewell to life. They would celebrate with the community, and then head to the highest point of a cliff and hurl themselves into the sea.

The people of Hyperborea worshipped Apollo, who it was said visited this far-flung land every nineteen years in order to rejuvenate himself. It was also believed that it was to here that Medusa was exiled.

The Hyperboreans, they said, were the first humans, happy giants.

Nietzsche wrote about them in *The Antichrist*:

"Let us look each other in the face. We are Hyperboreans – we know well enough how remote our place is. 'Neither by land nor by water will you find the road to the Hyperboreans': even Pindar, in his day, knew *that* much about us. Beyond the North, beyond the ice, beyond *death* – *our* life, *our* happiness . . . We have discovered happiness; we know the way; we acquired our knowledge of it from thousands of years in the labyrinth . . . We thirsted for the lightning and great deeds; we kept as far as possible from the happiness of the weakling, from 'resignation' . . . There was thunder in our air; nature, as we embodied it, became overcast – *for we had not yet found the way.* The formula of our happiness: a Yea, a Nay, a straight line, a *goal . . .*"

Freedom

Days passed and still Chelo did not come back. I would call her house in the early hours hoping that she would answer, but her parents always picked up. I was tormented by jealousy and doubt. Where was she? Was she with somebody else?

Nights were unbearable. The silence and the solitude made sleep difficult. Sometimes I would lie in Carlos's bed and read until dawn. Or I would go up to the roof, sit on the edge and look at the endless expanse of water tanks, clothes lines and antennas.

Only the presence of King and my grandmother's parakeets Vodka and Whisky stopped me losing my mind. Vodka, the female, was yellow, Whisky was pale blue. My grandmother had put a log in their cage, and the birds had carved it into a nest. The wood shavings from their day's labour would fall onto the floor of the cage, and Whisky would nudge them through the bars while Vodka went on pecking. The nest took a month to finish. For some time afterwards, Vodka did not emerge. Whisky anxiously hopped from perch to perch, picking up seeds and dropping them into the hollowed-out log.

One day we heard the clamorous high-pitched squeaks of four featherless chicks, two yellow, two blue, their eyes still gummed closed. For the first time in weeks Vodka emerged from the nest, fluttered her wings, then, taking some seeds and some water in her beak, went back to regurgitate food for her chicks. Whisky seemed to be in charge of keeping the place tidy, removing the fragments of eggshell from the nest and dropping them on the floor of the cage.

My grandmother had enjoyed watching the little chicks grow, and would sometimes feed them sugar solution with a pipette. Once their feathers had grown out she gave them to her cousins as presents, and from that moment, flocks of parakeets migrated through our extended family. By now, Whisky and Vodka must have had close to two hundred descendants, all condemned to live in cages fitted with two perches, a water dispenser, a log and some birdseed.

Every morning at daybreak, Whisky and Vodka would begin to chatter. My grandmother had always talked to them, hoping they might learn a few words, but nothing. Not "Hello", not "Pretty Boy", not even "Juan". Their morning chirruping had always annoyed me, but now that I was on my own, it made me feel less lonely. I too tried and failed to get them to talk.

One afternoon I decided to set them free. I took them out of the cage, carried them to the kitchen, opened the back door and set them on the back of a chair, perched between freedom and captivity. For a long while, they stayed motionless, unsure what to do. Vodka was the first to take to her wings. She fluttered through the kitchen and landed on the top of the cage. Whisky followed. After that I left the cage door open so they could come and go as they pleased. If they wanted to stay it was their own choice; if they wanted to escape, they could fly through the open windows. It was their right.

The parakeets hardly left their cage. They flew in circles around the living room, awkwardly avoiding furniture and ornaments. Despite the open back door, they never tried to leave. The furthest they ever went was my bedroom. They perched on my camp bed for a moment and almost immediately flew back again.

Morphine, an opiate first isolated in the nineteenth century by the German chemist Friedrich Sertürner, who named it *morphium* after the Greek god of dreams. It is used medicinally as an analgesic to relieve severe acute or chronic pain. Morphine produces feelings of euphoria in those who consume it, and over time became a recreational drug. It is highly addictive. Sudden interruption of consumption can trigger mild to severe symptoms of withdrawal. Morphine is a controlled substance.

Lysergic acid diethylamide, better known by the initials L.S.D. First synthesised by the Swiss chemist Albert Hoffmann in the late 1930s, L.S.D. is a psychedelic drug that affects the perception of reality and produces hallucinations similar to those experienced in dreams. L.S.D. was initially prescribed for psychiatric use and became popular as a recreational drug in the Sixties. Although medical research has produced no evidence that the drug causes lasting mental or physical harm, L.S.D. is illegal and classified as a controlled substance.

People had been dealing marijuana and cocaine in the barrio for years. The warren of alleys in La Modelito were perfect for trafficking. A dealer would lead the buyer down one alley, hand over the stash and then lead them out a different way. It was impossible for the buyer to create a mental map of where they'd been. Sales were monitored by armed lookouts on the rooftops. In case of any problems – inquisitive policemen, informants or disagreements with clients – these snipers would fire a warning shot. It was rare for them to have to fire a second shot. And rarer still for there to be fatalities. In this business, no-one wanted to have blood on their hands.

The market was controlled by the "Nazis". It was impossible to compete with them. Ruthlessly organised and vicious, they eliminated anyone who tried to muscle in on their territory. Their turf included vast swathes of Coyoacán, Benito Juarez and Ixtapalapa. Their leader, Pedro Jara, had cut a deal with the cops to keep the peace and if a new chief of police tried to shut them down, they would lash out with extraordinary violence, burning everything – buses, restaurants, pharmacies – and knocking over traffic lights and lamp posts. And the chief of police would have no choice but to revert to the original deal. With the "Nazis", keeping to your word was imperative.

Carlos's "merchandise" was L.S.D. and morphine. He used the word "merchandise" because it was a neutral commercial term, with no criminal connotations, and one that implied a serious, thriving business. The "Nazis" tolerated Carlos because he was not a direct competitor, and because it was extremely difficult to get hold of L.S.D. and morphine in commercial quantities.

Carlos considered himself to be a purveyor of unique substances. He marketed his business as a means of accessing "vital cognitive experiences", "journeys of perception", "altered states", and "creative hallucinations". Sensibly consumed, "none of the merchandise I sell causes health problems".

His clients didn't live in our barrio. The majority were from wealthy families. During his years at private school, Carlos had befriended rich classmates who thought of themselves as hippies. Now, they were to be the first link in the long chain of customers to whom Carlos sold his merchandise.

The business started up when Sean Page first arrived in the barrio. Carlos ran into him at La Escondida, the little grocery store at Retorno 202. El Loco was buying a six-pack of beer. Carlos noticed his tattoos and asked if he was a sailor. Sean said that he was a Vietnam vet, they got to talking, and ended up sitting on our roof until eight in the morning. It was the start of a close friendship conducted in Spanish, Spanglish and English.

Sean was renting a service room on a roof on Retorno 207. He had ended up in the barrio by accident. Queuing at the U.S. Embassy to get his Veteran's I.D. Card, he had run into a *chicano* who had also fought in 'Nam, and while they were waiting the guy mentioned that one of his cousins had recently been widowed and was renting a room in her house to make ends meet. After they left the embassy, they went to see the cousin. Sean thought the room seemed expensive and asked if he could rent the maid's room instead. She agreed and he moved in that night.

In no time, Carlos and Sean came to trust one another. In his tiny room on the rooftop, Sean showed Carlos his scars and told him about his chronic pain and his dependence on morphine. Sean took the ampoules of morphine out of the small fridge where he kept his food and showed them to my brother. Carlos asked if morphine was like cocaine. "No," Sean said. "It's much better." Sean expected Carlos to ask him if he could try a hit, but he didn't. The idea for a business venture was percolating in my brother's mind. He asked if he could have an ampoule to take to a coke addict he knew, to compare the effects.

A few days later Carlos brought good news: the junkie had preferred the morphine to cocaine and said that he would recommend it to his junkie friends. Carlos asked Sean if he would be willing to let him sell it, but Sean said he needed the morphine for his chronic pain.

"Don't you have some way of getting more?" asked Carlos.

"Yeah, in a hospital back in Texas."

"How many more?"

"Forty, maybe fifty amps."

"Could you get two hundred?"

Sean laughed. It was a ridiculous quantity, it would be impossible to get it across the border. Besides, where would they come up with the cash to pay for it?

"You find the morphine, I'll pay for it. And don't worry about customs. I'll give them a little backhander."

Sean was surprised by my eighteen-year-old brother's confidence. He knew nothing about Carlos's flair for business and his successful chinchilla breeding operation. Carlos saw morphine as a massive opportunity and intended to take it as far as it would go.

For help in setting up his new venture, Carlos turned to his friend Diego Pernía, known to everyone as El Castor Furioso, "The Angry Beaver", because of his buck teeth and his tendency to solve problems with his fists. Diego was a tall skinhead who'd briefly made ends meet by selling weed. He and Carlos had been friends since they were kids. Once an argument had turned into a brawl and Carlos knocked him out cold. The following day, El Castor Furioso appeared with a baseball bat looking for revenge and found Carlos waiting with his own bat. They looked at one another and burst out laughing. They never fought again, and for years they watched each other's backs, until the day that Carlos drowned, and Diego was arrested and sentenced to fifteen years in prison.

Sean and Carlos met him and agreed that Sean would travel to hospitals in Dallas and Laredo to try and get hold of the morphine ampoules. Diego would go with him, so he could discreetly pay off customs officials and look after the merchandise. Though it was a long detour, Sean felt that Acuña was the easiest place to cross the border unchecked.

Carlos handed over three thousand dollars to an astonished Sean. They had only known each other for a few weeks and already Carlos trusted him with his money. "I could steal it," he joked. "If you did, you'd be missing out on the best business opportunity of your life," my brother said.

It was not easy to get the morphine. The hospital porter in Dallas could only supply forty ampoules, and was terrified of getting caught if he stole any more. Sean and "the Beaver" drove to the military hospital in Laredo. As the pharmacist filled out his prescription, Sean leaned over and asked her if she could get any more.

"What do you mean?" the woman said, eyeing him narrowly.

"Thing is, I live in Mexico City and I don't want to have to come back all the time."

"So how many would you need?"

"Two hundred," El Loco said boldly.

The woman smiled sardonically.

"So, I'm guessing you're not planning on coming back for a hundred years, right?"

141

Sean shrugged.

"You do realise that ampoules are individually numbered and recorded?"

"Yup, I figured that."

"And you know that just asking me is a criminal offence?"

"Yup."

"And you know that if I supply you I could go to prison too?"

"Yup."

"So, if you know the risks I'm running, you'll know what it'll take to persuade me."

"I'd make it worth your while."

The woman leaned towards Sean and whispered:

"Meet me in the parking lot of Aguirre's Super Mart at six. I'll be driving a white Pinto."

At precisely six o'clock, the woman's car arrived, followed by a pickup with two guys in it. She parked and, without getting out, gestured to El Loco to come over. Sean approached warily. War had taught him to anticipate an ambush. He jerked his chin at the two men in the pickup to make sure El Castor Furioso knew they were there.

Sean stopped when he reached the car. The woman glanced around nervously.

"Didya get 'em?" Sean said.

"Are you a cop?"

"No, I'm not a cop."

"How can I be sure?"

Sean rolled up his sleeve and showed her the tattoo: his squadron name, the place and date where he'd been injured. The woman read it and then looked him in the eye.

"I've only got a hundred and twenty. It was all I could get."

"That'll do."

"Two thousand four hundred dollars," she said. "Twenty bucks apiece."

"What? In Dallas they cost ten bucks."

"Well, then go to Dallas."

The woman was about to turn the key in the ignition, but Sean stopped her.

"I've only got eighteen hundred on me."

"Come find me when you've got the rest."

The woman keyed the ignition and was about to drive off when Sean leaned through the window.

"Two grand. It's every cent I've got, but I'll buy more, I swear."

The woman stared out of the windscreen.

"Yeah, O.K., hand it over."

"Quid pro quo," Sean said. "Give me the ampoules."

"They've got the boxes with the ampoules," she said nodding to the pickup behind her. "You give me the cash, they'll hand them over."

Sean took out an envelope stuffed with banknotes and gestured for Diego to go over to the pickup. Diego planted himself in front of the two henchmen, who were just scared teenagers.

Sean handed over the envelope, the woman counted the notes and gave the guys in the pickup a thumbs up. The teenager behind the wheel handed the box to Diego and the two cars drove off while Sean and El Castor Furioso were counting the phials. There were exactly 119. One of the teenagers had obviously filched one. The two men smiled: they were in business.

Amaruq followed the trail in the snow. The tracks were not well defined: they were dragging their paws, which suggested that they were exhausted. Amaruq found no half-eaten deer. The pack had not been able to find any prey. The herds of wapiti had headed south in search of warmer climes. Why had Nujuaqtutuq led the pack so far north?

Amaruq was finding it difficult to forge on through the deep snow. His hands bled from dragging the sled, despite his thick leather gloves.

The muscles in his legs and arms ached from the effort. He could not abandon the sled with the furs and meat, his only supplies. With only two bullets left, he could not possibly survive.

Amaruq looked up at the sky. The lowering clouds threatened a storm. He set up his tent in the shelter of a grove of pine trees, secured the stays to the trunks, put his sled inside, lit a fire and thawed the furs he used as bedcovers, then tied up the canvas flap.

He could not sleep. Blasts of icy wind rocked the tent, slipping through cracks and freezing him to the marrow. The weight of the snow threatened to capsize the tent. Amaruq covered himself with the furs and wrapped his head in a half-frozen wolf pelt.

The storm raged for three days. A grey half-light blotted out the sun. The fierce winds made it impossible for him to build another fire, forcing him to eat raw, half-frozen wapiti that was difficult to bite off and chew. Sometimes, while he was trying to sleep, he would hear the low howls of the pack carried on the wind and would sit up and listen intently, unsure whether it was really the wolves or simply the howling wind.

Eventually, the storm abated. Amaruq peered through a crack and saw that the tent was completely encased in snow. Untying the flap, he found himself faced with a sheer white wall. He used a stick to clear a narrow passage, dragged himself from the tent and got to his feet. All around, the prairies were carpeted in snow. Amaruq climbed the mound next to the tent and gazed out at the vast horizon. Suddenly, sensing a presence to his left, he turned. Nujuaqtutuq, the big grey wolf, was staring at him from twenty metres away. Amaruq regretted having left his rifle in the tent. The man and wolf eyed each other for a few seconds and then Nujuaqtutuq turned and slunk away through the deep snow. Amaruq could just make out the rest of the pack in the distance, waiting for their leader.

Nujuaqtutuq must have been hungry. When the storm cleared, he had probably smelled meat inside the tent and come to investigate.

He was not frightened of Amaruq, which meant that the wolves had lost their fear, or, worse still, they were planning to attack. Amaruq went back to get his rifle and then set off to explore. The tent was surrounded by wolf tracks. They had outsmarted him again.

If Amaruq did manage to kill Nujuaqtutuq, the pack would probably disband. With the alpha male dead, the struggle for succession would split them into two or three groups. If the pack was thinking of attacking, killing the big grey wolf would reduce the threat. But killing him now would be difficult. With only two bullets and the snow almost waist deep, it would be impossible to creep up on the animal.

Amaruq set several traps around his camp. He heated water in a pot, defrosted hunks of wapiti meat to use as bait, placed them in the traps and then covered them with snow. Traps worked better when an animal had to dig to find the meat.

He secured them with chains to the trunks of the pine trees so that the wolves could not run off, dragging a trap with them. Escaping would mean that the wolf would have to gnaw off its own paw.

Night drew in. In the distance, Amaruq could just make out the wolves among the trees, slowly creeping towards him. They would be here soon.

My grandmother flattens herself against the wall in terror. The men in leather jackets rip open drawers and toss the contents on the floor. My grandmother asks them what's happening. "Shut up," Captain Zurita barks. I try to intervene. One of the cops grabs me and gets me in a chokehold. "Where did your grandson hide the drugs?" Zurita asks my grandmother. She doesn't know what to say. "Leave her alone," I say. The cop slaps me hard. "Don't talk to the *jefe* like that." They go into the bedrooms, pull clothes from the wardrobes, turn over the mattresses. "Where are the drugs, where's the money?" Zurita growls again. "I've no idea." They've already searched El Loco's place and found nothing. Now they are kicking him in the balls to make him talk.

El Loco won't crack. He's a soldier. A war veteran. Idiots. He's spent years tolerating pain. He's not about to crack. "Where are the drugs and the money?" "I don't know," I say again. They push my grandmother up the stairs. She is sobbing. "We'll beat her if you don't tell us," one of the officers threatens. "I told you, I don't fucking know!" I roar. My grandmother is still crying. Zurita goes over to her. All compassionate now. Tells her to calm down. Plays good cop. Asks her to *please* tell him where the drugs and the money are. "What drugs? What money?" My grandmother has no idea what they're talking about. From the kitchen comes the crash of plates and glasses shattering. An officer comes up the stairs. "We didn't find anything, *jefe*." Captain Zurita orders the other officer to let me go. "Leave the chickenshit kid alone. Let's get out of here." As he heads down the stairs, he jabs a finger at me. "If we find out that you do know where the money's stashed, I'll deal with you the same way I dealt with your brother." "You didn't kill him," I say to piss him off, "the Good Boys did." Zurita marches back up the stairs and punches me in the face. I collapse on the carpet. My grandmother screams: "He's just a boy!" Zurita smiles and then laughs. My brother is dead. And sooner or later he will pay for that.

Revennnje, Reventsch, Revensh,

    R

          E

               V

                     E

                           N

                                 G

                                       E

Revenge, revenge, revenge, revenge.

In the mountains of Transylvania, when a young unmarried woman dies, the town holds a wedding. Having died before her time, the *strigoi morți*, or imperfect soul, flies into a rage. It yearns to destroy the living before moving on to the next world. To bring her peace, a symbolic wedding is organised. Villagers dress the corpse in a bridal gown and ask one of the men from the village to act as the groom. The friends and family of the deceased wear their finest clothes. The marriage takes place. The groom says his vows, promising undying love and fidelity. At the end of the ceremony, a doll is placed inside the coffin to symbolise the children the young woman never had. The coffin is closed and lowered into the grave. The *strigoi* can depart in peace: her soul is now fulfilled.

Breath

Ten days without Chelo. She hasn't called me. My friends haven't seen her. I asked Pato to stand guard outside her house. Nothing. She has vanished. I rip down the poster of Raquel Welch from the ceiling above my bed. I want to think only about Chelo.

The parakeets have learned to be free. They flutter up the stairs to the bedrooms and quickly fly back to the living room. Still they don't dare go out into the yard. To them, an open door is an impassable barrier. King sleeps, snores, wakes, stretches, jumps up on me, drools, eats, drinks, sleeps, snores, wakes . . .

I've hidden all the clocks in the house. I don't want to know what time it is. I need only two units of time: day-night, light-dark. All the others – the seconds, the minutes, the hours – are irrelevant. For me, now, "time" is animal time. It doesn't matter when I wake or when I sleep. It is also ghost time. Insomnia makes it easier to commune with ghosts; it is their favourite time. They tell you their stories, you tell them yours.

I read Shakespeare, Rulfo, Faulkner. Their words resonate: revenge, death, passion, blood. Faulkner writes about a married woman who dies when her lover, a young doctor, botches her abortion. Scraping out her uterus, she bleeds to death. In the last line of his novel, Faulkner writes: "Between grief and nothing I will take grief." Really, William? You would take grief? Come and feel my grief, fucker. Feel the leaden weight of my dead. It would crush you. Get out of your grave, William, you fine Southern gentleman, I'm right here, waiting. Together we'll plunge into the cesspit of grief; after we climb out, then maybe we can talk.

Maybe you're right, Mr Faulkner. The stone eternally wants to be a stone and the tiger a tiger. I shall remain in myself. I would like to remain a tiger. With the blood of a stone. Powerful, unbreakable blood. Blood that does not spill or slip away, stone blood that scorns death. And yes, between grief and nothing, I will take grief, Mr Faulkner.

And you, Shakespeare, with your pathetic Hamlet, hesitating over whether or not to take his revenge. "To be or not to be." Read Spinoza, Shakespeare, it might do you some good, it would answer your question. Read Borges, your blind great-great-grandson. To be or not to be? To be, my dear Shakespeare. Always to be.

And what about you, Rulfo, bragging that your dead speak to you? Of course the dead speak. I hear them whispering every night, echoing around these walls. They won't let me sleep. My dead settle into their waterlogged graves. My parents, my grandmother and my sodden brothers, water pouring into their coffins. How do the dead ever get dry? Do they slowly turn into mud? Or do they shake themselves like a dog getting out of a pond? Come on, Rulfo, Faulkner, Shakespeare. Stay with me. Tell me something, I don't care, anything that might help me through these suffocating, stultifying hours.

Like a prisoner in his cell, I exercise every day. I stop reading, do twenty-five push-ups, pick up my book again, then another twenty-five push-ups. I do squats in the middle of dinner, run up and down the stairs, fifty, sixty times. I do lunges with King on my shoulders. I need to be strong. Out there somewhere, vengeance awaits.

I look at my arms, the veins bulging from the exercise. My heart pumps blood to my muscles. My blood. How many of those who gave their blood for me have died? How many have been brought to life within me? Whose is this blood that courses through my veins? How many of my unborn children are swimming in my blood, waiting for their moment? If I am silent, I can hear them breathing, hear them panting laboured breaths. Like tadpoles swimming blindly through my veins. What woman carries within her the missing half of my unborn

149

children? Will it be you, Chelo? Will my children dive into your belly to be conceived?

I breathe. My heart pumps blood to my biceps, my forearms, my hands. I feel it pulsing in my wrists. I drop to the floor and do some more push-ups. Rising and falling. One hundred. Push. Blood. Revenge. Love. My children. Chelo. Oh fuck, I miss her. God, how I miss her. Carlos. Papá. Mamá. Grandmother. I miss them all so much. And still they talk. They talk to me. And I beg them: please don't stop.

Postcard sent from Florence. Dated July 1969. Written by my parents.

"Carlos, *mijo*. This is Ponte Vecchio in Florence. It is so beautiful. The bridge was built in the Middle Ages. Merchants sold their wares there then, and they still do now.

Son, please think about going back to school. University can offer you so much in life. I know things are going well with the chinchillas, but still, please think about it. Much love, Papá.

We're having such a lovely time. It would have been so wonderful to have you here with us. We miss you. Never forget how much we love you. Mamá."

Postcard sent from Rome. Dated July 1969. Written by my parents.

"Juan Guillermo, my darling son. You would love this place. This is where gladiators fought tigers and lions. Just picturing it makes my hair stand on end. We've been eating pasta non-stop. By the time we get home we'll be horribly overweight. Your mother is already planning a diet. Nothing but water, she says. I love you so much. Hugs, Papá.

My long-haired little. Do you remember the Roman costume with the plastic sword we gave you when you were five? We couldn't get you to take it off. Being here in the Colosseum reminds me so much of you. Don't forget how much we love you. Mamá."

Thirty-six postcards to Carlos, thirty-six to me, twenty-four to my grandmother. A map of life before death.

Sean couldn't remember the name of the movie, but it was about G.I.s during World War II who dive into a river to get away from the Japs, and stay underwater, using reeds so that they can breathe. The Japanese scrutinise the water but don't realise that the American soldiers are under the surface, camouflaged by the algae.

"You're a soldier, do you think it's possible?" Carlos asked.

"I tried it once and I couldn't do it," replied Sean with a snort.

"It must be possible," my brother said.

They filled the bath and El Castor Furioso volunteered to go first. He climbed in in his underwear, ducked his head under, with a straw clamped in his mouth. Seconds later he popped up, coughing and spluttering.

"The water went up my nose," he said.

"Go under gradually and breathe slowly," my brother said.

Diego tried again, and again resurfaced gasping for breath.

"If you were a beaver, you'd starve," my brother teased him.

"Maybe, but these little teeth of mine have nibbled your mum's tits, cabrón," Diego retorted.

Carlos said nothing. He took off his clothes and practised breathing through the straw before getting into the water. He got into the bath, submerged himself and came up coughing. Sean and Diego laughed at him.

"Good going, Tarzan," Sean said.

"Not so much Tarzan as Cheeta," Diego said.

Carlos looked at them without a word and slid beneath the surface again. This time he managed to breathe through the straw. He lasted a minute before he emerged, coughing.

"It is possible, goddammit! It must be fucking possible."

They practised for hours. The problem was that they floated

and had to hold themselves under or hold each other down. But they managed. Eventually, Carlos managed to breathe through the straw for more than six minutes.

What had started as a game became a tactic. This was why Captain Zurita and his officers could never find them. Carlos reckoned that no-one would think to look in the water tanks. They practised in one of the cisterns and gradually perfected the technique. To keep their plan a secret, they would creep quietly across the roofs at night looking for suitable tanks. The best were those in which the water did not come all the way to the top, which had sloping sides so that they could hold themselves under, could be easily opened and closed, and were hidden behind walls near a spiral staircase so that, if all else failed, they could make a run for it.

They tested countless tanks, but most were constructed from asbestos and had rusty pipes. They finally settled on six, and Carlos assigned them. Sean would take the tanks belonging to the Padilla and Martínez families, Diego the Armendáriz and Carbajal tanks, and Carlos himself would use those on the rooftops of the Santibáñez and the Barreras. They arranged to meet on a different rooftop every morning at 3.00 a.m. Stopwatch in hand, they would time themselves leaping across the gaps between the houses, getting to the tank, opening it, getting inside without splashing, closing it and then breathing for at least fifteen minutes. The water level should be such that it covered only half their faces, so that they could bob up and breathe through their nose if necessary, then sink down and breathe through a straw.

They worked out the perfect length for the straws, calculated how long they needed to be so it would work in different tanks with different water levels, then cut straws of different lengths for the six tanks. They hid the straws in cigarette packets so no-one would connect them to their escape manoeuvres.

They swore never to tell anyone about their escape method. They became blood brothers. Each made a small incision in his left wrist and vowed never to betray each other. Carlos was the one who broke his word.

My life changed when I started middle school. I was used to marching during P.E., and showed up to class expecting "Right flank, about turn, quick march"; instead I met a teacher who would change my life: Fernando Alarid. When he saw how clumsily I bounced a basketball, he took me aside. "Come on, I'll show you how to do it," and with enormous patience guided me through it. "Bounce the ball with your eyes closed", "Dribble with both hands", "Now run with it". I became a great basketball player and Profesor Alarid gave me back the self-confidence that my primary school had crushed. Most of the teachers in my new school were like him, they wanted students to *learn*, they weren't fixated on discipline and punishment. The school welcomed pupils from the same social class, but the quasi-socialist attitude of the staff fostered an atmosphere of equality and respect. There were no spies here, no "safety patrols", no rule that you could only speak English during break. No self-righteousness. No parroting Beatles songs. No calling the female teachers "Miss". I felt liberated, reborn, and my academic performance improved considerably.

I stayed on at the Escuela Mexicana Americana when I reached high school. When my parents died, I was sorry to have to leave. Worried about my situation, the headmistress, Miss Salinas – the polar opposite of Miss Ramírez – called at my house several times to see how I was coping. She told me to take my time, that she and the other teachers would help me catch up, that there was no need for me to worry about school fees, that they would welcome me back with open arms.

After I'd been absent for two months, she suggested coming to see me, but I told her not to, I told her I was fine and said not to call again because I had decided I wasn't going back to school. She called four more times to try and convince me, until she finally gave up.

My friends decided to cut class to come visit me. They brought me tamales rojos and hot chocolate for breakfast.

"Hey, Cinco, why don't we all go to Chapultepec Park?" Agüitas suggested.

I was nicknamed Cinco because my birthday was May 5, 1955. And because five had been my average grade in elementary school.

"Yeah, we can go on the rides in the amusement park," Jaibo said.

I didn't feel like spinning upside down on the Kamikaze or rising and plummeting on the Crazy Rat. Sensing my reluctance, Pato suggested we go to the Natural Science Museum, the one Carlos and I used to visit when the school porter refused us entry for being too "filthy".

I hesitated. It would be a distraction, but it would also be painful. There was too much of Carlos in that museum. Just as there was too much of him at home, on the rooftops, in the streets, in the barrio, on Chelo's body.

"Come on, let's go," Pato said.

Did I really want to spend another day holed up with my ghosts, waiting to go mad?

"O.K., fine, let's go," I said.

We didn't take the bus as usual but a taxi. Taking a taxi was a luxury for families like ours, with our strained resources, but now that I lived alone I decided to splash out.

The museum was also known as "the domes" because the building featured nine brightly coloured domes, each housing a different exhibit: The Origins of The Universe, The Origins of Life, Invertebrates, Dinosaurs, Reptiles, Fish, Birds, Mammals and Ecosystems. We headed straight to Ecosystems, my favourite exhibit, with its huge dioramas of stuffed animals posed in front of painted landscapes. The icy Arctic plains were represented by a hulking polar bear defending its prey – a seal – from another bear, the forests by a wolf attacking a running deer, the mountains by a puma crouching on a rock, and the deserts by a rattlesnake poised to attack a kangaroo rat. Predators in the act of hunting, the boundary between life and death.

After two hours wandering through the museum, Pato and I sat in front of the wolf diorama while Agüitas and Jaibo went to find something to eat. Pato gazed at the scene: the fleeing, terrified deer was frozen mid-flight; the wolf, fangs bared, was about to bite its hind leg.

"I'd love to have Colmillo stuffed like this when the Prietos have him put down," he laughed. "Only, he'd be attacking a mechanic."

For some reason I'd assumed that Colmillo's execution ("being put to sleep" as his gutless owners would call it) would never happen.

"When is it?" I asked, anxiously.

"They're leaving tomorrow afternoon. I think the vet's coming round in the morning at nine."

"Are you sure?"

"Yeah, I know 'cos Fernando told me. The vet's taking the body away to be cremated."

I felt a hole open up in my stomach. They shouldn't kill him. They just shouldn't. Agüitas and Jaibo came back with some hotdogs and some tamarind-flavoured Boings. We walked out onto the terrace to eat. I didn't feel hungry, but gulped down the hotdog having barely chewed it.

We headed back to the barrio. My friends said their goodbyes and hurried home, expecting a telling-off for skipping school without telling their parents.

I went inside my house. King bounded up and slobbered all over my trousers. It was incredible how much drool that dog could produce. I poured some dry dog food into his bowl, gave the parakeets some birdseed, and went to bed, exhausted.

At 3.30 a.m. I was woken by Colmillo howling. I had no idea whether an animal could anticipate its death, but that night his howls sounded different – deeper and more melancholy. I sat up in bed. Colmillo wasn't calling to his invisible pack tonight, I felt – he was calling to me, begging me to save him.

I went to the Prietos' front door, rang the doorbell and kept my finger there. The loud rings could be heard around the block. After fifteen minutes, Mr Prieto appeared at the door in a tattered dressing gown, clearly bewildered.

"What's the matter, Juan Guillermo? It's nearly four in the morning."

"Don't kill Colmillo."

"What?"

"Don't kill him, I'll take him."

Mr Prieto looked at me pityingly.

"*Hijo*, the dog is uncontrollable."

"I don't care, I'll take him."

He shook his head.

"Juan Guillermo, that dog is capable of killing anyone who gets in his way."

"I can train him."

"No, lad, forget it."

"Don't kill him."

"We've made our decision, Juan Guillermo."

"I'm serious, I'll look after him."

"You can't be responsible. You're not even eighteen yet. If Colmillo attacks someone you'll be in serious trouble."

"I don't care, I'll figure it out."

"I'm sorry, son, but the answer is no. Now, I'm going back to bed and so should you. Good night."

He gave me an affectionate pat on the back, then turned and went inside.

I waited a few minutes, then rang the doorbell again. This time it was Fernando.

"What the fuck's going on, Cinco? You've woken up the whole family."

156

"I don't want you to kill Colmillo."

"I don't want this either, nobody does, but Papá has already decided."

"I can take care of him."

"Look, there's nothing anyone can do now. This is for the best, Cinco. The dog is completely wild."

He looked at me through the bars of the gate.

"And, please, don't ring the doorbell again."

He went back inside and I sat on the pavement and waited for the vet. I was not going to let them kill Colmillo.

The Xoloitzcuintli, 55r, is a breed of dog from Mexico that is completely hairless but for a tuft on the top of its head, with smooth skin that ranges from light to dark brown. Some have white or even pink patches. They are slim and graceful. In Aztec funeral rituals, it was traditional for Xolos to be buried with their masters.

According to Náhuatl mythology, when a person dies they go to Mictlán – the land of the dead – situated deep within the bowels of the Earth. The journey is long and it takes four years to complete in total darkness, during which the soul must face many challenges:

> Navigate a pass between two mountain ranges.
> Ford a river guarded by a snake.
> Pass through a place protected by the great lizard Itzchecaya.
> Scrabble over a vast heap of flint.
> Traverse eight icy deserts where the winds cut like a knife.
> Trudge across eight mountains where it snows without end.
> Cross the great river of Chiconahuapan.

This last is a raging torrent in death's impenetrable darkness. On reaching the banks of the river, the dead find their dogs waiting for them, wagging their tails, happy to be reunited. The soul then wades into the water, clinging to the back of its dog, who uses its canine wisdom to guide the soul through the swift rapids and across the river, safe and sound. When they reach the far side, dog and master continue together to the final resting place: Mictlán.

Those who, in life, have mistreated their dog will have no help crossing the river and are doomed to wander forever in the labyrinthine lands of eternal darkness.

Loneliness

The morphine ran out within a week. Having paid the pharmacist in Laredo twenty bucks an ampoule, Carlos and his friends had sold them on for seventy-five apiece. Word had quickly spread among young people eager for new experiences. Morphine provided a paradoxical mix of serenity and stimulation no other drug could provide. The customer base quickly expanded from the streets to the funk bars. In the seventies, experimenting with drugs was the norm, and many were prepared to go to extremes, even if it meant a brush with death. The more illicit the drug, the greater the interest in consuming it.

Carlos gave El Loco and El Castor Furioso eight thousand dollars apiece and sent them back to Texas. The pharmacists in Dallas and Laredo were skittish, scared of an impromptu stock check. To tempt them, Sean offered twenty-two dollars an ampoule. Despite this, the Dallas pharmacist could only procure thirty doses, and the woman in Laredo ninety – she suggested they try the military hospitals in Harlingen, Eagle Pass, Brownsville and El Paso.

Diego and Sean drove to Harlingen, where they tried to bribe the manager of the hospital pharmacy, who flatly refused. When they insisted, he threatened to report them if they ever showed their faces again.

In Eagle Pass they had better luck, and bought sixty ampoules at twenty-one dollars before setting off for El Paso – a twenty-hour drive – to the largest military base in Texas, and one of the biggest in the country.

Halfway there, near Langtry, Texas, they happened on a community of half-naked, free-loving hippies who spouted anti-bourgeois drivel as a pretext for filming their sexual excesses using a Super 8 camera.

They sold the home movies to a skin flick distributor in Houston to fill the community's coffers. Business seemed to be booming. They didn't consider themselves porn stars, simply "champions of sexual liberation and the beauty of the human form", and had no qualms about being filmed in multifarious sexual positions, threesomes, orgies and acts of sadomasochism.

Sean and Diego had no trouble getting laid. That night, in the glow of the campfire, in front of the whole community – including various children who wandered around naked – they had sex with two women with hairy armpits who reeked of sweat from weeks of not washing. The older hippies had fun flicking pebbles against their heaving buttocks and raucously celebrating when one of them howled as she came.

Sean offered to sell them some ampoules of morphine, but the guru objected: morphine was an army drug. He made them a counter-offer: "You can buy some acid, if you want."

Sean phoned Carlos from a petrol station in Comstock to ask whether they should spend some of the money on L.S.D., and Carlos immediately agreed – acid was highly sought after among the Mexican middle class – and told Sean to ask the hippies if they could buy more.

The hippies sold them a hundred tabs of acid for seven bucks apiece (they had bought them for four). Sean asked whether they could buy more. "Sure, man," the leader said with a smile, so Sean asked him to have a thousand tabs ready in a month's time.

They stashed the morphine and the acid under the back seat and drove on to El Paso. The military base was a sprawling, teeming hive of G.I.s, many of them about to be posted to Vietnam.

Sean got himself admitted to the hospital, claiming he was in rehab. Accustomed to dealing with homeless, unemployed Vietnam vets, military hospitals would accept anyone on condition that they presented their military I.D., a copy of their discharge papers and a recent prescription.

While in the clinic, Sean managed to get a one-month prescription for morphine, persuaded other veterans to sell him theirs, and tracked down nurses and porters willing to provide even more.

El Paso military base proved to be a motherlode. The pharmacy was huge, and there were dozens of employees just waiting to be bribed. In all, Sean and Diego managed to buy six hundred ampoules, a hundred and fifty bottles each containing six doses of liquid morphine, and four hundred and forty boxes each containing four doses in tablet form. A treasure ready to be distributed in the market.

There was no need to bribe customs officials since they crossed the Mexican border via a shallow ford at Latijas where there was no border post, then took a dirt track to Ojinaga where they joined the highway to Mexico City.

Carlos was thrilled with his friends' productivity. They had enough merchandise to satisfy demand for months, and, as a bonus, they could offer L.S.D., which, in the long run, turned out to be big business.

We are the Army of God, the Soldiers of Christ. We are His fist, His flaming sword, the instruments of His wrath.

Death to communists
Death to atheists, heretics and non-believers
Death to the Jews who betrayed Our Lord
Death to those who drug themselves
Death to those who prostitute themselves
Death to those who practise abortions
Death to those who denigrate or insult Our Lord Jesus Christ
Death to criminals
Death to those who poison, corrupt or infect our society

I swear to act in the service of Jesus Christ, Our Lord
I swear to obey the orders of my leaders

I swear to fight to the end

I swear to give my life to Jesus Christ and not fear dying in His name

Our Lord Jesus Christ, You slake our thirst, You feed us with Your body, enfold us in Your love, guide us through the darkness; we offer You our hearts. We belong to You. We are Your Army here on the Earth, Your sword, Your steel. In Your name we destroy sinners, those who betray, deny or disobey You. We are Your Army, Lord, and we will prevail.

During the night, Amaruq could hear the wolves circling the tent, their soft footfall, their panting breath. He could hear them growl and fight among themselves. He sat alert in the darkness, in his lap the rifle loaded with the two remaining bullets. He needed to be ready. He had never been attacked by wolves, but had heard stories of trap-setters and hunters who had been ripped apart alive.

He heard a dry crack and a howl of pain. One of the wolves had stepped onto a trap. He heard the chain clatter against the tree trunk as the animal tried to free itself from the steel jaws. Amaruq peered through a crack in the tent. He could see nothing in the darkness. The batteries in his torch had died. Three months away from civilisation had left him with no batteries, no flour, oil and salt, no bullets, and no fuel for the kerosene lamp. His nails had grown into claws, his hair was long, his beard tangled, his body stank of stale sweat, animal hide, grease and blood.

Amaruq listened to the frantic prowling of the wolves, the crunch of their steps in the snow, the rattle of the chain. One of the wolves came to the flap of the tent and growled, and Amaruq shouted in an attempt to scare it off, but still the wolf kept coming. Amaruq could not shoot blindly and risk wasting one of his last bullets. He yelled again. The wolf tore at the canvas with its teeth and the makeshift tent bowed. Amaruq shuffled backwards and shouted again, but still the wolf kept tearing at the fabric. Amaruq gauged the wolf's position and squeezed the trigger. The gunshot rolled like thunder across the plain. The bullet punctured the canvas and there was a crack of splintering bone and a piercing whine, then low growls as the wolf pack scurried away. After a moment, there was silence.

Through the long night, Amaruq did not sleep, on the alert in case the pack should come back. He heard the rattle of chains and the whimpering of the wolf caught in the trap. The wind whipped up and, with it, a bitter cold. Amaruq feared there would be another storm. He wrapped himself in the stiff, cold furs. The canvas of the tent was a frozen sheet. His breath was ice.

At dawn, Amaruq untied the flap, keeping his rifle cocked, ready to shoot. The wolf he had wounded might still be around, waiting to attack. He crept out and looked around. He could not see anything. Crouching in the snow he searched for the wounded wolf's tracks. There were no bloody paw prints, nothing but the bullet hole in the canvas. He glanced around at his traps. Nothing. Most were intact and there was no sign of wolves. He became anxious. He had heard a howl, the clack of the trap snapping shut, the rattle of the chain, the whimpers. He had heard the wolves prowling. But nothing. Not a single paw print.

Amaruq looked up at the overcast sky. A dirty yellow sun glimmered between the leaden clouds. The horizon was ringed with pine trees swaying in the wind, the prairies were hushed and white, a few carrion crows wheeled in the air. The snow-capped mountains rose up in the distance. Amaruq closed his eyes and began to tremble uncontrollably; perhaps he had been hallucinating. Had the wolves been real, or were they spirits leading him to his death? His grandfather had warned him that a man who spent too long alone in the snow would go mad and find himself chasing ghosts. Had he wasted one of his two remaining bullets on a ghost? Was he delirious, or close to death? What or who was Nujuaqtutuq? And those shapes in the distance, were they wolves or stones, plants or nightmares?

Amaruq looked down at his hands, flexing his fingers. He touched one of the pine trees, felt the rough bark, the needles. He felt. Perceived. No, he was not dead. He took a deep breath, feeling the icy air tear at his lungs. He did not care whether he was alive or dead, whether he was mad or not. He had to carry on: he had to keep going until he had killed Nujuaqtutuq.

I started going to the Good Boys' meetings every Monday and Wednesday. Jaibo came a few times, then stopped. I did as Carlos had asked and never disagreed with them again. I even tried to understand their view of the world. It was impossible, like trying to communicate with a foreigner from a distant era who spoke an incomprehensible language. Their logic was based on a simplistic reading of the Bible, every line or verse distorted and taken out of context in order to support their argument.

Each meeting began with one of the group members standing up and giving a talk on a particular topic. This was followed by a "discussion", where nothing was discussed; they simply became further entrenched in their bigoted beliefs. Finally, an "expert" would arrive to enlighten us. Most of these speakers were priests, or men or women who had devoted their lives to the church; some were more interesting than others, but all were equally fanatical. Their beliefs were contradictory. On the one hand, everything that happened was the result of Divine Will: "god willed it so"; on the other hand, the Devil was lurking everywhere, waiting for the opportunity to tempt Man and lead him from the path of righteousness. The Good Boys believed that the Devil was slowly leeching into the modern world, corrupting humanity and distancing Man from god. It was their moral duty to stop this. They were the vanguard of the evangelical moral army that would halt the Fall of Man.

One Wednesday after the meeting, Humberto asked whether I would do the next presentation. "Choose any subject you like," he said, "and present it on Monday. You have four days to prepare."

That night I talked to Carlos. I had been going to the meetings for five weeks, I said, and I was sick of it. He told me to be patient. "They're starting to trust you, just hang in there," he said. "Get the low-down and find out whether they're the ones who attacked my customers."

For my presentation, Carlos suggested the biblical story of David and Absalom. He told me that Faulkner had written a novel inspired by it. "And if Faulkner chose it, it's because it's ambiguous and intense," he said. "You'll see, it'll confuse them."

In the Bible story, Absalom sends his servants to murder his half-brother Amnon, who has raped his sister Tamar. For his crime, and because of issues of succession, Absalom comes into conflict with his father, King David, and raises a revolt against him at Hebron. It pains the king to be at war with his son. There is no ceasefire between the two armies. King David's followers find themselves at an advantage: Absalom is surrounded and tries to flee on a mule, and the mule walks underneath the thick boughs of a great oak, and his hair is tangled in the branches, and he is taken up between Heaven and Earth; and the mule he is riding walks away. Absalom is found by Joab, the king's commander, who orders his summary execution. When King David hears that his son Absalom has been killed, he greatly sorrows and goes into the chamber above the gate, and weeps; and as he goes, he says: "Oh, my son Absalom, my son, my son Absalom! Would god I had died for thee, Oh Absalom, my son, my son!" But Joab rebukes the king, saying that Absalom had been a fierce and implacable foe; this was no time for remorse, but for retaking power and regaining the respect of his subjects. Overcome with grief, but resolute, King David decides to retake command.

I told the story in the meeting. None of them knew this passage from the Bible, except Humberto, of course. Speaking in front of them made me nervous, perhaps because I was the youngest in the group – I was about to turn fourteen, while most of them were over twenty and Humberto was almost twenty-four.

As Carlos predicted, the Good Boys were utterly bewildered. They bombarded me with questions. Why had I chosen this story? What would Jesus have thought? Why did the death of the son who had waged war against him grieve King David so deeply? I didn't know what to answer. I told them I liked the story and had wanted to share it with them, but that I didn't know anything more about it. "The important thing," I declared, "is for everyone to draw their own conclusions."

During the break, while I poured a soft drink into a plastic cup, Humberto came up to me. "Congratulations," he said. "You couldn't have chosen a better passage. That is exactly how we should act. No matter how much it pains us, we must stamp out the root of evil, even if that means rebuking our fathers or our brothers. Soon you will understand our purpose. You are almost one of us." He patted my shoulder and went to greet the guest speaker, a wizened old priest.

"You are almost one of us." His words still echo in my mind. I wanted to shout, "I'll never be one of you", but I was such a good actor and my pretence was so perfect, that I did almost become one of them.

I call upon all the animals I have hunted and killed. In this moment, I summon you. Come to me; I need your strength. My wisdom comes from you. Your bodies feed my body, your life my life; your blood is my blood, your flesh my flesh. Your hides have kept me warm, your bones have been my tools. We have shared the day and the night, the cold and the tundra, the prairie and the forest. We breathe the same air, together circle the sun. I took your lives, your sacred lives, but now I need your spirits. I summon you. Come to me from death's dark lair. I need you all, every single one of you. You are my guides.

I am lost. I do not know where I am, or who is this wolf that I follow. I do not want to die alone in these silent wastelands. Animals I have hunted and killed, I need you. I summon you, bears, grant me your ferocity. Show me how to fight the blizzards, you kings of this icy kingdom. I summon you, caribou, brothers of my ancestors who fed the tribe to which I belong. I summon you, noble wapiti, who roam the grasslands and fight to the death for your females. Come and fill me with your ancestral lust for battle. I summon you, geese, to show me the way home, the shortcuts. I summon you, buffalo, for your powerful pace, so that I may recognise my enemies as you do yours. I summon you, wolves, for I must kill your brother. Help me be a wolf. Teach me to hunt so that I may hunt your brother, grant me your cunning, your senses of smell and vision. I want to become a wolf. Educate me in the art of your attack. I summon all those I have hunted and killed: ducks, coyotes, lynxes, partridges, hares, seals. Bring me the wisdom of your species, your instinct, your nature. I must kill the great grey wolf, only then can I return home and, if necessary, die. But now I need you. I summon all the animals I have hunted and killed.

167

Skeletons

Maddened by hunger, they frantically scurried around the cages. Those that shared cages viciously attacked each other, and the bucks – invariably the victors – devoured the does, leaving only a fragment of jaw or tail.

Trapped and weakened by starvation, the emaciated chinchillas lay on their sides and waited for death. The local cats slaughtered them and the chinchillas allowed themselves to be ripped apart, lacking the strength even to cower in a corner of their cage. My brother's lucrative chinchilla business had turned into a grisly abattoir.

It was Gumaro who came to tell us about it, three weeks after Carlos was murdered. "When can I go up and clean out the cages? It's disgusting, it's stinking out the whole street." In all the upheaval and the grief, my grandmother and I had given little thought to the chinchillas.

I went up to the rooftop. Gumaro was right: the smell was unbearable. The cages were a breeding ground for maggots and blowflies, which crawled through entrails and buzzed over the corpses. The few surviving chinchillas languished in their cages. Less than two metres from the cages lay salvation, in the form of a twenty-kilo sack of pet food whose smell can only have added to their torment. Prisoners whose only crime was owning glossy, much-coveted fur, they had been condemned to a slow, cruel death.

The Good Boys had not simply killed my brother; like a pebble tossed into a pool, Carlos's death rippled out in lethal waves. Death inciting death inciting death inciting death.

I ripped open the sack of food and placed some in the cages of the surviving chinchillas. The strongest ate hungrily, while the weaker animals lay with their legs in the air, staring at the food as though it were some distant, inaccessible place, before slowly dragging themselves to their bowls. I had to place the dry food in the mouths of some, and even then they didn't have the strength to chew. They had given up on life; or perhaps it had given up on them.

Of the 836 chinchillas, only fifteen survived. I gave one to each of my three friends and sold the rest to a pet shop.

Over time, the pile of empty cages rotted and corroded on the rooftop, like the rusted skeleton of some prehistoric animal.

At 7.00 a.m. I rang the Prietos' doorbell again. Mr Prieto appeared, his eyes thick with sleep; he was clearly in a bad mood.

"What is it, Juan Guillermo?"

"I've come for Colmillo."

"I already told you I'm not giving you the dog."

"You can't kill him."

"He's my dog, so I can do whatever the fuck I like, is that clear?"

"No."

"And stop ringing the doorbell, that's the third time you've woken us up."

"Let me have Colmillo and I'll stop ringing the bell."

Mr Prieto marched over to the fuse box and tripped the main switch.

"Fine, ring all you like, we won't hear it," he grunted, and slammed the door.

If the mechanic was prepared to burn the house down to kill Colmillo, I was prepared to burn it down to save him. I sat in the doorway and waited for the vet. An hour and a half later, Mrs Prieto came out and tripped the switch on the fuse box.

"Señora, can I talk to you?"

Without so much as glancing at me, she turned and walked away. A few minutes later Pato and Jaibo appeared.

"What are you doing here?" I asked them.

"Fernando said we could come to watch Colmillo being put down," Jaibo said.

"Why would you want to watch?"

"Just to see," Jaibo said.

Their morbid curiosity annoyed me. Pato pretended to be sensitive.

"I just came to say goodbye."

He was lying, he wanted to watch an animal die. Snapping the necks of hundreds of chinchillas was not enough for him.

"I'm keeping him," I said.

"You're keeping who?" asked Jaibo.

"Colmillo."

Pato laughed.

"Oh, really? And how are you going to keep him? You can't feed him the dog biscuits you give King, he only eats raw horsemeat."

It was true. Colmillo ate about four kilos of horsemeat a day. I hadn't considered how much this would cost, but I would manage somehow.

At nine o'clock precisely, the vet turned up. This was the man who had nursed Colmillo back to health after he'd been poisoned, after he'd been shot, after the attack with the Molotov cocktail. Now here he was, the Pentobarbital assassin.

As he was about to ring the bell, I said:

"There's no-one in. They've already moved."

"What?"

"They had to leave yesterday, they asked us to come and let you know."

The vet nodded at Colmillo, lurking at the back of the garage.

"So why is the dog still there?"

"We've decided to look after him."

Jaibo giggled.

"What are you laughing at?" I growled.

170

I wanted to punch him.

"This is a joke, right?" asked the vet.

"No, it's no joke," I said earnestly, but this just made Jaibo laugh more. Exasperated, the vet turned to ring the bell but I stood between him and the door.

"What are you doing?" he said, condescendingly.

"I already told you, they're not here."

The vet tried to get past me, but I stood my ground.

"You ring that doorbell and I'll fuck you up good."

The man looked at me, flustered.

"What?"

"Touch one hair on that dog and I'll break your jaw."

Pato laid a hand on my shoulder.

"Calm down, Cinco."

I shook him off and took a step towards the vet.

"Don't you dare touch him."

"Señor Prieto has asked me to do a job and I intend to do it."

Pato pulled me away.

"Forget it, *cabrón*."

The man seized the opportunity to ring the bell.

"I warned you," I said. I felt a black fury welling up as tunnel vision blacked out everything around me, and I focused on this man as though nothing else existed.

The man gave a mocking smile and rang the bell again. Fernando appeared and went to open the security gate. The tunnel vision tightened, so that I could see only the vet's chin; I let fly with a vicious right hook, but Pato got between us and the blow barely touched him.

I hurled myself at the vet, but Jaibo and Pato pulled me back and held on to me. Colmillo's barking and Pato's attempts to reason with me were a distant, muffled rumble. My whole body was focused on hitting that vet.

I slipped out of their grip and launched myself at him again. The vet grabbed his briefcase to protect himself. I threw several punches, knocking him to the ground. He scrabbled away and cringed behind a lamp post. Fernando came out and grabbed me in a choke hold while Pato and Jaibo clung to my waist.

With every second, the tunnel was growing darker and narrower. I tried to shake Fernando off by headbutting him, but he just tightened the stranglehold. Mr Prieto and Luis suddenly appeared and now there were five of them trying to restrain me.

I struggled furiously.

"Just calm down," Mr Prieto shouted in my ear.

It should have been the Prietos I was beating up, not the chickenshit vet who was just trying to do his job.

"They can't kill Colmillo," I shouted.

Fernando and Luis tried to get me on the ground, while Pato and Jaibo held my arms. Mr Prieto opened the garage gate and gestured to the vet, who had grabbed his bag and darted inside.

Who exactly was I trying to save, Colmillo or myself? What had triggered this blind fury? I was crushed by the weight of all my ghosts: a foetus bobbing in a mayonnaise jar, a brother drowned in a cistern, another strangled in the womb, my parents hurtling off a cliff, my grandmother passing away in silence, Carlos's killers walking around unpunished, an evil police captain, Chelo's disappearance, chinchillas rotting in their cages, parakeets afraid to fly free, my unsated lust for revenge, the blood of many people coursing through my veins, a numbed leg, scars: all this converged on one thing: Colmillo's life.

I lay sprawled on the ground, pinned down by four people. Pato crouched over me.

"Calm down, Cinco, calm down," he whispered, his knee pinning down one of my arms. I could hear Colmillo barking and growling.

I let my body go limp and Fernando and Luis got to their feet. As soon as they opened the door, I broke away from Jaibo and Pato and ran over to Fernando.

"Don't let them kill him."

"Jesus fuck, you think I want this? But what choice do we have?"

Pato grabbed me and pulled me back.

"He's right, Cinco."

The brothers went into the garage and locked the gate behind them. The vet was leaning against a wall, pale and breathless. He'd taken some gauze and surgical spirit from his bag and was dabbing at a cut on his chin.

Mr Prieto and his sons tried to muzzle Colmillo, but he twisted his head away, unsettled by the commotion and shouting. Eventually they managed to get the muzzle on and the three of them held the dog still while the vet rummaged in his bag and took out a syringe. He checked the dosage of anaesthetic, then went over to Colmillo and kneeled beside him. Panicked now, Colmillo tried to break loose, but Mr Prieto tugged on his chain.

Colmillo and I exchanged a look. That wolf-dog was mine and I was his. He never should have belonged to the Prietos. The vet grabbed a fold of flesh and prepared to inject.

"No," I screamed through the bars of the gate. "Don't kill him!"

This agitated Colmillo and he tried to extricate himself from Fernando and Luis's grasp.

"Stop it! Stop it!" I yelled.

Colmillo broke free, turned on the vet and headbutted him. The man fell over and the syringe skidded across the floor. Mr Prieto jerked the chain, but Colmillo jerked harder and ripped it from his hands. Colmillo leaped at the vet, pinned him against the cement floor and growled menacingly.

Luis and Fernando managed to pull their dog away from the vet and the terrified man scuttled off and crawled under Mr Prieto's battered Dodge Coronet.

Mr Prieto turned and glared at me furiously.

"You really want this dog, *cabrón*?"

173

"Yes, I want him," I replied.

He turned to his sons.

"Give him the dog."

Fernando looked at him, incredulous.

"What?"

"If he wants the fucking dog so much, let him have it."

Luis unhooked the chain from the post, wrapping it around his arm so that Colmillo couldn't escape, then he and Fernando led the dog to the garage gate.

"You're fucked in the head," Pato said, watching the approach of the hulking grey beast barely being controlled by his owners.

Mr Prieto opened the gate and Luis and Fernando let Colmillo out.

"He's all yours."

The moment he saw me, Colmillo bounded up, his muzzle hitting me in the stomach, winding me. He growled. What made me think I could control this animal?

"Could you take him round to the backyard?" I said.

"You want him, you take him," Fernando said, holding out the chain. I turned to Jaibo and Pato for help. Jaibo wound the chain around his arm as he had seen Luis do. Pato grabbed Colmillo's collar.

"O.K., you can let him go," I said.

The two brothers released the chain. Colmillo was mine.

I struggle to remember, but I can't. If there really is a hell, it is being unable to remember. I know Carlos stopped when he got to the door and said something to me, but I cannot remember what it was. Fuck! What did he say? I know he smiled and I watched him go. What did he say? These were the last words I heard him say, and had I known they were the last I would have stopped him and asked him to repeat them, slowly. He spoke the words and went out. Down on the street his enemies were lying in wait.

Carlos walked out, and I heard the front door open and my grandmother's voice calling: "Take care of yourself, *hijito!*" I was lying on my bed, reading, as my brother walked towards his final destination, to the water tank in which he would drown after being trapped in it for twenty-one hours.

I would give anything to have stopped him that morning and said, "Run for it, they're trying to kill you", but even I didn't know that this was the day they were going to kill him. The army of god, the assassins of god – yes, I'll always write god in lower case, because if he truly was god, Carlos would be alive and His hired assassins would be dead and there would be justice and I would still be able to remember Carlos's every last word.

Life is that line of light that hangs suspended between nothingness and nothingness

we leap from darkness into darkness

the stone eternally wants to be a stone and the tiger a tiger

we want to be perpetual light

but we gutter out

the tiger eternally wants to be a stone and the stone a tiger

in truth we are forever stones.

Cockroaches

Over time, Carlos and his partners found ways of cutting out the middlemen. Buying morphine from stock managers and military pharmacies was risky and made the product more expensive. Instead they went directly to the pharmaceutical distributors who didn't much care who they sold to. The price per ampoule fell by almost sixty per cent and their profits soared.

As for the L.S.D., they stuck with their original providers, the hippie porn stars. They had investigated other possibilities, but the hippies' wholesale price was much the same as that demanded by other distributors, and they were trustworthy, honest, polite and efficient. Negotiations were informal and quickly wound up, and the deal could be celebrated with a night of wild sex.

Although business was booming, Carlos felt they needed to take advantage of other possibilities. In their desire to rebel, the bourgeois teenagers were hungry for unique experiences, but their options were limited. Get stoned in some funk bar, get wasted at a clandestine rock concert or a private party in some mansion in El Pedregal – these were the only options. Once the band was playing, punters would take whatever was on offer: dope, coke, smack, booze, and under the influence they would dance, make out or meditate. Carlos sensed there was something missing, that this collective euphoria could be enhanced by using more imaginative locations. It was a niche that needed exploring.

The idea came to him while we were at a triple bill at Cine de la Viga, a huge, dilapidated cinema where it was common to feel rats and cockroaches scurrying between your feet. "I'm going to organise psychedelic screenings," he said. That same night he had a word with the manager, a short, chubby man who was constantly mopping sweat from his face. Carlos offered to hire the cinema every Saturday from 10 p.m. to 10 a.m. on Sunday. The manager tried to milk the opportunity. "In twelve hours, I could show five movies, and then there's the money I make from popcorn, Cokes, chocolate." He worked up an estimate based on having a full house for every screening. The cinema could hold eight hundred people, tickets for the usual triple bill cost Mex\$3 (one peso per movie); from this he extrapolated 800 customers × Mex\$5 = Mex\$4,000 + Mex\$2,000 to cover lost revenue from selling snacks = Mex\$6,000 a night. In addition, he wanted Carlos to cover the salaries of two security guards, a projectionist, two assistants, five ushers and the ticket clerks, as required by union staffing regulations.

Carlos laughed at the fat guy's chutzpah. "O.K., firstly, no-one goes to the cinema in the middle of night. Secondly, I've been to this fleapit dozens of times and I've never seen it full. Thirdly, the profit margin on the merchandise we're selling is much higher than on Coke and chocolate bars. So, here's my offer: I'll give you five hundred pesos a night plus a ten per cent cut of merchandise sales, and I'll cover fifty per cent of the salaries – you pay the other half out of your share. Do we have a deal, or should I go looking for some other fleapit?" The man asked for a day to think it over, explaining that most cinemas were government-owned and he only got the job because a cousin had contacts. He needed to talk to his cousin. "No way," Carlos said. "I don't have time to waste, and you're not discussing this with anybody. You've heard my final offer, take it or leave it." The manager took it.

Carlos was cautious about how he promoted these screenings; he was determined not to shell out a single centavo to bribe the cops. Corruption infuriated him. Sean suggested printing flyers, like the ones used to promote the funk bars and parties, but Carlos explained the risks: they couldn't print an address or a schedule without the police sniffing around. Besides, their merchandise was exclusive, so their events should be too.

They began a low-profile, word-of-mouth campaign, telling trusted customers about the "happenings" and suggesting they discreetly tell their friends about "a new way of opening the doors of perception". Within three weeks, they managed to enlist thirty-two guys and twenty-one girls, fine, upstanding kids who did not mind going to a cinema in a dangerous barrio. It smacked of adrenaline, adventure, transgression.

The first screening arrived. The entrance fee included twelve hours inside the cinema to watch the movie as many times as they wished, one hit of morphine or L.S.D., and their first shot of Black Bear vodka. Additional drinks cost extra.

Carlos bought a copy of "Jason and the Argonauts", the movie with the best special effects anyone had ever seen at the time. The projectionist was told to play the movie on a loop, with fifteen-minute intervals between each showing.

They set up tables in the foyer, with plastic cups and bottles of Black Bear vodka. Ushers brought people to their seats and served the drinks. Their chosen "merchandise" was handed to them at the ticket desk when they paid their admission. The security guards agreed to let Carlos know if they spotted any cops.

The first screening was a howling success. Watching "Jason and the Argonauts" – the fighting skeletons, Talos the bronze giant, Jason decapitating the Hydra – was the unique experience that Carlos had wanted for his clients. They clapped, they cheered, they clamoured for more drugs (and Carlos obliged at three times the normal price), they drank until they collapsed in the aisles, and had furtive sex among the balcony seats. A success.

The following Saturday, three times as many people showed up, and their response was just as enthusiastic: cheering, clapping, punters standing on their chairs and cheering Jason on, a few women dancing topless. Over the public address system, Carlos asked the viewers not to reveal the secret of "this grotto of freedom".

The screenings at Cine de la Viga attracted a faithful clientele. The cinema afforded an intimacy and a sensory experience that bars, private parties and concerts lacked. The public insisted that "Jason and the Argonauts" be the only movie. Nobody seemed to mind watching it again and again. It was the perfect movie to watch while tripping on acid. During the battle of the skeletons, people climbed on the seats and brandished imaginary swords. There were a few who had a bad trip – watched their hands melt, or huddled in corners, terrified that the heads of the Hydra would snake out of the screen and devour them. Those on morphine whooped every time Jason overcame an obstacle in his search for the Golden Fleece, while others dozed after fucking in the back row of the stalls. These high young people got a kick out of knowing the dialogue, the twists, the outcome of each battle by heart. The screenings were dubbed "The Argo Trip" and the participants "Jasons" or "Medusas".

Despite pressure from Sean and Diego, Carlos refused to roll out the idea to other cinemas. It might attract attention from bent cops or a corrupt politician, or tempt a greedy gang like the "Nazis", who trafficked in other substances.

Two hundred customers seemed like too many to Carlos, so he worked hard to keep the business off the radar. He kept a detailed record of everyone who attended the screenings: date of birth (no-one underage was admitted), address and phone number, whether they had previously attended or come on the recommendation of a friend. He created passwords and assigned each customer a secret number. If the name, password and number did not match, they were refused entry. Admission to the Argo Trip was as intricate as for a private members club.

Carlos ensured that the staff were paid generously to avoid disgruntled employees gossiping, increased the manager's percentage to keep him happy and quiet, appointed Sean as logistics manager and El Castor Furioso as security manager. He kept a close eye on every single detail, but one escaped him: he granted entry to a twenty-year-old dark-haired girl, beautiful and totally crazy. She was one of those girls that took two tabs of acid and ran topless through the aisles. She turned out to be a cousin of Josué, one of the Good Boys.

I was surprised by all the T.V.s: in the canteen, the communal areas, the warders' rooms, the hallways outside the cells. This was the difference between American and Mexican prisons. In Mexico, there were no televisions in prisons. Not one. American prisons seemed like a shrine to the goggle-box, with its rabbit's ears antennas. Mexican prisoners kept themselves entertained by playing cards or *rayuela*, or organising bare-knuckle fights. American prisoners would sit stupefied for hours watching inane game shows or insubstantial rolling news channels. In every other respect American and Mexican prisons were the same: the peeling paint, the smell of shit, the screaming, the suspicious looks, the cramped cells, the rats and the cockroaches, the concrete beds, the excruciating heat or cold, the broken fans, the prisoners with privileges, the racism, classism.

Sean ended up in a prison in Texas, while El Castor Furioso wound up in Lecumberri Prison in Mexico City. Both quickly adapted to prison life. Sean earned respect from the start as a Vietnam vet who had been wounded in action, spent time in the Mexican prison system and endured chronic pain without complaining about the lack of morphine. Nobody messed with him. El Castor Furioso quickly learned the rules in Lecumberri's notorious "Black Palace". Having grown up on the streets, he quickly identified the powerful gangs and their leaders, found a way to negotiate with them, and asked Pedro Jara for protection. The members of the "Nazis" in the prison backed him up. Pedro Jara asked nothing in return. Both men had grown up in the barrio of Unidad Modelo and that was enough for Jara.

Sean was offered the opportunity of serving the rest of his sentence in an American jail. His father persuaded a senator friend to broker a deal with the Mexican authorities, and the Texas public prosecutor's office agreed to let him serve out his sentence in one of its prisons. Sean went back to a country where he felt like a stranger, but fortunately ended up in a prison where most prisoners were Mexicans or *chicanos*, so he felt he was among family. He spoke Spanish to the other inmates and refused to speak English to the guards.

I was able to visit him in the minimum-security Texas prison. They even allowed me to see him in the prison courtyard, accessed via a warren of corridors, past guards' stations, workshops and dozens of blaring T.V.s. I asked Sean to help me get my revenge. He already had a plan to destroy Captain Zurita, one he intended to put into action as soon as he was released.

Diego managed to get himself transferred to the wing for white-collar criminals: crooked bankers, small-time conmen and extortionists, meaning he didn't have to share his cell with murderers and schizophrenics. His aggressiveness routinely led to punch-ups, but he survived thanks to his vicious street-fighting skills, or a timely intervention by the "Nazis". Even so, over time he was worn down by punishment beatings and learned to buy himself some peace and quiet.

I visited Diego a couple of times. It was difficult to get into Lecumberri Prison unless you were family, but I found a way. Having been sentenced to fifteen years because Captain Zurita had pinned a dozen bogus charges on him, Diego not only promised to help me get revenge, but vowed to devote his life to it as soon as he was released.

For three weeks he had been venturing deeper into increasingly barren terrain. He had not seen a single wapiti, deer or buffalo. His stock of meat was quickly dwindling and Amaruq divided it between bait and food. Though by now the wolves were starving and there was no prey, they sniffed around the traps without ever touching the meat.

Amaruq began to suffer nightmares and hallucinations. Several times, he encountered his dead grandfather in broad daylight, saw the old man scanning the horizon in search of the wolves, following their tracks, sniffing the icy morning air trying to detect their scent. He and Amaruq would spend the day walking together in silence. When exhaustion finally overcame Amaruq and he collapsed in the deep snow, his grandfather would go back to the sled, hack off two hunks of wapiti meat, grill them on a fire and bring them to him. The two men would sit on mounds of snow and chew them slowly. At night Amaruq would hear his grandfather whisper something unintelligible; he had not yet learned the language of the dead.

One afternoon, he spotted a dark shape sprawled in the snowy forest. Warily – his recent hallucinations had made him distrustful – he crept closer. It was a young, emaciated she-wolf, her skin stretched taut over her bony ribcage; she had been overcome by starvation. There were tracks around her body, including the unmistakable paw-prints of Nujuaqtutuq.

Amaruq spotted the rest of the pack slinking between the pine trees some three hundred metres away. He cocked his rifle and scanned for Nujuaqtutuq using the telescopic sight, but could not see him. Amaruq struggled to understand the big grey wolf: where was Nujuaqtutuq leading them if not towards certain death? This she-wolf was the first casualty.

Amaruq kneeled down beside her. Her fur was patchy from malnutrition, her breathing laboured, her body racked by shudders. Amaruq laid a hand on her back and she raised her head a little to look and then dropped it again. Amaruq drew his knife to kill the animal, but his grandfather stopped him. Amaruq turned to look at the old man. "Why?" he asked. His grandfather looked at him for a moment, then went to the sledge, fetched a trap and laid it about a metre from the wolf. Then he fetched another and another and placed them in a circle. Amaruq understood: the pack would almost certainly come back for her. Together, they finished setting the traps, then his grandfather vanished again.

Amaruq felt sorry for the wolf. By rights, he should put her out of her misery, but he needed to hunt Nujuaqtutuq by any means possible. The sun was beginning to go down. For the first time in weeks, the clouds cleared and Amaruq saw the sun set behind the pine trees. He put up his tent before it got dark. He could hear his grandfather softly singing outside. Amaruq wrapped himself in pelts and closed his eyes.

That night, there was no wind. Moonlight. Silence. The silvery silence of the prairies. Amaruq slept better than he had in a long time. He was sleeping soundly when he felt a hand on his shoulder, shaking him awake. He opened his eyes and saw his grandfather. Exhausted, he tried to go back to sleep, but his grandfather was insistent. Amaruq sat up and shook himself awake. The sun was rising. His grandfather untied the tent flap and pointed outside. Amaruq put on his coat of caribou hide and ventured out. Dazzled by the rising sun, he rubbed his eyes as his grandfather led him towards the pine tree. The she-wolf was dead now, and next to her was Nujuaqtutuq, caught in a trap.

Amaruq inched closer to make sure it really was the great grey wolf. Instantly, Nujuaqtutuq leaped at him, dragging the heavy trap clamped on his hind leg. All that prevented him from reaching Amaruq was a chain tethered to the tree, which he jerked with such force that he almost dislocated the leg, causing blood to spurt from the wound. Nujuaqtutuq turned and tried to bite the trap; his teeth cracked against the metal. This was no hallucination.

Amaruq went back to the tent for his rifle, loaded the one remaining bullet and walked towards the wolf, who was gnawing at his paw in an attempt to free himself. Blood reddened the snow around him, the shattered bone was visible beneath his bitten flesh. Nujuaqtutuq trained his yellow eyes on Amaruq and bared his teeth with a low growl. He was a magnificent and powerful animal. Amaruq raised the rifle, aimed at the wolf's head and released the safety catch. He took a deep breath as he gently squeezed the trigger, but just as he fired he felt something nudge the barrel. The bullet missed Nujuaqtutuq. His grandfather had deflected the shot. Amaruq turned, furious. "Why?" he screamed. They held one another's gaze for a few seconds and then his grandfather vanished between the rays of sunlight. Amaruq tried to follow, but found himself staring at the cold morning air. "Why?" he shouted again and the word echoed, unanswered, around the sprawling forests.

The blast did not perturb Nujuaqtutuq; the wolf still stood defiant. Amaruq had used his last bullet. Now he would have to kill the big wolf with a knife or with his bare hands. He would have to choose his moment.

The last words I heard my grandmother say: "Do you want me to make you some dinner?"

The last words I heard my mother say: "Look after yourself, we'll be back on Tuesday."

The last words I heard my father say: "Make the most of us being away and tidy your room."

The last words I heard Carlos say: "..."

Camping

Before the tragedies, my life was good. I enjoyed living in the barrio, made friends at my new school, had teachers genuinely interested in my education, got good grades, was brilliant at basketball and average at football, had a couple of girlfriends, learned a second language, was considering going to university, knew how to fend for myself on the streets and was earning good money helping Carlos with the chinchillas. But then came the plague of destruction, and the locusts of death devoured everything in their path.

When I lost my parents, one of my uncles – my mother's brother – insisted I go to live with him in San Antonio, Texas. He painted a rosy picture of an idyllic life: a family prepared to take me in, an excellent university, friends, outings. He was a good man and the offer was generous and sincere, but I couldn't see myself living in the United States. He was the only person who called me every week, worried whether I had enough money to survive, to pay the school fees, get around. My other aunts and uncles, who had been distraught on my behalf at the wake and the funeral, called a couple of times to see how I was, and that was it. They rushed the conversation: "Hi, Juan Guillermo, how are you?" "Not great." "I can imagine. It's tough, but you'll get through this. I'm devastated too, but that's life, you've just got to tough it out." "No, *tía*, that's not life." "Come on, *hijito*, you'll get through this. We'll try and come visit this weekend, or maybe next. Be a good boy and look after yourself." And they would hang up. I get it. What could they do when I told them I wasn't O.K.? Invite me to live with them? Lend me money? No. They had their own lives to lead and they didn't want to be infected with death. Not that I would have agreed to live with any of them anyway, they were strapped for cash as it was. Why make things harder? Two of my aunts and one of my uncles were raising kids of their own, all of them under six. What would they do with a seventeen-year-old orphaned to the marrow?

So yes, death burst into my life and ravaged it. But I was determined not to let it drag me under. Not me. No way.

It was colder than a witch's tit. The thermometer read -6°C and the Good Boys were stripped to the waist, doing their karate exercises. "Breathe from your diaphragm," Humberto said, bare-chested and looking as though he was in the blazing sun. "Cold is all in the mind, pain is all in the mind, defeat is all in the mind. Overcome them." Some of the boys were shivering uncontrollably, their lips purple, their skin livid. But they never grumbled. One protest could mean being excluded from the group. And that meant dishonour. Being a part of the Young Catholics Movement that exemplified the values instilled by their conservative families, defending their faith, fighting for Christian morality, all these things were a source of pride for them. They were thrilled at the notion of being righteous amid the moral decay.

According to Humberto, enduring the bitter cold made them stronger, the glacial mountain air purified body and mind. Exercise prepared them for battle. I watched from a distance, wrapped up warm in a Chiconcuac jumper. Agüitas had come with me, and complained steadily as he shivered. "Fuck! I don't know how I let you convince me to come on this bullshit trip."

The previous Wednesday, Humberto had come up to me after the meeting. "The last weekend of every month we organise a camping trip to Las Monjas, and we'd like to invite you and your friends." He made it sound fun: tents, campfires, trout fishing in the rivers, karate and judo classes, long chats, mountain treks, rock climbing, zip-lining. I knew it was all lies, another of his ploys to draw me in. Fanatical proselytising always dresses itself up in affability and affected smiles. I

187

accepted, not simply so that I could spy on them, but because there was something about their Christian zeal and incorruptible morality that fascinated me.

Of my friends, only Agüitas had agreed to come. He loved the countryside and he believed the lie I came up with to top Humberto's lie: "I think it could be a lot of fun," I said. It couldn't have sounded more phony. Who could have fun with this bunch of squares?

We arrived on a Friday afternoon. The Good Boys pitched eight tents, and assigned three people to each. Agüitas and I had a tent to ourselves, on the outskirts of the camp. Dinner was sweet pastries with watered-down milk. At eight o'clock Humberto ordered us to switch off our torches. Obediently, the Good Boys did as they were told. The campground was plunged into darkness. Over the next few minutes, there came a drone that grew steadily louder: the Good Boys were reciting the Lord's Prayer. Then, almost in unison, they ended with a resounding "Amen".

At 4.00 a.m. we were woken by Antonio blowing a whistle. "On your feet, it's breakfast time." Agüitas rolled over and crawled out of his sleeping bag. "These fuckers are crazy," he mumbled, as Antonio went on blowing his whistle.

The Good Boys emerged from their tents, lighting the way with their torches. Some collected firewood, others lit the fire or helped prepare breakfast: a huge pot of hot chocolate and several pans of scrambled eggs. They wore only white vests, with nothing else to protect them from the biting cold.

I decided to go out without covering up. Agüitas looked at me, bewildered. "Are you fucking serious, Cinco? You're as crazy as they are." "You think I'm going to let these guys think they're more macho than me?" I said. The cold hit me hard, but I tried to breathe the way Humberto had taught us and felt a warmth spread through my body.

After breakfast, a young priest celebrated a Mass that lasted nearly an hour and a half, with a sermon stuffed with parables and allegories.

The Good Boys shivered with feeling as he spoke, but the sermon was completely insubstantial, nothing but empty rhetoric.

When Mass was over, Humberto gathered us for a five-kilometre uphill run. We set off as a group. The chubby guys, like Josué and Lalo, soon lagged behind or started throwing up. Humberto, who was extremely fit, retraced his steps to urge them on: "Give it all you've got, don't embarrass us all. Run." He yanked their arms, forcing them onwards. Stumbling and tripping, the poor bastards had no choice but to carry on.

Nobody was allowed to give up. Nobody. I don't know how I hadn't realised that the Good Boys were an army in training. The paramilitary wing of the Young Catholics Movement. Humberto was the commander chosen to lead these clandestine death squads and everyone unquestioningly obeyed.

After the run, there was a difficult martial arts exercise. Agüitas and I were only allowed to observe. They were not just going through the motions, these were real attacks. They hit each other hard while Humberto roared, "Push through the pain! Pain is all in your mind!" Many of the boys had split lips, bloody noses, swollen faces, their feet were sore from the kicks. But they couldn't complain, so the injured would discreetly withdraw, some choking back tears, wipe off the blood and then carry on fighting.

At 2.00 p.m., they started to prepare lunch. "Breakfast like a king, lunch like a prince and dine like a pauper," the priest declared. For the Good Boys, eating "like a prince" meant boiling vegetables, rice and chicken legs in a huge cauldron. And that was it. Tasteless mush. Frugality and discipline.

The "entertainment" consisted of football matches played on the rocky ground. The trout-fishing, hiking and rock climbing were just empty promises. The Good Boys began and ended every activity with a prayer that always concluded with the words: "I will place my life in god's hands and be rewarded for my actions." Fucking murderers.

They didn't place their lives in anyone's hands and they escaped unpunished for their fanatical crimes.

On the bus home, Humberto sat next to me. We made small talk. He told me he wanted to run a marathon. "It's something I have wanted to do since I was a kid." I talked about how I used to want to be a professional footballer or a basketball player. He seemed interested. He asked if I was thinking about going to university and I said I was, told him I wanted to be a vet and a writer. He smiled. "Writing isn't always a good thing," he said, and I have never understood why. He talked about how much the group liked me, how quickly I'd become one of them. "You know a lot for a fourteen year old," he said. "You read the Bible and choose interesting parts." I didn't know where all this was leading. Why the compliments? Humberto glanced around to make sure nobody was listening, then whispered: "On the last Saturday of the month we meet to choose new members. It's a secret ceremony, nobody can know about it – not your brother or your friends. We want you to be part of the movement. We would be happy to welcome you," he said, and smiled broadly.

So this was the reason behind the compliments: they wanted to recruit me. I felt pleased with myself. My undercover spying had worked perfectly. Carlos would be proud. "Do I have to cut my hair?" I asked. Humberto smiled again. "Of course not. Jesus wore his hair long, like you. You can decide later whether you think it's necessary to wear it neater. Should we expect you on Saturday?" I nodded. Humberto squeezed my shoulder and gave me a benevolent smile. I stared out at the dark road. It was night.

It took a long time to get Colmillo into my house. Even three of us could barely control him. He snarled at us, growled, tried to break loose. Our hands were blistered from gripping the chain so tightly. The Prieto brothers laughed as they watched us tussle. "He's going to eat you alive," they snorted. The vet simply stood and watched, he didn't seem to be enjoying the show; in fact, even though I had punched him, he seemed to feel sorry for me. Mr Prieto came over. "Let the vet put him to sleep, *hijo*. You're never going to be able to handle him." He was a decent man. His concern was genuine. "No," I said stubbornly. "I'm going to look after him." Mr Prieto shook his head – I was clearly unable to control this fierce, indomitable beast. But I had vowed to save him and was not about to go back on my word. "The vet's right there, and I've already paid him – it's not too late to change your mind." "No," I repeated. Mr Prieto shrugged, walked back to his sons and urged them inside.

Colmillo didn't stop struggling even for a second. He had boundless energy. For almost an hour we sweated until we finally managed to get him into my garage. As soon as he saw King, Colmillo attacked. King raced up the stairs at top speed and Colmillo towed us along behind him. When we tried to restrain him, he changed course and crashed into the T.V., shattering the screen.

By now our hands were bleeding and still Colmillo twisted and turned, trying to attack, as we circled him. "I can't do this anymore," Pato said. "Me neither," gasped Jaibo. I was feeling exhausted too. "At least help me get him into the yard," I said. "I can't use my arms anymore," Pato wheezed, "maybe later, when he's calmed down." "O.K.," I said. "On the count of three, let go and run for it. And don't forget to close the door. One, two . . . three." Jaibo and Pato bolted, leaving me alone with Colmillo. For a moment, he seemed to calm down a little, but when I slackened the chain he turned to attack. He was still wearing the muzzle, so he just charged into my legs, almost knocking me over. He came at me again and I grabbed a chair to defend myself. I hunkered down, wound the chain around the table leg and dashed upstairs. Colmillo tried to follow but the chain held him back. I dragged King into Carlos's bedroom and closed the door behind us. I could hear Colmillo straining to break free, chairs toppling, glass shattering, plates crashing. Then, after a while: silence.

An hour later, I decided to check on him. Peering down from the landing, I saw Colmillo lying down. He finally seemed to have calmed down. Unable to escape the chain, he had dragged the dining table through the living room, wrecking the ground floor in the process. It would cost a lot of money to repair.

I went back to the bedroom. King was hiding in the bathroom. As soon as he saw me, he wagged his tail. I called him and he warily came and lay down on the bed. My hands were burning, my palms red-raw from Colmillo jerking on the chain. My arms ached so much I could barely lift them.

I lay down next to King. He was still nervous. He used to be as playful and confident as a pup, but had become timid and mistrustful since the stabbing. I was six when it happened. King had raced out of the house one night when we opened the security gate and headed across the motorway towards Río Churubusco. He was lucky not to be hit by a car. My father tried to follow, but King disappeared into the dark football pitches before emerging to prowl the alleys of San Andrés Tetepilco where he happened on a drunk. He bounded up at the man, eager to play. Thinking he was being attacked, the drunk man pulled a knife and plunged it into King's muzzle, almost cutting off his lip. King collapsed and rolled in the mud. We found out about the incident by following the trail of blood back to the drunk, who lay collapsed on a bench, still clutching the knife.

King had tried to run home, but having lost so much blood he passed out in a waterlogged field. My father found him hours later, unconscious and almost drowning. He carried the dog home, laid him on the back seat of his Mercury and took him to the vet. King needed fourteen stitches. The vet ordered rest. We moved King out into the backyard where he lay, unmoving, for days. One morning I went to see him and found a column of ants crawling over the wound and the inside of his mouth, carrying away pieces of the scab on his jaw. Furious at the thought that they were eating my dog, I trampled them. It took

King almost two months to recover. His lip was never the same again, it quivered when he breathed and made a snorting sound.

King and I lay on the bed for a while, drifting in and out of sleep. Several times, I was woken by the pain in my hands. After two hours, the doorbell rang insistently. Colmillo once again became agitated and started dragging the table around the room. I ran to my parents' room and opened the window. It was Fernando. "What's up?" I said. He held up a folder. "These are Colmillo's papers," he shouted. "Pedigree, the vaccination records and the documents from the vet." "Coming," I shouted.

I didn't dare go through the living room for fear of making Colmillo even more agitated. I climbed out onto the roof, into the Ávalos' backyard, jumped the fence and walked over to Fernando, who handed me the folder. I leafed through the papers inside. X-rays, medical reports, dates of vaccinations and leaflets in English about Colmillo's pedigree with recommendations about care, diet and training.

Outside the Prietos' place, removal men were carrying furniture to a van. "What time are you leaving?" I asked. "Four o'clock. They're just packing up the last few bits of furniture." We said nothing for a while. "Look after Colmillo," he said. "Sure," I said. "Come by and visit anytime." We hugged and Fernando walked back to his house. He never came back to the barrio and I never heard from him again.

I didn't know whether Colmillo would kill me. Whether he would kill King. Gobble up Whisky and Vodka. I didn't know what would happen if Chelo came back, opened the door with the key I gave her, and stepped inside only for Colmillo to eviscerate her. What would I do with one more death? There could be no more. There was no space left in the burial chambers of my mind. It was full. There was no room for Colmillo, that is why I had to save him.

Tame

A few months before Carlos died, a group of foreigners rented the Richards' house. Two long-haired athletic guys – one blonde, the other dark – who always wore jeans and a slim, pretty girl with powerful arms, pale skin and hazel eyes. All three were about thirty. We assumed the guys were football players and the girl was married to one of them. We could work out a little of what they said – a few words here and there. We knew they had taken a six-month lease.

At first, they were a mystery. Every day at noon, they would drive away in a white Datsun and not reappear until dark. One night, while we were shooting the shit on Mrs Carbajal's rooftop, we heard a roar from down in their yard. Peering over the edge we saw the girl playing with a tiger cub that was jumping up on her, gently nibbling her neck.

"Holy shit! A tiger!" Agüitas yelped.

She looked up and saw us spying.

"Hey! Do you want to come play with him?" she said in her foreign accent. We raced down from the roof, she opened the door and we ran out into the garden. Although it was just a cub, the tiger was magnificent.

"You can go closer," she smiled.

We inched closer. The cub looked at us then suddenly jumped up on Jaibo, who shrieked. Startled, the tiger cub scampered off and hid in a corner.

The girl's name was María, the guys were Braulio and João. They were animal tamers from Rio de Janeiro working for a circus that was in Mexico City for six months, which was why they had rented the house.

We started going round to their place to play with the tiger cub, and slowly got to know them. They often invited us for lunch. They cooked Brazilian food – moqueca de peixe and coconut shrimp. María would kiss both guys, without a flicker of embarrassment. They even admitted that the three of them slept with each other. Accustomed as I was to people in Mexico City being very reserved, I found her Brazilian directness incredibly attractive.

All three exercised every day: they went jogging at daybreak and lifted weights in the garden. João explained that they needed to keep in shape. "Lions and tigers know whether you're weak or strong. If they sense you're weak, they'll kill you."

They had travelled all over the world and were multilingual, and after only two months in Mexico they could hold a conversation in fluent Spanish.

One morning Braulio told us that they were going to practise their routine and asked if we wanted to watch. On Mondays, when the circus was closed, they used the time to correct mistakes and try out new routines. We jumped at the chance.

With no crowds, the big top looked cavernous. It could hold at least a thousand people. Braulio set up seats two metres from the huge cage, warning us not to get too close – with a swipe of its paw, a tiger could easily reach us through the bars.

"You can take the tiger out of the jungle, but you can't take the jungle out of the tiger," he said.

María and Braulio stood in the middle of the cage while João led in four tigers and four lions. You could clearly hear the harsh rasp of their breathing. Braulio cracked his whip, the big cats took their places on their stools and the rehearsal began. As the animal tamers cracked their whips, the circus cats jumped through hoops, balanced on balls and swapped stools, leaping through the air in unison.

João came out and sat with us while Braulio and María carried on.

"Like it?"

"It's fucking amazing," replied Pato. "Especially seeing them up close like this."

"Which one of you wants to come into the cage?" João asked.

"Not me, no way," Jaibo said without a moment's hesitation.

"Me neither," Agüitas said.

Pato and I looked at one another.

"I'll do it," I said.

João slapped my knee.

"*Vamos*."

He led me into the ring and told me to pay attention.

"Don't run, don't make any sudden movements, never try to run away, never look them in the eye and never turn your back on them."

I was starting to feel sick.

"Nothing can happen to me, can it?"

"Of course it can. To you, to me, to Braulio, to María. They could kill us all in five seconds flat. That's what makes it so thrilling. Do you want to stay outside the cage?"

I glanced at my friends. It was too late to change my mind now.

"No, I'll go in," I said.

João opened the gate, ushered me inside and then closed it behind him. Slowly, we walked to where María and Braulio were waiting. My heart was hammering. I could smell my own adrenaline. I could feel the big cats' breath, see the scars where they had slashed each other, make out the delicate shades of their coats, see the feral flicker in their eyes. I suddenly understood Braulio's words: "You can take the tiger out of the jungle, but you can't take the jungle out of the tiger." I understood Borges and Spinoza: the tiger eternally wants to be a tiger.

The animals studied me warily. I was an intruder. I turned towards the male tiger in front of me. He watched me intently. We stared at each other, less than a metre apart. The tiger crouched and leaned forward. His eyes narrowed. I looked away, careful not to turn my back, and retreated two paces, then looked at him again to show I was not intimidated. The tiger stood, motionless, glowering at me. Sensing the animal was about to pounce, Braulio cracked his whip twice and the tiger jumped to another stool.

I let out a sigh of relief. María came over and whispered:

"He was about to attack. You did exactly the right thing."

María cracked her whip and the lions and tigers began to circle the cage in opposite directions, almost brushing each other as they passed.

"Stand there. Don't move," she said.

João moved to the gate, opened it and ran his whip along the bars. The big cats trooped out. The tiger I had exchanged a look with paused and eyed me for a moment, then padded on.

"You're the first person to go inside the cage," María turned to me. "We've asked for volunteers in every country, but people are too afraid. Congratulations."

In fact it was incredibly stupid of them to invite me, and of me to accept. But I didn't regret it. It was the most terrifying experience of my fourteen-year-old life.

When Pato and I were walking home together, he asked what it had felt like, being in the cage with the lions and the tigers. I thought for a moment.

"Like we were all animals."

Pato gave a little laugh.

"You've turned into a real philosopher," he said. "But then again, you've always been a bit of an animal."

He clapped me on the back and walked away towards his house.

A lion does not wonder whether it is a lion. It is a lion.

His hands inside his gloves were numb, his vaporous breath formed crystals of ice in his beard, his lips were chapped. His head was battered by the cold night air. He did not care. He was keeping vigil over Nujuaqtutuq, his knife unsheathed in his hand.

The great wolf had curled up to protect itself from the snow that had been falling since sunset. The animal seemed placid but Amaruq was not reassured: this apparent calm might simply be a ruse.

Amaruq butchered the she-wolf and devoured hunks of meat and heart raw. He ate wolf so that he might become wolf. He did it while Nujuaqtutuq watched, to show that he was a predator and the wolf his prey.

At first light, a thick fog stole in. Within minutes, there was an impenetrable layer of grey. Amaruq could barely see a metre in front of him, and Nujuaqtutuq disappeared behind the dense fog. Amaruq gripped his knife. He did not know whether it was another of the wolf's tricks. Perhaps Nujuaqtutuq would slink around to attack him from behind. He turned around to look. The swirling fog was growing thicker still. Where was the great wolf?

Amaruq heard a low rumble from the mountainside. The snap of branches, the crunch of snow, the crack of boulders falling. Avalanche, he thought. Blindly, he stumbled towards the tree for protection and in doing so brushed against Nujuaqtutuq. The wolf's eyes were fixed on the approaching roar. Amaruq jumped back, fearing that the wolf would snap at him, but the animal ignored him.

The thunderous roar grew louder, and as it approached the wolf's every muscle tensed. Amaruq huddled behind the pine tree: if it was an avalanche, at least he would not be dragged far. It sounded as though the mountain itself was crumbling. Suddenly, Amaruq made out shapes charging towards them through the fog, a huge herd of stampeding wapiti being chased by Nujuaqtutuq's pack. In all that fog the wapiti could not see the trees, and they crashed into them. One bull was headed directly towards Nujuaqtutuq. Though chained to the tree, the great wolf bounded forward; the wapiti swerved, but was running so fast that it collided with the tree and fell onto its back. Nujuaqtutuq pounced, sinking his fangs into the animal's broken neck. The wapiti offered no resistance as it let out its last breaths.

The wapiti and the wolves hurtled past Amaruq in a maelstrom of hides and hooves, sending up flurries of snow. He could hear the howling wolves attack, hear the wapiti lash out with their hooves, the crack of antlers splintering against the trees.

The herd of wapiti disappeared into the fog, with the pack close behind, heading towards the prairie. The thunderous rumble faded. Amaruq felt defenceless. Maddened by the blood, the wolf pack could turn back to attack him. He heard a crack of bone and, peering through the fog, saw Nujuaqtutuq gorging on the dead wapiti's throat. Amaruq sensed a stealthy creeping; he could smell the wolf pack. He slipped his knife into his belt, grabbed a branch, hoisted himself into the tree and climbed as high as he could.

Amaruq listened to the struggle of the dying wapiti, the snapping jaws of the wolf pack, squabbling among themselves for precedence. He heard them eagerly devour their prey, the rip of flesh, the squelch of entrails.

This was where Nujuaqtutuq had been leading the pack: not towards death, but towards abundance. He must have known instinctively that the wapiti had sought refuge in the northern forests.

By mid-morning, the fog had dissipated. In the cold light of day, Amaruq could see no wolves, only scattered carcasses. A wapiti calf wandered through the pine trees, lowing for its mother. Amaruq jumped from his branch and fell face-down in the snow. Turning, he saw Nujuaqtutuq was still eating, his blood-smeared snout buried in the belly of the wapiti.

Amaruq scanned his surroundings to make sure there were no wolves nearby. Knife in hand, he went back to the tent, fetched a rope and made a slipknot. Some metres away, a wapiti with a broken back was trying to crawl away. Amaruq approached from behind to avoid being kicked, straddled the animal, grabbed it by the ears and slit its throat, slicing through the carotid artery. The wapiti groaned and the blood gushed. Amaruq left it to bleed out. With two wapiti he had enough meat to survive until he got back.

He moved towards Nujuaqtutuq, approaching him warily. The wolf pulled its snout from the belly of his prey and growled at him. Amaruq calculated the length of the chain tethering the wolf. He lassoed the leg of the wapiti with the slipknot and jerked it away from Nujuaqtutuq. He could not let the wolf continue to eat. If he was to kill the great wolf, he needed him so weak that he could no longer stand.

Amaruq heaved with both arms, inching the carcass towards him. Nujuaqtutuq clamped down on the ribcage with his powerful jaws. Amaruq wound his rope around a pine tree and made another knot for every centimetre he gained. The wolf did not give up, but struggled fiercely. Amaruq wound the rope around his arm, let himself fall backwards, levering with his legs. He pulled the dead wapiti closer. Still Nujuaqtutuq did not let go. Together, carcass and the wolf were so heavy that the task was almost impossible, but Amaruq was determined to take the wolf's prey.

Realising that his strategy was not working, Amaruq stood up again. Nujuaqtutuq quickly took advantage of this and tugged the wapiti towards him. Amaruq went back to his tent and returned with an axe. Careful to stay out of reach, he began to hack at the wapiti's carcass. Far from being intimidated, Nujuaqtutuq tried to attack, snapping at the air, but the pain from the leg caught in the trap forced him to recoil.

Amaruq cut the wapiti in half and then lassoed the remainder of the carcass, and was finally able to drag the butchered remains towards him. The wolf held fast with his jaws, but Amaruq would not give up.

Desperate, Nujuaqtutuq bit the trap to try and free himself, only to howl in pain as he bloodied his muzzle. Amaruq wasted no time; he hauled with all his might and lugged the remains of the wapiti away from the great wolf.

Enraged, Nujuaqtutuq lunged again and again at this man who had stolen his food, tearing his hind leg without managing to break free.

Both predators collapsed in the snow, exhausted. The battle had lasted more than an hour. Amaruq hung the pieces of wapiti from a

200

tree out of reach of wolves and bears. He had left Nujuaqtutuq with nothing. Now he had only to wait and see how long Nujuaqtutuq could hold out.

I walked nervously around the block several times before summoning the courage to ring the doorbell. Doing so would mean taking the deception way too far. I was starting to get bored with the whole thing, but at the same time the idea of penetrating the dogmatic world of the Good Boys was appealing. I stood in front of the door and hesitated. But for my brother's insistence, I would have long since given up my Trojan Horse project. It was 8.17 p.m. when I finally decided to ring the bell. I remember the time because Mr Belmont was driving past in his blue Opel with the windows down, and I could hear the tinny voice of the radio presenter: "It's seventeen minutes past eight, here on Radio Mundo, music fans, and I'm going to leave you with the song 'Rosas en el Mar', by the beautiful Massiel."

Antonio opened the door and eyed me disapprovingly. He was wearing a black cassock, tied at the waist with a thick cord. "The appointment was for eight sharp." "I got held up," I lied. "If you want to come, you can't be late." I felt like saying: "I don't want to come, you fat shit," but instead said: "Then I'll see you next time, I guess." He opened the door and ushered me in.

He led me to the basement, where the lights were turned off and the space was illuminated by a kerosene lamp and two flaming torches mounted on the wall. The Good Boys, all dressed in black robes, were sitting in a circle. Humberto was in the middle, looking grave. "You have interrupted our devotions," he snapped. "I'm sorry," I said. He gestured for me to join the circle between Josué and Saúl, waited for me to sit and then bowed his head and continued to pray.

The devotions lasted several minutes. This time they weren't muttering Our Fathers or Hail Marys, but prayers I couldn't make out. When he'd finished, Humberto raised his head and looked at me again.

201

"Welcome," he said. Then he spoke to the rest of the group. "Brothers in Christ, as I told you I have invited Juan Guillermo to join our flock. He has shown constancy and discipline, and though he does not attend Mass, and knows little of religion, he has demonstrated devotion to Catholic morals and made an effort to integrate into the group and study the Bible."

He waved his hand. Two boys set up a folding table and covered it in a cloth of purple velvet embroidered in gold, with a large cross and four smaller crosses: the Jerusalem cross.

Humberto watched in silence and, when the table had been set up, took his place behind it. The others remained in the circle. "Juan Guillermo, take two paces forward." I did so. "We are a tight-knit group and when someone decides to join the Movement, it is for life," Humberto continued. "We defend each other and we safeguard our families. We have deemed you worthy of joining, which is why we invited you here. If you do not think yourself equal to these commit-ments, you may refuse. We will not take your refusal badly, but will pray that the Lord Jesus Christ may send you a sign of love and hope, so that you may accept in the future. But if you should decide to join us, know that this bond is sealed in blood and to break it is considered treason. Not against us, but against god the Almighty. No-one should dare forsake the brotherhood. I will ask you three times, and if you respond "yes" each time we will rejoice and accept you with open arms. If, even once, you answer "no", we will mourn and anxiously await the moment when you are ready to say "yes" with joy and certainty. Now, Juan Guillermo, do you consent to join the Young Bridegrooms of Christ, to submit to our rules and devote your life to the service of Our Lord?"

I said nothing for a moment. They stared at me, expectantly. I wanted to shout NO, loudly, definitively. Make them see that I thought their movement was sick and ridiculous.

"Yes," I said.

"I will ask a second time: do you consent to join the Young

Bridegrooms of Christ, to submit to our rules and devote your life to the service of Our Lord?"

Abso-fucking-lutely not. Jesus, fuck! Why did I feel this morbid need to say "yes"?

"Yes," I said.

"For the third time, Juan Guillermo: do you consent to join the Young Bridegrooms of Christ, to submit to our rules and devote your life to the service of Our Lord?"

Final chance. Final. Humberto's eyes bore into me. I stared back evenly. Almost fourteen and about to sign up to a life sentence. I've said "yes" twice. Desperate to prove my manliness. I can't back down. "No" is not an option. Morbid fascination. Machismo. Infiltration. Pretence. Curiosity. Sentenced to life.

"Yes," I said.

The word was followed by a long silence. A faint smile played on Humberto's lips. "We welcome you. Now you must seal your entry into the Movement in blood."

The Good Boys broke the circle, rummaged in a box and took out dark hoods which they placed over their heads before returning to their places. Humberto was the last to don his hood.

"Take off your shirt," he ordered.

"What for?"

"From now on, your duty is to obey. Take off your shirt."

I took it off. One of the other boys took it and laid it on the table, neatly folded.

"Kneel."

What had I got myself into? Fuck. I kneeled down.

"Confess."

I had never made my confession. I had a vague idea of what it entailed: kneel in a wooden box and tell the priest your sins, no matter how trivial. But these boys were not priests and I didn't think they had the right.

"I thought people were supposed to confess to a priest?"

"Obey. We are your brothers now. Christ is listening, so you'd better not lie."

I made up enough to satisfy their need to pry into my private life: lying to my parents, larceny and petty theft, sinful, unfulfilled desires (if they only knew about Fuensanta . . .).

They listened attentively – or so I supposed, it was impossible to know what they were thinking under their hoods. When I'd finished, Humberto took a whip out of the cupboard and stood behind me. "Be strong as Christ was strong, endure as Christ endured the scourging by his enemies, the Jews," he said and started to whip my back. I cried out at the first stroke. After the third, I fell flat on my face. He whipped me three more times. My back was burning.

"You have been cleansed," he said.

I lay on the floor as they once again formed a circle. "Get up," Humberto said. I struggled to my feet; every movement was agony. Humberto stood in front of me.

"You have shed your blood for us, just as Christ did on the cross to save us from sin. You are now our brother. Welcome."

That night, I looked at the weals in the mirror. Six long bloody slashes. I soaked a towel in surgical alcohol and laid it across my lacerated back to disinfect it. The pain kept me awake all night.

Humberto was a great deal more sophisticated than we were. There I was, playing at being Carlos's spy, when in reality the whole thing had been an elaborate trap patiently orchestrated by Humberto. Humberto knew we were atheists, he knew all about our Argo Trip at Cine de la Viga, he knew Carlos dealt drugs, that he was an enemy to be destroyed. He also knew Carlos was armed and knew how to fight. The fight with Antonio had proved that. He knew Captain Zurita had tried and failed to arrest him. He knew that I was lying, that I didn't agree with any of the ridiculous beliefs they professed. He had used me. Without realising, I had become a double agent. He feigned smiles, enthusiasm, apologies, invitations, speeches. He knew how to impress, how to manipulate. We had fallen into his trap. In my defence I can cite my youth, my naivety. I was too young to realise what he was doing. But I was stupid and Carlos was arrogant. We never considered the consequences. We never sized up the enemy. And for that we paid dearly.

Etymology of Events (Part One)

ABANDONMENT: to be left alone. Derived from Old French *a bandon*, to place oneself in someone's power.

GOD: deity. From the proto-Indo-European *deiwos*, god, from the root *dyeu*, brightness.

ASSASSIN: murderer. From the Arabic *hashishiyyin*, plural of *hashishiyy*: hashish-users. A group of murderers who acted under the influence of hashish.

INTIMATE: close. From the Latin *intimus*: inmost, innermost, deepest.

PENETRATE: infiltrate. From the Latin, related to *penus*, the innermost part of a house where food is stored to keep it safe from thieves and animals.

JEALOUS: fear someone will take your beloved. From the Late Latin *zelosus*, from *zelus*, zeal, fervour, from the Greek *zelos*.

ANIMAL: living organism capable of breath and movement. From the Latin *anima*, breath, soul.

EMBRYO: a living being in the process of gestation. From the Greek *embryon*, literally "that which grows".

ENEMY: adversary, foe. From the Latin *in-*, not, + *amicus*, friend.

SUFFOCATE: to be unable to breathe. From the Latin *suffocatus*, past participle of *suffocare*, to choke.

SACRIFICE: to forgo, to offer the life of a creature to a deity, to kill. From the Latin *sacrificium*, from *sacrificare*, to make sacred.

INJURY: wound. From the Latin *iniuria*, wrong, injustice, insult, unlawful violence.

ADMIRE: respect. From the Latin *admirari*, regard with wonder, from *ad* + *mirari*, to wonder.

206

OBSCURITY: absence of light. From *ob*, over, + *scurus*, covered, from Proto-Indo-European root *(s)keu-*, to cover, conceal.

PASSION: strong and barely controllable emotion. From the Latin *passio*, suffering.

COMPASSION: to feel sorrow at the suffering of another. From the Late Latin *compassionem*, I share your suffering.

SAVAGE: indomitable, primitive, fierce. From the Late Latin *salvaticus*, alteration of *silvaticus*, wild, literally "of the woods".

TREASON: profound betrayal, a breach of trust, to deliver someone to their enemy, from the Latin *traditio*, I deliver, hand over.

CHAOS: disorder. From the Greek *khaos*, abyss.

Search

The cinema business generated extravagant profits. The income from vodka sales alone was double that of the chinchilla business. At every screening, at least two hundred and fifty tabs of L.S.D. were sold at six times the cost price. At the time, drug trafficking tended to be from the Third World to the First; this was the reverse. The merchandise was produced in the United States or Europe and imported into Mexico. This fact filled my brother with pride: Mexicans buying from Americans rather than the other way around.

Word of mouth became the most effective form of marketing. While most people were smoking weed or snorting coke, Carlos's clients had access to a more select experience. For middle-class Mexican kids, the notion that they had some connection with Vietnam vets by taking morphine or with the avant-garde by dropping acid made them feel rebellious and unique. And in a capitalist system, rebellion was – as Carlos had understood – a valuable commodity. One that Carlos knew how to label and market. He persuaded his customers that true rebels were those who stepped into the world of morphine and L.S.D. and left behind the pedestrian world of weed and cocaine.

Private universities fuelled the meteoric growth of the business. Well-heeled students with anti-establishment inclinations paid promptly and in hard cash. Additionally, terrified by the prevailing authoritarianism of the period, they kept a low profile, eager to avoid trouble with a regime that ruled with an iron fist. Some clients could be difficult, tried to avoid paying, became hysterical if a deal was delayed, called at all hours, pestered, resorted to blackmail. It was customers like these which led to Carlos carrying a knuckleduster in his pocket and a knife in a sheath up his sleeve. In most cases, Carlos could placate them by talking to them calmly. If that didn't work, the threat of a beating was usually enough to silence them. Only a handful of times did he have to resort to physical violence. A broken nose or a black eye would dissuade them from causing any further trouble. After all, this was the era of peace and love. For these young rebels the enemy was the *system*, not guys like my brother who provided access to the doors of perception.

With success came the danger of conspicuousness. Carlos became more cautious. He decided it was reckless to have Sean and Diego cross the border and ferry the merchandise for fourteen hundred kilometres. They had only to be stopped once for the authorities to be able to disentangle the labyrinthine system of supply, distribution and sale that he had created. Instead, he persuaded the hippies in Texas to buy morphine from the American distributors, in addition to supplying acid. He didn't mind paying extra. Dealing with only a single supplier was worth it.

He also persuaded them to get one of the group to transport the merchandise to Mexico. They chose a shy, innocuous blonde guy, cut his hair short and dressed him in preppy clothes so that he wouldn't attract attention. He looked like just one more exchange student coming to live with a Mexican family to learn Spanish.

His name was Bill Cone and he hailed from Seguin, Texas. His appearance belied his formidable intelligence and his ability to extricate himself from risky situations. He spoke flawless Spanish, but pretended not to understand when customs officials interrogated him about his luggage. He gave them a moronic gringo grin and they waved him through: anyone as stupid as he seemed couldn't be smuggling.

Bill would catch the Líneas Anáhuac bus from Piedras Negras to Mexico City, and when he arrived would take a taxi from the bus station to one of five hotels approved by Carlos, where he would patiently wait for the pickup. Carlos had a number of couriers – including

Jaibo – who had no idea what was in the Kleenex boxes wrapped in brown paper and sealed with packing tape. The unwitting couriers would walk past cops and police stations so calmly that nobody ever suspected anything.

I first met Bill at my house. He spoke Spanish with a neutral accent and perfect pronunciation. He was friendly and cultivated. Like Carlos, he was a fan of Hendrix, Blake, Rulfo, Faulkner, Nietzsche. Once the handover was done, Bill would check out of the hotel and move into Sean's room for a few days – where he dressed in his hippie threads, wore his necklaces and bracelets, and would shoot up morphine, take an acid trip. He was a strange sight in tie-dye shirts and jeans, with his military buzz-cut. Before returning to Texas, he would change back into his Mormon missionary clothes.

I liked Bill, until I found out that he was one of the many guys Chelo had fucked.

The sale-and-distribution system operated like clockwork. Carlos chose the Jesuit-run Universidad Iberoamericana as the base of operations ("Jesuits are the only atheists who believe in god," he used to say). A lot of his customers were students there, mostly in Communications, History or Literature.

Carlos never directly touted his merchandise. He would sit in the cafeteria chatting about history, literature, cinema, art and politics with professors and students. His broad knowledge charmed them. He could argue about existentialism with philosophers, and Hemingway or Buñuel with connoisseurs. He could recite by heart poems by Rimbaud and Verlaine – the favourite poets of the pretty female students he regularly screwed.

When invited to dinners or private parties, he would discreetly bring up the subject of drugs – "You know, true rebels are people who . . ." – and talk at length about the chemical, psychological and neurological changes produced by morphine and L.S.D., how they created a breach in the fabric of reality that allowed you to see it from unexpected angles. "The system warps your way of seeing the world," he would argue, persuasively. "Morphine and L.S.D. make it possible to reclaim your original viewpoint, your identity." These young people were fascinated by my brother's theories and charmed by his erudite digressions. He would give them a couple of hits for free and get them hooked, turning them into regular customers.

Once Carlos had created a solid base of consumers at the Universidad Iberoamericana, he moved on to other, much more conservative private universities run by religious institutions. "Opium is the religion of the people," he said, misquoting Marx. Here, too, he relied on his wit and knowledge. He could hoodwink reactionary professors with his wide-ranging knowledge of the Bible. If necessary, he would cite chapter and verse and pretend to be devout.

I went with him a few times and had fun watching him brazenly reel them in. Once, he was barred from an extremely religious university after telling a group of students over coffee: "God is like Santa Claus, something you believe in until you're eight. After that, praying to god is as ridiculous as expecting a fat grey-haired man in a sleigh drawn by reindeers to leave you presents under a tree." One of the female students – a devout believer with a taste for morphine – reported him to the board of directors. Although Carlos denied the incident, they discovered he was not enrolled at the university and denied him access. It hardly mattered; by then he had a long list of customers – including the outraged believer, who continued to buy from him and would occasionally roll around with him in seedy motel rooms.

Business at Cine de la Viga continued to grow steadily. In the course of fourteen months, Carlos, El Loco and Diego had encountered no serious setbacks. There had been no overdoses, no paranoia, no panic attacks, not even any brawls. Occasionally someone would start looking for a fight only to be calmed down by the peaceable spirit of the community.

Additional screenings were scheduled for Friday nights and the results were just as successful. In my honour, Carlos screened "Fantastic Voyage" with Raquel Welch, my favourite pin-up, about a group of scientists who are shrunk to microscopic size and injected into the body of a dying diplomat. In a race against time, they travel through his bloodstream in a minuscule submarine to break up a clot in his brain and save his life.

If the morphine freaks loved "Jason and the Argonauts", "Fantastic Voyage" was the perfect movie for acid heads. It was a metaphor for what they were experiencing: an impossible adventure inside their own bodies. The tiny vessel bumps against the walls of veins, silently passes nerve endings, becomes lost among neurons, is attacked by white blood cells, and is propelled by the powerful pulse of the heart.

Delirious and excited, customers started coming to both screenings. Nothing like a weekend devoted to the sensual pleasures of drugs and movies. Watching the same movie in the same place with the same people made them feel secure. A brotherhood of junkies.

The problems started one Saturday at dawn. Four revellers were heading back to their car on Calzada de la Viga. As the driver opened the door, they were surrounded by four men in hoods carrying baseball bats. Petrified, the four moviegoers put their hands up. "Take whatever you want," the driver pleaded, only to have a baseball bat smash into his face, shattering his nose and sending him flying. The other three, still tripping, thought maybe they were hallucinating, but a series of brutal blows quickly dispelled the psychedelic effects. As they lay on the ground they were beaten to a pulp of blood and broken bones. Before leaving, one of the attackers bent down and said: "We're going to kill junkies like you, and the dealers who supply you. Tell your friends that they must change, because God has sent us to drive the merchants from the temple." He stood up and the attackers ran off.

A couple of the moviegoers were left with broken arms or legs, all had cracked ribs, one had a fractured skull and the driver's nose and jaw were broken. All four were hospitalised and required surgery. The savagery of the beatings indicated a blind fury. Their parents decided not to inform the police. Their children had confessed their addiction to L.S.D. and morphine and they didn't want a scandal. None of the four informed on Carlos or his partners, or mentioned the secret cinema screenings. Sean went to visit them in hospital and they reassured him that they wouldn't rat on him.

Carlos was worried, but hoped it was an isolated incident. It wasn't. On the Monday afternoon, he had a call from the cinema manager. In a quavering voice, the man asked him to meet him in the cereal aisle in Gigante. Though it was a strange request, Carlos agreed. When he arrived, he spotted the nervous manager hiding behind a stack of Corn Flakes. When Carlos approached, the manager glanced around to make sure nobody was listening. A police captain named Zurita had paid a visit and told him he knew about the midnight screenings, the drugs, the booze and how much money they were making every night. "He asked for a fifty-thousand-peso down payment for not having me banged up," the fat man said, and whined: "You promised there'd be no problems." Carlos thought for a moment. "He's not going to send you to prison. He's got no evidence, no-one has raided the screenings. Go home and ask your cousin to give you two weeks' holiday and then assign you a different cinema. Don't go back to Cine de la Viga." The fat man was sweating. "But you said—" "Forget what I said," Carlos interrupted. "Now do what I tell you. I promise you'll be compensated for the inconvenience." Then he turned and walked away down the aisle.

The fat man did not do as he'd been told. The next day he went to Captain Zurita and cut a deal. In exchange for immunity, the fat man handed over the papers for his brand-new Volkswagen Combi and gave up Carlos, Sean and Diego.

Captain Zurita was surprised that such a profitable and clandestine operation was being run by three twenty-something punks. It wasn't in his interest to arrest them if he could extort money from them instead. He assumed the cinema screenings were the only business Carlos and his accomplices had going. He didn't realise that it was only a minor outlet within a complex narcotics enterprise.

Captain Zurita sent my brother a message via the fat manager: he would allow the cinema screenings to continue on condition that they gave him sixty per cent of their revenue from ticket sales. Carlos agreed. After six more screenings, when the day came for him to meet Zurita and hand over his percentage, Carlos disappeared. Captain Zurita was livid and it was then that the game of cat-and-mouse on the rooftops began, the police officers going undercover as buskers or street cleaners, the interrogations of neighbours and customers, the cars parked outside our house waiting for Carlos to appear. Their inefficient and clumsy pursuit.

My father wondered how it was possible for airplanes to fly. My mother wondered whether television waves, the images of newsreaders and presenters and football matches, passed through her body and lodged between her cells.

My father wondered how much animal remained in a football made of pigskin. My mother wondered how much animal remained in the human species.

My father wondered how mankind had managed to harness electricity to make a bulb work. My mother wondered how a car engine could use exploding petrol to make the wheels turn.

My father wondered whether dinosaurs had breathed the same air he now breathed. My mother wondered whether dinosaur meat was edible.

My father wondered about the teenage girl with the pointy nose and the almond eyes. My mother wondered about the black-haired boy who was always staring at her.

214

My father wondered whether the girl had a boyfriend. My mother wondered whether the boy found her attractive.

My father wondered how he might approach her. My mother wondered whether she should talk to him first.

My father wondered where she lived. My mother wondered whether her father would take to my father.

My father wondered what she looked like naked. My mother wondered whether he would get fat when he got older.

My father wondered whether she had bad breath in the mornings. My mother wondered whether he stank when he came home from work.

My father wondered whether she would like a pet dog. My mother wondered whether she could invite her parents to dinner on Thursdays.

My father wondered whether she would be good with money. My mother wondered if they would have enough to get by.

My father wondered whether a man who had been beheaded could still hear. My mother wondered whether it was worth bringing children into such a brutal world.

My father wondered whether a murder victim could forgive. My mother wondered if a rape victim could get revenge.

My father wondered what his first child would be called. My mother wondered what her last one would be called.

My father wondered whether he should tell us about Santa Claus. My mother wondered whether she should admit that her mother was an alcoholic.

My father wondered whether he should brake as he drove into the bend. My mother wondered whether this was her last moment alive.

Ever since he was a puppy, Colmillo had lived alone in a cramped space. During the day, he lay by the metal post to which he was chained. He didn't doze like other dogs, but peered through the railings at the street. When anyone came too close, he would get up and growl.

215

The Prietos rarely took him for walks. Even when muzzled, he caused trouble. He would attack people, cats, dogs, cars – anything that moved. He could put a deep dent in a car door. For his exercise, the Prietos preferred to take him to the football fields and let him run, always on a long lead.

Colmillo's whole life took place within a two-metre radius. Not that this stopped him from killing several cats. Colmillo would leave pieces of raw meat on the outer edges of his perimeter and hide in his kennel, patiently waiting for a cat to approach the bait. As soon as it was distracted, Colmillo would pounce. His jaws would close around the head and you could hear the skull cracking as he crushed it. He would devour them, skin and all. Carlos often joked about giving Colmillo a cut of his chinchilla profits for killing so many stray cats.

The Prietos had bought Colmillo by mail order. In the sixties, American magazines like "Outdoor Life" or "Field & Stream" ran advertisements by animal breeders offering dogs, cats and rabbits, as well as exotic pets like tarantulas, snakes, crocodiles and monkeys. Mackenzie Breeders, based in Mayo in the Yukon, offered wolf-dogs and pureblood wolves. "Buy a wolf-dog or wolf from us. Bred from grey wolves crossed with Alaskan Malamutes, our wolf-dogs are 25%, 50%, or even 75% pure grey wolf. For those brave enough, we also sell pureblood wolves." They discussed the characteristics of the cross: "Wolf-dogs are strong, companionable, magnificent and playful. Ideal for families. Once you've had a wolf-dog, you'll never want another breed."

Fernando, who like many in the barrio was passionate about hunting, saw the advertisement in "Outdoor Life" and asked his father for a wolf-dog for his birthday. Mr Prieto thought it was a good idea. They had owned demanding breeds before, a Doberman and a Great Dane. He assumed that, having trained such stubborn breeds, training a wolf-dog wouldn't be too difficult. He sent a letter asking for details.

After two months the reply came: the wolf-dog or pureblood wolves cost $150. It wasn't possible to ship to Mexico, but the animal could be transported to anywhere in Canada or the continental United States. The buyer should specify the desired percentage of wolf blood.

Mr Prieto sent a money order and the address of a cousin in Brownsville, Texas. A month later, the cousin called to tell him the puppy had arrived safe and sound. They smuggled him over the Mexican border in the boot of a Ford Mercury and took him to the train station in Matamoros, Tamaulipas, where he was put in a cage usually used for fighting cocks and sent to Mexico City as cargo.

They hadn't reckoned on the slow Mexican train network. Due to a derailment, the train carrying Colmillo spent hours stalled in the desert at San Luis Potosí, leaving the dog trapped in a cage, surrounded by sacks of flour and fertiliser, with little air and no water, at temperatures that reached 40°C. Colmillo, then only a month old, suffered serious dehydration and pulled through only because of his genes and his will to survive.

I went with the Prietos to the train station. Colmillo was lying in the cage unconscious and gasping for breath. They took him to the vet (the one who, years later, was his would-be executioner), who put him on an intravenous drip, in a room with a fan to lower his body temperature. Colmillo took weeks to recover. We visited every day. At first he just lay limply in the corner of the cage, but gradually the vet built up his strength, feeding him milk and later raw horsemeat. I loved feeding him. I would take a little ground meat between my fingers and Colmillo would lunge, his sharp incisors leaving teeth marks on my hand.

Fifty days later the Prietos took him home. The father tried to train him as he had his previous dogs. With Colmillo, nothing worked. Not shouting, not beating him with a rolled-up newspaper, not even lifting him up precariously over their heads. Colmillo destroyed the roses the mother had painstakingly cultivated, chewed on the hose, jumped on the car and ripped off the windscreen wipers, and, worst of all, attacked anyone who tried to stop him. At eight months, he bit Luis's arm. As punishment, Mr Prieto beat him and chained him to a metal post in the yard. Still, Colmillo savaged anything within reach. Mr Prieto gradually shortened the chain until Colmillo was confined in a tiny space where he had now lived for three years and ten months.

At 7.00 a.m., I resolved to go downstairs. As soon as I opened the bedroom door, King ran and hid in the bathroom. When my parents first bought King they thought they were getting a fearless guard dog who could scare off burglars. King was a wonderful dog – obedient, calm, playful – but fearless he was not.

I crept downstairs as slowly as possible so as not to attract Colmillo's attention. The ground floor looked as though a tornado had swept through it where he had trailed the table through the living room. Six of the ten dining chairs were broken, the china from the cabinet had been smashed, food was strewn over the floor, pots and pans were scattered around the kitchen. Colmillo had shattered the glass door leading out to the yard and ripped the plywood walls of my bedroom to shreds. Every corner, every piece of furniture, was soaked in urine. The carpet was covered in dogshit. I couldn't see Whisky or Vodka, and assumed they had escaped through the broken glass door, but then I found them, huddled and terrified inside their hollow log.

I knew that Colmillo couldn't eat while wearing a muzzle, but he'd bite me if I took it off. Perhaps it would be best to get hold of the vet, apologise and ask to have him put down? At the Prietos he'd been chained up day and night; with me he would permanently have to wear a muzzle. What was the point in keeping him?

Colmillo was lying under the table. He didn't try to stand up when he saw me. Hugging the wall, I inched barefoot towards the kitchen, careful not to step on dogshit or broken glass and crockery. I filled a saucepan with water and set it down close to him. I took the parakeets' cage and headed back upstairs. As soon as I started to go up the stairs,

Colmillo stood up, went over to the saucepan and managed to drink through his muzzle.

I set the birdcage on Carlos's bed and went into my parents' room to find the Yellow Pages. María, João and Braulio would know how to manage the savage beast prowling around downstairs and I needed to find a number for the circus where they worked. Being a touring circus, it wasn't listed. I phoned a famous Mexican circus where a man with a gravelly voice gave me a Russian phone number. "They're in Moscow," he said. "That's the agent's number." I had no idea how to call Russia, what prefix I should use. I called Pato and asked if he knew. "Sure, *cabrón*, I call Russia every fucking day. You dial who-fuck-knows-four-three-three and they put you straight through," he giggled.

After two hours I gave up and called the Mexican circus again. The same man answered. "So, did you get through to the Russkies?" I told him that I hadn't. "So what do you want?" he asked. "Do you have lion tamers?" I said. "Are you kidding? We don't take lions to children's parties," he laughed. "I need someone to help me train my dog." The man was silent for a few seconds. "You need a dog trainer, not a lion tamer," he said. "But he isn't a normal dog, he's a wolf-dog." "How old is he?" "Four." "And he's yours?" "Yes," I said, "but I only got him yesterday and I can't control him." "Sorry, we don't take on that kind of work, but if we did, we'd charge a fortune." This time I was silent for a moment. "If you can tame him, I'll pay anything you ask. If you can't, I'll give you fifty pesos just to come take a look at him." The man laughed again. "O.K., *chamaco*, I'll send over our best lion tamer. Give me your address and be prepared to shell out about three thousand pesos."

I sit in front of the mirror. I don't see myself, only him: Juan José, my twin. We talk. He tells me about darkness; I tell him about light. He tells me about the person he never got to be, and I tell him who I have been. He describes the world from the inside out; I describe it from the outside in. He stares at me from a body with no scars; I stare at him from a scarred body. Juan José struggles with death; I struggle with life. Juan José stopped. I . . . advanced? Juan José is steeped in silence; I in noise. I dream, he is a dream.

Every birthday, I thank him. For not killing me, for allowing me to kill him. Juan José was born a ghost. I am a living ghost. Juan José's house hovers in the air, mine is stranded here on earth. Juan José is wind. I am dust. He perceives, I feel. He watches me and in doing so watches himself. I am who he never came to be.

Every day when I look in the mirror, I remember him. His absence is presence. Juan José, my brother.

In the mountains of Serbia, it was believed that witches killed infants. They flew over their cradles and stole their lives away. That's why villagers sometimes name their male sons Vuk, meaning "wolf". That way the witches, who fear wolves, will not dare to attack them.

Tunnels

Legend has it that in the city of Kapilavastu, in the foothills of the Himalayas, a child was born and he was named Siddhartha Gautama. They say he burst into the world, not from his mother's vagina, but from her right side. His birth astonished his contemporaries and from his very first moments Siddhartha was considered to be special.

A caesarean, from the Latin *a caeso matris utero*, meaning "cut from the mother's womb", referred to the removal of a baby from a mother who died during childbirth. "*Si mater praegnans mortua sit, fractus quam primum caute extrahatur*": "If a pregnant mother dies, the fruit of her womb should be carefully removed as soon as possible." Those born by caesarean section explode into life from the tomb their mothers have become. The inverse of my mother's experience with Juan José, when she became my brother's coffin.

Over time the caesarean evolved, and it wasn't only used to remove babies from their dead mothers, but to save mothers and infants from certain death if the baby was awkwardly positioned, or there were potentially fatal risks. This was the case with Julius Caesar, the great Roman emperor.

If the difficult passage through the muscular tunnel of the uterus helps to prepare those born naturally for the rigours of life, does this mean that those who are born by caesarean are at a disadvantage? Is the pain of being born necessary in order to confront life?

I picture the moment of my birth. A corpse is floating next to me. Poisoned, I frantically search for a way out. My mother doesn't know what is happening in her womb. She feels weak, feverish. She is rushed to surgery. She is anaesthetised. A surgeon marks a line across her pelvis, makes an incision with a scalpel, cutting through skin, fat and muscle. He slices into her womb. Blood gushes. Without hesitation, the doctor puts his hand into the bloody opening and pulls out my brother's corpse. A minute later, he delivers me from the swamp where I lie submerged. I am rescued by the slash of a knife. Did this brute violence leave me less well prepared for life? Did it make me rougher, tougher, or more delicate?

When I turned eleven, my mother showed me the scar on her lower belly. It was not a neat, straight scar. The surgery had been rushed and the incision was crude. "This is where you came out," she said. My eyes followed the jagged white scar from end to end. "*A caeso matris utero.*"

It was my mother who told me the stories of Siddhartha and of Gaius Julius Caesar, so that I might identify with great men and feel as though I belonged to a glorious dynasty. My mother. How glorious could an emergency caesarean have been if one twin emerged alive and the other dead, one triumphant and the other defeated?

For three days the wolves circled the campsite, feeding off the remains of the dead wapiti between the pine trees. Amaruq was forced to hide in the tent and keep a fire burning outside the flap to ward them off. But through gaps in the canvas he could see various male wolves adopt a submissive posture before Nujuaqtutuq. At a growl from their leader, they would meekly roll belly-up. Even with his leg mangled and caught in a snare, Nujuaqtutuq still ruled.

The pack would spend the day lazing around the great wolf. At night they would howl. Nujuaqtutuq, though weakened by his wound, would stand and howl with them. Surrounded on all sides, Amaruq did not leave the tent for days. He ate strips of wapiti meat which he cooked on the fire outside the entrance to the tent. He was convinced that they would not attack for as long as the fire blazed. To feed the flames, Amaruq would force open the frozen flap and place branches on the fire. Fortunately, he had collected firewood some days earlier, and stacked it beside the tent. To fetch more fuel, he would arm himself with a flaming branch to ward off the wolves, collect what kindling he could and return to his refuge.

At moments of extreme exhaustion and ennui, Amaruq would ask his grandfather to guard the door and feed the fire while he drifted in and out of sleep, babbling in his dreams. He began to confuse night with day, day with night, a confusion brought on by exhaustion and delirium. He would wake with a jolt, fearing the fire would consume him, or the wolf pack enter the tent and devour him.

One morning, he looked out and the pack had disappeared. He stayed inside the tent, keeping watch to be sure that they had gone. At midday, he heard a roar. Peering out, he saw a cougar feeding on one of the wapiti. Ten metres away, Nujuaqtutuq was watching the big cat's every move, braced to fight.

The cougar ate until it was full. When it had finished, it dragged the wapiti carcass to the foot of a pine tree and used its paws to cover it with snow. Then the big cat looked at Nujuaqtutuq, bounded away and disappeared into the forest.

Amaruq knew that the cougar would only have dared to come so close if the wolf pack was gone. He scaled a tree to check. The icy branches were slippery and he almost fell, more than once. With great effort he reached the top and straddled the thickest branch, wrapping his legs around it. He scanned the horizon. The wolves were nowhere to be seen. Why had they left?

Amaruq climbed back down, collected more firewood and stacked it by the tent. Nujuaqtutuq watched him. More than once, their eyes met. The wolf was not yet ready to surrender, but Amaruq's strategy was beginning to work: the spreading gangrene was weakening Nujuaqtutuq.

Amaruq lit fires at the four corners of the tent. Snowflakes began to fall, carried on the wind. He looked up. Clouds covered the sky. A heavy snow was coming. In the shadows, Amaruq saw Nujuaqtutuq go to the foot of the pine tree to protect himself from the approaching storm.

Amaruq went into the tent and closed the door. Another long night on the icy prairies, roaming along the brink of madness.

He was from Oaxaca. He was chubby, with childlike features. He would have been about twenty-eight. The alcoholic and divorced lawyer (on whose property I'd cut my leg) had hired him to do the cleaning, the laundry and the cooking. He wore skin-tight jeans, gaudy T-shirts and sandals. He was an efficient and responsible worker. In less than a week he had sorted out the neglected garden and thoroughly cleaned the mucky yard. He planted rose bushes, chrysanthemums, night-blooming jasmine, calla lilies. He cleaned the windows, painted the walls, mowed the lawn.

In the afternoons, while we were playing football in the street, he would be watering the vines – or at least pretending to. In his tight jeans and lime-green T-shirt, he would watch us out of the corner of his eye. At first he feigned timidity and would greet us with a neutral "Afternoon, lads". Soon he would make the occasional comment, "Nice goal!" or "D'you think it's going to rain?", and attempt to make conversation.

One day he came up to us. "Hey, we've seen each other around but I haven't introduced myself. I'm Enrique, but I prefer to be called Quica. Nice to meet you." Pato leaned towards me and whispered, "Fag." Enrique or Quica was standing in the middle of the street, one pedicured foot pointing out in front of him. He had heard. "Don't be so rude," he said. "That's *no* way to treat a lady." We laughed and decided we liked Quica.

Enrique felt he was "a beautiful young woman trapped inside the body of an ugly man". He gave up pretending to water the vines and now sat on the kerb every day and watched us play. He would applaud our best moves with girlish enthusiasm. "Let's go, boys!" he would shout. He made no attempt to hide his homosexuality, he flaunted it.

At ten to eight precisely, he would say goodbye. "See you later, guys, I'm off to cook dinner for my boss." And swaying his hips in an exaggerated swagger, he would close the gate and head into the house.

Rumour had it that the lawyer's wife had divorced him after she caught him sexually abusing one of their sons one night. He didn't seem like a paedophile to us, but when it came to alcohol who knew what monster could be unleashed.

Agüitas swore he had once seen the guy kissing the lawyer through the window. We didn't believe him. Days later Pato bluntly asked Quica if he and the lawyer fucked. Quica smiled flirtatiously. "A lady never tells," he replied.

Quica's girlish boldness became increasingly provocative: surreptitious looks, sexual innuendoes, furtive fumbles. The crude attempts at seduction and the groping began to bother me. I kept my distance. His innocent, flirtatious maiden routine no longer seemed funny. I stopped speaking to him or paying him any attention. "Are you annoyed with me, Cinquito?" he asked, haughtily. I wouldn't even look at him. Enrique could be as womanly as he liked, I didn't care. It was his need to get in with us at every opportunity that irritated me. Agüitas and Jaibo, however, seemed hugely entertained. They laughed hysterically at his double entendres, and found it hilarious when he blew us kisses. Jaibo even seemed to enjoy the fondling. "Do you think you might be gay too?" I asked him. "No fucking way," he replied immediately and contemptuously. "It just seems like you enjoy it a lot," I shot back. "You're a dumbass," he said.

One afternoon Quica came up to Mrs Carbajal's rooftop with us. He drank beer with Agüitas and Pato. After the fourth beer, his gaze became mawkish and lecherous. He stared at me so insistently that I challenged him: "What the fuck are you looking at?" It was hardly likely that a twenty-eight year old would be intimidated by a thirteen-year-old boy. "You've no idea how much I want to kiss you when you're angry," he said, smiling. "Go fuck yourself," I said. Jaibo laughed derisively. Quica looked at him. "I love it when you laugh like that." Then, to the four of us, he said: "You should all have sex with me. You'd love it. I'll do things to your dicks that no girl ever could. I'm a wild pony, I'll give you the ride of your life," he said, without a hint of embarrassment. I felt uneasy around Quica even when he was sober, but when he was drunk, his brazenness made me furious. "I only ride mares," I snapped. "Are you staying here?" I said to Pato. "No, let's go." He got up and the two of us walked away. Being thirteen and incredibly horny, Jaibo and Agüitas stayed with Quica.

The following day, Jaibo told us that Quica kept up the sexual advances all night, and told them not to worry. "Nothing bad will happen, I just want to do some things that women do," he said to them. Two hours and ten bottles of beer later, there on the rooftop, Enrique, from San Mateo Tlachihuacán in Oaxaca, took their virginities. He kneeled in front of Agüitas, pulled down his boxers and started to give him a blowjob. A bewildered Jaibo stood and watched. Confused and excited, Agüitas leaned back against the clothes lines and came almost immediately. Enrique swallowed it all. When he had finished, he peeled off his trousers and told Jaibo it was his turn. He pulled the boy towards him, rubbed himself against him, tugged down his boxers and grabbed his penis. "Put it in me," Quica said, bending over and exposing his ass. Jaibo started to tremble. He didn't know whether he was turned on or terrified. "Go ahead, put it in," Enrique insisted, smearing saliva around his anus. Jaibo grabbed him by the hips, penetrated him, and Quica pumped until he came. "Didn't you find it disgusting?" Pato asked. "No," Jaibo said ingenuously. "It felt really good." Pato couldn't hide his disgust. "Seriously, Jaibo? Cinco was right, you're such a fag."

Jaibo didn't think it had anything to do with being gay. "Quica is the fag, he let me put my dick inside him. That doesn't make me a fag.

Anyway, he's basically a woman. He has the body of a woman, the ass of a woman, he walks like a woman and thinks like a woman."

Mortified, Agüitas refused to see us for weeks. He had satisfied his arousal and that was it. He didn't want jokes or judgement. Jaibo had sex with Quica a few more times – once in the lawyer's bed, where he found proof that the two were lovers. A jar of Vaseline, some condoms on the bedside table and the fact that Quica referred to him as "my man" was enough to confirm the relationship.

Neither Agüitas nor Jaibo slept with a woman until many years later, when they were nearly twenty, though neither of them showed any sign of being gay after that. In fact, probably to compensate, they became so obsessed with women that they hardly talked about anything else.

They called him Father Pepe. His full name was José de Jesús María Revilla del Campo. Bald, heavy-set, red cheeks. He always wore a black cassock and a white collar. Friendly and good-natured, he went from house to house in the neighbourhood inviting families to sign their children up for catechism classes and urging them to come to Mass. He was persistent. If he didn't see a family at Mass, he would visit until he'd persuaded them. "A community united in Christ is a powerful community," he would say. He had the tenacity of a vacuum-cleaner salesman. His aim was to get every child in the neighbourhood to come to classes on the sacred doctrine.

The persuasive powers that had been so effective in the fifties began to fade in the sixties. Attitudes changed fast. More cosmopolitan and educated, the parents in the barrio were not easily won over by Father Pepe's homilies. My parents were among those who clashed with him. Try as he might, he could not prevail against my father's categorical refusal to send his children to be educated in a religious dogma he didn't believe in.

After ten tiresome visits, my parents decided to stop answering the door. Still Father Pepe didn't give up. He would ambush my father anywhere their paths happened to cross: in the street, at the Popo-Sur 73 bus station, in the supermarket. My father avoided him. The priest would justify his evangelical harassment: "If a sheep should be lost, it is my obligation as a priest to bring it back into our Lord's fold." When my father insisted that he wasn't a believer, Father Pepe would retort: "You may not believe in god, but god believes in you."

Tired of his lectures, my father confronted him one Sunday as we were on our way to have tacos at La Cabaña. Father Pepe saw us from a distance and hurried across the road.

"I'm so happy to see you all here together," Father Pepe said. "I'd love to sit and chat with you."

"We're in a bit of a hurry. We want to get back in time to see the bullfight."

"Come on, *hombre*, just a minute to talk about god," said Father Pepe with his pedlar's enthusiasm.

"Please, sir, I beg you not to bother us." (My father would never address a priest as "father". "'Father' means my father, and I am a father to you and your brother, and that's it," he would often say.)

"Forgive me for being a nuisance," Father Pepe apologised, "but my mission is to guide you into the house of god."

My father glanced at Carlos and then my mother, then turned back to the priest.

"I believe in god."

"Really? You told me you didn't."

"I believe in the great god Quetzalcóatl," my father said, just to annoy him.

The priest smiled mockingly.

"You're joking, of course."

"No, it's no joke. I believe in Quetzalcóatl, our creator."

The priest laughed.

"Ha ha. So you're telling me that you believe in a feathered serpent who wears a loincloth?"

"Ha ha," my father sneered. "And you're telling me that you worship a long-haired man in a loincloth hanging from a cross?"

The priest's expression suddenly hardened and turned sour.

"Be very careful what you say," he warned.

"If you don't mock my god, I won't mock yours," replied my father.

Father Pepe stalked off with a red face, and hurried down the avenue. My father watched, satisfied. Perhaps that was the last time he would bother us.

He never came back to the house, and never importuned us again. If any of us bumped into him, Father Pepe looked at us scornfully and kept walking.

The priest met with defiance from other parents, who also rejected his relentless proselytising. His genial disposition turned to bitterness. Agüitas and his family, who went to Mass every Sunday, told us that in his sermons Father Pepe called for a boycott, and denounced the heretics in the barrio. "Do not speak to them, do not help them, do not sell to them, do not spend time with them. Do not allow your children to play with theirs, your wives to talk to theirs. If they wish to set themselves apart, so be it. But let them be truly apart. If they reject our Lord Jesus Christ, then we should reject them. Let them feel our censure."

Few among the faithful obeyed the priest's orders. Believing in god didn't mean causing trouble with your neighbours. Father Pepe became infuriated. His flock refused to obey him. Allowing heretics to thrive in the parish contaminated the rest, he thought, this was why drug use was on the rise, why young girls were promiscuous, why people were increasingly rude and selfish.

Father Pepe considered several options to strengthen the faith of the community. After some deliberation, he decided the best option was to focus on the young. From there, several strategies arose. He set up a choir to bring girls and boys into the church through music and "wholesome fun". He increased the hours of catechism classes and brought two more priests to the parish to help with his evangelical mission. He introduced a "youth Mass" for those under twenty on Saturdays at 10.00 a.m. His sermons attempted to kindle the love of Christ in them. An effective orator, he spoke of the heroic feats of the crusaders defending the faith, the suffering of martyrs at the hands of the non-believers, the vicissitudes suffered by missionaries spreading the word of god to remote regions. He encouraged young people to organise themselves to save Christianity: "Become the knights of the new Crusade, share the love of Christ with the world, devote your lives to defending the faith." The results were clear: young, committed people, ready to be a barrier against moral degradation and heresy. No more blasphemy, no more materialism, no more enemies of Catholicism.

According to Father Pepe's plan, these young people should behave generously, respectfully, responsibly. He never could have imagined the Frankenstein's monster his youth organisation would become. The "Good Boys", as he called them, were divided into various groups. Those in the choir were innocents only interested in singing and organising harmless parties to raise funds for charitable activities in the parish. Others became missionaries and set about visiting poor communities to offer help and share Christ's message, or decided to enrol in seminaries in the hope of becoming priests. Still others banded together in an intolerant and fanatical brotherhood. Young People Committed to Christ was founded by Humberto and Antonio, together with Ricardo, who died from leukaemia when he was eighteen.

This brotherhood belittled the other groups that had emerged from Father Pepe's initiatives, considering them insipid, weak and incapable of defending Catholicism. They thought those in the choir were as immoral as the heretics who cared only about hooking up and having parties under the hypocritical guise of promoting a love for Christ.

231

The missionaries, they felt, were deserting the true battlefield, ignoring the true enemy: the barrio and their heretical neighbours. They looked down on the seminarians. "We need soldiers of Christ, warriors ready for battle, not men who are locked away and sheltered," Humberto would argue passionately.

At first, Father Pepe thought highly of the ardent and devout spirit of the Young People Committed to Christ, but he was concerned by their contempt for the other groups. He tried to persuade them to soften their position. Humberto confronted him. "You taught us that the only true path is the one that leads to Christ. And now you want us to be pushovers?"

Father Pepe did not get a chance to curb the ruthlessness of the Young People Committed to Christ. After twenty-two years in the barrio, he was transferred by the powers-that-be to a parish in Chihuahua. He tried to stay and requested that the transfer be reconsidered; he wanted to demonstrate his influence in the community, his work in defending the faith and the vital nature of his youth projects. His superior was unequivocal: "The Tarahumara people need you." Overnight, he vanished.

If his replacement, Father Arturo, didn't have the same charisma or charm, he made up for it with determination and despotism. Laconic, tight-fisted and much more conservative, he was tall and bony, with a permanent grim scowl. He wore sunglasses day and night. Javier Arturo Magaña Pérez was from Cihuatlán del Monte, a cluster of ranches about half an hour from Lagos de Moreno, where he had been a parish priest serving several congregations. In his sermons, he viciously attacked "the enemies of the church": those who tempted others to "stray from the true path of Christ". His diet was unvarying: every day, for lunch and dinner, he ate poached fish with vegetables and a bread roll, and drank water with lime.

No sooner had he arrived, than Father Arturo reversed the majority of Father Pepe's initiatives. He disbanded the choir, which he deemed trivial, and condemned the use of frivolous music in the church: "Monkey music has no place in the house of god." He cancelled the church's social and charitable activities in working-class areas because they "reeked" of communism. "The church has a spiritual responsibility to help the poor, which is why we provide them with encouragement and hope, but it should not be distributing resources to the criminal or the feckless, and certainly should not squander money intended for improvements to the church or priestly life," he said in one of his inflammatory sermons. He cancelled the youth Mass. He thought the concept of Mass "by age groups" was absurd. "Families ought to come together and celebrate the love of Christ together. It is crucial that parents, children and grandparents experience the joy of the Eucharist as a family tree, not as loose leaves." He offered moral and financial support to the Young People Committed to Christ, considering the group to be the vanguard in the reconquest of the Christian faith. He helped them organise and put them in touch with the powerful Young Catholics Movement, the most reactionary organisation in the country, whose headquarters happened to be located in Lagos de Moreno.

Father Arturo financed the Good Boys' activities. He suggested they use the Crusader's Cross as their emblem, and the habits and cowls they wore at their clandestine meetings were his idea. He guided them towards ever more radical positions. He often met Humberto to discuss the group's tactics and the actions they ought to take.

I didn't know him very well. I heard about his sermons from Agüitas, to whom I hadn't spoken once since I had joined Young People Committed to Christ. And it was through him that I discovered the terrifying depths of Catholic fanaticism.

Probability of dying in an airplane crash: 1:30,000
Probability of dying in a car accident: 1:140
Probability of dying in a dog attack: 1:150,000

Probability of dying in a shark attack: 1:300,000
Probability of drowning: 1:1,000
Probability of dying from heart disease: 1:5
Probability of being murdered: 1:250
Probability of dying from a lightning strike: 1:10,000,000
Probability of both parents dying in a car accident:
Probability of a 71-year-old woman dying of a heart attack
    and nobody noticing:
Probability of your brother drowning:
Probability of dying from a wolf-dog attack:
Probability of the woman you love coming back:

Ancient Norse mythology spoke of a frozen place, foggy, dark: Hel. It was located in the depths of the earth, beneath the world of the gods and of humans and it faced north. It was the land of the dead. It was governed by the goddess Hel, daughter of Loki and the fortune teller Angrboða, both of them evil beings. Hel was half-alive, half-dead. Her torso was alive, but her violet legs were eaten away by death.

The realm of Hel was the final resting place for the dead not admitted to Valhalla. The evil, the perverse, murderers and those falsely pledged were damned to Hel. To get to Hel many landscapes had to be crossed.

1) The entrance to the realm of Hel was through a gloomy cave called Gnipahellir, set into steep and dangerous cliffs.
2) Past Garmr, a ferocious hound (some say a wolf) with a blood-stained chest. Garmr was the first guardian of Hel's gate.
3) Through the fierce currents of the river Gjöll, as knives rained from the sky.
4) Across the bridge spanning the Gjöll, whose roof dripped with molten gold.
5) On the other side of the river, a path descended towards the north, protected by the pale maiden Móðguðr.
6) The gates of Hel slammed shut behind all those who passed through.

7) Upon the gates stood Gullinkambia, the golden-combed rooster which would crow to wake the inhabitants of Hel and herald the events of Ragnarök.

8) In the deepest part of Hel was Elivdnir – "Sleet Cold" – the hall wherein Hel, goddess of the underworld, ruled alone, surrounded by ghosts.

The Hel of Norse mythology became the Hell of the ancient Anglo-Saxons: the place where sinners were condemned to carry out their penance.

Garmr was much feared, and savagely guarded the gates of Hel. Some of the Eddas, including Völuspá, mention another guardian: Fenrir, the wolf, who presided over a barren fenland.

Fenrir was the eldest son of the god Loki and the giantess Angrboða, and had a wolf's form. It was believed that he and his family would destroy the Nine Worlds. And so the gods attempted to bind him with chains. But Fenrir was so powerful that he shattered the chains. Fearful, the gods sent a messenger to the realm of the dwarves, asking them to forge a chain whose strength could restrain him. The dwarves fashioned a chain called Gleipnir, which, though soft, was sturdy; it was wrought from the sound of a cat's footsteps, the beard of a woman, the roots of mountains, the breath of a fish, and the spittle of a bird. Fenrir was chained to a rock called Gioll, in the depths of the earth.

Nobody approached Fenrir. Even the gods feared him. Only Týr, the god of war, dared to approach and feed him. Enraged that he could not break the chain of Gleipnir, Fenrir bit off Týr's hand.

According to legend, the great wolf would loose his shackles at Ragnorök, the great battle in which the giants would fight the gods. Fenrir, making common cause with the giants, would attack, kill and devour Odin, only to be slain in vengeance by Odin's son Viddar.

Garmr and Fenrir, a dog and a wolf, both in chains. Guardians of the underworld. Dog and wolf, fierce annihilators. Garmr, with his blood-smeared chest. Fenrir, devourer of gods. Fenrir and Garmr, dog and wolf in chains.

Fenrir.

Garmr.

Wolves

The doorbell rang early, at 6.30 a.m. King and I had slept in Carlos's room again. In the early hours, Colmillo had re-embarked on his reign of destruction. What was left to break, he broke that night. Finally, around dawn, he stopped.

I had only just managed to fall asleep when I heard the grating screech of the doorbell in the distance. I decided to ignore it and pulled a pillow over my head. Again and again, the doorbell rang. Half-asleep, I got up, put on my flip-flops and went downstairs. Colmillo was in the living room, staring at the door. He had destroyed the flimsy plywood walls of my bedroom and shredded the blanket, the mattress and the bedsheets. The scraps now littered the carpet, which was soiled with excrement and urine.

I went to the garage to open the gate. Outside was a heavy-set man in his fifties with long unruly hair and a thick moustache.

"Morning," I said. "What are you selling?"

The man looked me up and down, stopping for a moment to stare at my frayed pyjama trousers.

"You're gonna be using those pyjamas as dusters pretty soon."

He was right: they seemed more like rags than pyjamas, but I thought his comment was ill timed.

"What are you selling?"

"Did I wake you?"

"Yeah."

"Good. You ought to be out in the fresh morning air."

"I went to sleep very late."

The man didn't seem to be listening.

"So where's the dog?"

Half-asleep, I didn't understand.

"What dog?"

"The one you want tamed."

"You mean the circus sent you?"

"Yep."

The man didn't look as though he could tame anything. He was the opposite of João and Braulio. He looked more like an eighteenth-century German composer than a tiger tamer. Still sceptical, I said:

"*You're* the tamer?"

"I'm the guy who trains the tamers. So, yes, I'm a tamer."

I couldn't imagine this fat little man wearing tight-fitting sleeveless costumes like my Brazilian friends. He took a card from his shirt pocket and handed it to me.

SERGIO AVILÉS DE LA GARZA

ANIMAL TRAINER

TAMER OF LIONS & TIGERS

BIOLOGIST

Below were multiple addresses and three telephone numbers with different international codes. The addresses were Mexico City; Saltillo, Coahuila; and Houston, Texas.

Avilés jerked his chin.

"So, this beast, is he in there?"

I nodded.

"You want me to come inside, or would you prefer I give you advice from out here?"

Hesitantly, I opened the door. This guy couldn't possibly be a tamer. Maybe he had overheard my conversation with the man with the gravelly voice and had come here to rob me.

Without another word, Avilés stepped inside and I followed. In the doorway to the living room, he stopped to assess the damage.

"You don't need a tamer, you need carpenters, plumbers, glaziers and someone to clean up this pigsty," he said, smiling.

His comment didn't amuse me.

"I'm going to clean things up and fix them myself."

But he was no longer listening. He was carefully studying Colmillo. He took two steps towards him, then turned back to me.

"Who told you this was a wolf-dog?"

"His owners. They bought him mail order from a breeder in Canada."

"Well, they lied," he said. "This is no wolf-dog."

"Sure it is, they even sent certificates."

"Take my word for it, this animal is not a wolf-dog."

I felt a knot in my stomach: a myth was about to be shattered.

"So he's an Alaskan Malamute?" I said, hoping that at least he was a sled dog.

"No, he's not a Malamute, or a Husky, or a German Shepherd, or any other breed."

"So what is he?"

"That's a purebred wolf," he said confidently.

Either he was mistaken or he wasn't an expert at all.

"He *is* a wolf-dog," I said.

"No, this is an example of *Canis lupus occidentalis*, the Canadian timber wolf, also known as the Mackenzie Valley wolf. It's the largest subspecies of grey wolf, weighing up to eighty kilos – which is more or less what he weighs," he said.

Avilés spoke like an entry in the *Encyclopaedia Britannica*.

"How long have you owned him?"

"Two days."

Apprehensive about the intruder, Colmillo began to growl.

"Where did he come from?"

"He belonged to some neighbours, they wanted to have him put down."

240

Avilés leaned against the wall and thoughtfully stroked his moustache while evaluating Colmillo's devastation.

"I think that might have been for the best."

Colmillo didn't take his eyes off the man.

"Did they have him locked up or chained up?"

"He was chained up, all the time."

"From what age?"

"Since he was a puppy."

Avilés looked at Colmillo again.

"I doubt I'll be able to get very far with him," he said, "but I'll try."

He glanced at the stairs.

"Are your parents still in bed?"

"I don't have any parents."

He looked at me doubtfully.

"What do you mean you don't have parents?"

"They were recently killed in a motorway accident."

Avilés's face changed.

"Who lives here with you?"

"I'm alone."

"Alone? How old are you?"

"Seventeen."

"You have no siblings, no grandparents?"

"No."

"Nobody?"

"I have a boxer, a couple of Australian parakeets . . . and Colmillo here," I said, nodding at the wolf.

"What's your name?"

"Juan Guillermo."

"Juan Guillermo, do you have a job? Are you at school?"

"Neither."

"How do you plan on keeping him alive?"

"I have savings."

"Did they tell you how much I charge?"

"Yes."

"You'll be able to pay me?"

"I'll pay if you manage to tame him."

Avilés smiled.

"The chances of that are practically non-existent, and it would in any case take a long time."

"I'll pay if you tame him, otherwise, I won't."

"Four thousand pesos."

"They said three thousand."

"They told you wrong."

"I only have two thousand."

Avilés looked at Colmillo. Through the muzzle, his lupine eyes glowed.

"Honestly, I think you should donate him to a zoo, or have him put down."

"No, I'm keeping him. Can you tame him or not?"

"I don't know. As pets, wolves aren't usually a problem, they're meek and obedient, but if they're not socialised as puppies they become aggressive. It's difficult to tame them as adults. Truth is, I think it would be a waste of my time and your money."

"I don't care about money," I said, decisively.

"But I care about wasting my time. This could take months, and I have a lot of work on."

He walked over to the stairs and sat on the second step. Colmillo's eyes followed him, and he kept growling.

"I'll make you a deal," he said. "I'll come every day for ten days and teach you how to tame him. That'll cost you a thousand pesos."

"What if I don't manage to tame him?"

"That's your problem, not mine. Deal?"

I nodded. Avilés offered me his hand and I shook it.

"Deal."

Avilés got up and walked to the furthest point Colmillo's chain would allow him to reach. He beckoned me to join him.

"He's an alpha male. A leader. He's used to doing whatever he wants. He needs to learn that you're in charge."

"Colmillo a leader? He's spent his life chained to a post."

"He knew they chained him up because they couldn't handle him. Wolves aren't stupid, they know when they're stronger than those around them."

Avilés pointed at Colmillo.

"Never show fear again," he said.

I wanted to see what Avilés would do if Colmillo wasn't chained up. He picked up a chair from the floor, held it like a shield and slowly walked towards Colmillo. He took four steps and, on the fifth, Colmillo bounded and hit the chair with such force that Avilés nearly fell, but he managed to hold firm. Colmillo lunged again and once more Avilés withstood the blow.

He turned to me.

"Your turn, Juan Guillermo."

I took the chair.

"Don't even think about backing away."

Holding the chair, I stepped forward. Colmillo looked me in the eye for a few seconds and then attacked. The impact nearly ripped the chair from my hands. I tried to get my balance, but Colmillo attacked again, hitting me in the stomach with such force that it knocked the air out of me. I dropped the chair and tried to take a step back, but Avilés stopped me.

"Never back down."

I tried not to move, but Colmillo leaped and knocked me onto my ass. If it hadn't been for the chain, his muzzle would have smashed my face.

"Stand up, pick up the chair and go again."

Colmillo was strong and vicious. I got up and again tried to take a step back, but Avilés laid a hand on my shoulder.

"Hold the chair and stand in front of him."

I picked up the chair, holding it like a shield, and took two steps forwards. Colmillo lunged again, and again the blow knocked the chair from my hands. I was at his mercy. He charged into my thigh. I felt a shooting pain, thought he had broken it.

"Stand firm!" Avilés shouted.

I tried to stand firm, but Colmillo doubled back and charged at the same leg. I tumbled onto my back, my head hit the floor. Maybe Avilés was right, maybe Colmillo couldn't be tamed.

Avilés gripped my shoulders and dragged me a few metres from the wolf.

"Very good," he said, and helped me to get back on my feet, which I barely managed. The pain in my leg was agonising.

"I need you to do this day and night, any time you get a chance. Got it? That is the first lesson."

Day and night? I'd need to be able to stand first.

"I think my leg's broken," I said.

"No, nothing's broken. Learn to endure the pain," he said, impatiently. "And if it breaks, you will have to endure that too."

He lifted his shirt. His stomach was criss-crossed with scars.

"I have been attacked by six tigers and four lions. One of them ripped my belly open with one swipe and my guts fell out. Even then I had to stay standing. When I tell you to endure, it's because you have to."

Avilés nodded towards the chair.

"Again."

I limped over to the chair, picked it up and faced Colmillo. No sooner had I crossed the line into his territory than he lunged. I tightened my grip. The blow shook my tensed arms, but I managed to keep hold of the chair.

"Take another step towards him," ordered Avilés.

I took a step, and Colmillo leaped again. I clasped the chair against me. It shuddered from side to side, but I held on. Colmillo launched two more attacks in quick succession. The second sent me flying. Desperately, I clutched the chair to protect myself. Colmillo jumped on top, slamming it against my shoulder. Instinctively, I lashed out, hitting Colmillo with the chair. He yelped in pain and retreated.

"Good, very good!" exclaimed Avilés.

Colmillo didn't attack again. I struggled to my feet and went to sit on the stairs. My leg and shoulder hurt as if I'd taken a beating.

"First lesson learned," said Avilés. "I'll be back first thing tomorrow. Don't forget to do this night and day. Don't give him any water or anything to eat. He needs to learn that he's dependent on you."

He clapped me on the back and smiled.

"I think you might regret this. See you tomorrow."

He turned and left. Colmillo and I glared at one another. Blood trickled down his nose and dripped onto the floor. Throwing himself at the chair repeatedly had left a wound.

I slowly climbed the stairs. King was lying on the bed. He wagged his tail. I sat down and took off my trousers. An enormous bruise extended over half my leg. I could barely move. If I wanted to master Colmillo, I would have to endure the pain. There would be much, much more. I fell back on the bed, closed my eyes and drifted off.

I continued to go to the secret meetings every Saturday. I didn't dare tell Carlos or any of my friends. Breaking the vow of silence would mean serious consequences, as Humberto never tired of warning us. "If someone tells their mother, their brother, their cousin, their best friend who we are and what we do, he will pay, and not just him, but all those whom he has told."

It was no empty threat. Several incidents demonstrated that Humberto was serious. I put two and two together about an attack that took place in the barrio: a year earlier, Shrimp's mother, a widow, had been found unconscious in her backyard. Nobody knew who had attacked her, but Shrimp – his real name was René and he'd once belonged to the group – moved away with his mother and his two sisters. They didn't explain the reason for their sudden departure. They simply left and never returned.

Nobody could understand why a defenceless woman had been so viciously beaten. After Humberto's warning, I understood: Shrimp had talked too much.

The Saturday sessions took on a frightening tone. They would begin with a chant, but these were not just prayers, they were rants about vengeance, death, Christ, soldiers, retribution. Anyone who faltered and interrupted the flow of these "prayers" was disciplined with shouts, slaps, even punches to the face.

"We are an army and we shall behave like an army," is how Humberto justified the assaults. "We are soldiers of Christ and for Him we endure our pain." Those who were punished had to bear it in silence. There could be no weakness, no complaints. Obedience was everything. Unity and discipline, for the good of the army.

Despite his brutality, Humberto was charming. He listened attentively and made every member of the group feel important. He worried about their well-being, and their families. He offered advice and spiritual counsel. His feverish, moralistic speeches roused them. Humberto knew exactly which buttons to push.

With me, Humberto was friendly and thoughtful. He often asked me to come with him to buy things: stationery, pens, soft drinks, crisps. As we left the supermarket, he would slip chocolates into my pocket. "To take home." I would try to give them back, I didn't want to be in his debt, but he would insist. "Please don't take away the pleasure of sharing something with you."

I'm sure that most of the Good Boys joined the group because they were pushed into it by parents or grandparents. They agreed to accept the rules and the harsh discipline because they wanted to be accepted, to be recognised. Humberto knew how to persuade them. After a few months, his alternating tactics of cruelty, charm, discipline and friendliness bore results. The young men ended up believing that they were "Soldiers of Christ" whose duty was to defend "true Catholicism" with their lives. They began to follow the unspoken rules regarding the uniform: beige trousers, white long-sleeved shirts, cropped hair.

Even I was tempted to change the way I dressed, to shave my hair. I felt an urgent need to belong, to be accepted by Humberto and the others. Their ideas seemed absurd, but Humberto's strategies of persuasion gradually began to take root in my adolescent mind.

I began to obey his orders, answer his questions, accept his dogmas. Deep down, I wanted to think that I wasn't really part of the group, that there was a line between me and them. I didn't realise just how implicated I was until the night I told Humberto how Carlos always managed to evade the police.

During the night, he heard the wolf howl. Long, deep howls punctuated by silences that were as long and as deep. All this silence worried Amaruq. He laced up his boots and opened the tent flap. He took a torch, lit it from the fire and walked towards the foot of the tree to check that Nujuaqtutuq was still there. The sleet made it difficult to see and he fumbled in the darkness, trying to get his bearings. He made slow progress in the snow. He waved the torch from side to side until he saw the great wolf lying next to the tree trunk. Amaruq realised he had come too close and tried to backtrack, but in this deep snow it was impossible to move quickly. Nujuaqtutuq leaped up and attacked. Amaruq managed to hit him in the snout with his torch. Confused by the flames, the wolf fell back into the snow. He tried to attack again, but was held back by the chain.

Exhaustion had prompted Amaruq to do something foolish. How could he have left his tent in the middle of the night with no weapon, no lantern, while a wolf pack was prowling the forest? Why had he come so close to Nujuaqtutuq? He looked at his left arm. It was bleeding. The wolf had bitten him. In the light from the torch, he examined the wound. His caribou-leather parka was ripped. Blood was gushing. He went back to the tent, took off his parka and rolled up his sleeve. The wolf had buried his fangs close to his elbow, the wound was a through-and-through. He used the torch to try to cauterise it, enduring the pain of his burning skin until the bleeding was under control. Then he rubbed the wound with snow to clean it.

He pulled on his parka and lay down. It took him a long time to get to sleep. Pain pulsated through his arm, numbing his hand. Now he and the wolf were brothers. The wolf's saliva and his own blood had been mingled. Yes, that wolf was his master, had made Amaruq lose his mind, had led him all the way to the icy tundra of the frozen north. Amaruq had lost all sense of danger, had allowed his supplies to run out. He had come to the frontier of death itself.

He should kill Nujuaqtutuq as soon as possible, eat his flesh, wear his skin, make a knife from his bones. He needed to see like Nujuaqtutuq, to sense like Nujuaqtutuq, to breathe like Nujuaqtutuq.

Amaruq slept until mid-morning. When he emerged from the tent, the sun was already at its zenith. The sleet had stopped and there was not a single cloud in the blue sky. He looked at his wound. His forearm had swollen to nearly double its normal size. The charred flesh flaked away in small black chunks when he rubbed it with his fingers. Through the four puncture wounds made by the wolf's fangs he could see deep into his arm. He was lucky the wolf had not ripped it off.

He looked around. There was no sign of the pack. Between the pines, the ground was littered with dead wapiti covered by a blanket of frost. He walked over to Nujuaqtutuq and sat in the snow just beyond the chain's reach. The wolf growled, but Amaruq did not move. The wolf sprang, but the chain stopped him a few centimetres from Amaruq's face. They stared at one another, their eyes level.

Amaruq could smell the acrid breath from the animal's snout. The wolf bared his teeth, but the man remained impassive. Amaruq leaned forward, bringing his face closer, and began to speak. "Prepare to die, Nujuaqtutuq. Look at the sun. Listen to the crows caw. Feel the snow beneath your paws. Say goodbye, your final hour is at hand."

The pack did not return. They must have followed the herd of wapiti. Better to hunt and eat fresh meat than to keep gnawing at hard, frozen carcasses.

As days passed without anything to eat and only melted snow to drink, Nujuaqtutuq began to weaken. Still defiant, he growled whenever Amaruq came near. Amaruq paid him no heed, but came and sat close by him. Once, Amaruq reached out and patted the animal's head. The wolf did not try to bite. He let the man stroke him gently.

Starving, and with a gangrenous leg, the great wolf began to waste away. Amaruq made a spear with which to kill him. He used a knife to whittle a sharp point on a long maple branch. As soon as Nujuaqtutuq could no longer stand, Amaruq would spear him through the heart to grant him a quick death.

Amaruq made an incision in the wound in his arm and dipped the tip of the spear in the gushing blood. Nujuaqtutuq had offered up his saliva; now it was his turn to make an offering. He would kill the wolf and commingle their blood; each would be master of the other. In this life and in those that came after. His grandfather's prophecy would come true and Amaruq could die in peace. He just needed the great wolf to lie on his flank, starving and weak, so that he might spear him.

The traveller had heard that in the midst of the desert there was a magnificent oasis overflowing with riches. He asked how he might get there. He was directed into the vast desert. "Keep walking until you find it." The traveller set off on foot. For years, he wandered across the dunes in the blazing sun. He encountered long caravans of camels, and the blue men – the Tuareg – carrying salt. He saw lions prowl among the dunes, lizards burrow into the sand, snakes slither on the slopes, a scimitar oryx trotting among the mirages. He happened on the bleached skeletons of those who had come before him. He survived on dates and insects. Drank his urine and stagnant water from pools under palm trees. He suffered from diarrhoea and fever. He spent freezing nights beneath the Sahara's star-flecked vault. The noonday sun burned his lips and his eyelids. His feet were covered in blisters. He did not stop until he reached the promised oasis. Weak, crawling on his hands and knees, he dragged himself to its gates. Here was the oasis, the magnificent oasis of which he had been told. The traveller soon realised that he had arrived back at the place whence he had set out.

Encounters

They found Quica's corpse lying face down on the deserted basketball courts. Some kids stumbled on it one morning when they went to see what their dog was snuffling at. At first, they thought he was a drunk and poked him with sticks to see if they could wake him up. He didn't move. They realised he was dead when one of them crouched down and looked at his face, horrified to see the dried-out eyes and the bloody mouth. Terrified, they raced home to tell their parents.

The news quickly spread through the barrio. My friends and I went to look, with a dozen curious neighbours. The livid body lay beneath one of the hoops. Enrique's eyes stared out into the distance. I wondered if the image of his killers' faces was seared onto his retinas; perhaps some future technology might one day allow the final images seen by murder victims to be recovered.

According to the news the next day, his skull had been crushed by a blunt object. The reporter blamed the crime on "sordid affairs between faggots". I felt sad about his death. If he hadn't harassed us, I might have liked him more. He wasn't a bad guy; he'd been funny, easy-going and hard-working.

Captain Zurita led the investigation, and began by questioning everyone in the barrio. No-one had heard screams that night or noticed anything out of the ordinary. Only one man said that his dog had barked solidly through the early hours of the morning.

The cops didn't find fingerprints, or bloody footprints, or any trace of the weapon used. The alcoholic lawyer who Enrique worked for swiftly paid Zurita to shut down the case. He didn't want to be caught up in a scandal involving queers – his divorce and the accusations of child sexual abuse were more than enough. The lawyer insisted he knew nothing beyond the fact that Enrique had worked at his house.

No-one came to claim the body. Zurita called the leader of San Mateo Tlachihuacán council to find out if he knew Enrique's relatives. Nobody knew who he was, or, if they did, they didn't admit it. Within four days the investigation was over, the case was closed and the murder was forgotten. Not just because the lawyer had paid to make it go away: Zurita didn't want to waste his time investigating the murder of some faggot *mixteco* from Oaxaca.

For two weeks, the corpse lay in a drawer at the mortuary. From there it was taken to U.N.A.M.'s School of Medicine and used for students practising dissection. Medical students cut into his fatty tissues, the flaccid muscles, the slack, penetrated rectum, the broken skull, the bloated face. A John Doe who wound up being cremated in the university incinerators. His ashes tossed into a garbage can, exposed to the elements, to hungry dogs, amid rotting vegetables, plastic bags, broken bottles. No ceremony, no funeral. No proper send-off. Another crime unpunished, just like so many others.

Confused by their sexual experiences with Enrique, Agüitas and Jaibo didn't know how to react to his death. Should they feel satisfaction or grief, anger or compassion? Agüitas thought Quica deserved to die for messing around with kids like him. It took him a long time to recover from the trauma of his fulgurant blowjob. What would he tell his children? "My first sexual experience was a small, fat guy sucking my dick." For months Agüitas's reaction was ambiguous, a mixture of guilt and anger. In the end, anger won out, and the conviction that he had been manipulated while under the influence of alcohol into allowing Quica to unzip his pants, take out his cock and, in a brief, blurred incident, change his whole life. He would feel the humiliation of those two minutes for years to come.

Jaibo mourned Quica's death. In his mind, there was nothing twisted about his relationship with Quica, he didn't feel abused or violated. He and Quica had hung out together, Quica had never forced him to do anything, he didn't feel his masculinity had been threatened. The way he saw it, Quica was "basically a woman, with a woman's body, a woman's ass and a woman's mind. Besides," he declared with macho pride, "I was the one sticking my dick in him."

Record of happy moments:
- King recovering from his stab wound.
- My parents giving me a tortoise for my fourth birthday.
- Learning to swim all by myself, aged three.
- Winning the trophy for "best player of the season" at a secondary school basketball tournament.
- Stroking Fuensanta's pussy.
- My father teaching me to ride a bike.
- Profesor Alarid noticing me in my first P.E. class.
- Scoring a goal from the halfway line when I was twelve.
- Hearing Hendrix for the first time.
- Reading Faulkner.
- Seeing "The Vikings" for the first time.
- Carlos teaching me to fight.
- Beating the crap out of that fat fucker, Brand, who wouldn't leave me alone at secondary school.
- My mother sewing up my ripped Atlante T-shirt.
- My grandmother warming my bed with an iron at night.
- Watching colour T.V. for the first time round at the Tenas' place.
- Our team, Los Canes, beating Retorno 304.
- Jumping from the highest point of a footbridge over the Río Churubusco into the overgrown grass and not breaking a single bone.
- My father taking me hunting for axolotls and crayfish.

- My mother making a picnic that we ate out in the yard.
- Carlos winning the 800 metres at school sports day.
- My parents giving me a Scalextric set when I turned eight.
- Going with my father to Tlaxcala and Puebla, just the two of us.
- My mother taking Carlos and me to the beach in Tampico.
- Taking a trip in a glass-bottomed boat in Caleta, Acapulco.
- My father taking me rabbit-hunting in La Marquesa.
- When Vodka and Whisky had their first chicks.
- Tasting avocado for the first time when I was four.
- My parents taking us to San José Purúa where we paddled in the hot springs.
- Diving in the spring water cave in Agua Hedionda.
- The whole family taking the train to Monterrey.
- Hunting with Carlos on my cousin Pepe Sánchez's ranch in Coahuila.
- My parents taking us to the Uruapan National Park.
- Speeding downhill on my bike and not crashing.
- The day I realised I was taller than my dad.
- When I had my first wet dream.
- The first time I got paid for butchering chinchillas.
- Seeing a naked girl for the first time, when I was five.
- The book of animal pictures my mother bought me when I turned seven.
- Sunbathing on the roof of the church.
- Swimming in the cold river in Las Estacas.
- Scrabbling up the Pyramid of the Sun in Teotihuacán.
- Learning to body surf the crest of a wave.
- Killing a wild boar with my bow and arrow, when I was thirteen.
- Seeing "Viento Negro" on T.V.
- Reading Rulfo's *The Burning Plain and Other Stories.*

- The first time I was inside Chelo and felt her wetness.
- Knocking out four people during a brawl at a football match.
- When I see photos of us, together.

Even after he'd cancelled the cinema events, Carlos's business continued to run smoothly. The screenings had brought in a lot of money, but the biggest profits came from the sale of "merchandise". The core of the business was the customers, and Carlos thought it was important to protect that. He visited each of his biggest clients, convinced them not to talk to the cops and persuaded them to strengthen their business relationship with him and his partners. In the repressive, authoritarian environment of the time, the strategy worked: the police, the army, the riot squads represented "the enemy", the corrupt, outdated system. As Carlos summed it up: "It's us against them." None of his customers ratted him out.

This intensive P.R. campaign bought Carlos time. The longer the "network", as he called it, remained active, the more power and opportunity for him and his partners. My brother's mistake was refusing to do a deal with the cops. It was his deep-rooted hatred of corruption that led to his downfall.

After Carlos cheated him out of the promised hush money, Captain Zurita became obsessed with arresting him. He never did. Again and again Carlos, El Loco and El Castor Furioso managed to escape, hiding out inside the rooftop water tanks, breathing through straws. And even if Zurita did arrest them, what charge could he bring? Carlos knew he was risking a few months in prison, but Zurita could never build a case against them. He had never raided their screenings and nobody was prepared to testify against them. What evidence could he come up with? Obviously, they could be arrested on a trumped-up charge – this was common practice in the Mexican judicial system – but Captain Zurita didn't really want to bang them up, what he wanted was his cut of the profits. He wouldn't make any money if the traffickers were banged up. Besides, if Carlos was already reluctant to pay off the police, he'd be even less inclined to do so from a prison cell.

Zurita and his team had no idea of the size of Carlos's business, or the vast profits. Uncovering the network my brother had created took a long time. Although Zurita was a seasoned extortionist in underworld circles, his ability to detect and control crime among the moneyed classes was limited. As a police officer, he was well aware that his authority meant little when dealing with the son of a wealthy businessman or a high-ranking politician. Without orders from someone higher up the chain, he couldn't investigate students at a private university. And no-one was likely to order such an investigation. The privileged looked out for one another. He could arrest a hippie, as long as he didn't take things further than demanding a small "contribution" to avoid a scandal, or giving the kid a few slaps to scare him. There was nothing more they could do. No police cells, no visible injuries, no handcuffs, no beatings.

As for girls from wealthy families, they were completely off-limits. The rules for the police were like those for hunters: no females. Or at least not pretty, well-dressed bourgeois girls. One of Zurita's captains had paid the price for daring to arrest one for smoking weed on the street. He placed her in a holding cell and left his men to guard her. During the night, three cops got drunk and raped her. The captain found her the following morning, dumbstruck, blood streaming down her legs. He tried to protect his men, insisting that she had been in that state when she was picked up. The girl turned out to be a senator's daughter. Needless to say, there was a painstaking investigation and the truth was uncovered. The captain was personally forced to execute the offending officers. He took them to a wasteland in Tláhuac and shot them. One of the officers was a friend. "You're godfather to my son," he begged. "Don't do this." But the captain had no choice. He emptied the clip into the man's head, just to shut him up.

The captain himself didn't go unpunished. He'd arrested an

underaged girl from a powerful family and locked her in a cell without notifying her parents. She had just turned sixteen. The brutal rapes destroyed her womb, leaving the girl sterile and traumatised. The senator ordered his henchmen to break the captain's arms and legs with a hammer. He was left seriously injured and dismissed from his post. Now lame, suffering from chronic pain and with limited mobility, he ended up selling newspapers on street corners.

No, Zurita was not about to do something that foolish. Let the pampered teenagers take drugs, brawl in the streets, kill each other if they wanted. He would intervene only if an order came directly from Olympus. In other words, only if asked by the President, a government minister or a senator.

Carlos's network operated within a rarefied zone that was off-limits to Zurita. That was why it took him so long to uncover. The clue that led him to the motherlode came almost by accident. A Universidad Iberoamericana student tripping on acid was seen walking naked along Avenida Taxqueña at 7.00 p.m., babbling incoherently and gesticulating wildly as he weaved between lanes, insisting that he had to climb a waterfall of molten clouds. He was arrested and pushed into a police car. The moment the cops heard his name, they panicked. The boy was the son of a director of a state-run company, the President of the Republic's brother. The boy was the nephew of Zeus himself. They couldn't let him wander around naked, but they certainly couldn't take him to a police station. Terrified, they put in a call to Captain Zurita, since he was chief of the local precinct.

Zurita arrived, calmed the boy down, wrapped him in a blanket and sent someone out to buy him clothes. He helped the boy to dress, then took him to a private clinic run by a friend, where he was registered under a false name to protect his identity. Three hours later, since the boy was still obsessed with climbing the waterfall of molten clouds, Zurita called his parents and told them. "We're keeping him under observation to make sure he doesn't harm himself." The parents arrived, whisked the boy out through the back door of the clinic, bundled him into an ambulance with two private doctors and took him home. As the ambulance pulled away, a motorcade of cars with tinted windows followed.

Grateful for Zurita's sympathetic handling of the incident, the boy's father gave Zurita five thousand Mexican dollars and ordered him to track down whoever had given his son "that poison". Since commands from Mount Olympus could not be ignored, Zurita brought in dozens of students from private universities for questioning. Knowing they were untouchable, the students didn't rat on Carlos, giving evasive answers and false leads; but despite their caution, they gave Zurita just enough information for him to realise that he wasn't dealing with a notorious gang or with high-level traffickers like the "Nazis", but with a network run by only a handful of people.

After weeks of investigation, he finally came up with three names: Juan Carlos Valdés, Sean Page and Diego Pernía. Zurita could hardly believe it. The network seemed too complex to be run by the three guys from Unidad Modelo who had organised the cinema screenings. Where were they sourcing the morphine and the L.S.D.? How was it being transported? Who was bankrolling them? How had they managed to infiltrate the private universities? How had they managed to stay under the radar? Who was protecting them? It didn't make sense. It couldn't be them. Or at least not just them.

Zurita pressed on with the investigation, convinced that someone powerful must be backing them. But for all his efforts he couldn't come up with anyone else. Juan Carlos Valdés, Sean Page and Diego Pernía were running the network alone. Zurita was furious with himself and his officers. A trio of amateurs had set up a highly profitable business in a zone he controlled. He resolved to redouble his efforts. He was going to bring Carlos and his partners down. He was in no doubt about that.

*

I woke up at 11.30 a.m., sweating from the hot sun streaming onto the bed. King was sleeping next to me. As soon as he realised I was awake, he stood up and wagged his tail. I patted him and he licked my face. Vodka and Whisky had abandoned their cage and were perched on a window ledge.

I sat on the edge of the mattress and felt my bruised leg. The muscles throbbed and ached. I struggled to my feet. One of my legs was excruciatingly painful, the other was completely numb. I slipped on my trousers and my shoes. King watched from the bed. I grabbed his collar and tried to pull him towards me, but he resisted. I tried again, but King pulled back with all his strength. There was no way I would persuade King to come downstairs while Colmillo was still there.

I opened the window to let air into the room. The parakeets shuffled to the edge of the window frame. I nudged them, encouraging them to fly away. They pecked my fingers gently, but did not dare take wing. I pointed at the trees. "Fly over there," I said. They simply tilted their heads and settled in a patch of sunlight to keep warm.

I went downstairs and found Colmillo lying under the table, watching warily. Deciding to follow Avilés's instructions, I picked up a chair and walked towards him. His eyes followed me, sizing me up, and when I was about three metres away he got to his feet, ready to pounce. Three metres was enough for him to pick up speed and attack with great force, so I took two more steps forward. Colmillo began to growl, but remained completely motionless. I gave him no time to attack, but gripped the chair and, with a yell, I charged, hitting him in the snout. Not only did Colmillo not recoil, he leaped forwards, forcing my hands back and slamming the chair against my chest. I stumbled. Colmillo charged again, sending me sprawling. Lying flat on my back, I used the chair to shield my face. Colmillo growled and climbed over me. I knew enough to know that Colmillo was adopting a dominant position, and this was something I couldn't allow. As he tried to pin me down with his front paws, I punched him again and again in the snout, rolled out from beneath him, scrabbled to my feet, grabbed the chair and brought it down on his head. The dog reeled. Again, I hit him with the chair, which shattered, and went on screaming and hitting him with the back of it. Colmillo leaped at me again, and rammed my left thigh. I fell heavily and an excruciating, sharp pain shot through my leg as though it had been ripped off. Colmillo stood up on his hind legs and pounced, his snout hitting me on the jaw with a sickening crunch. As quickly as I could I crawled away, out of his reach.

Colmillo continued to growl, his whole body tensed. I felt something viscous in my mouth and spat out a mouthful of blood. The dog was bleeding too. There was a cut on his snout and his canines were blood-smeared, there was a wound to his head and a gash across his ear. I wasn't going to let him get the better of me.

On all fours, I crawled to the precise point the chain allowed him to reach. Our eyes were locked, our breathing ragged. For a long moment, we stared at one another, and then the wolf turned and lay down under the table. As Avilés had suggested, I was going to deprive him of food and water. He was completely dependent on me, so I would give him food and water only when he obeyed. I had to show him that I was in charge.

I hobbled into the kitchen. Another bruise was blossoming across my thigh. I couldn't believe the agonising pain. I took milk from the fridge and poured myself a bowl of cereal, then sat down to eat it in front of Colmillo. I wanted him to see that I was free to do as I pleased and he was not; it was a distinction I planned to reinforce every single day.

We stared at each other as I finished my cereal. I went back to the kitchen, washed the bowl, grabbed a sack of dog biscuits and headed upstairs. I fed King and took him up onto the roof to empty his bladder and his bowels. Having been housetrained as a puppy, he was incapable of shitting in the house.

It was a cold, clear afternoon. The trees swayed in the gentle breeze. The traffic flowing along Río Churubusco rumbled in the distance. I started my workout with a hundred push-ups, then grasped an overhead pipe to do some pull-ups – six sets of six – finishing off with a few wide-grips.

When I'd finished, I lined up the rusting chinchilla cages and hurdled them, using only my good leg. I didn't stop until I was exhausted. I put my head under the outside tap and ran the cold water until my hair and my T-shirt were sodden, then sat propped against the wall and dried myself in the sun. King lay across my lap and we both fell asleep.

At about 8.00 p.m., I was woken by the sound of the doorbell. I opened my eyes. King was gone. I whistled but he didn't reappear. The doorbell kept ringing. I lazily stood up and peered over the roof. It was Sergio Avilés. "Be right down!" I called. Avilés glanced up and smiled.

Heading downstairs, I saw King lying on Carlos's bed. He seemed happy to see me. He started following me downstairs, but then, suddenly remembering the wolf, froze on the step, turned tail and trotted back to Carlos's room.

I opened the front door. Avilés looked weary. The wind tousled his dishevelled hair.

"Have you had dinner?" he said without preamble.

"No," I said.

"How about tacos?"

I nodded.

"Come on then, let's go."

I was still wearing the sodden T-shirt. I felt cold.

"I need to change. Can you wait?"

"Sure I'll wait, I came to fetch you, didn't I?"

I went back inside, put on a fresh T-shirt, a sweater and some sneakers, grabbed my wallet and my keys and headed out. I wasn't sure why Avilés was inviting me to dinner. I had only met him that morning. I hoped that he wasn't going to turn out to be a creep.

We had pork tacos at Don Cipriano's. I was amazed by how much fat Avilés could gobble down without pausing for breath. He scoffed pickled pig-skin tacos one after another, popping them into his mouth like cherry tomatoes. Grease dripped from the tortillas. I ordered pulled-pork tacos.

'Why do you live by yourself?" he said through a mouthful of half-chewed taco.

"I like it."

"You don't have any brothers or sisters?"

This question threw me. I wasn't sure whether I should tell him about what had happened to Carlos. I hesitated.

"I had a brother, but they killed him."

Avilés put down his taco and looked at me.

"Who killed him?"

"Some fucked-up neighbours."

"Are they in prison?"

"No, they're still wandering the streets."

He picked up a paper napkin and wiped the grease from his fingers.

"It's not good for you to live on your own," he said.

"Why?"

"It just isn't."

"I've got King and Colmillo," I said.

He sighed, and for a long moment stared silently at his plate. Then he looked up.

"What are you living off?" he asked.

"Some savings that my parents left me."

"And how long are they going to last you?"

"Long enough."

He fell silent again, picked up the half-eaten taco and devoured it.

"Did you do what I told you with the wolf?"

"Yeah."

He pointed to the bruise on my chin.

"The bruise there, that was him?"

I nodded. He chuckled sympathetically.

"He'll give you a lot more before you're done. That's what this is about. I still think it would be best if you gave him away or had him put down."

He wiped his hands again and took a gulp of horchata.

"So, aside from the stuff I've told you to do, he needs to see you going about your daily routine. Prove to him that he has no control over your life, that you're stronger than he is."

"I proved that today."

Avilés shook his head.

"You'll prove that you're the stronger when you take off the muzzle and the chain. Right now, he's shackled and defenceless. The hardest part is still to come."

I swallowed. He was right. Dominating an unchained, unmuzzled Colmillo was going to be a very different challenge.

"Growl at him, piss wherever he pisses. Show him the house is *your* territory and you intend to defend it," he added. "I'm not kidding."

He took another drink of his horchata and asked for the bill.

"I'm not going to charge you a peso," he said, "and I'll come by every day until you've tamed that fucking wolf."

"I don't want you to work for free."

"O.K., come to the circus every now and then, help me clean out the cages. You can pay me that way."

The waiter brought the bill. I reached for my wallet but Avilés stopped me.

"I'm paying," he said firmly, taking out a bill and handing it to the waiter.

He finished his horchata and turned back to me.

"And I'm not gay, if that's what you're wondering. I love women. That's why I became a lion tamer, to impress them. If I could, I'd have women for breakfast, lunch, dinner and every snack in-between. And that's why I'm divorced; I like women far too much."

We walked back towards the house, beneath the towering electricity pylons, the cables buzzing above our heads. Neither of us said anything.

When we reached our street, he climbed into a brand-new Maverick parked outside the Ávalos' place. The guy was obviously earning good money; those cars were fucking expensive.

"I lost my parents when I was a teenager too. I know how it feels, not having anyone you can count on," he said. I was beginning to notice that Avilés had a habit of blurting out information completely out of the blue. He rolled down the window.

"See you tomorrow," he said. "Oh, and try to sleep as close to the wolf as you can."

He gave a cursory wave, turned on the ignition and drove off, crossing the street and heading towards Avenida Oriente 160.

Etymology of Events (Part Two)

ADDICT: dependent on something, generally a drug or other substance. From the Latin *addictus*, assigned, handed over. In Ancient Rome, those who could not afford to repay debts were called *addicti* – "debt slaves" to those whom they owed. It is thought that slaves given to victorious military leaders were also considered *addicti*. An addict is "a slave to . . ."

GENUINE: authentic. From the Latin *genu*, knee. In Roman times, soldiers returning from a long war and finding their wives with a recently born child could choose whether or not to recognise the child as their own. To acknowledge paternity, the man would place the baby on his knee, thereby recognising it as legitimate.

ACCIDENT: unforeseen event. Derived from the Latin *accidere*, from the prefix *ad*, to, and *cadere*, to fall.

MAMIHLAPINAPATAI: a look shared between a man and a woman when each wishes that the other would initiate something that they both desire but both are too afraid to begin. The inability of a man and a woman to express what they truly desire. From the Yaghan language spoken by the indigenous peoples of Tierra del Fuego.

MATTAQTUQ: to release a dog from its harness. To set it free. From the Inupiaq language spoken by the Inuit peoples in northern Canada.

DESIRE: to wish or long for, the wish that something will happen according to one's intentions. From the Latin *desiderare*. Ultimately derived from *de sidere*, "from the stars", to await what the stars will bring.

GAINISG: a small god who dwells in the sedge and reeds around lake-shores and marshes, and who, before a storm, bewails the coming deaths. From the Gaelic.

AYANMO MI: my destiny. From the Yoruba, a language spoken by West African tribes, principally in Nigeria.

KUNMARNU: an avoidance phrase used as a substitute for the given name of anyone who is dead. From Manyjilyjarra, a language spoken by the indigenous Manyjilyjarra people of Australia.

DRAUGR: a mythological creature capable of surviving death. From Old Norse meaning "to walk again".

Victories

Gainisg, god of tempests, you who mourn those yet undead, why did you not warn me of the vortex of deaths that would drag me under? I beg you, tell me how many more deaths are yet to come. Warn me so that I may face them.

Gainisg, god of reeds and marshes, answer me. Where am I submerged? What is this mire of endless days? This passing of time without time, this life without life, this plenitude of absences, this emptiness?

Gainisg, who foresees death, from whom do you receive the names of those about to depart this life? You must know so much to weep so much for them, it must pain you to foresee their deaths. You watch them as they walk, smile, dream, love, eat, kiss, embrace, awaken, and then, all of a sudden, know with certainty that all this will soon dissolve in the fine mist of oblivion. Gainisg, tell me: where is the boneyard where all that we have experienced lies buried? Where are my mother's caresses, my father's hugs, my grandmother's kisses, my brother's words? They cannot simply disappear, Gainisg. How can a whole life disappear with death? In that unfathomable fog of death, surely something must remain, some fragment of what once was.

God of lakes, tell me where I might find my dead. I long to see them once more. I feel a burning need to find them. I have so many questions to ask, so much to tell.

Gainisg, wake them from their slumbers, rouse them so that they might once more feel the wind, might once more speak to me. And if you will not bring them back, I beg you, Gainisg, stop the torrent of death. Stop this tidal wave that is drowning me. I am begging you.

*

After eight days caught in the trap, Nujuaqtutuq was looking increasingly weak. His shivering skin clung to his ribs. His survival instinct led him to eat snow, roots, even clay. The bare minimum needed to keep him alive. The wolf wanting to remain a wolf.

In the afternoons, Amaruq would sit facing the animal, scraping the last traces of fat from wapiti skins or lighting a fire to keep warm. The wolf would stare at his sworn enemy, waiting for the man to make just one mistake so that he could attack and kill him. He would devour him in an instant, thereby satisfying his ravening hunger and his thirst for vengeance. Both would die, Nujuaqtutuq in the claws of the trap and Amaruq between his jaws.

Three more days passed. The great wolf began to deteriorate, his body ravaged by anaemia. His eyes clouded over. His tongue dried up. Amaruq could see his grandfather kneeling before the wolf, the old man stroking the animal's back to calm him. The wolf looked up and their eyes met. Amaruq's grandfather whispered something and Nujuaqtutuq once more rested his head in the snow. The grandfather got up and went to sit on a tree trunk.

In the afternoon, a light breeze sprang up. Amaruq glanced up at the sky. Rays of light pierced the dense clouds. "Death is coming," he murmured to himself and turned to look at the wolf. Nujuaqtutuq's breathing was ragged, he could not hold out much longer. In a few hours, Amaruq would run him through with the spear, pushing it into the hollow where the foreleg met the chest to skewer his heart. In less than a minute, the wolf would be dead.

As darkness began to fall, Amaruq went back into the tent and sat down on the frozen pelts. He was overcome by a wave of melancholy. He was but a step away from defeating his wolf-master. The following morning, the very reason for his existence would be focused on the great wolf's chest. The moment the beast died, Amaruq's destiny would be fulfilled. He would take on the wolf's name. He would search for his grandfather in the icy wastelands of death to tell him:

"I am now Nujuaqtutuq, the untameable." He would wear the name with pride. Amaruq, transformed into the great wolf.

He tried to sleep, without success. Outside, the wolf lay wounded, his leg a bloody pulp, almost comatose from starvation. Yes, Amaruq had defeated him. He had hunted the beast across valley and mountain, he had forded rivers, endured the cruel winter, the lack of supplies, he had come close to madness and suffered hallucinations. The wolf had duped and tricked him, had fought him for the wapiti. Amaruq deserved this victory: every moment, every minute had been hard won. But did victory mean he had to kill the wolf?

For much of the night he lay awake, falling asleep only shortly before sunrise. He dreamed of the first woman he had ever been with, a prostitute from Keno who had been pale, blonde, very tall, about eighteen – the same age as he was. The blonde woman had told him her name was Lucy. She undressed casually, as though he were not there, as though she were waiting for the water to heat up to take a shower. He found her brazen nakedness intimidating. He thought her much too beautiful for a man like him. He had closed his eyes. She sat on his lap and kissed his eyelids and they had made love for hours. They found that they liked one another, and met up on several more occasions. After a time, the woman stopped charging him, and they began to go out together for coffee or for dinner.

One day Lucy arranged to meet him in a hotel room. She told him she had been offered a job as a waitress in a café in Banff and that she could not pass up the prospect of a proper job. They made love and, between orgasms, she sobbed and sobbed. They said their goodbyes and he watched her walk away. He never saw her again. In the dawn light, inside his tent, Amaruq dreamed of the moment when she kissed his eyelids before she left. The dream was so vivid that, when he woke, he could still feel her skin beneath his fingertips.

Amaruq crawled out of the tent. Infinite snowflakes hovered in the chill morning air. He walked towards the place where Nujuaqtutuq was lying, limp, gripped the spear and warily crept forward until he was only a couple of paces away. The great wolf tried to stand, but his legs buckled and he collapsed.

Snow began to fall more heavily. The wolf turned his head towards Amaruq. There was nothing in his eyes now, nothing but the emptiness of those who know that death is coming. Amaruq raised the spear, ready to deliver the fatal blow. Aiming for the hollow behind the left foreleg, he took a deep breath, tightly gripping the shaft of the raised spear. He looked around for his grandfather. He scanned the terrain but could see nothing except sheets of snow falling between the trees, could hear nothing but the snow's silence. Man and wolf were utterly alone. Amaruq thrust his body forward, his every muscle tensed, prepared to kill. The wolf prepared to die. Then their eyes met and, slowly, Amaruq lowered the spear.

The wolf turned his head to see what was happening. Amaruq bent down, picked up the trap and prised opened the jaws. He freed the fractured leg and examined it. The deep gash went through the muscles, and the bone was black with rot.

Amaruq went back to the tent, and fetched some rope. He tied Nujuaqtutuq's hind legs together, careful not to aggravate the injury. Then he tied the animal's front paws. The wolf offered no resistance. Amaruq slid his hands under the body and unsteadily picked up the animal, carried him into the tent and gently laid him on the ground. He covered the wolf with one of the wapiti pelts, then cut small chunks of meat and placed them near the animal's snout. It took some time before Nujuaqtutuq reacted, but eventually the wolf opened its mouth and accepted a piece of the food, swallowing with difficulty. He ate a few more pieces and then closed his eyes, exhausted. Amaruq left the tent. He needed to talk to someone, to ask whether he was right to allow the wolf to live, whether in doing so he was betraying his hunting spirit. He roamed the prairie searching for his grandfather. There was only snow and silence. Not even a god to ask for advice.

That night we wore our robes and our cowls. The prayers went on longer than usual. Once again, there were furious tirades and hymns promising penance and death.

When the ceremony was over, Humberto told us to remove the cowls. He walked along the line we had formed. Some fearfully lowered their eyes as he passed. Midway along the line, he stopped and began to speak. "After months of investigation we have finally discovered the names of the three enemies of god." He took a whiteboard from the cupboard and wrote:

Profesor José Luis Cedeño. Retorno 207 #49. Works at the Universidad Autónoma de México. Communist.

Mr Mario Arias. Retorno 202 #8. Shopkeeper. Nonbeliever.

Mr Abraham Preciado. Owner of a grocery store, La Españolita. Formerly of Hacienda de Guadalupe #857. Jew.

The first step in someone being labelled an "enemy of god" was an anonymous "alert" from a member of the group. At the end of our Saturday meetings, everyone was given a piece of paper and an envelope and if any of us suspected someone of promoting anti-Catholic ideas or behaving immorally, we would write down the name, seal the envelope and slip it into a padlocked metal box to which only Humberto and Antonio had keys.

More often than not, the slips of paper were left blank, but if they came across one with a name, Humberto and Antonio would consider the suspect, and – in absolute secrecy – order an investigation. This was carried out by three members selected by Humberto, each acting alone without knowing the identity of the other two. Those chosen took an oath not to speak of the investigation to any other member of the group.

If the investigators provided irrefutable evidence incriminating the alleged "enemy", the process moved on to the third step: the "resolution". Humberto would assess the evidence, decide whether or not the accused was an "enemy of god" and take the matter to Father Arturo. If Father Arturo gave his consent, Humberto would inform the rest of the group. Then came the final stage: the "defence". Humberto would ask the group whether anyone had information that might mitigate or even refute the charge. To lie in the defence of an accused was forbidden and considered a heinous betrayal that might warrant severe punishment. If, however, convincing evidence was advanced in defence of an accused, then further investigations would be undertaken until a final verdict was reached.

"Does anyone have anything to say in defence of Profesor Cedeño?" Humberto asked.

Profesor Cedeño was known in the barrio as a serious and polite man. Some of his students visited his house, mostly long-haired guys who wore necklaces and medallions. Raymundo, a scrawny boy with a long face, gingerly raised his hand.

"I know Profesor Cedeño. He's a friend of Papá's."

"And what has that got to do with anything? He's a communist."

Raymundo swallowed hard.

"But he believes in Christ and he goes to Mass."

"Just because he goes to Mass it doesn't mean that he's not a communist. He teaches Marxist theory and atheist socialism at U.N.A.M.," Antonio spat.

The evidence against Cedeño was piling up. Raymundo made one last-ditch attempt.

"He's a good man. He's my sister's godfather."

Humberto strode over and stopped a few centimetres from Raymundo.

"Being a good man and believing in Christ is not enough. Maybe corrective measures are needed to remedy his communist beliefs."

Intimidated, Raymundo stammered his response.

"Yes, maybe."

"Corrective measures" meant a beating, the most lenient punishment in the arsenal of the Good Boys.

"Cedeño will be punished," Humberto announced to silent nods from the group.

Nobody raised a hand to defend Mario Arias. He had moved into the barrio only six months earlier. His crime was that he had renounced his Catholic faith and become a Jehovah's Witness. He had said as much to Father Arturo when the priest came by to welcome him to the congregation and invite him to attend Mass. Humberto decided to spare him corrective measures. "He still believes in Christ. But if any of you hear him insulting the Catholic religion, let us know immediately." Arias was sentenced to a process of supervision.

Abraham Preciado was a bitter, cantankerous man of seventy-five who ran his shop, La Españolita, with his wife Elsa, who was equally unpleasant. Until now, no-one had realised that he was a Jew, since he had a Spanish surname. When Father Pepe had invited him to Mass, he explained that he had arthritic knees (he used a walking stick) and preferred to worship god at home for fear that his inability to kneel might offend. He even asked the priest to bless his shop, and Father Pepe happily agreed. This is how Don Abraham managed to hide his religion and avoid the persecution he'd suffered since childhood.

As far as the Good Boys were concerned, all Jews were enemies of Christ: "The Jews crucified him, they rejected him. They try to control us, they think they're superior but they're scum," Humberto said during one of our meetings.

For years, no suspicions were raised about Don Abraham and his wife. They were simply two bad-tempered old people who served behind the counter every day from 7 a.m. to 9 p.m. Monday to Saturday, and a half-day on Sundays. They constantly yelled and screamed at their only employee and refused to serve anyone whose appearance or clothes they found offensive. "We don't sell to people like you, boy" they would say. It didn't matter if the customer begged; Abraham and Elsa wouldn't even look at them.

Their high-handed manner provoked a lot of animosity among the neighbours, but since the only other shop in the area was Gigante, which was out of the way and open only from 10 a.m. until 7 p.m., emergency supplies were invariably bought from La Españolita. At a twenty-five per cent mark-up, of course.

It was Josué who discovered that Don Abraham and Doña Elsa were Jews. One of his classmates, a Jewish boy called Grinberg, had mentioned that his aunt and uncle lived in Modelo. "Are they Jewish?" Josué asked. "Of course," Grinberg said. "Señor Abraham is my father's cousin. He and his wife run La Españolita, the shop opposite the church."

Josué immediately informed Humberto. The name Preciado didn't sound Jewish to them, since they knew nothing about the difference between Ashkenazi and Sephardic Jews, and Preciado was a Sephardic name.

Humberto chose three boys to investigate the couple. In less than three weeks, they discovered the location of the synagogue they attended far away in Polanco, the name of the rabbi they went to for advice, and the names of every member of their extensive family. Abraham and Elsa were practising Jews who were active within their community.

In the pantheon of the enemies of Christ, being a Jew wasn't considered especially serious and, in general, they were simply sentenced to "supervision". But several other factors counted against the Preciados: their surly manner, their greed and their penny-pinching. Humberto considered them typical of the Jews who had slain Christ and therefore deserving of severe corrective measures. "We're going to teach them the humility and the generosity that are expected of a devotee of any religion."

Nobody raised a voice in their defence. It didn't matter that they

274

were an elderly couple who worked from dawn to dusk every day. It did not matter that they had lived among us for years, that we had known them since we were kids. No. The decision had been made and nobody was about to question it.

ENEMIES OF GOD:

1) Those who do not profess the one true religion. Penalty: supervision. If aggravated by offences against Christ or the Catholic faith: corrective measures.
2) Those who convert from Catholicism to another faith. Heretics. Penalty: supervision. If aggravated by affronts against Christ or the Catholic religion: corrective or severe corrective measures.
3) Atheists and agnostics. Penalty: severe corrective measures. If aggravated by insults to god or jokes about the Catholic faith: elimination.
4) Communists. Penalty: severe corrective measures. If aggravated by attacks on religion or jokes about the Catholic faith: elimination.
5) Those who consume drugs or alcohol in excess. Penalty: severe corrective measures.
6) Promiscuous women or those who prostitute themselves. Penalty: corrective or severe corrective measures.
7) Those who steal, or are guilty of fraud, extortion or corruption. Penalty: severe corrective measures.
8) Those who practise abortion. Penalty: severe corrective measures.
9) Kidnappers. Penalty: elimination.
10) Sodomites, rapists and those who corrupt members of their own sex. Penalty: elimination.

11) Those who poison society by trafficking in drugs or
    illegal substances. Penalty: elimination.

Supervision: the guilty party is to be closely watched for any offences in thought, word and deed that constitute an affront to the Catholic faith or the teachings of Our Lord Jesus Christ.

Corrective measures: corporal punishment carried out by members of the group using only fists, elbows, feet, knees.

Severe corrective measures: harsh corporal punishment is meted out by members of the group, this may include the use of blunt objects: bats, sticks, bottles, pipes, chains.

Elimination: summary execution of the wicked individual, preventing any further harm. In addition to those weapons used in severe corrective measures, firearms and knives are permitted.

Bible verses selected by Humberto and displayed in framed posters on the walls of the room where the Young People Committed to Christ would meet (none of the verses actually mentions Christ):

God judgeth the righteous,
And god is angry with the wicked every day.
If He turn not, He will whet his sword; He hath bent His bow and
    made it ready.
Psalms 7:12

Wait on the LORD, and keep his way, and He shall exalt thee to
    inherit the land: when the wicked are cut off, thou shalt see it.
Psalms 37:34

Woe unto them! for they have fled from me: destruction unto
    them!
Hosea 7:13

A man also or woman that hath a familiar spirit, or that is a
    wizard, shall surely be put to death: they shall stone them with
    stones: their blood shall be upon them.
Leviticus 20:27

1. And I heard a great voice out of the temple saying to the seven
    angels, Go your ways, and pour out the vials of the wrath of
    God upon the earth.

2. *And the first went, and poured out his vial upon the earth; and there fell a noisome and grievous sore upon the men which had the mark of the beast, and upon them which worshipped his image.*

3. *And the second angel poured out his vial upon the sea; and it became as the blood of a dead man: and every living soul died in the sea.*

Revelations 16:1–3 The Seven Cups

3. *Thus saith the Lord GOD; I will therefore spread out my net over thee with a company of many people; and they shall bring thee up in my net.*

4. *Then will I leave thee upon the land, I will cast thee forth upon the open field, and will cause all the fowls of the heaven to remain upon thee, and I will fill the beasts of the whole earth with thee.*

5. *And I will lay thy flesh upon the mountains, and fill the valleys with thy height.*

6. *I will also water with thy blood the land wherein thou swimmest, even to the mountains; and the rivers shall be full of thee.*

Ezekiel 32:3–6

For without are dogs, and sorcerers, and whoremongers, and murderers, and idolaters, and whosoever loveth and maketh a lie.

Revelation 22:15

Justice

I watched as Avilés's Maverick disappeared into the winding streets. I went back inside and turned on the living room light; Colmillo was lying under the table. I picked up a chair and sat a few metres from him. He watched me suspiciously. Although Avilés had recommended challenging him as often as possible, I was too bruised and too exhausted to try.

I looked around at the ruins of the ground floor, then got up and went over to the rubble that remained of my bedroom. I hopped over the demolished partition. My clothes were scattered all over the floor – underwear, trousers, socks. The only thing still hanging in the ruined wardrobe was a shirt I'd kept that had belonged to Carlos.

I started to clean up the mess, piling books onto the bed and arranging them in alphabetical order. As I cleared the floor, I happened on the folder Fernando had given me, containing Colmillo's information. Avilés was categorical that he was a pureblood wolf. I wanted to see if there was any proof.

I sat on the bed and leafed through the documents. The first page was a record of vaccinations, stating that Colmillo had been vaccinated against rabies as a puppy and been given the annual triple vaccine since then. Every two years he'd been vaccinated against distemper. Next to each entry was a date and a vet's signature. Colmillo was up to date.

There were photos of Colmillo in an envelope. Some from when he was a puppy, others more recent. From the photos, it was hard to believe that this tiny puppy would grow up to be the whirlwind that had destroyed my house. Then I found an English leaflet with a cover depicting a snow-covered prairie with a wolf in the foreground. It looked like a poster for an old Rin-Tin-Tin movie. Mackenzie Breeders, Exotic Pets. I opened it. It recounted the history of the breeding centre. A man named Mackenzie had found a wolf caught by a legendary Inuit trapper, and had taken the animal to a huge enclosure he'd built so that the wolf could roam freely. He first mated it with a she-wolf, and then crossed the offspring with purebred female Alaskan Malamutes. Mr Mackenzie decided to put the pups up for sale. It was a success. The brochure featured several photographs of the centre, showing a huge number of wolves and wolf-dogs, and the Malamutes used for cross-breeding.

Attached was an instruction sheet for how to care for the recently purchased pet.

> Congratulations, you have bought a purebred wolf. Please read the following instructions on how to care for your pup so that it will adapt to its new environment.
>
> 1) Wolves are sociable creatures. It is important that your pup spend a lot of time with your family, and that you play with it as often as possible. DO NOT tie it up or leave it in a confined space, which can adversely affect its sociable nature and result in an aggressive animal.
> 2) Be firm with your pup. Never allow it to disobey. If it is unruly or defiant, you should reprimand it. It is crucial that the animal recognises you as the alpha male.
> 3) Make sure your pup gets at least an hour of exercise every day. It is important that the animal be able to roam freely and interact with people. A wolf needs to know that it belongs to a pack – your family is now the wolf pack.
> 4) Take time every day to train your pup. Teach it to respond to simple commands: to sit, lie down, walk to heel and defecate only in permitted places. Your pet must follow your lead, not the other way around.

5) Do not feed the wolf raw meat, since doing so will awaken its hunting instincts. Meals should consist of cooked meat with bones for the animal to chew. We also recommend dog biscuits.

6) As far as possible, allow the wolf to spend time with you inside your home. When wolves are lonely, they become anxious. Let it lie next to you while you are cooking or watching television. It is essential that the wolf feels involved in family activities. We recommend socialising the wolf with other dogs, taking care to curb any aggressive behaviour. Spending time with other dogs will reinforce its sense of belonging to a pack.

   If you follow these instructions, your puppy will grow up to be an easy-going, reticent, playful and obedient pet. There is no reason why a wolf should behave aggressively.

No-one in the Prieto family knew any English. Had they read the instructions, Colmillo's problems could easily have been avoided. Everything they did was the opposite of what was recommended: they kept him chained up, left him alone in the garage, fed him raw horse meat, never exercised or trained him, never allowed him into the house, and never shared anything with him. Colmillo had become aggressive because he'd been deprived of space, of freedom, and of a social environment. Avilés's identification had been spot on. Now we would see whether those mistakes could be undone, whether Colmillo's temperament could be improved.

I leafed through the rest of the documents. The last was a piece of parchment with florid handwriting detailing Colmillo's limited pedigree. It listed only the names of the sire and the dam; there was no way of knowing who Colmillo's ancestors were since he was descended from wolves captured in the wild rather than animals bred in captivity. The sire was called Nujuaqtutuq (the leaflet explained that it was an Inuktitut name meaning "The Untameable"), the dam was Pajamartuq

281

("She Who Bites"). A stamp and a notarised signature authenticated the pedigree.

I left the debris of my former bedroom, sat on the last unbroken chair in the living room and stared at Colmillo. How different we were. Through his veins flowed the blood of a line of purebred wolves; through mine flowed the blood of countless donors. The pure and the impure. I was excited at the thought that I had a wolf living in my house. I felt a powerful desire to tame him, to make him my companion, to convince him that we belonged to the same pack.

There was no time to be lost. Although my leg was still throbbing with pain, I got up, picked up the chair and, without a second thought, I charged.

tell me god – if you exist – why are you so wrathful? those words carved in stone, brimming with rage, where did they come from? and if we are made in your image and likeness, why does it anger you that human beings are so like you?

tell me god, are you the one who orders the killings? are you the one who commands that atheists like me be murdered? do you approve of those who claim to be your soldiers? or do they act of their own free will?

tell me whether the age-old wrath in the bible is yours, tell me to whom you dictated the fearsome utterances that appear in your holy book? are these ruthless commandments yours? why this urge to spill blood, to destroy, to leave bodies scattered over the land to be devoured by beasts? why do you threaten so?

and you, Christ, surely you came to change the world? to forgive, to fill us with love? were you truly the son of god? or are you god? god the father, the son and the holy spirit? your father wrote one section of the book, did you come to rewrite it? if you are truly one god, is this a contradiction? a correction? did you regret your previous commandments?

come, christ, and put a stop to this. to this gang of murderers devoted to defending your name. they wield your name like a banner of death and destruction. they misuse it, spatter it with blood – or was it you who handed down the death sentences? you, who preached about love and harmony?

holy spirit, I imagine you as a gentle breeze, a purifying wind. are you the breath of the loathsome army that kills in your name?

god, did your burning finger mark out my brother for death? did you reach down from the heavens and seal his fate? tell me. reveal yourself. have the courage to reveal yourself to me and explain or justify his death. who did my brother ever hurt? he never forced anyone to take drugs. surely you are the one who is always talking about free will? surely their bodies were theirs to do with as they chose? or do all the bodies in the world belong to you?

how many people have you ordered to be killed, lord? you cannot simply order killings, cause so much destruction and sit serenely on your heavenly throne, unpunished.

answer me or I will assume that you do not exist. speak now or forever hold your peace. but if you say nothing, you will simply be confirming that you are only a puff of smoke, that you never existed, that you are nothing but an excuse to be used by criminals. in other words, you are a fictional character, the product of diseased minds. come or go, manifest yourself or disappear, but stop being some pathetic excuse for a gang of killers.

too much death and fear has been caused by gods. if you exist, bring comfort and happiness. ensure that no-one murders in your name. that no-one robs, kidnaps, rapes, judges or condemns. do not allow it. check the killer's hand right now. mankind yearns for peace. let us make a deal and live in peace. you, us. in peace

The lashing blizzard made it hard to pull the sled. The great wolf, though scrawny and malnourished, was still heavy, and then there was the store of meat, the tent and the pelts. Dragging the sled uphill through the trees left his hands blistered and his muscles aching. He could not stop. When spring came, the snow would melt and he would no longer be able to pull the sled. It would become impossible to keep moving.

Amaruq had lost all sense of time and space. He trudged resolutely southwards, heading towards where he knew was home. He trekked through unfamiliar terrain, convinced that at any moment he would recognise the mountains, the rivers, the wilderness.

The wolf grew stronger. His eyes once again began to glitter, his lips to drool, and he stopped panting. Though his legs were still bound, Nujuaqtutuq was strong enough to try to bite Amaruq. Once, while pulling the sled, he had come too close and the wolf had snapped, ripping away a piece of his trousers. To stop him from attacking again, Amaruq tied a rope around his neck.

Amaruq feared another wolf pack might attack. They had not yet encountered any wolves, but if a roving pack were to scent an injured wolf, they would inevitably attack. Amaruq would not be able to fight them off. He was exhausted, he had no gun, only a spear and a knife to defend himself. It would not be a fair fight. He also feared that they might be attacked by a bear, a puma, even a wolverine. It had been a harsh winter: a wounded animal and a feeble man were easy prey.

At night, Amaruq would pitch the tent among the pine trees where he felt more sheltered, then drag the sled and the wolf into the thicket and set fires in a circle to ward off animals. Leaving Nujuaqtutuq in one corner, next to the tent flap, Amaruq curled up in the corner furthest away from him, sleeping with his knife by his hand in case the wolf managed to break free.

The winter felt like the longest and darkest he had ever known. The bitter cold grew harsher, the icy wind clawed at his face as he trudged on. He was reluctant to muffle up, he needed a clear line of sight to watch for predators. Sometimes, he was tempted to head across the prairie, an easier trek since he would not have to weave between the trees, but he knew it would be a fatal mistake; it would make him an easy target. Among the trees he could protect himself, shelter behind a trunk or climb a tree.

Now and then as he travelled his grandfather kept him company and Amaruq would ask him to tell stories. But the grandfather walked in silence or sang softly, almost inaudibly. Amaruq would complain. "Talk to me, make the day's labour a little easier to bear." But nothing. Snow. Wind. Whispers.

He came to the shores of a broad river. The water was frozen solid. He could not remember crossing it. Which way was he headed? Did this river lie to the east, to the south? He gazed up at the sky, searching for the sun to get his bearings. It was covered by a veil of cloud, but he could still calculate from its glare. He was right, he had been heading southward. So where had this river come from? He did not recognise these banks, these wide meanders. He had not crossed a river of this breadth. He turned and looked behind him, confused. He had never strayed before. What was happening? He took a deep breath and tried to calm his panic. He knew that in the icy tundra people were liable to get lost when they panicked and made rash decisions. They would find themselves going in circles, plunging deeper and deeper into a labyrinth, not stopping until they died from hunger and exhaustion.

Amaruq walked along the banks and studied the landscape. He looked around for some sign that he had forded this river. Nothing looked familiar, not a copse of trees, not a mountain or a valley. While he had been hunting Nujuaqtutuq he had forgotten the golden rule: stop every hundred metres and look behind you, because the landscape you see ahead is not the same as the landscape you leave behind. Now he was paying the price.

Amaruq did not dare cross the frozen river. It was very wide, and if the ice was not strong enough to bear their weight, he and the wolf would fall through it and drown, towed beneath an ice sheet by the current.

He decided to head downstream to find a place where it narrowed. He walked for several kilometres before rounding a bend and coming face to face with a herd of wapiti. As soon as they sensed him, they bolted. After about eighty paces, they stopped and turned back. Hundreds of pairs of eyes studied this man wrapped in pelts and the wolf lying on the sled. One of the bucks let out a loud grunt and the herd turned as one and ran across the frozen river.

The pounding of hooves on ice echoed around the valley. Amaruq watched as they disappeared, then moved to the spot where they had crossed. There was not a single crack in the ice. He pounded it with his fist. It felt solid. He decided to go two hundred metres further, to avoid the stretch that they had trampled.

Unsettled by the presence of the wapiti, Nujuaqtutuq squirmed anxiously on the sled, and Amaruq loosened the rope around his neck so that he would not hurt himself. The wolf craned its neck, turning back towards where the wapiti had disappeared. Amaruq waited for the wolf to calm, then decided to cross.

He cleared the river without any difficulty. The sled skated smoothly across the ice. Amaruq was grateful; the pain in his legs and his back was excruciating, to say nothing of his blistered, bleeding hands. When they reached the other side, Amaruq left the sled by the bank and collapsed into the snow. He watched as a flock of crows flew overhead and landed on the branches of a tree. He heard the bugles of the wapiti as they moved further and further away. Exhausted, he fell asleep.

It was night when he woke, and he was frozen to the marrow. He stood up and looked around. In the darkness, he could just make out the sled and the wolf. He had made yet another mistake: he had fallen asleep out in the open, without any protection from predators. He could feel the first symptoms of hypothermia: the headache, the numbed fingers, the stupor. He walked over to the sled, unpacked the tent and set about pitching it. His deadened fingers made it difficult to drive stakes into the ground and tie the guy ropes. The tent was unsteady.

He lit two fires, hauled the sled into the tent, and then, half-asleep, walked past Nujuaqtutuq. Seizing the opportunity, the wolf sank its teeth into his ankle. Amaruq howled in pain. The wolf's fangs had gone deep, blood was spurting. Amaruq picked up the spear and beat the wolf several times on the head with the handle, screaming: "I'll kill you, I'll kill you!" The wolf whimpered. Feeling his grandfather grip the spear, Amaruq stopped beating and whipped around. He was sick of the old man's ghost. "I'll kill you too," he said. He snatched the spear from the old man's hands and hit out at the empty air, until eventually he collapsed, utterly drained.

Nujuaqtutuq had now bitten Amaruq twice. Wolf spittle, human blood. Miserable and humiliated, forced to defecate and urinate where he lay, the wolf had taken his revenge. Amaruq sat down and examined his wound. Blood was still flowing fast. He fashioned a tourniquet, then tightened and released it every twenty seconds. The bleeding began to slow. He placed burning embers on the gash to cauterise it, clenching his jaw at the pain.

He took a hunk of wapiti meat and set it by the fire to thaw, then cut it into pieces and fed it to Nujuaqtutuq using the spear. Man and wolf ate in silence. When they had finished, Amaruq extinguished the small fire inside the tent and settled down to sleep.

Reflections on the enemy as I sit on the rooftop:

"Do not fight your enemy. Let him make the critical mistakes. He will defeat himself. Sit calmly and watch the river. Sooner or later his corpse will float downstream."

"The most difficult enemy to defeat is the one you see in the mirror every day."

"Revenge is a matter of precision."

"Do not allow emotion to fuel your urge for vengeance. Bide your time; the moment to act will come."

"If your enemy is spoiling for a fight, all too soon he will meet the rival who will kill him. It may be you, it may be someone else."

"Allow the enemy to believe he has defeated you, then attack when he least expects it."

"When walking through a jungle waiting for a lion to attack, never forget to look down: the enemy may disguise himself as a snake."

"Your enemy will always believe that he is on the side of right and you are in the wrong."

"The most implacable enemies know both your weaknesses and your strengths; they have been close to you, they have watched you."

"You may be someone's enemy without realising. They will attack and you will not know when or why."

"Battles are brief, wars are long. It does not matter how many battles you lose; the war goes on."

"The enemy should find you prepared."

"Watch out for the traitor in your midst."

"Our greatest defeats and our greatest victories are private. We alone know when we truly win or lose."

"Do not squander your energy hating the enemy, focus on defeating him."

"Your enemies believe the gods are on their side."

Chess

He moved his rook, threatening my bishop. There was no way for me to protect it. If I moved the bishop, his pawn would advance to K6, pinning my king. Father Arturo smiled, satisfied. I had taken two pawns and his knight; he had taken two knights, a rook, four pawns and a bishop. I was being trounced.

Humberto had asked me to go with him to the shops and on the way back suggested we stop by the church. He led me into the warren of little rooms behind the vestry where Father Arturo lived with another priest and two nuns who looked after them. There were three small, spartan rooms. A tiny living room with a television, a table and a kitchenette crammed into thirty square metres.

We had to wait for fifteen minutes to see Father Arturo. "He's at prayer," one of the nuns said as she let us in. When he finally appeared, he greeted me politely. "I've heard a lot about you," he said, squeezing my arm. I had pictured him as a solemn, austere man, but Father Arturo was easy-going and even had a sense of humour. But it felt strange to talk to someone who never took off their sunglasses. Humberto treated the priest with an almost obsequious reverence, hanging on his every word.

Father Arturo gestured for us to sit next to him on one of the threadbare sofas. He offered us café de olla freshly prepared by one of the nuns. "It's the finest coffee you'll ever taste in your life," he said. I took a sip. It was delicious, with hints of cinnamon and just the right amount of brown sugar. I glanced at the chessboard on the table. "You play chess?" he asked. I nodded. I had learned to play when I was eight by studying the description in the *Encyclopaedia Britannica* of how each piece moved. My father had refined my knowledge of the game, and we'd played often. When I was nine, I finally beat him. I thought he'd let me win, but no, I really had beaten him.

"What's your favourite opening?" asked Father Arturo. I didn't know what he meant. The only one I knew was Scholar's Mate. "I don't have one," I replied. "I like the Spanish Opening," he said. He gestured to the table. "Fancy a game?"

In the first game, he began by advancing the queen's knight. I was used to my father and Carlos always beginning by advancing the king's pawn. I didn't know how to counter this opening and, within a few moves, he had control of the board and delivered a resounding checkmate. In the second game, I was forced to concede after losing both knights, a rook and a bishop. Father Arturo was famous for the time he spent studying openings, defences and attacks.

"Do you know who Capablanca was?" he asked as we replaced the pieces on the board. "Sure, a Cuban grandmaster. He was a world champion," I said. "Do you know how he lost the championship?" I shook my head. "José Raùl Capablanca was a genius. Probably the best chess player who ever lived. An exceptionally gifted man, but . . . he led a dissolute life. He liked drinking and partying. The time came for him to defend his title against Alexander Alekhine, a methodical, disciplined Russian player. While Alekhine was studying his opponent's weaknesses, Capablanca spent his time sleeping with loose women – some of whom, they say, were paid by Alekhine. No-one expected Capablanca to lose, but after forty games he was defeated. Having had little sleep, he couldn't focus and was mentally and physically unable to carry on. Alekhine refused to grant him a rematch and remained the world champion for years."

Though I found the story interesting, I had no idea where he was going with it. "There is a lesson to be learned there, Juan Guillermo," he said, emphasising my name. "You have to decide whose side you're on, the winner's or the loser's. You should side with Alekhine, not people like Capablanca. Do you understand?" He smiled, satisfied, and slapped my thigh. "You did the right thing in joining us. Because we will prevail. But you have to remain loyal." He brought his face close to mine. His breath smelled foul, as though he never brushed his teeth. "It's no coincidence that Humberto's mother was the one who saved your life. Can you begin to comprehend the scope of god's mystery?"

He stood up and smoothed out his cassock. "If you'll excuse us, Humberto and I have things to discuss." They went into the priest's bedroom and closed the door. The nun brought me another cup of café de olla. This one didn't taste quite as good. Perhaps because I could still taste Father Arturo's fetid breath. To this day, the memory of it makes me shudder.

I waited for Humberto for almost an hour. When he finally emerged, he smiled and said, "Father Arturo liked you a lot." We hardly spoke as we walked back. As he left me outside my house, Humberto looked me in the eye. "Sunday, ten o'clock," he said. "We're counting on you."

José Raúl Capablanca collapsed at the age of fifty-three, felled by a stroke as he walked into a restaurant and asked someone to help him take off his coat. He died in hospital some hours later. To this day, he is admired and respected as a brilliant chess player, a man of exceptional natural talent.

Alexander Alekhine was found dead sitting at a table in his hotel room at the age of fifty-three. He died as he was eating alone. The autopsy attributed his death to a heart attack. Someone suggested he'd choked on a piece of meat. Conspiracy theories claim he was poisoned. Some versions of the story claim that Alekhine was an anti-Semite and a Nazi sympathiser. In chess circles, he was called a coward for refusing to allow Capablanca a rematch for the title.

I am, and always will be, on the side of the Capablancas of this world.

*

I woke up on the living room carpet, with Colmillo lying a few metres away. I tried to move but felt a shooting pain in my leg. Colmillo lifted his head and looked at me. I couldn't think of a better way to greet him than "Good morning, asshole".

I had gone downstairs during the night to challenge him, a brutal struggle that lasted more than an hour. I lashed out at him with the chair and he attacked more than once, snapping at the same leg as before, this time with such force that I couldn't move. Sprawled on my back, I managed to hit him twice more, forcing him to retreat. I crawled backwards and we stared at each other. Then, exhausted, I feel asleep.

Colmillo got to his feet. Blood trickled from his chops. He was also suffering from last night's bout. I stood up. Colmillo growled. I picked up the chair as if to smash it over his head. That was enough to silence him.

I went to the fridge and grabbed the remains of a rotisserie chicken Pato had brought me three days earlier. I pulled off a leg and a thigh, warmed them up on the stove then went and sat in front of Colmillo. As soon as he smelled the food he got up, his every muscle tensed, clearly half-mad with hunger. He stared at the chicken and then suddenly lunged at me with such force that he pulled the table behind him. I only just managed to shuffle out of the way. I stood up and circled him, never turning my back on him. Colmillo strained, dragging the table behind him. Whenever he came too close, I kicked him in the nose. He paused, now chary of me. We glared at each other.

I picked up the chicken leg and started to eat. When I'd finished the drumstick, I tossed him the bone and Colmillo pounced. The muzzle made it impossible for him to eat the bone and, frustrated, he began shaking his huge head from side to side. He turned and looked at me, his eyes filled with rage rather than a plea for mercy. I ate the thigh, exaggerating my enjoyment to provoke him. Afterwards I went upstairs to Carlos's room.

More shit and piss. I'd had to leave the rooftop door open for King. Being completely housetrained, the boxer had shat in the shower, trying to aim for the drain the way Carlos had taught him to do in the backyard.

I tore off a piece of toilet paper, picked up the shit and tossed it into the toilet, then turned on the shower to wash away the urine. The poor dog was still terrified. He refused to let me out of his sight, even when I took a shower. Although usually desperate to avoid getting wet, King sat in the corner of the shower, oblivious to the splashes of water.

I closed my eyes and allowed the hot water to run over me for half an hour. The jet of water eased the pain in my leg and shoulder a little. The doorbell rang as I was getting dressed. It was my three best friends. I opened the door. As he stepped into the room, Pato stared at the destruction. "Colmillo did this?" he said. I nodded. There was almost nothing left for the wolf to destroy.

"Let's take a walk," Jaibo said. "You guys go ahead," I said. "No, we came to take you out," said Pato, "so we're not going anywhere without you." They suggested we walk to Buenavista station. Ever since we were twelve, we'd fantasised about hopping the freight trains like a bunch of hobos. We even tried once, but Jaibo fell onto his back and cracked a rib. When my father found out, he was furious. As a teenager, he and his friends had done the same thing, but one of his friends slipped as he was jumping between the cars, fell onto the tracks, and the train ran over him, severing both legs. Depressed after the double amputation, he holed up in his room, where he died a year later.

My father had made me promise never to do it again. But now that my father was dead, there was no promise to keep, and to be honest, the thought of falling between the cars and being crushed didn't much bother me.

We walked to the station and stood on the platform, choosing a train. The first to leave was headed for Saltillo. We studied the motionless freight cars, trying to decide how best to get aboard. Then we walked along the tracks, jumped the fence and hid behind a stack of barrels, waiting for it to pull out.

The train rattled as we jumped on and quickly clambered into a wagon filled with sacks of maize. As the train left the city, we sat on the edge of the wagon, staring out. The landscape changed from woodland to scrubland, to desert. Huizaches and prickly-pear trees were dotted across the plain. Startled by the passing train, hares bounded away, while mournful doves fluttered across the sky.

The freight train stopped in villages and sometimes in the middle of nowhere. Five hours later, as we were pulling into Querétaro, we decided to get off. The train began to slow and we jumped down as we pulled into the railyard. We were spotted by guards, who started to give chase. Weaving between the freight cars, we eventually managed to lose them.

We spent the afternoon in downtown Querétaro, eating enchiladas from a street stall and wandering through the alleyways, squares and parks. I was struck by the purity of the light, the deep blue of the sky, the dazzling white of the clouds.

When the sun began to set, we headed back. We stood next to the train tracks on the outskirts of the city in the middle of a dust storm. A freight train roared towards us at high speed, and we waited until the engine had passed, then ran alongside it. Pato and I grabbed the railing of the steps and heaved ourselves up onto a boxcar. Agüitas and Jaibo nearly missed it completely, but eventually managed to scrabble into a wagon loaded with sand.

We found ourselves in an open car filled with huge rolls of sheet metal, lay down and fell asleep. Halfway home, we were woken by the rainstorm. In less than a minute we were completely drenched, since there was nowhere to shelter. We simply lay there, letting raindrops splash onto our faces.

The train stopped several times, and each time we heard the metallic shrieking of brakes as the mechanical beast of burden shuddered to a halt in the curtain of rain. Each time it pulled away again the engine jolted and the wagons rattled.

Snaking its way through the hills, the train headed down towards the urban sprawl. We pulled up at a platform in Vallejo, an industrial area in Mexico City. Still sodden, we climbed down and wandered past huge warehouses through a warren of deserted streets prowled by rangy, hungry dogs, the pavements strewn with garbage and fetid black pools. We were unfamiliar with the area, and met no-one who could give us directions.

We wandered in circles, shivering from the cold. Jaibo told stories about Tampico to keep us entertained. Stories of fishermen cast adrift for weeks on end on the high seas, of ships' captains who spoke unintelligible languages, of oil slicks rolling like huge black waves on beaches, of blazing cargo ships that lit up the night sky, of red tides that left shoals of fish and crabs rotting on the sand.

Finally, we stumbled out onto a busy street, where we hailed a taxi. We arrived back in the barrio around midnight, exhausted, wet and cold, and went our separate ways. When I arrived at my place, there was a note taped to the front door:

> I dropped by to see if you wanted dinner. I brought some biscuits from a Chinese café – I left them inside the gate. Eat them with melted butter, they're delicious. Today's lesson in dealing with Colmillo: howl, bark, growl, talk, sing to him. Wolves are very vocal. Try to communicate with him. I'll stop by for dinner tomorrow. If you can't make it, let me know.
> Sergio

I went in and looked around for the bag. Avilés had left it by the hosepipe in the yard. He'd obviously had to squeeze between the bars to leave it there. He'd left me four biscuits. Forgetting about the melted butter, I gobbled one up then and there.

I groped my way into the dark house, and, turning on the light, found Colmillo standing, staring at the stairs. I turned and saw Chelo, sitting on a step.

Zurita had never laid eyes on my brother before they pulled his bloated body from the water, his mouth hanging open, water spewing from his lungs, his face purple, his eyes fixed on the metal cover that had prevented his escape. Zurita was surprised by his height, his curly hair, the colour of his eyes. Kneeling down, he looked at Carlos, then turned to Humberto.

"Is this him?"

"Yes, that's Carlos Valdés," Humberto said.

"A handsome fucking bastard." Zurita got to his feet. "Could have been an actor."

Cops and Good Boys were huddled around the body. I tried to creep closer. Two cops barred my way, but Zurita signalled for them to let me pass. My brother looked as though he was trying to say something, as though he was mid-sentence, but no words came, only water. I was determined not to cry, especially not in front of his killers. "We rid the world of a plague," Humberto said. I whipped around. He was standing a few metres from the edge of the rooftop. I imagined charging and shoving him over the edge. The cops must have realised what I was thinking from the look on my face, because two officers barred my way. It didn't matter, sooner or later I would kill Humberto.

"What a tragic accident," Zurita said to me. Humberto and Antonio smirked. An accident? This was the word Comandante Adrián Zurita used to describe my brother's murder in his report. "For reasons we have been unable to discover, Juan Carlos Valdés was hiding in a rooftop water tank whose lid became wedged shut, preventing him from escaping. Death was the result of drowning. The corpse showed no signs of assault or anything else that might suggest foul play."

Just as the bodies of chinchillas used to twitch after they had been slaughtered, so my brother's body spewed water and bile. "That was no accident," I roared at Zurita. "That is something to be determined by the coroner," he said, sarcastically. Out of the corner of my eye, I saw Agüitas and Jaibo watching from the Ávalos' rooftop. They were sobbing. I wanted to scream at them to stop crying, to run and fetch the gun from Sean's house, to toss it across the gap between the rooftops so I could gun down the twelve disciples of evil gathered around my dead brother.

I looked around warily. The cops barring my way were momentarily distracted. I glared at Humberto, then dodged past the cops and charged. When I was two metres away, I hurled myself forward and headbutted him. I heard his nose shatter and it started to spurt blood. I grabbed him around the waist and was forcing him towards the edge of the rooftop when Antonio got me in a chokehold and threw me to the ground. Josué and two other Good Boys raced forward and lashed out, kicking me in the ribs, the stomach, the balls. I lay there. Zurita and his men did nothing to stop them. Humberto crouched down and brought his face close to mine. "*Non nobis, Domine, sed nomini tuo da gloriam,*" he whispered as his blood dripped onto my T-shirt. Then he got to his feet and walked away across the rooftops, followed by his acolytes.

One of the cops walked over to where Carlos's body lay, took off his jacket and laid it over my brother's face. I struggled to my feet, furious and still aching from the beating. I grabbed the officer's jacket and tossed it into the puddle of Carlos's vomit. I wanted to force them to look at the ugly rictus of death, I never wanted them to forget the face of this man whose murder they had failed to prevent. I wanted this vomiting corpse to haunt their nightmares.

Down below, an ambulance pulled up. Three paramedics raced up the spiral staircase. Before they reached the body, Zurita intercepted them and whispered something to them. All three listened closely. One of the paramedics bent over the corpse, pressing a finger to my brother's carotid artery in search of a pulse, as though Carlos were just

298

playing dead, just waiting for a sign to jump to his feet and carry on with his life.

Zurita ordered the paramedics to take the body. I stood in their way. "Someone from the public prosecutor's office has to come," I told them. "They need to file charges." Zurita turned back to me, exasperated. "So now you're a lawyer, *pendejo*? I give the orders around here."

The paramedics lifted my brother onto a stretcher and clumsily carried him down the spiral staircase, while taking care not to let the body slip off and tumble into the Martínez family's yard. A number of neighbours watched from their rooftops.

They arrived downstairs with the body. "They'll take him to the station and from there to the morgue in Xoco," one of the officers told me. The cop who had laid his jacket over Carlos's face came over. "Was it your brother they killed?" he said. I nodded. "I'm really sorry. But those fuckers are going to pay some day, you'll see."

I peered over the edge of the roof. A crowd of onlookers had gathered around the ambulance and the paramedics had to clear a path to lift my brother into the back. They turned on the siren and, slowly, to avoiding knocking down the rubberneckers, they pulled away.

The great novelist Honoré de Balzac tried to explain the causes behind love at first sight. He concluded that as blood courses through our bodies it creates magnetic fields, which manifest as heat, glow and radiance. These fields project aeroluminous alphabets, unique to every individual.

These ciphers, unintelligible to most people, can be understood only by those with a similar alphabet. When two individuals have similar alphabets, they can read each other clearly. They are inevitably drawn to one another, they understand each other perfectly. This is love at first sight.

It is a pity that the chances of meeting someone with an aeroluminous alphabet similar to our own are pretty remote.

Ice

Sunday. 10.12 p.m. It's bitterly cold. We creep in silence, hugging the walls and fences. My heart is pounding. The balaclava makes it hard to breathe. I'm clutching a baseball bat. I can feel the grain of the wood, the smooth varnish. What am I doing carrying a bat, heading out to beat up two old people? I can see Humberto's eyes through the holes in his mask. I cannot tell what they are saying. They are two dark slits. We stop outside the house. "The old Jew is going to pay dearly," Antonio says. It is so dark that I can't see a thing. The Good Boys spent the past week smashing all the street lights with catapults. They've made the street so dark that there can be no witnesses.

We get ready to go inside. Humberto pats me on the back. "Good luck," he says. Good luck? We're about to beat the shit out of a defence-less old couple and he's wishing me luck? Humberto gestures for us all to gather around and whispers his final instructions. "This is a corrective measure," he warns. "We are not here to kill them." This is the first time I've heard him explicitly use the word "kill". How many times did Humberto say "we're going to kill him" when referring to my brother?

Humberto and the others bless themselves, muttering in hushed voices: "By the sign of the Holy Cross, Amen." Humberto looks at the front door. "Ready?" he hisses. "Ready," the others answer. Not me, I'm not ready. How could anyone be ready for something like this? Felipe jemmies open a window. One by one, they crawl inside. While I wait for my turn, my fingertips trace the letters engraved on the bat: "Louisville Slugger".

We creep through the dark living room, avoiding the furniture, trying not to stumble or make any noise. I'm finding it hard to breathe. God be with us. Soundlessly, we tiptoe upstairs. I can't stop shaking. Humberto nods towards a door. The bedroom. Antonio steps forward, throws it open and gropes for the light switch. The elderly couple are in bed. When she sees us, the old woman screams. She is wearing a striped nightgown. The old Jew clambers out of bed and stands looking at us, bewildered. The assault begins.

He set himself the task of covering two kilometres a day, although sometimes he barely covered four hundred metres. The snow lay so thick that, even wearing snowshoes, he sank into it at every step. The effort of pulling the sled had reduced his gloves to frayed strips of leather. His bleeding fingers were numb from the cold. The wapiti meat froze solid and now had to be left on the fire for some time before it could be eaten. As Amaruq grew weaker, Nujuaqtutuq grew stronger. At any moment, the great wolf might break his bonds and escape. Amaruq still did not know quite why he was keeping the animal alive. His grandfather had to know of some plan made by the gods to stop Amaruq from killing the wolf.

The canvas tent was wearing thin from the ravages of the long journey. Here and there were holes that let in icy blasts of air. It was difficult to sleep, and insomnia made him lethargic. His body exuded a foul smell. Perhaps he was already dead and did not realise it.

Amaruq lugged the sled through valleys and ravines, scaled mountains and sheer rockfaces. Still he did not recognise his surroundings. Again and again he chastised himself for not making a mental map of this remote, unfamiliar terrain. In the distance he saw another herd of wapiti and headed towards them. As soon as they sensed him they scattered, raising drifts of snow that climbed into the air to form a white whirlwind. Ghosts of the prairies.

Dragging the sled to where the wapiti had been, he saw he had reached another broad, frozen river he could not remember crossing.

He gazed at the far shore. It looked familiar. He was getting closer to home.

He tested the ice to make sure it would bear the weight of the sled. It was a thick layer. He slowly made his way across, careful not to slip – the last thing he needed was to break an arm or a leg, or be otherwise injured in a fall. When he reached the other side, he trudged on.

Driven by the pressing need to get home, he quickened his pace. It was something he had seen sled dogs do after a long journey. Even if they were utterly exhausted, the moment they sensed they were close to home, they would run as fast as they could. Some would die within from the gruelling effort, curl up behind the igloos and peacefully succumb. Amaruq slowed his pace, there was nothing to be gained by hurrying.

The landscape he was passing through grew increasingly familiar. He headed for a clump of pine trees, pulling the sled with him, and settled on a place to pitch the tent. When he got there, he found his grandfather sitting on a mound of snow, honing a knife. "What are you doing here?" Amaruq asked. The old man turned and smiled. "I think the question is, what are you doing here?" The grandfather jerked his knife towards a tree trunk on which Amaruq could see grooves made by the chains he had used to secure the trap to catch Nujuaqtutuq. Further off lay the skeleton of the wapiti that had smashed into the pine tree. On the right, the ribcage of a female wapiti poked through the snow. Amaruq felt sick. He had come full circle. It was impossible, he had headed south. Due south. How could he have gone astray?

Abandoning the sled, he strode over to confront his grandfather. "Guide me home," he ordered. The grandfather gestured to the surrounding forest. "Perhaps this is your home, perhaps that is why you have come back." Amaruq looked around. "I cannot survive here, I have no bullets, no matches, the tent is falling to pieces, my gloves are in tatters, the food has run out." "Stop whining," the grandfather growled. "Our forebears' forebears learned to survive in places far

303

more hostile than this. Be a man and wrest from this land all that it will give." The grandfather turned to leave. Amaruq stopped him. "At least leave me your knife. It's sharper than mine." The grandfather handed it to him. "I'll give it to you," he said, "but this knife will be of no use to you in this world."

Without a word, Chelo led me to the bed in my ruined room, taking me by the hand and leading me past the broken furniture. She turned off the lights, swept everything off the mattress and lay down. She held out her arms for a hug. I didn't want to hug her. "Where have you been?" I said. "Come," she said. It was the first word she'd uttered. The very sound of her voice simultaneously reminded me how much I loved her and how much she'd hurt me. "You just disappeared," I said. She thought for a moment. "I'll tell you about it later. Come here." I was consumed with jealousy. Chelo had no right to show up out of the blue and ask me to hold her without explaining herself. "Who've you been sleeping with?" She looked up at me. I could just make out her eyes in the darkness. "I'll explain everything later, I promise. But come, please." The words were like a knife in my belly. Her evasiveness obviously meant she'd been sleeping with other people. I felt as though I was going to be sick. Why does it hurt so much, the image of another man's penis penetrating the woman you love? Why this terrible vulnerability, this terrible feeling caused by this woman, your homeland, having been sullied by others? The desecration of another man's semen. I stood, paralysed. There she lay, the woman who had left me, the woman I had prayed would come back. I couldn't touch her now. I couldn't. "Tell me, please," I said. Let her tell me straight out if she has slept with someone else. Let the wound come now, a swift, precise machete-blow, not a slowly seeping pain. "I'll tell you later," she said again. She rose from the bed, wrapped her arms around me and laid her head on my aching shoulder. Pain upon pain. In the darkness, I could see Colmillo, chained, watching us. Maybe I should set him free, take off his muzzle. King used to playfully jump on top of us when we made love; Colmillo could rip us to pieces. Let his fangs put an end to my suspicion, my uncertainty. Let us be devoured by the beast.

Chelo began to kiss me. Who would have thought a kiss could cause such sadness? So much sadness. She peeled off my wet clothes, folded them carefully over a chair, went into the bathroom and fetched a towel to dry me. Each time she towelled part of me, she kissed it. Seeing the bruises on my legs and my shoulder she said, "What happened?" I jerked my chin towards Colmillo. She stared at the wolf and the damage he had wreaked, then returned to drying me. She seemed unruffled by the fact that the house had been laid waste to by a wild animal, as though it were nothing out of the ordinary.

"Can I stay the night?" she asked. I nodded. She took off her clothes and, still standing, we began to make love. Wrapping her arms around my neck, her legs around my waist, she clung to me. With my aching legs, it was hard for me to bear her weight so I threw her down on the bed. I came very quickly, long before she was even close to orgasm. "Thank you," she said. "For what?" "For coming before I did." I'd always thought she liked having multiple orgasms before I came, it never occurred to me that she might want me to come quickly. She snuggled against my chest and we fell asleep.

I woke in the early hours to find Chelo no longer in bed. Looking around the living room, I saw her sitting naked on a chair, faintly illuminated by the moon, humming softly to Colmillo. The wolf listened, his ears pricked. The tune seemed to have a calming effect on him. I lay and watched her.

She stopped humming and walked over to stroke Colmillo. He lowered his ears and, once she was in range, he attacked. Terrified, Chelo tried to retreat, but Colmillo butted her in the stomach and she fell back onto the fragments of the television strewn across the floor. I leaped out of bed and ran over, picked her up and carried her away as the wolf prepared to attack again.

In the darkness, I negotiated the splintered partition walls, laid her on the bed and turned on the light. Her right foot was bleeding. A shard from the television screen had gashed the sole. I checked the wound to see if there was any glass inside. She whimpered as I parted the side of the gash. The gushing blood made it difficult to see. I went into the bathroom and fetched some toilet paper to clean the cut. There was no glass. Chelo started to laugh. "And I thought they were exaggerating when they said he was wild."

Here on the ruined ground floor, on sheets smeared with blood, surrounded by walls sprayed with Colmillo's urine and the stench of shit, I found Chelo's nakedness more moving than ever. Fuck! Why did I love her so much?

We made love again and she hummed a tune that grew sadder the closer she came to climax. As she came, she whispered in my ear, "Juan Guillermo, Juan Guillermo." She shuddered in my arms, her belly quivering against mine, her hands gripping my shoulders. When the muscles in her thighs relaxed, she pulled away from mine, rolled over and curled up with her back to me. For a few seconds she panted, until she got her breath back. Without turning, she murmured, "I missed you." I could have said, "If you missed me so much, why did you disappear for more than two months? Why didn't you come by, why didn't you phone, why couldn't you spend just one night? Just one, Chelo. That's all I wanted. One night. Please tell me, Chelo, did you sleep with other people? What were their fucking names?" But all I said was "I missed you too". I wrapped my arms around her until we fell asleep.

Humberto and Antonio are sitting facing me. Humberto seems worried. "You went too far," he says to me. "We all hit him," I counter. "You hit him hardest," Humberto says. "It doesn't matter," says Antonio. "He deserved it." The old Jew has ended up with a limp, his hip smashed by baseball bats. He finds walking difficult and painful. Humberto is pleased by my fury. "I didn't expect it, you really let fly."

I can't bear the guilt. I'd just turned fourteen and already the guilt was suffocating me.

I'm not the one who dealt the blow, I'm sure. "It'll be our secret, Juan Guillermo. We won't tell anyone you did it," Humberto says. "I didn't whack him on the hip," I say. "We all saw you, but don't worry, we're in this together."

At what moment, at what precise moment did I become one of them? It's true, I did hit him. But it wasn't me who put him in that state. It was the rain of blows from the others.

The wife is still in hospital. She hasn't said a word. The doctors say she will make a full recovery. Abraham Preciado and his wife Elsa. I will never be able to forget their names. How many times would I need to apologise? How many?

I can't sleep, I can't eat. I'm terrified. The others pretend to try to calm me down. "We had to do it, it was god's will," Antonio says. Was this really god's will? Did god command us to beat a defenceless old man as he lay on the floor? Humberto squeezes my shoulder. "Don't worry. You keep our secrets, we'll keep yours." He stands up and smiles. "See you next Saturday."

My father who art below,
Buried next to my mother,
Hallowed be thy name and thy memory.
You who dwell in dust,
with my mother and
my brothers,
send me a sign
that you can hear me,
guide me,
a woman is circling me,
a wolf lies in wait.
They are life, father,
the planks to which
this castaway
must cling.

Please, send me a map,
a compass,
a ship,
a sea,
a river,
books.
A South,
a North,
an East, a West,
a horizon,

a future
towards which to steer.

My father who art below,
give me counsel,
free me from uncertainty,
give me air, wind,
I am stifled by this present.
I need you, father,
you, mother,
you, grandmother,
you, my brothers.
I need
your words,
the memory of your love,
the memory of us together,
father and sons,
stillborn son,
murdered son,
protective mother,
gentle grandmother,
send me a sign
that you can hear,
a compass,
a ship,
a sea,
a river,
books.
A South,
a North
an East, a West,
a

horizon,
a future,
towards which
t
  o

    s
     t
    e
     e
      r

Words

In my third year in secondary school, a few months before Carlos died, my Spanish teacher, David Barraza, set us a task: "Choose ten words you think would be essential during a natural disaster to communicate with others and survive." It sounded like a simple exercise. It wasn't. The whole class spent two hours trying to choose ten words, with little success. When the bell rang, none of us had finished. We were told to finish it as our homework.

That afternoon, I wrote down dozens of words. I ruled out most abstract nouns: ideology, uneasiness, expectation, etc. I decided to choose those that encompassed sheer survival: food, shelter, water. Next, I chose linking words: you, me, us. Lastly, those that gave a sense of humanity: love, friendship, happiness, sadness. In the end, I was satisfied with what I considered to be a realistic selection.

The next day, the teacher asked us to read our ten words aloud. Two classmates I thought of as shallow and superficial went first. Both lists were almost identical to mine: food, drink, home, us, you, love, friendship, happiness, sadness. One had included the word "parents" and the other "clothes". The rest of my classmates read out their lists which were also much the same, with minor differences: journey, pain, medicine, money, fear.

I was starting to feel like a fool. We had all fallen for the same clichés. Maybe it was because of the way Profesor Barraza had phrased the task: choose words that would allow you to survive. It was true that words like drink, shelter, food, clothes, you, us and love made it possible to quickly and clearly connect with others.

The teacher wrote the words on the blackboard and the number of times they'd come up. It seemed as though my words were destined to join my classmates'. I refused to be another redundant statistic. I started scribbling words in no particular order, anything that might save me from these anodyne clichés.

"Your turn, Valdés," Profesor Barraza said. He was one of my favourite teachers, along with Fernando Alarid. He was young and thinking about a career as a writer. He was talented. He read his stories to us in class. They had narrative tension, power, imagination.

I stood up and began to read the list I'd created through free association: nothing, everything, rescue, abandon, danger, forgiveness, calm, animal, tame, wild. When I'd finished, Barraza smiled. "Why are those words essential for survival?" he asked. I extemporised: "Because everything else I can express with signs or pictures." Barraza smiled again. "I don't agree, but you're the only one who knows what you need in your life in order to survive," he said, and launched into a discussion about the importance of creating a language that allowed us to communicate efficiently in periods of crisis.

He congratulated the group, because the majority – from which I with my extemporised list was excluded – had created a precise linguistic framework in just ten words. Profesor Barraza added two points to that month's grade for everyone in the group, "except for you, Juan Guillermo, we'll talk later." I assumed he was going to fail me.

As I was leaving class, he stopped me. "Why do you try so hard to be different, Juan Guillermo?" The question caught me off guard. I didn't want to be different, I just didn't want to be the same as everyone else. "I'm just trying to be myself," I said. Barraza patted me on the shoulder. "You'll get a pass this month," he said. "Because?" I said. "Because literature is the search for an individual language, it involves rupture, originality, and you achieved that. Ten out of ten." He clapped me on the shoulder again and set off across the yard.

*

After four weeks, the meat ran out. Amaruq looked around as he chewed the last hunk. He had set several traps in a wide circle in the hope of catching something – he did not care if it was a wolf, a lynx, a bear, even a crow. They needed food, but nothing had fallen into his traps.

It was mid-March, but it felt as though winter would never end. The interminable cold, the driving snow, the wind blustering day and night. Storms had ripped the canvas of the tent, which now fluttered in tattered shreds. The guy ropes snapped during a blizzard and Amaruq had to venture out in the dark to retie them, to stop the tent from being swept away by the wind.

Then one morning the sun rose, the sky was clear, there was not a single cloud on the horizon. After weeks of grey, overcast skies, the brightness was unsettling. Spring has finally come, he thought. It was time to try again to return home.

He collected the traps, packed up the tent, rolled the furs and stowed them on the sled, and laid Nujuaqtutuq on top of them. The wolf had lost weight, so carrying him was not difficult. Since supplies were scarce, Amaruq had been carefully rationing the meat. At first, he had given the wolf equal rations, but as time passed he had reduced this to little mouthfuls. Amaruq needed to preserve his own strength so that he could hunt for both of them.

He set off. His grandfather had not reappeared since giving Amaruq the knife. Amaruq was unsure whether he had offended the old man, or whether he had simply returned to the land of the dead. Just in case, he waved farewell and headed south.

He decided to take a different route. He could not afford to stray again. Calculating that the wide, frozen river was to his left, he turned right, to the west, towards the soaring mountain range. It would be difficult to climb, but from the peaks he would be able to survey the horizon and find the railway line that would lead him home.

When he reached the foothills some days later, he recognised them as the ones he had seen from the station. The snow-capped peaks, the dense pine trees that ended where the sheer rockface began, the crags, the granite cliffs. He studied the various routes he might take, and decided on the north face. Where the slope was gentler, where he could drag the sled up most easily. He would begin his ascent the following morning.

As he was pitching the tent, he spotted a herd of mountain goats near the summit. "White ghosts," his grandfather used to say, "the most difficult of animals to hunt. Only when you have killed a buck can you call yourself a true hunter." Amaruq would try to kill one with his spear, show his grandfather how good a hunter he was, how skilled he was at negotiating cliffs.

He slept better than he had in a long time. The wind had died away and it did not snow. Even Nujuaqtutuq slept soundly. The great wolf snored so loudly that he woke Amaruq, who leaped to his feet in alarm, thinking the wolf was attacking. When he realised the sound was simply his snoring, he laughed out loud.

The following day, he began the ascent. It was a difficult climb. Viewed from below the trail looked undemanding, but he often found the path blocked by rocks or cavernous ravines. He looked around for side trails and finally found a path that seemed less steep. He walked for a long time before sitting down in the snow to rest. He had been hauling the sled uphill for more than six hours. Gazing down, he saw the frozen river he had crossed some weeks earlier. It weaved in wide meanders, sometimes east to west, sometimes north to south. It was clear now how he had been confused and crossed it twice in the same direction.

He continued to climb until he reached the mid-point of the slope, and began to circle the peak. The trail became increasingly rocky, making it harder to pull the sled. More than once, he came close to giving up, but he knew that he could only get his bearings from the summit.

He reached a hollow and, exhausted, decided to pitch camp. He put Nujuaqtutuq inside the tent, took his spear and set off to explore the precipitous terrain of the mountain goats. He walked for about a kilometre, then sat on a rock. In the distance, he saw two bucks and four does. They bounded up the steep rockface. If they missed their footing, they would plummet five hundred metres, but this did not seem to worry them. They leaped from one escarpment to another without hesitation.

He watched for a long time and realised they were heading towards a small valley near the summit. He turned and ran, weaving between jagged rocks to cut them off. He reached the edge of the valley. He threw himself on his belly and crawled through the wind to a promontory in the middle of the valley, where he hid and waited for the goats to approach. It was two hours before they appeared, and beginning to get dark. The largest buck led the herd to the edge of the valley, near a trail by which they could escape. The does lay down to sleep while the bucks remained standing, watchful.

Amaruq lifted his head just enough so that he could see them; he bided his time until the bucks lay down. Night drew in. Amaruq waited for the moon to rise and illuminate the valley. He dozed for a while, in spite of the bitter cold. As soon as the sun had set, the temperature had begun to plummet. Just after eleven o'clock, the waning moon appeared. The faint glow was enough. Amaruq glanced around and, using the peaks and crags as reference points, calculated the goats' position.

He crawled from his hideout, his spear by his side, and crept towards them. From time to time, he stopped and lay in the snow for a few minutes, worried that he might startle them, then inched forward until he was within fifty metres of them. To spear a buck he would need to be thirty metres closer. It seemed impossible. One of the does fretfully got to her feet and sniffed the wind. Amaruq lay motionless, trying not to breathe. The goat took a few steps, snuffled, and after a moment lay down again.

It took an hour for Amaruq to crawl to within twenty metres of the goats. His hands were numb from the cold, he could hardly hold the spear. He crept a little closer and, calculating exactly where they were, slowly got to his feet. He could not see the goats. As he surveyed the valley, he saw only a white blanket of snow. He checked his bearings: the peak to the left, the crags in the centre, the cliffs to his right. This was the spot where the goats should be sleeping, but he could see nothing but snow and more snow. Hearing a clatter of stones, he turned and saw the goats some two hundred metres away, leaping nimbly along the steep cliff. At what moment had they stood up and bolted?

Frustrated, he headed back. It took almost four hours to reach the camp. Dawn broke. Drained, he lay down and fell asleep.

We slept in each other's arms. I woke before Chelo. I gazed at her naked body and ran my hand along her back. I studied her smooth skin, trying to discern some aeroluminous alphabet that would tell me why she had disappeared, but all I could see written on her skin was my love for her. And at the same time the heartache caused me by her promiscuity, her mysteries, her secrets. My mother always said "everyone has the right to their secrets". Maybe, but those who suffer because of those secrets have a right to know them. The unknowability of the person you love is a terrible thing. Those secret places that erode our trust, our confidence, our certainty and end up destroying us. I had already been destroyed once.

Chelo woke up smiling and stroked my face. "You're a handsome fucking bastard," she said. The words cut through me. Zurita had used those same words to describe Carlos. She stretched and asked what the time was. "Eight fifteen," I said. "I've got Anatomy and Physiology at ten, I'd better get a move on," she said.

Naked, she got out of bed and, slipping on her shoes to protect her feet, hopped over one of the ruined walls of the old partition. As she did so, Colmillo started to growl. Chelo smiled, as though the wolf would understand this gesture. She made her way around the edge of the room to the kitchen. "D'you want some fried eggs?" she called. "Sure," I said. Suddenly, our relationship felt familiar again.

I slipped on my own shoes and, naked, padded over to the kitchen table. Chelo served the eggs and sat down next to me. Sitting naked in the ruins of the ground floor, dipping tortillas into our yolks, we looked like survivors of a tsunami who had lost all their possessions.

Chelo dressed without bothering to shower. "I want to smell like you all day," she said, kissing me on the lips. She made to leave. I asked her not to go. "I'll be back tonight," she promised. I didn't believe her, and as soon as she was gone I was overcome with anxiety.

Still naked, I sat facing Colmillo. As Avilés had suggested, I barked and howled. Colmillo tilted his head, trying to understand what I was doing. I didn't give up. I kept my vocalisations going until Colmillo lifted his head and howled, still wearing his muzzle. Together we howled a discordant symphony.

When I stopped, he stopped too. We sat in silence. At first our eyes were locked, then we broke off and each went about our business. Colmillo scratched his neck with his hind leg and I set about cleaning up the mess.

For hours I picked up excrement, washed down urine-spattered walls, swept up shards of glass and crockery, moved furniture, scrubbed the dirty carpet, and yet it didn't look as if any progress had been made. The doorbell rang. I wrapped a towel around my waist and opened the door. It was Avilés. "You taking a shower?" he asked. "No, I was picking up," I replied. "Picking who up?" he quipped and laughed at his own joke. "Let's eat," he said. He didn't seem to care that he'd caught me half-naked. "Now?" "Of course, it's lunchtime. Get dressed and let's go."

We went to a seafood stall in La Viga market. Avilés ordered for both of us: scallops, an oyster cocktail, seared octopus, chargrilled fish.

I hadn't eaten such delicious food in months. Avilés scolded me for mashing the avocado over the octopus, rather than slicing it. "Food has to look good to taste good." I ignored him. Unsettled by Chelo's reappearance, the last thing on my mind was slicing food.

"What's up with you?" Avilés asked. I turned to look at him. Why would this stranger care about my life? Why did he take me out for lunch, for dinner, buy me biscuits? What did he want? I asked him that. Avilés thought for a moment before he answered. "I handle six tigers. Five of them were born into captivity. The other was caught in India as a cub, the poachers killed his mother. When he came to us, he was a hostile animal who attacked anyone who came near him. I gave him all my attention, I fed him. Just that. I didn't try to tame him, to domesticate him. In time, we started to get along. He was an orphan, like me. Today, Tito would kill for me. If another tiger tries to hurt me, he defends me. You and I both belong to the community of orphans, that's why I come to visit you – since we're both orphans and we could look out for each other, but if it bothers you I won't come by again."

His long answer rattled me. The concept of a "community of orphans" gave me a new perspective on my own situation, on the fragility of growing up without parents, and in my case without siblings or grandparents. He was right, we had to look out for each other. "No, it doesn't bother me, I just didn't understand why you come round," I said. "And now you do?" I nodded, then we went back to our food.

As we drove back, Avilés played a tape of *canto cardenche*. "This is the closest thing we have to the blues in this country," he explained. "These are the songs sung by cotton pickers working the fields in Coahuila. They sing a cappella, one voice for every furrow."

The song was raw and melancholy, a heartfelt lament. "When I was a kid, my papa took me to hear them. Most of the singers were old men with calloused hands and weather-beaten faces creased from the

318

sun. I keep a tape of *canto cardenche* with me to remind me of Papá."

I asked him how his parents had died. "My mother had a stroke while we were eating dinner. She died right there, at the dinner table. My father committed suicide a year later, on my fourteenth birthday. But I'd rather not talk about that stuff."

We got to the house, and he came in to see Colmillo. "He's dehydrated," he said. "His nose is dry. Have you given him water?" I hadn't. Disconcerted by Chelo's return, I'd forgotten all about Colmillo, about King, about the parakeets. I filled a bucket and set it down next to Colmillo, who lapped thirstily through his muzzle.

"I better go up check on my dog," I said. I had left him in Carlos's room for more than twenty hours. When I opened the door, King anxiously jumped on me. In desperation, he had clawed the paint off the door. This time he had shat on the bed rather than in the shower. I grabbed him by the scruff of the neck and yanked him to the bed. "You don't do that here! No!" King broke free and cringed under a chair. Now he not only had to deal with the terrifying wolf downstairs, but the only member of the family still living had abandoned him.

Feeling guilty, I called him over. King approached me warily, but when I kneeled down and stroked him, he licked me and wagged his tail. I called to Avilés to come up and told him how frightened King was of Colmillo. I asked him what I should do. "I don't know . . ." he replied. "My job is to tame wild animals, not turn spineless animals into brave ones." He crouched down and looked at the dog. King licked him, covering him in drool, like he'd done to me. Avilés played with him and, once King seemed to have relaxed, lifted him over his head and carried him down the stairs.

King struggled to get free, but Avilés held on tight. When they were close to Colmillo, Avilés turned the dog's head so they were face to face. King started to tremble. Avilés set him down and King dashed back upstairs to hide in Carlos's room.

319

"I'm afraid there's no cure for your dog," Avilés said smiling, as he watched King scarper. He pointed at Colmillo. "Try taking off his muzzle. If he attacks you, leave it on until he's starving. When he's weak he'll submit to you."

The anonymous letter read:

"The Supreme Commanders and Knights of the Most Serene Order of Cuckolds, convened in Open Assembly, in the presence of the venerable Grand Master of the Order, His Excellency D.L. Naryshkin, have unanimously named Mr Aleksandr Pushkin coadjutor to the Grand Master of the Order of Cuckolds and Historiographer of the Order."

Alexander Pushkin, the admired Russian poet, read the letter with mounting indignation. He, a cuckold? His wife an adulteress? Of notoriously choleric disposition, Pushkin vowed that whoever had committed the offence would pay with his life. He suspected Georges d'Anthès, a French official who served in the Tsar's Guards at the court, who had been adopted as his heir by Baron van Heeckeren, the Dutch plenipotentiary to the Russian court. D'Anthès had been known to flirt on several occasions with Pushkin's wife, Natalia Goncharova, a woman famous for her beauty and her elegance, with whom the short, unprepossessing poet was desperately in love.

Without troubling to confirm his suspicion, Pushkin challenged d'Anthès to a duel. The plenipotentiary attempted to dissuade him, but Pushkin would not be swayed. In an effort to avoid the duel, d'Anthès proposed a solution that would allow them both to emerge with dignity: d'Anthès would marry Natalia's sister, Ekaterina, and in doing so prove that he harboured no lascivious desire for Natalia.

Pushkin considered the gesture an act of goodwill. The wedding was arranged and the duel cancelled. But the two men had not counted on the sender's malice. Another letter arrived suggesting that Natalia was having an affair with d'Anthès. Incensed, Pushkin became convinced that d'Anthès had taken advantage of his marriage to Ekaterina to stay close to Natalia, and, by sending Van Heeckeren an insulting letter, forced d'Anthès to defend his adopted father's honour by challenging Pushkin to a duel.

Preparations were made. All those involved in the duel were taking a serious risk: the Tsar had forbidden duels, and any breach was punishable by execution. If the duellists survived, they would be hanged. Witnesses and seconds were to be stripped of all privileges and potentially incarcerated.

The threat of legal sanction did not prevent the duel. On January 27, 1837, at 4.30 p.m., the duellists met in a remote location near St Petersburg. Their seconds handed each man a pistol loaded with only one bullet. The rivals took twenty paces, turned, and at the appointed signal d'Anthès – a soldier of considerable experience – fired first, wounding Pushkin in the stomach. The poet fell, bleeding, in the snow. Although in pain, he managed to get up and shoot his rival, the bullet grazing his right arm and ribs. Pushkin's wound was mortal, the French soldier's was not.

The poet was taken by sled to a hospital in the city, where doctors strove for two days to save his life. But the bullet had damaged vital organs and Pushkin, the obstinate duellist, died.

Thirty thousand people attended his funeral. A requiem Mass scheduled to take place in St Isaac's Cathedral was moved by the authorities to a small church, in order to avoid unrest. Pushkin was buried at midnight in an unmarked grave to prevent the proletariat from using the death as a pretext for rising up against the Tsar.

The Tsar stripped both Baron van Heeckeren and d'Anthès of their Russian titles. D'Anthès was not condemned to death, but was banished and returned to France, where he lived into his old age and pursued a successful career in his country's army. After she was widowed, Natalia married an officer in the Imperial Guard.

Contemporary accounts suggest that the duel was a plot orchestrated by van Heeckeren together with officials close to the Tsar, who considered Pushkin's popularity and his subversive nature a threat to the regime and decided that the safest option was to get rid of him. They took advantage of his volatile temperament to whip him into a rage, so that he would find himself facing an opponent better skilled in handling weapons. The conspiracy theory has never been proved.

Alexander Pushkin is considered the finest poet in the history of Russian literature.

Saturday

I continued to go on Mondays and Wednesdays to the Good Boys' absurd meetings, where we were treated to soft drinks, crisps and guest speakers with fanatical views. This was how we came to meet the anti-abortionist doctor who showed us "The Silent Scream", a documentary with footage of the fragments of a foetus scraped from a uterus using a curette; a Holocaust denier named Cordero; and a woman who claimed that she communed with angels.

In one session Father Arturo personally denounced an atheist–Jewish conspiracy to take over the world: "Behind them looms the Devil himself," he said. "We cannot afford to let our guard down." The two greatest enemies of the Catholic faith, he insisted, were heathen governments which turn people against the Church, and those in society who poison and corrupt the young with sex, drugs and alcohol. Both had to be battled with equal determination and we had always to remember that evil could lurk in our every action.

As he said his goodbyes, Father Arturo brought his lizard-like face close to mine. "Important decisions are approaching and we hope you are on our side. Can we count on you?" he asked. I didn't know what to say, but I nodded. He pinched my cheek and left with an icy smile.

The following Saturday, we wore our habits and cowls as usual and the prayers and the pledges to destroy our enemies began. When we'd finished, Humberto told us to take off our hoods and brought out the board. "We have the names of our new enemies," he said, gesturing to the one name already written on the board:

Margarito Rosas. Retorno 108 #46. Taxi driver. Heretic.

Humberto glanced at me before writing out the other names:

Sean Page. Retorno 207 #20. Ex-soldier. Poisoner.
Diego Pernía. Retorno 201 #2. Unemployed. Poisoner.
Juan Carlos Valdés. Retorno 201 #85. Unemployed. Poisoner.

He read the names aloud. I felt the skin on the back of my neck prickle. Was that what Father Arturo had meant, when he'd asked, "Can we count on you?" Without taking his eyes off me, Humberto asked if anybody could present any arguments in defence of the accused. I raised a hand. "I can," I said. Humberto sneered. "You know the rules, Juan Guillermo, you cannot defend a close family member or their accomplices," he warned.

"My brother hasn't done anything," I continued. Humberto fixed his gaze on me. "Our investigations have conclusively proven that he is guilty, as you know better than anyone." "Guilty of what?" I asked. "Your brother has poisoned hundreds of young people, including Josué's cousin. He sells them drugs, he even provides a space where they can consume this poison. Are you really saying you didn't know?"

Humberto turned to everyone else. "Does anyone have anything to say in defence of the accused?" Everyone was silent. "If there is no defence, we move on to the next stage," he said. "No," I shouted, "don't hurt them!" Humberto turned to Antonio. "Do they deserve our forgiveness?" he asked derisively. Antonio shook his head. Humberto turned back to me. "I'm sorry, but we will have to decide on the appropriate punishment."

Carlos and I had fallen into their trap. Humberto had spent months laying it. He'd built it piece by piece, set the bait, and we'd clumsily fallen into it. The "can we count on you?" was the alleyway, the point of no return. As soon as the meeting was over, I went to speak to him.

"Please don't do anything to them."

"They deserve it," Antonio said.

"I can convince them to stop."

"It's far too late," declared Humberto. "You should have done it sooner."

"I didn't think what they were doing was so bad."

"It's as bad as it gets. It's thanks to people like them that an entire generation is mired in evil," Antonio said. "And it's only because you are one of us that we are not accusing you of covering for them."

"I imagine you are aware of the punishment they deserve?" Humberto said.

The punishment for "poisoning" was elimination. I started shaking. I was afraid. Not for me. For my brother, for El Castor Furioso, for El Loco.

"Please don't eliminate them!" I begged.

Humberto brought his index finger to his lips. He looked down as if he was contemplating it and then he looked back up at me.

"We might be persuaded to reduce the punishment to a corrective measure, but we would need certain information in order to do so. Do you understand?"

"Like what?"

"We need you to tell us where they hide when the police chase them."

This was Carlos's most closely guarded secret, the one I could never tell.

"I don't know," I said hesitantly.

"Well if you don't know, find out. In fact, if you haven't told us in three days, we will be forced to administer a corrective measure to your parents. We know what time they leave work, what time they come home, what route they take."

"My parents have done nothing wrong."

Humberto looked at me with hatred in his eyes.

"Your father insulted Christ, he mocked Father Pepe. Did you think we had forgotten? Besides, if your parents produced a son like Carlos, they are more than guilty. Listen carefully: if you even think about telling them to run away or anything else, we will leave him in the same state we left Enrique, your friends' little girlfriend."

Antonio looked disconcerted. They exchanged a look.

"Don't worry," he told Antonio. "We can count on Juan Guillermo, can't we? You left the old Jew like a broken toy, we know what you and all of us are capable of."

He took two steps towards me and quietly said:

"There is no alternative. You tell us where they hide, or you deal with the consequences. If you don't tell us soon, we will apply a simple corrective measure, but if you dare mention a word to them, we will kill your whole family. And you know I mean it. If you tell us now you won't run the risk of getting cold feet."

I could have accepted the three days' grace they offered, bought some time, warned my parents of the danger, told Carlos to strike first, I could have found a gun and shot them all, I could have done so many things; instead I did only one:

"They hide in the water tanks. Sean and Diego in the ones that belong to Mrs Carbajal, the Santibáñez and the Martínez families. My brother hides in the one belonging to the Barreras or the Armendáriz one."

"How do they hide?"

"They use straws so that they can breathe while they're underwater. They can stay there for a long time."

Humberto smiled. That damn smile.

"You just saved their lives. You were right to tell us, this shows we can count on you. You can go."

The nausea crept up my oesophagus, I felt like I was about to explode. I turned around and left as fast as I could. As soon as I got through the door, I vomited.

*

Several times, he tried to hunt the goats, but he never got any closer than a hundred metres. At the first sound, the slightest sense of movement, the goats bolted. However difficult it might be, Amaruq had to kill one. He had no choice. The lack of food was starting to defeat him. Going back down the mountain to lance a moose or a wapiti meant finding them first, which would take weeks, and in his state of malnutrition it would be impossible.

Nujuaqtutuq grew hungrier and more desperate every day, snapping at anything within reach: the rope, the sled, the canvas of the tent. Amaruq found some old bones, the femur and pelvis of a dead goat. He scraped them with his knife, mixed the parings with snow and ate them, then threw what was left to the wolf who gnawed on them.

Amaruq set up the tent under a large rock to avoid an avalanche sweeping them away. As he was working, he heard a distant rumble. He spotted a helicopter crossing over the grasslands at low altitude. It was the first sign of life he had seen in months. The helicopter turned towards the mountain, flew past the cliffs on the north face and then left it behind. Amaruq watched it until it disappeared.

A few days went by, and without food Amaruq and the wolf became weaker and weaker. Amaruq decided to take the risk and hunt the goats. He tied a rope around a protrusion on one of the rock faces, wrapped it around his waist and lowered himself down until he was hanging over the very narrow pathway that the goats took from the cliffs towards the valley.

Amaruq hung there for four hours, hidden behind rocks. As the sun began to set, he heard a clatter of stones. The goats were returning from grazing and were heading to where they rested at night. Amaruq could not see them, but their bleating sounded nearby. His heart began to race. A nanny goat with a kid passed below without noticing him and kept walking slowly towards the valley. Behind her two more does and a young buck appeared, walking calmly along the path.

Amaruq slowly raised the spear and aimed it at the gap where he expected the male leader of the herd to appear, but instead a large doe emerged. Amaruq knew this was his chance. The doe continued along the path. Amaruq smacked his lips and the female stopped to look towards where the noise was coming from. Amaruq threw the spear, which pierced the goat's side. When she realised that she had been injured she recoiled, and then scampered off towards the valley. Amaruq could see a stream of blood running down along the goat's white fur.

Amaruq did not move. He needed to wait at least an hour so that the goat would bleed out. If he went looking for her too soon, she might get scared and bound away between the boulders where it would be impossible to find her. An hour went by. Amaruq untied the rope and carefully lowered himself. The path was only around forty centimetres wide. One foot wrong and he would plummet into the precipice. He went to inspect the place where his spear had hit the goat. He saw drops of blood mixed with chunks of ground-up grass. He cursed his poor aim: he had hit her in the stomach. Ten centimetres closer to her shoulder and the goat would have died in a matter of minutes, suffocating from the perforated lung. But now it would take her at least five hours to die, and following her tracks would be difficult. Intestinal matter would block up the wound and the blood would stop flowing. He would have to get down on his hands and knees to look for the small red drops.

He decided to postpone the search to the following day and go back to the camp. He made a detour so as not to scare the herd. The less pressure he put on the injured goat the better. He could only hope that she would sleep with the others and that she would eventually die from septicaemia, caused by intestinal bacteria entering her bloodstream.

He was exhausted by the time he arrived at the campsite. He had remained still for so long that the sun had badly burnt his face, and his ribs ached from the pressure of the rope straining against his chest. He lit a fire by whittling some dry sticks. He melted some snow to drink and placed a pot of water next to the wolf. Nujuaqtutuq barely had enough strength to lift up his head to drink. Amaruq watched him. "Good night," he said.

He woke up early to track the wounded goat. He took several twigs to mark the places where he found blood. He started where she had been wounded. At first, the goat left many bloody splatters, but they became increasingly small and scarce. After a hundred metres, he lost track of her. Not one drop. He came back to look for the twig that marked the last place he had found one. He walked in increasingly large circles so as not to leave any ground unexamined. After two hours, he found a piece of bloody stomach matter. The goat hadn't collapsed in the valley, she had headed for the cliffs. This was the worst possible scenario. Unsteady on her feet and close to death the goat could tumble four hundred metres into the void.

Amaruq continued to search. He found the spear. It was covered in blood, bits of digested grass and white hairs. It had gone all the way through the goat. A few metres away, Amaruq discovered a puddle of congealed blood. This meant that the goat, weakened by haemorrhage and infection, had lain down before continuing on. She could not be too far away.

After looking for signs of blood for hours, Amaruq spotted the goat in the distance. He advanced slowly through the rocks towards the chasm. She was trying to protect herself on the cliffs. She knew that standing on a narrow path halfway down a cliff face minimised her chances of being attacked by a puma.

Amaruq needed to intercept her before she got there. If not, getting hold of her would be complicated. He turned around and ran as fast as he could with the spear in his hand. He needed to circle the pinnacles and cut off her path. If the goat became scared and escaped towards the valley it did not matter, but it was crucial that he distance her from the precipice.

Weakening, Amaruq wasn't able to keep up the pace. He kept stumbling and had to stop several times to catch his breath. When he reached the crossing where he thought he would catch her, she was nowhere to be seen. Amaruq was afraid that she had fallen. He peered down towards the bottom of the abyss but could not see her.

He walked towards where she had come from. He could not find her. Inch by inch, he examined the ground in search of blood. Nothing. He retraced his steps to the place from which he had started. Then he walked in a straight line to where he had seen her for the last time. A little further along he found her tracks and some small traces of blood. The trail was marked out in the snow and led to the cliffs. But then the goat had turned around and done something unusual for a wounded animal: she'd started to climb up towards the rocks. It was more common for them to avoid the effort of climbing slopes in order to save energy.

Amaruq asked himself the fundamental question that all hunters must ask themselves: if he was a goat, what would he do? He must forget the behaviour of all the animals he had hunted in the past and concentrate on this goat and its unpredictable decisions.

He scanned the snowy peaks, the granite crags, the dips, the ravines, the pinnacles. Where would she feel safest? The obvious place was somewhere near the cliff edge where she would be safe from attack, but Amaruq ruled this out. Having been speared, the goat would not be able to leap or to keep her balance on the small rocky promontories. Another possible refuge was one of the crevices. She might lie down in a cave and feel protected. And could slake her thirst from the pools of water where the ground had thawed. When they sustain stomach wounds, animals become thirsty. The fever brought on by septicaemia and internal haemorrhaging causes them to quickly dehydrate.

Amaruq eventually reasoned that the goat must be hiding between the rocky outcrops near the peak. He was right. He found drops of blood along the rocky slope. The goat had climbed the enormous rock formations. Amaruq tried to climb up, but the slippery ice made it

331

impossible. The rock had no ridges he could grip to pull himself upwards. The only way of getting to the top was up the mountain's north face, which was far less steep. But it would take at least five hours. He studied the position of the sun. Night was going to fall soon. He decided to tackle the climb the next morning. He would wake up before sunrise to give himself enough time to climb up, find and kill the goat, skin it, butcher it and return to the campsite with the meat.

That night, while he warmed himself at the fire, he felt ashamed. He had cheated the magnificent wolf. He had left him stuck in the trap's jaws for days, allowing his leg to steadily rot. He had defeated him with starvation. He had lugged him from place to place, tied to the sled, immobilised, humiliated, thin, malnourished, furious, subjugated. For what? He promised himself that if he did not manage to catch the goat he would set him free. Although this would mean certain death. With his right leg unusable and skeletal he would be unable to hunt, and if he were to bump into other wolves, they would certainly kill him. Perhaps the best thing would be to sit next to him and wait until both of them died of hunger and cold. At least that would be fair. Or free him and allow the wolf to eat him, to devour him piece by piece. At least that might make up for the long weeks of indignity to which he had been subjected.

He stroked Nujuaqtutuq's back and lay down by his side.

Mirrors

When Humberto's grandfather died, my parents went to the wake. When they offered his mother their condolences, she responded with incoherent ramblings. Her father was a tyrant, he never spoke to her again after she got pregnant, he had kicked her out of the house, he was a ruthless father, thank you so much for coming, did you find somewhere to park your car?

My parents listened to her disjointed verbal diarrhoea. She knew she wasn't making any sense and she apologised between sobs. My parents just hugged her and whispered, "We are sorry for your loss."

They looked for Humberto, thirteen years old at the time, to offer him their condolences too. They found him alone in a corner. "Are you alright?" my father asked him. Humberto turned to him, his eyes filled with tears, his face gaunt, and shook his head. No, he wasn't alright. Not alright at all. He had lost the only person who'd provided him with any order or stability.

My father tried to console him by putting his arm around him, but Humberto slipped out of his grasp. "I want to be alone," he said. My father moved away. "Come and find us if you need us," he said. Humberto didn't even look at him.

My parents said goodbye to the mother and a few of the other bereaved family members. Before leaving, my father spotted Humberto. He was on his knees, praying silently as he wept. At what point did that fragile and vulnerable boy become the uncompromising and fanatical Humberto? From what reserve of hatred did his discipline, his talent for manipulation, his cold blood, his murderous fanaticism come?

She kept her promise and returned at 8 p.m. that night. As soon as she came through the door she kissed me on the mouth. "I missed you so much," she said. We went into the house. After Avilés had left, I'd thrown myself again into cleaning up. I had swept, washed, scrubbed and tidied. Apart from my completely destroyed bedroom, the ground floor looked habitable again.

Chelo smiled as she looked around. "You clearly haven't stopped," she said. That night she seemed happier than usual. "I'm starving, I haven't eaten all day," she said. I offered to make her nopales with grilled panela cheese.

We went into the kitchen, closely observed by Colmillo, who didn't take his eyes off Chelo. She slumped into a chair. "I'm exhausted. I had an Organic Chemistry exam today, it's my toughest class." And just like that, she chattered away about her day when all I wanted to know was why she'd disappeared and, consumed by jealousy, if she'd been with other people.

We finished eating and she suggested we take a shower together. We stayed under the water for half an hour. She asked me to massage her back to "get rid of the knots". At the end, she made me endure an ice-cold rinse. "To firm up the skin," she insisted. I hated that she did that. Cold water always put me in a bad mood.

When we got out she wrapped herself in a towel and brushed her hair in front of the mirror. I saw my life with her flash before my eyes. Waking up together, having breakfast together, showering together. But the jealousy demon immediately mounted an offensive. I imagined other men looking at her naked body as she brushed her hair, touching her, penetrating her.

We lay down naked in my parents' bed. Only the bedside lamp was on. She stroked my face and wiped away a drop of water that was slipping down my forehead. "You're still wet," she said, smiling. I couldn't take it anymore. The uncertainty was strangling me. "Why did you disappear?" I asked her straight out. She stroked my face again, looked me in the eye and began to tell me. "I don't know why, but every now and then a wave of sadness hits me. It's happened ever since I was twelve years old. I don't feel like eating, going out, talking. I hide in my room, I close the curtains and get into bed. I feel drowsy day and night. I wake up out of breath and I feel like my heart might stop beating at any moment. When I was fifteen, I took a whole bottle of aspirin, a bottle of muscle relaxants, ten sleeping pills and a lot of tequila shots, because I was desperate. I wanted to pass out until the sadness was gone. I ended up in hospital where, miraculously, they saved my life. Once I was discharged, my parents took me to see plenty of doctors. None of them could explain my suicide attempt. One of the doctors recommended electric shocks, another that they put me into a psychiatric hospital. Luckily my parents didn't listen to them and let me go back to my everyday life. I promised them I would never hurt myself again, but the sadness still hits me so hard sometimes that I really do want to die. Luckily it's happening less and less as time goes on, but when we buried Luis and later when I told you about Carlos, it all came back. It was like a giant hand squeezed all the life I have out of me. That's why I chose to study medicine, because I hope that one day I might understand what this is."

Her story completely threw me. If anything defined Chelo it was her joy and exuberance. It sounded like she was describing someone else. I couldn't imagine her depressed. She was the antithesis of sadness. She smiled when I said this. "It's part of the rollercoaster ride," she said. We were both quiet. "Can your sadness be cured?" I asked. "No, but it can be controlled. Although occasionally, once you get to a certain age, it disappears. I hope that happens to me."

She took my hand and kissed it lovingly. I couldn't help but ask the second question. "Did you sleep with other people?" She gazed at a fixed point, as if she was looking for her answer in the corner of the room, then turned to me. "Why do you want to know?" she asked. "I need to know, I have to ask." She said nothing for a moment. "Yes," she said. "I slept with other people."

Amaruq woke up before sunrise and lit a fire for warmth. Hunger had kept him awake much of the night. Several times he had been woken by dreams of food to find his stomach aching, his whole body trembling with the fear that he might die. His trousers were falling down and he had to tie a rope around his waist to keep them up. To alleviate his hunger, he chewed on some dry twigs and spat them out. They tasted bitter and earthy, but at least they somewhat resembled food.

When the sun began to come up, he picked up his spear and went out to look for the goat. He stopped to observe the clear sunrise. It was cloudless, the horizon red. "Blood of the gods," his grandfather used to call it. Again he heard the propellers of a helicopter, but this time he could not see it. He followed a path that he could tell from the quantity of small droppings had been much used by the goats. He stumbled over and over again. His torn boots made it impossible for him to take firm steps, and in order to straighten himself up he supported himself on the spear.

He walked for a kilometre. The path disappeared under a heavy blanket of snow, which, in the heat of the sun, was in danger of becoming an avalanche. He needed to cross exactly at its breaking point. He considered alternative routes to the pinnacles where the goat was hiding. The most viable one would mean going back down to the skirt of the mountain, going in a wide circle and climbing up a sharp incline. He decided to continue.

He tested every footstep, to avoid breaking the fragile equilibrium of the snow's crust. He had seen devastating avalanches triggered by minor causes: a falling stone, a clap of thunder, an animal's footsteps. Once he saw a flock of wild sheep disappear beneath a wall of snow set off by an old ram trotting along. The snow under his feet had slowly begun to slide before gathering speed. It only took a few seconds to bury all the sheep that were grazing at the bottom of the hill. The ram remained at the top, startled by the white explosion.

Amaruq had watched the avalanche swallow the sheep. The old ram bleated, calling his missing flock. Only the echoing mountain answered him. He was a magnificent creature, with horns that curled round on themselves almost twice. Amaruq would have shot him, had he had his rifle on him.

Amaruq had dug into the snow in search of the buried sheep. Each one would provide thirty kilos of meat and strong leather for coats. He managed to dig out five. Three of them had obvious fractures and ruptured intestines. He kept shovelling and found a young ram, still alive. He had survived in a cavity within the snow. Amaruq pulled him out. The ram lay there for a few minutes, stunned. Then he got up, looked around and staggered away along a path.

It took Amaruq an hour to cross the ice sheet's two hundred-metre breadth. At one point it felt like it was about to crash down on top of him. Although he was extremely cautious, a small chunk of ice broke away under his foot. The snow above it shifted as it settled, but there was no avalanche.

He reached the pinnacles where he thought the goat had taken refuge. He carefully climbed down. The frozen rocks were slippery, he could easily plunge to his death. He peered through the cracks and in a distant gap he glimpsed a flash of white fur: the goat.

He climbed down to get in from the other side. He used his boots to dislodge ice from the overhang so that he could get a better grip. Eventually he got to the cave where the goat was hiding. He crawled in on hands and knees and found her lying there panting, her side bloody. Amaruq lifted his spear and slowly approached her. The goat turned towards him. Just as Amaruq was about to kill her, she jumped up and leaped through a crack.

Amaruq rushed after her. He crawled beneath the rocks and

glimpsed the goat climbing up the pinnacle. Amaruq circled to intercept her. He clambered over a ledge and when he reached the top they suddenly stood facing one another. The goat turned and began to descend diagonally. Amaruq ran after her, but just as he was about to catch up with her they both slipped. Amaruq tried to hold on to the smooth rock, but it was impossible and he kept sliding down towards the precipice. Both of them slammed into another pinnacle and plummeted down. Amaruq heard his bones crunch as he collided with the sharp rocks.

They rolled and rolled until they ended up low down the mountain. The goat was by his side, dead. Her mouth hung open in what looked like panic. One of her horns was broken, blood was pouring from her nose. Amaruq tried to get up, but he couldn't move his arms or legs. He had landed facing up, towards the clear blue sky. He could see the dead goat out of the corner of his eye. It wasn't the large male he had wanted, but he had managed to kill a goat with a spear. His grandfather would be proud of him.

It was difficult to breathe. He inhaled deeply and as he exhaled he coughed up blood. He was convinced that his ribs were broken and had punctured his lung. He had imagined many times the place where his life would one day come to an end: in a bed, as an old man; struck by hypothermia during a snow storm; attacked by wolves in a meadow; hidden away and starving inside his tent; drowned in a river. Never had he imagined a broken spine at the bottom of a mountain.

With difficulty he turned his head, to take a look at the place where his life would end. A cluster of pine trees on the mountainside on his left, a snowy slope on his right and the cliff edge he had fallen from just in front of him. "A good place to die," he told himself.

He thought of Nujuaqtutuq. He would also die, tied up at the top of the mountain. It distressed him to think of the slow agony that awaited him, his master, his god. No, the grey wolf did not deserve to die like that, dehydrated and starving, but now nothing could save them. Their fate had been decided by the mountain. That was what his actions and his will had determined. He had trapped the wolf, tied him to the sled and dragged him for all those kilometres, only for both of them to end up dead. Their spirits would move on from this life and pass through to the next, together. They would guide one another through death's vast territories.

Again Amaruq coughed up bloody phlegm. He knew that the smell of his blood and the dead goat would attract predators. If one was going to eat him, let it be a wolf. That way he would feel more at peace with himself.

He watched the sun go down behind the line of pine trees. Its rays filtered through the branches. A flock of crows flew over him. He heard stones rolling. Up at the top of the mountain, the rest of the goats were leaving the cliffs and heading towards the valleys to sleep.

It got dark. It got colder. Amaruq could only feel the cold on his face; his rigid body was numb from the neck downwards. The waxing moon appeared on the horizon. He heard the howling of a pack of wolves a long way away. Close by, an owl hooted. He started to count the stars in the sky. His father had insisted on his learning maths. He'd sat down many times to teach him how to add, subtract, divide and multiply. "That way they cannot cheat you when you buy or sell," he told him. "Practise at every opportunity. Count, add, multiply." Now Amaruq wasn't counting the stars for practice, but to remember his absent father. His mother who had hummed Inuit songs to him. His half-brothers who had played with him once. His grandfather.

The cold made his teeth chatter. This had never happened to him before. His father had taught him that breathing deeply helped you to tolerate the cold. "When the air enters the lungs, heat blooms in our bodies." The wound in his side was causing his left lung to deflate. He could hear it bubble with every breath.

He kept counting the stars. He closed his eyes when he got to a hundred and eighteen. Then he multiplied them by two: two hundred and thirty-six. Then he divided them by three. His mind was not capable of doing more mental arithmetic. A profound fatigue came over him. He concentrated on Nujuaqtutuq. He hoped that the wolf would die with the same calm he felt now.

In Ancient Greece and the civilisations that came after, physicians based their diagnoses on the bodily fluids, the humours of the human body. Humours did not merely govern disease, they also determined character and possible mental disorders.

The four humours were:

Blood

Yellow bile

Phlegm

Black bile

Each humour was linked to a season of the year. Blood to spring, moist and warm. Yellow bile to summer, warm and dry. Black bile to autumn, cold and dry. Phlegm to winter, cold and moist.

Black bile was called *melan* (black) and *kholé* (bile). To be melancholic meant you suffered from black bile. The term was associated with madness, as it was believed that black bile affected the mind and provoked extreme reactions in the body. Bloody black faeces, dark and bitter vomit, these resulted from melancholia.

Although to begin with the word melancholia indicated spells of madness, with time its meaning changed, and it was used to describe the sombre moods of those who, exhausted by bursts of insanity, were left thoughtful, depressed and fearful.

Today the term melancholia is used to describe a profound state of sadness. It is the black bile that clouds our spirits, the liquid darkness that flows through our bodies. The night concealed within us.

Afternoons

I was fourteen years old and believed that Humberto would keep his word. I was too naive to read the signs, to realise that he'd no intention of keeping it, that he'd long ago taken the decision to kill my brother.

Humberto made a pact with Comandante Zurita. Knowing that the police commander was desperate to catch them, Humberto offered to hand them over if he let them "eliminate" one of the three. Zurita agreed. A dead criminal was irrelevant. His only concern was delivering results to the President's brother.

Carlos was reckless. He thought that sooner or later Zurita would stop harassing him. He didn't understand that the enemy wasn't the cops but the Good Boys. I wanted to warn him about the plan to give him a "corrective", but was too afraid that Humberto would follow through with his threat to kill my parents and my grandmother. I was consumed with the guilt of keeping it a secret. I couldn't eat, sleep or pay attention in class.

One afternoon I couldn't take it anymore. I told Carlos about the secret meetings on Saturdays, the attack on Don Abraham and his wife and the punishment they were thinking of inflicting on him and his partners. I warned him about what they'd threatened to do if they found out that I'd told him, and I begged him to leave the city with his friends as soon as possible.

Carlos played down the threat. "They went after Don Abraham because they're cowards, but they wouldn't dare take me on." "They're killers, they killed Enrique," I told him. Carlos believed another version: that the lawyer had him killed after Quica tried to blackmail him in exchange for not revealing their affair. I told him that it was they who beat his clients to a pulp. "I thought as much," he said. I begged him not to confront them. Carlos shook his head. "If war is what they want, war is what they will get."

I decided not to go to the meeting on Wednesday, afraid that my nervousness would give me away. I was naive to think that they wouldn't come looking for me. The next day, while Carlos and I were feeding the chinchillas, the doorbell rang. Carlos looked over the edge of the rooftop. Humberto and Antonio were waiting at the door. "Your little friends are looking for you," he said.

I went down to open the door. I tried to keep my composure. Humberto looked me in the eye. "Why didn't you come yesterday?" he asked. "I had a headache," I lied. "We want to talk to you," he said. "About . . .?" I asked, feigning calm. "A few details. But not here, let's go to the courts." This was a concrete quadrangle on a field that lay beneath enormous electricity pylons, where there'd once been basketball hoops and a children's playground, but which was now an abandoned wasteland. The rusty, broken hoops hung from rotting wooden backboards. Grass had grown between the abandoned seesaws and the swings. There were piles of rubbish. Rats. Cockroaches.

They'd murdered Enrique on the courts. I thought they might kill me there too. "Why there?" I asked. "So that nobody bothers us," replied Antonio. We were about to leave when Carlos appeared in his flip-flops. Since Zurita's incessant harassment, he never left the house by the front door. He would go across the rooftops and emerge from another house. He and his friends never repeated a pattern that Zurita's men could predict.

"What's up?" he greeted them. Humberto's face changed. "How are you, Carlos?" he asked him, with a false smile. I noticed Carlos had his knife hidden in the sleeve of his shirt. "Very well," my brother replied. "And is Juan Guillermo behaving himself?" Humberto slapped me on the back. "Yes, he's a good boy." My blood ran cold. "A good boy" –

just hearing it repulsed me. "Where are you going?" Carlos asked. "To take a stroll around the courts," Humberto replied. "I'll join you, let me just put on my plimsolls," Carlos said, and went inside.

Humberto turned to me, his jaw tense. "Did you say anything to him?" I shook my head. He smiled, impassive and cold. "You'd better not have," he threatened.

Carlos came back. "Let's go," he said, and peered at the cars parked on the street. He knew exactly which ones belonged to the neighbours and which didn't, and he'd memorised all of their number plates. To begin with, Zurita sent people to watch him in the typical undercover police car: a Dodge Dart with tinted windows. They were so easy to identify that when the cops left them parked up to go and eat, we'd write "dopey cops" with our fingers on the dusty boots. Zurita had since refined his strategy and started sending old, run-down cars such as Volkswagen Sedáns, Opels and Renaults. He hoped that they would go unnoticed, but Carlos recognised them immediately.

We headed to the courts, talking about Vera Caslavska and Natasha Kuchinskaya, the beautiful Czech and Soviet gymnasts who had competed in the Olympic Games the year before. Antonio announced that they didn't watch athletes from communist countries, especially not girls wearing scanty clothing. "Well, you missed out – they're unbelievably hot," Carlos said.

When we arrived at the courts, it was obvious that my brother's presence made Humberto feel uncomfortable. Had Carlos known that they were planning to kill him a few days later, a fight would have broken out and he'd have beaten them senseless.

Carlos pointed to the spot where Quica's body had been found. "Do you guys know who killed him?" he asked, just to provoke them. "No," said Humberto. My brother made another attempt. "You know what I heard?" I thought he was about to reveal what I'd told him. "I heard his boyfriend had him killed because he was trying to black-mail him," he said. "A lot of homosexuals are killed by guys they've slept with who can't accept that they're fags." This subject seemed to disturb them. "Well, they get what they deserve," Antonio said.

I heard the sound of a car engine. My brother turned around. A suspicious white Volkswagen Sedán was approaching from Retorno 206. "See you," he said. He walked up to the gate outside Víctor Vargas's house, jumped up to grab the top of it and then pushed himself over to the other side. That had been his last chance to stop the countdown towards his death.

As soon as he'd disappeared, Humberto turned to me. "How much did you tell him?" "Nothing," I replied. I exchanged a look with Antonio. "Your brother interrupted us, we couldn't speak to you about what we want you to do," he said. "What?" I asked. "Buy thirty sacks of cement and take them to Humberto's rooftop." "What for?" I asked. "I'm thinking about building a room up there," Humberto said. "So why don't you buy them yourselves?" Antonio stood in front of me. "You don't ask, you obey." "And where am I going to get the money to pay for it?" "You'll have to find it," Antonio said. Humberto signalled for them to leave with a flick of his chin. They walked away along Retorno 206 and stopped to talk to whoever was driving the Volkswagen that had just arrived.

"I slept with two other guys," Chelo says. I feel as if I'm about to throw up. The pain turns into vomit. I stand up and go to sit on the stairs. Where is there to hide when the woman you love confesses to having been with other people? I hold my head in my hands. Why? "A crime of passion"; that's what they call the irrepressible desire to kill the person you love the most. Kill her so that you feel a little less dead. The vomit stings my throat, it's about to spill out. She comes over to me, naked. She sits down next to me in silence. I want to hit her, hug her, kiss her, stab her, make love to her. My heart, where is my heart? This murky emptiness I feel inside, is that my heart? Heart turned to mud. Mud and more mud. I vomit. I vomit mud. "Forgive me," Chelo

345

begs me. She reaches out her hand to touch me. I turn away. "I didn't know how to get rid of this sadness," she says. Every word crushes my insides. So then, Chelo, tell me, does a dick between your legs help get rid of the pain? With other men's dicks? A knife-dick inside of her, the knife-dick that stabs me now. I ask her: "Does a dick between your legs help get rid of the pain?" She looks at me. She reaches out her hand again. I shuffle as close to the wall as possible so that she can't touch me. "I needed someone," she explains. "If you needed someone why the fuck didn't you come to me?" I demand to know. I feel the mud-vomit at the back of my mouth. The pain runs through me from head to toe. My stomach bubbles. It runs along my back, and descends through my spine. Mud and more mud. "I didn't come to you because you were sad too." Idiot, what would she know about my sadness? She, the wooden plank of my shipwreck, is now pulling me down by my feet and submerging me in the sea. Deeper and deeper. Drown, motherfucker. "Fuck, didn't it occur to you while you were fucking other assholes that finding out would kill me?" Chelo says nothing for an eternity. Vomit on my tongue. "Forgive me," she says again. "I didn't think it would hurt you so much." No? You didn't think so? What world are you living in? "I regretted it as soon as it was over," she says. Ahhhhhhhh! She needed to fuck two different people before realising how much she regretted it. Every word that comes out of her mouth accelerates my collapse. The building inside me implodes. I feel the bricks fall with a crash into the puddle of mud that my guts have become. Boiling sludge, splashing lava. I want to tell her to get out, to never come back, but there she sits, naked. The woman I love. "You hurt me, you know?" she tells me. Hurt her? All I've done is love her, furiously. "Oh yeah? How exactly?" She looks me in the eye. "Because I'm in love with you." "What a fucking lie!" I shout. "If you were in love you wouldn't have been with anyone else. You wouldn't have left me and gone looking for other dicks." She doesn't take her eyes off me. "Forgive me," she repeats, "but I didn't think we stood a chance. We spoke about it. We both knew this wouldn't last." I feel the urge to grab her by the neck and pull her towards me. To tell her: Listen, you idiot, if you are in love with me then you stay with me. With me. Do you understand? W-i-t-h m-e. Why would you get involved with anyone else if you love me? But I can't even speak. I'm drowning. I turn and throw up. A sea of mud explodes from the bottom of my intestines. Pure pain. The mud runs down the stairs. Fuck! Surrounded by so much death, this love is dying. This vomit is the cemetery of my love. There it goes, liquefied, a jumble of sadness, jealousy, fury, passion. "Are you alright?" she asks. Four semesters of studying medicine every day and she can't even tell when someone is seriously unwell. I get up, naked, and lock myself in Carlos's room. I lie down on the bed and hug King. The anxious dog licks my face. This is why people love dogs so much, because they ask nothing of you, they're living cuddly toys offering abundant love. Lazy dogs that get fed in exchange for being emotional crutches. Theirs is a lovely job. I pull King tightly to me. Chelo knocks on the door several times. "Juan Guillermo, please open the door. I beg you." I don't open it. I don't want her and the two men smeared all over her to come in. I don't want her stink of other men's semen, her mouth covered in other men's saliva, her fondled breasts, her penetrated vulva. No, Chelo, I can't open the door, you aren't alone, you are with those two assholes who ruined you. You, the woman I love.

For an hour there's only silence. I know she's out there, waiting for me to open the door. I hear her get up, go to my parents' room, get dressed and then go downstairs and leave the house. I hold King even tighter. The dog knows exactly how to do its job as a professional consoler. He licks me and cleans the mud-vomit from my chin and chest. He devours my pain. My dog, my faint-hearted and mediocre boxer. All that remains of my family, the remains of a happy world. King survived them and is still here with me. Terrified, fearful, but with me, covering me in his smelly saliva, the evidence of his limitless love. I wait a few minutes to make sure that Chelo has gone. I come out of Carlos's room naked. Not a sound can be heard in the house. I turn on the light and go downstairs. Colmillo watches me from beneath the table. I look at the ruined walls of my bedroom. I remember my father putting them up. I was sitting on a chair, watching him. My leg sewn up with twenty stitches. My father hammers. The nail penetrates the chipboard. My father climbs onto a chair. He tightens the screws that hold up the door. He builds a room for me, his injured son, where I lived until the arrival of the whirlwind *Canis lupus.*

I walk into my destroyed room. I empty drawers onto the camp bed. I find a photo of my family in Acapulco. We are all smiling, apart from my grandmother, who looks hot and uncomfortable. I am five. Carlos is twelve. My father in his swimming trunks, my mother wrapped in a towel. I keep searching. My grades from primary school. Red numbers: Grammar 5, Spelling 5, Maths 5, Civics 6, Geography 5, Natural Sciences 5. There's a reason why they call me "Cinco". I find a signed photograph of Horacio Casarín. The great football idol, the explosive and dangerous goal scorer from my father's time. I find a note from my mother in one of my notebooks: "Son, you need to work harder at school. We know you can. Pay more attention in class. You will see you'll get better grades. I love you very much. Your mother." I miss my mother. I need her advice, her love, her presence. Within the stack of papers is the list I wrote in David Barraza's class:

Nothing,
everything,
rescue,
abandon,
danger,
forgiveness,
calm,

animal,
tame,
wild.

I feel overwhelmed: the words I'd randomly chosen three years ago seemed to predict what lay ahead:

Nothing–Everything.
My life had swung between everything and nothing. That is how existence is perceived when death devastates you. Everything–Nothing. Live or die. With me or against me. Love or hate. Shakespeare, my friend, so much sense hidden in Hamlet's doubt: "To be or not to be."

Rescue.
In the shipwreck of death that I became, rescue became my daily affirmation. Save Colmillo to save myself.

Abandon.
Abandon who I was? Abandon Chelo? Hate her for being such a slut? Or, like my father asked me to: abandon the hatred, the vengeance, the poison of the past? What should I abandon?

Danger.
What dangers should I be protecting myself from? Those who murdered my brother and would come for me? Becoming a killer myself? Losing myself in the swamp of self-pity and shame? Getting used to death and forgetting about life?

Forgiveness.
Forgive Chelo? Forgive myself? Forgive death for its brutal interruption? Forgive Carlos's murder? Forgive my parents for abandoning me? Forgive the killers' god? Really forgive?

Calm.
How could I be calm at my seventeen years of age, when I was so completely alone? How could I be calm enough to look Humberto in the eye before killing him?

Animal.
Which animal should I identify with? Which animal loves? Which has its vengeance? Which forgives? Which fights to the death? Which is invincible? Which is the wildest?

Tame.
I cannot allow anything or anyone to tame me. I cannot let my dead family lash me to the mast of their ghost ship. I will not be tamed.

Wild.
I will be the Untameable. They will not stop me. If I need to have my vengeance, I will have my vengeance. If I have to forgive, I will forgive. If I have to love, I will love. If I have to give up, I will give up. If I have to fight, I will fight. It's clear to me that life – not death – is guiding my decisions. I will devote my life to life, always to life.

I am still sitting on the bed. I miss Chelo. Her absence gnaws away at me. I hate her, I love her. I get up. I decide it's time to free Colmillo. I take my knife and walk towards him, naked. If he attacks me, I will attack him. If he bites me, I will stab him. If he wants to kill me, I will kill him. If he offers peace, he will get peace. As soon as I get close he straightens up. He's terrifying. I advance slowly. Colmillo doesn't attack. He seems weak. I get behind him. Nervous, he turns and tries to lunge at me. I leave the knife on the table. I grab his collar and hold him still. I don't know where the strength comes from. I undo the straps and pick up the knife again. The muzzle falls to the floor. I have taken the first step towards freeing him. I keep holding on to him with one hand. If he tries to bite me I'll slit his throat. I warn him, speaking into his ear: "I will kill you, *cabrón*." He opens his mouth, his canines gleam. I'm naked and he could emasculate me with one bite. I grip the knife and retreat with caution, without turning my back on him. Colmillo watches me, menacingly, but he doesn't attack. I go to the kitchen. I take out the remains of the rotisserie chicken. I return to the living room and stand in front of him. Colmillo fixes his gaze on me. I put the chicken on the floor and take two steps back. Colmillo looks at the chicken and then at me. He fears me. The wolf fears me. The combined effect of hitting him with the chair and his hunger and thirst has forced him to surrender. At least for now. Avilés's strategy for taming him is working. Colmillo cautiously inches towards the chicken. He looks at me again. He really fears me. He lowers his head and begins to eat. He devours it in seconds. I go back to the kitchen. I take out ham, bread, cheese. I take it to him. He guzzles it down. He's still hungry. Of course, he hasn't eaten in days. I serve him insipid dog biscuits in King's bowl. Colmillo finishes them. I serve him again. He finishes them. He finishes half a fifteen-kilo sack. I fill the bucket with water. The wolf drinks and drinks. I walk around him. I stand next to him as he drinks, I grab his collar and take off the chain. Colmillo is free.

I sit down on a chair. Colmillo knows he is free. He walks around the ground floor. He lifts his leg to pee into a corner. Only a small amount comes out. He investigates unknown areas. He goes to the garage and comes back. He comes up to me, he sniffs me. I pick up the knife. If he so much as growls at me I'll run it through his skull. He gets close to my genitals. He sniffs them. He raises his head and looks at me. Then he goes back to exploring the house. I exhale.

I sit there for two hours watching the wolf's comings and goings. After wandering around the yard and the kitchen, he lies down underneath the table. He dozes. I think about Chelo, the promiscuous woman I love. Twenty years old and more than twenty men have fucked her. Should I love such a whore? Or in Viking terms, should I love such a desirable woman? A couple of idiots fucked her just to pass the time, they don't love her. Pure transience scorching my land: her. I feel nauseated, plundered. They can screw other women. This woman is unique to me. To you fucking assholes, she is just a body into which you can masturbate. A sack into which to empty your white excrement. Why did you allow it, Chelo? Once again, I feel the mud rise inside me. The boiling mud scalds my oesophagus, it bubbles inside my intestines. I can't deal with the jealousy anymore. I don't want to imagine the faces of those who slept with her. Not even my brother's, flat against her belly. I hate Chelo, I love her.

I walk towards the stairs to go up to the bedroom. The wolf stands up and follows me. He can't go upstairs, King would be terrified by his scent alone. I pause on the fifth step and with my hand signal for him to stop. Of course, Colmillo does not obey. He's a wolf, not a boxer. He comes up behind me. Climbing stairs is challenging for him. He stumbles. An unfamiliar surface. I hurry to shut the door to Carlos's bedroom, where King is. I hear my dog scrabble towards the bathroom. He must be petrified. Colmillo sniffs the door. He knows that inside there's a dog that has submitted to him without even seeing him. Metres away, he has detected adrenaline impregnated with fear. I go to my parents' room. The wolf follows me and comes in behind me. He wanders around the room and pees on the walls. I go to each place and pee there too, just like Avilés suggested. I pee on the carpet. He has to know this house is my territory and there is no way I will give it up. Colmillo smells my urine. He lifts his head, looks at me, and leaves. In the hallway, he stops in front of Carlos's room. He pees on the door and continues his rounds. He moves quickly from one place to the next. He returns to the hallway and I see him stop at the top of the stairs. He looks at them. Their symmetry must seem like a challenge. He disappears from view. I get into bed. I close my eyes and think of Chelo. A few hours ago she was lying by my side, naked. The light filters through the curtains. The sun is about to come up.

Etymology of Events (Part Three)

Words derived from Inuktitut:

AJUSTITSIJUQ: one who frees an animal from captivity.

AQASILI: the farewell said by one leaving to one who is staying.

NINGIUSUK: a woman who has casual sex.

ARIUTTAQ: rejected by a loved one.

PAARSAITUQ: those who separate and take different paths.

NIKANARTUQ: one who has died and is still missed.

ANIRNANGIRNIQ: a last breath.

PAINNNGUITUQ: to miss somebody.

NUUTSUITUQ: motionless.

NUQARTATUQ: he who does many push-ups or pull-ups, does exercise.

NIRLUNGAJUQ: a watchful animal.

ANGUTIUSUGIJUQ: one who thinks himself capable of attacking many things.

Day

Robert Mackenzie woke at 4 a.m. He needed to get ready to travel across the long mountain range. He sat up in his camp bed and lit his Coleman lantern. He put on two layers of underclothes, two pairs of trousers, two sweatshirts, a jumper and a goose-down jacket. The weather forecast said it was -25°C. Despite spring's imminent arrival, the cold was not letting up. The construction of the oil pipeline in north-eastern Canada had been suspended because of the harsh winter. Luckily the storms and blizzards had stopped. Sunny days were forecast for the next two weeks and work had started up again.

Robert emerged from his tent and headed towards the hall that housed the canteen. A flurry of workers and trucks passed each other on the muddy tracks. The activity in the camp never stopped. Divided into three eight-hour shifts, hundreds of men worked day and night. The generators powered colossal towers that lit up the camp.

Construction took place in several stages. First they tore down the forest with bulldozers and saws, to free up the land. The felled trees were taken to the sawmill. Then the excavators dug the trench that the pipeline would run through. In the third stage, tract trucks brought the giant tubes which cranes would place in the hollow. In the fourth, a group of solderers joined and sealed them, and in the fifth, the diggers covered the duct with earth.

Robert did not join the queue in the canteen, where dozens were waiting to be served. He went directly up to the bar. When they saw him, the other workers moved out of his way. He was one of the most respected managers. Robert asked for coffee, scrambled eggs and a slice of bread. He picked up his tray and went to sit down in the section reserved for the executives. Alex, his assistant, and Jack, the pilot who was taking them across the mountain range, were waiting for him.

As soon as they had finished eating breakfast, Alex unfolded a map on the table. Robert studied it carefully. The construction's progress was marked in red lines and the possible routes they could follow were in green. These were divided into five. One followed the edge of the mountain range, and that was the one they planned to explore that day. They calculated that the day's journey would take them around nine hours.

"We'll leave in fifteen minutes, I don't want to be coming back in the dark. They should get the topographers' helicopters ready too, so they can leave as soon as we call them," ordered Robert.

"Yes, sir," Jack said, and went to get the helicopter ready.

Robert was the engineer in charge of deciding the oil pipeline's route and carrying out topographic and land studies. He knew the area better than anyone. He had studied in Vancouver and his ancestors were the Scottish explorers in whose honour the vast territory had been named Mackenzie.

The helicopter took off at daybreak and flew over the forest. They had had to change the route of the pipeline. Months of planning had had to be tossed aside because of problems with the indigenous land-owners. Now they had to start from scratch and establish an alternative course.

Robert was leaning towards the route that ran alongside the mountain range. Excavating the rocky ground would be arduous, but Robert had thought about continuing the pipeline on piling. Yes, it would be more expensive, but they could use the wood from the felled trees to make the posts, and besides, it would make it easier to fix any leaks or cracks in the pipe. He needed to convince the company's administrative board of the advantages of this possible route.

The helicopter flew at low altitude, only a few metres above the tops of the pine trees. Alex and Robert took notes. Every stream, lake, hill and valley was recorded in the logbook. Even the herds of wapiti or caribou they saw. They needed to avoid building the pipeline in grazing or hibernation areas, as the reverberations from hooves hitting the ground could eventually damage the pipes.

They flew over a meadow and headed towards the mountains. Robert made out a wide river and a herd of hundreds of wapiti running away, frightened by the noise of the propellers. He noted down the co-ordinates of their location and the helicopter continued on its journey. They made a turn and a pack of coyotes fled between the pine trees. Alex touched Robert on the shoulder and pointed at the ground. It looked like a human being was lying sprawled on the snow next to a mountain goat. Robert asked Jack to circle as low as possible. The pilot avoided a few pine trees, lowered the helicopter and hovered in the air so that they could inspect the area. The wind created by the blades lifted the snow around the two bodies. It was difficult to see through the snowy whirlwind.

"Yes, it's a man," Alex confirmed as he looked through his binoculars.

"Is he alive?" Robert asked.

"I don't know. He isn't moving."

"Land as close as you can," Robert ordered Jack.

The helicopter landed in a clearing. Robert and Alex put on their snow shoes and started walking towards where they had seen the man.

Along the way, they came across a couple of coyotes who bolted. When they got there, they saw the man and goat lying in puddles of frozen blood. The coyotes had begun to eat one of the goat's flanks. Robert kneeled down next to the man. He was bleeding from the mouth and you could see some bite marks on his neck. The coyotes had tried to devour him.

"Can you hear me?"

The man only looked at him.

"Can you move?"

The man did not seem to understand him. His features were Inuit, but his blue eyes, long hair and long, almost reddish beard were in stark contrast to the rest of his face.

Robert looked at the goat and then at the man. He looked up towards the cliffs at the top of the mountain. "They must both have fallen from up there," he said to Alex. It was a miracle that the man was still alive.

"Let's take him to the camp," Robert said.

The man made an effort to speak.

"Nujuaqtutuq."

Neither Robert nor Alex understood what he was trying to tell them.

"'Niujaq usu'?"

"Nujuaqtutuq," repeated the man.

Robert and Alex exchanged a look.

"Is that your name?" they asked him, gesturing with their hands.

The man shook his head.

"Nujuaqtutuq," he said again.

"What is Nujuaqtutuq?" asked Alex.

The man turned his head towards the mountain.

"There," he said in his heavily accented English. "Nujuaqtutuq."

Robert took out a pen and a notebook, and wrote as he repeated, "Nu-juaq-tu-tuq?"

The man nodded.

"Tell the other helicopter to come here," Robert ordered.

Alex took the radio and spoke to the other pilot.

"You'll be alright," Robert said to the man, in an attempt to comfort him.

The man smelled of animal, blood, bait, sweat, meat. He lifted his head to look beyond them and began to speak in Inuktitut.

"Are you there?"

"What did you say?" asked Alex.

"You left," the man said in his language.

Alex and Robert turned around. There was nothing there.

"I think he's hallucinating," Robert said.

They could hear the other helicopter's rotors.

"Help is coming," Alex said to the man.

The man looked at him.

"Nujuaqtutuq."

"Yes, we will look for Nujuaqtutuq."

The man turned his head and spoke again to someone in Inuktitut. Robert turned around to look. Nothing. Just the pristine mountain air, the rows of pine trees, the foothills.

Alex went to examine the goat. Within the intestines half-eaten by the coyotes he could see the wound the spear had made in its stomach.

"I think he was hunting it," he said to Robert.

Robert took out a handkerchief and wiped away the blood trickling from the man's mouth.

"What's your name?" he gestured.

"Amaruq," the man said.

"Amaruq?"

"Amaruq Mackenzie."

Robert was surprised to discover this mixed-race Inuit bore the same surname he did. In the distance, he could see the other helicopter landing.

"Amaruq, we will take you to a hospital soon."

The topographers arrived. They carried a canvas stretcher. They lifted him, trying to move him as little as possible. The man spat blood. He seemed to choke, but as soon as they placed him on the stretcher he breathed normally again.

The four men carried him through the pine forest. The blue-eyed Inuit didn't stop repeating the same phrase in Inuktitut.

"Let me die here. Let me die here."

They ignored his pleas. The four of them hurried through the deep snow until they got to the helicopter. They laid him across the back seats and strapped him in with rope.

"Die here," the man echoed.

In their flurry of activity, the men did not hear him speak. They closed the doors and the helicopter rose up between the pine trees.

Robert saw it go and then turned back towards the mountain. Who or what was Nujuaqtutuq?

Carlos said goodbye. Standing in the doorway of my bedroom, he said something I didn't catch and then left. I was lying on my bed, engrossed in a book. A few minutes later I heard shouts and, going out onto the street, I saw Carlos, Sean and Diego being chased by four undercover cops. The white Volkswagen Sedán I had seen at the basketball courts the week before was stopped halfway down the retorno with its door wide open. A cop, crudely disguised as a hippie in a black wig, pulled his gun and aimed, but didn't shoot. Carlos and Sean bounded over the Rovelos' wall while Diego hurdled the Richards' fence. The cops seemed to give up. I watched Carlos as he weaved across the rooftops. It was the last time I saw him.

I assumed the police pursuit had been abandoned when Carlos and his friends disappeared on the rooftops. I went back inside, still uneasy at having seen the cop pull a gun. I sat on my bed, glad that Carlos had made his escape. A few minutes later the doorbell began to ring insistently. I opened it to find Pato, his face deathly pale. "What is it?" I asked. Pato was panting for breath. "They've fucked them over, trapped them inside the water tanks, weighed down the lids with the sacks of cement we carried up there," he said. I didn't understand what he was talking about. Humberto had said the cement was to build a room up on the roof. "What do you mean trapped them?" I asked. "They're going to drown them," Pato said.

Comandante Zurita had made a deal with Humberto in order to trap Carlos. The police would patrol the streets, the Good Boys the

360

rooftops. Humberto dispatched his people to keep watch on the rooftops, day and night, working in eight-hour shifts. He didn't care whether they missed school, or were exhausted from lack of sleep. He personally took several shifts, keeping watch in the early hours.

As soon as they saw Carlos and his friends crawl into the water tanks, the lookouts raised the alarm. Within minutes, Humberto and the others arrived and quickly heaved sacks of cement on top of the water tanks. More than a hundred kilos on each lid.

Pato and I ran to the Barreras' house. The Volkswagen and a police car were parked out front. Mrs Barrera was arguing with one of the officers. We tried to go in, but the cop stopped us. "Where do you think you're going?" Mrs Barrera intervened on our behalf. "Don't speak to these young men that way." The cop looked at her menacingly. "I'll speak to whoever I want however I want, you old bitch." The woman bowed her head, humiliated, and the cop turned back to us. "Now you brats can fuck off."

We turned and ran to the Armendáriz house, jumped the wall and tore up the spiral staircase to the roof. The water tank where my brother was hiding was four houses away. From the rooftop of the Martínez place, Jaibo and Agüitas were shouting at Humberto to let him out.

Dodging cables and wires, we reached the Barreras' rooftop. I walked over to Humberto. "What the fuck are you doing? He's going to drown!" Humberto smiled, the sinister grin of a ventriloquist's dummy. "Nothing is going to happen to him," Humberto said. I moved closer. Felipe and Antonio blocked my path. "You promised it would be only a corrective measure," I said, desperate. Humberto smiled again. "It *is* only a corrective measure, to make him learn." I banged on the water tank. "Carlos, are you O.K.?" He couldn't respond, the water had risen all the way to the top.

In a bound, I was on top of the tank, pushing one of the sacks of cement over the side. When I tried to move another, Antonio and Josué grabbed my ankles and pulled me to the ground.

I struggled to my feet. "Leave," Antonio growled, "unless you want us to do the same to you." There were ten of them. It was impossible to fight so many. I raced down the spiral staircase and into the house. I rushed to the bathroom and turned on the taps in the sink and the shower. I flushed the toilet and jammed the ballcock so the water would keep flowing. Pato caught up with me. "We have to empty the tank," I screamed.

We ran around the Barreras' house, Pato turning on the taps, the shower and the bath while I raced to the kitchen and opened the tap in the sink and then went into the yard to turn on the hose. Mrs Barrera was terrified. Over and over she asked what was going on, why was her house crawling with cops and Good Boys? I could only say: "They're trying to kill my brother."

As water gushed in the bathrooms, the kitchen, the yard, I desperately hoped that the tank would empty faster than it filled, giving Carlos a moment to breathe. Josué leaned over the roof and, realising what we were doing, alerted Humberto, who calmly turned off the house's stopcock. The water tank began to fill again.

"No water's coming out, they've closed the stopcock," Pato shouted. I went to check the bathrooms. Only a trickle dripped from the taps. I raced from the Barrera house back to mine, took the steps to the roof four at a time, ran to the kennel where Carlos hid his .22 and grabbed it. I would shoot at them from there. I rummaged in the kennel and under the cages, searching for the bullets. The chinchillas squealed in fear.

Pato caught up with me and, seeing the rifle in my hand, snatched it away. "What are you doing?" "I have to save Carlos," I said. "Not like this, don't be an idiot," he said and put the rifle back where I had found it.

I glanced around. On the Padillas' rooftop, three Good Boys and a cop were standing around the water tank, whose lid was weighed down with sacks of cement. Later I found out that Sean, who was hiding inside, had been able to breathe only because the tank had a small leak, which stopped it from filling up to the top.

A patrol car screeched into the street, siren blaring. In the Prietos' backyard, Colmillo began to howl. A deep howl, filled with pain, as if the wolf could sense that death was near.

"Crito, we owe a cock to Asclepius; pay it and don't forget." These were the last words of Socrates, before his heart was paralysed by the hemlock he had drunk. His student Plato recounts the words in his *Dialogues*.

Meletus, a young poet and religious fanatic, had accused Socrates of "failing to acknowledge the gods" and of "corrupting the youth of Athens". Socrates could have avoided the trial, but he refused. He did not think he had done anything wrong and therefore thought he had nothing to fear. The charges were brought against him, and after each side had presented its arguments to the court he was found guilty. Of the five hundred and fifty-six dikasts – male jurors chosen by lot – two hundred and eighty-one voted against him and two hundred and seventy-five for him. He was sentenced to death by only six votes.

Throughout the trial and until the very end, Socrates remained serene. The death penalty was carried out by compelling Socrates to drink hemlock, a powerful poison. Socrates asked Crito – whom the authorities had tasked with carrying out the sentence – how he should proceed and what symptoms to expect. Crito told him to drink from the cup, and then "you have only to walk about until your legs are heavy, and then lie down, and the poison will act". The disciples watched in horror as Socrates "raised the cup to his lips, and quite readily and cheerfully [. . .] drank the poison".

Socrates walked around the room. After a few minutes, just as Crito had predicted, Socrates felt his legs begin to fail him and he lay down. Coldness began to spread through his body. Crito said: "When the poison reaches the heart, that will be the end." Socrates had a revelation, and that was when he asked Crito to sacrifice the rooster. "The debt shall be paid," Crito said. "Is there anything else?" There came no answer.

Upon his death, Crito pronounced: "Such was the end, Echecrates, of our friend; concerning whom I may truly say that, of all the men of his time whom I have known, he was the wisest and justest and best."

To this day historians do not know what became of Meletus.

Death

I opened my eyes. Still half-asleep, I saw Colmillo by my bed, watching. I tried to move slowly, feeling for my knife, but as I did so the wolf growled. I lay motionless and closed my eyes so that he would think I was asleep. Immediately, I regretted doing so – if Colmillo was going to attack, I needed to give myself time to react. I opened my eyes again. Colmillo was thirty centimetres away, staring at me. What would Avilés do in this situation? He'd told me wolves were vocal animals. I growled loudly, something that visibly disconcerted Colmillo. I growled again and he turned and left the room.

I closed the door. The knife was lying on top of what had been my mother's bedside table, next to a jar of face cream, a bottle of aspirin and a book by Papini. I'd left my clothes in Carlos's room. I didn't dare venture out naked with Colmillo outside. In the early hours, in a state of euphoria, I had set him free. Now I had to deal with the consequences, knowing he was prowling around the house without a muzzle.

I decided to wear something of my father's. Anything that would fit, since he was ten centimetres shorter and his feet were two sizes smaller. When my parents died, my aunt asked which clothes I wanted them dressed in for the funeral. "Whatever they were wearing when they died," I said. "But their clothes were ruined. They won't be presentable. Go find something appropriate," she said. "Presentable" – I brooded over the word for hours. Presentable for whom? For ghouls who wanted to prise open their coffins? For maggots? For my father, I picked out a pair of jeans and a blue shirt, for my mother, a flowery print dress. My aunt was scandalised. "You can't dress them as if they're off on holiday!" She felt that I should have picked out a black suit for my father, and a sober dress for my mother. "I'll dress them however I like," I said, and that was how they were buried.

I tried on my father's shirts and trousers. The only things I could find that would fit were a pair of sweatpants, a T-shirt, a leather jacket and his flip-flops. The leather jacket was thick. If Colmillo did bite me, at least it would provide a little protection. I grabbed the knife and a belt with a heavy buckle so I could hit him if he tried to attack. I left the room. The wolf was nowhere to be seen.

I went into Carlos's room and closed the door. The parakeets were perched on top of their cage. As soon as they saw me, they started singing. Once again, I had forgotten them. I fed them some birdseed, and when I went into the bathroom to fill their water bottle, I found King huddled in the shower. I called to him, but he didn't move. Only his tail wagged a little. As I crouched down to examine him, he licked my hand. His eyes looked watery and yellow. I tried to pull him to his feet, but he couldn't stand.

I needed to take him to the vet, but without a car that was impossible. I couldn't carry him to the bus stop or down to La Viga to hail a taxi. The only solution I could think of was to call Chelo. Her mother answered. "Chelo is at college, she won't be long," she said. "How long?" I asked. Chelo's mother said she would be home for lunch at about 2 p.m. I swallowed hard. The only family I had left was dying in the shower. "Señora, can I ask you a favour? My dog is very ill and I don't have a car to take him to the vet. Could you help?" She said she would pick me up in ten minutes.

I peered over the banisters to check where Colmillo was, and saw him sniffing around the ruins of my bedroom. Soundlessly, I tiptoed back to King, picked him up and carefully carried him into what had been my grandmother's bathroom, whose window opened onto the spiral staircase that led to the roof. I couldn't carry him out through the front door, Colmillo was bound to attack us.

With King slung over my shoulders, I clambered up the stairs, almost dropping him more than once. Reaching the flat roof, I zigzagged between the clothes lines and the television aerials before climbing down the Ávalos' staircase. Coco, the eldest boy, was in the kitchen. I asked him to open the door and he did so without a second thought. In the barrio, neighbours sometimes appeared unexpectedly in each other's backyard. Nobody was surprised to find someone wandering through their garage or coming through their front door.

When Chelo's mother arrived, Coco helped me carry King to her car. I laid him on the back seat. "Where are we taking him?" I told her to drive to the university, to the Emergency Clinic of the Veterinary Department. This was where a couple of neighbours, Jorge Padilla and Rubén Rodríguez, had studied.

Chelo's mother floored the accelerator, swerving to avoid buses, pedestrians, cyclists. In less than twenty minutes we had arrived at the university campus. She pulled up in front of the clinic and I carried King inside. We were greeted by a young student who ushered me into a consulting room, where I laid King on the table. The student disappeared and came back with one of her tutors. "I'm Dr José Sánchez Martínez. Can you tell me exactly what's wrong with your dog?" "He can't stand up," I said. He asked me about changes to his diet or his environment. I explained that I'd brought a wolf to live in the house and that King was terrified. "A wolf?" he asked, sceptically. I nodded. "Wait outside, we'll examine him."

I waited in a small room where Chelo's mother joined me once she had parked the car. We sat on orange plastic chairs. "Chelo told me you'd ended up looking after Colmillo, said he's wreaked havoc in the house." I turned, surprised. Chelo had talked to her about me? "Yes, he is a little wild," I said. "What about you, how are you?" she asked. "I'm O.K." "Are you sure?" Of course I'm not sure: your daughter broke my heart, my parents, my brother and my grandmother are all dead, in a couple of months I'll run out of money and have to sell the furniture and probably the house in order to survive, my friends are all at school so I rarely see them, my dog is lying in the next room, dying, I feel completely alone and there's a huge wall barring any hope for the future. "Yeah, I'm sure," I said.

A silence descended. Somewhere, a clock loudly ticked away the passing seconds. "Do you know Consuelo was ill?" she asked suddenly. I nodded. "It was very hard. When she has these episodes, it's like she disappears into a black hole," she said. The metaphor perfectly described what I'd felt: that Chelo had disappeared into a deep hole, into some place where I couldn't reach her. "She trusts you," she added. "You need to take care of each other." Of course, we'd take care of each other. The lonely orphan and the crippled manic depressive. We made a lovely couple.

The woman excused herself. "I need to get going, Juan Guillermo, I have to make lunch." I thanked her and walked her to the front door. As she left, I stood and watched a group of guys playing flag football in the car park. I was still watching when the vet called my name. "We've examined your dog," he said gravely. "He's suffered a serious heart attack, it's very unlikely he'll recover." In that moment, I realised how much I loved King, how much I would miss him. "Can't you operate?" I asked. "I'm sorry, there's nothing I can do." I began to feel queasy. Once again, death was circling me. "Could he have had a heart attack because he was scared?" I asked. The doctor took a moment before he answered. "It could have been triggered by any number of factors." My grandmother often used the phrase "scared to death". And it was true, fear could kill you. A cousin of mine died of a heart attack while walking down the street when someone pointed a toy gun at her.

I was overcome by guilt. Locked in Carlos's room, terrified of Colmillo, huddled in a tiny bathroom with no means of escape, King had still been able to smell the wild animal downstairs that could rip him to pieces, and the stress had caused his heart to fail. My need to save Colmillo was about to claim its first victim.

"I can only suggest we put him down," the vet said. At least he didn't use the hypocritical phrase "put him to sleep". I kept insisting that they operate. The vet looked at me kindly. "There is irreversible damage to the heart muscle, I'm afraid there is honestly nothing to be done."

I decided to take King home. If he was going to die, let it be because he could not carry on, rather than from a lethal injection. I asked the student if I could call a cab. "Sure, but they take a while to get here," she said. She handed me a number and let me use the telephone. I called. The dispatcher told me I'd be waiting around forty-five minutes. I phoned my friends, who were now home from school, and asked them to help me carry King back up to Carlos's room when I got home.

King was brought into the waiting room, barely able to move. According to the vet, the damage to his heart was preventing him from getting enough oxygen. I laid him across my lap while we waited for the taxi.

Ten minutes later, an old Ford 200 pulled up outside. A student in a white coat got out, and came into the clinic. "Juan Guillermo?" she asked. I nodded, thinking she was another student. "We came to collect you," she said, and nodded towards the car where Chelo, also wearing a white coat, was sitting in the passenger seat. We looked at each other. She got out and came towards me. "How's King?" she asked. When he heard her voice, King began to wag his tail. She bent down and stroked him. "He's had a heart attack, he's dying," I said.

We carried King to the car and laid him on the back seat and I climbed in beside him and patted him soothingly. He licked my fingers. Standing by the open door, Chelo took my face in her hands. "Please forgive me," she said. "I don't ever want us to be apart again." She kissed me on the lips, closed the door and climbed into the passenger seat as her friend started the car.

He heard footsteps in the snow. The animals, whatever they were, were moving quickly through the darkness. Amaruq tilted his head and, a few metres away, spotted a pack of coyotes, barely visible in the moon-light. The wild dogs would devour them. Amaruq clicked his tongue to try and scare them, but this simply made them more curious. Fearless, the coyotes came closer. One began to rip the goat's belly with its teeth. Coyotes prefer to begin with the intestines, the softest and easiest part to rip from a carcass. Amaruq listened to the chewing. Several more coyotes joined the feast and began to fight among themselves. Amaruq could hear them growl as they attacked one another.

A male pup driven away by the others continued to circle the goat carcass, trying to get close enough to snatch a mouthful, but the other coyotes would not let him. He crept towards Amaruq and sniffed his boots. Amaruq tried to whistle to scare him off, but could manage only a faint puff of air. The coyote continued to prowl around him, sniffing his face. Amaruq made a guttural sound he hoped was men-acing, but still the coyote pup continued to sniff. Amaruq could feel the animal's teeth on his neck. He jerked his head from side to side to shake him off, but the coyote did not give up. He tried to scream, but no sound came.

The coyotes were joined by others. One started to gnaw on the back of his head, another bit his leg. Before long the animals were once again fighting among themselves. Amaruq watched as they growled and snapped at each other inches from his face. Just before daybreak, they retreated a few paces and began to howl.

When at last the sun appeared over the horizon, Amaruq heard a distant sound. The coyotes fell silent, their bodies tensed. As the sound came closer, they darted into the clump of pine trees. Amaruq looked up at the sky and saw a helicopter circling, heard it land in a clearing between the trees. Then there were voices, and, at last, the scent of other humans.

Two men came up to him. Amaruq knew that he had no chance of surviving. His body was unresponsive from the neck down. He tried to indicate where they could find Nujuaqtutuq, but they did not understand his language. They were talking so much it made him dizzy. "Save Nujuaqtutuq," he tried to tell them, but they did not understand.

He heard a familiar voice. He tried to lift his head to see where it was coming from. The men were in the way. "I am here," his grandfather said. Now he could see him more clearly than ever. Amaruq realised that being close to death meant that they could communicate more easily. "How are you feeling?" asked the grandfather. "Bad," said Amaruq. The grandfather said something else, but he couldn't hear him over the chattering of the men.

He heard another helicopter approaching. Where had this swarm of helicopters come from? More men arrived. More noise, more talk. Why would they not leave him alone? They lifted him onto a stretcher. It hurt where the coyote had gnawed his head. The men talked among themselves. Amaruq could not understand them. He asked his grandfather to come with him. The grandfather smiled. "No, you do not need me."

The men took him away on the stretcher. Amaruq saw the tops of the trees, the profound blue of the morning. Amaruq loved belonging to the Earth. How he would miss living on it. He turned towards the mountain and whispered "sorry" to Nujuaqtutuq for humiliating him. "I will see you in the next life," he said.

They loaded him into the helicopter. The helicopter rose into the air. He was Amaruq of the skies. The man in the clouds. The man close to the gods.

My brother has been trapped inside the water tank for hours. Despite my pleading, Humberto refuses to let him out.

"He must learn," he argues.

He bangs his fist on the outside of the water tank. Carlos responds with another bang.

"See? He's fine."

"He will drown."

"When he starts pounding over and over, we'll know he can't take it anymore."

The presence of patrol cars and cops causes a commotion in the barrio. The neighbours gather around. They want to know what's going on. Various adults intercede on behalf of my brother and his friends. Among them is Pato's dad. The police threaten him: "If you choose to get involved in what doesn't concern you, you'll have to face the consequences." One of them opens his jacket and shows him his gun. Frightened, the neighbours withdraw, one by one. There is nobody left to ask for help.

Pato's father leaves, taking his son with him. Agüitas's mother orders him to go home immediately. Agüitas does so, in tears. Only Jaibo and I remain.

Humberto's mother can't believe what her son is doing. She tries to talk to him. Humberto refuses. "Please leave, señora," one of the Good Boys says. "Your son doesn't want to see you." The woman insists and walks towards him. A cop shoves her away. She sees her son in the distance, staring at her impassively.

At 8 p.m. that night they decide to let Diego out. Several cops surround the tank. As soon as they open the lid, he comes out, gasping for air. A cop pulls him by the hair and he falls onto his back two metres below. His right shoulder blade fractures. You can hear the bone break. The cops don't care. They push him down face first and handcuff him.

"You're fucked," says one cop to him.

Diego looks him in the eye, still gasping for air.

"For now," he replies defiantly.

The answer earns him a flurry of blows. Diego heroically tries to resist, despite his broken shoulder blade. They push him down a spiral staircase and drag him to a patrol car.

"Bird one is in the nest," a cop says into his radio.

I am relieved to see Diego. It means they will soon free Sean and my brother. Two more hours go by. The Good Boys don't seem to be in a hurry.

373

I climb up to the rooftop again. It's cold and the Good Boys have lit a fire to keep themselves warm. Carlos must be freezing in the water. I look for Humberto. He's leaning against a corner. The fire lights up his face. I ask him once again to let Carlos go and remind him of his promise that he would only administer a "corrective".

"We decide when it's time to let him out," he says irritably.

The moon appears on the horizon. The recently conquered moon. Two astronauts bound across the surface of the moon while my brother is drowning inside a water tank. Half the world is watching them while my brother is alone inside the water tank. The moon lights up the rooftop. It is midnight. Sean and my brother have been underwater for fourteen hours.

A cat walks towards the chinchillas. I spot it from a distance. I run at it, to scare it away. I can't let it kill even a single one; death cannot be in the air around us tonight.

At 1.18 a.m., while the astronauts are collecting lunar samples, I see the beam of a torch on the Padilla rooftop. They're circling the tank in which Sean is trapped. Again, I run across the roof terraces. As I arrive they're pulling him out. Sean can hardly move, he's frozen solid. He frantically gasps for air. The cops pull his hands behind his back and handcuff him. They insult him. Sean doesn't answer. He looks them straight in the eye. He has fought wars. He has endured pain and injury. He has nothing but contempt for these men. The cops beat him for looking them in the eye. He falls to his knees. He looks weak. They drag him along the ground, scraping his knees until they bleed. Sean asks his captors to let him climb down the spiral staircase on his own. They agree. One cop walks in front, two behind, with three Good Boys making up the rear. Sean takes six steps then stops. The cop at the front turns and growls, "Keep moving." Sean lashes out with a vicious headbutt, sending him sprawling, leaps over the cop and races down the stairs, but just when it looks like he might escape, he trips and tumbles down the last few steps. The cops catch him and beat him again. A baton-blow to his jaw knocks him unconscious.

They toss him into the patrol car. One of the officers calls it in. "Bird two is in the nest." They take him away. "Bird three", my brother, is still trapped in his watery prison. The moon disappears.

Carlos has now been trapped for eighteen hours. It starts to rain. The cops go in search of shelter, but the Good Boys remain steadfast. They are god's army. Humberto has taught them to endure harsh weather, hunger, thirst. I stand out in the rain. I need to show them that I can endure more than they can.

At six in the morning the rain stops. The cops come out from their shelters. A fat one comes up with a thermos of coffee and disposable cups. The cops share them out. They offer some to the Good Boys. They decline, they don't drink coffee.

The sun rises as Comandante Zurita arrives, flanked by four officers. He greets Humberto warmly. He has been bragging to his superiors about his trophies – Sean and Diego – and has been congratulated. He took them alive, ready to be tried and convicted. No more young drug addicts. The end of their narcotics trade. Efficient policing.

Zurita looks at me. He must know by now that my brother is about to be executed, I can see it in his eyes. But I still have hope. I walk over to the water tank, look for some sign of compassion, some evidence of the merciful god the Bible talks so much about. But there is no such thing. There is no god, no mercy. Only an army following the orders of an angry, spiteful god.

The cops have been up all night and look tired. Zurita and Humberto quietly confer, and then Humberto has a word with Antonio and Josué. They are planning something. I see my friends standing on the neighbouring rooftop. They have gone against their parents to stand with me.

At 8.58 a.m. Humberto walks towards the water tank, stands on a pile of bricks, grabs the stopcock and breaks it. The tank begins to fill. Humberto climbs down from the bricks and watches as the water overflows. "Carlos is going to drown!" I scream and run towards the tank only to be stopped by the Good Boys. I try to shake them off, but they overpower me. Water is gushing into the tank. My brother is drowning. Carlos is desperately pounding on the walls. Zurita watches, unconcerned. Water starts to spill out. Water. Carlos has no air. "Get him out!" I scream. Still the water flows. No air. Pounding. Carlos. No air. Water. Pounding. More pounding. My brother is drowning. Dying. I howl. Nobody moves. Water. Suffocating. Agüitas is sobbing. Pato is begging. Jaibo is pale. My brother. Dying. Zurita. Humberto. Them. The killers. Water overflowing. I break loose, run towards the tank. They tackle me. I fall. I hear the pounding. Carlos's life slipping away. Water. Kicking. 9.03 a.m. Carlos. Struggling. Kicking. Pounding. No air. Choking. I scream. Still the water spills out. My brother is drowning. Life. End. Water. Death. Death. 9.05 a.m. Death. Silence. The water is still flowing. Streaming over the flat roof. Carlos's life. Trickling away. His body's final throes. Humberto. Killer. Water spreading. Carlos floating. Drowned. 9.07 a.m. Water is spilling. Carlos is no more. A bloated corpse. Water. My shoes are sodden. Death. My shoes

are sodden

A woman's name betrays me.
A woman aches all through my body.
JORGE LUIS BORGES

Voids

The helicopter circled the mountain several times. Robert, Jack and Alex carefully scanned the slopes, until they spotted a camp located almost at the summit. Robert peered through his binoculars. There was no sign of life, but they decided to check the tent.

Jack landed in a valley three kilometres from where they'd seen the camp. Robert and Alex climbed out. The day was cold, despite the dazzling sunshine. Robert slung a rifle over his shoulder, Alex took the radio and they set off. The snow was heavier than expected. It required considerable effort to make headway. Robert had no idea what the man meant when he said "Nujuaqtutuq", but it was better to investigate.

They came to a precipice. To reach the camp they would have to navigate a narrow path running along a sheer cliff face. There were few things that Robert feared, but one of them was heights. Since childhood he had suffered from vertigo. Just imagining tumbling into the void as the man and the goat had made him tremble. In his mind, the terror of falling was much worse than any other death: worse than being burned, devoured, drowned.

The trail used by the mountain goats was no more than half a metre wide. They would have to sidle along, clinging tightly to the rockface. Robert stopped and surveyed the terrain. The mere sight of the abyss left him paralysed. What was the point in risking their lives like this? Alex set off first. Robert could not afford to show weakness in front of his subordinate, but the thought of negotiating a hundred metres of steep cliff face was too much.

"Let's find another way."

"This is the shortest route," Alex said.

Robert looked down again. If he were to lose his footing, the fall would take several seconds. He felt physically sick as he imagined being suspended in the air, then crashing against the rocks.

"No, we'll find another route," he said, but Alex had already disappeared around a bend.

Robert took a deep breath and put one foot on the path. Piles of stones and snow made it even more precarious. Hesitantly, he took one step after another, struggling not to look down. He stared straight ahead, as his father had taught him, feeling his way by testing the ground ahead. Out of the corner of his eye, he caught a glimpse of Alex, whose quick, surefooted gait simply made him more nervous. He came to an overhanging rock. He would have to crawl underneath if he was to get past. Robert froze. He could not crawl. He might lose his balance and fall to certain death. He looked back at the distance he'd already covered. Almost twenty metres. The prospect of going back was as terrifying as carrying on. He started to shake uncontrollably. He was tempted to plunge over the edge, if only to put an end to the terror and the vertigo. Or to stay where he was and wait for the helicopter to come and rescue him. He looked down. It felt as though the void was pulling him. He pressed himself as close as he could to the rock face. His jaw clenched. He eyes closed.

"Are you O.K.?" Coming back to look for him, Alex found Robert standing there, rooted to the spot, halfway along the path. Robert shook his head.

"Don't panic," said Alex.

Robert was hyperventilating. What must Alex think of him? What would he tell the dozens of workers back at base camp? That he was a coward? It embarrassed and terrified him.

"Open your eyes," Alex told him. "You'll see, everything's alright."

Robert opened them and looked to his right. Alex was standing on the lip of the abyss. Far from bringing him relief, Alex's presence made Robert feel even more frightened.

"Get away from the edge!" he shouted.

Calmly and deliberately, Alex walked towards Robert.

"Honestly, it's fine," he said, offering his hand. "Let me help you, hold on to me."

Robert reached out and grabbed the hand.

"Now, very slowly, lean forward and bend your knees."

Robert obeyed and slowly managed to pass the overhang.

"We'll take it one step at a time, I won't let you go," Alex assured him.

It took almost an hour to cover the remaining eighty metres. When they reached the other side, Robert was shattered. Sweat trickled down his forehead. He swallowed hard, his throat dry. He turned back and gave a nervous laugh.

"I did it! I did it! I did it!"

It was the first time he had ever conquered his fear, yet he still felt weak. Without Alex's help, he would not have been able to move an inch. He made him promise not to tell anyone.

They headed east and found the campsite in a hollow near the summit. The tent was ripped, tattered shreds flapping in the wind. The frayed guy ropes barely held it up. Around the embers of a fire, they found pieces of chewed twigs. Crawling into the tent, Robert came face to face with a huge wolf tied to a sled next to a leather sack, some pelts, a bolt-action rifle and some crude snow shoes.

He pointed to the wolf.

"Nujuaqtutuq."

The wolf looked emaciated, one of his hind legs was ruined, his coat was dull and slashed with cuts, his eyes listless, his nose dry. Dehydration. Robert crouched down to examine the animal.

"Careful, he might bite," Alex called.

No, this wolf could not bite him, he was severely malnourished and close to death. What was the animal doing tied up on a mountain peak, far from its natural forest habitat? Why had the man dragged it here?

"Should we put him out of his misery?" asked Alex. "He's dying."

"No, let's take him with us to base camp."

"How will we get him down?"

Robert nodded towards the sled.

"We can drag him down to the foothills and radio Jack to pick us up."

They piled the man's scant belongings onto the sled and made sure the wolf was securely strapped on. Then they radioed Jack and told him to land the helicopter on a plateau on the eastern face.

Together they dragged the sled, their progress hampered by the boulders and the snow. They marvelled that one man had managed to lug something so heavy to the summit. Several times, they had to stop to catch their breath. They radioed Jack for help. Between the three of them they managed to load the sled into the back of the helicopter and take off.

They reached base camp at nightfall and moved the wolf into a pen next to the sled dogs. The moment they smelled the wolf, the huskies began barking furiously.

Robert cut the ropes that restrained him, but the wolf did not have the strength to stand. He lay staring at the barking dogs on the other side of the fence. Robert kneeled down to inspect the animal's leg. It was badly broken, ulcerous, and gangrene had begun to set in. He would get the vet to examine him when he came to check on the dogs and draught horses the next day.

Robert set a bowl of mince and a bucket of water in front of the wolf, then left, locking the gate and heading for his tent. One of the young doctors stopped him. "I've been looking for you."

"What is it?"

"The man just died," the doctor said.

"See if you can track down his family, or someone who knew him. His name is Amaruq Mackenzie."

"Yes, sir." The doctor turned and left.

Robert felt a profound need to discover who this man had been.

Their shared surname was more than a coincidence. It was a sign, perhaps. Blood calling to blood. He would look after Amaruq's body and the injured wolf. They were his responsibility now.

My friends were already waiting when we got back to the house with King. Chelo's friend left and the four of us carried King up to the roof and set him down. I went into the house to see if I could find Colmillo. He was dozing beneath the dining room table. He seemed to have chosen this place as his lair. He stood up when he saw me. I walked slowly towards him, and he allowed me to get close. I stretched out my hand and stroked his head. He looked me in the eye. I was afraid. Cautiously, I took the chain and attached it to his collar. Colmillo did not take his eyes off me. I retreated, never turning my back on him, and went back upstairs. Colmillo watched me leave then calmly lay down underneath the table.

We carried King down to Carlos's room and laid him on the bed. He licked our hands gratefully. He looked terrible. Pato hugged him and Agüitas naturally shed a few tears.

My friends left via the roof and the spiral staircase. They were terrified of Colmillo, especially now that they knew he was a pureblood wolf and was allowed to roam free. No matter how many times I assured them he was chained up, they never dared leave by the front door.

I was alone with Chelo. We lay down, she on one side of King and me on the other. I told her everything: what the vet had said, how he had suggested putting King down. "I'll make him better," Chelo said. "I'll talk to my cardiology tutor. He'll be fine. You'll see."

As Chelo stroked his back, King fell asleep and began to snore. This made Chelo laugh. At every snore, she giggled. She reached a hand across King and stroked my face. "Do you forgive me?" I looked into her eyes. "You promised not to sleep with anyone else while we were together," I said. She continued stroking. "I know, and I'm sorry, I swear, but when I get depressed it's like someone else is making decisions for me." We lay quietly for a moment. "I want to be with you," she said. "I promise I'll be faithful to you forever." I didn't believe her. Sooner or later her compulsive promiscuity would prevail. "I can't trust you," I said. "Maybe not right now, but I'll do whatever it takes to win your trust again." She climbed over the sleeping King and wrapped her arms around me.

We lay there in silence until darkness fell. We did not kiss, we did not make love, we did not touch. I was grateful that she didn't try. King's snoring stopped. I was afraid that he was dying. I pressed my ear against his chest to listen to his heart. It was beating irregularly. Thump-thump followed by a prolonged "whoosh". I told Chelo. "Could be arrhythmia," she said. King did not wake. He must have had many sleepless nights, consumed by terror, waiting for the wolf to attack. Perhaps his fearfulness dated from the night he had been stabbed. A trauma he would never forget. Or perhaps he was just easily fright-ened. Now, with us lying next to him, he could sleep in peace.

Chelo walked into the bathroom without switching on the light. In the darkness, I heard the stream of urine and a discreet fart. Grow-ing intimacy. When she reappeared, she warned me about the risk of disease. "The bathroom is covered with King's piss and shit. We need to disinfect the whole place or it'll be teeming with germs." She had said "we need", as though my house was hers too. I didn't like her assumption that we were reconciled.

She sat on the edge of the bed. "Can I stay the night?" "No," I said. She stood up, kissed me and then paused. "Do you want to see me again?" I wanted to say "Of course I want to see you, I want you to stay here forever, to sleep here today, tomorrow, Monday, for the rest of our lives. I want you to keep using the plural, keep talking about 'us'. I want us to make love for days, to lie in bed, to have you kiss me, hug me, naked, and never leave"; but between two people who love each other, jealousy becomes a stone wall. A wall that casts a shadow over everything.

"Call me if you want to see me again," she said, then kissed me on the lips and left the room. I heard the front door close. I turned on the light. King was still asleep. I went downstairs to feed Colmillo. There was shit and piss around the table again. A tidal wave of excrement.

I gave him dog biscuits with some leftover rice and six raw eggs. I unhooked the chain and took his food out to the backyard, hoping that he would follow. This was where he would be living from now on.

Smelling the food, Colmillo came outside. The yard was very small, but he would quickly learn to climb the spiral staircase and enjoy the open space and the view from the rooftop. I shut the door. Colmillo glanced at me for a moment, then went back to his food.

I picked up the shit and scrubbed the urine stains with soap and water, then I disinfected the whole place. Chelo was right. It wasn't just the unbearable smell, there must have been germs everywhere. It was a miracle I hadn't caught typhoid or dysentery.

When I went back up to the bedroom, King was awake. He tried unsuccessfully to get up. I sat next to him, stroked him, and he lifted his head so that I would scratch under his chin. That and having his back rubbed were his ultimate pleasures. He drifted off again. Afraid that this might be his last night, I slept with my arms around him.

A woman's name betrays me
A woman aches all through my body

A woman's body betrays me
A name aches all through my body

A woman's name pains me
A body betrays all through my body

A body's name betrays me
My body aches all through a woman

A woman's name aches all through my body

A name eternally wants to be a name

A body eternally wants to be a body

A woman eternally wants to be a woman

A name eternally wants to be a woman

A body eternally wants to be a woman

A woman eternally wants to be.

A woman's name betrays me
A woman aches all through my body

Among the Jola people in Senegal, when someone dies, the body is carried on a bier by four men. An elder from the village – the *asaba* – begins the ritual of *kasab*, the interrogation of the deceased, during which he asks these questions:

"Did someone or something kill you?"

"Was it a disease?"

"Did you disobey one of the spirits?"

The deceased responds with vibrations that can be felt by the men carrying the bier. If it moves up and down the answer is "yes", if it moves side to side it means "no". Swifts movements mean truth, slow movements mean lies.

Finally, the *asaba* asks the question most likely to cause anxiety in the deceased: "Should you have died?" The men who carry the body await the answer. If the sway is gentle, the answer is "yes, I should have died". A violent shake means that the deceased believes their departure to have been unjust. Bitterness consumes them and they desire to take vengeance on the living. The *asaba* tries to comfort them: "We wish for you to be at peace. Yes, you should not have died, but your death allows for the resurgence of life."

The deceased becomes calm, comes to realise that the living are not responsible for their death, and departs without causing harm. But if the departed was murdered, they cannot be at peace until the guilty party is punished. The *asaba* asks: "Who killed you?" The dead body rocks and the name of the killer resonates through the arms of the bearers, who repeat it aloud. The crowd turns on the named person.

It doesn't matter if they protest their innocence. The dead man has spoken their name and they must be punished.

The deceased coldly watches as their killer is whipped and cast out. Satisfied, they go in peace.

Bodies

Carlos's bloated body arrived at the undertaker's six days after his death. He'd been sliced from end to end and sewn up with crude stitches. An autopsy had been carried out, as though there was any doubt that he had drowned.

My grandmother, usually cheerful and talkative, became taciturn. She was never the same again. She blamed herself for not taking care of Carlos, as though he was still a child. It angered her that I didn't shed a tear. She didn't understand that there are many ways to weep: clenching fists, grinding teeth or lying awake at night.

King was also affected by my brother's death. His was a hyperactive grief. He raced up and down the stairs, and in and out of Carlos's room, leaped up on every visitor, slobbered over the sofa, the walls, the dishes, anything that had a trace of Carlos's scent. He didn't sleep in his bed, but lay in the garage facing the door, waiting for Carlos.

Only family and close friends came to the wake. Many people, concerned at being associated with a "delinquent" and imagining police harassment and gossip, decided to stay away.

Comandante Zurita suggested to Humberto, Antonio, Josué and Felipe that they leave the city for a while. The rest of the Good Boys holed up in the houses of relatives who lived in distant neighbourhoods. Although there was little possibility that they would be prosecuted, there had been numerous witnesses to Carlos's murder and Zurita suggested it would be unwise for them to stay in the barrio. The real truth was that Zurita wanted them gone. A major drugs ring had been busted and he wanted to take the credit in the eyes of the president's family.

Father Arturo immediately washed his hands of all responsibility. He visited my uncles and my grandmother, told them how sorry he was about Carlos's terrible "accident". He staunchly defended the Good Boys, said that they had done no more than tell the police where the "poisoners" were hiding, claimed that – regrettably – the lid of the water tank had got stuck and that Carlos, unlike his accomplices, had not been able to get out in time. He distanced himself from the events and even insisted he did not know precisely what had happened.

All lies. His constant contradictions, his familiarity with the details of the murder, his every word proved that he had been involved. The church authorities were informed and, less than a month after Carlos's murder, Father Arturo was relieved of his position at the Iglesia del Espíritu Santo and transferred to a parish in an isolated village in Zacatecas. The authorities shielded him from scrutiny and from any semblance of a police investigation. Meanwhile, Father Arturo made sure that Humberto and his acolytes were protected in parishes throughout Jalisco, where he still had influence.

Comandante Zurita was promoted and given the title General Coordinator of Criminal Police Investigations, a prestigious role that offered more opportunities for corruption. As his influence grew, he was able to exert more power over petty thieves, drug dealers, pimps and prostitutes. The criminal network was at his service. He had no truck with rapists, murderers or armed robbers. They caused too much trouble for meagre returns, so he had them executed. After being caught they were taken to abandoned lots and shot in the head. Then they were thrown into the sewers. That was how he placated the great and the good and justified his appointment.

Once the funeral was over, I went back to school. I didn't say anything to my teachers. I made up something about my grandmother being sick to explain the days I'd missed. That was it.

In the morning, I'd wake early and catch the Popo-Sur 73 bus, which dropped me on the corner near my school. On the bus, I sat in silence. Other people's conversations irritated me. I was adamant that the rest of the world should be mourning my brother too.

Only one word echoed through my mind: revenge. In class I would close my eyes and picture the moment when I would make everyone involved in my brother's murder pay with his life. I was fourteen years old, and my dream was to grow up to be a silent, ruthless killer.

After Carlos died, I often went to look at the water tank. The family had replaced it with a new one and left the old one lying in a corner of the rooftop. They refused to drink, to wash or to cook with water from the tank in which Carlos had been drowned.

I would climb into the empty tank and try to imagine how my brother had suffered. I wasn't being morbid, I needed to understand what had happened, to somehow clear my conscience. In those days, most water tanks were asbestos – before anyone knew it caused cancer. They were grey, hulking things and, inside, when you shouted, it made a muffled echo. The tank seemed a good metaphor for the womb. Did my brother Juan José scream soundlessly as he was strangled by the umbilical cord?

I found the straw my brother must have used to breathe. It was yellow, about nine centimetres long, and cut in half. It was through this narrow tube that my brother had clung to life, had taken his last breaths, before spitting it out, his whole body gasping for air.

I couldn't keep it. There was too much pain in those nine centimetres. But I could not throw it away. In the anatomy of his murder, this little tube contained Carlos's whole universe: the cinema screenings, the acid and the morphine, the atheism, the books, Chelo, Humberto's malevolence, my parents, King, my grandmother and me. I put it back where I found it. Let the wind, the rain or a stray cat decide its fate.

By the time my parents came home from Europe, I had more or less processed Carlos's death. They had not. They returned to the brutal absence of their elder son. Their grief once again stirred up the chaos inside me. I went back to my trance-like state, to wandering around the house in silence, to sitting mutely on the bus to school. My mourning was back at square one. Once again, I had to deal with the pain and the rage.

It was a small thing that made it possible for me to escape that cobweb of death: a basketball game. Mr Alarid had set up an annual tournament with teams from each class. Just before Carlos died, our third-year group B team, had reached the finals. To get there, we had beaten every other team in the middle school, as well as high school teams from the fourth and fifth years. Now we were to face the sixth-year team. They were eighteen, we were fourteen. And although I was taller than any of their players, they were stronger, faster and more experienced.

The final took place a fortnight after Carlos's death. I was depressed and in no mood to play. I asked to stay on the bench, even though I'd been in the first five throughout the tournament. By the time I went on, in the third quarter, they were thrashing us 46–18. I don't know how my grief spurred me on, but I played the best game of my life. I scored forty-five points – forty-five of the fifty-six points my team scored in the second half. I scored from the halfway line, I scored backward shots, hook shots, fast breaks, bank shots. We won 74–73 with a basket I scored from the difficult corner two seconds before the whistle. I was voted player of the season.

Buoyed up by victory, I managed to shake death off for a few days. At school, I suddenly became a celebrity. My triumph was written up in the school newspaper. Teachers held me up as an example of courage and dignity. Mr Alarid even suggested I try to secure a basketball scholarship at a U.S. college. But it was just an illusion. Gradually, a trickle of sadness eroded the thin carapace of victory and I came crashing back to the suffocating reality of life without my brother.

Like the rusty chinchilla cages and Mr Belmont's wrecked pigeon loft, the water tank on the Barrera rooftop lay abandoned like a beached whale. A greyish, hollow mass that rotted with time.

The water tank was taken over by feral cats. One afternoon as I passed, I heard mewling. I peeked in and a cat hissed at me. A litter of seven kittens was blundering around, blindly searching for their mother's teats. In the belly of the grey whale that devoured my brother there was life. Life.

Lying in the back of the helicopter, Amaruq stared through the window at the sky. A blue, translucent sky. As a boy, his father had told him that, after death, the good and righteous went to heaven. His Inuit grandfather had told him that, after death, the good and righteous departed for the icy tundra, which would be teeming with caribou, wapiti and seals. His father told him that, after death, the good and the righteous were reunited with a merciful and loving god in heaven. His grandfather told him that they travelled to meet living gods: Earth, Water, Sky and Wind. His father had told him that there was but one true god. According to his grandfather, the sky was the heart of the gods.

Amaruq regretted having fathered no children, so that he might know which of them had been right and which of these gods were real. He would have said nothing to his children about gods. Without the burden of beliefs handed down from generation to generation, the children would carry within them the new gods, the true gods, the profound gods.

The swaying of the helicopter made him drowsy. He closed his eyes and began to drift off. He was exhausted, having been kept awake by the cold night air and the coyotes. He opened his eyes again, afraid that these might be his final moments. He did not want to miss them.

The helicopter landed. Amaruq could no longer see the sky, which was blotted out by tall towers, machines and pine trees. The door opened. Several men came towards him. One leaned into his face. He could smell toothpaste on his breath. He spoke to him in English. Amaruq could not understand. They brought a gurney, lifted him onto it, took him to the large tent they used as a field hospital and laid him on one of the beds.

He was examined by several young doctors. One examined his pupils with a penlight. The glare was painful, but the doctor was holding his eyelids open, so that he could not close them. Another used a needle to prick his fingertips, testing his peripheral reflexes. A third auscultated his chest while another administered an intravenous saline solution. The young men were medical students, working as interns in the field hospital. They argued over a diagnosis. Amaruq wished they would stop their incessant bickering. He wished he had never been brought here. He wished he had died in the mountains. He longed for a silent death. Now he had to endure the prattle of a group of young men who pawed at his numb, broken body. The thought of dying in this dark, ugly place while outside the sun was shining horrified him. He wanted to die in the snow, close to the earth, not in some hospital bed. In Inuktitut, he asked to be taken back to where they had found him. The young men asked each other what he had said, but no-one could decipher the words.

After they had poked, prodded and manhandled him for half an hour, the senior doctor arrived, accompanied by a nurse. He asked the interns a few questions, listened attentively to their answers and then, delicately, unhurriedly, examined Amaruq. Amaruq appreciated his calm.

The doctor asked for a chair and sat down next to him. Using gestures and speaking slowly, using an occasional word of Inuktitut learned from an Inuit labourer, the doctor explained that he had suffered a spinal fracture, a number of broken bones and a punctured lung. They would transport him by helicopter to a hospital in Whitehorse for surgery. Amaruq refused. He knew it was hopeless. The doctor produced a syringe and used the Inuktitut word for "sleep" to ask whether he wanted to be sedated. Despite the excruciating pain, Amaruq chose to remain awake, to be as alert as possible when death came for him.

Amaruq became anxious at the thought of what they would do with his remains. His grandfather had told him that, in his tribe, the dead were wrapped in caribou hides and left face up on the icy grasslands so that their spirits could gaze at the sky. He did not want to be buried in a wooden box, beneath layers of earth, in a white man's cemetery. His spirit would be trapped.

"I want outside," Amaruq said in broken English. The doctor signed that his condition was critical and it could kill him. Amaruq pleaded in Inuktitut. He wanted to be taken back to the mountain, he did not care if he was devoured by coyotes or became carrion for crows, he simply wanted to leave this place, he could not bear to die surrounded by strangers.

The doctor understood. Leading the interns out of the tent, he explained the dying man's wishes and told them that he intended to honour them. If anyone objected, they should say so. The youngest argued that it was immoral not to treat someone so ill. Another said it would be a breach of professional ethics, that their duty as doctors was to save his life, that the patient should immediately be flown to the hospital at Whitehorse, even though he had refused treatment. The doctor told them there was nothing to be done, this was the patient's decision and they had to respect it. "That's not what I was taught at university," the youngest said. "That may be," the doctor replied, "but life teaches you other things."

Though they still disagreed with the decision, the students, followed by the doctor and the nurse, carried Amaruq to the woods. Dozens of curious labourers watched as they crossed the campground. They passed the line of trucks waiting to collect the dug-up earth. Amaruq could hear engines, voices. He could smell exhaust fumes, engine oil, the labourers' sweat.

They took him to the bank of a nearby river. The students gently laid the stretcher at the foot of a steep grove of pine trees and headed back to the hospital. The nurse and the doctor sat on two boulders.

Amaruq could feel the wind on his face, could hear the water lapping against the riverbank, the branches of the pines swaying in the breeze, the dripping of a melting icicle, crows cawing in the distance, birds trilling. At the top of a pine tree, a red squirrel bounded from branch to branch. The sounds of this life began to fade, making way for the sounds of the next. Amaruq needed to concentrate, he did not want to miss a second of his own death. He wanted to be ready for the shudder before the final moment. He had seen it in dying animals. They would lie still, their eyes wide, and then suddenly their flanks would start to quiver. They would look about, searching for the last place to settle their gaze. Then their muscles would tense, they would let out a long breath, and their limbs would grow slack as life evaporated. Amaruq wanted to feel that rippling tremor, to decide what to look upon as he died.

Darkness began to draw in and, with it, the bitter cold. The doctor signalled to Amaruq that they had to take him back to the hospital. Amaruq shook his head. "I'm sorry," the doctor said in English, "but we can't stay." Much as he wanted to respect Amaruq's wishes, the doctor could not risk being accused of causing death by negligence. Hypothermia could kill this man and he would be legally responsible.

The nurse went to look for the students and returned after a few minutes. They carried Amaruq back to the tent. The puddles in the wheel ruts had frozen and they had to be careful not to slip. The trucks were still lined up, engines idling. The night shift had begun. People were coming and going. Amaruq watched them. Dark figures framed against the light that blazed from the towers, flooding the camp. Sounds, smells, murmurs, shouts.

At the hospital, they lifted Amaruq back onto a bed. This time he was not alone. There were two labourers in the tent, one in the bed opposite, the other four bunks away. One had had his fingers crushed while repairing a tow truck's engine, the other had fallen from a freight truck and landed on his back. The first man was discharged without much delay. Among the workers, severed fingers and a bloody bandage were considered a badge of honour, a proof of diligence and hard work. Although in pain, the labourer felt a sense of pride. The other man had been concussed, but was recovering quickly.

The doctors lit the lamps. Amaruq saw the gas mantle catch light. Coleman lamps, his grandfather used to call them. In his house, they had been a luxury lit only when he had important visitors like trappers, hunters and fur traders; people like his father.

As he watched the mantle blaze, Amaruq was reminded of child-hood evenings spent watching his mother and grandfather and their guests. Suddenly, he felt his scalp prickle. Death, thought Amaruq. A shudder ran down the back of his neck. He tried to say something, but choked on the words. He could hear distant sounds. Involuntarily, Amaruq's head began to arch backwards. He strained to keep his eyes on the Coleman lamp. His grandfather, his father, the station, the wolves, the grasslands, the mountains, the snow. Countless memories, all focused on the blazing mantle. He exhaled, tried to inhale again, but no longer had the strength. The doctor noticed and rushed to help him. It was too late. Amaruq's face was already tilted towards the sheets, his eyes still fixed on the gas lamp. The doctor made a cursory examination, then covered Amaruq's body with a blanket. "Go tell the engineer," he said to one of the doctors. The young man left and the doctor turned to look at the clock that hung from one of the tentpoles. In a notebook, he wrote: "Amaruq Mackenzie, March 15, Time of Death: 19:18."

According to accounts by twentieth-century anthropologists, when a child died, the Amahuaca people native to the south-eastern Amazon basin would place the remains in a large cauldron and boil them until the flesh fell away from the bones.

When the mixture had cooled, the mother would take out the bones and grind them into a fine powder which she mixed with corn flour until it formed a shapeless dough. When she had finished, she would devour the dough between sighs and sobs.

Once the mother had performed this ritual, the rest of the tribe would take the boiled flesh and bury it. Meanwhile, the mother would withdraw and weep as her son or daughter returned to the belly whence they had come.

Mothers

The woman walks along the street. Stops. Turns. Comes back. She is obviously nervous. She doesn't know I'm watching from the rooftop. She turns around again, then turns back. She approaches my house. Stops in front of the door. Rings the bell. Glances up and down the street. It takes a while before someone comes to the door. Since Carlos died, everything takes a while in my family. As though death has disrupted our internal clocks by seventeen seconds. Mine is also disrupted. It takes me a while to answer questions, to wake, to swallow, to drink, to piss, to think. Seventeen seconds behind standard time.

She waits uncertainly. This is the woman who saved my life. Who reacted quickly and took me to the hospital. If it weren't for her, I'd have bled out right there on the pavement. She doesn't see me. If she looked up she'd see me watching her. My mother opens the door. They look at each other. You can see the seventeen-second delay in my mother's eyes. The woman asks if they can talk. My mother thinks for seventeen seconds, then nods. They stand there, not talking. The woman has asked if they can talk but both are silent. In their different ways, both have been left orphans by their sons. Or widows by their sons. The mother of the murderer visits the mother of the victim. They understand each other. They know what it means to carry a child. These women, who give life, who nurture life, stare at each other. They are enveloped in the plastic film of death. A transparent but impenetrable barrier. The woman summons the courage to say: "I'm so sorry." Although she speaks in barely a whisper, I hear her. My mother looks at the mother of the man who murdered her son and is lost for words. "We both lost a son," the killer's mother says, "because mine is dead to me." My mother stares at her, it is obvious that she was not expecting this. She swallows hard. She is on the verge of tears. She balls her fists to stop herself from crying. The woman continues: "I can't forgive myself for what my son did to yours. I'm dying inside too." My mother cannot speak. For some time now, words have formed a knot inside her. They are snarled inside her. I watch from the rooftop. Eventually, my mother manages to say a few words. Words filled with pain, with grief. "Why did he do it?" she asks the murderer's mother as though somehow she might know the reason, and somehow the woman answers: "He did it because, in him, god is a disease."

The woman knows her son behaves as he does because of his hatred of her. She knows this hatred began to take root when she was fucked by a man on a beach in Acapulco. "El Basta", the bastard son of an unbalanced, promiscuous woman, an only child cosseted by his dyspeptic grandfather who constantly judged his daughter. "God is a disease with him." My mother looks at the woman and, without a word, steps forward and puts her arms around her. My mother cries. Her back is racked by sobs. The woman cries too. They hold each other tight. I am the sole witness to their solidarity. Which carries a greater burden of pain? The murderer's mother's anguish must have been unbearable, for her to find the courage to face the mother of the man her son had murdered. She did not come to justify, she did not come to beg forgiveness on his behalf. She came to share her grief, to console the mother who lost a son because of hers. The women part. They dab their tears. The woman takes a step back and says goodbye. They do not touch again. With their embrace, they said all they needed to say. My mother watches her walk away.

Three years later my mother would die with my father in a car accident. A few months later, the mother of the murderer would loop a rope over a beam in her house and secure it with a knot. She would climb onto a chair and tie the rope around her neck. She would take a deep breath, kick the chair away and hang herself. Some days later, my enemy would return to the barrio for her funeral. The one diseased with god. My enemy. Revenge within my grasp.

At 6 a.m., the doorbell rang. I woke to find King in my arms, still alive and snoring loudly. Looking at the clock, I assumed it was Avilés. I was right. As soon as I opened the door, he smiled. "You had breakfast yet?" Of course I hadn't had breakfast. Only a lunatic like Avilés would think anyone has breakfast before 6 a.m. on Saturday morning. "No," I replied. "Do you like fishing?" I nodded, not understanding why he was asking. "I'm taking you fishing for breakfast," he said. The thought of fish for breakfast wasn't exactly appealing, but he was so enthusiastic that I agreed.

We climbed into the Maverick and took the motorway towards Toluca. We stopped just outside Mexico City at La Marquesa, a national park nestled between forests and streams. It often snowed here, and when we were kids my father would take us here to play in the snow. We had even seen a group of French competitive anglers (from a town called Barcelonnette) "seeding" the streams with rainbow trout so that they could fish for them on Sundays.

Led by a man called Donneaud, they showed up with thousands of fry in huge plastic bags of water oxygenated by aquarium pumps powered by the car's cigarette lighter. We walked over to watch them being freed. As soon as they emerged from the bags, the tiny trout swam towards the shadowy waters by the riverbank and drifted there, facing upstream. Being natural predators, they would wait in the shadows for their prey to head downstream. In less than ten seconds, the small fish had obeyed their hunting instinct.

I assumed that Avilés would park near one of the streams and take out rods and hooks, but instead he drove to a wooden cabin by the side of the motorway with a sign that read: YOU FISH, WE COOK. As we got out of the car, two women appeared. Avilés was clearly a regular, because they greeted him affectionately.

I thought the women would lead us to a stream where we could fish for trout; instead they took us to a little muddy pond where five bamboo poles with hooks and sinkers were propped against a wooden fence. "Take your pick," Avilés said. I chose a rod and he chose another. He stretched out his arms and breathed in deeply. "You have no idea how much I love being in touch with nature," he said. In touch with nature? The motorway was less than fifty metres away. Trailers, trucks and cars hurtled past at ninety kilometres an hour. For my father, being "in touch with nature" meant driving down remote dirt tracks until the car could go no further, then hiking for kilometres into the forests up in the sierra. For Avilés, it was enough just being fifteen minutes from the city.

One of the women brought us soft bread rolls. We moistened scraps and threaded them onto the hooks, then cast our lines into the pond full of trout fattened with chicken feed. After only two attempts, I reeled in an enormous trout that weighed a kilo and a half. Avilés caught a smaller one. He called it Small Fry, because it was the perfect size for a frying pan. The women weighed them and asked if we wanted them fried, battered, barbecued or cooked in foil. Avilés asked for his in foil, I asked for mine to be grilled.

We sat at a patio table overlooking Lake Salazar, ringed by wooded hills. Avilés asked about Colmillo. I told him I'd taken off the muzzle and the chain. "He didn't attack you?" he asked, incredulous. "No," I replied. "Congratulations, I didn't think you'd be able to control him. You've proved to him that you're the alpha male."

The trout arrived. They'd grilled mine over pine coals and the pink flesh was flavoured by the smoke. Avilés's came wrapped in aluminium foil, steamed with carrots, onions and chilli. I preferred the taste of mine, it was a truly delicious breakfast.

A young woman came over selling plastic cups of crayfish. As children, Carlos and I used to catch them and keep them in a bucket of water collected from the same stream. Chlorinated tap water would kill them, so whenever we had to refill the bucket, we used rain-water. When startled, the crayfish would dart backwards, propelled by their tails. They reproduced quickly, and we would usually end up with more than two hundred. Later, in the countryside with our parents, we would return them to the stream where we had caught them.

Avilés bought two cups and handed one to me. "How are things going?" he asked. "Going," I answered. "Better or worse?" I didn't know what to say. They couldn't get any worse, but I wasn't sure they were getting better either. My future was too murky to be intuited.

There was too much lime on the crayfish, but Avilés didn't seem to care. He gobbled one after the other. "And how's it going with your girlfriend?" he asked. I had never thought of Chelo as my girlfriend. Back in the seventies, the word referred to someone you had formally asked, "Will you be my girlfriend?" If you didn't ask, the relationship wasn't official. Maybe that's what had gone wrong with Chelo and me. "Not going," I said. "Why?" he asked. Should I tell him about my "girlfriend" being unfaithful? About the two guys she'd screwed? About her clinical depression? Yes, I should. This was my chance to drain some of the poison flowing through my veins. "Because she hooked up with other guys," I said. Avilés looked at me, perplexed. "What do you mean by 'hooked up'? Dated? Kissed?" I took a moment to answer. The thought of saying the words "she fucked other guys" made me feel sick. Black vomit scalding my throat. "She slept with them," I said. Avilés must have sensed my pain, because he squeezed my forearm. "Shit, man," he said.

We were quiet for a while. "Did she tell you or did you find out from someone else?" he asked. "She told me." "Well, at least she had the guts to tell you to your face. Did she apologise?" I nodded. "D'you think she meant it?" I didn't know. "Look, the real question isn't whether or not she meant it, it's whether you choose to believe her."

We headed back to the city. On the way Avilés stopped to buy a sheepskin, the kind you use as a rug or to throw over an armchair. Getting back into the car, he tossed it to me. "Here you go, a little present – now you can have a wolf in sheep's clothing," he said, cackling uncontrollably at what he thought was another brilliant joke. Then he opened the glovebox and pulled out a cassette. "Here's another present," he said. He slotted it into the tape player. It was a recording of grey wolves. Howling, barking, growling. He had bought it from one of the circus clowns, who collected sounds from the natural world. Avilés suggested I play it to Colmillo and watch his reaction.

We got back to my place. I thanked him for breakfast and the presents. As I got out, Avilés stopped me. "You've got more guts than you think," he said, smiling. "I'll be in touch the day after tomorrow."

After he drove off, I went up to Carlos's room, brought down the cassette player, set it on the kitchen counter and opened the door to the yard. Colmillo was lying under the outside sink. The moment he heard the lone wolf's howls, he stood up. It was the first time he had ever heard one of his own kind. Curious, he tilted his head to one side and began to growl anxiously.

I stopped the tape. Colmillo kept looking expectantly towards the door. I pressed fast-forward. A group of wolves howling. Colmillo joined in. At last, he had a pack he could howl with.

I let the tap play for half an hour. Colmillo reacted differently to the recording. I'd never noticed before how expressive his face was. Avilés had referred to him as "your wolf". I'd never thought of Colmillo as mine, he was more like an unmanageable guest who had destroyed my house and would leave at some point. For the first time, I considered our relationship. Colmillo was just as much my wolf as King was my dog. He depended on me for his survival. Unlike King, he did not offer unconditional affection and loyalty, but he was a perfect example of nature that cannot be tamed. King was a comfort to me, whereas Colmillo challenged me. And if anything could rouse me from my stupor, it was definitely that crazy wolf.

403

I turned off the tape player, went up to my parents' room, picked up the phone and called Chelo.

Robert was convinced that Amaruq belonged to his clan. Over the radio, he asked the secretary in the Whitehorse office to contact his cousins and uncles, to ask whether they knew Amaruq or had heard of him. "If they don't know who he is," he added, "call up every Mackenzie in the phone directory."

The doctors pressed him to make a decision about Amaruq's remains. They could not be kept in the tool store, wrapped in a blanket for want of a body bag. It was so cold that the body had not yet begun to decompose, but the weather was beginning to turn, and one balmy morning was all it would take for decomposition to set in. If he could not track down a family member who would claim the body, it should be buried in an unmarked grave.

Robert pleaded for more time. He did not want Amaruq to be buried without his loved ones having time to say goodbye. It was agreed he could have forty-eight hours, after which, if no-one had claimed the body, it would be sent to Cooper for burial.

Robert gave orders that the vet was to wait for him, regardless of how late he arrived back. The vet visited only every two weeks, and Robert did not want him to leave without examining the emaciated wolf, who was still unable to stand up.

He took off again in the helicopter and flew over the mountains. With every flight, he became more convinced that the oil pipe should run alongside the mountains. Many disagreed, arguing that avalanches or landslides might break the pipes, leading to oil leaks or uncontrollable fires. The losses to the company could be enormous. To counter this objection, Robert suggested that the slopes be shored up with containment walls, and he designed a system of automatic valves to control the flow of the oil. When others argued that this would add to the cost, Robert pointed out that the current route was sixty kilometres

404

longer and consequently more expensive. The board of directors and the C.E.O. were weighing up the pros and cons of each proposal. The decision was edging closer and Robert urgently needed to present his argument.

Robert enjoyed his work. Within two years, this pipeline would reach Vancouver, fulfilling southern Canada's energy needs. He had been involved in the construction of other pipelines and understood their impact on the lives of those who lived in towns and cities, understood that every home, every kitchen, every car owed much to his efforts and that of the hundreds of workers and engineers, something that gave them a deep sense of satisfaction. But in exchange Robert had paid a high price: he saw little of his family, he had missed his children's first words, their first steps, their school events. His wife was tired of singlehandedly caring for their children – taking them to the doctor, waking early to make breakfast, helping with their homework, refereeing their arguments, putting them to bed – and exhausted by the daily household chores: the washing, the cooking, the ironing. She and her friends called themselves "Pipeline Widows".

Robert, too, was beginning to feel worn-out. His work involved a constant battle – in winter against the snow, rain, cold and risk of pneumonia, in summer against the heat, humidity and mosquitoes that brought diarrhoea, dysentery, fever and parasites. Often, he returned from his expeditions long after dark, drenched and freezing, with no time to shower or even rub down his body with a hot flannel; still shivering, he would strip off his clothes and get into bed because the working day began at 5 a.m.

When he returned from his mission, Robert immediately went in search of the vet and told him about the wolf and the circumstances in which they'd found him. The vet was amazed by the story. In the years he had spent living among the indigenous peoples of northern Canada, he had never heard of anyone trapping a wolf alive, tying it to a sled and hauling it up a mountain.

Examining Nujuaqtutuq, the vet found signs of malnutrition and acute anaemia. The animal's muscles had atrophied from lack of movement, the right leg fracture had not healed, the tendons were ruptured, and there were early signs of gangrene.

When Robert asked what he could do, the vet looked down at the wounded wolf with his bald tail and protruding ribs as he lay lifelessly on the floor. "Put him down," he said. "I don't see much chance of him surviving." Robert shook his head. "That's not an option," he said. "What else?" The vet suggested he might be fed and hydrated intravenously and later given minced meat, milk and eggs. The necrotic tissue could be debrided and the leg put in a cast in the hope that the fracture might heal. The wolf would have to be kept away from the dogs. In his weakened state, any infection could kill him. Even then, the vet insisted, he felt sure that the wolf would die. Robert knew the animal would fight. There was no doubt in his mind.

Boxers originated as a hybrid of two now extinct breeds: the Bullenbeisser, meaning "bull-biter", and the Old English bulldog, bred to control cattle in slaughterhouses and farmyards.

Both breeds were also used for hunting. The Bullenbeisser was capable of defeating wolves in fights to the death. The Old English bulldog could grip a wild pig three times its weight in its powerful jaws, until the hunters arrived to spear it.

Bullenbeissers were large and powerful dogs, similar in size to the Argentine dogo. With brown-striped fur, they were descendants of the war mastiffs in the Roman army. Old English bulldogs were different from contemporary bulldogs: taller, stronger and more agile, nothing like today's chubby-cheeked dogs which pant heavily after the smallest exertion.

Boxers were first bred in Germany in the late nineteenth century by Friedrich Robert, Elard König and Rudolph Höpner, who were attempting to produce a loyal and affectionate guard dog of medium size, with a muscular, symmetrical body. In cross-breeding, they favoured docile, gentle specimens and avoided aggressive or disobedient animals. Boxers quickly became popular as a perfect family dog: good with children, calm and placid in temperament, yet always prepared to defend their master.

By the early twentieth century, the Bullenbeisser and the Old English bulldog had died out. Dog breeders focused on producing obedient, manageable specimens, and cross-bred them so many times that the earlier breeds became extinct. Today, they can be seen only in rare photographs or drawings of the period.

Re-encounters

You are holed up in your house, Humberto, alone with your hatred and your fear. You dare not go out, the ghosts have left you with no choice but to lock yourself away. You stare at the beam from which your mother hung herself. Her suicide note left you devastated, guilt is eating away at you, fuelled by your religious fervour, you are slowly falling apart. Your fear is palpable. Anyone seeing you from a distance would recognise it. You are lost. And you are terrified, Humberto, you are terrified.

Your god is being asphyxiated. You and all those who murder in his name have sucked up his oxygen. He cannot breathe. He flounders and gasps. He is wasting away. Now that you need him, he cannot answer. He is a weak and shrivelled god. Go on, summon the paltry remains that you call god. Call him, demand that he show himself. Let's see whether your prayers are answered, whether they can stop the rot of your mother's bloated corpse.

Humberto, the world keeps spinning, and, as it spins, winnows the chaff of time. The past slithers from the depths, lumbering like a great baleful lizard, sinking its teeth into the present. Or maybe you thought that the past remains forever buried in the graveyard of history? You fool. The past reappears when you least expect it, and yours is daubed with blood and death. This body over which you sit keeping vigil, this hanged woman you hated while she was alive, this purple, swollen face, this is your past, and it has caught you up. Or maybe you believed your uncompromising judgements of your mother would have no consequences? Maybe you believed she could endure your sanctimonious splutterings unscathed? Fool! Your hatred killed her.

Let's see who is the stronger now, Humberto. I am rising from the pits of agony. You have only just begun your descent. Soon, you will understand what it means to be caught in the quagmire of death. And there I will defeat you, Humberto. There, in the underworld, we will fight to the death and I will vanquish you. I will destroy you and your god. I will destroy you both.

When she picked up the phone, Chelo did not give me a chance to talk about us. She launched into an explanation of how she had been studying King's problem and how she had talked to her tutors about possible treatments. Like the majority of crossbreeds, she explained, boxers were prone to various genetic defects, including a predisposition to heart disease known as "boxer cardiomyopathy" which could result in fainting, arrhythmia, tachycardia, congestive heart failure and even heart attacks. The condition could be aggravated if the dog experienced acute emotional stress. Stress, she said, caused the arteries to contract, reducing blood flow to the heart, forcing the body to release adrenalin and speeding up the heart rate. It was this combination of factors that had caused King's heart failure.

She rattled off the diagnosis like a professional. She was convinced that, with the right treatment, King could recover. She hung up before I could say a word, and fifteen minutes later she showed up with cortisone injections and propranolol and amiodarone tablets. She was relieved to find that Colmillo no longer lived in the house but out in the yard. "If King is to get better, we have to remove the cause of his stress," she said.

We went up to Carlos's room and found King on the bed. He wagged his tail but was not strong enough to get up. Chelo asked me to hold him while she injected cortisone into his rump. She fed him half a tablet of propranolol and one of amiodarone, clamping his jaw shut until he swallowed. The cortisone would ease the arterial swelling and improve blood flow to his heart, propranolol – a beta blocker – would limit the uptake of adrenaline, and the amiodarone would control the arrhythmia.

Chelo wrote the dosages on a piece of paper and gave it to me. "You need to give him half a propranolol three times a day, and one tablet of amiodarone morning and night. I'll come by to give him the cortisone injections," she said, stroking King's back. "He won't die, I promise you."

We lapsed into silence. She reached out to touch me, but I pulled away. She smiled sadly. "I love you, Juan Guillermo," she said. We were silent again. Beside us, King was panting. Thirteen years of living side by side. My dog. I looked at Chelo. The afternoon light streaming through the window lit her face, making her eyes seem greener. There was so much I wanted to say, so much I wanted her to feel, so much rage and love, so much confusion and uncertainty, yet all I could come out with was an idiotic question: "Do you want to be my girlfriend?" She smiled. "Are you really asking?" I nodded. She burst out laughing. "Wow, it sounds so corny." I wasn't sure whether I should laugh too. My proposal was both preposterous and entirely necessary. "Yes," she said softly, "I want to be your girlfriend." She moved closer and took my hand. "Nobody's ever asked me that before," she said. "I always assumed I'd tell the first guy who did to go fuck himself, but, thinking about it, it's the nicest question I've ever been asked." Then a thought occurred to her, her expression changed. She was serious for a few seconds, then looked intently at me. "And do you want to be my boyfriend?" she asked. "Yes." "So does this mean you forgive me?" No, I would never forgive her. And this was how we would spend the rest of our lives together, traces of pain distancing me from her. It was as though my homeland had been invaded by an enemy army that had left a trail of ruin and devastation. Yet, in spite of everything, it was still my homeland. No, I could not forgive her. Nor could I ever stop loving her. My life would be more painful without her than with her, even if it were haunted by the spectre of her promiscuity. "No, I don't forgive you," I said. Chelo said nothing for a moment. "I swear I'll never hurt you again," she said.

She stayed for the rest of the afternoon and helped me clean the house. She took her clothes off, keeping on only her shoes so as not to cut the soles of her feet. I didn't feel able to take off my clothes. I needed more time to recover our lost intimacy.

I watched her as she swept the floors. She hummed a tune, intent on her work. She was thin. During her last bout of depression, she had barely eaten. Her ribs protruded; her buttocks had lost some of their roundness. Yet she was beautiful. Incredibly beautiful.

"I want my little potion," she said, throwing her arms around my neck. I wanted to kiss her, hold her, never let her go. I wanted to hit her, push her, throw her out of the house. We made love. I lifted her up, laid her on the dining table and, without undressing, I pushed into her. She clung to me as she climaxed. I didn't come. Consumed by jealousy, my body refused to respond.

That night, Chelo got dressed to go. As she buttoned her blouse, she turned and said: "Can I ask you a question?" I nodded. "What happened to Carlos's savings?" "What savings?" I asked. "The money he earned from the chinchillas and from selling 'merchandise'," she said, using the word Carlos always used. "I think he spent it," I said. She shook her head. "No, he didn't spend it. A few weeks before he was murdered, he showed me his bank statements. He'd deposited the money in a bunch of different banks so that if he was caught they wouldn't find it all." I had no idea what she was talking about. The sums Chelo was talking about sounded astronomical, but a quick calculation of the earnings of both businesses proved the numbers tallied. It was a fortune.

She asked if my parents had claimed it. "I don't think so," I said. "They never knew about Carlos's business ventures." I should claim it, she insisted, otherwise the banks would keep it.

We searched Carlos's room for the bank statements. Our search disturbed King, preventing him from getting to sleep. He kept turning to look at us. He would close his eyes, snore a little and then wake again. We tried to work as quietly as possible since, as Chelo reminded me, it was important he not be stressed.

We emptied the drawers of Carlos's clothes, leafed through all his books, checked the pockets of his jackets and trousers, climbed on chairs to check the top of the wardrobe, lifted the carpet to check for cubby holes, searched the sleeves of his L.P.s, opened the tins where he kept pencils and pens, even took down the bathroom mirror. Nothing, not a trace of any bank statements.

I was afraid that Comandante Zurita and his men had found them. Maybe, even now, Zurita was squandering Carlos's millions. Chelo thought it was unlikely. Carlos had told her that my parents and I were his sole heirs, so court proceedings would have been necessary to appropriate his assets. The money had to be in the various banks where Carlos had lodged it. If we could find deposit slips, bank statements or any official document, I could insist that they return his savings. If we could not find any documentation, Chelo suggested we visit the nearest banks and ask whether they held an account in Carlos's name. Getting them to reveal confidential information would be difficult since their profits depended on their secrecy and strict rules. I doubted that they would be keen to give back the money three years after Carlos's death.

In the end, we admitted defeat, switched off the lights and left King to sleep. It was almost midnight. Chelo asked if she could stay the night. It was late and it was raining. I said yes.

We went into my parents' room. She undressed and slipped between the sheets, laid her head on my chest and fell into a deep sleep. I lay awake. So many thoughts were running through my mind. I listened to King's snoring, to Colmillo's restless pacing in the yard, to Chelo's gentle breathing. I had to find some way to remake myself. To build a future over the ruins. I wanted this woman who was sleeping next to me to be by my side forever.

At 6 a.m. I shook Chelo and asked whether she had a lecture at seven. "Yes," she said sleepily, kissing me on the mouth. She was at her most lovely first thing in the morning, never sweeter or more affectionate than when half-asleep. I loved her smell, unmasked by soap or perfume.

She clambered out of bed, phoned a friend to pick her up and then stumbled into the shower. I made scrambled eggs and brought it up to the room where I found her brushing her hair. When she saw the tray on the bedside table, she covered my face with kisses.

After breakfast, she went to give King his injection. He was still lying on the bed, but had got up in the night to pee in the shower – a sure sign the treatment was having an effect.

We heard Chelo's friend honk her horn. I walked her to the door. She took my hand as we went down the stairs. When we got to the hall, she cradled my face in both hands and kissed me. "Don't forget that I'm your girlfriend," she said. She walked towards the car, turning as she reached the door. "I'll be back for lunch at two o'clock." She got in and waved through the window.

I went back upstairs to feed the parakeets, but they were gone. I searched the house. They were nowhere to be found. I went into my parents' room. Chelo had left the window open. Leaning out, I spotted Vodka and Whisky perched in the branches of a cedar tree on the central reservation that ran down the middle of the avenue. I was thrilled to see them out there, free. They had finally ventured beyond the confines of the house. I put some birdseed and a bowl of water on the sill, and left the window open in case they decided to come back.

The vet reset the broken bones and put a cast on the leg. Nujuaqtutuq remained perfectly still as the bandage was applied. A cannula was inserted into his left foreleg and an I.V. drip hung on a stand next to him. The vet calibrated the infusion rate to ensure Nujuaqtutuq was kept hydrated and fed glucose. Before he left, he stressed how important it was to get the wolf to eat.

Robert went to the camp kitchen and prepared a batch of minced meat, then went back and, squatting down next to Nujuaqtutuq, pushed small balls of the mixture between his jaws. Weak as he was, the wolf barely managed to swallow three. Robert covered him with a blanket and left the pen.

As he was heading back to his tent, he was stopped by Alex, who told him they had found someone who thought they might know Amaruq. The secretary had put him in touch with Kirk, a distant cousin, who said he remembered being taken as a boy by his father to meet a blue-eyed Inuit and his mother. He did not remember their names or where they lived, but he was sure that his father would. His father, Charles Mackenzie, had moved to a lakeside cabin near the Alaskan border and there was no way of getting in touch with him. Robert asked Alex to contact the Mounted Police and request that an officer be sent out to find him and, if possible, bring him to the camp.

Back in his tent, Robert set about reviewing the work reports for the past months. Tomorrow was an important day: the C.E.O. and the board of directors were flying in to the camp to decide on the best route for the pipeline.

Robert had prepared conscientiously. Each of the various proposals was accompanied by folders containing detailed studies. He was familiar with every aspect of the proposed route, the costs, the viability, the forests to be traversed, the topography, the average wind speed for every week of the year, the native fauna that might be affected by the pipeline. He was aware that his plan had met with intense resistance, but could not understand why people who were less well informed should question his work.

The meeting with the C.E.O. and the board was heated. His recommendations were fiercely opposed by the financial consultants, who reiterated the risk of avalanches or landslides that could cause a pipe-

414

line set on piles to burst. Robert was irritated. It was obvious that they had not read the topographic report, or the plans for the retaining walls. What was the point of him slaving over the proposal for months and months, if he was going to be questioned by a string of desk jockeys? He had personally covered every metre of the possible routes. By helicopter, by dog sled, by snowmobile, on foot and on horseback. Why had the consultants not discussed the proposal with the field engineers who, like him, worked on the icy plains and mountain ranges, rather than take the word of pen-pushers in heated offices hundreds of kilometres away?

Robert argued forcefully, rebutting their criticisms point by point. His folders of detailed reports put his opponents to shame and made it seem as though they were merely inventing objections. Eventually, the consultants gave up and the directors were convinced. His preferred route was chosen, and the C.E.O. congratulated Robert on his precise and solid arguments. The camp would begin the process of relocation the following day so that work on the new route could progress.

Robert stepped out of the conference tent. It had begun to snow and already a layer of white powder had settled on the earthmovers and the trucks. He heaved a sigh of satisfaction. He had taken the objections to his proposal personally, but in the end he had prevailed.

He climbed aboard a snowmobile and headed back to see Nujuaqtutuq. He had to prepare the wolf for the imminent move. He picked up the animal, laid him in the basket, loaded it into the snowmobile and rode back to his tent. He set the basket down next to his heater. The wolf lay very still. Robert pulled up a chair and sat watching him. "Nujuaqtutuq," he called softly. The wolf raised his head slightly, looked at the man for a moment and then lay down again.

Actaeon so loved hunting that he had bred a pack of eighty blood-hounds to help him corner his prey. One morning, he and his companions set off into the woodland with the hounds. For hours they tracked deer without success until, exhausted, the huntsmen decided to rest.

Refusing to admit defeat, Actaeon continued the hunt alone. Aimlessly, he roamed the woodland trails until he came across a pool of crystal-clear water. There, he surprised Diana, goddess of the forests and the hunt, bathing, surrounded by her nymphs.

Actaeon stood and gazed upon the naked goddess. Seeing the hunter, the nymphs cried out in fear and quickly covered Diana's sacred body. Still Actaeon did not withdraw, so captivated was he by the beauty of the goddess. Diana reached for her spear and her bow to punish this man for his audacity, but they were on the edge of the pool, beyond her reach.

Incensed, she splashed him with water from the pool, and raged: "Now you can tell the story of seeing the goddess naked – if you can still speak." No sooner did the droplets touch him than Actaeon underwent a metamorphosis. His ears grew longer, antlers sprouted from his head, his hands and feet were transformed into hooves.

Actaeon took flight, covering a great distance, marvelling that he was so swift in his speed, not knowing what had befallen him. Exhausted, he slowed his pace, and went to drink from a stream. Seeing his reflection in the water, he realised with horror he had been transformed into a deer. Hearing his dogs baying, he thought that they were coming to his aid. He quickly realised his mistake: the pack was hunting him. Terrified, he tried to run, but had gone no more than twenty paces when his hounds caught up and snapped at his legs. Actaeon tried to cry out to them to stop, but the only sound that came was the grunt of a stag. He kicked out to free himself, but the hounds surrounded him until he fell. In despair, Actaeon watched as his friends arrived to goad them on. He called for help but once again made only a faint bleating sound. The dogs ripped him to pieces alive. He suffered a horrifying death.

Hearing the snapping jaws tear insolent Actaeon limb from limb, Diana smiled, satisfied. No mortal now could boast of having seen her naked.

Car

The phone rang the moment Chelo left. "I found your parents' car," Pato said when I picked up. "Where?" "In a breaker's yard in Ixtapalapa." After my parents' accident, the car was impounded by the Policía Federal de Caminos pending the investigation. In all the confusion of identifying their bodies, buying coffins and engaging a funeral director, I had forgotten to claim it. Only days later did I remember and, when I phoned to find out where it was, the Policía Federal de Caminos gave evasive answers and told me to "call again tomorrow". I gave it up as a lost cause, but Pato promised he would find it.

Every day for weeks he called the police, who were as vague with him as they had been with me. Armed with the details of the model and the licence plate, Pato took buses to every breaker's yard and car pound. It was a Herculean task, and one for which I will always be grateful. The owners of the breakers' yards offered little help, in fact they did their best to frustrate his search. After a certain period, any impounded car became "subject to public sale". In other words, the owners could strip them and sell off the parts.

Pato found the car in a corner of a scrapyard known locally as "La Ford". The car was crammed between two school buses. One was little more than a rusty shell; the other had been involved in a head-on collision, and the engine had burst through the bonnet, twisted and tangled like spilled entrails.

The windows of my parents' car were broken. Rain had rotted the fabric seat covers. There was a stagnant pool in the footwell. Pato told me the car stank. He didn't think I should go see it. He had found it upsetting, and could only imagine how much it would distress me to see the last place where my parents had talked, breathed, lived. "Give me the paperwork. I'll get it released and have it taken to the mechanic," he said. I refused. Painful though it might be, it was my moral duty to claim it.

We caught the bus on Avenida Ermita and headed into the most dangerous area of Ixtapalapa. The "Curve", the district where "La Ford" was located, was surrounded by shanty towns and rubbish tips. Dangerous slums. I taped my knife to my wrist and slipped a knuckle-duster into my pocket, just in case.

The bus ride took almost two hours. Avenida Ermita was lined with trucks on their way to Puebla, and the bus stopped on every corner to pick up passengers.

The gate of "La Ford" was located near the top of a hill. Behind the railings, the breaker's yard stretched endlessly downhill, the rusted skeletons of hundreds of cars and buses piled on top of each other in the waterlogged ground. On the surface of fetid puddles floated blue-grey oil slicks.

We walked in. Pato asked one of the workers where we could find "Santaclós", the guy who ran the place. A hulking man with shoulder-length hair and a long, thick beard appeared. Even from five metres away, the stench of alcohol, sweat and greasy food was overwhelming. He asked if I was the owner of the vehicle. I told him I was the only child of the owner, who had died with my mother in that very car. He asked me for proof of ownership. I handed him a photocopy. I wouldn't have dared wander around this barrio with the actual papers, it would be like carrying a blank cheque – though it seemed unlikely that anyone would want a car with a crushed roof, flat tyres and broken windows.

Santaclós examined the photocopy. He had huge fat hands and the fingernails and the creases on his palms were black with grease. There was enough food in his beard to feed a family of mice for weeks. He looked like he'd never washed in his life.

"Sorry, kid, I can only release the car if you bring the original documents," he said. I told him I only had the photocopy. "Gonna be tough to let you have it then, 'less you're feeling frisky." I had to be "frisky" to the tune of a hundred pesos. The fat man plucked the notes from my hand with his greasy fingers and grinned. "Guess this should be enough to treat me and my buds here to a barbecue and a couple of brews."

He walked over to a corrugated iron shack with a T.V. aerial sticking through the roof and outside it the back seat of a pickup truck acting as a makeshift sofa. The fat man settled himself on the "sofa". Pato told me this was his office.

We walked between rows of wrecked cars, some piled on top of each other, each with its own tragic story. How many fathers, sons, friends, sisters had died inside them?

We reached my parents' car. Just seeing it left me gasping for breath. I felt dizzy. I hadn't thought it would hit me that hard. I leaned against one of the school buses, my legs shaking. I had thought it would not affect me, that enough time had passed, but seeing the car like this, destroyed, in the middle of a muddy scrapyard surrounded by junk, was like a punch in the gut.

Pato grabbed my arm. "You want to go, Cinco?" I shook my head. "Give me a couple of minutes, I'll be fine." My mother had taught me how to breathe to calm down: "Breathe in for a count of six and out for a count of six."

I straightened up and approached the car. There were still shards of glass on the dashboard. The steering wheel was twisted to the right. A plastic keyring with a scorpion inside it hung from the rear-view mirror. My father had bought it in Durango. I was lucky nobody had stolen it.

Hardly had my parents hurtled off the cliff than the people who lived near the crash site showed up to rob them blind. They didn't care that my mother was lying dead, that my father was choking on his own blood, the steering wheel lodged in his chest. They looted anything they could find, stealing their shoes, their suitcases, the spare tyre, my father's jacket, my mother's sweater.

I grabbed the keyring from the mirror and stuffed it into my bag. I turned around. The buckled passenger door was open. I ducked under the crumpled roof and opened the glove box. There was the vehicle licence and the remains of a bar of chocolate, perhaps the last thing my parents ate. The chocolate was dusty and a little mouldy, but I took a small bite. I felt as though I was communing with them.

We went back to Santaclós and asked if he knew of someone with a tow-truck so that we could take the car away. He said that for another hundred pesos he'd tow it to whatever repair shop we chose. I haggled and in the end he accepted fifty.

Santaclós hooked up the tow bar, and a few pieces of bodywork fell onto the muddy ground as he hoisted the car. Pato gathered them up and put them inside the car.

The three of us climbed into the front seat of the tow truck. Fat Santa took up half the space, leaving Pato and me wedged against each other. Since it was a manual, whenever Santa wanted to change gears Pato had to lift his legs and flatten me against the door. And then there was Santa's unbearable reek. Everything about him was rancid: his breath, his hair, his beard, his armpits. The stench was so strong it seemed almost solid. The roof of my mouth felt oily, and it made my nose itch.

We pulled up outside Retorno 104, a workshop that belonged to El Güero – a blonde, blue-eyed, well-built guy from Los Altos de Jalisco. He was a distant cousin of Father Arturo, whom he loathed. El Güero had once been a professional second-division footballer, but had had to give it up because he had problems with booze. He would have been penniless, but his skills as a car mechanic helped him back on his feet. He married, gave up the booze and set up the workshop. He was proud of his talent for fixing wrecks.

Santaclós unhitched the car, wheeled it into the workshop and drove off, leaving a pestilential cloud that took several minutes to dissipate. El Güero and I had already agreed that he would fix the car, then we would sell it and split the profits fifty-fifty. I almost regretted it. How could I let a stranger drive my parents' car, their death carriage? But on the other hand, what masochistic urge was tempting me to keep it?

El Güero walked around the car several times and squatted down to examine every dent. He ran his hand along the rough metal surface and wrote notes in a small notebook with a pencil. "She's going to be difficult to fix, this one," he said. "Needs repainting, a lot of work on the chassis, a new engine, a new rear axle, and that steering wheel will need to be fixed." "What are you saying?" I asked. "That I wouldn't make a profit even if I sold it as new." We made a new deal: we would split any profit sixty/forty.

Pato and I head home. On the way, we don't say a word. We get back. I invite him in. He pretends he's got homework. A lie. Grief is weighing on him. Seeing the car my parents died in has again taken its toll. I insist. He accepts. I open the door. He goes ahead while I lock it behind us. When I catch up, I see that he's standing in the hall, staring at the floor. I don't understand what's happening, but then I see Chelo naked, standing by the dining table. "I told you I'd be back for lunch," she says defensively. Pato, embarrassed, quickly turns and tries to leave. I stop him. "Did you see her naked?" He nods. This guy is my best friend, my brother, but I want to rip out his eyes and toss him into the yard for Colmillo to rip to pieces. "Why did you look at her?" I fume. "How the fuck did I know she'd be in here naked?" Hearing us, Chelo starts to laugh. I want to kill them both. Pato laughs too, still staring at the floor. I feel like hacking his head off and using it as a football; then I start laughing too. Chelo goes upstairs to get dressed. Pato stays for lunch.

*

Charles Mackenzie – Uncle Chuck – arrived at the camp as the sun was setting. After tracking him down to his remote cabin, the Mounties had driven him in a squad car to Beaver Creek. From there he took a bus to Bear Crossing, where he was picked up by the helicopter that brought him to the camp. Twenty-two hours after setting out, he finally arrived. At no point did the police tell him why they needed him.

He was taken to see Robert. The two men had met once or twice at family reunions. Uncle Chuck was Robert's father's second cousin, but he'd always been known as Uncle Chuck. He had made a fortune as a fur trader. In the early days, he sold the pelts to wholesalers, but later he exported them himself, to the U.S., to Mexico and to Europe. He had retired a couple of years earlier, leaving the business to his children, and moved into the out-of-the-way cabin with his wife.

Robert had been packing for the move while he waited. In a few hours, they would strike camp and relocate thirty kilometres to a plain by the river. Heavy snowfall had hindered their relocation, but it was essential that they move soon to avoid delays to the work.

Robert and Chuck greeted each other warmly. If there was one thing that mattered to the Mackenzies, it was their family solidarity. Anyone who shared their surname was welcomed with open arms and offered a place to stay. Chuck looked curiously at the injured wolf lying life-lessly inside the tent. "What's with the wolf?" he asked. "That's what I wanted to talk to you about," Robert said.

He led Charles to the tool shed where Amaruq's body had been stored and pointed to the figure wrapped in blankets. "We found him badly injured in a valley near the summit. He died in the field hospital. His told me his name was Amaruq Mackenzie. I don't suppose you knew him?" Shaken by the mention of the name, Chuck brought a hand to his forehead and breathed deeply. Seeing his distress, Robert asked, "Who was he?" "He was my son." Chuck went over and uncov-ered the body, which was perfectly preserved by the cold. Chuck studied his face. Yes, this was his son. He had the same red hair as

Chuck himself, and the delicate features of his mother. The sweetest woman Chuck had ever known. They had never fought or even argued. She had never demanded anything of him. Not money, not time, not even his attention. She was always happy to see him, to make love to him and hold him, naked, on the nights he visited her house next to the railway station. Chuck had come close to leaving his wife and family for them. When he realised that he would never leave, he stopped visiting. He did not write or offer an explanation. He simply disappeared, and for years this decision weighed on him.

Robert did not pry. Chuck was married to Aunt Rosie, they had three children together, why make him uncomfortable? He explained that they had found Amaruq with a fractured spine next to the body of a mountain goat. It seemed likely that the man had been hunting and both had tumbled into the void. He told him that they had found the wolf in Amaruq's tent and asked if Chuck knew why Amaruq would drag the wolf up a mountain on a sled. Chuck said he had no idea, but that the name Amaruq was an Inuktitut word meaning "wolf".

As they left the shed, Chuck confessed that he hadn't seen Amaruq since the boy was twelve years old. He told Robert about the day he had taken his other children to meet the boy – one of the happiest days of his life. Seeing them all together, he felt relief. The children had played together happily. The problem came on the way home, when his three children bombarded him with questions. Who was this boy? Why had Chuck taken them to meet him? Why was he so affectionate with the boy's mother? Chuck knew that if his wife found out she would never forgive him, she would leave and move back to Calgary. He did not want to be separated from his children, and, in his way, he loved Rosie. He chose the family of four over the family of two. He deserted the woman he loved and stayed with the one who was already by his side.

Robert asked what they should do with the body. Chuck said it should be sent home to his mother so that she could bury him. "And if she's dead?" Robert said. "Then I'll make arrangements." Chuck explained that he wanted to take the wolf back with him. If his son had captured the animal, there had to be a reason, one that his mother would probably understand. Robert told him that they were currently in the process of relocating the camp but that in the morning he could let him have a truck and a driver, to take the body wherever he directed them.

They spent the night in Robert's tent. Although exhausted from his journey, Chuck could not sleep. Over and over, his mind whirled with images of Amaruq as a child, and of his lifeless face. He tossed and turned on the camp bed, grieving for the child he had abandoned.

At 3.00 a.m. they were woken by the men responsible for relocating the camp, who asked them to vacate the tent so it could be struck, and the furniture and equipment packed up. The two men went and sat at a table that had been set up so senior managers could rest while labourers pitched the new camp. It was very cold and fires had been lit to keep them warm.

In the artificial glow of the floodlights, men, machines, trucks, horses and dogs began to move off. Chuck watched as dozens of people trudged through snow and mud while he warmed his hands around a mug of coffee.

At 4.00 a.m., one of the move coordinators came to tell them that the new camp was ready. They climbed into a truck and were driven along a muddy trail. The sky was cloudless now, and moonlight suffused the snow-covered prairies.

At daybreak, Alex came to tell Chuck that a driver and a truck were waiting for him, and Nujuaqtutuq was in a cage in a trailer. They had fitted him with a sled dog harness, to which a chain could be attached if the wolf needed to be taken out.

Robert and Chuck went to the newly erected field hospital to ask the chief medical officer for Amaruq's death certificate and the necessary permits for transporting a body. In the sprawling territories of the Yukon, it was not unusual for human remains to be moved from one place to another, and it was not always easy to find a coffin, so the authorities made it lawful to transport a corpse without a coffin if a doctor had certified that death was due to natural causes. The doctor wrote up a detailed account of Amaruq's injuries and the circumstances in which he had been found, making it clear that death had not resulted from homicide or neglect.

The body, wrapped in blankets, was placed on the flatbed of the truck and secured with ropes. Robert prepared to bid farewell to Chuck. The two men shook hands, then Chuck opened the truck door and got in. Robert looked from his uncle to the shapeless form lying in the bed of the truck. Just as Chuck was about to close the door, Robert waved for him to stop. He could not let him travel alone, could not send him off with a driver to deliver the body of his son as though it were a piece of cargo. "I'll drive you," he said. "Wait a minute."

Robert quickly went to the tent the C.E.O. used as an office. The secretary said he was in a meeting. "Tell him it'll only take a minute, please." The C.E.O. ushered Robert in, puzzled by the urgency. Robert explained that the wounded man found in the mountains had turned out to be the illegitimate son of one of his uncles and that he wanted to go with his uncle to bury the body. He asked for a month's leave, arguing that work was already twelve weeks ahead of schedule.

The C.E.O. agreed and instructed the secretary to give him money for the journey. Robert thanked him for his generosity, left the tent and went to say goodbye to Alex and Jack. He told them he would be back soon and asked that, in his absence, they make sure that his route was followed precisely. The three men hugged and then Robert climbed into the cab. The truck pulled away. They had two hundred and fifty kilometres of dirt road to cover before they would reach a highway.

The car travels along the highway it goes around a

                                                  c
                                                      u
                                                        r
                                                      v
                                                    e
                                          and
                                  my
father loses control.
                              The car
              Z
                  i
                          g
                  Z
          a
                  g
                          s

And my parents

H
      u
            r
                  t
                      l
                          e

towards the

p
r
e
c
i
p
i
c
eeeeeeeeeeeee

The car smashes into the rocks and

          rolls and
             rolls and
                rolls and
                   rolls

until it STOPS.

Silence...........................

My mother dies.   My father is dying.

Silence.

Local

villagers

arrive and

                              s

        d   u
     n   r
       u   r

                    o

them.

They pillage and plunder them.

My father suffocates and he chokes chokes chokes chokes
chokes chokes

                         chokes

They take everything. They care about nothing. Everything for (nothing).
                    (   ) x everything
                           X

        My father watches them. His eyes pleading. Begging for help.
                         Spitting BLOOD.

            They carry on. Looting. My father cannot believe it.
He is dying and they are stealing. He s dying and they ar ste l ng.
                 He is dy ng and th y r s al g.

Until

My father   d   i
              e   s.

The villagers finish l o o t i n g.

And they   leave.

                  leaving my dead parents
                 (my dead parents are left)

429

alone

Letters

I picture her writing the letter. She finishes it. Reads it. Tears it up. Writes it again. Tears it up again. Throws the scraps into the toilet. No-one need know about the confusion she is feeling. She writes again. The handwriting seems alien, a stranger writing in an unknown hand. The strokes are uneven. The cross of the T lists to the right, the tail of the Y curls, the E is a castrated C. As hard as she tries to control her hand she cannot. She trembles as she traces the pen across the paper. She can no longer bear the guilt, the lies, the fights, the hatred, the fleeting moments of happiness, the infatuations. She was daughter to the wrong man and later mother to the wrong man. Why are there so many wrongs in her life? A misshapen family tree twisting upwards and downwards.

And the cancer. The damn cancer. Cells in revolt against the rest of the body. Black, mutinous, infecting healthy tissue with their deadly and irrational rebellion. Cancer of the uterus, the same uterus that sheltered the young man to whom she is now writing, the womb in which the killer grew, the boy diseased with god. Did her son infect her with evil? Was he the beginning of the cancer, the mutant cell that infected all the others?

At what point did Humberto become a stranger? Why did he constantly revile her? She had never done any harm to anyone. Yes, she had slept with drunk men who had beaten and belittled her, who had beaten and belittled her son. Yes, she worked long hours in order to support them, and in doing so had abandoned her son. Yes, she had turned a blind eye to the secret meetings Humberto organised in the basement of her house, never imagining that they might be a breeding ground for fanatical killers. Yes, she had got pregnant aged sixteen to a man whose name and face she cannot remember. Yes, she had tried to abort the child sired by the shadow that had mounted her in an alcoholic haze. But she was not wicked. No. It was life that had caused her to stumble so often, spreading chaos, pulling her this way and that, it was life that had led to all the booze, the dope, the sex, the men, the beatings, the semen, the sweat, the blood. But none of these things justified such rage. She did not deserve her father, or her son, or this cancer. Nothing she had done justified her father calling her a whore, her son calling her a whore, the women who knew she was not a whore calling her a whore.

She writes her last letter to her son-judge-executioner-murderer. It is protest, retribution, revenge, a settling of scores. She wants to rub his nose in the shame she feels at being mother to a murderer. To leave no doubt in his mind that she hanged herself because of him, through his fault, through his fault, through his most grievous fault.

(*here son take the daggers of my last lines I hope they cut you that you bleed that they bury themselves in your guts that every time you breathe they rip your liver your intestines your kidneys your pancreas son I leave to you my last words I hope they poison you scald your throat burn your entrails drain you of blood I bequeath to you suicide may you be crushed by my broken body may my vacant staring eyes remain etched in your memory I leave you these lines I leave you my corpse Humberto your time will come it will come.*)

Chelo had planned a romantic lunch. The table was decorated with tulips and she had made fillet steak al tequila, an old recipe of her grandmother's, and chocolate mousse. Neither Pato nor I mentioned the emotional turmoil of recovering the car in which my parents had died.

Chelo was gentle, sweet, attentive. She kissed and hugged me. She made jokes. She made us laugh. Her happiness dulled my sorrow and the rage I felt that Pato had seen her naked. Chelo had the ability to make me feel both at peace and permanently at war.

Pato left at seven. I walked him out. "Promise you won't get annoyed if I say something?" I nodded. "Chelo's really pretty." I felt like punching him in the face, but Pato smiled, gave me a hug and walked down the street.

When I went back inside Chelo was washing the dishes. She had taken her clothes off again and was humming. Pato was right, she was very pretty. "Come here," she called. I walked over and she put her arms around me. "I don't like to be away from you," she said.

We went upstairs to give King his medicine. His condition had visibly improved; he was a far cry from the death's door predicted by the vet at the university clinic. With an effort, he managed to stand up and take a few steps.

We went to my parents' room. A soft drizzle began to fall and Whisky and Vodka fluttered in through the window. Chelo was excited to see them come in from the street. "Look at them," she said, thrilled. I hadn't mentioned that the parakeets had finally ventured outside. They always came back when it rained. I was pleased to know they came and went between the cedar tree and the house.

She asked me to take off my clothes too. I still felt stabs of jealousy, and taking off my clothes meant taking her back. But I needed to feel as close to her as possible. I undressed and got into bed. She slipped under the sheet and started to kiss my chest, my stomach. I was overcome with doubts. Had she done this with the other men she had slept with? I told her to stop. She peeked out from under the sheets. "Did I do something wrong?" "I don't want to," I said curtly. "Do you want me to go?" "No," I replied. Chelo kissed my cheek, lay down on the far side of the bed and soon we were both asleep.

I woke in the early hours. Chelo wasn't in bed. I called out, thinking she might be in the bathroom, but there was no answer. I switched on the light. Her clothes were neatly folded on the chair. I padded downstairs naked and found her in the dark, staring through the window at Colmillo. "He doesn't deserve to be shut up out there," she said. Hearing her, Colmillo turned to look at us. "No, he doesn't," I said.

I took her by the hand and led her into the dining room. "Climb up on the table," I said. She looked at me, puzzled. "Why?" she asked. "I'm going to let him in," I said. "What if he attacks me?" I turned and looked out at Colmillo. "I'll kill him." She was clearly sceptical. "Trust me," I said. Chelo got up onto the table and sat in the middle of it, terrified.

I fetched my knife, then opened the door for the wolf. He loped in, sniffed me up and down, circled the kitchen, and when he lifted his leg to piss in the corner I shouted, "No!" Colmillo looked at me defiantly and did it anyway. I picked up a chair. Colmillo backed away. He'd learnt to respect me when I was holding the chair. His head lowered, he continued to explore. He seemed to pick up Chelo's scent, because he looked up and noticed her on the table. Chelo curled into a ball to protect herself. In a single bound, Colmillo could attack her.

I warily put myself between them. Colmillo had to learn to respect her, and I needed to force him to do so. I climbed onto the table and put my arms around Chelo. Colmillo circled the table, never taking his eyes off us. "Would you believe me if I said this was a turn-on?" Chelo asked. I looked at her. "I know it sounds ridiculous, but it's true." I parted her legs and slipped two fingers inside her vagina. She was wet and started to moan. Colmillo stopped to watch us, his head right at the edge of the table. I removed my dripping fingers and held them out to him. He sniffed them. Yes, it probably sounds stupid, even dangerous, but I was turned on too.

I laid Chelo back on the table and continued to finger her until she climaxed. Chelo stifled her moans, she didn't want to provoke the wolf. She pulled me to her. I slipped inside her and we came together. Chelo hugged me and started to sob. "Please, tell me what I can do to make

434

you forgive me." I wanted to say so many things that I couldn't put into words. I kissed the scars on her legs. To kiss them was to kiss her past. Kissing the last time that she made love to Carlos, kissing that plunge into the void when she misjudged the distance between the rooftops. I was kissing her pain, her aborted child, the legs that had wrapped themselves around those of other men. Kissing the penetrated woman, the woman who had hurt me, the unfaithful, promiscuous woman. Accepting her, hating her past, loving her present.

Gradually Chelo calmed down and stopped crying. I got down from the table. Colmillo, bored with watching us, was lying underneath. As soon as he saw me, he got up and sniffed me. I cupped my genitals with one hand. I had no desire to discover that the combination of our fluids would awaken his predator instinct and give him the urge to emasculate me in one bite.

I fetched some slices of ham and some minced meat and threw them out into the yard. Colmillo followed the food outside and I closed the door. I went back to Chelo, helped her down from the table and, hand in hand, we went up to my parents' room.

They covered the first hundred kilometres slowly, following the dirt track that ran parallel to the oil duct. It was a narrow trail with sections that were flooded or covered in snow. All along the route, labourers were soldering the last joints in the pipes while others covered the finished pipes with earth. They lived in small camps – two or three tents and a canvas awning that served as kitchen and canteen.

Every night, one of the groups would invite Chuck and Robert to eat with them and stay the night. They stretched out on camp beds with five or six workers and ate beans, eggs, game, tinned fruit and honey. It was a long time before Robert managed to get to sleep. He was accustomed to sleeping alone, and the snoring of the other men kept him awake.

Every night they would take Amaruq's body from the bed of the pickup truck and lay it on the back seat to avoid attracting predators or vultures. Fortunately, the weather was no warmer and the body remained frozen.

It was slow work, navigating the rutted, muddy path. They were constantly getting bogged down and having to use a winch to free the pickup. It could take a whole entire day to cover fifteen kilometres. On nights when they had not reached a camp, they pitched a tent and ate jerky or cooked the wapiti they had been given by one of the labourers over a fire. They fed Nujuaqtutuq the minced meat Robert had prepared for the journey.

By day fifteen of their trip, the wolf was showing signs of improvement. He was strong enough to stand up and began to prowl the cage. When Robert approached, the wolf would try to bite him. Chuck laughed heartily. "A wolf will always be a wolf."

Nujuaqtutuq seemed more active at night. Even with his front paw in a cast, he would pace up and down, bumping against the bars of the cage. Once, in the early hours, a nearby pack of wolves began to howl and Nujuaqtutuq joined them. When he heard them, Robert loaded his rifle in case they came too close.

Provisions and meat were hung high in a tree, far from wherever they pitched their tent, so no bear could climb up and take it. Bears had no fear of humans, and would be attracted by the smell of food. They would pitch the tent next to the pickup and light several fires for protection.

Despite these precautions, a grey bear came within five metres of the tent one night. Chuck and Robert could hear Nujuaqtutuq growl and the bear grunt. Robert saw the huge shadow it cast on the canvas. He signalled to Chuck to keep quiet. If the bear sensed them, he might charge. Robert grabbed the 30-06, aimed it where he estimated the bear's elbow to be and pulled the trigger. He heard a hoarse roar and then a snap of branches as the bear ran up the mountain. For several minutes, the animal's moans echoed around the forest and then silence.

436

The next day they found some spatters of blood just outside the tent. Following the trail, they found a dead she-bear on the banks of a stream, with a bullet wound in her neck. In principle, Robert was against killing females, but he had had no choice. He knew of bears that had entered tents and killed the sleeping occupants. Two friends of his had died that way.

They skinned the bear, cured the hide with salt and ash and stretched it on sticks to dry it in the wind and the sun. They kept the meat to eat. Chuck claimed to have at least fifteen recipes for stewing sweet bear meat, and grumbled about not having the right ingredients.

They reached Windy Pass. Here, the going was dangerous. The narrow road snaked along the edge of a gorge, and stretches were often blocked by rockslides or avalanches. Robert had mapped out the road himself. Construction had taken a year as the sheer rock face had to dynamited before they could use the bulldozers. One of the earth-movers had tipped over the edge of a cliff. Luckily the driver had managed to jump clear before the huge machine slid six hundred metres to the bottom.

Chuck did most of the driving on this stretch. Robert's fear of heights left him paralysed, with the vehicle only centimetres from a sheer drop. Occasionally the pickup would skid on an icy patch and slide towards the ravine. Chuck would pump the accelerator and the handbrake simultaneously to avoid losing traction.

When they came across boulders in their path, they used a heavy iron bar to lever them and roll them into the gorge, listening to the splintering of pine trees as the boulders plummeted.

At night, they would pitch the tent in the middle of the narrow road, careful to choose a sheltered stretch unlikely to be struck by a rockslide. One night, Robert woke to find that Chuck was gone. He got up to go looking for him, and found him in the back seat of the pickup with Amaruq's head on his lap. He was sobbing inconsolably, a bottle of whisky in his hand. Robert heard him whispering to his dead son, asking him for forgiveness, explaining why he had abandoned him, telling him about his life and the lives of his half-siblings. Robert was moved by the sight of his uncle. He must be feeling so much guilt and pain.

It took them four days to cover the forty kilometres of Windy Pass. When he first glimpsed the wide expanse of flat ground up ahead, Robert breathed a sigh of relief.

That night, they camped on the bank of a wide river. They gave Nujuaqtutuq a bucket of water and a hunk of bear meat. "The good thing about the cold," Robert said, "is at least we don't have to deal with the flies." It was true. In summer, the area teemed with mosquitoes and flies. Food could not be left out. In less than two hours, flies would lay their eggs and it would be writhing with maggots. In summer, it would have been impossible to transport Amaruq's body without it becoming infested.

They stretched out and Robert quickly fell asleep. Chuck crept out of the tent, spread a canvas tarp on the ground beside the pickup, brought down Amaruq's body and laid it on top. He uncovered his son's face and stared at it in the starlight. A few short days ago, this body could breathe, could speak, could think. His son. What had he been doing for all these years since he last saw him? Chuck had never stopped thinking about Amaruq or his mother. Every night, before he fell sleep, he would talk to them in Inuktitut: "Good night my dear wife, good night my dear son." To avoid hurting his family, he had hurt them, and he had hurt himself.

Chuck swigged from a bottle of whisky. In the middle of the night, he got up, drunk, and wandered over to the cage. The wolf growled as soon as he approached. Without attaching the chain to Nujuaqtutuq's harness, Chuck opened the gate. "Go on," he said. If the wolf wanted to escape, he would escape. Warily, the wolf padded out, sniffed at the air and caught a whiff of carrion. He limped towards the dead body, brought his nose close and snuffled. The wolf could run off into the grasslands, he could gnaw on the bones of the man who had subdued him, he could attack Chuck. Instead, he circled the body twice and lay down next to it. Chuck buried his face in his hands and began to cry.

According to Sigmund Freud in his essay "Totem and Taboo", a reverential fear of contact with the dead exists in diverse cultures. In Melanesia, someone who has touched a corpse is forbidden from using his hands to eat and must be fed by another member of the tribe so that death does not enter his body. For the Toaripi people of New Guinea, "a manslayer must not approach his wife and must not touch his food with his fingers". It is the same with the Shuswap in eastern Canada: "widows and widowers have to remain segregated during their period of mourning; they must not use their hands to touch the body or the head".

For some peoples, it is forbidden to utter the name of the deceased. To do so is to invoke death and puts the living in danger. This constraint, writes Freud, is imposed among people as distant from each other as "the Samojedes in Siberia and the Todas in South India, the Mongolians of Tartary and the Tuaregs of the Sahara". In other tribes, they change the names of the dead so that they can speak about them without the risk of invoking death.

Freud also mentions various rituals for appeasing the dead enemy: "When the See-Dayaks of Sarawak bring home a head from a war expedition, they treat it for months with the greatest kindness and courtesy and address it with the most endearing names in their language." The Choctaw and Dakota people of North America mourn the death of their enemies as courteously "as if they had been friends".

In all of these cultures, death is a breath that floats above men and women, waiting for the smallest lapse in order to penetrate the bodies of the living. Dishonouring an enemy killed in combat, calling a dead person by name, eating with one's hands after touching a corpse, these all become invitations to death, they open the door.

Death. The great shadow, the immeasurable light. Death.

Rope

"Over there – that's Goyo Cárdenas," Diego said, nodding at a man strolling through the prison canteen. Cárdenas was a serial killer who had strangled four women with a rope and buried them in his garden. Dubbed "The Tacubaya Strangler" by the media, he became so infamous that people sold on street corners replicas of the rope he'd used. He had been banged up for several years now. Serving a life sentence, he was the most famous inmate in Lecumberri Prison. It was hard to believe that this scrawny guy who looked like a pen-pusher was a cold-blooded killer.

"They should shoot the fucker," Diego said with a sneer. Cárdenas was coolly wandering through the general population. Warders talked and joked with him. Cárdenas hardly smiled. Serious and guarded, he responded to others with exaggerated politeness. And, yes, you felt like punching his little round glasses through the back of his skull.

I woke early that Sunday to go see Diego in prison. It was visiting day, so a line had started to form by 6.00 a.m. By eight it already snaked around the block. Middle-aged women carrying baskets of food, teenagers visiting their fathers, wives, brothers, parents, friends, and then there were the cronies, stooges and people hawking cigarettes, dope and booze to smuggle inside. More than four hundred people waiting in line.

There was a second, all-female line for conjugal visits. I wasn't sure why they were called "conjugal visits" – aside from two or three women who looked like they might be married to inmates, the profession of the other women was pretty obvious from the way they chewed gum and swore like sailors, from their short skirts, bleach-blonde hair and inch-thick make-up over deep wrinkles or pox scars. Prison rules prohibited prostitution, not for moral reasons but for reasons of hygiene. An inmate with gonorrhoea, herpes or syphilis could cause an epidemic among the prison population. Although prostitutes were technically barred, if you greased the right palm, you could bring in an elephant, if that happened to be your sexual predilection.

From what Diego had said, few inmates could afford to pay for sex, so the prison was full of "boyfriends": weak, skinny guys, or unfit chubby ones, who allowed themselves to be fucked not because they were gay but because they had no choice. If they resisted, they would be beaten. If they kept resisting, they'd be castrated, and if they still kept resisting they'd be killed.

There were many ways to speed up the process of getting in. You could pay one of the many "coyotes" who milled around outside, wearing cheap, sweat-stained suits, who offered their services as "agents". Their sole advantage was knowing the duty officer who granted access via a side door to anyone willing to pay. Another option was to pay the "placeholders", penniless women who showed up at 5.00 a.m. and later sold their place in line to the highest bidder. The "placeholders" sat on wooden crates, wrapped in black shawls to keep warm. They charged up to thirty pesos depending on how close they were to the front of the queue. A third option was to pay "compensation" to whoever was in front of you in the queue. "Do me a favour, I'll give you fifty centavos." Most people agreed. You could save about two hours by paying "compensation" to people along the line.

If you had serious money, you could go to the front of the queue, slip the guard a hundred-peso note and go sit at a reserved table in the middle of the visitors' area without even being searched. The people who chose this option – mostly wealthy visitors who came to see political prisoners or white-collar criminals – were greeted by insults and a chorus of hisses and boos from those who'd been waiting for hours.

Although I could have paid a few pesos' "compensation" to those ahead of me, I decided to wait in line. My savings were rapidly depleting. It wasn't just the money I spent on myself; keeping Colmillo and King in food was not cheap, so I queued with everyone else.

To kill time, I chatted to a family who had come to visit the grandfather who was serving forty years and, according to his daughter, had already served twenty-eight years, nine months and two weeks. He had been convicted of murder – although he continued to protest his innocence. He had woken up one morning after a night on the tiles drinking pulque with a knife in his lap and blood on his clothes. Lying next to him was a stranger with thirty stab wounds to the chest. He was arrested and charged with murder. The grandfather could remember nothing, and was banged up without ever finding out exactly what had happened. Years later, the daughter said, a friend had confessed to the stabbing. The uncorroborated confession had not been enough to exonerate the grandfather. "My grandad's a nice man," his ten-year-old granddaughter told me.

I was sodden by the time I got into the prison, having spent three hours waiting in the incessant drizzle. At the gate, I was interrogated. Visiting rules had been tightened and Diego was classed as a Category 3 prisoner: "high-profile or dangerous". This was the sort of shit you had to put up with to save a few pesos.

Once inside, I was told to wait in the canteen. I saw the grandfather and his family sitting a few tables away. He did not look like "a nice man", far from it. It was still etched on his face, the blood from the man he'd stabbed to death twenty years earlier.

It was another fifteen minutes before Diego showed up. Since he hadn't been expecting a visitor, he had been sleeping in his cell. He was delighted to see me. He asked if I had any money to buy ham sandwiches and a couple of beers so we could have lunch together. I paid five times what I would have on the outside. Food was sold by a woman "authorised" by the prison governor, which explained the hike – the governor pocketed eighty per cent of her profits.

I came back to the table with the beers, the sandwiches and a soft drink for myself. Diego asked if I knew where Zurita was working these days and I said he was still a high-ranking officer in the Policía Judicial. "I'm going to beat the shit out of that fucker when I get out," Diego growled.

Diego was twitchy, glancing around him nervously. "I'm going to have to say you're my little brother, otherwise these guys will think I'm a faggot and you're my boyfriend, and if that happens, I'm fucked," he muttered, nodding at a group of inmates who were leaning against a wall, watching. Three of the "Nazis" had left the prison, so the protection they'd afforded him had diminished.

I asked about Carlos's bank accounts and Diego explained how they had managed their finances: seventy per cent of the profits went to my brother, with fifteen each to Diego and Sean. Carlos divvied up the money with total transparency, checking every deposit and every expense. Although they were all free to do whatever they wanted with their share, they set up a joint account in which they all deposited small amounts. This was the "dummy" account. If they were ever arrested, they could give up this account and protect the rest. Needless to say, this account had immediately been seized.

Diego didn't trust banks so kept all his money in cash, except for the deposits into the dummy account, and the apartment he bought in Juárez – the one asset he didn't lose. When he had been arrested, Zurita searched his house and found wads of cash inside the lining of his clothes, in plastic bags floating in the cistern, in envelopes taped under the tables. The very places Diego assumed were foolproof were typical hiding places. Diego lost everything he had saved. Carlos, on the other hand, had opened accounts with various different banks – nine or ten, Diego thought, though he could only remember four: Banco de Londres y México on Insurgentes Sur, Banco de Industria y Comercio on the corner of Calzada de la Viga, Banco Nacional de México on Calzada de Tlalpan and Banco Industrial on Avenida Taxqueña.

I asked where I could find the paperwork for the accounts, since no statements ever came to the house. Diego grinned. "Carlos would never have put his family at risk, so the accounts aren't listed at your address." According to Diego, some were registered to the business address of the Jewish fur trader who bought chinchilla pelts from him.

Five or six years earlier, I'd gone with Carlos to a textile factory in the city centre to pay the merchant a visit. I remembered a vast workshop with dozens of women sitting behind sewing machines stitching dresses. Behind them were huge rolls of fabric of every colour and texture. It was impossible to hear above the clatter of the machines, so we had to shout. The trader was medium height, with long hair and glasses, and boasted about the size of his biceps, claiming he could arm-wrestle any of his burly workmen. Neither Diego nor I could remember his name or the location of the factory.

When I said goodbye to El Castor Furioso, he suggested I come and visit more often and – if possible – bring newspapers and magazines. "I've no idea what's going on in the world," he confessed. Just before he left, he glanced around to make sure none of the thieves locked up in there could hear and whispered, "Lend me a hundred pesos." "I've only got fifty," I said. "That should be enough to get these bastards off my back for three months," he said, nodding towards the wardens. He'd already explained that he had to bribe them every week to avoid being put on toilet duty. "Make like you're tying your shoelaces, drop the cash on the floor and leave." I did as he asked. As soon as I dropped the note, Diego covered it with his foot. I walked away quickly. When I looked back, I saw him still sitting at the table, his shoe still covering the note, then, after a few seconds, he bent down and stuffed it in his sock.

I walked out into the cold Sunday afternoon. The rain had stopped and the sun was peeking through the clouds. After less than an hour and a half, I had cabin fever. How did prisoners last longer than three days?

I got the hell out of Lecumberri as fast as possible, as though I might be tainted. Arriving back on Reforma, I saw people strolling in their Sunday best, couples kissing on benches, taxis picking up passengers, people coming out of taco joints, a kid clutching a goldfish in a plastic bag. This was the world Diego was missing, the one he wanted to make up for by reading newspapers and magazines. The world those prisoners had lost. Diego was behind bars for dealing drugs while a group of fanatical killers were walking free, living in comfort.

Those who saw her in the days leading up to her suicide said she was wandering the streets, talking to herself. Not babbling, not crazy, just mumbling to herself. She had lost a lot of weight and looked haggard. I had run into her one afternoon and said hello. She had mumbled, "Hello, Juan Guillermo," and walked on, preoccupied. The woman who had saved my life was planning to end her own.

Nobody in the barrio suspected what was about to happen. Nobody saw her at the hardware store buying the six metres of rope she used to hang herself. No-one could have guessed what the doctor discovered in her X-rays: two tumours in the uterus, a smaller one on the bladder and three more on the liver. No-one could imagine what was going through the mind of this outgoing woman who gradually retreated into herself. This woman who, with every passing day, became more withdrawn. The murderer's mother, spattered with hatred of her son and his god. The woman sullied by god, a god that snuffs out desires and throttles the will to live.

Jaibo said he had last seen her go into her house on Thursday afternoon. The postman claimed he had given her the mail at noon on Friday. The milkman said she had paid him on Saturday. Various people vied for the title of "last person to see her alive".

She had been sufficiently self-possessed to throw the rope over a beam, secure it, tie a slipknot, climb onto a chair and put it around

447

her neck. The forensic officers could not say precisely when she kicked the chair away, the final moments when her legs thrashed and jerked, but they estimated that she had been dead for more than three days. Perhaps she had spent hours deliberating on the best moment to hang herself before going through with it. Perhaps she had woken up, gone downstairs and taken her life. Perhaps she had sat up all night, staring at the rope in her hands until the early hours.

For three days, she had twisted in the wind. The window was open and rain had soaked the carpet. A neighbour had discovered the body. Having not seen the woman for days, and getting no answer when she knocked, she persuaded a nephew to climb over the back fence and open the door. She had walked in, never expecting she would find Humberto's mother, in a white nightdress, hanging from a beam, her tongue lolling.

She was wearing one slipper, the other one had dropped onto the floor. Three feral cats had crept through the window and were circling the body. A feast almost within reach. Horrified, the woman did not scream or run outside to call for help. She shooed the cats away, picked up the fallen slipper and placed it on the dead woman's foot, smoothed the nightdress, then sat on the sofa and waited for her nephew to come back with two cops he found sitting in a squad car on Calzada de la Viga.

The officers climbed out of the car and carelessly wandered into the house, without thinking to check whether there was evidence of murder. They were shaken by the sight of the hanged woman, her tongue lolling. They were rookies, this was their first corpse. They radioed the station and the station called Zurita.

Comandante Zurita and his squad arrived and conducted a meticulous examination, taking care not to contaminate the scene. They found no evidence of a crime. The house was tidy. Clothes had been recently laundered and lay folded on the bed, dishes had been washed and put away, the floors were clean and polished. The only incongruous details were that woman hanging from the beam, the open window and the rain-soaked carpet.

None of Zurita's officers dared touch the body. Some because they were superstitious: to touch a suicide might bring bad luck; others because they were nauseated by the livid skin and the foul smell; still others because they were religious: suicide was a sin against god and the sinner deserved no compassion.

Zurita climbed up on the chair, took out a knife and cut the rope. The woman tumbled onto the wet carpet, landing awkwardly so that her knickers and her crotch were exposed to the prurient gaze of some of the officers.

She had prominently placed her last letter on a top shelf in the living room, with the envelope inscribed: "For Humberto". According to the neighbour's nephew, Comandante Zurita read the letter through several times, then slipped it into the envelope, put it back on the shelf and slumped on the sofa, his face pale.

Humberto sent someone out to buy the cheapest coffin – a cheap pinewood crate, little better than cardboard. The timber was unvarnished, there were no brass handles. Spend money on his mother? Absolutely not. In Humberto's eyes, his mother was an accursed woman, even in death. Only an unstable, whorish, fool of a woman could have hanged herself, sticking her tongue out at those who found her.

In the letter, she blamed Humberto for her suicide. (Comandante Zurita told one of the officers, who told his nephew, who told Agüitas, who told me.) It was a pitiless letter for a ruthless man.

Humberto arrived home some days later and holed up in the house, sitting vigil. No-one was allowed to visit: those who took their own lives had to be hidden from view. They were shameful. Pusillanimous. An affront to god.

Alone, he kept vigil. With his dead, with his letter, with his god. Alone. With the rain, the reek of death, the smell of mouldering carpet.

Alone. With his rage, his guilt, his pain and his confusion. Alone. Locked away. The scene was set for me to kill him. Revenge was a few short steps from home.

Waking at dawn, Robert crawled out of the tent. He could not see Chuck anywhere and, as he searched, he came upon Nujuaqtutuq, lying next to the body of Amaruq. The wolf got to his feet. Robert saw that the chain was not attached to the harness. He picked it up and tried to get close, but the wolf bared his fangs. Robert backed away, the wolf watching him intently, and when he was far enough away, the animal lay down next to the body again.

Robert found his uncle asleep in the pickup and shook him awake. "Did you let him out?" Robert gestured to the wolf. Chuck nodded. "Why?" asked Robert. Chuck shrugged. He stank of whisky. "Don't know." Robert looked at the wolf. He was worried the animal might attack them, but he did not want Nujuaqtutuq to run off. In his weak and crippled state, if he encountered a wolf pack, they would tear him limb from limb. They had to get him back into the cage. They decided to wait for Nujuaqtutuq to settle down, then they could try to lasso him.

They wandered off a little way. Nujuaqtutuq lay next to the corpse and, after a while, lowered his head. Seizing the opportunity, Robert crept around behind the pickup, but just as he was about to throw the rope Nujuaqtutuq got to his feet and turned to face him. Man and beast stared at each other. Suddenly realising that Chuck was approaching from the other direction, Nujuaqtutuq turned and growled. Robert took two paces forward and managed to get the lasso around him. Nujuaqtutuq bit at the rope, attempting to get free, but stumbled and fell. Chuck took his chance and lassoed the animal's leg. Together the two men restrained the wolf, led him back into the cage and, once he was inside, clipped the chain to the harness.

They set off across the vast open plains and, two hours later, they reached a paved highway – if such a narrow, rutted, potholed road could be called "paved". As they headed south, they had to stop several times to clear the road of snow. There were few other vehicles, but when they encountered one they stopped to chat with the driver. In such desolate terrain, it was important to share information about the state of the roads. There were few obstacles ahead, they were told, just a few patches of ice and snow and the body of a moose that had been run over.

After fifty kilometres, they stopped at a small town to get petrol. Robert asked to use the telephone to call his wife, Linda. He didn't intend to tell her about the trip he was taking. No sooner did she hear his voice than she launched into a monologue about the kids, her friend's problems with alcoholism, the work needed on the house, the new grocery store opening in Whitehorse. Whenever he phoned, Linda would give a detailed account of her weekly activities before asking her husband how he was. She spent her life in a world of children and of women as lonely as she was, trapped in a banal and stifling routine, without Robert to share it with. Robert briefly told her he was fine, that the company had settled on his preferred route, that the weather was improving so work could begin. In the twelve minutes they spent on the phone, she had spoken for eleven.

Hanging up, he headed back to the pickup where the petrol station attendant, a stocky mixed-race man with slanted eyes and a shock of hair, was peering curiously at the wolf in the cage. It was the biggest wolf he had ever seen. It was a shame the animal was in such bad shape, he said, since he owned a bitch and would have loved to cross-breed.

As night drew in, they set up camp in a hollow just off the highway. A cold front had moved in, making the roads dangerously icy. They were in no hurry and it wasn't worth taking risks. The train station was seventy kilometres away. The total distance must have been about four hundred kilometres. Robert calculated that from the place where they found Amaruq to his house it was around one hundred and

451

eighty kilometres as the crow flew. What was Amaruq doing so far from home? What was his story?

Robert thought about his two sons and his daughter. In his own way, he had abandoned them. True, his work demanded long absences, but his children did not understand that and they resented him. Sometimes, six months would go by without his seeing them. Last winter, when weather had delayed the work on the pipeline, he had spent a long stretch with them. It had been such a harsh winter that the children barely left the house. He had felt trapped and frustrated. The children's shouting, their constant commotion, which he had initially enjoyed, ended up irritating him. He found his wife tiresome. Her constant need to talk and talk while all Robert wanted was to read in peace or take a nap. She was graceless in bed, vigorously pumping her pelvis against him to get aroused and sometimes hurting him. She was also timid. She didn't like him to see her naked and she never bared her breasts. She was embarrassed by the flab and the stretch marks left by her pregnancies. And yes, Linda was a good woman, devoted to her children, but she was possessive and narrow-minded. After a month of sitting at home, Robert was desperate to get back to work, but he had to endure another seven weeks of forced coexistence. It changed his mood. He began to reprimand the children for no reason, and say "Shhh!" to Linda when she wouldn't stop blabbering.

When he got a call summoning him back to work, he left as soon as possible, unable to stomach any more family time. Now he missed them, missed his daughter's smell, his son sitting on his lap with a colouring book, his eldest daughter telling him all about her daily adventures. He even missed Linda. Much as she annoyed him, he loved her and she put up with his long absences.

They made better progress that morning. They drove further south and the roads improved. After a few hours, they reached the junction of the narrow road that led to the train station. Chuck asked Robert to pull up for a minute. In revisiting his past, he was faced with two possible scenarios: he would see the loving woman he had abandoned thirty years earlier, or he might discover that she, too, was dead. Both would be difficult to handle. He took a deep breath. "Let's go."

When they arrived, Chuck told Robert to park behind the house. Stepping out of the car, he surveyed the cabin, remembering. The same rusty mailbox, the porch looking out onto the forest, the wrought-iron benches. He had helped build this house, laying logs with Amaruq's grandfather. He had secured the roof beams, made the window frames. Though a little more ramshackle, the cabin was just as it had been when he left all those years ago. He walked up to the door and rapped with his knuckles. Robert stayed back, out of respect. From inside came the sound of footsteps. The door was opened by an Inuit woman, who exchanged a glance with the blue-eyed, grey-haired man standing on the threshold. They stood for a moment in silence, then she stepped aside and ushered him in.

Animals

I arrived home from Lecumberri at two o'clock and, opening the door, I heard a man's voice. I found Avilés and Chelo sitting at the dining room table. "*Hola, mi amor*," said Chelo, "we have a visitor." It was the first time she had called me "my love". I walked over to them. "I had no idea your girlfriend was so beautiful," said Avilés. He nodded to a large platter on the table. "I brought lunch." The platter was filled with maguey worms, grasshoppers, ant eggs, stink bugs, iguana meat, grilled field rats and green turtle eggs, delicacies Avilés proudly told us he had found in a city centre market. Chelo pulled up a chair next to her. "Come and sit down beside me. We've been waiting for you."

We stuffed ourselves. Everything was delicious. Chelo wanted to try everything. I had always assumed she was a fussy eater, but I was wrong. When it came to food, she was the all-terrain four-by-four of gourmets. She was not disgusted by anything and had no problems eating tacos stuffed with live wriggling stink bugs.

Avilés was being flirtatious, and Chelo laughed at all his terrible jokes. He teased, he quipped, he recounted stories. Though I knew he was just enjoying being the centre of attention, I felt absurdly jealous. Chelo could clearly tell, because she was affectionate and kept her arm around me the whole time.

Chelo was fascinated by Avilés's job as a lion tamer and bombarded him with questions. Where did he get the animals? How many times had he been mauled? Why had he decided to do this for a living? Avilés answered with a combination of modesty and boastfulness. When he asked what her favourite circus act was, Chelo admitted she'd never been to the circus. Avilés and I were surprised. My parents used to take us all the time when we were kids. Although it was expensive, they thought circus shows were important for our education. To them it was a metaphor for courage and risk-taking, two qualities they believed were essential to life. Chelo's parents – who were rather more conservative than mine – considered it a vulgar, gruesome entertainment. "They're toying with life, which should be sacred," they argued.

Avilés was not surprised that her parents had forbidden her to go. He told us of the countless times he had heard parish priests urge villagers not go to the circus: the clowns made a mockery of authority figures, the trapeze artists exposed too much flesh, magicians practised dark, demonic arts "and they accuse animal tamers of stirring up bestial instincts," he said with a chuckle.

He asked whether we wanted to go to the afternoon show with him. "I'd love to," Chelo said eagerly. We climbed into the car and headed for the big top. Avilés parked behind some tents and told us that he had to go change for the show, but Paco, his gangly assistant, would look after us.

There was a long queue at the ticket office. The circus was clearly popular. Paco took us on a tour backstage. Chelo gawped in amazement at a man training a quintet of French poodles. With a click of his fingers, the dogs stood on their hind legs and hopped into line, one behind the other. Another man was feeding an elephant huge fistfuls of lettuce. A baby chimpanzee wearing a nappy was clinging to a woman in a leotard.

After the tour, Paco led us to a caravan and tapped on the door. Avilés opened with a loud "Come in!" We trooped inside. He was dressed in a nineteenth-century outfit, a red frock coat, black trousers, a white shirt and black leather boots. To be honest, I was impressed.

As we walked back to the big top, he reached through the bars of the cages and stroked the tigers and the lions, talking to them gently and calmly. A lion nuzzled his hand, encouraging Avilés to scratch behind his ears. A tiger purred like a kitten when Avilés called his name. If the animals respected the Brazilians, they worshipped Avilés.

Avilés suggested we go and take our seats, "the best in the arena", and they were. Front row, in the middle of the ring. From here, we could hear the roar of the elephants parading around the ring, the smack of the trapeze artist's hands grabbing the wrists of his partner after a perilous triple somersault, the ragged breathing of an acrobat crossing a tightrope.

Chelo watched each act, spellbound. The finale belonged to Avilés. Lions and tigers filed into the ring. Avilés's act was similar to the one I had seen the Brazilians do, but with one exception: he did not have a whip or a chair. A gesture of his hands was enough to make the big cats obey. I was awed by his command over them. His every movement exuded elegance. Who would have thought that a short chubby man with a shock of hair like a dead German composer could effortlessly handle such ferocious animals?

He closed his performance with an age-old trick: placing his head between the jaws of a lion with a thick mane. For ten endless seconds he held it there. The lion could easily have ripped his head off, but it barely moved. When, finally, Avilés took his head out, the audience went wild. Chelo kept saying "Fucking hell! Fucking hell!"

When the show was over, Avilés's assistant drove us home. We arrived back in the middle of a downpour, climbed out and raced to the door, drenched and cold. We immediately went upstairs and got into the shower where we stood for a long time, kissing beneath the scalding spray.

Naked, we slipped under the sheets and flicked off the lights. Our whole day had been filled with animals, those we had eaten and those we had seen at the circus. Chelo began to string sentences together using the word "animal". She would come up with one, then I would come up with another. The game ended when she suddenly sat up in bed and stared at me. "I love you, you animal," she said, stroking my face. "I really do love you." I clung to her. Her body was warm and soft.

456

There was no doubt about it, there in her nakedness, in her embrace, I was home.

How many days before she hanged herself did Humberto's mother buy the rope? How much did it cost? How did she know which one to choose? Where had she kept it? How had it felt, the first time she held it in her hands? Were her hands shaking as she tied the knot? Did she feel a pang of regret as she kicked the chair from under her? What was her last thought? Did she say anything in the second before she died?

The mother listened as Chuck explained how her son had died. He had to struggle to find the words. It had been years since he had spoken the Inuktitut he had learned from them. Once they were out of his life, he had gradually forgotten it. The mother spoke little English. A few words here and there. Yet despite their lack of words, the weight of their grief was palpable.

They went out to the pickup truck. The mother unwrapped the blankets and stared at the body for some moments, gently wiping away a spot of mud from her son's forehead. She asked Robert and Chuck if they could carry him into the house. They brought him in and laid him on a camp bed. The only bedroom in the house had been the mother's; Amaruq had always slept in the living room. Amaruq had gone out hunting one morning, she explained, and never come back. She had been waiting for months. Chuck told her about Nujuaqtutuq, how Amaruq had captured the wolf alive and hauled him on a sled to the summit of a mountain. "Nujuaqtutuq." The woman repeated the name to herself, then explained that this had been the last word her father had uttered before he died, two years earlier.

The woman offered to make them something to eat. Chuck translated and Robert tried to make an excuse, feeling it would be somehow inappropriate to sit down to eat with them with their dead son lying a few metres away, but Chuck warned him that refusing would be considered an insult.

The woman went to the stove to heat up a pot of venison stew. Chuck took a seat at the table but, when Robert moved to do the same, the woman gestured for him to sit on a different chair. This was where Amaruq had always sat, Chuck explained.

The woman served up the stew on blue enamel plates, setting the last one in front of Amaruq's empty chair. Chuck asked how she had managed to survive without her son's help, and she explained that she had been selling to the few buyers who still occasionally stopped by the small stock of wolf and bear hides Amaruq had brought back from previous hunting trips.

Robert enjoyed the stew. She had made it with bear fat and herbs, a refined combination of strong flavours. When they had finished, the woman took away the plates and plunged them into a basin of soapy water.

Robert thanked her for the food, then told Chuck he would go and wait outside so they could speak alone. Leaning against the back of the pickup truck, he contemplated the view. The railway tracks snaked away across the snowy plains. The station was little more than a platform with a room attached. Freight trains stopped there to pick up cargoes of wood, furs and meat and leave supplies of sugar, salt, flour, batteries, matches and petrol. People from the surrounding small villages would gather at the station, waiting for the train to arrive. Amaruq's mother sold them coffee and hot food while Amaruq used to exchange animal hides for bullets or traps.

Robert remembered his train stopping at this station, remembered the endless procession of goods being loaded and unloaded. Perhaps Amaruq's was one of the nameless faces he had seen.

Chuck emerged from the house and called to Robert. "Kenojuac wants to sit vigil for her son tonight, and wait until tomorrow to decide what to do with his body. I hope you don't mind." Robert said he was happy to stay for as long as necessary. Chuck went back inside. Hearing the name for the first time, Robert thought it sounded strange. Kenojuac.

He parked the pickup inside a shed next to the train tracks, filled a bucket with water, set some meat down on the ground, then opened the cage. When Nujuaqtutuq padded out, Robert tied the chain up to a post. With a glance, the wolf sized him up and then went to eat and drink. Having ensured that the wolf could not escape, Robert closed the door to the shed and headed back to the cabin.

They had laid out the body in the living room and dressed it in fresh clothes. Amaruq was wearing a pair of sealskin trousers, a wolfskin coat and boots of caribou leather. An old .30-30 Winchester repeater was laid across his chest. Kenojuac was sitting beside the body with Chuck standing next to her, one hand on her shoulder.

Robert stood in the doorway, keeping a respectful distance. The woman was sobbing, a silent, suppressed keening. Amaruq had spoken very little since his grandfather died, Kenojuac told Chuck, he had become reclusive, but this did not explain his long trek into the northern territories, the wolf lashed to the sled, the camp at the mountain summit.

That night, Robert slept in a corner of the living room next to the hearth. Chuck slept with Kenojuac in the bed where, thirty-seven years earlier, Amaruq had been conceived. Robert could hear them talking, but did not understand what they were saying. After so many years apart, would they make love? Did she hate him, had she forgiven him, did they still love one another?

As night wore on, the cold gradually seeped into the room. Robert got up to pile more logs on the fire and, turning around, found himself face to face with Kenojuac. "Nujuaqtutuq," she said, gesturing that she wanted to see the animal. Robert picked up a torch and together they headed out to the shed, moving silently through the darkness, their feet sinking into the snow.

As they stepped inside, Robert shone his torch on the wolf. Nujuaqtutuq's eyes gleamed yellow. Kenojuac moved closer. The wolf watched her guardedly. She spoke to Nujuaqtutuq as though he were a person. When she was closer than Robert thought was safe, he took her arm and signalled that the wolf might attack. She pulled her arm away and walked on, murmuring to Nujuaqtutuq without pausing for breath. When she was within reach of the wolf, Robert took her arm again, but she managed to slip free. She took the torch and trained the beam directly on the wolf's face. Dazzled, the animal froze. Taking two steps forward, she reached out and patted his head. Nujuaqtutuq sniffed her arm, then suddenly lunged. Robert only just managed to pull her to safety. The woman was not frightened in the least. She stood in front of the wolf, scolding him loudly and angrily.

The wolf growled, his body tensed. Kenojuac shone the flashlight away from his face. She retreated a few steps without turning her back on him, handed the torch to Robert and left the shed.

The following morning, Robert told his uncle about the incident. Chuck explained that Kenojuac was convinced that her father – Amaruq's grandfather – had metamorphosed into Nujuaqtutuq and that this was why her son had followed him such a long way. Robert thought the idea absurd, dangerous even, and asked Chuck if he believed her story. Chuck said only that he respected her beliefs.

Kenojuac asked them about the place where they had found Amaruq. Robert described the hollow near the summit, the pine forests, the soaring cliffs, the snow-covered peak. Kenojuac suggested that they travel to the mountains to the west and choose a similar spot to bury Amaruq. If her son had chosen to die at the foot of a mountain, then at the foot of a mountain was where his soul should rest for eternity.

She asked what they had done with the carcass of the goat. Robert said they had left it for the coyotes. Kenojuac said she wished they had kept a scrap of the animal's hide to lay in the grave next to Amaruq.

The goat had been his companion in death; they should travel together into the next life.

They wrapped Amaruq's body in a bear hide and laid him in the bed of the pickup. They packed away the tent, sleeping bags, supplies, cans of petrol, water and whisky. The woman asked if they could bring Nujuaqtutuq. The wolf seemed much stronger now, and it was a struggle for Chuck and Robert to get him back into the cage.

Chuck and the woman decided to sit in the bed of the pickup truck. Despite the bitter cold, they wanted to make this final journey with their son. They set off for the mountains, the sun behind them.

"You eat like an animal"

"He's as strong as an animal"

"They treat him worse than an animal"

"We love like animals"

"He fights like an animal"

"They fuck like animals"

"You make noises like an animal"

"You smell like an animal"

"Like an animal, he slaughtered her"

"He walks like an animal"

"She lives like an animal"

"Don't be an animal"

"You're like a tame animal"

"Killer! Animal!"

"Your animal scent turns me on"

"We may be human, but first and foremost we are animals"

"I love you, you animal"

The roar of god, the panting of his mastiffs, the devious scheming of the almighty, **the** insipid creatures, the obscene fury, the insurgents, the indomitable, the invisible reprisals, the great rage, the memory of rebels, the quirks of war, the flag hoisted at half mast, the interminable mourning, the breaches, the retreat, the **steadfastness** of those who resist, the renegades from paradise, the excuses for murder, the ecstasy of free will, the cry of victims, the poisonous vapours, the sweat **of** god, the massacre of the innocent, the suffocating guilt, the crack of bones, the flayed skin, the clash of warriors, the giddiness of those born to die, the vulnerable **men** against an all-powerful god, the guerrilla pitted against the army, the joy of the murderers, the baleful god, the folds of death, the nostalgia of the newborn, the nothingness, the purification of light, the lost galaxies, the subversive word, the scarlet verb, the presumptuous god, the presumptive gods, the fire of Prometheus that **lights** up the world, the dread of freedom, the misdeeds of the fornicators, the condemnation, the meddling god, the shattered harmony, the sacrifice of the unbound, the bitter vengeance, the contagion of the infected, the redemption of the pariahs, the bodily fluids, the vaginal fluids, the semen of the god, the tears of men, the women penetrated, the suffocated embryos, the umbilical cord, the women loved, the mother-countries, the men who love them, those brought before the courts, **the** magnanimous humanity, the miserable humanity, the expansion of the universe, the irreconcilable gods, the confutation, the ineffable, the relative absolute, the castigation of the vanquished, the lees of blood, the solemn burial, the screams, the entrails, the excrement, the suicide, the wiles of treachery, the clotted hatreds, the lines of bodies, the return to **earth**, the dusty battles, the forbidden pathways, the mud, the rain, the fire, the sky, the sun in flames, the plaintive lament of the wounded, the swift spear, the shattered skull, the fluttering of bloodstained shirts, the millstone of the drowned man, the gasp, the uprising of men, the triumph of the insurrectionaries. Men.

Mountains

After a couple of attempts, I managed to get Sean on the phone. "What's up, *cabrón*?" he said in a heavy north Mexican accent from the Texas prison where he was serving out his sentence. I briefly told him my life story. He was happy that I had stopped Colmillo from being put down and was looking after him. He was less enthusiastic about my relationship with Chelo. He seemed to disapprove. "Be careful," he said, "you know she's a bit of a slut." It hurt to hear him say that. It was hard enough dealing with my own jealousy without having to hear him talk about her like that. He seemed concerned about King's health. "If he dies, cremate him and scatter his ashes over Carlos's grave. Your brother loved that dog."

He told me he would probably get early release for good behaviour. He was desperate to get out. He found life in prison unbearably monotonous. The same spaces, the same people, the same food. He refused to watch T.V. with the rest of the inmates – "It's a fucking lobotomy" – preferring to stay in his cell and look at the view through the bars.

I asked about the Jewish fur trader. Sean couldn't remember his name, but he remembered the building where Carlos used to deliver the furs – a four-storey building, the front painted pistachio green, with a window display of various fabrics, wedding dresses, school uniforms and crocheted baby clothes. He could not remember the precise street, "but it's in the city centre", he said confidently.

I asked what he had done with his money. "Bought myself a house in Ciudad Acuña, a ranch in Del Río, and put the rest in a bank in San Antonio." He told me he thought he might lose the ranch, because the U.S. government might seize it as the proceeds of criminal activity.

He had already cut a deal with the D.A. to hand over some of his earnings from drug dealing as a condition of his transfer to the United States. Even if the property was forfeited, Sean's finances when he was released would be enough for him to live comfortably for the rest of his life, "probably the rest of my grandkids' lives," he added.

"How did you make so much money?" I asked. "We had a huge client base," he said, explaining that they might still be in business if they had been prepared to do a deal with Comandante Zurita, but Carlos had refused. "It's a pity," he said, "because the network never stopped generating profits." He told me how much he used to make in a week. It was outrageous.

We hung up. "I love you, bro," he said by way of goodbye. I smiled, picturing him in his prison filled with T.V. screens, surrounded by Mexicans and chicanos, sweating through 40°C in summer, shivering through -10°C in winter, staring through the bars of his cell at the rolling Texan plains.

I was stunned to discover just how much property and money Sean had amassed. Carlos's business had obviously been much more profitable than I'd imagined – and Comandante Zurita had pocketed a fortune when he appropriated Diego's share. Just thinking about the amounts made me dizzy. Carlos's assets must have been sizeable, inconceivable. I was not about to let the banks keep it, even if it meant fighting them for the rest of my life.

Robert drove for four hours along a dirt road that often disappeared beneath the snow and undergrowth. When they came to the end of the road, he parked in a clearing at the foot of the mountains. They climbed out of the truck. Kenojuac studied the peaks, pointed to a remote spot and told Chuck they should walk towards it.

Kenojuac set off, determined to find the perfect spot for a grave. For an hour and a half, she walked unwaveringly, then stopped and scanned the sheer cliffs. She asked Robert whether this looked like the place

465

where they had found Amaruq. Robert nodded. The same granite rock face, the same snow-capped peaks, the same forests. The woman took a few more steps forward, then pointed to a depression in the snow. "Here," she said in Inuktitut, using twigs to mark off an area.

By the time they returned to the clearing, it was nightfall. While Robert pitched camp, Chuck and Kenojuac collected wood and built a fire. The woman set wapiti meat to roast on a stone slab she placed over the fire. After they had eaten, she and Chuck went into the tent while Robert climbed into the sleeping bag and lay down on the back seat of the pickup.

Sometime around midnight, a pack of wolves began to howl nearby. Robert sat up and listened. He loaded the rifle and got out of the truck. If the wolves came close, they might attack Nujuaqtutuq, or even them. He shone the torchlight around him. A few snowflakes drifted through the beam of light. After a few minutes of searching and seeing nothing, he went back to bed.

At sun-up, when Robert woke, Kenojuac was already hunkered in front of the fire making breakfast. Wisps of smoke rose into the chill mountain air. Robert greeted her in English and she replied in her own language.

When Chuck emerged from the tent, the three of them settled around the fire to eat. Chuck told Robert that Kenojuac wanted to set Nujuaqtutuq free. Robert shook his head. There was a wolf pack close by; if they set Nujuaqtutuq free, he was likely to be ripped apart by the other wolves. "I get what you're saying," Chuck nodded, "but she's still convinced Nujuaqtutuq is her grandfather in animal form and she wants to free him." Robert, who was sceptical even of his family's Catholicism, thought the idea was absurd. Even so, he had to accept the woman's decision: it was her son who had captured the wolf and she should decide its fate.

Kenojuac opened the cage and Nujuaqtutuq warily slunk out. "Go!" Kenojuac shouted in Inuktitut. The wolf bared his teeth. The woman

466

was not afraid. "Go now," she repeated. The wolf stared at her for several seconds, then turned and limped towards the forest. Robert watched worriedly as the animal headed into the pine trees, towards what he believed was certain death. With the cast on his leg and the cumbersome harness, he would find it difficult to hunt or fight.

They laid Amaruq's body on his old sled, and Chuck and Robert tied ropes around their waists so they could drag it. Kenojuac walked on ahead, deciding the route. It was hard going. When they encountered rocks, streams or drifts of snow, they had to lift the body from the sled and carry it over the obstacles.

It took five hours to reach the spot that Kenojuac had chosen for the grave. She and Chuck made a circle of stones and set the body in the centre. As they peeled away the bearskin, the body, which had thawed a little, gave off a fetid odour. Robert turned away until the smell had dissipated.

Amaruq lay facing the sky. His ashen skin had the texture of cardboard. The blood from the wound on his neck had formed a thick scab. His eyelids, half-open, revealed dully lifeless eyes. Flesh transforming into not-flesh. Into rock, root, snow, gas. Into death.

Kenojuac kneeled down beside him, collected a handful of snow and rubbed it over her son's neck until the traces of blood had disappeared. She stood up and began to sing. Chuck prayed silently, his head bowed. When they had finished, the three of them collected stones and branches and together built a cairn over the body to deter scavenging animals. They set the sled and the old rifle next to it as a memorial.

Chuck and Kenojuac headed down the mountain while Robert stood in silence, paying his respects. As he turned to go, he saw Nujuaqtutuq watching from fifty metres away.

I had only two snippets of information that might help me track down the fur trader: a description of the textile factory and a vague memory of what the man looked like. I asked my friends to help me find him. We took the Popo-Sur 73 bus to Calzada de Tlalpan and the metro from there to the station at Pino Suárez. When we reached the city centre, we wandered around aimlessly looking for any shop that sold fur coats. We asked a couple of cops, who directed us to Calle Corregidora, where there were numerous clothes shops but none that sold furs, and nobody there seemed to know where we might find them. One of the managers said the only place he had seen them for sale was in Palacio de Hierro, a huge department store on Zócalo, the main square.

Palacio de Hierro sold only leather jackets and the sales assistants had never heard of a chinchilla. We left, disheartened. Tracking down the fur trader was going to be harder than I had thought.

We spent the next three days commuting to the city centre. Exceptionally loyal, my friends skipped school to come with me. Pato, ever the methodical one, searched through the phone book and called several shops, but none of them sold chinchilla fur.

We trudged up Cinco de Mayo, along San Juan de Letrán and down Avenida Madero. Nothing. In every shop, we were greeted by shaking heads. It seemed as though we would never find it unless we had a stroke of luck. In one of the shops someone asked us: "Have you tried Avenida Izazaga?"

Izazaga was a broad avenue filled with workshops that made clothes and textiles, most of which were Jewish-owned. We covered it twice from end to end, but the buildings all looked the same and at least fifteen had pistachio green facades. Drawn by the bargains, crowds thronged the shops. Delivery men bustled about, lugging huge rolls of fabric. Vans were piled with dozens of dresses. "We'll never find anything in this crowd," said Jaibo.

We decided to visit every shop with a green frontage. In the first five we had no luck. In the sixth I asked the man behind the counter if he remembered a Carlos Valdés who years ago used to sell chinchilla furs. He said he didn't know him. I asked if he knew a Jewish fur trader, medium height, who liked arm-wrestling labourers. The man grinned. "Ha! You must be talking about Simon Bross," he said, and gave me directions to his shop.

The moment I stepped inside the store I remembered it. A few bald mannequins in the window triggered my memory. Yes, this was the place. The flowery floor tiles, the fabric samples hanging from the walls, dresses on the shelves. I went towards the till. "Is Mr Simon Bross here?" I asked the stony-faced woman behind the counter. She lowered her glasses and scrutinised my face. "May I ask what it concerns?" she asked brusquely. "It's personal," I replied. "If it's personal, you can call on him at home. He only deals with business matters here." "I don't know where he lives," I said. "In that case, Mr Bross clearly does not know you and has no reason to speak to you, sir." I was taken aback by a woman in her fifties speaking so formally to me, a boy of seventeen. "He doesn't know me," I ventured, "but he knew my murdered brother." When she heard "murdered", her expression changed. "What was your brother's name?" she asked. "Carlos Valdés." She looked me up and down. "The guy with the chinchillas?" I nodded. "You don't look much alike," she said gruffly. "Wait here."

The woman asked a girl to take over behind the till and headed into the back of the store and up some stairs. Agüitas nudged me in the ribs. He liked the look of the girl. She was dark-skinned and pretty. Agüitas approached her. "Hello," he said. "What do you want?" she said, her curt response putting an end to his advance in under five seconds. "Nothing, thanks," Agüitas said, turned to look at the window display as though he found the *quinceañera* party dresses fascinating. Jaibo laughed. "Nice one."

The woman reappeared. "Come with me," she ordered. We followed her. Agüitas turned to look back and the girl gave him a coy smile. Confused, he wasn't sure whether she was teasing him or genuinely flirting. We mounted the stairs, past a floor where dozens of women

469

were working at sewing machines. Memories came back to me. The smell of sweat and cigarettes, the babble of women's voices, the deafening clatter of their machines.

We came to a stockroom piled with enormous bolts of fabric and the woman led us to an office at the back. She suggested I go in alone, leaving my friends to wait on some rickety chairs.

Nervously, I walked into the office. When he saw me, Simon Bross got up and greeted me warmly. "How are you, Juan Guillermo?" I was surprised that he knew my name. I had not mentioned it to the woman. Over time, I would learn that Simon Bross had a prodigious memory and could recall the names of people he had met only once.

He gestured for me to sit. On the shelves behind his desk I spotted the names of authors Carlos loved: Rulfo, Faulkner, Nietzsche, Sartre, Baroja, Stendhal, Balzac, Hemingway. Novelists from the time of the Mexican Revolution such as Ferretis, Azuela, Urquizo, Martín Luis Guzmán. It was strange to see the books here, in a textile factory in the city centre, surrounded by sewing machines, bridal dresses and school uniforms. Bross asked if I read as voraciously as Carlos. "Not as much as him, but those . . ." I gestured towards the books behind him, "I've read most of them." He smiled sadly. "Your brother used to talk a lot about literature, philosophy and cinema. He was a brilliant young man. You have no idea how sad I was to hear about his death."

Bross had introduced Carlos to psychology and philosophy, given him books by Kierkegaard, Wittgenstein, Freud, Hegel, Marx, Plato, Aristotle. I had no idea that there had been a mentor–student relationship between them.

Bross had changed his last name from Abramovich since it was difficult to pronounce in Spanish. His second surname was Soriano. His father was an Ashkenazi Jew, he explained, his mother a Sephardi. He and his siblings had arrived in Mexico from Poland as children. They had not endured the Nazi terror, but their grandparents, their uncles, their aunts and their cousins had all died in the concentration camps.

Bross was funny and easy to like. Within ten minutes, I felt as though we had known each other for years, and that, despite the difference in our ages, we might become the best of friends. I asked him if he knew anything about Carlos's bank records. "I have them here," he said. "I've been waiting a long time for someone to come for them. Carlos did give me your home number but when I found out about his death and tried to call, it was out of service." It was true, my parents had had our number changed after we started receiving anonymous calls, disembodied voices telling us that they were going to kill us and we would burn in hell with Carlos.

Bross opened his desk drawer and handed me five folders stuffed with bank statements, neatly organised by branch and date. The earliest statements were from 1966, when Carlos started the business, and the last was dated a week before his death. These alone represented a considerable fortune. And there were still statements from four or five other banks I needed to track down. "You'll need a lawyer to deal with this, because the banks won't hand over the money just like that. They'll fight tooth and nail to keep it." I explained that I had hoped my brother's death certificate and my birth certificate would be enough to collect the money as his only heir. Bross shook his head. "Those people won't give you a single peso."

Bross was aware Carlos had other accounts, but he didn't know with which banks or where the statements were sent. He offered to help with the formalities and negotiating the lawyer's fees.

As I was leaving, he pulled three books off the shelves and pressed them into my hands. *The Green House* by Mario Vargas Llosa, *The Wild Palms* by William Faulkner and *The Eagle and the Serpent* by Martín Luis Guzmán. "Have you read these?" he asked. I shook my head. "Read them, and when you've finished, come back and see me to discuss them." The two of us walked out of his office and I introduced him to my friends. Bross repeated each name and surname, instantly memorising it, and warmly shook their hands.

My friends asked if they could look at the books. Jaibo took the one by Vargas Llosa, read the first page and handed it back to me. "I don't understand a word," he said.

Worms

If you'd read Freud, Humberto, you'd know that among honourable tribes, when they kill an enemy, they pay homage to him, they lavish him with attention. They know that if they do not do so, they may be impregnated with death's viscous slime. Or maybe you were naive enough to believe that those who kill can get away scot-free? Of course not. Those who sow death reap death. Do you know what a screwworm is? I'm sure you have no idea what I'm talking about. Let me explain. The screwworm fly lays its eggs in open wounds in cattle. One after another the larvae hatch and feed on living flesh, biting into it with their minuscule teeth. It's a sickening sight. You see a strong, powerful bull strutting across the prairie. As you get closer, you notice a white pulsating mass on its flank. Closer still and you see worms writhing inside the wound. They devour muscle, nerves, fat. They puncture life. They dig out flesh, deepen the wound to make room for more eggs, more larvae, leaving a trail of blood and clots. Within weeks, the bull will weaken and will eventually collapse.

Cochliomyia hominivorax is the scientific term. The mere word "hominivorax" is terrifying. Did you realise that the stench of death which clings to murderers like you attracts invisible death flies? They buzz around your head, land on your shoulder, drink from the corners of your eyes. They lay eggs in your heart, on your skin, in your brain, in your eyes. Over time, these small white ovules develop into the larvae that will feast on you. Humberto, you may not be punished for your crimes, but you can never escape unscathed. The ravening larvae are there to remind you of your murders. From afar you can sense the mass of worms eating away at your soul. Look in a mirror, fool. Look closely. They gnaw at your tongue, slither through your eyes, burst out through your parted lips.

You must know, you son of a bitch, that death ripples outwards. It creates waves that devastate everything in their path. To kill one is to kill many. Yes, Humberto, many. You killed my brother and that killed my grandmother and my parents. You killed my brother and in doing so you killed your mother. Your own mother, Humberto. The woman who regretted giving birth to you. If only one of those sinister doctors had stuck a curette into your mother's womb and scraped you out, piece by piece. You are living proof that abortion should be legal. The political campaign slogan should be: "NO MORE HUMBERTOS. YES TO ABORTION."

By now you must have realised that you will never be free of the dead woman for whom you sit vigil in your house, the shameless, drunken woman to whom you owe your life. Her tentacles are long. Maybe you believed that by running off to the land of the Cristero Rebellion your minions would protect you, that nobody could get to you, that you would be beyond the reach of justice? You felt indestructible, invincible. But who was it who found you in your bolthole? It was death, Humberto. Death sniffed out your worm-eaten soul, you fucker. The mother now rotting in a cheap coffin tracked you to your hiding place. She found you and dragged you out by the hair. And you were stupid enough to think you could escape.

Humberto, butcher of the cross, righteous killer, staunch defender of a murderous morality, just like the bulls infested with screwworms, you too will soon fall lifeless to the ground. The worms will annihilate you. You will be nothing but a piece of putrid meat, a pestilential soul. The time of the worms has come. You will be devoured. The time has come, Humberto, for my revenge. I am coming for you. I will look you in the eyes as I kill you. It will be just the two of us. You won't get away. You have run out of escape routes. I am coming for you, Humberto. My revenge has arrived.

Chelo got home after a long day of lectures just before dark, made herself dinner, washed the dishes and went upstairs to my parents' room. The window was open. The light rain suddenly turned into a downpour. Chelo closed the window, then went into the bathroom to brush her teeth.

As the cloudburst raged, Whisky and Vodka fluttered from the cedar tree to the window, not noticing it was closed. The light in the bedroom meant they did not see the glass. Whisky soared through the air and smashed into the glass, dying instantly, his neck broken. Vodka managed to slow down in time, lightly grazing the glass. Whisky lay lifeless on the windowsill. Vodka perched beside him, bedraggled in the cold night air.

Chelo later told me that as she was rinsing out her mouth, she heard a soft thud, but never imagined it might be the birds crashing into the glass.

When I arrived home and went up to my parents' bedroom, the first thing I noticed was the closed window. I asked Chelo if the parakeets were inside. She looked worried. "I don't think so," she said. Opening the window, I discovered Whisky's blue body on the sill and Vodka shivering next to him.

I gently picked them up and brought them inside. There was nothing I could do for Whisky, but I wrapped Vodka in a towel and set her next to a heater. She died a few hours later.

I was furious with Chelo. I laid into her for forgetting that the parakeets came and went through the window. She tried to defend herself. For days she had been staying up into the early hours studying for her exams. She was exhausted, she hadn't realised her mistake. Over and over she apologised as I screamed at her, I couldn't take any more death, still less when it was caused by stupidity. King was all I had left now, and he might die at any moment. I was bereft of life, death was all around me.

Chelo slumped on the bed, inconsolable. Looking at the lifeless parakeets on the towel, I thought of my grandmother, remembered how she used to chatter to them in the mornings, how she scratched their heads gently, cradled them in her hands. Fuck! I couldn't believe those two little birds were such a fundamental part of the memories I had of my family.

Eventually, I calmed down. Everything would have been fine if it hadn't been for the sudden downpour. If it had only been a light drizzle, the parakeets would have sheltered in the cedar tree. It was sheer bad luck that the rainstorm had coincided with Chelo's exhaustion.

Chelo suggested we wrap them in tissue paper, place them in little boxes and bury them. I refused. I could not endure another funeral. I'd had enough of solemnity and fanfare. They were parakeets, not human beings. Yes, I had been fond of them. For years they'd been part of our daily lives. But to bury them would be to make too much of their death. No more brutal wounds, no more voids in life.

Without thinking, I picked up the parakeets, the cage and the sack of birdfeed, and climbed up to the roof in the driving rain. In the darkness, I stroked their stiff bodies by way of a goodbye and laid them on the ground. The cats could come and eat them. What better grave than to feed a living creature, rather than ending up melding with the mud and roots and worms and bacteria, like my parents, my grandmother and my brothers.

I put the parakeets' cage on top of the rusted chinchilla hutches. In a few months, Vodka and Whisky's former home would be a mass of tarnished wires, one more element of the rooftop's rust-red landscape, one more vertebra of the prehistoric skeleton.

The morning after the funeral, they headed back, and the men decided to go hunting to stock up on fresh meat.

Kenojuac suggested they head for the meanders upstream where moose were plentiful. They loaded an old canoe into the back of the pickup, one that Amaruq's grandfather had fashioned from maple wood, whalebone and sealskin decades earlier. They drove down a dirt track to the river, unloaded the canoe and set off, paddling slowly, staying close to the riverbank. In front of them, a few beavers splashed through the water and disappeared beneath the surface. At a bend in the river, they spotted a young moose who was scrabbling in the snow. Chuck thrust his oar into the water to slow the canoe, Robert raised himself onto his knees and aimed the rifle, steadying himself against the prow. The canoe drifted for a few metres and then stopped. Robert trained the crosshairs on the animal's knee. The moose must have caught their scent because it lifted its head in alarm. "Now!" Chuck hissed. Robert gently squeezed the trigger. The bullet hit home, the moose shuddered, stumbled a few metres and then collapsed in the snow.

Although a young buck, the animal weighed four hundred kilos. They butchered and deboned the carcass and transported the meat back to the pickup. They stretched the hide over the frame of the canoe so it would air as they moved, then drove back to the house.

They parked up next to the shed, used snow to wash the meat, packed it inside a bear-proof container and put it in a store two hundred metres from the station.

Kenojuac called them to lunch. Robert ate in silence, brooding. He still felt bitter that the woman had insisted on freeing Nujuaqtutuq. Though he had warned her that freeing the wolf amounted to a death sentence, she had insisted, and now Nujuaqtutuq was in danger.

When they had finished eating, Chuck asked Robert if they could talk in private. They went outside and walked a short distance away. Chuck gazed out towards the horizon and sighed. "I need to stay a little longer," he said. "I hope you understand." "How much longer?" Robert asked. "I don't know. You can go, I'll find my own way back." Robert said he could wait, he was in no hurry, his proposed route for the pipeline had been approved and discussions about the extension would not start for at least two months, so he had plenty of time.

Robert moved his belongings into the shed. He would treat his time here as a holiday, get some rest, consider his next steps. He promised his uncle he would keep his distance and not interfere. They agreed that Robert should go into town to buy food and petrol. Chuck tried to give him a hundred-dollar bill towards expenses, but Robert refused.

He set out for Mayo, the closest settlement, ninety kilometres away. It was a one-horse town with a population of two hundred and a scattering of houses at the confluence of two rivers. In the town's only shop, the fruit and vegetables were half rotten. It was difficult to find fresh produce. Locals bought up everything as soon as it was unloaded from the trucks. What little made it onto the shelves was already beginning to rot.

He also bought flour, sugar, salt, matches, beer, cask whisky, rice, cigarettes, batteries and some tinned food. In the Yukon, tinned food was essential not only to survive the harsh winters but the humidity and the flies in summer months. He picked up three boxes of 30-06 cartridges, mantles for the gas lamps, four litres of white spirit and two fishing rods with reels, forty-pound line, bait, lures, floaters, sinkers and hooks. And a few animal traps. If he could catch wolves, foxes, coyotes, pine martens or beavers, he could sell or trade the pelts for extra money.

He filled five sixty-litre cans with petrol, since he could not keep coming back to fill his tank. Five cans should be enough for two months' travel around the region.

Back in the shed, he stored everything in a dusty cupboard, then went outside and drank a beer as he contemplated the sunset. Whorls of smoke from Kenojuac's chimney rose into the chill air. In the distance, he heard a wolf pack howling. He thought of Nujuaqtutuq and his inevitable death. If the wolves did not kill him, starvation would. He decided to go look for him. He had found him for a reason and he shouldn't just leave him to his fate.

He loaded the tent into the back of the truck, along with some spare cans of petrol, his sleeping bag, provisions and his rifle with the boxes of ammunition. He had no idea how long it would take to find Nujuaqtutuq and bring him back. He had enough to last at least three weeks.

He climbed into the pickup and set off towards the mountain.

m
 a
  g

  g   **m**   s   s
  o   **m**   g   **t**
   t   **m**   **a**   **a**   t   **o**
  s   **m** **agg**ots s   o   **g**
    g   s   **g**   **g**
  m   **a**   g   g a   **oa**   m
  m   o   **m**   **a**   **o**   **m**   **t**
 a   g   t   a   t   s   s
    g   m   s   s   **g g**
  a   **g**   a   **g**   t   **o**
   m   **o**   g **gg**o**t**s
       t

   mag   g   ots m **a**   **g**
             a
         g
       g   **g**
     o   **g**
      t   o
     s

Banks

The bank's legal representative read through the document several times. When he had finished, he set it down on the desk. "There have been no transactions on this account for three years," he said, "consequently, the account holder must be present in person for it to be re-activated." Simon shot a sidelong glance at our lawyer, Octavio García Allende, who smiled mockingly. "Either you're a retard or a real son of a bitch," he said. The official looked offended. "There's no need to be insulting," he protested. "Did we not make it patently clear that the account holder died three years ago?" Simon said with a sneer. The official looked at him contemptuously. "No, that was not made clear." Simon jabbed the death certificate with his finger. "I would have thought this made it clear." The official picked up the document again. "The certificate alone is not enough; it must be duly notarised by an attorney." Octavio García Allende leaned towards the man. "This is a *certificate*, sir. That means that the relevant authority has *certified* it as a legally binding document." "How do I know it's not a forgery?" the bank official said haughtily. "The death notice was duly filed with the authorities," García Allende said. "You can go see for yourself." The man shook his head. "I don't have time, and besides, that's not my job. Bring me a notarised death certificate for Señor Carlos Valdés, together with a copy of his will, also duly notarised. Once we are in possession of those documents, we will accept the application to change the name of the account holder to the beneficiary."

Bross had been right. The banks would do everything in their power to avoid returning the money. Every bank official demanded notarised certificates and documents that were impossible to find. It was absurd.

481

I left the bank discouraged. García Allende and Bross tried to cheer me up. It was going to be a complicated process, but there was definitely a way of resolving the issue. The lawyer was frank. He wouldn't work for free. If he managed to retrieve the money, he wanted fifteen per cent of the total. He explained that usually he charged forty per cent, but because I was a friend of Simon Bross, he would give me a discount. I asked him if we had to sign a contract and he said that a handshake would be enough.

While it is usually a good idea to be honest with a lawyer, I had told García Allende that the money in the accounts was the profit from Carlos's fur business. I didn't dare tell him that most of it was the profit from drug dealing. I was afraid that if the banks somehow found out, they would share this information with the authorities in order to expropriate the accounts.

I was in two minds about the money. I had no intention of letting the banks keep it, let alone the government. I didn't want it to be fought over like pigswill by a herd of corrupt politicians. But, tainted as it was with death and devastation, would the money truly make me happy?

Simon Bross invited me to lunch. He was in high spirits. He told funny stories and stopped to chat with whoever he met, be it a cook, a street cleaner or a businessman. He was genuinely interested in human beings. He would ask complete strangers about their families and their jobs, and would sometimes cross the line into brazenness. Are you faithful? Do you and your wife still sleep together? Have you ever stolen anything? Do you have homosexual tendencies? Far from being offended, people answered honestly; they felt they could trust him. Bross was not judgemental. With question after question, he would burrow deeper until a secret was revealed: married industrialists having illicit affairs with factory workers; kleptomaniac housewives stealing from their families; men who had screwed their brothers' wives on the kitchen table while the family was eating Christmas dinner;

teenagers who admitted putting rat poison in coffee they made for their mothers. The dregs of morality, a cesspool of furtive acts.

Initially, Bross had heard nothing about the circumstances of Carlos's death. He had found out by chance four months later, and – ludicrously – had been told that Carlos drowned in a swimming pool. With his talent for interrogation he wheedled the truth from me. I even told him about Carlos's other "businesses", the psychedelic movie screenings, Comandante Zurita's obsessive pursuit, the Good Boys' warped faith and how Carlos was murdered because of my indiscretion.

Simon was distressed to hear how my brother had died. It was clear that he thought highly of Carlos, he was distraught. He pushed his plate aside. "I'm not so hungry after hearing that," he said, and sat lost in thought for a long time.

We went back to the factory and Simon took me to a warehouse on the fourth floor. He opened a crate. "Just arrived from Alaska," he said. They were wolf pelts, lush and silky. He draped them over a beam. "The best fur comes from wolves trapped in winter," he said. He used the fur to tailor overcoats that he exported to the U.S., Spain and France. He used the brand name "Pietro Castelli", leading his customers to believe they were hand-stitched by Italian masters, when in fact they were designed and made by two seamstresses from Oaxaca. Bross laughed loudly. "Pietro Castelli, just imagine!"

I told him I had a wolf at home, and explained how I'd rescued Colmillo. Bross asked if I found seeing the furs disturbing and I said no. I asked if he would sell one to me so that I could see how Colmillo reacted to it. He offered me one as a gift, explaining that all the pelts were chemically treated and had no scent, so it was unlikely Colmillo would have any idea what it was.

As I headed home that night, commuters on the metro were startled to see a wolf skin draped over my shoulders. Once home, I hung it on the sill of the window that opened onto the yard. Colmillo sat up and stared at it intently. Seconds later, he pounced. Though I tried to jerk it away, it was futile. He snatched it from me and ripped it to shreds, leaving tattered scraps of fur scattered all over the yard.

Robert headed towards the mountain, driving through the night. As he crossed a plateau, the headlights picked out dozens of pairs of eyes in the darkness. It was a herd of wapiti migrating north. He stopped the truck and climbed down to study them through his binoculars. There were more than a hundred of them, eyes glinting between the trees. He drove slowly along the dirt track, his window wound down so he could hear them padding through the snow.

His familiarity with the route meant he had been able to avoid the muddy potholes and snowdrifts, and he arrived sooner than he expected. He parked the truck in the same clearing. He lit a fire, roasted some moose jerky over the coals, and when he had finished eating went to sleep in the truck.

At sunrise, he spread out the canvas tent and used it to bundle up the sleeping bag, the gas lamp, his provisions, the cooking essentials and the lanterns. He secured the bundle with a rope that he tied around his chest so that he could drag it through the snow and the brushwood. He took his rifle and his binoculars and set off towards Amaruq's grave.

He moved between the trees. His beard and his moustache froze in the glacial dawn air. Spring was already three weeks old yet winter had not relented. The wind and the louring clouds heralded another cold front.

The ground was frozen solid, causing Robert to slip several times. As he crossed a rocky outcrop, he stumbled and wrenched his left ankle. He did not try to break his fall, choosing to use his hands to protect the rifle. He lay for a few moments, unable to get up. He feared the ankle might be fractured, which would mean almost certain death. After examining the injury, he realised it was only a sprain. He struggled to his feet and hobbled on.

Four hundred metres from the grave, he scanned the area with his binoculars, searching for Nujuaqtutuq. He saw a grey mass beside the cairn. The wolf was lying next to the grave. Was he protecting the body? Eating it? What was it that tied Nujuaqtutuq to the dead man?

Robert decided to pitch camp at some distance, so as not to disturb the wolf. When this was done, he grabbed the rifle and some rope and took up a position on a nearby hill where he had a better view of Nujuaqtutuq and the surrounding area.

After watching for an hour, Robert decided to approach. The wolf had been lying motionless for some time. Robert crept closer. He would have to lasso the wolf and immobilise him if he planned to take the animal back with him. Only in his care would Nujuaqtutuq survive. But the wolf seemed to have regained his strength. Despite the badly healed fracture, the festering wound and the harness, the wolf had managed to walk several kilometres to the grave. Capturing him would not be easy.

Crouching low, Robert crawled forwards until he was within thirty paces. Sensing him, Nujuaqtutuq got to his feet. Man and wolf stared at one another. Robert readied the lasso and walked warily towards the animal. The wolf watched for a few seconds, then turned and loped into the forest. Robert watched as he disappeared between the trees. He knew it would be futile to follow.

He walked towards Amaruq's body. It was still covered by stones. The wolf had made no attempt to eat it. For some inexplicable reason, Nujuaqtutuq was keeping vigil. Robert could not understand. For a moment, he toyed with the idea that the old woman was right: the wolf was a transfiguration of Amaruq's grandfather.

He sat a few metres from the grave and waited, hoping Nujuaqtutuq would come back. Hours passed. Untroubled by Robert's presence, a flock of crows came and settled on the mound. Through the gaps between the stones, they began to peck at the face, ripping off small pieces of flesh. Robert wanted to chase them away, but it was pointless. Sooner or later they would return to devour him.

The crows fed for a while and then suddenly took to the wing, startled by something nearby. A wolverine scurried towards the grave and began to worry at the corpse. With its front paws it managed to scatter the stones, then it sank its teeth into Amaruq's chest. The wolverine could rip the body limb from limb. For Nujuaqtutuq to come back, the corpse had to remain intact. Once it was dismembered, it was likely that the wolf would lose interest.

Robert stood up and shouted, trying to scare it off, but the wolverine, which had only just noticed his presence, raised its head and growled. Robert knew that wolverines rarely retreat; if it was growling it would doubtless attack. Robert fired a shot into the air. Unperturbed, the wolverine menacingly continued to advance towards him. Robert aimed at its head and squeezed the trigger. The wolverine fell dead.

Robert skinned the animal. It was not a fine pelt, but it was tough and would make a satchel or a pair of gaiters. He set some of the meat aside and buried what remained some distance from the grave so as not to attract other predators, such as pumas or the wolf pack roaming the forest.

The cold became unendurable and still Nujuaqtutuq had not reappeared. Robert decided to leave and come back the next morning. After he had walked two hundred metres, he turned back. The wolf was staring at him from between the pine trees, close to the grave. Robert smiled. Nujuaqtutuq had been watching all along.

Robert carried on walking and the wolf went and lay down again next to the corpse.

What is the best day to commemorate the dead? Should we visit the cemetery on the day the deceased was born or the day he died? My parents decided to celebrate birthdays. Every year we went to the cemetery to visit our dead. My parents were atheists, they did not believe in life after death. They did not go to the grave to talk to the spirit of Carlos, or the corpse of Carlos. They went to commune with the various iterations of Carlos that still lived in their memories. The Carlos they had cradled when he was born. The Carlos who had taken his first steps at eleven months, clutching my mother's finger. The Carlos who had broken a tooth falling off his bicycle at the age of ten. The Carlos who had gone on work trips to Puebla and Tlaxcala with my father. They felt a connection to this Carlos, the one who, in their hearts, had never stopped being their son. Not the one lying dead and mute in the grave, squeezed between Juan José and my grandmother in their home of clay and roots.

I used to sit on the neighbouring grave. I would speak in a soft voice, not just to Carlos, but to Juan José and to my grandmother. My cramped dead in their home of mud and roots. Those words must have released some of my sadness because I would return home feeling lighter.

A few months after my parents' death I was faced with my father's birthday. The night before I tossed and turned, debating whether or not to go to the cemetery. Chelo noticed I was restless and asked what was wrong. I explained, and asked if she would come with me. She gazed at me and took me in her arms without a word. I wanted to pull away, I wanted her to say "yes" or "no", but she pulled me closer and started to sob. I didn't understand her desolation. It was my father we were talking about. My sadness, not hers. Tears streaming down her face, she stammered: "They're all buried there, aren't they?"

Now I understood why she was crying. Carlos was buried next to my parents and my grandmother. Visiting my father's grave meant visiting Carlos's. She hadn't come to the wake or to the funeral. This would be the first time she had to face my dead brother. I was thinking about my father and she about Carlos. My jealousy, once again. My brother coming between us.

Once she had calmed down, she asked me not to go. My parents' death was too recent, she argued, I wasn't ready to face it. Deep down I knew it was she who wasn't ready.

We slept naked in each other's arms. Bitter jealousy coursed through me. I had a terrible night. Plagued by nightmares, jolting awake. I got up, went to the bathroom and splashed cold water on my face. I dressed quietly so as not to wake Chelo, tiptoed downstairs and went outside. The sun was only just coming up. I stopped a baker who was walking along the street with a basket balanced on his head. I bought some sweet cocol rolls and a few conchas. He gave them to me in a paper bag, still warm. They had obviously only just come out of the oven. I ate a cocol as I walked to the bus stop at Colonia Sinatel, on the far side of Churubusco. I reached the cemetery at 9.00 a.m. I wandered the labyrinthine paths of this tomb-clustered landscape. Crowded together, pretentious, tasteless. Broken, dirty, cracked, looted.

A man was watering flowers in the portico of a stately family mausoleum. In the distance, a young mother clutched a small boy's hand. Both were dressed in black. She was wearing dark glasses, the boy a ridiculous suit with shorts.

I came to the grave where my family was buried and stopped ten metres away to catch my breath. My father's birthday. He and my mother had planned their European trip to be the greatest adventure of their lives; in the end it had been a tombstone to their guilt. They had made the trip to celebrate my father's forty-fifth birthday and my mother's forty-second. Now, in this grave, they were celebrating what would have been his forty-eighth journey around the sun.

I sat on the headstone of the next tomb. I couldn't utter a word. Not a single word for my dead. Perhaps Chelo had been right: I wasn't ready for this.

Feeling a hand on my shoulder, I turned. It was Chelo. She smiled sadly and, without a word, sat down next to me. She stroked my arm. Noticing the paper bag, she took out a cocol and laid it on my father's grave. "Happy birthday," she said. I was touched by the gesture. My beloved girl talking to my beloved father. She took my hand and rested her head on my shoulder.

An hour later, we left the cemetery. We caught a taxi and rode in silence. I rolled down the window. The wind buffeted my face and tousled Chelo's hair.

When we arrived back, I paid for the taxi and we got out. I brushed Chelo's tangled hair away from her face. She kissed my fingers. "I love you more than anybody, more than ever," she said. "I hope you know that." And without another word, she walked off down the street.

Wounds

As night drew on, it got increasingly cold. However tightly he pulled the sleeping bag around him, Robert could not stand it. It was impossible to sleep. He crawled out of the tent and piled more wood on the fire. He drank sickly sweet coffee to warm himself up. He was about to crawl back inside the tent when he heard a noise in the distance. He got to his feet, holding his breath the better to hear. He could make out growls and barking. The wolves were killing Nujuaqtutuq.

With his rifle at port arms, he ran towards the sound. More than once, his sprained ankle made him stumble and he fell face first into the snow. He scrabbled to his feet and kept running. He was putting his life at risk; the enraged wolf pack might attack him too.

When he reached the site of Amaruq's grave, he saw shadows circling. He swept the clearing with his torch. Eight wolves were attacking Nujuaqtutuq. One had him pinned on his side, another was gripping his neck. The harness offered some protection, and Nujuaqtutuq was putting up a fight, but it was obvious he was at a disadvantage.

Robert kneeled, holding the torch against the barrel of the gun to light the scene and, peering through the telescopic sights, trained it on the wolves attacking Nujuaqtutuq. It was difficult to take aim amid the swirl of snapping jaws.

He aimed at the wolf nipping Nujuaqtutuq's throat and fired. The bullet went wide, but the sound of the shot made the wolves pause. Robert quickly reloaded and fired again. He hit one of the wolves in the chest and it staggered backwards, howling and rolling in the snow.

Robert fired again and another wolf collapsed. At the sound of the

490

gunshot, some of the wolves ran into the forest, but others remained, surrounding Nujuaqtutuq. Robert feared they might circle and attack him from behind. He reloaded the rifle, leaning against a tree to cover his back.

The dark shadows flickered back and forth. Robert scanned the area again with the torch. Two wolves had once again latched on to Nujuaqtutuq. Robert squeezed the trigger, hitting one of them in the rump, and the wolf began to run in circles, snapping at the wound.

He fired three more shots, killing another wolf and sending the rest scattering. The beam of the torch fell on Nujuaqtutuq, lying in a bloody heap. Robert decided to wait a moment before going to him. The fight, the adrenaline, the gunshots had almost certainly incensed the wolf pack and they might be circling, preparing to attack again.

Robert waited out the rest of the night, resting against the tree trunk, numb with cold and inactivity, the safety catch of his rifle off so that he could shoot quickly if necessary. When dawn finally broke, he saw the carcasses of the wolves he had shot, and he could make out the rest of the pack, lying in wait among the pines. Leaning back against the trunk, Robert aimed at what he assumed was the alpha male and gently squeezed the trigger. The bullet hit the wolf between its eyes, and it crumpled into the snow. The others retreated a few metres, then stopped. Robert trained the sights on a she-wolf and took a shot. She fell, wounded, managed to crawl a few metres with her broken spine, then lay inert.

Nujuaqtutuq, badly injured, tried in vain to stand up. Robert walked towards him. His back, his haunch and his throat were streaked with deep gashes. The harness was in tatters. Blood gushed from his wounds. Robert slipped the lasso around the wolf's head. Nujuaqtutuq tried to shake it off, but he was too weak, and he lay where he had fallen until he lost consciousness. Robert bound his paws and, bending down, slipped his arms under the great wolf, lifted him onto his shoulders and started walking.

They passed the grave. The stones had been scattered, the corpse was half-eaten, the entrails hanging out, the limbs badly gnawed. Nujuaqtutuq had fought to defend Amaruq in death; now it was unlikely the wolf would survive.

Robert carried the wolf back to the truck, stopping several times because of his swollen ankle. The whole area was a dark, livid bruise. Taking out his lighter, Robert heated his knife to sterilise it, then made a small incision to drain the clotted blood, squeezing until it was almost gone. Then he cleaned the wound with snow. The swelling subsided and Robert walked on.

They reached the pickup, the wolf still unconscious, his head hanging limp, his tongue lolling from his mouth. Robert laid him on the back seat, removed the remains of the harness and covered him in a blanket. His own jacket was soaked in blood. The wolf would not hold out much longer.

Robert climbed into the cab, glanced back at the bleeding wolf and started the engine. He would save him. He had to save him.

García Allende, the lawyer, told me to come see him at his office. The lawsuit we were about to bring against the banks was ready, but there were certain requirements we had to attend to before a judge would allow it to proceed. Despite the fact that I would turn eighteen in a few weeks, I had to appoint an adult as my guardian. As a minor, I was not entitled to instigate legal proceedings, nor to hold a bank account. A trust had to be set up if we were to recover the money.

I asked García Allende whether there was any way for my guardian to defraud me. He said he thought it was unlikely, given that the moment I turned eighteen I would be legally entitled to manage my own assets. In addition, he proposed including a clause preventing any money transfers.

García Allende suggested I name a family member as my guardian, since this would speed up the process of the lawsuit. If there was no family member I felt I could trust, either he or Simon Bross would be happy to stand as my guardian, but I needed to make a decision quickly.

I went outside and sat on a bench on Alameda Central, near the lawyer's office. I considered my options, which I had already narrowed down to five: one of my mother's brothers, one of my father's sisters, García Allende, Simon Bross or Sergio Avilés. I ruled out my uncles. The only one I trusted lived in Texas and would not be able to come and go during the legal proceedings. My aunts all tended towards the melodramatic and, besides, they had shown little concern for me when I found myself completely alone. I barely knew García Allende, and if anyone would know how to cheat me it was a lawyer. Simon was a decent man, he had cared about Carlos and I had no doubts about his integrity. Sergio had shown more concern for me than any of my family. Being an orphan himself, he understood the fragility, the rage and desperation that came with the title.

I felt a strange sense of guilt, as though I would be betraying those I did not choose to be my guardian. Simon was a skilled businessman – who better to advise me about money? Avilés had become a father figure to me, with no ulterior motive beyond wanting to keep me company and look out for me.

I wandered around the park, past balloon sellers, *merengueros*, women cooking gorditas on hotplates and harried office workers hurrying back after lunch. In one corner of the park, a gypsy had a dancing bear. The gypsy played a tambourine while the Russian black bear stood on its hind legs and swayed half-heartedly. A monkey in a red frock coat and a top hat scurried through the crowd with a cup for coins. The bear seemed docile, and performed his routine without any hint of discontent. The monkey, on the other hand, gesticulated anxiously. When someone tossed a coin into the cup, the monkey ran and stood in front of the next person. If they gave nothing, his face would contort, he would stare at the cheapskate and then turn back

493

to his master, whom he obviously feared. The gypsy would signal to him to insist and the monkey would tug at the punter's trousers. If that didn't work, he would glance again at his owner, who would gesture for him not to give up and the monkey would beat on the man's ankles until, to general hilarity from the crowd, he was forced to give him a coin. The monkey would shake the pewter cup, making the coins tinkle, and look for approval to his master, who would throw him a peanut as a reward.

The show finished and the crowd dispersed. The monkey scampered over to his master and nimbly climbed onto his shoulder and the whole troupe headed down Alameda to another corner to repeat the act. The bear trudged wearily, swaying from side to side as passersby dodged past.

Seeing the bear, the money and the tamer seemed to be a sign. I leaned towards choosing Avilés. This chubby little guy had looked out for me, he cared about my problems, he knew my girlfriend and he was a part of my life.

I felt obliged to go and see Bross and thank him. Perhaps he wouldn't mind that I had chosen Avilés to be my guardian, but, out of courtesy, I felt that I should tell him in person.

His shop wasn't far from Alameda so I went on foot. I got there in under ten minutes. I asked the woman at the till if I could see him. With a smile, she asked me to wait for her there. She was certainly treating me differently from the time before. She soon came back and told me that Mr Bross was waiting for me in his office. She led me to him. On the way there, we passed two orthodox Jews in traditional black dress coming out of Bross's office. One wore a hat and the other a kippah. I had never seen Jews dressed that way. The woman left me at the door and asked me if I would like a soft drink, water or coffee. I asked for a coffee.

Simon welcomed me with a smile. "Those are my uncles, can you believe it?" he said, pointing towards the orthodox Jews who were leaving by the stairs. "They are frightening," he said, and roared with laughter.

He told me that his uncles had been living in Mexico for years, but that they barely spoke Spanish. I asked him what language they spoke. "Yiddish," he answered, "our people's ancient tongue that evolved in Central Europe. We are a community rooted in our traditions." As he spoke to me about Jewish culture and history, I began to feel dizzy. Simon asked me if I was alright. No, I was not alright. I had become another link in the chain of hatred against the Jews. I forgot about the bank accounts and my choice of guardian. The only words I managed to say were: "Do you know Abraham Preciado?" Bross suddenly looked grave. "Yes, I know him. He's the shopkeeper who was beaten senseless and left practically paralysed," he said. I swallowed hard. I felt the world spin faster. "I was one of the guys who attacked him."

As he crossed the rice fields, weighed down by the load on his back, an Indian peasant came across a cobra. He raised his machete and decapitated it in one swift movement. The headless body writhed in the mud and the man continued on his way.

Half an hour later as he returned along the same path, now rid of his burden, he saw the snake's body still writhing. Crouching down, he examined the snake. The head lay next to the body and the man decided to pick it up. As he did so, the decapitated head, in a reflex action, bit his left hand. The peasant tried to prise it away, but the fangs sank deeper into his flesh, releasing all their poison.

The terrified man knew that the only way to escape death was to cut off his hand. Raising his machete, he struck a blow but, already weak from the poison, he succeeded only in slashing his wrist. Again and again, the man swung the machete until finally the hand was severed, the cobra's head still clinging to it.

Glancing around, the farmer saw his village in the distance. He stumbled towards home until he fell face down in the mud. In vain, he tried to struggle to his feet. With difficulty, he managed to roll over, turning his face towards the sun. A few bees buzzed above him. He could feel pressure on his lungs. He was panting for breath. His heart was beating irregularly. He felt thirsty. He licked his lips. He gazed up at the sky, felt the wind on his face. He turned his head towards the ground and closed his eyes for the last time.

Streets

Agüitas was the first to deliver the news: "Humberto's mother killed herself." At first I thought it was one of his ill-judged jokes. "Come outside," he said. I opened the porch door and stepped out to look. There were three police cars in front of Humberto's house. A group of neighbours was crowded around the front door.

"Let's go up to the Barreras' rooftop," he suggested. Pato and Jaibo were already up there, he said, and you could see the woman hanging from the beam. Some hours before, forensic officers from the Ministerio Público had arrived and – purely out of professional zeal – had strung up the body again so that they could "analyse" the crime scene. "Why do you want to see her?" I asked Agüitas. He looked at me as if the answer was obvious. "But . . . it's Humberto's mother," he argued, as though this was reason enough for me to go with them. "What difference does that make? She saved my life," I said. Agüitas didn't know how to respond. Angrily, I told him to leave her in peace. He promised to go up to the roof and persuade the others to leave. Of course, he didn't and the three of them stayed up there until someone from the forensics team took the body down.

The death of Humberto's mother weighed on me. Again and again, I saw her hands, the long, slim fingers stained with nicotine. I remembered the afternoon she had driven me to the clinic, chain-smoking as she hurtled through the streets. From the back seat where I was lying, I could see the swirls of smoke reach the roof and then disperse around the car. I could remember the smell of my blood, her floral perfume and her menthol cigarette. I remembered her hand stroking my forehead to calm me down, her hand tossing the cigarette out of the

497

window, her hand squeezing my thigh while we waited for the doctors to arrive and stop the haemorrhage.

Her car had been drenched in my blood. It had been Humberto himself who washed down the back seat and the plastic mats. He scrubbed with a damp cloth until the stains faded. He wrung it out in a bucket and poured the bloodstained water down the drain.

Robert drove rapidly along the track. If he wanted to save Nujuaqtutuq he would have to be treated soon. The wolf, unconscious on the seat, was bleeding heavily from the neck. Robert had to stop to press down on the wound with his hand. The blood stopped flowing, but as soon as he took the pressure off it surged again.

Robert was distracted and the pickup skidded around a curve and drove straight into the snowy ridge. Robert got out to check the truck. The wheels were submerged, the snow was level with the body-work. Getting it out of there would take hours. Carrying the wolf to the house would be impossible. He was at least seven kilometres away.

The wolf needed to be treated by a vet immediately, and he didn't even know if there was one in the area. It seemed likely that Nujuaqtutuq would die. Robert decided to act. He carefully lowered the wolf from the truck and lay him down on the snow. His tongue was hanging out of his mouth and his pulse was almost non-existent. Robert examined the wounds. Seven in total, of which three were serious. The most severe was his torn neck, which would not stop bleeding.

Robert scrubbed it with snow. He poured some whisky on it to disinfect it and opened the wound with his index finger to make sure that it permeated the deepest tissue. He would need to cauterise the wound to stop the bleeding. He pulled out a pair of tongs and two bullets from his toolbox. He sprinkled the powder around the lesion and then lit it with a match. The powder burst into flames and the blood stopped flowing.

With a fish hook and fishing line he sutured the wound. He sewed in a zigzag anchored with double stitches, as he had been taught to do by a hunting guide from the Kajú tribe. Finally, he sprinkled on salt as an antiseptic. He did the same with the other wounds.

Robert washed the bloody residue off his hands. He put Nujuaqtutuq back in the pickup and wrapped him in several blankets. The blood loss meant his body was incapable of generating heat, and maintaining his body temperature was crucial. The wolf's breathing was ragged, with long gaps in between, a sign that he was dying.

Robert collected firewood. He surrounded the pickup truck with bundles of it, sprayed them with petrol and lit them, intending to melt the snow to release the tyres. The wind began to blow. The flames crackled and the smoke rose in waves. Exhausted, Robert sat down next to the fire. His strategy was working. The snow was melting.

He dozed for a while and when he woke up the fire was almost out. Robert stood up and shovelled away the remaining snow from around the wheels until the pickup was free. He climbed behind the wheel and turned the key in the ignition. The pickup skidded across the muddy ground, and would have caused Nujuaqtutuq to fall off the seat had Robert not reacted quickly and grabbed hold of him.

He passed the train station and kept going. He kept driving until he got to the town. He asked about a vet in the gas station. There wasn't one in town, but there was a vet who lived on a cattle ranch a hundred and twenty kilometres west. They gave him instructions on how to get there.

He drove along the asphalt road until he came to a dirt track that crossed a vast plain and turned to the right. A few Angus bull calves stood huddled around hay bales for warmth. They turned as he passed and followed him for a few steps, mistaking the truck for the one that delivered their food.

A few kilometres further on, Robert came upon dozens of dead, skinned wolves and coyotes hanging from a barbed wire fence. There was one every ten metres. Only their tails remained, and they fluttered in the wind. Crows had plucked their eyes out, leaving empty sockets. Their desiccated bodies gave the landscape a grotesque air of foreboding.

Robert had seen such things before. Farmers often hung dead wolves and coyotes from fences to frighten the animals, to let them know the fate that awaited them if they attacked the livestock. He had even met a hunter who made his living killing them. Using a cry that imitated the squeal of a dying rabbit, he lured them. As the predators approached, the hunter crouching in the undergrowth would aim for the head so as not to damage the fur. Farmers paid him a fee per kill, and he sold the furs to traders.

The farmhouse, barns and storehouses were situated in the middle of the immense plain. There were no mountains visible in the distance, nothing but a vast snowy expanse, a far-off forest and the grisly musical stave created by the wolves and coyotes hanging from the wires.

Robert parked next to a garage and headed towards the house. He knocked on the door. A large man with reddish-blonde hair, large hands and a red face opened the door. Robert introduced himself and the man mumbled his name, but Robert didn't catch it and he was embarrassed to have to ask him to repeat it. Robert took him to the pickup to show him the injured wolf. The vet laughed. "You want me to treat vermin?" Robert nodded. The vet gestured towards the wolf and coyote corpses on the fence. "I killed all of those, they're a plague," he said. He didn't understand why Robert wanted him to save it. Several local farmers had been bankrupted by wolves attacking their animals. They were the enemy and had to be exterminated, before they left the region in ruins.

Robert explained where they had found him and why he had decided to rescue him. He offered to pay whatever he charged. The vet laughed. It wasn't about the money. He was a specialist in bovine livestock and not a skilled surgeon. He asked him again, why did he want to keep that foul creature alive?

They moved Nujuaqtutuq to a table in the garage, between a

500

tractor with a disassembled motor, agricultural equipment, cans of oil, discarded tools and hay bales stacked against the wall. The vet examined the wolf. "Who sewed him up like this?" he asked Robert. "I did," he replied. "Well, you did a good job, I don't know why you came to see me," he said laughing. He noticed the long scar on his right leg. "This wolf got caught in a big trap," he declared. The man could recognise the uneven lacerations from the iron jaws, from the depth of the gash and the damage they caused. In general, trappers killed wolves they caught with a bullet from a .22 rifle in the back of the skull. Nobody ever thought of trying to tame one. They were useless.

The vet confirmed that the wolf was in a deplorable state. "I doubt he will survive for long, but let's give it our best shot," he said. He cut the fishing line stitches, shaved off the fur, introduced a tube to the affected area and flooded it with antiseptic solution. Then he removed the pieces of damaged tissue, applied iodine solution around the edges and sewed them up with surgical thread.

Robert asked if there was anything else he could do. "He's lost a lot of blood and that's what's killing him," said the vet. "And how can we fix that?" asked Robert. The vet laughed again. "What for? It would be better just to let him die." "How can we cure him?" Robert repeated. "With a transfusion, but where are you going to find wolf blood?" "If I do find some, can you do the transfusion?" The vet wasn't sure whether Robert's obstinacy was admirable or absurd. "Yes," he said, mockingly.

Robert drove back towards the town, once more passing the line of hanging corpses, which looked even more barbaric in the gloaming. Did this dangling boneyard truly deter wolves and stop them killing the bull calves?

He drove along the fifteen-kilometre track and turned onto the paved road. It was nearly dark by the time he reached the town. He went straight to the petrol station and asked the manager about the mixed-race man who had helped him a few days earlier. He had gone home. His shift ended at three in the afternoon. The manager told him his name was Parson, though he was better known as "Bull", and gave him directions to where he would find him.

On the outskirts of the town Robert found a shack built with wooden planks, with a sheet-metal roof. Dark, dense smoke rose out of a chimney. Three thin dogs came out to bark at him as soon as he got out of the pickup. Robert pretended to pick up a stone to throw at them. The dogs ran away, but continued to bark from a few metres away.

Robert jumped over some muddy puddles and knocked on the door. Inside he could hear a radio playing and a baby crying. Nobody answered. The dogs continued to bark. He went to the truck and honked the horn several times. After a few minutes, an indigenous woman opened the door with a baby in her arms. "Is Bull here?" Robert asked. The woman looked him up and down and called into the shack. "Someone wants you out here!" She went back inside without another word.

Bull came out barefoot and a little drunk. He stopped in the doorway. "What do you want?" he asked abruptly. The dogs were still barking and the man shut one up with a kick. The dog ran away with a howl and the other two hid behind a clapped-out car. "Do you remember me?" Robert asked him. He shook his head. "I had a wolf in a cage. You told me you would have liked to cross him with your female wolf." The fat man smiled. "Yes, now I remember." He walked towards him, apparently unconcerned about his feet getting wet in the icy puddles. "You have the wolf with you?" he asked, gesturing towards the back of the pickup. "No," replied Robert, "but I wanted to see yours."

The man led him along a passageway walled with planks of wood and barbed wire. A plastic doll missing eyes and an arm had been thrown into the mud. The fat man picked it up and threw it over the other side of the fence towards an empty plot of land. When the dogs saw him coming their tails disappeared between their legs and they scampered away underneath the car.

They walked into a backyard enclosed by a rudimentary log fence. There was a chicken-wire cage on one side. The wolf was curled up and tied to a post; she had scabies and was severely malnourished. Her left ear was missing and her tail had practically no fur left on it.

The wolf turned, then stood motionless, staring at them. Robert asked if she had a name. The man smiled. "Pajamartuq," he replied. He raised his arm, lifted up his jacket and revealed a scar. "It means animal that bites," he said, "and here's the proof." The marks of the wolf's canines were clearly visible in his flesh. "I'll buy her," Robert said. The fat man shook his head. "She's not for sale." "How much do you want?" Robert asked, as if his answer meant nothing. "She's not for sale," he repeated. "My wife is very fond of her." Clearly not *very* fond of her, Robert thought, if she was kept in these conditions. "I'll give you fifteen dollars," he offered. The fat man laughed good-naturedly. "Farmers pay ten dollars for 'em when they're dead." "I'll double it," Robert said. "Twenty bucks." The man immediately declined. "Like I told you, she's not for sale." Robert persisted. "Twenty-five." The fat man leaned back against a fence post. "A hundred bucks if you want her, I won't take less." Robert took out his wallet and handed him two twenty-dollar bills. "Here, this is the most I can offer." The man looked at the money and then at the cage. "This is a pureblood wolf. My grand-father caught her. She's worth a hundred," he declared. Robert put the notes back into his wallet. "O.K., never mind, shame we couldn't make a deal. Good night." He turned and headed for the corridor leading to the pickup. The man shouted, "Sixty dollars and she's yours." Robert kept walking. "Fifty," he shouted. Robert turned around. "Forty, not a cent more." The man thought for a moment. "O.K., forty. Take her."

Bross listened in silence to my story about attacking Don Abraham. "How old were you when this happened?" he asked. "Fourteen." "People do a lot of dumb things when they're fourteen," he said. I asked his forgiveness for my part in the attack. "He's the one you need to ask for forgiveness, not me," Bross pointed out. "I couldn't even look him in the eye." "If it comes from the heart, he'll forgive you," Bross said, and offered to come with me to see him.

I told him that Humberto's mother had recently killed herself and that I was sure he was coming back to the neighbourhood. I was ready to kill him and nothing could stop me from taking my vengeance. My tone of voice must have convinced Simon that I was going to go through with it. He looked at me, his expression serious. "The fundamental question you must ask yourself is what you want: vengeance or justice?" I said that the only way to achieve justice was to get my vengeance. Simon shook his head. He stood up, looked for a book among the shelves behind his desk and sat back down again. "Listen," he said, and started to read:

"Vengeance means causing the same amount of damage to the other that they inflicted, or more. Vengeance can generate a spiral of violence, since it provokes new grievances and incites the other side to attack again. Justice does not just try to repair the damage, but to assuage the fury unleashed by the offence. Justice is achieved by the verdict – as objective as possible – of a social institution not related to either side."

Simon paused and lifted his finger to indicate that I should pay careful attention. "The desire for vengeance poisons the soul; the desire for justice relieves it." He closed the book and looked at me. "Do you know who wrote this?" he asked. "I don't know," I said. "Albert Rosenthal, a Nazi-hunter whose parents, wife and four small children were killed by the Nazis. He didn't kill a single one of his family's murderers. He captured them and handed them over to the authorities alive so that they could be put on trial." I smiled sarcastically. "And here in Mexico, what authority is going to put these killers on trial? The police helped them kill Carlos," I said. "Here the system is rotten." Simon got to his feet, faced a window and looked out over the neighbouring yards. "I understand," he said, without looking at me. "It's difficult not to want vengeance when your neighbours, people you have known since you were a child, spent time with, played with, kill one of yours. That is precisely the history of my people."

He gazed out of the window for a while, then came and sat down in the chair next to mine. "Will you allow me to give you some advice?" I nodded. "If you want revenge, go after Humberto but not the police." "Why?" I asked him. "The police chief was just doing his job. You shouldn't take it personally." I couldn't believe Simon would say something like that. Not take it personally? How was I supposed to take it? "He's a corrupt fucking cop, a piece of shit," I spat. "Listen to me," Simon said. "People like him always get what's coming to them. He'll come to a bad end, take my word for it. Don't be foolish enough to go picking a fight with him." It was true, attacking Zurita would mean attacking the system, and the system would ruthlessly crush me.

He handed me the book. "Read it before deciding what to do." It was called "On Forgiveness". I said goodbye and left. As I walked away, I regretted not thanking him for his offer to be my guardian, but I was sure he would understand my decision to choose Avilés.

I went into a coffee shop. I ordered a bísquet with butter and a café con leche. I sat down to read the book. The opening story was sickening. Rosenthal's four children, the eldest of whom was only eight, had been slaughtered and incinerated in concentration camps. His family had suffered persecution and barbarism, and he felt a terrible guilt that he had not suffered at their side. His life had been spared because a Nazi commander separated him from his family and sent him to a different death camp. When the Russians triumphed on the Eastern Front, Rosenthal had been liberated. When the war was over, he had tried to rescue his family, only to discover that they had been utterly annihilated.

Suddenly faced with the horror, Rosenthal had plunged into a spiral of self-destruction. Alcoholic and depressed, he hoped vodka would quickly kill him because he did not have the courage to kill himself. One morning he woke up covered in vomit having drunk himself into a coma with a trio of fat, toothless whores. He had no idea where he was, beyond the fact that it was a filthy room in a city only just recovering from the devastation of war. He glanced out of the window. In the streets, people just like him were wandering, not knowing where they were going. Naked and malodorous, he sat down on the bed. If one of his children had survived, if they had seen him like this, what would they have thought? That he had become a vagrant, a loathsome thing. No: his child would not have been able to look him in the face. He would feel ashamed. The enemy would have won on every front. Rosenthal decided that he could not allow the enemy to win.

The first thing he did that morning was take a shower and wash his clothes. He realised that, to deny the enemy his victory, he had to purge himself of the thirst for revenge. He could not live with the poisonous impulse to cause injury and death. He knew he needed a goal on which to focus, and that goal was to track down his family's murderers and deliver them to justice. He realised that, to be truly free, he had to forgive. To forgive, in order to purify himself of the emotional filth that vengeance brings with it; to forgive, to escape the mire of bitterness and self-pity. To forgive.

Having read these lines, I snapped the book shut. No, I would not forgive. Why had Bross given me this book? Reading it was doing me more harm than good. I could not absolve my enemies. My family rotting underground, my whole life slashed from end to end, the entrails hanging out, no future, no hope, and Bross naively believing that this book might help me. Who did he think he was to even suggest it?

I paid and stormed out of the café in a rage. It was dark and only the occasional car was driving through the centre. I ripped pages from the book and tossed them into the gutter. Rosenthal and his forgiveness could go to hell. And so could justice. In this corrupt country, where impunity reigned, there was room only for vengeance, and I would have mine.

"Before you embark on a journey of revenge, dig two graves."

CONFUCIUS

Path

Far from healing me, Rosenthal's book made me feel sick. An antidote distilled into a poison. Word by word, drop by drop, I became intoxicated. Rosenthal, the Jewish Hamlet. His entire family is murdered and, like that Danish milquetoast, he wonders whether or not to take revenge. They must both have had maple syrup running through their veins. Rosenthal's determination to cling to justice is unnatural. Vengeance seethes in our blood. It is real, palpable, innate to our species, entrenched in our nature. Justice is a system invented by the piranhas of pain – cops, judges, lawyers – who lurk below the surface for their victims to fall in, so they can dart over and devour them. With their needle-like teeth, they rip away hunks of human suffering. Justice serves only to feed rapacious scavengers with more victims. Justice is the source of corruption, a scam. Beneath the thin veneer of civility and decorum, the rot spreads. It is enough to lift the carpet to see the putrid dumping ground where thousands of murderers enjoy freedom and robust good health. That is why vengeance exists. To sweep them away. To clean up that malign and rancid swamp. Vengeance sanitises, it purifies. An eye for an eye, a tooth for a tooth. *Lex talionis*, the unalloyed wisdom we inherited from desert tribes. Justice is the recourse of the weak, of those incapable of confronting those who have destroyed them. They leave to others the task of purging evil. Vengeance is the weapon of the strong and the bold. Vengeance is the only way out. My only way out.

The body of Humberto's mother was not taken to the morgue, no post-mortem was performed as required by law in cases of violent death (yes, suicide is a violent death). None of the legal or forensic measures required to discount the possibility of murder were carried out, there was no attempt even to comply with basic public health guidelines by disposing of the body as quickly as possible. Of course not. The body never left the house. Humberto's henchmen did a shady deal with Zurita to ensure the authorities left the body undisturbed. The terms of the deal remain a mystery. All decisions about what to do with the remains and when were left to Humberto.

His return was inevitable. He would creep home at the weekend, at dawn, under cover of secrecy and darkness. The coward must have been afraid. He would not arrive without taking precautions, or without a security detail. (Will you show up in this neck of the woods alone, faggot? Will you have the balls to face that protruding tongue, that livid skin, those bulging eyes, that bruised neck? Will you be able to endure the shame of being the son of that promiscuous-failed-prostitute-successful-suicide-victim-who-came-close-to-aborting-you? Or maybe the guilt will eat away at you and you will weep with regret. You know I am waiting for you, don't you? Don't take too long, because I'm here, waiting to kill you face to face.)

Chelo tried to dampen my desire for vengeance. She had also grieved over Carlos's death and hated Humberto and the Good Boys. But vengeance wouldn't make Carlos come back, it would snatch me away from her instead. "I don't want you to end up in prison, or dead," she said anxiously. She was consumed with the fear that she might lose both of the Valdés brothers. Of loving and losing us.

Chelo did not want to understand that such a thirst for blood pulsed through the heart of the man she loved. "Killing a killer turns you into a killer," she told me. Sure, it would mean lowering myself to Humberto's contemptible level, but I couldn't allow that scumbag to enjoy another second of freedom. From his watery grave, my drowned brother clamoured for revenge and nothing and no-one would stop me from getting it.

509

I promised Chelo that my vengeance would be silent and discreet, that no-one would know anything until after it was done. By the time the police found out, she and I would be far away. "You don't fucking get it!" she shouted. "I don't want you to be a killer." I asked her to go back to her house. She refused; she didn't want to leave me on my own. We argued for hours until, exhausted and disheartened, she agreed to leave. "If anything happens to you, I will hate you for the rest of my life," she warned. She left in a black rage and I padlocked the door to make sure she couldn't get back in.

I decided to spy on Humberto's house from my parents' bedroom. I pushed to the window the reclining armchair my father used to sit in to read. I placed it at an angle so that I could see the street. I prepared myself for a long wait. Water, food, blankets.

I had counted the exact number of steps to his house. A hundred and forty paces in a straight line along the street. A hundred and fifty-two if I went across the rooftops. I devised a strategy. I had to reach his house without being seen. I could creep down stealthily from the roof, knife him repeatedly and escape across the rooftops without leaving a trace. I would have to be precise; to stab him in the chest without thinking about it. Without giving him the chance to cry out or defend himself. To act decisively, unthinkingly.

Humberto did not show up on Friday night. All quiet. No movement. I peeled off my shirt and started doing push-ups. I tried to get to two hundred without stopping. After a hundred, I was exhausted. My arms were shaking. Still I kept going until I had finished. I needed to be strong, my hand needed to plunge the knife deep into his guts, four, five, six times.

He didn't arrive the next day either. Inside the house the dead woman lay rotting in the cheap pine coffin her son had bought her. The only people who came close were some neighbours. They stopped by the door, whispered to each other and left.

The night passed. My eyes were heavy and I nodded off a couple of times. To wake myself up I went to the bathroom, splashed cold water on my face and went back to my spot to check the street with my binoculars. Nothing. Not a trace of Humberto.

At 1.00 a.m. I opened the window to get some fresh air. I could hear a drummer practising the solo from "In-A-Gadda-Da-Vida" somewhere far away. His neighbours must have hated him. It would be impossible to sleep for the pounding of those drums. I wouldn't have minded if the noise had been coming through my wall. To me, Ron Bushy's drum solo had always sounded like a heart beating frantically after a sudden rush of adrenaline. Almost a metaphor for what was going on inside me at that moment.

The neighbourhood drummer made frequent mistakes, he seemed incapable of synchronising the kick drum to the tom. Despite the ham-fisted, amateur performance, I liked the way his mistakes emphasised the solo's anarchic nature. The guy didn't stop. He played the solo over and over from start to finish.

At 2.30 a.m. the drummer fell silent. Once again it was quiet and the street was empty. King peeked his head out of Carlos's room, still afraid of Colmillo's ubiquity. I called him and he hurried towards me. I rubbed him behind the ears and he rolled around happily. Venturing outside Carlos's room must have been an emotional and physical challenge for him.

King lay down by my side. He kept looking anxiously towards the door. My ever-faithful dog. Even with his damaged cardiac muscle and his nerves destroyed by the wolf, he dared to come out just to show how much he loved me. After a while, he could no longer bear the strain. Fearfully, he got to his feet, his tail between his legs, and went back to Carlos's room.

I closed my eyes and slept for a while. The sound of a car woke me up. A police car passed under my window and stopped in front of Humberto's house. Two cops got out and positioned themselves in the area, watchful. I looked at the clock on the wall: 4.27 a.m.

A Dodge Dart with Jalisco number plates slowly circled the retorno and parked behind the police car. One of the cops went over to speak to whoever was in the passenger seat. A couple of minutes went by. My heart was beating fast. Was Humberto inside the car?

The Dodge Dart pulled away and disappeared. If Humberto was in the car something must have made him suspicious. Maybe it wasn't him, just an advance party of his people making sure there was no danger. My enemy. So close and yet so far. I pressed myself against the window, scrutinising the smallest movement, never lowering my binoculars for a single second. The tingle of vengeance coursing through my veins.

After half an hour another car arrived, a yellow Rambler that also had Jalisco number plates. It was escorted by the Dodge Dart. Both cars stopped next to the police car. Josué and Antonio got out of the Rambler, both with pistols tucked into their waistbands. They exchanged a few words with the cops, then went back to the Rambler. After a few minutes one of the back doors opened and Humberto emerged. He looked around warily. Then he turned towards my window. He looked straight at me for a long while. I stepped back from the glass, although I didn't think he could see me from where he was. Humberto spoke to Antonio, then pointed towards the end of the retorno. He studied the street once again. He turned and went into the house alone. Antonio and Josué climbed into the Rambler. They left, followed by the police car, leaving the Dodge Dart parked in front of the door.

Humberto had arrived on Sunday at 4.38 a.m. His countdown had begun.

Robert drove back to the ranch with the wolf inside the trailer. Exhausted, he dozed off for a moment and had to swerve to avoid driving off the road. He had been awake for so long, it was difficult to remain alert. The wolf corpses hanging on the fence seemed even more ghostly in the moonlight. He pulled over to have a closer look.

He walked through the snow and stopped in front of them. It was a cold night and a thin layer of ice encased the dried-out flesh. The skulls bare. Canines exposed. Death's face smiling out across the snowy plains.

Robert wanted to test the she-wolf's reaction when faced with the frozen mummies. Perhaps she would be scared, or at least agitated. Robert manoeuvred the pickup so that the trailer faced the fence. He got out and shone his torch on the corpses, the beam of light casting macabre shadows. Curled up in a ball, the she-wolf paid them no attention.

Lamps had been lit in the windows by the time Robert got back to the ranch. A glimpse of civilisation in the middle of nowhere. He parked in the courtyard. An ochre metal rooster on the roof spun in the wind. The moon had turned the silent plain silver. He went into the garage to check on Nujuaqtutuq and found him stretched out and unconscious between some sacks of cattle feed. For a moment he thought he was dead, but he relaxed after he saw that he was breathing. He went to get some blankets from the pickup and wrapped him in them to protect him from the frozen ground.

He knocked on the door of the house. It was opened by a haggard, lanky girl of about twelve wearing a threadbare nightgown covered in pink roses and a flannel dressing gown. Almost a ghost. Robert asked her if her father was around. The girl looked him up and down and went back into the house.

The vet appeared. He asked mockingly if he had managed to find any wolf blood. In response, Robert took him to see the she-wolf in the cage and shone his flashlight on her. The wolf raised her eyes, then curled up again. "This wolf is just as fucked as the other one," the vet said. "If I take blood from her, I'll bleed her dry." Both wolves were clearly suffering from acute anaemia, he said, but if Robert wanted

513

he could take half a litre of blood from the bitch and transfuse it into the male, though it was unlikely that she would survive. Robert shook his head. It would not guarantee Nujuaqtutuq's survival and it put the female's life at risk.

The man went into the house and came back with some steaks. He opened the cage in the trailer and threw them inside. The wolf sniffed the food suspiciously, then began to devour it. "Where did you find this filthy wolf?" the vet asked. "I bought her," Robert replied. "Her name is Pajamartuq." The vet smiled disdainfully. "They named that rat?" He couldn't believe that anyone would treat those vile animals like pets. If it were up to him, he would exterminate the entire wolf population.

Robert asked for permission to pitch his tent in front of the house. The vet invited him to stay with them. "We have a spare room," he said, "and my daughter's already made dinner." The man had three children. Two girls and a boy. All three were pale, quiet and thin. They seemed to be the offspring of someone other than the ruddy-cheeked vet. Their conversation was limited to "yes", "no" and "thank you". They were taciturn, unlike their loquacious father. Robert wondered whether they might be autistic, or be suffering from some genetic disorder. The way they dragged their feet when they walked, eyes fixed on the floor, their exaggerated politeness, their use of monosyllables, the hair hanging down in front of their faces, the milk-white skin.

The house was large and spartan. Three bedrooms and a rudimentary bathroom. Robert was given the bedroom belonging to the boy, who would sleep with his father. Patricia, the eldest daughter, filled a bathtub for him with buckets of water heated in a copper kettle.

Robert hadn't bathed in days. He soaped himself three times and, after rinsing himself, lay soaking in the tub until the water was cool. He shaved, ran his fingers through his hair and went down to the dining room. The three children were standing behind their chairs, waiting for Robert to arrive before they sat down. The vet gestured for Robert to sit at the head of the table opposite him. After Robert sat down, the children took their places.

A roast joint of meat sat steaming in the middle of the table. It had been cooked by Patricia, who was in charge of making dinner every day, while her younger sister made breakfast. Patricia served everyone and covered the meat with gravy. Then they held hands to pray. Robert was taken aback by these children. They didn't chatter amongst themselves and they couldn't speak unless their father invited them to do so. They didn't jump onto the table to grab things. Their behaviour was the polar opposite of his own children, who almost had to be dragged to get them to sit down at the table. And Robert realised that he preferred them that way, a little rebellious, not submissive like the vet's.

The children seemed wrapped up in their own thoughts as they ate. They rarely looked up to interact and when their father asked them questions, they replied in quiet, timid voices. As if they weren't there at the table, their father began to talk about them. He told Robert that his wife had died giving birth to the youngest child, that raising them had been gruelling and providing them with an education difficult. The school was far away in town, so he had decided to teach them how to read and write himself. When the town acquired a run-down school bus that picked up children from remote places, he refused. He wouldn't allow his children to travel in that thing and, furthermore, he thought the teacher (who he had known since they were kids) was an idiot. The kids were better off with him. The three of them worked on the ranch once the lessons imparted by their father were finished. Patricia milked the cows. The other two mucked out the stables and fed the bull calves. They came back at night completely drained. The man told Robert that they were easier to teach when exhausted. As soon as they turned four, they had to spend three working hours a day in the field, including Saturdays. It didn't matter if the weather was grim, if there were storms, or it snowed. It was their duty to obey.

515

Robert found the vet's educational methods disconcerting. It had never occurred to him to put his small children to work. Their obligation was to study and their reward was play. It seemed the vet had a different idea. He had nobody to help him look after them and his only option was to keep them busy. There were no women in the town willing to come out all that way to work as a nanny. Besides, the man didn't want a feminine presence taking the place of his absent wife, which was why he had never considered remarrying. "Look at them," said the vet with pride, "they look healthy. They are polite and courteous, they can read and write and they know how to earn a living." Patricia exchanged a glance with her sister. Robert saw it and she, embarrassed, looked down.

After dinner, the vet asked Robert if he had enjoyed the dish. Robert replied that the meat had been a little tough, but well seasoned. The man laughed loudly. "That was wolf meat," he said tauntingly. Robert was irritated, not because it was wolf, which he had eaten before, but because of the vet's provocative trick. "As long as it's not mine," said Robert, surprised by the way he so naturally referred to Nujuaqtutuq as his. The man smiled. "He's too thin and foul-smelling to grill."

Robert said goodnight and went up to his room. He fed the iron stove in his room with logs and lay down on the bed without getting undressed. It had been weeks since he had lain on a mattress and he quickly surrendered to sleep.

A sound woke him up at midnight. He opened his eyes and saw Patricia, dimly lit by the light from the fire. She was watching him in silence. Robert was overcome with tiredness and barely managed to mumble, "Do you need something?" She didn't answer. She looked at him for a few seconds longer, then left. Robert assumed she had come to leave him more logs and went back to sleep.

He woke late. He looked out of the window and saw that the sun was almost at its highest point. In the distance, he saw the vet's pickup moving along one of the ranch's trails. Several herds of cattle were scattered across the plain. It was a clear, sunny day.

He washed his face in a basin. His muscles ached and his hands were blistered. His ankle was still swollen. He sat on the bed and massaged it for a few minutes. He turned around to put on his boots and on top of them found a note, filled with clumsy spelling mistakes: "Help uss pleeeze."

King Maharatha reigned over a prosperous territory in India. He was renowned for his good governance and his concern for his subjects' well-being. Maharatha had three sons. The elder boys helped the king with his royal tasks, while the youngest, Prince Mahasattva, distinguished himself by helping the poor.

One day, the king and his children decided to take a journey into the forest. They travelled by elephant and covered many kilometres before they reached a riverbank where the king ordered them to pitch camp.

The following day, the three sons prepared to go hunting. They took their bows and arrows and headed into the mountains. They climbed until they reached a cave and, looking inside, they saw a tigress feeding her two cubs. The tigress was weak from hunger, since she refused to leave her cubs to hunt, and could barely lift her head.

The brothers took aim at the mother's heart. Prince Mahasattva stopped them. If they killed the tigress, the cubs would die unprotected and their evil deed would be punished in this life or the next.

Knowing that the cubs would suck the remaining life from the tigress and that her death was inevitable, the elder brothers decided to leave. Prince Mahasattva told them to go on ahead and promised he would soon catch up with them. The brothers left and the prince kneeled beside the dying tiger mother. His entire existence had been filled with happiness, he had never wanted for anything, and yet when he had tried to be kind, it had never been enough. This was the perfect moment to make a sacrifice. He would give up his body to feed the tigress so that she might survive and watch over her cubs.

With a sharp bamboo stem, he cut the veins on his wrists, brought them close to the tiger's muzzle, and she began to lick the blood. Gradually the tigress grew stronger and managed to get to her feet. She looked at the man and attacked him without mercy. The prince heard his bones crack between the beast's powerful jaws and smiled as she ate him alive.

When they noticed that Mahasattva had been gone for a long time, his brothers returned to the tiger's lair. To their horror, they found only scraps of his clothes, his bones and a pool of blood. Bitterly regretting having left him alone, they picked up what little remained and headed back to the camp. Sobbing, they told his parents the terrible story. The king and queen fell to their knees. Imagining the terrible pain their son had experienced as the tiger devoured him made them faint.

In honour of his good deed, Mahasattva was reborn in the heavenly reign of Tushita. From his ethereal position, he saw his family's suffering. He explained that he had offered himself to the tiger and had died with great joy. The family understood Mahasattva's sacrifice and started to act with charity and generosity so they might join him in the heavenly kingdom.

His parents placed the fragments of Mahasattva's bones and hair in a chest encrusted with seven precious stones and over it they built a stupa to honour his memory. It is believed that, centuries later, Prince Mahasattva was reincarnated as the Buddha.

His grave, in the mountains of Nepal, is revered as one of the most sacred Buddhist shrines. Thousands make the pilgrimage every year to venerate the relics of Prince Mahasattva in the place where it is said he sacrificed himself to feed the tigress.

Skies

Humberto has been locked up in his house for three days. Is he too busy making plans to bury his mother? Is he talking to her? Is he asking that mute, stinking corpse for explanations? Is he suffocating in her gases? Or did he shoot her up with formaldehyde so she wouldn't rot? What was Humberto plotting?

The Dodge Dart is parked in front of the door during the day. At night, the Rambler takes its place. Men I don't recognise guard the house twenty-four hours a day. They are young and they wear crucifixes around their necks. Short hair, patent leather shoes, fine wool trousers, white shirts. These Good Boys are not from the city. They wear barely concealed pistols beneath their clothes. They ask the neighbours if they can use their bathrooms. They ask for glasses of water. Stoic, they stand most of the time. Sometimes they doze in the car. They don't dare touch Humberto's doorbell. It seems he has forbidden them to bother him. They are there to look after him, not annoy him. Antonio and Josué have turned up a couple of times. They speak to the lookouts for a few minutes, hand them bags of food and soft drinks and then leave again. Zurita's men come by too. They drive slowly down the street in their patrol cars, take a look, then continue along their way.

I cannot wait any longer. Humberto might go back into hiding in the skirts of his protectors' robes, those virtuous priests and their tendency to side with miscreants. If he should escape, I will not be able to find him. I need to act fast; there can be no mistakes. I have seen what prison is like, I have no desire to spend the rest of my life locked up with the dregs of society.

Crouching behind the Barreras' water tank, I keep watch on

Humberto's house. His mother's coffin has been set in the middle of the living room, where she hanged herself. Four altar candles burn, one at each corner of the coffin. My enemy is pacing nervously. He sits, he stands, he comes and goes. It's that gnawing sensation, the death maggots have begun to consume him.

I spend all afternoon watching him, then Humberto draws the curtains. I can no longer see him. I don't know whether he is eating, whether he is asleep or awake, whether he has managed to stop pacing. I count the steps to his house again. I have memorised the route. I could cross the rooftops blindfolded. I know every wire, every television aerial, every inch of space between our houses. I could be struck blind and still walk there without hesitation.

I decide the time has come. I prepare to kill him that night. I strap the knife to my wrist and practise drawing and lunging in a single movement. I hone my technique. The knife slides into my hand in milliseconds. Humberto will not know what lightning bolt has stabbed his abdomen. I'll drive it in and twist, rip open his insides. I picture his stunned expression, his white shirt dripping blood, his hands struggling to hold back the intestines as they spill onto the floor.

I observe Humberto's guards. At six in the afternoon and six in the morning they change shifts. By midnight they are tired and nodding off where they stand, more asleep than awake. I decide to attack at 1.00 a.m. At that time, nobody is on the streets and his defenders will be dead on their feet.

Chelo knows that the time has come for me to take my revenge. She calls and, sobbing, begs me not to go through with it. "Please, don't." I hang up. She calls back but I don't answer. As well as padlocking the front door, I have bolted the door to the roof. There is no way for her to get in.

I take a nap. I take the phone off the hook and switch off the electricity in the house. I don't want anyone to bother me. I don't want my friends to come looking for me. I don't want Avilés to turn up

521

unexpectedly. I am going to kill Humberto, this is the only thing I should be thinking about.

I wake up four hours later. My teeth and jaw hurt. I must have been clenching them in my sleep. I stretch. I want to lengthen my muscles, make them flexible, prepare them for the attack. I look at the clock. Five hours left until vengeance. I look at the street. Both guards are in their places, upright and steadfast. Humberto must have prepared them for this. "Cold does not exist, hunger does not exist, tiredness does not exist." They are outsiders, they don't know the neighbourhood. They are probably oblivious to the fact that I could sneak into Humberto's house from the rooftop. In all the time I have been watching them, not once have they looked up. I will be the ghost that killed their leader.

I keep the lights off in the house. There is no trace of my presence. I am going to see King. He lies in the darkness. Snoring. I sit down next to him and stroke him. He does not wake up. His ears tremble. He shivers in his sleep. He must be dreaming.

I go down to Colmillo. He should be my ally. I should let him into Humberto's house and let him rip him to pieces as soon as he sees him. Eat him alive. Chew on his guts. Colmillo looks hungry. I throw him a few shank bones and he crushes them like biscuits.

The hours pass by slowly. I walk in circles around the living room. I slide the knife down my wrist again and again. With practice, it has become an extension of my arm. My hand turns into steel, the steel into my hand. In my mind, I rehearse the exact place where I should bury it. In the centre of his solar plexus. And once inside, I will shred his liver, heart and lungs.

I think about using one of the old woollen balaclavas my father bought us in La Marquesa when he took us to play in the snow. I try it on. It feels tight, but it covers my face completely. I look at myself in the mirror. Only my eyes are visible. I take it off. I decide not to cover my face. I want Humberto to see me, to know who his executor was.

I am executing him, not murdering him. Execute: kill the killer and justice prevails.

The hour draws near. I watch them through my binoculars. One of the Good Boys has got into the car. The windows are steamed up, a sign he has been asleep for a while. The other is leaning against the door. He looks sleepy. His eyes are closed. His mouth is open.

Midnight strikes. I sit down in the dining room and pick up the old brochure that contains the itinerary of my parents' trip to Europe. I read it just like my father did the night before they left for Madrid. "Europe within your reach." Something my family had dreamt of since my great-grandparents' time: the Colosseum, the Eiffel Tower, Big Ben, Plaza Mayor. History's Disneyland. I read: "comfortable buses", "expert guides", "three-star hotels", "breakfast included", "tours to the main attractions".

I go to my room and pick up the linen shirt my parents brought Carlos from Italy. I put on the shirt he never wore. The shirt my parents carefully chose in a Florentine market. Egyptian linen, the vendor told my parents to convince them of the item's quality. Dressed as Carlos, I get ready to avenge him. I put on a brown jumper. I need to wear something dark to camouflage myself as I cross the rooftops.

I strap on the knife and cover it with my sleeve. I put a knuckle-duster into one trouser pocket and a switchblade in the other. My temples throb. My breath is ragged. I can't stand it. At 12.28 a.m. I climb the spiral staircase to the rooftop. The night is clear and starry. It's cold, and there's a light breeze. The cedar tree in the middle of the road sways slightly.

I head towards the Garzas' rooftop, climb down their stairs, jump to the pavement and come out at Retorno 202. I turn around, walk behind my street and get to Río Churubusco. There is nobody out, only a couple of street dogs scampering along the pavement. I walk to the Martínez house, jump the fence and climb up to the rooftop. From the Martínez rooftop to Humberto's house was eighty-six steps. I take a deep breath and go. I pass Mrs Carbajal's house, sixty-two steps, fifty, across the Montes de Oca house, thirty-seven, twenty-one, walk over the Rovelos' rooftop, eighteen, fifteen, six steps. I get to Humberto's spiral staircase. I go down the stairs without making a sound. No lights are on. The kitchen door is locked. I try to open a window. I can't. It's locked. I notice the second-floor bedroom window is half open. I climb the staircase again. I shuffle along the ledge, sticking as close to the wall as possible until I get to the window. I pull it open. I peer inside. I can't see anyone. I enter the house.

Robert sat there on the bed with the note in his hands. Why was Patricia asking for his help? Was her father a perverted monster who forced her to do unspeakable things? Did he beat them? Sexually abuse them? Enslave them? Robert was confused. The children were strange and extremely timid, and the vet was eccentric and boisterous, but he did not seem like an evil man. How should he help them? And who? The whole family? Or just the children?

He opened the door and found a plate with some bread and slices of ham. The fact they had left his breakfast outside his room intrigued him further. Why was the man being so hospitable? It was true that in regions with such punishing weather people tended to help one another, and survival often depended on a helping hand. But this didn't seem to be the case here. Was the vet expecting a more generous payment for his services or was it a way of covering up his sinister behaviour?

He sat down on the bed to eat and when he finished, he went downstairs. Nobody was home. He washed his plate, dried it with a cloth and placed it with the rest of the dishes piled up next to the sink.

He went out to check on the wolves. The female was still curled up in the cage and she barely looked at him as he approached. Robert slipped a few slices of ham between the bars, but the wolf didn't make any attempt to eat them.

He went to the shed and couldn't find Nujuaqtutuq. He feared the vet had killed him and that his body would be hanging from the wire fence, shivering in the wind. Worried, he climbed into the pickup and drove along the endless tracks, searching for the man. It took him a while to find him. He eventually located him on a remote part of the ranch. He was unloading hay bales to feed a herd of eager bull calves.

Robert got out of the pickup, ready to confront him, but the friendly way in which the vet greeted him soothed his nerves. "Good morning," the man said to him, smiling. "Did you sleep well?" Robert nodded and the vet slapped him on the shoulder. "I'm glad." Robert spotted Patricia further away, spreading hay across the snow with a pitchfork. Their eyes met for a moment and then she looked down.

Robert asked about Nujuaqtutuq. The vet told him he had gone to examine him that morning and had found him close to hypothermic shock because of the intense cold. He had laid him down next to the smokehouse behind the shed so that the embers would warm him up.

Patricia came over. As hard as Robert tried to find some clue in her expression that would explain the note, she never looked up. The vet told him they were thinking of going back for an afternoon snack around five, and that if he got hungry, he could find bread and cold cuts in the pantry.

Robert climbed back into the pickup. Patricia watched him drive off, and, as soon as he was some distance away, went back to helping her father spread the hay. Robert observed her in the rear-view mirror. He would find the right moment to ask why she had asked for help in the middle of the night.

Robert drove directly to the smokehouse. Nujuaqtutuq was still unconscious. He laid a hand on the wolf's back. Nujuaqtutuq felt cold, and Robert could feel a steady tremble under his skin. He did not feel hopeful. It was unlikely the wolf would survive.

He picked him up and carried him into the house, placed him next to the chimney and lit a fire. He needed to elevate his temperature by whatever means possible. Bringing him inside would doubtless annoy the vet, but he had run out of options.

He sat down and looked at him. What would he do with him if he managed to recover? He certainly couldn't free him, it was obvious that other wolves would attack him immediately. Should he take him home and keep him in a cage in the backyard? No, that wasn't an option either. He would be putting his wife and children at risk, and nobody in Whitehorse would find it amusing if the wolf escaped and wandered the streets, ready to attack anyone in his path.

If any animal in the folklore of the Yukon settlers represents evil, it is the wolf. It has always been described as a malicious and treacherous animal; some even attribute demonic traits to it. Only in a few First Nation legends is the wolf considered a superior and wise being, a hunter admired for its resistance and tenacity. But to others, as to the vet, it was a foul animal that deserved to be annihilated. Truth be told, Robert had paid wolves scant attention. They did not interfere with the working of the oil pipeline, like wapiti or caribou. The first time he'd seen wolves was when he'd seen a pack devour a female wapiti alive. They attacked as she was giving birth. Her calf had not yet fully emerged when they ripped it in half. The wolves bit the mother's legs and she collapsed in the long grass. Lying there, the wapiti watched with tired eyes, seemingly waiting for the pack to finish her off. She occasionally looked back to see wolves pull out her intestines. The wolves ate voraciously, indifferent to the suffering of their prey. This was nature red in tooth and claw, but the scene did not perturb Robert. He found a certain beauty in the contrast between the serenity of the wapiti and the frenzy of the wolves as they fought among themselves for mouthfuls of meat.

As soon as Nujuaqtutuq recovered, they would have to part ways. Robert thought about taking him to Vancouver zoo or finding an animal reserve. He would do the same with Pajamartuq, the miserable, maltreated wolf who was waiting, deceptively meek, for the opportunity to snap her jaws.

He got up to look for something to drink. In the cabinet he found a bottle of hand-distilled Canadian whisky. A rustic label said it had been made in Saskatoon. Robert opened it and a pungent whiff of alcohol made him turn away. It smelled more like disinfectant than a drink. Even so, he poured himself a glass. He needed to relax. The first gulp left a strong taste in his mouth, and the alcohol burned his oesophagus. Once his palate became accustomed to it, he noticed the aftertaste of corn combined with bitter notes of rye.

Bottle in hand, he went back to sit by the chimney. The wolf's breaths were laboured; there were gaps of several seconds between one inhalation and the next. It seemed as though his lungs could collapse at any moment. Robert noticed that one of his wounds was oozing and he poured some whisky over it. He drank what was left in his glass and then served himself again. He leaned his head on the back of the chair and closed his eyes.

In Bucovina, a region in eastern Romania, there are many Orthodox Christian monasteries. The majority of them were founded in the fifteenth century by Ştefan cel Mare (Stephen the Great), who led the Christian resistance to incursions by the large Turkish army, which his army defeated despite a distinct numerical disadvantage. Hundreds of years later, Ştefan was canonised a saint for his successful defence of Christianity.

The murals on the walls of Voronet monastery, built on his orders, are covered in byzantine frescos. On the western facade, symbols of heaven and hell, good and evil, stand out.

To represent the resurrection of souls, Romanian old masters chose to paint images of beasts with human body parts emerging from their snouts. A hand emerges from a wolf, a head from a bear, a shoulder from a lion.

Men devoured by beasts – having suffered one of the worst deaths imaginable – are resurrected from out of the animals' gastric juices and digested food, to continue their journey towards eternal life.

Hunters

It is dark inside the house. Not a single light on the top floor is on. I don't know the layout of the rooms or where Humberto might be. I grip the knife and grope my way around the bedroom. Every step is cautious. Vengeance is close, very close. I move around something bulky and touch it to find out what it is. A sewing machine. The mother mended strangers' clothes here, desperately trying to earn a few extra pesos to pay for her treatment. I make out a chair in the darkness. I walk around it and reach the door. As soon as I open it a crack the nauseating stench of the corpse surrounds me. It makes my stomach turn. I cover my nose and mouth. I struggle not to vomit. I attempt to control my gag reflex and keep still, hoping to get used to the smell.

It takes me a few minutes to compose myself. I could never have imagined such a stink. It impregnates my saliva, my taste buds. I am desperate to spit out this repulsive slick that tastes of death. I leave the room. I walk along a passageway. A street lamp dimly lights the photographs hanging on the walls. I can't see who is in them. I keep walking towards what I think is the main bedroom. I grab the doorknob with my left hand and slowly turn. I push, but it's locked.

Perhaps Humberto is inside, waiting with a gun in his hand. I press my ear against the door to listen. I can hear nothing but the distant yowl of cats fighting on one of the rooftops. I slowly retreat. I head towards the stairs. The fetid smell sharpens. The house is bursting with death's gases.

I descend one step and stop for a few seconds. Then another and again I stop. This is how the Sioux hunted. Every step, complete stillness. "The act of being invisible to your prey", they taught their children. "Make sure it thinks you are earth, grass, another bush, a wind blowing from the north. You must become nothing and be everything. The deer should not suspect that you have killed it until it sees one of your arrows buried between its ribs." That is what I want to be now: "invisible to Humberto", for him to know that I have killed him only once he is down, writhing in pain on the ground, and I get up close to tell him: "It was me."

I have walked down five steps and as I reach the landing I notice a flickering light on the wall. It is coming from the altar candles on the corners of the coffin. I get ready to walk down another step when I hear a sound. I stop, my right foot in the air, paralysed. I grip the knife harder and hold my breath, ready to kill. I expect to find myself face to face with Humberto, to have to jump on him as soon as he appears on the staircase. Two minutes go by and I hear nothing more. I lower my right foot and put it on the next step. I must be invisible, I repeat in my mind. I descend, moving as slowly as a praying mantis. Another sound. I stop. I want to hear more clearly, but my beating heart booms in my eardrums, drowning out everything else. I want to ask the old Sioux how to control this throbbing. The drumming is so deafening that I worry Humberto can hear it from metres away. I swallow, trying to dull the adrenaline's brutal effect. Impossible. Nothing can slow this beating, or the trembling, or my uneven breathing.

I descend another step. In the seventeenth century, the Zen monks would instruct the warriors: "Do not concentrate on your sword or on your enemy's sword, or on his hand or yours, or on your movements or his. Suspend your thoughts, let your mind go blank and allow your body to flow during battle." Easy for a Buddhist monk to say, training a fighter inside the peaceful walls of a monastery.

The amber light of the altar candles shudders. Something or someone has made the flame gutter. I freeze. "Don't think, flow with your surroundings, don't think, flow," I repeat. I take another step downstairs. There are three more to the ground floor. My muscles, my tendons, my bones, they can't take much more. My body is tense, made of wire. And the smell, that damn smell of death. The nausea, my veins about to explode, the knife in my hand. I should be invisible, I should flow. I should slice open Humberto's guts, turn him into a cloud of gas, a piece of fetid meat. I should send him into the dark well of nothingness, where everything is black and there is no light, no god.

I reach the penultimate step. From there I can see part of the living room. I spot the coffin; three of the altar candles are lit and one has gone out. I can't see Humberto, but I know he must be huddled somewhere, waiting to die or kill. I carefully look around. Nothing. I must be invisible. I descend the final step pressed against the wall. My heart slams. I look around the corner. My eyes pass over the living room. I spot a bare foot. There he is, the son of a bitch. I hide in the alcove. He hasn't noticed me, I am invisible. He doesn't know I am only a few paces away. I could creep up behind him and plunge the knife between his shoulder blades again and again. I could wait until he turns around and bury the steel into his chest and tell him: "Here I am, *pendejo*, welcome to your hell." My heart. Slam. My heart. Slam.

I look again. This time I see all of Humberto. He is kneeling with his back to the coffin, his arms flung open, his naked back torn, blood flowing. On the floor lies the whip he has lashed himself with. The wounds are deep. It looks as though he has been flaying himself for hours. The walls and the carpet are spattered with blood. He holds in his hands the rope his mother hung herself with. I hear a faint sound. Humberto is praying. The fool still dares to pray.

I walk towards him warily. The carpet muffles my footsteps. The smell of putrefaction is unbearable. In the corner of my eye, I see the coffin. The lid is half open and I glimpse the dead woman's swollen face. I get even closer. Humberto is still lost in his prayers. He doesn't sense me. I am invisible. I stand just behind him. I raise the knife, ready to sink it into him. I say his name to make him turn around, so I can kill him face to face. "Humberto."

*

Robert dozed for a while in the chair, sluggish from the whisky and his fatigue. The sounds of doors and voices woke him. He stood and looked out of the window. The clouds were reddening with the last of the sun's rays. A flock of thrushes flew across the horizon towards a far-away pine tree. He saw the vet heading towards the house with his two youngest children. He was surprised to see that it was Patricia who was parking the truck in the garage. He needed to find a moment alone with her so that she could explain her request for help.

He supposed the vet would be irritated to see Nujuaqtutuq inside the house and he had prepared a speech to explain himself. The man walked through the door, took off his heavy jacket and hung it on a hook next to the entrance. He spotted Robert standing next to the chimney and greeted him with a loud "Everything alright?" Robert nodded. The man looked at the frail wolf. "Is he dead?" Robert shook his head. The vet walked towards Nujuaqtutuq. He squatted down to examine his wounds and pressed his index finger against his carotid artery to check his pulse. "He is still very weak," he said, "but his wounds are starting to heal." Then he brought his nose close to the animal's back and looked at Robert. "This whisky isn't easy to get hold of. It would have been better to use surgical spirit." Robert felt he should apologise, but the man was already serving himself a drink.

Robert asked him if he had a problem with his keeping the wolf inside the house. The vet smiled. "It's a terrible example to set for my children, and the truth is it's like inviting the devil to stay. But you've brought him inside now so never mind about taking him out." Patricia came in and handed her father the keys to the pickup. The man put them in the pocket of his overalls and settled down on a sofa next to the window. Robert thought it was improper for the man to sit down in his clothes still covered in earth, straw and manure. He would never do such a thing. This was a rule first laid down by his great-grandparents and passed from generation to generation: you do not sit on the furniture in the living room or dining room while wearing work clothes and you certainly do not lie on the bed, and you of course take off your muddy boots before coming into the house.

The vet looked out across the prairie as he sipped his whisky. Robert looked for Patricia out of the corner of his eye, but she and her siblings had gone up to their rooms. The vet was still gazing outside, engrossed. Robert wanted to say something to him, but he suddenly realised he couldn't remember his name. He seemed to be of Scottish origin, like himself. To own such a huge amount of land his ancestors must have arrived centuries ago. The ranch must have been at least two hundred thousand hectares. How many of them had been snatched from native tribes? How much bloodshed had that land seen?

Robert tried to work out if there was something not right about the man, anything that could explain Patricia's urgent plea for help. Apart from his obvious lack of cleanliness and manners, and his loud hoots of laughter, he didn't notice anything out of the ordinary. A farmer like any other.

The man invited him to sit down next to him. Robert settled down in the adjacent chair. The fabric of the sofa the vet was sitting on was smeared with dry mud and bits of straw. Clearly the vet often sat in that spot after getting home from work.

The man finished his whisky, got up to fetch the bottle and filled his and Robert's glasses. "A friend of mine gives his geese this whisky for fifteen days before killing them. You can't imagine the flavour it gives the meat," he told him. "On the fourth day, the geese start racing towards my friend as soon as they see the bottle. After drinking some they stagger away and end up on their backs in a corner of the pen," he said laughing.

The man drained his glass in one gulp, poured himself another and polished that off too. He didn't seem at all drunk. It was as though he were drinking lemonade. He pointed out of the window towards the cattle walking along the fence and through the afternoon shadows. "One day I'll buy a barrel of whisky and get them drunk to see what the meat tastes like," he said with a chuckle. Robert asked if he had any kind of social life with his neighbours. "What neighbours?" he said with a laugh. He gave the impression that he found life as a friendless widower amusing, that this lonely existence with his three depressed children did not trouble him at all.

Patricia came downstairs with her sister, and without looking in their direction they went into the kitchen. Robert excused himself, claiming to want a glass of water. He went in, got a glass and served himself some water from a jar. He approached Patricia. She turned to look at him nervously. "Why did you leave me that note?" asked Robert. She looked towards her father in the living room and then at her sister, who was slicing an onion. "I'm going for more firewood," Patricia told her. Her sister nodded and returned to her task. Patricia picked up her coat and a torch and opened the door. Before leaving she looked at Robert, and with an almost imperceptible nod she gestured for him to follow her.

Patricia walked towards a barn. Robert waited a few minutes before catching up with her. He checked that the vet hadn't noticed him go outside. The man was still staring out of the window, deep in thought. Robert had gone out without a coat and felt the piercing cold as soon as he stepped outside. He pulled up his shirt collar to protect himself.

He got to the granary. Patricia was pretending to gather firewood. As soon as she heard him come in she shone her torch in his face. The light was blinding him so he covered his face with his hands. "Are you alright?" he asked. She lowered her torch and Robert took a few steps closer. "Why do you need help?" Her breathing was agitated. It was obvious she was working up the courage to speak. "Tell me," Robert insisted. "My father," the girl said and then stopped. "What about your father?" She seemed to be choosing her words carefully. "My father isn't well," she said, looking towards the barn door as if to make sure nobody was listening. "In what way?" Robert asked. Patricia took a deep breath and continued. "Sometimes he talks to himself and stops eating and acts like we aren't there and he leaves the house and doesn't come home for days and when he comes back he locks himself in his room and doesn't come out and then he grabs his rifle and shoots the walls and punches himself in the face and breaks the doors down and shouts and threatens us and then he cries and asks for forgiveness and talks to himself again and his voice changes and he moves his hands a lot and he scares us so much, so much," she said in a rush, as if pausing for even a second would prevent her from going through with it.

Robert noticed the girl was shaking. He wasn't sure if he should go over and console her or keep his distance. "Does this happen to him often?" he asked. Patricia told him that her father had had a crisis just a few days earlier. Robert asked if he had ever hit them or sexually abused them. Patricia said no to begin with, but then admitted he had hit them before, that several times he had given them bruises or bloody noses. She asked Robert to take her father to see a doctor or to stay and protect them, because she could no longer bear to live with the fear of seeing him so out of control. Robert asked her what his name was. "I don't know," said the girl. "What do you mean you don't know? He's your father," said Robert, incredulous. "I don't know," said Patricia. "Sometimes he's John, other days he's Joe or Mark. His name changes all the time." Robert asked her what his surname was. "Sycamore, I think. I'm not sure," she replied.

Patricia picked up a few logs and hurried out of the barn. Robert watched the light disappear into the blackness of the night. He stayed by himself for a while, to allow what the girl had told him to sink in.

He was about to go back to the house when the vet's voice cut through the darkness. "Do you intend to believe everything she told you?"

Martín Luis Guzmán was a brilliant Mexican writer and intellectual, and is considered to be one of the best Spanish language prose writers of the twentieth century. He was also a man of action. During the Mexican Revolution, he joined forces with Pancho Villa, the dazzling and bloodthirsty general.

Guzmán maintained such close ties with Villa that he essentially functioned as his private secretary. Because of their close relationship, he was a privileged witness to the general's decisions and military tactics. He vividly captured this in two of his best works: *Memoirs of Pancho Villa* and *The Eagle and the Serpent*. The second is a collection of stories about the revolution from the perspective of Villa's supporters. In the book, Guzmán tells a tale titled "Pancho Villa at La Cruz". He and Llorente, a friend and comrade, go to see Villa in the train carriage from which he issues his orders. The general is highly agitated. Maclovio Herrera, one of his most trusted men, has mutinied. Villa cannot believe it. "But he is my son in arms!" he exclaims, aggrieved. His emotional state leaves an impression on Guzmán: "He is so sombre that just the sight of him fills us with dread. The flashes of his eyes suddenly revealed to me that men belong not to one single species, but to many; and that from one species to another, within mankind, there are impassable distances, worlds irreducible to a common term, capable of producing – if from one world, you were to look into the depths of the world opposite – the vertigo of *the other*." Villa furiously paces the carriage. The commander of the troops that fought Herrera's followers asks in a telegram what should be done with the hundred and sixty prisoners who surrendered. Villa is indignant at being asked the question. They are traitors and must be executed as soon as possible. Villa instructs the telegraphist to send the order to bring them to justice without delay. The telegraphist nervously taps: "Shoot them immediately." The fate of a hundred and sixty men, transcribed in the tap-tap of the machine.

The order sent, Villa sits down on a chair. He is clearly uneasy. "He scratches his head, as if he wants to kill an internal, cerebral itch – the itch of his soul." Llorente plucks up the courage to declare that he thinks he has made the wrong decision. Villa confronts him: "Tell me why you disagree with my order." Llorente argues: "Because the report states, general, that the hundred and sixty men surrendered." Villa does not understand. In his obstinate and coarse view, a captured soldier is a dead soldier. Terrified, Guzmán timidly intercedes in Llorente's favour. Villa obliterates him with one look. Known for his scant tolerance for being questioned, the general could send them off to face the firing squad. Villa demands an explanation. Guzmán tries to articulate it as well as possible: "General, those who surrender spare the life of the other, or others, since they renounce their pledge to die fighting. And therefore, he who accepts their surrender is obliged to allow them to live."

Something in this explanation touches a moral spring within Villa. He stands next to the telegraphist and dictates: "Stay execution of prisoners until further notice." The telegraphist taps urgently. Once again, the fate of one hundred and sixty men hangs on the tap-tap trilling across the telegraph wires. There is no immediate response. There is no way of knowing if the distant outpost has received the revocation. Time passes, there is a growing anxiety. The delay could mean the death of dozens of men. Villa is overcome with panic. Moments earlier, he was determined to execute the "traitors", now he wants to save them. Other messages come through, but nothing to indicate that the countermand has been received. Half an hour goes by. Tension builds until the telegraphist finally announces that the commander

537

of the column has stayed the mass execution. Villa exhales, relieved.

Llorente and Guzmán spend the afternoon with him. The incident is not mentioned again until nightfall, when Villa says goodbye. "And thank you very much, my friends; thank you very much for the business with the telegram, and the prisoners."

Revenge?

I call his name a second time but he does not turn around. He continues to pray with his back to me and his arms open. The third time I say "Humberto" he turns to look at me with a lost expression on his face. It's not what I was expecting. I get ready to plunge the blade into his face and he looks back at me without even raising his hands to defend himself. "Get up," I order him. Humberto stays prostrate. I kick him in the stomach and he doesn't react. His stupor is disconcerting. "Motherfucker, I'm going to kill you!" I shout. Humberto only looks at me in response. I was expecting resistance, not this bland, pitiful attitude. I kick him again, this time in the jaw. He falls back. "Defend yourself for fuck's sake!" A buried instinct for fighting surfaces and he wraps his arms around my legs in an attempt to topple me. It's a weak shot and I easily slip out of his grasp. I toss the knife aside and jump on him. I slam my fist into his face with all of my strength. His nose cracks. His lip is split. His gums are bleeding. He barely tries to defend himself. He slaps like a little boy. I beat him furiously. His face is a viscid mass of blood and shattered bone. He makes no effort to shield himself. He takes punch after punch. My knuckles are bleeding. Despite the pain, I do not stop. I keep pounding until I lay him out cold.

I get to my feet, spattered with blood. I am horrified at who I have become. My breath comes as a growl. My fists are swollen, broken. I am shaking with rage. My enemy lies, inert. I could kill him now. I could beat him, strangle him, stab him. I could douse him in petrol and set him ablaze. I could torture him until the pain kills him. But I know I will not kill him. I can't, I simply can't.

It is clear that Humberto has had a complete emotional breakdown.

Infected with the poison of his mother's suicide and his own crimes, he has descended into madness. I can see it in his eyes. They are bottomless, lifeless. There was nothing and no-one to hold him back.

Humberto snorts, choking on the blood pouring from his nose. He coughs up bloody saliva. I lay him on his side so he doesn't suffocate. He breathes a little more easily. A wave of the corpse's stench washes over me. Impossible to get used to that reek. The nausea comes back, my stomach turns. I don't understand how Humberto has tolerated this smell for days. The windows are shut. I open them and stick my head out. The cold night eases my urge to vomit. I try not to make any noise. A few metres away on the street are two armed men, ready to kill.

I go in search of ice, I need to ease the swelling around my knuckles. I enter the kitchen. It's a dump. The tap is dripping. Dirty dishes in piles. Rotting leftover food. More foul smells, more fermented and putrid air. I open the kitchen windows. Let the wind carry away the death that engulfs the house.

I take a tray of ice cubes out of the freezer. I tip the cubes into a cloth and wrap it around my fist. They burn. The ligaments are swollen. I think my right metacarpus is fractured. My hand is a purple ball that I can barely move.

I go back to Humberto. He pants noisily and his eyes open and close. I turn him face down. His torn back is a mass of blood and sores. He's whipped himself with all his strength. The wounds are beginning to weep. It's frightening to think he did this to himself in his desperate need to subdue the death worms.

I speak to him, but he stares back at me, dazed, from within his fog of semi-consciousness. I take the rope his mother used to strangle herself and tie him up. My hands are swollen and clumsy, so this takes me a while. I tie his wrists and ankles together and make sure that the knots around his arms are tight. He is immobilised. To stop him screaming, I gag him with the cloth I used to wrap my bleeding knuckles. Icy, bloody water is still trickling from it. Humberto will taste my blood.

I don't know when exactly it was that Humberto broke down, whether he was already halfway there by the time he came home or whether his mother's corpse gradually insinuated its way into him, tearing him in two. What I had pictured would be an epic struggle became a grotesque beating. I expected a fierce contender, not this puppet petrified by remorse and fear. But I need to remain vigilant. The vicious, manipulative, opportunistic Humberto might return, the one with the sinister grimace of a killer, the one diseased with god.

I don't know what to do with him. For three years my greatest fantasy has been stabbing him to death. Over and over, I practised knifing him. But now I realise there is no trace of a murderer in me. There is no part of me that considers killing him. But although my lust for vengeance has abated, it is still alive. Humberto cannot go unpunished. I mustn't let him become sane again, so that he can go out and preach his homicidal dogma. His urge to moralise and his twisted idea of god must end.

I am exhausted. My pent-up desire for revenge has ended up crushing me. So much adrenaline, so many late nights spent planning the perfect revenge, imagining the evisceration of my enemy, have turned it into a solid mass that is impossible to bear. I realise that I am on the verge of crossing the thin line separating me from madness. I need to calm down. Think clearly.

I step out into the tiny garden in front of the house for some fresh air. A street lamp illuminates a withered rose bush and the parched, yellow lawn. Even out here the putrid stink is overwhelming. I breathe deeply to try and calm down, but my heart is racing. I see the passage I walked down to get to the Good Boys' meetings. I curse the day I agreed to attend.

I have no plan B. There are no shades of vengeance, no halfway points. Reconciliation is not an option. It's vengeance or nothing. The total destruction of the other or the eternal bitterness of seeing him walk free. Now I am trapped in my enemy's house. With no vengeance and no alternative plan.

I listen to the hooting of one of the owls that nest in the Quiroz family's tree. During the day they are still, camouflaged between the branches. At night, they catch rats or birds. The silent beating of their wings cuts through the air. It doesn't matter how dark the night, they swoop directly on their prey. I wish I were an owl and could see where I needed to go in the darkness. What the fuck am I going to do?

Robert could barely make out the vet in the darkness, he was an ill-defined silhouette in the frame of the door. The man walked slowly towards him. "I don't think it's right that you speak to my daughter alone," he said. For a moment Robert was concerned the man could be armed. "She asked me for help," Robert explained. He groped around in the dark for a tool or a pitchfork to defend himself with. "Help doing what?" the man asked. "That's what I wanted to know. That's why I wanted to speak to her," Robert said. "And what if she is lying to you?" Robert found a shovel leaning against the sacks of food and grasped it. "She told me you have problems." The vet snorted. "Do I look like I've got problems?" he asked. "I'm not the one who thinks so," said Robert.

The vet stepped closer. Robert steeled himself in case he was attacked, or noticed a weapon glimmer in the darkness. The man's breath smelled strongly of alcohol. He had obviously drunk a few more glasses of whisky. "What exactly did she tell you?" he asked. "That your personality changes, that you never use the same name." The vet sighed. "My name is John Sycamore. I can show you my birth certificate. I didn't change my name like she told you." "I believe you, John," Robert said, emphasising his name.

Neither of them spoke. His ragged breathing was loud. Listening to his profound exhalations, Robert could sense how hurt he was.

"What else did she tell you?" the vet asked. Robert wasn't sure he should reveal any more of what Patricia had told him. He could put her in danger. "Why don't you speak to your daughter instead?" he suggested. "I offered you my house, my food and my friendship," the man said accusingly. "Don't you think I deserve to know?"

Robert considered how best to respond without offending him. "Apparently you do strange things." The vet switched on a torch and, just as Patricia had done earlier, shone the beam directly into his face. Robert covered his eyes with his left hand and prepared to lash out with the shovel in his right if the man decided to attack. "What strange things?" John said. Robert turned away to escape the glare. "Please could you stop that? I can't see." The vet lowered the torch, and in the brief flash of light Robert noticed that he had no weapon, but he did not let go of the shovel.

"I didn't mean to upset you by speaking to your daughter," Robert said. The man appeared to relax. "I just want to know how much she told you." They heard a faint sound. The man shone the torch around the barn and followed the sound. He kicked some straw and a field rat scurried out and disappeared. Following it with the torchlight, he watched to see where it hid. He crept silently towards it and then stamped on the straw with force until he heard a squeal. The man flattened his boot against the floor then bent down to pick up the crushed rat, which was still convulsing.

"Take it to the wolf, it's fresh meat," he said and handed it to him. Robert held it by its back paws. They felt cold and smooth. The vet shone the torch around again, searching for more rodents. "My children don't understand the things I see and hear," he said. Robert turned to face him. The light bounced off the floor and cast strange shadows on his face. "Like what?" Robert asked. "You wouldn't understand 'em either." The man gazed at a fixed point, immersed in thought. "I'm tired of people judging me, including my children. The only person who ever understood what I see and hear was my wife, and even then only after she died." Robert was surprised. "After she died?" The vet lifted his torch and shone it into Robert's face again. "Like I said, you wouldn't understand." This time Robert endured the light in his eyes without covering them. "Perhaps I would understand if you explained it to me." The vet shook his head and shone the torch on the rat hanging head down from Robert's hand. "Let's give it to the wolf."

They left the barn. The night was getting colder. They walked in silence. The vet walked ahead, the beam of light jumping from one side of the path to the other. Ice had formed in the middle. Robert walked along the snow-covered edge to avoid slipping. Still wary, he had brought the shovel with him. He regretted not having brought a coat or gloves. The handle of the shovel was so cold it stung his hand and the icy wind buffeted his back and neck.

They approached the cage and John shone the torchlight on the she-wolf. She was upright and lowered her head as soon as she sensed the light. Robert stuck the rat between the bars. Pajamartuq tugged on it with her teeth and devoured it. The vet laughed. "This wolf is a rativore. You should leave her in the barn to get rid of the rats."

Pajamartuq looked terrible. Her recovery would take time. Feeding her plenty of fresh meat would help, as would finding a large space where she could exercise. As with Nujuaqtutuq, setting her free was not an option. Her physical condition was not good enough for hunting or facing a pack. It was obvious that "Bull" had kept her in that tiny wire cage ever since she was a puppy.

The vet switched off the torch and pointed to the snow-covered prairie. "Close your eyes and listen," John ordered. Robert obeyed. A cow mooed in the distance. The rusty rooster on the roof of the house squeaked as it turned in the wind. A loose sheet of corrugated iron clattered against one of the posts holding up the metal structure that served as a garage. "Did you hear?" John asked anxiously. "Yes, I heard a cow moo, the rooster spinning up there and a sheet of metal banging against another," Robert answered. The vet looked disappointed. "No, that isn't what you were supposed to hear. But I can't tell you what it is. You would think I was crazy, just like everyone else."

Robert had only come face to face with madness once in his life. A schizophrenic worker whose personality transformed for weeks and whose voice would abruptly change. The vet was somewhat eccentric, but there was nothing to suggest the catastrophic picture painted by Patricia. Perhaps his episodes were alcoholic outbursts or bouts of depression over his wife's death. But was it bad enough to merit a plea for help?

"What should I have heard?" asked Robert. "Nothing," said the vet. Neither of them spoke. After the tense encounter in the barn, Robert thought it would be unwise to spend another night with them. "I think I will sleep in the tent until the wolf recovers," he said. "I won't interfere in your affairs again."

Robert was about to return to the house to get his things, but John held his arm to stop him. "You know why folk think I am crazy?" he asked, and, without waiting for a response, said, "Because I see and hear dead people." Robert smiled faintly. "I'm serious." "I believe you," Robert said. The man pulled him along, urging him to follow him onto the prairie. They stopped after walking several metres through the black night. "This is where I hear them," John said. Robert could hear nothing but the rumble of the wind. Maybe the man was crazy, perhaps the whisky had brought on hallucinations. John picked up on his incredulity. "I'm a shaman," he said without hesitation. "Patricia says you sometimes lose control," Robert told him. The man turned to him. "I do, when the spirit of the dead enters me and I fight to cast it out." John's words made Robert wary. Madness certainly seemed to be rearing its head. "You still don't believe me, do you?" John asked. His previous experience with the schizophrenic worker had taught Robert not to contradict those suffering from psychotic episodes. "I believe you." The man smiled. Despite his strange behaviour, he remained in a good mood. "Do you know why I decided to treat your wolf?" John asked.

"No, I don't." The vet pointed out across the prairie. "Because he asked me to." Robert turned towards the blackness. "Who?" "Amaruq," John replied confidently. "He's out there, can't you hear him?" Robert looked out again into the darkness and felt a shiver travel down his spine.

I walk in circles around the small garden. I need to make a decision. I peek through a crack in the gate. The two Good Boys are talking, leaning against the car. I can't make any mistakes.

I go back into the living room. Humberto moans, his eyes are open. He isn't fully conscious yet. I've destroyed his face. His cheeks are puffy. His nose is broken. His left eyebrow is split. His eye is half-closed and purple. His forehead is bruised.

I close the windows. The stench rapidly intensifies. The air becomes unbreathable. The corpse is pumping out the vapours of its decay. The pestilence has pervaded every corner.

I crouch down next to Humberto. "Can you hear me?" He doesn't respond, he just looks at me. I'm worried the beating has damaged his brain and that he will be a vegetable for the rest of his life. "Do you know where you are?" Humberto watches me, bewildered. I ask him again. He looks around and nods. I breathe out, relieved. At least he understands where he is.

His small, rodent-like eyes shine from within his tumefied face. A trapped, fearful rat. Not a vestige left of the "soldier of god" who barked orders, who bore pain and extreme temperatures, whose smile was full of hatred. It's as though he has been replaced by someone who looks exactly like him.

My hand hurts. I try to open and close it to encourage the blood to circulate but the pain won't let me. I feel it with my other hand, looking for a fracture, but it's too inflamed to feel any bone.

The smell of death penetrates my taste buds, it makes my eyes itch. It's so thick in the air it feels as though it's dripping. I feel it trickle down me. Death's sweat. When I was a teenager, a human skeleton hung from a wooden frame in my high school classroom. Because of the shape of its hips and its bone density our anatomy teacher concluded it had belonged to a young man. We dressed it with hats, jumpers, ties. One classmate knitted him a scarf and another pinned a carnation to his sternum. Amused, we even named him: Rogelio. What would happen if I brought this corpse to school with me? Would someone dare to dress it, wrap a scarf around it? Who would mess around with a body that oozes liquids, whose dry and pallid eyes look back at you, whose bloated tongue still lolls from its mouth, whose distended stomach looks about to explode, convulsed by gases, making noises, erupting with maggots and flies? I challenge a school to put a recently deceased corpse next to the blackboard. Who would be brave enough to dress it up? Who would make jokes? Could anyone endure the terrible fury of death, as I do now from a metre and a half away?

I can't take it anymore. I stand up and quickly open the windows. The wind makes the curtains flap and the reek disperses a little. I can finally breathe. I spot a record player on the table and some L.P.s next to it. It's French music: Serge Gainsbourg, Charles Aznavour, Yves Montand, Edith Piaf, Jacques Brel. An unusual musical selection for a lower-middle-class Mexican woman. On the record player is a 45 r.p.m. record by Jacques Brel. Four different versions of "Ne me quitte pas".

I let the room air a little longer. I close the windows and press play. The needle drops into the groove. I turn down the volume, but Brel's aching, pain-filled voice is still clear. The record must have been exposed to the sun, since the sound skips with every revolution and the needle jumps. How many times did Humberto's mother listen to Brel's song while she was deciding to hang herself?

I can't take the smell any longer. I leave the living room and climb the stairs. Upstairs the air is more breathable. I can faintly hear Brel's music playing. I lean against the wall. Such a strong desire for vengeance and now I have no idea what to do. Perhaps, as Confucius once said, I should have dug two graves. Brel's song ends and a few seconds later it plays again. The record player stays in repetition mode. The needle will play it over and over again.

I go to the mother's room. I push the door three times until it opens. I close it and fall onto the bed. On a table there are several perfectly folded blouses and dresses. The carpet is immaculate. The decorations are perfectly symmetrical. There is not a single stain or speck. The neatness and attention to detail stands in sharp contrast to the chaos and confusion of the woman's life, and the disarray of dirty plates and leftover food that Humberto has left in the kitchen. Zurita and his men did break into the bedroom, but (I knew this because Agüitas told me) they didn't touch a thing. It wouldn't have made any sense. Why rummage around, mess everything up, break things, if she had clearly explained her reasons in her letter?

I suppose Humberto didn't dare go inside that room. His swarm of guilt must have stopped him. I imagine him paralysed in the doorway, unable to cross the threshold. He must have remembered the men he saw leave that bedroom when he was a child. He probably remembered the smell of sex, alcohol, sweat, semen and vaginal fluids that came from it. Remembered his mother's moans of pleasure, the snores of the lover of the moment, the voices, shouts, blows. Remembered the Sunday mornings when his mother would sit alone on the bed, wearing her tattered nightgown, with no-one to open her legs and climb on top of her and come as fast as they could inside her. He must have imagined her looking over and over again at the pale shadows on the X-ray films, the tumours the doctors warned her were gnawing away at her healthy tissue. Imagined her writing her letter, her hand trembling, her lost gaze. Imagined her crossing that very same threshold to go down the stairs towards the chair and the noose.

Exhausted, I close my eyes and fall asleep. I wake up jittery. There is no clock to tell me how much time has passed. I turn off the light and get out of bed. I go down the stairs. "Ne me quitte pas" is still on repeat. I see Humberto lying a few metres from where I left him. He dragged himself halfway to the front door where he now lies, snoring.

The smell, the music, the killer. Nausea. I turn around and resolutely head upstairs, cross the sewing room door to the spiral staircase and walk home across the rooftops.

Between the trees, the sun is beginning to glow. I take a deep breath.

Karl von Clausewitz sat on the edge of the bed. Once again, his throat and lips felt dry. His forehead was sweaty. His body was weary. There was a sharp pain in his gut. Cramps. He had survived infinite battles, hand-to-hand combat, bombardments, cavalry charges. Ever since he was twelve and his father enlisted him in the Prussian army as a corporal, he had endured war's most extreme hardships: cold, insomnia, wounds, prison. He had come close to death several times. The cannonball that exploded a few metres away from him and blew his companions to pieces. The bullets that flew past his ears as he led his battalion through the mud and killed dozens of his soldiers. The nights when the temperature reached -10°C and he and a few others were trapped in the trenches for a week, with no supplies, water or ammunition. Now Von Clausewitz, the brave combatant, was languishing in his bedroom, a prisoner of a deplorable disease: cholera. For a soldier of his calibre to die halfway through a bout of diarrhoea and spasms seemed to him a great humiliation. He wished he could regain enough strength to allow him to venture once more onto the battlefield and die from a bullet to the chest, not slowly from bloody bowel movements and a delirium-inducing fever.

Von Clausewitz called to his wife, Marie. Shouted for her to bring more water and salt. The doctor had recommended he take half a tablespoon to encourage fluid retention. The woman hurriedly appeared to help him drink, dabbed his brow with a handkerchief. She then emptied the chamber pots filled with liquid excrement which she would wash and return in anticipation of her husband needing to fill them again. Even four chamber pots were not enough for the general.

Von Clausewitz watched her leave. His wife must love him so much to endure such abominations and, above all, his terrible moods. He had abandoned her for long periods to go and fight. Despite his absences, Marie von Brühl, daughter of a prominent Turingia family, showed great pride in her husband. Not only had he been one of the courageous soldiers who fought in the Rhine campaigns and the Napoleonic Wars, he was also a great military thinker and theorist who would run the Prussian War Academy in the mornings and write a long treatise called *On War* at night.

Von Clausewitz drained the glass of water completely, despite his doctor's instruction that he take only small sips so as not to overload his injured intestines. The thirst was unendurable and small sips did nothing to relieve it. He went to lie down, but the pressing urge to vomit forced him to kneel over the one remaining chamber pot. He threw up the water he had just drunk. Most of it splashed onto the floor. Damn it, it was happening again. He should follow the doctor's orders and limit his intake of liquids. Frustrated at his own foolishness he slapped his forehead. Why won't you bloody learn, he said to himself. He tried to straighten up. He had seen several of his soldiers die of cholera on the fertile fields on the border with Poland. Many of them perished on bended knee after ejecting the contents of their stomachs, lacking the strength to get to their feet. Undoubtedly a humiliating pose. No, he refused to die this way, on his knees over a chamber pot.

He pulled himself up using the bed's headboard and climbed back up onto the mattress as best he could. He held in further retches to avoid staining the sheets. It was difficult to breathe. He closed his eyes. Perhaps he could at least sleep a little.

Marie returned to the bedroom. She saw that the floor was covered in vomit. She left the clean chamber pots on the floor and ran to check on her husband. He was stretched out on the bed with his eyes open, staring at a fixed point. The woman ran off in search of the servants. One of them tried to revive him, but there was nothing to be done. Von Clausewitz had succumbed to cholera.

He died on November 16, 1831 at fifty-one years of age. Von Clausewitz left a solid body of written work which Marie published after his death. His treatise *On War* still exerts great influence within contemporary military theory and action.

Fragments from *On War*, Book 1:

"We see then that there are many ways to one's object in War; that the complete subjugation of the enemy is not essential in every case."

"War, that is, the hostile feeling and action of hostile agencies, cannot be considered to be at an end as long as the will of the enemy is not subdued also."

"The result in war is never absolute."

"If we desire to defeat the enemy, we must proportion our efforts to his powers of resistance. This is expressed by the product of two factors which cannot be separated, namely, the sum of available means and the strength of the will."

"War is the province of danger, and therefore courage above all things is the first quality of a warrior."

"War is the province of physical exertion and suffering. In order not to be completely overcome by them, a certain strength of body and mind is required, which, either natural or acquired, produces indifference to them."

"War is the province of uncertainty: three-quarters of those things upon which action in war must be calculated are hidden more or less in the clouds of great uncertainty. Here, then, above all a fine and penetrating mind is called for, to search out the truth by the tact of its judgment."

"Two qualities are indispensable: in the first place an intellect which, even in the midst of this intense obscurity, is not without some traces of inner light which lead to the truth, and then the courage to follow this faint light."

War

Although the vet insisted that he continue to sleep in his son's room, Robert decided to move into his tent. He put it up on the other side of the path, a hundred metres from the house. He thought it wise to keep his distance from John Sycamore, or whatever his name was. Especially after the litany of premonitions he'd recited out by the prairie. One struck him as chillingly uncanny: he warned him not to travel by helicopter. "You will die in a fire. The aircraft will crash and explode among pipes and hundreds of workers. There will be many deaths." It was obvious how John knew Amaruq's name and that he often travelled by helicopter: he had already told him the story about how and where he had found Nujuaqtutuq. But he did not remember mentioning where he worked or having described the construction camps for the oil pipeline. The man continued: "You will soon leave your three children orphaned." He hadn't spoken about his children either. How had he deduced that he was a father of three? Robert felt unnerved by these premonitions, a blend of alcohol, madness and delirium.

Deeply absorbed in his role as a shaman and unbothered by the cold which intensified by the minute, John's performance went on and on. He insisted that these were warnings from the spirits. "I am only the messenger," he said with such gravity that it bordered on the ridiculous, or, worse still, on the psychotic.

They went back to the house. John got out another bottle of whisky and urged Robert to sit and drink some with him on the porch despite the icy wind coming from the north. At first Robert refused, he couldn't bear to be outdoors for another minute, but the man was so insistent that he decided not to antagonise him. The vet fell into a chair on the porch. Robert had one glass for warmth, but John knocked back half a bottle and passed out in his chair. Robert knew that if he left him outside he could get hypothermia. But carrying him into the house would be impossible. The man must weigh a hundred and forty kilos or more. Robert went into the house, found some blankets and covered him up.

Robert put on his coat, put up the tent, then returned for Nujuaq-tutuq and took him with him. He was concerned that John might wake up and decide to kill him during one of his episodes. He carried him to the pickup and placed him in the back. Then he fastened on the trailer. He shone his torch into the cage. The female wolf, curled up in a ball, looked at him with desperation. He thought he saw rage in her eyes, after years spent locked up in tiny spaces. Robert knew that if he stretched his hand out towards her she would bite him.

He parked the pickup at the camp. He threw a piece of meat at the wolf, filled her water tray and covered the cage with canvas to block out the wind. He lay Nujuaqtutuq down in one corner of the tent. Exhausted and nervous, he wrapped himself up in his sleeping bag and went to sleep.

His dreams were filled with vivid images of fire, accidents and death. He woke up several times, anxious and short of breath. Although they were absurd, John's words were troubling him. He sat up to try and calm down. Nothing that man said could be true. Nobody could predict the future. His grandfather, an extremely religious man, often said that the Bible condemned to death fortune tellers and sorcerers. When Robert asked why, his grandfather replied: "Because they foster disquiet." His flood of nightmares had shown this to be true.

He was still distressed from his last nightmare. He took deep breaths to try to calm down. He, a man of no faith, a strong believer in science, shouldn't allow the rantings of a drunk schizophrenic to cause him alarm. But what if there was a small chance his premonitions would come true? After a while he composed himself and went back to sleep.

In the early hours, he heard hurried footsteps crunching across the snow. Half-asleep, he straightened up and grabbed the rifle as a precaution. A silhouette appeared against the canvas. Robert waited for a few seconds before he heard Patricia's voice. "Sir, please come with me." Robert opened the door. Patricia was standing in front of him, wearing only a nightgown, a dressing gown and a pair of slippers. Her breathing was erratic, and her exhalations stood out against the frozen plains, lit up by the moon. "What happened?" Robert asked her. The girl pointed towards the house. "Give me a minute," Robert asked. He put on some boots and a jacket. He had barely emerged from the tent when, without another word, Patricia started running. Robert caught up with her and grabbed her by the shoulders. "Tell me what happened." She looked at him, distraught. "My father," she said and then started running again.

I get back to my house as the sun is rising. My temples are still throbbing. My mouth is dry. My hands hurt. I feel a knot in the pit of my stomach. My clothes are impregnated with the smell of a corpse. I take them off and put them in the washing machine. I add detergent and half a bottle of one of my father's aftershaves, English Leather.

I come out of the bathroom naked and go to feed King. My dog sniffs me and then backs away, afraid. I leave him his plate of food and go downstairs to Colmillo. He behaves the same way. He puts his tail between his legs and hides under the sink. Their instinct has told them to stay away from me. My skin stinks of death.

The doorbell rings. I peek discreetly through the curtains. It's Chelo. She looks worried. I am tempted to open the door. I need to hug her, kiss her, listen to her voice. Lay my cheek on her lap and let her caress me. I need to sleep entwined with her, as close to her as possible. But no, she shouldn't get involved. This is my vengeance, and mine alone.

She keeps ringing the bell. I decide to get into the shower so I can't hear it anymore. I close my eyes and let the water run down my body.

I scrub myself with soap several times to get rid of the smell. As soon as I turn the water down in the shower I can hear the distant sound of the doorbell again. When I get out it has finally stopped.

Wrapped in a towel I go down to the garage. I find a dozen notes that Chelo has slipped under the gate. It seems she has come a few times. In one, she begs me not to take revenge. In others, she berates me for having disappeared. In all of them she expresses her profound love. "I love you, I love you, I love you." Should I believe her or not?

I get dressed and put on a little of the remaining English Leather. Smelling like my father calms me down. I flick through the first volume of *On War*. I'm desperate for the clue that will help me make the right decision. I try to find it in Von Clausewitz, who knew what it meant to kill, and for someone else to want to kill you. I am not looking for an infallible answer. Just a hint towards an escape route, any one at all. I read:

"There are many ways to one's object in War . . . the complete subjugation of the enemy is not essential in every case."

And immediately afterwards:

"War, that is, the hostile feeling and action of hostile agencies, cannot be considered to be at an end as long as the will of the enemy is not subdued also."

I am confused by Von Clausewitz. On the one hand, he says I don't necessarily have to defeat my enemy; on the other, that my war will not be over until he is crushed. I couldn't crush him any more than I have. By now his trousers are probably covered in faeces and urine, and he must be dehydrated, hungry, raw from the beating. How else could I crush him?

The third quote shatters any hope I had of finding an answer:

"The result in war is never absolute."

Fuck. Never absolute? Then what is the point in all that effort, all that risk? Does this mean that if I let Humberto live he could kill me? Do I have no option other than to destroy him, by which I mean kill him? I stand up, dejected, and begin to read the quotes out loud. Perhaps this way some secret message hidden inside the guts of these sentences will reveal itself. Nothing. I jump to the third volume of *On War*. In long digressions, Von Clausewitz expounds on how to attack and defend rivers, mountains, swamps, forest, but provides no illuminating revelation.

I delve into Carlos's library. I find *The Art of War* by Sun Tzu. I open it in the hope that a Chinese soldier from two thousand four hundred years ago can provide some guidelines on how to proceed.

I flick through it and in Chapter XI, "The Nine Situations", verse 65, I find:

"If the enemy leaves a door open, you must rush in."

I keep reading, and immediately afterwards, in verse 66, it says:

"Forestall your opponent by seizing what he holds dear, and subtly contrive to time his arrival on the ground."

I jump to the following chapter, XII, "The Attack by Fire", and in verse 19 I read:

"If it is to your advantage, make a forward move; if not, stay where you are."

And finally, verse 57 of Chapter XI lifts my spirits:

"Place your army in deadly peril, and it will survive; plunge it into desperate straits, and it will come off in safety."

Sun Tzu clears up the picture. I still don't know what to do, but I know I can't remain paralysed. My enemy opened a door, his actual or apparent madness, and I should take advantage. I have the upper hand and I should dominate him physically and, above all, emotionally. I will not kill you Humberto, but you will regret killing Carlos.

I should get ready. I need chloroform, gauze, a surgical mask, alcohol and air freshener. I leave the house via the rooftop. I scurry between water tanks until I reach the end of Retorno 201. I come down through the Ruiz house, walk to the corner, climb the steps of Chorizo's house and then walk along the row of rooftops on Retorno 207. From there

I can see Chelo's house. I don't know if it's possible at seventeen to be sure you have found the love of your life, but in this moment I believe it, I am absolutely convinced.

I go down the spiral staircase to the alleyways leading to the back of the Centenario school and take the road that brings me out on Retorno 204. I walk towards Avenida Emiliano Zapata, pass the church and keep going towards La Viga. I turn a corner and get to Gigante. Dozens of people jostle each other in the enormous supermarket. I scurry along, trying not to bump into anyone I know. I quickly buy the things I need.

I walk through Modelito's alleyways to get home. From the corner, I can just make out the two Good Boys guarding Humberto. They are clearly unaware that I have my enemy tied up inside. A lumpen sack that snores, pisses and shits itself. I surreptitiously open the door and slip inside.

I grill a chicken breast and make a salad. There are hours to go until I return to Humberto. I eat lunch, then to kill time I sit in the dining room reading old *Popular Mechanics* magazines that my father collected. I can't concentrate. The pressure builds minute by minute. I do push-ups and sit-ups. I go up and down the stairs. I try to stay active. If I stop, I might explode.

I keep moving until I feel exhausted. Ridding myself of excess energy calms me down. Worn out, I sit down to watch T.V. in my parents' room. It's black and white, not colour like the Tenas'. I watch "Bonanza", dubbed by Puerto Ricans. It's amusing to hear cowboys from the American West speak in Caribbean accents.

I fall asleep. I wake up to King licking my hand. Startled, I react by kicking him in the nose. The dog squeals and scampers unsteadily into Carlos's room. Paranoid, I look around the room. I realise that there is nothing and no-one that is a threat to me.

I switch off the television. My jaw is aching. I must have been grinding my teeth in my sleep. I look out of the window. Two new sentries are guarding the house. They are both blonde, with close-cropped hair. They look like yokels from Los Altos de Jalisco. "Blondes from the Backwoods" my grandmother used to call them. They can't be more than twenty. They look vigilant, and make no effort to hide the weapons at their waists.

It's 8.00 p.m. I should wait until the small hours. I need to keep myself busy somehow or the tension will turn my brain to mush, the grey matter will trickle out of my mouth and nostrils, leaking desperation and anxiety.

Only half an hour has gone by. I'm tempted to turn on the T.V. and lie down to watch gringo shows. But I can't take this anymore. Sun Tzu's orders: "If you hold the advantage, take a step forward, if not, stay where you are." At 9.00 p.m. I get up and get ready. It's time to return to Humberto's house.

"Quem deus vult perdere, dementat prius"
"Whom god would destroy, he first makes mad"

Madness

Despite the fact that she was only wearing slippers, Patricia ran fast. It was hard for Robert to keep up. The fragile girl ran through the thick snow without stumbling, while his feet sank. She stopped several times to wait for him. They got to the house. Patricia opened the door then stopped, motionless, on the threshold. Robert caught up with her and stood next to her. In the glow of the kerosene lamps John was pacing the living room stripped to the waist, babbling incoherently. The windows were broken and some of the furniture had been smashed to pieces. The curtains fluttered in the icy breeze. From the top of the stairs, the two younger children sat watching the scene in terror.

Patricia began to hyperventilate. Robert was not sure whether to try and calm her or to placate the man, who was panting heavily as he paced. Robert stepped towards him. "John!" he said. The man turned to look at him as though staring into empty space. "John, sit down there, please," Robert said, gesturing to the sofa by the window. John's face changed and he strode towards them threateningly. Robert placed himself between him and his daughter. "Everything's fine," he told him. The man exhaled loudly. There were some slashes on his pallid torso, and rivulets of blood were trickling down his chest, his back, his belly. "Please sit down," Robert pleaded. With a nod, he gestured for Patricia to go into the kitchen. The girl obeyed and hid behind the table. John fixed his gaze on her and murmured something unintelligible. Robert looked at the children on the stairs. "Go to your rooms," he said and they immediately obeyed.

"John, you need to sit down," Robert said again. The man turned and surveyed the destruction. He seemed disoriented. His features softened and he staggered towards a window, stretched his hand out to touch one of the broken panes still hanging from the frame. He pressed his finger against one of the shards. "Careful, you could cut yourself," Robert warned him. The man jerked his finger away, jabbered something incoherent and walked over to the armchair Robert had indicated. He sat down and scratched at one of the gashes on his chest, pensive.

Robert calmly turned to the kitchen and called Patricia. She approached cautiously. "I need you and your brother and sister to put on some warm clothes and come downstairs as quietly as possible," he whispered. Obediently Patricia scurried past him and slowly climbed the stairs, anxious that they should not creak and attract her father's attention.

Robert approached John. "Are you alright?" he asked. The man didn't reply, he was immersed in piercing his flesh with his fingernails. Robert was about to sit down on the sofa next to him, but John put his hand on the seat to stop him. Robert took a step backwards. John looked at him, his eyes full of menace, then turned to look outside again.

The children silently came down the stairs. Robert jerked his head for them to go outside. They walked to the door and pulled on the coats hanging from the hooks. John watched them with a bitter expression. Seeing his father's steady gaze, the youngest child froze. "Where are you going?" John bellowed. Robert quickly intervened. "They're coming with me." The vet shook his head. "Get over here," he ordered. The children made to go over to him, but Robert signalled for them to stay put. "They're coming with me," he repeated firmly. John stood up. Robert turned towards the children. "Go wait for me in the tent." The children were stupefied, waiting to see what their father would do. "Now!" Robert urged. Patricia pushed them out of the door and as soon as they were outside, they began to run. John watched them out of the window and smiled. "Look at the little beasts. They don't know how to run in the snow." Robert looked out. The two smallest ones kept tripping and falling flat on their faces, then would get up and fall again a few metres on. "You ought to abandon them on the mountain," he said to Robert. "They're useless. Good-for-nothings." He sat down again and resumed his mutterings.

Robert found the children waiting in the tent. They were huddled in the far corner from where Nujuaqtutuq lay. Robert shone his torch at them. They stared back at him, dumbfounded. The boy had bumped his head and had a small graze on his forehead. Robert moved to check on him, but the boy flinched. "Are you alright?" he asked. The boy was silent. Robert went to the pickup and brought back a sleeping bag and some blankets. He rolled out the sleeping bag. "You two get in here," he said to the younger ones and then pointed out his one to Patricia. "You sleep in that one."

Robert switched off the lamp. In the moonlight that leached through the canvas, he could see that their eyes were open. "Everything's going to be O.K.," he said, without much conviction. What was he going to do now? Patricia's call for help had been more than justified. John was an out-of-control maniac who had suddenly erupted. Robert didn't know what to do with the children. Should he take them to the police and file a report or leave the family alone?

Robert wrapped himself in the blankets and tried to go to sleep. The children were whispering to each other. He was tempted to tell them to be quiet, but he resisted. They needed to give voice to their fear, support one another. He listened to them for a few minutes until, suddenly, he fell asleep.

The sun was already up when Robert was woken by the sound of an approaching vehicle. He sat up, alert. He opened the door and saw John's truck approaching. The light of the sun reflecting off the snow dazzled him. He heard the vehicle stop and a door open. He quickly searched for his knife and hid it in his back pocket. "Robert," the man called to him, "can you come here?" "Coming, give me a second," he replied. As he put on his boots he turned to look at the children. The younger ones were asleep but Patricia was watching him attentively. He attempted a soothing look and then got up to leave the tent.

John was standing in front of his truck waiting for him with some folders in his hands, wearing a shearling coat and jeans. "Good morning," Robert greeted him. John did not respond. He seemed preoccupied, his gaze fixed firmly on the ground. After a few seconds, he managed to say a few words. "I need to talk to you," he said, without looking up. "What about?" asked Robert. John straightened up, took two steps forward and offered him the folders. "Take them," he said. Robert made no attempt to take them. John insisted. "Please," he said, without lowering his outstretched arm. "What are they?" The man looked out towards the horizon. "I can't carry on," he said. "I just can't." He stood pensively for a moment. "I am not a good father," he said and offered Robert the folders again. "I beg you to take them." Robert took them, but just as he was about to open them John stopped him. "They are the deeds to the ranch. There is a document in there that cedes to you a third part of the land and the livestock and another in which I grant you legal custody of my children." "What are you talking about?" Robert said. "My children will be better off with you," he insisted. "Everything is laid out there." Robert shook his head. "I won't allow this. You don't know me, you know nothing about me." The vet looked at him. "Please take care of them." And with that he turned and walked back towards his truck. Robert rushed to intercept him. "I won't do it," he said, and handed back the folders. John pushed them away and opened the door to climb into his truck. Robert berated him. "Those children are your responsibility, not mine. They are your children, dammit!" Unperturbed, John started the engine without closing the door. "Take care of them," he said. He pressed the accelerator and drove away quickly, skidding on the ice. Robert watched as he disappeared across the plains, until the truck became a tiny dot. Then he turned back to the tent. Patricia was watching him, her expression blank.

*

Just as I thought, Humberto reeks of urine and shit. The house stinks even worse than before. The dead woman keeps releasing torrents of fumes. Brel's songs are still on repeat. Lovely soundtrack for the scene: still life with son.

I turn off the record player. I spray air freshener in every corner of the living room, using the surgical mask to protect my face. The scent of lemon and lime serves only to accentuate the fetid smell of death and putrefaction. I throw open the windows. There is not a breath of wind, the miasma lingers in the living room. It's difficult to believe that Humberto didn't throw up sooner.

Unable to endure it any longer, I go out into the garden. I retch from the nausea. I rip off my surgical mask and stuff it in my pocket. I can't leave any evidence. I gaze up at the moon. The night Carlos was killed, there were two men bounding across its surface. We defiled the moon and for what? What was achieved by that epic journey to the barren shores of the Sea of Tranquillity? I stare at the moon and my hatred for Humberto is reborn.

I go back into the house. Humberto has dragged himself up against a wall. He looks at me and mumbles something through his gag. I don't know what he's trying to say. I squat down in front of him. "What do you want?" I ask him. He opens his mouth. The knot has given him sores. "If I take it off, you won't shout?" Humberto nods, docile.

Out of caution, I close the windows – he might start screaming for all he's worth. I grab his feet and drag him into the kitchen. The gashes he made on his back must be exacerbated by the friction of the carpet, because he writhes and whimpers. I lay him next to the refrigerator and barricade the door with a chair. "You'd better not scream," I warn him. I get behind him and untie the rag. As soon as he is able, he runs his tongue over the sores the gag has left at the corners of his mouth.

I prop him against one of the shelves and pour a glass of water. I try to get him to drink, but he turns his face away. I try again, and again he refuses. He's in a bad state, his swollen right eye can barely open. His broken nose makes it impossible to breathe so he gulps air through his mouth. His piss, shit, blood and pus contribute to the pervading stench. The staggering variety of odours emitted from deep within the guts of the human body. "Aren't you going to drink some water?" I ask. Humberto turns his face away. He must be dehydrated, yet he's adamant. Perhaps he wants to die.

I pull up a chair and sit facing him. A cockroach crawls from under the stove and scurries along the walls until it finds a crack through which to escape. An absurd notion occurs to me: I have turned Humberto into my own Gregor Samsa. A cockroach, an insect that deserves to be squashed.

I begin to feel ashamed. In my defence, I could claim to be the executioner of an executioner. Perhaps what Humberto needs, in the language of the Good Boys, is to learn a lesson. A punishment for his arrogance. Only someone as arrogant as he could believe that he was acting in the name of god, an invented being. If, as the faithful allege, god is all-powerful, why can't he defend himself? Can he not send down scorching bolts of lightning, or sweep away those who offend him in a tsunami? Is god so tiny and insignificant that he needs the protection of his minuscule and feeble subjects? Too many questions, too many deliberations. The leeches of vengeance begin to suck away my sanity.

I kick the sole of Humberto's foot. "Are you going to drink or not?" He ignores me. I kick him again. "Look at me," I order him. He keeps looking at the floor. A thought seems to cross his mind because suddenly he smiles. "What's so funny?" I ask. He turns to me. "Are you going to kill me the way your brother and his friends killed that Oaxacan faggot?" His question catches me off guard. "What?" Humberto smiles. "Did you really not know, *pendejo*? Or are you just playing dumb?" It's the first time I've ever heard him swear. "Go fuck yourself," I say. "They beat that little queer to death with a bat. Didn't

Carlos tell you?" "Go fuck yourself," I say again. "That fat slob was playing girlfriend to you and your friends, wasn't he? Your brother didn't like that, that's why he killed him." I'm close to attacking him again. "Shut the fuck up, *imbécil*," I shout. "Your brother murdered a scumbag and we killed the scumbag that killed the scumbag," he says with an evil, inane grin. I pick up the rag and try to stuff it into his mouth. He throws himself onto the ground in an attempt to stop me. I stamp on his face. Once, twice, three times. I split his lips, crush his nose again. I bend over him. "My brother wasn't like you," I say into his bloody face. "That's what you think," he says. Despite the flowing blood, the idiot grin is still firmly plastered on his face. I stop resisting. I take the jar of chloroform, empty half of it onto a wad of gauze and press it to his nose and mouth. Humberto squirms. No matter how hard I press the chloroform pad to his mouth, it doesn't seem to do to Humberto what it did to the rabbit we anaesthetised in a biology class before we dissected it. I pour more onto the gauze. I press it into his face. I'm covered in his blood. Humberto coughs uncontrollably, but does not pass out. I've added another perfume to the bouquet of stenches, as if the lemon and lime weren't enough.

The chloroform makes me dizzy and though I haven't managed to render him unconscious, at least he is as dazed as I am. I lift his head, squeeze his neck with my left hand to immobilise him and with my right stuff the cloth all the way into his mouth. He chokes and is suffocating. I don't care. I keep pushing until he shuts up.

I leave him there on the floor and sit down in the chair. I know that Humberto is just playing mind games. I don't understand the way his thoughts lurch back and forth. Sometimes he seems engulfed in madness, but then he turns back into the cold and cerebral manipulator he has always been.

I switch off the lights. In the dark kitchen, all I can hear are Humberto's irregular breathing and the dripping tap. I decide to go and explore the basement. Since Carlos's death, it has become a recurring feature of my dreams. Images of those Saturday meetings come back to me again and again: the hoods, the habits, the hissed prayers, the board on which Humberto would write the names of those he'd sentenced.

I walk down the stairs, ready to face this place. I need to purge what it represents, eradicate it from my dreams. I turn on the light. It's completely different: the posters with the biblical phrases have disappeared, the folding chairs, the table. In their place are stacks of discarded furniture, dusty boxes tied with rope, artificial flowers missing their petals, and old newspapers and magazines. The only remnant of its dark past is a broken part of the crucifix with Christ's bloody, cracked feet. I pick it up and examine it. The splintered wood tapers to a point. It looks as though his mother smashed it against the wall until it broke to pieces.

I take the piece of crucifix to throw at Humberto's feet, so he can see what has become of the anachronistic, ridiculous cross of his crusades. I go back up to the living room and as I head towards the kitchen I hear a sound. I turn and see a shadow slowly creeping downstairs. I look around for the knife. I tossed it somewhere out of Humberto's reach and can't see it in the darkness. I clutch the jagged piece of crucifix, ready to use it as a weapon, and hide in the furthest corner of the living room.

The shadow continues to descend the stairs. I get ready to attack.

La Parguera is a fishing village located on Puerto Rico's Caribbean coast. It's famous for its colourful floating houses built over the mangrove swamps, and for the phenomenon of bioluminescence in two of its bays.

During the night, if you disturb the water, dinoflagellates (tiny one-cell organisms) emit phosphorescent light. The spectacle attracts hundreds of tourists who cruise around the bays in glass-bottomed motorboats while divers stir up the water, causing a blue beam of light to glow in the darkness.

There are a number of species other than dinoflagellates which are bioluminescent: fireflies, certain bacteria, fish, worms and snails, to name a few. It's caused by the interaction of the luciferin and the luciferase. The luciferase is a molecule and luminescence occurs when the enzyme catalyses the oxidation of the luciferin.

Both substances owe their name to Lucifer, a name the Romans gave to Venus, the morning star, which appears in the sky as the sun is rising. In ancient times it was also used to refer to humans who radiated light and kindness, and it was not until centuries later that Lucifer became the name for the devil, as a metaphor for the luminous being who fell from heaven, and of course, from divine grace.

Scientists named them "luciferin" and "luciferase" in honour of the original meaning of Lucifer: bringer of light.

Lucifer

After the man drove away in his truck, Robert returned to the house with the children. They refused to go inside. They stood at the door, surveying the damage. The sofas were torn, the dining room table was shattered. There were drops of blood all over the floor. The youngest was scared and began to cry. In an attempt to comfort him, Robert promised he would look after them, and would never let anything bad happen to them.

Robert asked them to go upstairs and gather up their belongings. Robert opened a desk and found various papers with John Sycamore's name and signature on them. They tallied with those on the documents the man had handed him.

He went out to pack his things. He went into the tent and kneeled down to examine Nujuaqtutuq. He was still unconscious, but his breathing was more regular. The wounds were healing and there were no signs of infection. Robert wrapped him in some blankets, picked him up and carried him to the bed of the pickup truck. Then he hooked Pajamartuq's trailer onto the truck and went back to the house.

Since they had no suitcases, the children piled the few clothes and toys they owned into cardboard boxes. Robert prepared sandwiches, filled canteens with water and put some bread, cold meat and biscuits into a basket. He lifted the children into the pickup and they departed for Kenojuac's house.

They drove alongside the fence decorated with dozens of wolf corpses until they turned onto the paved road. The children looked back at the ranch disappearing in the distance.

Kenojuac and Chuck were astonished to see Robert arrive with three children and the two wolves. Bewildered, they walked over to the pickup. Robert explained everything to Chuck: who the children were, the reason why they were travelling with him, how difficult saving Nujuaqtutuq had been and where he had found the female wolf. Chuck translated for Kenojuac, who approached the children and touched their heads with tenderness. "Welcome," she said in her broken English.

Kenojuac settled the children into her living room. She brought in several bearskins so that they could sleep on the floor. She baked walnut wheat rolls and warmed up milk for them, sweetened with maple syrup given to her by a fur trader.

After dinner, the children went to bed. Kenojuac lit the fire and covered them with caribou hides. As soon as the woman left them, the youngest one began to cry. He wanted to see his father. Patricia lay down by his side and put her arms around him to console him. Robert got up to comfort them, but his uncle stopped him. It was important for the children to get these feelings off their chests and reassure one another. A while later, all three were asleep.

Chuck and Robert went over John Sycamore's documents by candlelight, checking them line by line. Everything indicated that the transfer of one third of the farm and the custody of the children were legally valid. They checked the signatures in the documents against those in the papers Robert had found in John's desk. They matched. The deeds seemed to be in order. The property was perfectly defined and the heads of cattle, buildings and agricultural tools were inventoried in detail. It was obvious from the flawless wording of the documents that John had prepared them long before, with the guidance of a legal expert. Despite his schizophrenia, he was sufficiently lucid to realise the profound damage he was causing his children. He must have been waiting years for the opportunity to leave them with the first person to gain his trust.

Robert felt uneasy about the man's radical decision. Just like that, he had left his children in the hands of a stranger. And what was he

573

supposed to tell his own family? "Hello, they're going to live with us." It would be a drastic change for his wife and kids, and of course for him too. How could he convince his wife to agree to this new family life when he complained about spending even a few weeks in the house? Besides, the vet's children had had little education and their protracted isolation would make it difficult for them to integrate, not just with his family, but with society as a whole. On the other hand, he was convinced that he should take on this new responsibility. He needed to care for these children, he needed to educate and protect them.

In the country's southern cities, the legal process for adopting children was long and tedious. It was different in the Yukon and in the Northwest Territories: the inhospitable conditions in which the inhabitants lived – fierce snow storms, a lack of hospitals and doctors, a dearth of supplies, extreme weather – caused early and sudden deaths. Small children would suddenly be orphaned and their survival depended on the willingness of neighbours or relatives to take them in and raise them. The long bureaucratic process of official adoption risked leaving children in limbo. This was why, in the Yukon, a letter such as the one signed by the vet was enough.

Robert watched the children sleeping, wrapped in the caribou hides. He didn't even know the names of the two youngest. He took one last sip of his coffee, said goodnight to Kenojuac and his uncle and headed to the shed. He went out and stood for a moment watching the train tracks that crossed the plains. As he contemplated the vast snowy horizon, he felt certain he had made the right decision. He would no longer live in Whitehorse, and he would resign from the company. He would move to the farm as soon as possible. He would get his children to work, not out of duty, but as a game. He wanted them to enjoy the countryside, to leave the protective bubble in which their mother had raised them. He wanted them to herd cattle through the snow, to sleep out of doors. To grow up breathing cold air, to run around outside whenever they wanted. To hunt and fish for food, to know the names of every animal, every plant, every insect, every star, every constellation. To be bitten by mosquitoes and black flies in summer. To know how to skin and butcher an animal. To know how to light a fire without matches, and cook whatever they could forage on the mountain. To know where to find wild berries. He didn't want children who were isolated and silent like the vet's, but the time had come to put an end to their suffocating life in the small city, where their mother kept them indoors all winter for fear of them catching a cold. Let them get ill, let them cough, run a fever, create antibodies. Let them grow hardy in the cold weather and the forests, the meadows and the mountains, teach them never to be afraid of anyone or anything.

He would stop agonising. The decision had been made. He walked towards the barn and, in the moonlight, he saw Nujuaqtutuq. The wolf was standing in front of the door, eyes fixed on him.

The shadow has stopped on the stairs. I grip the broken piece of crucifix. The splintered wood is sharp enough to use as a dagger. If it's Zurita and his men, I won't let them arrest me. I have no intention of setting foot inside a prison. If it's the Good Boys, it doesn't matter how many there are or how heavily armed, I'll fight to the death. I am ready for anything.

The shadow comes closer. I keep still so as not to reveal my presence. I don't know if it's only one person or if more are following. I crouch down as low as possible and look towards the stairs. Whoever it is stops just before reaching the last step. The smell of the body must be a shock. Perhaps they are about to vomit. The shadow continues its descent and finally comes into the living room. I get ready to attack. I stand up, wielding the crucifix. I step forward and just as I'm about to jump on the shadow, I see Avilés, lit by the dim light from the altar candles. He is the last person I was expecting to see. Rage is boiling inside me. What's he doing here?

Avilés looks around him, disconcerted. Perhaps I should stay still and wait for him to leave. He steps forward and looks into the coffin. It's obvious he can hardly control his retching. I notice his gun. He is pointing it in front of him, ready to use it. I worry that he'll shoot me if he doesn't recognise me in the dark. I call to him. "Sergio, I'm here." He peers into the corner, looking for me. I walk towards him and indicate his gun. "It's me, don't shoot." Avilés doesn't lower it. "Are you alright?" I emerge into the light. "Yes." Avilés makes sure it's safe then tucks the gun into his belt. "I can't take this smell anymore," he says. He covers his mouth with his hand, opens the door to the garden and goes out.

Avilés leans his forehead against the wall. He breathes in deeply, trying to contain the vomit. I open the window. He hears the squeaking hinges and turns to look at me. He straightens up and peers through a crack in the gate. He watches the Good Boys talking among themselves. He quietly creeps away from the gate and comes back into the living room. "Did you kill that guy?" he asks me in a low voice. "No," I reply. "So what did you do with him?" By way of an answer, I turn and go into the kitchen and Avilés follows me.

I switch on the light. Humberto is lying on the floor, staring into space. Lit by the ceiling bulb, the signs of the beating are more glaring. Avilés stares at the lump lying at his feet, covered in urine and shit, stinking of chloroform and with a rag stuffed in his mouth. He crouches down and examines the wounds on his face. He turns to me. "Well, you didn't kill him, but you came close."

I explain that Humberto doesn't want to drink water or eat anything. Avilés puts his face close to his. "Is that true?" Humberto doesn't respond. Avilés takes hold of his chin and turns his face. "You don't want to drink water, Lucifer?" The word "Lucifer" flips a switch in Humberto's fanatical subconscious. Furious, he starts kicking, but Avilés and I avoid his legs. He drags himself along to try and get to us, but we move around him until he gets tired. He snorts fiercely through his broken nose. He is suffocating. He looks on the brink of pulmonary failure.

Avilés provokes him again. "Come on, Lucifer, drink some water." Humberto lifts up his upper body and tries to headbutt him. Avilés dodges him. Humberto falls back and his head smacks against the floor. It obviously hurts, because he moans. Avilés leans towards him again. "You are dehydrated," he warns him. "Whether you live or die is up to you." Humberto doesn't even look at him. Sergio signals for me to leave the kitchen with him. I switch off the light, leaving Humberto alone in the dark again. Avilés climbs the stairs and peers into each room. "Where can we talk without this smell?" I point to the mother's bedroom, at the end of the corridor.

I close the door and we sit on the bed. The stench isn't as intense in the bedroom and there is still a faint floral aroma in the air that dilutes it. "The things you make me do, *cabrón*," says Avilés. He doesn't seem very happy to be there. He picks up a photo of Humberto's mother from the bedside table and examines it. "She must have been very beautiful, this woman. Look at her lovely calves." I look at the image. It would never occur to me to notice a woman's calves – least of all when their owner is fermenting in gases downstairs. Avilés places the photo back on the bedside table and turns to me. "What do you think you'll do?" he asks. "I don't know," I reply. Avilés looks at me, incredulous. "You have a guy in the kitchen beaten to a pulp and you don't know what to do with him?" I shake my head. "What's your plan?" he asks. His question stings. "I don't have one," I confess. Avilés rubs his forehead. He squeezes it as though it might give him a good idea. "We can't just leave him there. As soon as the police find him they'll stick us behind bars." He speaks in the plural. I want to tell him that this is my problem and I can fix it on my own, but the truth is that I'm relieved by his solidarity.

Avilés comes to the conclusion that I have no choice other than to leave the city and hide for a long time while things cool down. "Go somewhere far away, and once you are in a safe place we can make an anonymous call and tell the police about Humberto." The idea of abandoning my house and leaving everyone behind is upsetting, but there is no other option. I hate the thought of running away like a rat, just like Humberto and the rest of the Good Boys did after killing Carlos. It seems cowardly, but I want justice for my brother and I won't get it inside a prison cell.

Avilés asks if I've got enough savings to survive for at least a few months. I tell him I haven't got much left. "I can help you while you find a job," he proposes. I am touched by his generosity. Avilés keeps surprising me.

We say nothing. We can hear a radio playing somewhere far away. I recognise the voice of the host from Radio Capital's "Vibrations". He is talking about Hendrix. "The soundwaves from his guitar reverberate in our cerebral cortex, expanding the universe of the human species." It's my favourite radio programme, despite the presenter's convoluted and baroque style. Avilés insists that I pack and leave as soon as possible. He suggests I go to Jorge Jiménez's ranch in Zaragoza, Coahuila. Jorge is an actor friend of his from there, with whom he often goes hunting. He agrees to call him and is sure he'll let me stay as long as I need to. "He and his mother Luz Divina, they're very decent people. They'll be good to you, and you can be sure that nobody will find you there."

A sinking feeling takes over. The idea of a life on the run makes me nauseous. I tell Avilés I'm worried about King and Colmillo. "I'll look after Colmillo, and Chelo's already agreed to look after King," he explains. I ask him if Chelo knows I might run away. "Of course," he replies. "She's ready to meet you wherever you go. She's waiting for you on your roof, worried sick."

I can hear the chords from Hendrix's "Hey Joe" playing on the far-away radio. I mustn't forget to take his records with me. My whole life in 33 r.p.m. I need to listen to them always. They're relics of the identity I am hours away from losing.

Avilés asks if there is anything I need to do before I leave the city. I

578

tell him about Carlos's bank accounts and the lawyer's plan to gain control of them. I confess that I've been thinking of making him my guardian and guarantor of my trust fund, but that I haven't told him yet as there are still a lot of legal formalities to get through.

He asks how much money we're talking. I give him an estimate. He asks me to repeat the number. I say it again, figure by figure. He looks at me, astonished. "That's an incredible amount of money. Your great-grandchildren will be able to live off that." Avilés thinks the lawyer's tactics are impractical and ineffectual. "That will take years," he declares. He asks me if a lawsuit has been filed against the banks. I tell him it hasn't. "Time has run out," says Avilés, "we need to resolve this quickly." I ask him if he can think of any other way of recovering the money. "No, but we'll have to come up with something."

He decides to leave. I go to help him climb through the window, but to my surprise he's much more agile than I thought. He slips through the window, climbs up the stairs, and then I lose sight of him in the dark, as he makes his way to the roof. I know that I should follow him in a few minutes, but decide to go down to the kitchen again. It's my last chance to face Humberto.

I go into the kitchen and switch on the light. He is awake and looks at me with fear in his eyes. I've abused and overpowered him, he's unrecognisable behind his purple, swollen face. I kneel down beside him. I would like to know exactly what's going through his mind. In which of his lobes is his coldness, his pathological tendency to manipulate and murder, in which part of his brain does that insane and vindictive god live? I let him know I'm getting out of the city, that my plan is to leave him tied up and gagged, that it's possible that several days will go by before they find him, and that he must drink water and eat. He looks back at me with dry, glassy eyes, like the fish on their beds of ice in the supermarket. Clear symptoms of dehydration. I can't leave him in this state. He could be dead in less than a day.

I lean towards him. "You will drink water. Whether you want to or not, understood?" He just looks at me absently. An inexpressive vacuum. I take out the rag. He doesn't move. "Lucifer," I say, to see if it livens him up. This time he doesn't react. He remains indifferent. I lift him and lean him against the base of the sink. I pour a glass of water and bring it to his lips. He makes no effort to drink it. I raise his chin and start pouring the water into his mouth. He doesn't reject it. He accepts it gulp by gulp until it's finished.

I grab a slice of bread from the fridge, cover it with a slab of cheese and fold it. I jam it between his teeth and he begins to chew, almost out of habit. The maniac from a short while ago is gone, to be replaced by a flaccid character, devoid of willpower. He swallows and takes another bite. He chews with his mouth open, the cud sliding between his tongue and the roof of his mouth. He's a domesticated animal. A docile cockroach. Having desperately wanted him dead, I'm now feeding him so that he doesn't starve. The vengeance paradox.

Humberto finishes the bread. I give him another slice, which he also devours. I force him to drink two more glasses of water. I gag him again. He puts up no resistance whatsoever.

Taking care not to hurt his head, I drag him slowly by the feet to the living room so that he doesn't have to lie on the cold kitchen floor. I leave him on the carpet, by the side of the coffin. The stink is unrelenting. It's omnipresent. I turn on the record player. The needle glides along the groove in the vinyl. Whoever finds Humberto will do so with Brel's music in the background.

I squat down in front of him. "See you in hell, Lucifer." I don't know if he's heard or understood me. He shows no emotion at all. I look at his face. I etch it into my memory. I will remember him not as the triumphant, depraved Humberto who smiled as my brother drowned, but as this puppet I defeated, whose will I snatched away.

I blow out the candles. I don't want Humberto to topple one of the candelabras as he drags himself along, sending the house up in flames and burning himself to a crisp. I go up to the top floor, clamber out of the window, climb the spiral staircase, and reach the rooftop. It's a cold early morning, and at last I can breathe air that is free of death and putrefaction.

Departure

Robert sat down at the table with the children and tried to explain to them as calmly as possible what the situation was going to be from now on. He told them their father had asked him to look after them. He told them about his family, his three children, his wife, and that the idea was for them all to live together on the ranch and that all they needed to do was take the documents their father had left behind to the local authorities to make the adoption official.

The three of them watched him in silence. Robert asked them to tell him their names and what they would most like to be called. The smallest one's name was also John, but he preferred to be called Johnny. The middle child, Maria, chose Mary. Patricia asked to be called by her name, exactly as it was.

Johnny asked if he would ever see his father again. Robert began to formulate an answer, but Patricia interrupted him. "No, he will never come back," she declared. Taken aback by the conviction of her answer, Robert asked her how she could be so sure. "He told me many times that he'd leave one day and never come back," she replied. Robert thought about what they'd gone through with their father, the nightmares that would follow them forever, how much pain and fear they had collected over the years.

Tears began to roll down Johnny and Mary's faces. Patricia pulled down the sleeve of her jumper and mopped up their tears with it. "It's what Papa wanted," she told them. "Did he die?" asked Mary. Patricia shook her head. "No, he just went far away." Her answer distressed the children even more, and they quietly wept.

Robert felt so much for them. The three of them must have been terrified. John may have been an alcoholic schizophrenic who put them through terrifying moments, but he was their father, the only one they'd known. Now they were facing the vertigo of uncertainty. Thrown suddenly into the outside world, a place their father had never allowed them to see.

Robert told them they would leave for Whitehorse in one or two days. Until then, they were free to do whatever they wished – play, sleep, eat. Patricia said they wanted to see the wolves. Robert agreed and that seemed to cheer Johnny and Mary up.

The night before, when Robert had come across Nujuaqtutuq at the entrance to the barn, the wolf had not tried to run away. Meek and frail, he had allowed Robert to lasso his neck and made no attempt to escape or to bite him. Robert tied him to the wall and called Chuck over. "He came back to life," he said. "Quite the miracle," added Chuck. The wolf's recovery defied belief, let alone his ability to stand up.

Robert and Chuck restored an old corral to keep the wolves in. They reinforced it with boards so there were no gaps they could escape through, and raised the height of the fence so that they couldn't jump over it. They installed wooden boxes filled with scraps of fabric and fur so that the wolves had some shelter. Neither one of them seemed in a fit state to bear the cold and they needed to be protected.

They put the male in first. Nujuaqtutuq sniffed the posts and, managing to cock his leg with difficulty, urinated on them. Even wounded, he marked his territory. Robert drove the trailer with the female into the corral and opened the door. He thought that, as the charier and more reluctant of the wolves, she would hide in a corner, afraid of the male. What happened was quite different. The female got out of the trailer, and she and Nujuaqtutuq looked at each other. He was probably the first wolf she had seen since she was a pup. Curious, she approached. He bared his teeth. Accustomed to leading a pack, he must have been unsettled by this female's incursion into his new territory. Although she had spent no time among wolves, Pajamartuq submissively lowered her head, accepting that, inside the corral, the male was the one in charge. Nujuaqtutuq sniffed her for a few seconds and then, reassured of his status, lay down against the boards.

Robert took the children to see them. They found them lying down next to each other inside one of the wooden boxes. The children watched them through the fence. "They're pretty," Johnny said, used to seeing them skinned and hung along the trail to the ranch.

The big wolf straightened up. Even maltreated, thin, covered in scars, he was imposing. "What does 'Nujuaqtutuq' mean?" Patricia asked. "It means 'Wild One', in Inuktitut," Chuck said. Patricia reached through the planks to stroke him, but Robert stopped her. "They may seem tame, but they're not. They could rip your hand off. Don't do that again." Robert's words alarmed the children. The wolves looked so gentle.

Robert and Chuck decided to head into town to meet the local authorities, and asked Kenojuac to look after the children. The two men climbed into the pickup and left. Kenojuac went into the house, picked up a Winchester 94 calibre 30-30 rifle and gestured for the children to follow her towards the river. Despite the fact that she was elderly, they found it difficult to keep up with her. The woman walked confidently through the snow, avoiding the mounds and hopping nimbly across the streams.

Close to the river, the woman spotted footprints. She walked slowly and brought her finger to her lips, instructing the children to keep silent. She followed the trail through the snow and about a hundred metres along they spotted a lynx running ahead of them. The woman took a shot, but missed.

They kept going. When they got to the edge of the river, Kenojuac went up to the water, which still had chunks of ice floating on the surface, and tugged on a chain. Something heavy must have been on the other end because she struggled to pull it towards her. Patricia rushed to help her. They pulled between the two of them, until suddenly

584

something furiously splashed in the water. Pulling the chain hurt the girl's hand; she was frightened and stepped back. Whatever was thrashing in the water was enormously strong.

Patricia saw a flash of brown, which then disappeared back into the water. After a tug of war, they managed to bring the animal close to the riverbank. It was a beaver caught in a trap. The beaver was injured, but even so it attacked them as soon as it set foot on dry land. Kenojuac moved and fell backwards onto the frozen mud. The beaver leaped towards her, but Patricia managed to stop it by whacking it in the mouth with a branch. Kenojuac got up. The beaver tried to dive back into the water, but the woman clung on to the chain. She asked the three children to help her. They did so, afraid all the while that the beaver would turn around and sink its sharp front teeth into them.

The beaver was not able to get back below the surface of the water. Kenojuac picked up the branch and hit it on the head, hard. The beaver was stunned, and the woman took the opportunity to deliver several more blows, one after another. The beaver flipped over and floated belly-up.

Between the four of them they pulled the beaver to shore. It lay motionless on the snow. Kenojuac picked it up by its tail. It was enormous, an old male with thick fur. Four more of that size would be enough for a proper coat.

They walked along the river. The children took turns carrying the beaver. Johnny and Mary could barely manage it. Kenojuac had placed several traps all along the river, one every two hundred metres. In the next four there were no beavers, but in the fifth they found a small one that had drowned. Kenojuac took it out, tied its legs together and threw it over her shoulder.

Kenojuac had placed the traps close to the beaver dams. She attached the chains to tree trunks or rocks and half-buried the traps in the snow or mud. Since beavers were herbivores, there was no point in using bait, which is why the woman studied their routes between the dens and the trees they gnawed on to build their dams.

They found one more beaver and then began their journey back to the house. Patricia carried the last one they had found, and her siblings carried the large male between them. Kenojuac, rifle in hand, looked around her in search of prey. Her sight was failing her, so she didn't spot a deer among the pine trees that the children pointed out to her.

Despite the cold, their exhaustion from carrying the beavers, the long walk through the snow and their sodden shoes, the children returned content. They had rarely explored beyond the confines of the ranch. The new landscape, the semi-frozen river, finding out how the traps worked, the damp smell of the beavers' fur, hearing the woman's strange language – they were excited by all of it.

They skinned the beavers. The woman put the skins on one knee and with a small knife scraped away the remaining fat and muscle. Then she butchered them. She saved the fat in a container and separated the fillets from the front and hind quarters. She put the ribcage, neck and head onto the stove to make soup with. She gave the hearts, livers and lungs to the children and pointed towards the corral where the wolves were kept, so that they would feed them.

The children rushed to take them the innards. Mary and Johnny threw theirs in, but Patricia offered Nujuaqtutuq a piece of liver in her hand. The wolf came up close and when he was only a few centimetres away Patricia opened her hand and let the meat fall to the ground. Nujuaqtutuq looked briefly into her eyes. She was not afraid. "Nujuaqtutuq," she whispered. The wolf looked at her for a more few seconds, then lowered his head, took the piece of liver in his mouth and carried it a few metres away to eat.

Chelo was waiting for me on the rooftop with Avilés. She looked upset. As soon as she saw me, she blurted: "You're a fucking moron!" Angrily, she told me how worried she'd been, convinced that something terrible had happened to me. I tried to take her in my arms, but she pulled away and told me again that I was a moron. She was furious. Avilés tried to pacify her. "There's nothing to be gained by insulting him, there are decisions to be made. Do you understand?" Sergio's words worked. Chelo came over and wrapped her arms around me. She cried on my shoulder. "I thought they'd killed you," she said. I squeezed her tight. Avilés left us alone on the rooftop. Chelo couldn't contain herself. I kissed her tears and we stood with our arms around each other until she calmed down.

We went into the house. Avilés suggested I pack my suitcase now, so that we could leave immediately. We could stay at his place while we figured out how to get the money out of the bank accounts. Chelo decided to come with me to Coahuila. I tried to convince her it would be best if I left on my own, so that I could get settled in. Once she'd finished her medical degree, we would see. She refused. She would come with me wherever I went. She insisted I mattered more to her than her studies. I thought about taking off without her. Why should I condemn her to the life of a fugitive? Why smear her with my frustrated vengeance and its consequences?

I persuaded Avilés to let us stay in my house one last night. Avilés agreed and lay down on my parents' bed, his gun by his side in case he needed it. Chelo helped me pack. I packed enough clothes for a month, my Hendrix records, Carlos's lumberjack shirt, the file with Colmillo's papers in it and the presents my parents had brought us from Europe.

We went up to Carlos's room. As soon as he saw me, King's tail started to wag and he jumped on top of us, covering us in drool like always. Chelo was delighted. "He's doing so well," she said. I started to choose which of my brother's books to take with me. If I could have, I'd have taken them all, but I'd have needed a van to transport them.

While I put them into the suitcase I looked around me. The mirror in which Carlos used to see his reflection peering back at him, the clothes he wore, the records he listened to, the posters that decorated his room. I turned to Chelo. "What if I become Carlos?" Chelo looked at me, confused. "What are you talking about?" she asked.

Without answering her I went to knock on Avilés's door. He opened the door wearing only his boxers with a gun in his hand. His chubby legs were extremely pale. A deep scar ran across his thigh. "What would happen if I turned up at the banks as Carlos?" I asked him. "What are you talking about?" he said sleepily. "If I go to the banks and tell them that I am Juan Carlos Valdés, could I take the money out of the accounts?" Avilés thought for a moment. "Do you look like him?" "Yes, a lot," I replied. "We need two pieces of official I.D. with your photo," he said. "We look very similar in our military service records," I told him.

I went back to Carlos's room. Chelo was waiting for me in the doorway. "What's happening?" "I am going to impersonate Carlos," I said and hurriedly explained my plan. She didn't understand. I moved past her and started rummaging through Carlos's drawers. I found his military service record and took it to Sergio, who studied it. "Well you're not exactly the spitting image of him, but it's probably close enough," he said.

Avilés told me he had a contact in the Ministry of Foreign Affairs who helped him get passports at short notice whenever they hired new circus employees and needed to tour overseas. He thought that if they gave the civil servant enough of a bribe, we'd quickly be able to get a fake passport.

Avilés insisted we should leave before sunrise and he sent us off to get ready. Chelo and I got into the shower and, despite the urgency, made love under the water. Then we hurriedly got dressed and went downstairs with my luggage. Chelo agreed to stay with King while we went for the passport; we would meet at Avilés's place later.

Avilés parked his Maverick in the garage. We threw my suitcases into the boot and, between us, carried King downstairs and out to the street. The dog was petrified. He writhed in terror as we carried him through the ground floor. Once outside, he was calmer. Chelo clipped him to a lead and walked a few steps with him. He sniffed a fence, a drain, a doorway. I hunkered down to say goodbye. I put my arms around him, he licked me a couple of times, then I got up.

Chelo hugged me tight. "Take care," she said. She gave me a long kiss. She pulled away and turned to go. I watched her walk away with King. Avilés pulled me out of my daydream. "Hurry up," he said.

I went to fetch Colmillo and found him curled up under the sink. He got up and padded towards me warily. I never stopped fearing him. I knew it was important to remember that he was capable of killing me in seconds. I squatted down to put on his muzzle. He shook his head in an attempt to stop me. I rubbed his neck to calm him until he allowed me to place it on him. I attached the chain and led him outside.

I lifted him onto the back seat of the Maverick. Avilés asked me to make sure Colmillo faced the rear windscreen, so that he couldn't attack. I left him in the car for a while, to let him adjust to the confined space. Colmillo tried to turn around, but the front seats made it impossible. After a few minutes, he decided to lie down. When Avilés got into the car, Colmillo became uneasy; his hackles bristled. I stroked him until he was calm and lay back down. "Let's go," Avilés said.

I opened the gate. The sky was beginning to brighten. A street cleaner in an orange uniform was sweeping up rubbish and dry leaves with a broom made of twigs. A flock of sparrows woke up on a cedar tree's branches. The milk truck drove along the street. It pulled up in front of several houses to swap the empty glass bottles neighbours had left by their front doors for fresh ones full of milk. Mr Belmont passed us in his blue Opel, on his way to work. He greeted me with a nod and drove on. The little things in the little world of my street.

Avilés drove out of the garage and stopped a few metres away. I locked my front door. I took a few steps back and looked at it. I might never see it again. For a second, I was tempted to forget the whole thing and go back inside. Let Zurita and his men come for me. I could arm myself and fight them to the end.

"Let's go," Avilés said. I looked at Humberto's house. His guards were watching the door. I got into the car and we left. The sun was rising.

Remoteness

The government official in Mayo did not need to see the documents. He knew that John Sycamore was ill, madness seethed beneath his affable personality. He had once encountered him on the main road in the middle of a snowstorm, gesticulating wildly at an imaginary companion. He had tried to help, but John had become so enraged that he had left him alone in the storm.

One afternoon, the vet had showed up to ask whether it was possible for his children to be taken into care by a state or religious institution. John realised how much his mental health was affecting them. The official explained that it was possible, but that the children would have to go to Whitehorse where there was a small orphanage that took care of the children of loggers who died in sawmills and those of indigenous parents who succumbed to epidemics. He would be required to undergo a medical and demonstrate that he was incapable of raising his children for health reasons. The official informed him that mental illness was unlikely to be considered proof of incapacity.

The vet asked until what age the orphanage would look after the children and was told that once they turned thirteen they would have to leave and fend for themselves. Resources were scarce and the government could not afford to take care of teenagers. John ruled out the idea of putting them into the orphanage. His children should never be separated. He asked if he could give them up for adoption. The official told him that this was a more viable option and helped him fill in the necessary forms, the very ones that Robert was now handing back to him.

"You can refuse," the official told Robert, "and even if you refuse you can still keep a third of the ranch. They are two separate issues." Impossible. Robert was incapable of taking any part of the children's inheritance. He replied that he was prepared to adopt the children on two conditions: that the children themselves agreed to it, and that if the father came back he could not rescind his decision. The official explained that neither condition could be met. Firstly, being minors, the children could not legally agree to anything. Secondly, John had the legal right to seek custody of the children – although, having given them up voluntarily, it would require a court hearing that, in the official's opinion, John was likely to lose. It was up to Robert to decide whether or not to accept.

"I accept," he said categorically. On behalf of the Federal Commissioner of Yukon, the official stamped the forms granting Robert Mackenzie custody of Patricia, Maria and John Sycamore. A third of High Plains ranch was transferred into his name and he renamed the property Mackenzie Plains ranch. He had a new branding made to mark his own livestock, and it was decided that Robert would manage both ranches until Patricia was of legal age.

Robert left the office, a wooden cabin, in a bittersweet mood. He felt selfish for having accepted the large parcel of land, but John Sycamore's documents did not allow him to turn down the right of ownership of the ranch, the outbuildings or the livestock. John had made the handover to Robert legally bulletproof, so as to force him into a moral commitment to the children.

On the other hand, agreeing to adopt them gave him a profound sense of well-being. He knew that he would have to permanently live with his wife, that he would become frustrated with her and the six children milling around the house and that he would yearn for the vast, unspoiled landscapes he once explored to determine the routes for his pipelines. He was also sure that he would quickly tire of the routine of livestock farming and the flat plains of the ranch. But he had the feeling that his life needed this change of direction, that some new and precious meaning would come from cohabiting with his wife and their now six children. He felt inspired to rise to the challenge of educating three children who had spent years imprisoned in a tense and isolated environment. He did not share his parents' religious fatalism, which made them see god in everything that happened, but he was convinced that life had led him there for reasons that only time would reveal.

He walked to the river. A barge was gliding slowly upstream. Eighty years earlier, this river had attracted hundreds of gold and silver prospectors desperate enough to cross the surrounding mountains in search of a concession, only to end up stranded in this savage land, with few resources, living in abject misery. Defeated, the fortune hunters emigrated and left the colonists and the Na-Cho Nyäk Dun people in peace. Now Mayo was a tiny one-horse town of only three hundred inhabitants. Half of them were white, and the other half were indigenous or mixed race.

Chuck caught up with him and they watched the flowing water in silence. Chuck had rowed along this river several times. He used to tie up his canoe to the bank, put up a flagpole he'd carved from a long and slender maple wood log, and raise a yellow flag, the signal for the native Canadians that a fur buyer had come. Groups of them would arrive in canoes filled with all kinds of pelts: beaver, pine marten, wolf and bear. Negotiations would go on for hours. The bargaining wouldn't be over until both parties closed the deal. Chuck traded bullets, flour, salt and sugar. He paid for large batches of the highest quality furs with Winchester 30-30 calibre rifles, the object which was most valuable to the First Nations peoples. After a week, he packed up his camp and travelled a few miles upstream. He would unload the cargo there in Mayo and drive it to Dawson, where his wife was in charge of selling it.

"I envy you," Chuck said to Robert. "At least you know what you're going to do." Robert smiled. "And you? What have you decided?" Chuck pointed towards where the Mayo and Stewart rivers converged. "I am going to try and unite two rivers," he said with a chuckle.

Later on, they arrived back at the train station. Kenojuac had made a stew from the beaver meat and some salmon fillets she and the children had smoked.

It was a fresh, sunny afternoon, and they decided to bring out the table so they could eat outside. The children seemed excited. Johnny told the story of that morning's hunt. Mary regularly interrupted him to add details, such as the musky smell of the beavers, or the calm waters of the dam.

Robert was relieved. The children were gradually becoming less silent and withdrawn. If they continued like this, it wouldn't be too difficult to integrate them into the family, or at least that was his hope. Robert explained to them that the adoption was official. That from now on he and his wife would be their parents and they would live alongside their three children like siblings. They would build a bigger house on the ranch so that they could all fit, but for now they would settle into their current house. Johnny asked if he should lend his toys to the other children. Only if he wanted to, Robert told him. Mary was worried about whether or not they would buy new clothes. Robert assured her they would. Patricia asked about the wolves. Would they kill them to hang on the fence, like her father had, or set them free? Robert told her they would do neither. The wolves were physically very weak, they were incapable of surviving in the wild. He declared that Nujuaqtutuq and Pajamartuq would be part of the family and that they would build a large enclosure where they could live comfortably.

Robert told them they would set off early the next day for White-horse. He asked them to wash and put on clean clothes. Chuck translated for Kenojuac, and she got up to put a water basin in the hearth. She poured the water into a tub in the back room for the children to bathe in.

Robert and Chuck collected the dirty plates, washed them in a bucket and, when they were done, left the house. The sun was dipping behind the mountains. Chuck brushed the snow off a broad sawn-off trunk that served as a bench and sat down. He gazed at the train tracks and the ramshackle wooden station. "It's such a shame the train hardly stops here anymore," he said. "You have no idea how many people used to swarm around the carriages. Stevedores, merchants, settlers, fur traders, farmers, gold panners. They loaded and unloaded packages, boxes, sacks of corn and wheat, barrels of oil, bundles of bearskins. This place provided for the whole region. Now look," he said, and pointed towards the rotten wooden walls, the broken glass, the rusty benches. Nowadays the train only stopped briefly in this ghost station on Tuesday and Saturday nights, but in happier times it had stopped there six times a week. Gold fever came to an end and with it the town's prosperity. The villages founded by the prospectors slowly dwindled until all that was left were ruins. They left a legacy of cheap alcohol and venereal disease that decimated the indigenous tribes. It took years for the sweeping forests to recover from the wounds caused by the dozens of frenzied excavations.

Chuck pulled out a packet of tobacco, emptied a little onto a sheet of rice paper, rolled a cigarette and lit it with a gas lighter. He took a drag and blew out the smoke. A small white cloud climbed up in a spiral and then vanished in the wind. Robert breathed in the acrid smell of the tobacco. It reminded him of his childhood. His grandfather liked to smoke the strongest tobacco there was. "It cleanses the blood," he would say as he inhaled. Robert imagined the smoke travelling through arteries, sweeping away impurities as it went before it was blown out of his mouth. His father smoked too. He preferred a lighter and smoother tobacco. "A cigarette is company when you're on your own," he would say. Aged ten, Robert tried to take a drag from a cigarette. It irritated his throat so much that he couldn't understand how his father and grandfather could take any pleasure in inhaling the burning smoke. It was a long time before he tried again, one icy night in the mountains, when one of the guides offered him a cigarette to warm him up. He never developed an addiction, and smoked only when the cold was bitter and the proximity of the lit end to his face gave him a warm, peaceful sensation.

He felt like a cigarette now. He asked his uncle for some tobacco and rolling paper. He rolled the tobacco, lit it and breathed in deeply. He felt the smoke rush into his lungs and he released it slowly. Yes, a cigarette was another way of feeling less lonely. He looked at the moon peeking out between the pine trees. "We are leaving early tomorrow," he told his uncle. "Will you come with us?" Chuck shrugged. "I don't know," he replied.

When they returned to the house, the children had already bathed and were ready to go to sleep. Robert looked at them all wrapped up in furs, looking scared. This was going to be a big enough change for him, but they were truly diving into the unknown. He promised himself he'd be loving and affectionate with them. He would be patient and understanding. That very day they had become his adopted children. There was no turning back.

He sat by them and told them a story about his journeys as an explorer. The children listened attentively. Afterwards he tucked them in and said goodnight, lightly touching their heads with his hand. He went to sit down at the table with Chuck and Kenojuac. They weren't speaking. She had her head bowed, and his uncle looked thoughtful. Robert realised that his presence was making them feel uncomfortable so he left and headed for the shed.

Robert lay down, worried. He had to convince his wife and kids to accept these children. He knew Linda would welcome them. She was a good woman and a good mother. And his children would eventually adapt. He turned off the oil lamp and closed his eyes.

In the early hours, Nujuaqtutuq began to howl, a howl amplified by the absence of any wind. Robert sat up in his camp bed. Other wolves were responding from afar. Perhaps it was the same pack that had attacked him a few weeks ago.

Robert sat and listened to it. The moon was beginning to drop towards the horizon and soon the sun would come up. He decided not to go back to sleep. He prepared the cage for the wolves. He hooked the trailer onto the tow ball and secured it with a chain, then he returned to the shed to pack up his belongings. They would travel all the way to Whitehorse without stopping. He would take the children directly to his house. He would leave them to play with his children while he explained everything to his wife. Then he would go to his company headquarters to hand in his resignation. He was certain that, although he was leaving of his own accord, the company would acknowledge his many years of hard work and give him a significant severance payment.

He went to the house as soon as the sun rose. The children were already having breakfast, chatting excitedly. Taciturn, Kenojuac was heating up a pot on the stove. Robert blurted out a loud "good morning" and as soon as the children saw him, they fell quiet. It felt like a bad sign. He must still seem intimidating to them. He needed to be more intimate and warm. He sat between Patricia and Johnny. He joked with them, then asked if they were ready to leave.

Before answering him, the three siblings looked at one another and then Patricia nodded.

They loaded up the pickup truck. Chuck and Robert tied up the wolves and got them into the cage with difficulty. They only just fit. Perhaps Robert could find a bigger trailer in Mayo, a second-hand one of the kind used to transport packs of sled dogs.

Chuck came out with some bundles and threw them into the bed of the pickup truck. He and Robert looked at each other. Chuck swallowed and turned back to the house. He hugged Kenojuac, kissed her, and then quickly climbed into the vehicle and shut the door.

Robert and the children said goodbye to the woman. Her faint smile only made her look sadder. The children turned and walked to the pickup truck and squeezed themselves into the seat between Chuck and Robert. Johnny had to sit between Patricia and Mary with his knees pulled up, so that Robert could change gears.

They drove off and followed the track to the highway. Chuck turned around to look back at the woman standing in the doorway as she vanished into the distance.

"Bring four passport photos and five gold centenarios," said the man behind the counter. Avilés smiled and told him that last time it had been taken care of for far less than that. "I'll give you one," Sergio offered. The passport official shook his head. "If you want them for today, pre-dated and stamped, it has to be five." They haggled for ten minutes before agreeing that we would give him one centenario and three one-ounce silver libertad. The guy set a deadline of 1.00 p.m. for bringing him the birth certificates and the coins if we wanted the passport that afternoon.

For the photographs, I brushed my hair so it looked similar to Carlos's. I studied my facial expressions in the mirror, trying to replicate his: an easy smile, a gaze that was practically a wink. Even in photos for official documents, Carlos looked seductive. We went to a small photography studio on the ground floor of a building around the corner from the Ministry of Foreign Affairs in Tlatelolco. My photographs looked almost identical to the ones on Carlos's military service record. Avilés approved. Then we stopped by a jeweller's in the city centre owned by an acquaintance of his, who sold us the gold centenario and the libertad.

We arrived at the passport office shortly before 1.00 p.m. The guy jerked his chin to signal to us to wait outside. We waited in the hallway. The little man emerged, walked past us and went into the toilets. We followed him. "Did you bring it?" he asked as soon as we walked in. Avilés nodded and handed him two silver coins. "And the rest?" the official asked. "You scratch my back, I'll scratch yours," said Avilés.

A few hours later, the little man handed us the passport. To avoid raising suspicions at the banks by presenting a brand-new passport, we had it dated nine months earlier, and added a few Mexican entry stamps to make it look as though Carlos had been travelling during that period.

We'd arrived at Avilés's house very early that morning. It was a one-storey mansion with a large garden in the centre of San Ángel. I never imagined that a tamer's salary would be enough to buy a property of that size. Avilés noticed my surprise. "I'm also one of the circus's owners," he said.

We put Colmillo into a large cage where Avilés usually housed lion and tiger pups, and went inside. A sleepy woman let us in. "Doña Natalia, this is Juan Guillermo," Avilés said. She offered me her little bird-like hand and I held out mine. "Nice to meet you, young man." Avilés asked her to take me to the guest room. I followed her with my suitcases until we reached a bedroom at the back. There were countless photographs on the hallway's walls. Avilés with Julissa and César Costa, with El Santo, Charlton Heston, Jean-Paul Belmondo, Lyndon B. Johnson. Avilés in New York, Rome, London, Rio de Janeiro.

We left early to open an account in my name at a different bank from those that Carlos had used. The plan was to withdraw the funds from all the accounts using certified cheques and then transfer them into the new one. We went to the only branch of the Banco Mercantil de Monterrey in the city, a regional bank based in the north-east of the country, which would make it difficult for Mexico City banks to reclaim the money we would deposit there. I applied to open an account, but although I was only two months away from turning eighteen the bank wouldn't allow it. For a minor, the only option was a "savings book", intended for children and teenagers who wanted to save small sums each week. When they came of age, they could withdraw the total together with the minimal interest accrued. The manager lectured me about the importance of saving and urged me to put away at least ten pesos a week. I smiled, imagining his reaction when I deposited millions into my little book.

Avilés also opened an account. If for some reason I was not allowed to deposit such large amounts into my "savings book", we would put it into his. He made a point of telling me that he would return every centavo. I told him that I trusted him entirely.

When we left the passport office, I called Pato from a public phone. I'd asked him to watch Humberto's house. He told me nothing unusual had happened. I warned him that things would begin to happen soon, that he had to be vigilant. I gave him Avilés's phone number and asked him to call me as soon as he knew anything.

I hung up and then handed the receiver to Sergio. He put a twenty-centavo coin into the machine and dialled the 06 emergency number. A woman answered. "Emergency services, how can I help you?" Avilés reported that there was a powerful corpse-like smell at number 45, Retorno 201, in Unidad Modelo. When the woman asked for his details, he hung up.

In a few hours, perhaps a few minutes, Humberto would be found bound and gagged. When this happened, Zurita would give the order to release the hounds. Knowing him, he would not give up until he had tracked me down and locked me up. Staying in the city and try to outwit the banks was risky. But I had no intention of running off to the Coahuila desert with no money or resources.

Avilés dropped me off at the house and went to do his act at the circus. I lay in bed in my room. The walls were thick and blocked out any external noise. I closed my eyes and fell asleep. Hours later I woke up to someone knocking on the door. I felt dopey, unsure of where I was, with a sandy feeling in my eyelids. "Young man, young man," Natalia said. I got up and opened the door. The tiny woman pointed to a telephone at the other end of the hallway. "Phone call for you." I walked over to it and picked up the receiver. "Hello?" "Something big is happening," said Pato. "Zurita got here about two hours ago with

600

lots of cop cars." I covered the mouthpiece and took a deep breath. The roulette wheel had begun to spin. Sooner or later the ball would land on my number. "You there?" Pato said. "Yeah," I said, "I'm here." "The cops are going from house to house questioning the neighbours," he continued. I asked if my name had been mentioned. "Not as far as I know," he said, then added, "not yet." Fuck! Why did he have to say "not yet"? "If I hear anything else, I'll call you back," he said and hung up. I hated how vulnerable his phone call had left me feeling. I felt like a prisoner. Pursued. Hunted.

I stood next to the telephone. Natalia peered around the kitchen door and told me she had made quesadillas for dinner. I said I'd be there in a minute. I looked at the photos on the wall. One of them featured an incredibly young Avilés with a huge dead male lion at his feet. He was surrounded by a group of Maasai warriors in traditional dress. A spear rested on the animal's side. It was bleeding from a wound in its shoulder. From the picture it was clear that Avilés had killed it.

Avilés arrived while I was eating dinner, still in his tamer's costume. He fell back into a chair. "This work just gets more and more tiring, my body can't take it anymore," he said. I told him about Pato's phone call. He tried to calm me down, telling me that Zurita would not try too hard to find me, I wasn't a hardened criminal he could extort, so he was not likely to waste time and money tracking me down. I disagreed. Zurita would come after me for one simple reason: to stop me getting my revenge on him. "That's true. Men like him don't like stray bullets," he said.

No, Zurita and the Good Boys were never going to let this drop. Not because of Humberto, that was the last thing they cared about, but because I had broken an unwritten rule: victims could not become aggressors, and, if they did, they were declaring war.

Signals

Anxiety about what was around the corner kept me awake. Exiled, orphaned, on the run. Colmillo began to howl, once again summoning an invisible pack. A few dogs echoed him. Despite the waistcoats knitted by their lady owners, the collars strung with little bells, the ridiculous haircuts, the genes of those pampered, innocuous pedigree dogs recognised the call of the primeval howl. The chorus of barks carried on for almost an hour. From the unbearable yaps of the miniature Schnauzer to a St Bernard's baritone growl.

I went to the garden to check on Colmillo. The leaves of the giant ash tree rustled in the wind. The branches creaked. An ocote pine swayed from side to side. A narrow stream coming from some rundown barns flowed through a gully. The house must have belonged to a wealthy family towards the end of the nineteenth century, their country property where they reared cows, chickens and pigs. Colmillo had been housed in what looked like the old stables.

I crouched down next to the cage and Colmillo padded over. We looked at one another for a few minutes. Once I left for Zaragoza it was unlikely that I would see him again. Surrounded by so much death, I had become certain that what was present in our lives could be lost from one second to the next, that there was no guarantee that anyone or anything was permanent.

I went back to bed and slept for a couple of hours. Avilés woke me up at six banging loudly on the door. "Get up, we have to be at the first bank by eight thirty. Come and have breakfast," he shouted from the other side of the door, then I heard his footsteps disappear down the hallway.

Avilés was waiting for me in the kitchen with a mug in his hands. "This is chocolate atole, a Coahuila recipe," he said as he handed it to me. He'd turned on the stove. The kitchen was old; the walls were covered in Talavera tiles and there were clay and copper cooking pots everywhere. I sat at the table while he cooked eggs with dried beef. We decided to visit the Banco de Londres y México on Insurgentes first, where the second-largest portion of Carlos's money had been deposited. I could live worry-free for years if I managed to recover this sum alone. We agreed that Avilés would introduce himself as my legal representative and I would give my finest impersonation of Carlos.

We arrived at the bank at 7.45 a.m. "Always best to be punctual," Avilés said. Was arriving forty-five minutes early really punctual? We leaned against the back of a 1952 Mercury, identical to the one my father had sold to be able to pay our school fees. Far from bringing me down, seeing it sparked a defiant urge to fight. It was time to break the vicious cycle of self-pity that had ended up strangling and destroying my family. I wouldn't be defeated again. I wouldn't give another inch.

At eight o'clock, the bank's employees began to arrive one by one. The security guard on duty opened the door for each of them and closed it again behind them. At 8.30 a.m. precisely, Avilés walked up to the door, but the guard blocked his path. Avilés showed him his watch. "It's time," he said. Confused, the guard turned to look inside, and one of the cashiers signalled for him to let us in.

We asked an assistant if we could speak to the manager. She stared at us as though we'd asked to speak to the president of the republic. "He's busy. How can I help?" she said disdainfully. "I would like to close my account, señorita." "You don't need to bother the manager for that," she said. "Take a form, fill it out and queue at any window. They'll look after you." She looked down at the papers on the desk and I placed a hand over them. She looked up again, irritated. "Señorita, tell the manager that Juan Carlos Valdés would like to speak to him." "And?" she said haughtily. "And that I would like to withdraw the three million four hundred and thirty thousand pesos I have on deposit here." The woman studied me for a few seconds, then turned to Avilés, waiting for him to confirm what she had just heard. "Is he serious?" she asked him. "Yes, completely serious, and I would be grateful if you could treat my client with some respect," Avilés said. Still incredulous, she looked me up and down. She got up and went to consult a chubby man wearing a lopsided hairpiece. He pointed towards some drawers. The woman rummaged through a few folders and took out one. Together, they perused it, the man occasionally glancing at me out of the corner of his eye.

The chubby man emerged from his office and greeted me. "Señor Valdés, what on earth have we done here at the bank to make you want to close your account? Please, come through to my office. I would like to present you with our plan to secure the highest possible returns for your money." The man looked pale. This was clearly one of his most important accounts. Losing it would be a black mark on his reputation as a manager and a blow to the branch's finances.

He asked us to sit down in his office. He promised me an "unbeatable interest rate for your money, and a personalised service". He apologised for the "assistant's insolence" and promised I would never be treated that way again. I explained that I needed to withdraw the entirety of my assets because I was moving abroad. In an attempt to convince me not to flee the country – or his bank – the manager began to rattle off nationalist clichés. "Don't go – there's no country like Mexico", "'Made in Mexico' means well made", "You'll end up like the Jamaicón Villegas, homesick and out of place", etc. I smiled and shook my head. The decision had been made, I had found a job with an American company. I took out my wallet and my false passport and placed them on the desk. "My identification." Avilés leaned towards him. "We would like a certified cheque for the total of the savings, please." The manager made one last-ditch attempt to keep me as a client. "If you stay, we can offer you a complimentary stove." Avilés laughed. "Why would he want a stove?" The manager claimed that it would take two to five working days to issue a certified cheque. He probably thought that this would give me enough time to reconsider the stove. Avilés refused to accept this. "That's a lie. Whenever I've closed an account, they've handed the money over instantly." The manager realised he had no choice but to issue the cheque. He picked up the phone and dialled an extension, and just as he was giving instructions I interrupted. "I would prefer the money in cash." In unison, Avilés and the manager turned to me, disconcerted. "I don't believe we have that amount of money in the vault, and besides, are you really intending to walk around with that fortune? Aren't you afraid you might get robbed?" I coolly told him I wasn't. The manager stood up. "Let me see how much we have. The branch cannot be left with no reserves of cash." He was about to leave when I grabbed his arm. "I'll accept dollars or centenarios," I said. The manager looked at me, confused. "If the bank charges commission," I said, "I'm happy to pay it. Or a personal commission for yourself, of course, if that helps." The little man slapped my back and headed towards the safe.

As soon as the manager had left, Avilés upbraided me. "Are you crazy? Your ridiculous demands are going to get us found out. You're behaving like a bank robber." I smiled. "I want something more solid. Once the alarm is raised, it won't matter how certified that cheque is, I won't be able to cash it."

We left the bank with two bags. One containing forty thousand dollars, the other containing one million two hundred thousand pesos in hundred-peso notes. Avilés and I each managed to fit ten coins into our trouser pockets. The balance was covered by a certified cheque. Minus the manager's commission of three thousand dollars for facilitating a cash transaction.

Avilés didn't stop grumbling. "You're nuts, totally nuts." We got to the Maverick, parked three blocks away. We threw the bags into the boot and Avilés drove off at full speed. He was paranoid, and couldn't stop checking his rear-view mirror. I was euphoric. Without any lawyers, lawsuits or time-wasting I'd recovered a considerable portion of Carlos's money. And yes, I did feel like a bank robber.

Avilés refused to go to another bank without stashing the bags in his house first. We hid them inside a shed in a corner of the garden filled with old junk, and buried the coins by a wooden fence. Then we went to deposit the cheque in Avilés's account. Suspicious, the bank cashier checked the amount over and over again. She held the cheque up to the light to make sure it wasn't fake and asked the other cashiers to look at it too. After much toing and froing, she handed us the corresponding receipt. Another million and seven hundred thousand pesos guaranteed.

Once we had left the bank, we both breathed a sigh of relief. We'd been afraid that someone in the chain of bank employees might discover our scam and call the police. Technically I was not committing fraud – the money belonged to me – but I had acquired the money through fraudulent means. I didn't care, though; the banks played dirty too.

Carlos had saved seven hundred and eighteen thousand pesos with the Banco de Comercio. I thought the manager might also try his best to keep hold of me as a client, but he didn't hesitate to give us part of the money in pesos, part in the form of a certified cheque and the rest in dollars. He said it was a shame I didn't want to continue with the bank and wished me luck with my job abroad. He wouldn't accept a "commission" and asked the security guard at the entrance to escort us to the car, giving us his card in case we required his services in the future.

Avilés and I thought the manager was laying a trap so that he could rob us – that he'd found us out and asked the security guard to force us to hand the money back at gunpoint. But no, the guard walked us to the car, made sure nobody suspicious was loitering nearby and then politely said goodbye.

We got into the Maverick, stunned. The speed and ease with which they had handed over the money meant the banks' central offices hadn't informed their branches of García Allende's request for Carlos's money to be given to me. They simply hadn't taken the request seriously. I was surprised that it only took a couple of fake pieces of I.D. to recover in a few hours what could have taken years, had we taken the legal route.

We hid the cash and the dollars in Avilés's house and deposited the new cheque. It was 11.00 a.m. and I'd ensured my financial security for the rest of my life. Avilés suggested we take a break, but my adrenaline level was through the roof. I didn't want to stop. I convinced him to try one more bank. Reluctantly, he agreed. We headed to the Banco Industrial, where Carlos had saved two million and eighteen thousand pesos.

The branch was located around the corner from the Galaxia and Géminis cinemas. We parked the car in front of the box office, which was closed, and walked to the bank. We went in and asked to speak to the manager. "May I ask who wishes to speak to him?" the receptionist replied. "Juan Carlos Valdés." The woman dialled a number and asked us to wait for a few minutes, the manager would be with us as soon as he had finished with other clients.

Half an hour passed before the woman instructed us to go to the desk at the rear of the bank. A couple of elderly men, the clients the manager had been dealing with, passed us on their way out. When the manager, a man of average height with curly hair who couldn't have been older than thirty-five, saw us coming, he got up to greet us. "Please, take a seat," he said. We sat on the plastic chairs. "How can I help you?" he asked. I handed him the account statement. "I would like to withdraw all of my funds," I said. He took it and studied it carefully. He handed it back. "Of course, with pleasure. May I see your I.D.?" I placed the military service record and the fake passport on his desk. "Is this gentleman your father?" he asked. "I am his legal representative," Avilés said. The manager opened the passport, studied it carefully and then placed both documents in his desk drawer. He looked up and studied my face. "You're not Carlos," he said. "Of course he is," Sergio snapped. The manager smiled contemptuously. "Oh no, he's not – not unless the dead can come back to life."

In Abyssinia they were called *kabbazah* or "squeezers". They were women of the Oromo people, who had strengthened the muscles in their vaginas to such a degree that they could straddle a man and make him orgasm without moving. Slave traders would pay a fortune for a *kabbazah*.

They were written about by Richard Burton, an English explorer and the first European to enter the sacred city of Harar in the mid-nineteenth century. The white men and the Christians who had attempted to do so before had been tortured to death for their audacity. Born in England in 1821, Burton spoke twenty-nine languages and almost forty dialects. He studied religions in depth and could debate the Qur'an with authority. He wrote several books chronicling his journeys. He translated *A Thousand and One Nights* into English and co-translated the *Kama Sutra*. Together with Lieutenant John Hanning Speke, he set out on an expedition in search of the source of the Nile. Early in their journey, they pitched camp on the Somali coast where, one night while they were sleeping, they were attacked by Somali warriors. One of the attackers drove a javelin into the left side of Burton's face which went straight through both cheeks, breaking four of his teeth and the bones in the roof of his mouth. Speke was left injured, with many stab wounds. The skirmish over, and with the spear still stuck in his face, Burton walked a long way in search of help. They both survived the massacre and were sent back to England to recuperate.

Speke and Burton returned to Africa to accomplish their mission of finding the source of the Nile. Their contrasting personalities meant that they often clashed. Burton liked to integrate into the communities they encountered: he wore their clothes, learned their languages, slept with their women and studied their myths and customs. Speke was completely the opposite: an arrogant man who looked down on native peoples.

For various reasons, they parted ways halfway through the journey. Guided by the information Burton had elicited from locals, Speke reached the edge of a vast lake and concluded that he had found the source of the Nile. Speke shared the news with Burton when they next met and they celebrated together.

Speke returned to England. For health reasons, Burton could not go with him, but they agreed that Speke would wait until he returned so that together they could present their findings to the Royal Geographical Society.

Upon arriving back in England Speke declared himself to be the sole discoverer of the source of the Nile. He became famous for it, publishing a number of papers on the subject. On his return, Burton was furious to hear of his companion's selfishness, and mounted a campaign to discredit him. The British association for the Advancement of Science proposed a public debate at which Burton and Speke could set forth their arguments. The day before the debate, Speke died from a self-inflicted injury while out shooting: a bullet to the chest. It was never determined whether the weapon had been discharged accidentally as he climbed over a wall, or whether it was suicide.

Burton left behind a vast body of work including stories of his travels, translations, diaries and even treatises on fencing. After his death his wife Isabel, encouraged by her Catholic confessor, decided to burn all the documents she considered to be "indecent": meticulous descriptions of the sexual organs of various ethnicities; comprehensive accounts of sexual mutilations, such as the removal of the clitoris or the emasculation of eunuchs; detailed descriptions of the sexual practices Burton engaged in; and his diatribes against the English civil and military authorities.

Despite the destruction of so many of his papers, more than sixty of his works were published. His writings were key to understanding a diverse range of cultures, and simultaneously helped to open up unexplored regions to voracious British expansionism. Burton epitomised the rare combination of erudite academic and man of action. By diving deep into the unfathomable and sweaty human experience, Burton established a reputation as one of history's greatest adventurers.

Hell

His name was Eduardo Martínez Solares. He had been one of Carlos's clients. He became addicted to morphine, lethargic for days at a time from its effects. He had problems at work, and his girlfriend left him because of it. He suffered withdrawal symptoms many times, and even stole to buy more fixes. He loathed his addiction and blamed Carlos for it. My brother denied all responsibility: "I only open doors, you decide whether or not you walk through them." Carlos helped him beat the addiction by supplying him with a methadone treatment designed by U.S. military doctors to help veteran addicts, which Sean got hold of at an airbase. Despite his help, Eduardo didn't forgive him, and never would. "Meeting him was the worst thing that ever happened to me. He sent me to hell."

For a while, they saw each other often. "I even considered him a friend," Eduardo said. Eduardo had convinced Carlos to put the money in that branch, even advised him on how to make sure that the police couldn't trace the accounts. It was his idea to deposit the money with different banks.

Eduardo spoke loudly, unconcerned by who might hear him. Avilés and I looked around. All it would take to screw us over was one person overhearing and telling the police. He asked me if I was Carlos's younger brother. I nodded. "Well it's up to you to clean up his mess," he said threateningly. "He has nothing to do with it," interrupted Avilés. "He got involved as soon as he came here for the fucking money." He turned to me. "I'm going to fuck you over." I didn't believe he was as tough as his act. He was just bluffing to try and get something out of me.

I asked him to hand me back my documents. "No," he said bitterly.

612

Avilés once again tried to mediate. "What do you have to gain by screwing him?" Eduardo looked me up and down. "I'd be screwing him the same way his *pendejo* brother screwed me."

I felt my anger ignite. "Fuck you," I said furiously. "Excuse me?" said Eduardo. "Go fuck yourself, and you'd better not insult Carlos again." Avilés put his hand on my chest to try and calm me down, but I pushed it away. "Be careful what you say," Eduardo warned and looked towards the two security guards by the door. I spotted a letter opener on the desk and grabbed it. "By the time they get here, you'll be dead," I threatened. Eduardo lifted up his jacket, showing us the handle of his semi-automatic pistol. "I doubt that. You and your friend would die first." Avilés opened his jacket. He had a pistol too. "I don't think so. I think it would be best if we all calmed down."

Avilés asked me to leave him alone with Eduardo. I tried to refuse, but he ordered me out with a look on his face that made it impossible to object. I got up and stood a few metres behind Eduardo's desk. I hid the letter opener up the sleeve of my shirt, in the same way that I usually hid my knife. I counted the steps: twelve. If the situation got out of control and Eduardo tried something with Avilés, I was three seconds away from slamming it into his neck.

Avilés and Eduardo spoke for a few minutes. As he talked, Avilés gently moved his hands. It reminded me of the way he directed tigers in the cage. He looked calm. Avilés said something to Eduardo that made him laugh. Sergio gestured to me to come back. As soon as I sat down, Eduardo apologised. "I'm sorry, I didn't realise both your parents had died." Far from comforting me, his words made me want to stab the letter opener between his C2 and C3 vertebrae. What the fuck did he care if I was an orphan or not? I was trying to shed the weight of orphanhood and Avilés was using it as a cheap trick to pacify this idiot Eduardo. "It makes no difference if I'm an orphan," I replied. Avilés stopped me, afraid the tension would escalate again. "Eduardo and I made a deal," he declared.

I turned down every one of Eduardo's terms. In exchange for not accusing us of fraud and for handing us the money in cash, he asked for half the money in the account. Avilés tried to convince me to agree, but I refused. There would be no deal. Eduardo turned to look at me. "I have you by the balls," he said with conviction. "You haven't got shit. You still haven't realised I have nothing to lose," I replied. Eduardo tried to defuse the threats. "I can help you get the money from the other accounts," he offered. "I already have enough. And you can keep the passport."

I got up to leave. Avilés looked at me in astonishment. "Shall we go?" I said. Avilés exchanged a glance with Eduardo and then got up too. "Wait," Eduardo stopped me. "How many banks have you withdrawn from?" I was about to tell him it was none of his business, but it occurred to me that he might know about Carlos's other accounts. "How many should I be withdrawing from?"

Eduardo revealed four accounts I knew nothing about. He told me he had the list at home, with their account numbers and the amount deposited. Carlos had trusted him with it when their relationship was still solid. Eduardo assured me he was friendly with three of the managers of those branches and that he could make sure they handed over the money, no questions asked, and in whatever way I wanted: cash, centenarios, dollars, travellers' cheques or certified cheques. For his services and for the "serious damage your brother inflicted on me and hundreds of others", he asked for compensation in the shape of thirty per cent of the total. I offered him the percentage I'd decided to give García Allende: fifteen per cent. He tried to negotiate, but I didn't back down. In the end, he accepted. He'd be pocketing a significant figure. We agreed to go to the other banks together, and he insisted there was no time limit for claiming the money. He handed me back my documents and we shook hands to seal the deal.

Despite the negotiation with Martínez Solares and the fact that I finally knew which banks the missing accounts were with, I felt deeply uneasy. Eduardo had revealed yet another dark side to my brother. How many others had got hooked on L.S.D. or morphine and despised him for it?

Avilés noticed I was gloomy. "What's wrong?" he asked. "I don't know if I want that money," I replied. "My brother poisoned so many people." I immediately realised I'd used the same word the Good Boys had used to sentence him to death. A delayed product of my brainwashing.

Avilés got me to sit down next to him on the stairs leading up to the Galaxia cinema. "At university," he began to say out of nowhere, as he tended to do, "an immensely fat man we nicknamed 'The Atom' taught us chemistry. He thought that in order to learn chemistry we needed to recite Shakespeare: 'Hamlet', 'Macbeth', 'King Lear'. Out of everything we read, it was a passage from 'Antony and Cleopatra' that left the deepest impression on me: a messenger delivers the news to Cleopatra – the queen of Egypt – that Antony, the man she is hopelessly in love with, has married another woman. Cleopatra flies into a jealous rage and attacks the messenger: 'What say you? Hence, Horrible Villain! or I'll spurn thine eyes like balls before me; I'll unhair thy head: Thou shalt be whipp'd with wire, and stew'd in brine.' Shaken, the messenger only manages to say: 'Gracious madam, I that do bring the news made not the match.' Do you understand what I'm trying to tell you?" I didn't know what to say so I said nothing. Avilés continued. "Your brother never forced or tricked anyone into trying morphine or L.S.D. He only delivered the news, he did not make the match."

Avilés's argument was identical to the one Carlos used to deny any responsibility. "But he gave them the drugs," I argued. "Fortunately, yes," Avilés said. "Why?" I asked, surprised. Avilés thought about his response for a moment. "Most people come to the circus with the expectation that a lion might rip me to shreds. They yearn for a tragedy, anything to take them out of their incredibly boring lives even for a moment. They are dying to see my guts fall out, my head mashed

615

between the jaws of a lion. They long to have something to tell their incredibly bored grandchildren." He paused, licked his lips and continued. "The bourgeois teenagers who bought drugs from Carlos were sick of living inside that thick, congealed boredom. And yes, that idiot manager told you his sob story about hell and everything his morphine addiction destroyed, but his real hell is going to be spending the next thirty years of his life sitting in that incredibly boring office until he becomes an incredibly bored pensioner. So stop being ridiculous and let's get every last centavo from every single one of those banks, because there's no reason why you should make those bored millionaires who own them any richer than they already are."

Africa

On September 18, 1970 at 11.00 a.m., Jimi Hendrix was found unresponsive in his rented Kensington apartment by his friend Monika Dannemann. He was taken to Saint Mary Abbott hospital, where he was pronounced dead. The death certificate named two probable causes: the inhalation of vomit and his intoxication from barbiturates, although there was "insufficient evidence of the circumstances".

Jimi's death was followed by those of Janis Joplin and Jim Morrison, the great rock trilogy. The three of them had plenty in common: a cocktail of substances, young bodies worn away by drugs, alcohol, lack of sleep, excess. All three were twenty-seven years old. Yes, they spent their lives shielding themselves from the boredom Avilés was talking about: catalysts, tunnels, rivers, avenues, paths, trails. But weren't the people who provided them with these substances responsible for their deaths?

Carlos never considered morphine and L.S.D. to be "lethal" drugs. On the contrary, he saw them as beneficial. Morphine helped war veterans such as Sean cope with chronic pain, and L.S.D. provoked a state of profound contemplation, it was a porthole to underlying realities inside the mind. Why had some found peace with morphine while Eduardo had found hell?

Martínez Solares's bitterness made me realise that Carlos's money came with an army of enemies. As soon as they found out about the scam and the fortune's illegal source, banks would send their teams of lawyers after me to get it back and teach me the harshest lesson possible, which would almost certainly involve a long prison sentence. Many of Carlos's old clients would blame him for their addictions,

617

and would be ready to take it out on me. Zurita would try to extort money from me, and the Good Boys would pursue me until they found and probably killed me, just like they killed Carlos.

I needed to protect myself. García Allende, the lawyer Bross had recommended, was competent but way too straight-laced. Maybe it was because I never gave him the whole truth that he hadn't been able to come up with a more solid plan. But to find him again now and tell the truth about the source of Carlos's savings and the reasons for his murder was no longer an option. Especially not after scamming the banks. García Allende would never trust me again. I needed to find somebody powerful, somebody who could stand up to every one of my new enemies.

That afternoon I grabbed a stack of bills, stuffed them into my trouser and jacket pockets in four equal parts and asked Avilés to take me to the offices of Ortiz, Arellano, Portillo & Associates. If any lawyer was going to be able to protect me, it would be Alberto Ortiz. Avilés knew who I was talking about. He described him perfectly: "Ortiz would be the gold medallist in the 1500 metre freestyle, swimming through sewage." King of the drains and the gutters. A cross between a hyena, lion, eagle and a snake.

When we arrived, the receptionist asked us if we had an appointment. "No," I said, "but I need to see him." She said it was impossible without an appointment. I told her I was sure this case was going to interest him. She dialled a number and a few minutes later another woman appeared, who walked straight up to Avilés. "Good afternoon, my name is Clara, I'm Mr Ortiz's personal assistant. How can I help you?" Avilés smiled and pointed to me. "It's him you need to speak to." She asked my name and the reason for my visit. I told her I would only speak to Ortiz about the matter and that my family had been one of his clients a few years ago. Clara insisted I tell her the reason why I was there. "It's about a murder, the death of my parents and a great deal of money." She looked at me. "Let me see if Mr Ortiz can see you now."

Dozens of certificates attesting to the professional qualifications of the firm's partners adorned the walls. The photos taken with presidents, governors, syndicate leaders and senators confirmed the power that hung in the air between the studded leather armchairs, the walnut desks and the shelves where old law, history and politics books could be glimpsed behind frosted glass. An original oil painting by José María Velasco showing Mexico City at the end of the nineteenth century and a self-portrait by Hermenegildo Bustos decorated the stairway, intended to demonstrate both purchasing power and good taste.

Half an hour later Clara came back. "Mr Ortiz is willing to see you for ten minutes between nine and eleven this evening," she said. It was five o'clock. We would have to wait for at least four hours. I suggested to Avilés that we go and entertain ourselves somehow, and come back at eight. "No, it would be better to stay in case he finishes early and leaves." I suggested he go and come back later. He refused. "There's no show at the circus today, so I have the night off." He picked up the Excélsior he found on the table and began to flick through its pages. Not long afterwards he was sprawled out on the sofa, asleep. He snored loudly. The receptionist and I couldn't contain our laughter at every snort.

I got up to look at the books in the cabinet. Among them was one by an author Carlos and I had heard of but whose books we'd never managed to find: Richard Burton. In front of me were the two volumes of *Wanderings in West Africa*. I asked the receptionist if I could open the cabinet. She produced a key, opened it and then went back to take a phone call. I flicked through the volumes. They were first editions in their original jackets, published in 1863 by Tinsley Brothers. Next to them, I found *First Footsteps in East Africa, Or, An Exploration of Harar*, published by Longman, Brown, Green and Longmans. All three smelled of real books. The paper had a rough texture. You could feel the life of the tree it came from. They must have been worth a fortune.

I looked at the receptionist. She was not watching, busy as she was taking notes and talking on the telephone. I considered shoving the books down my trousers, waking Avilés and taking off with these literary treasures. I was tempted, but it wasn't worth making another enemy, especially not one of Ortiz's standing.

I pored over them for a while and then put them back. Two men who looked like politicians came into the office. The receptionist glanced at Avilés with embarrassment. She asked them to follow her and wait in a meeting room. When she came back she called me over. "Could you wake him up? I don't think it looks very good for the firm." She was right. Coming in to see a guy snoring with his mouth open couldn't have been a great advert for the notorious lawyers.

I shook Avilés awake. He was dazed and the first thing he said was, "Aren't you hungry?" The receptionist giggled. Avilés stretched and got to his feet. "I'm going to go and get something to eat, I won't be long," he said, then left without another word.

As soon as Avilés walked out of the door, the receptionist dialled a number. Clara came down two minutes later. "Mr Ortiz can see you now." I asked if we could wait until Avilés came back, it wasn't even seven. "I don't think so. Mr Ortiz has a free moment now," she said. "Are you coming or not?"

I followed her up the stairs to the second floor. There were several meeting rooms and offices upstairs. The one I was led into was enormous – it had a lounge area with a couple of sofas, a carved oak table with eight chairs, and at the back there was a desk the size of my bedroom. More photos and old books. Original paintings by Ernesto Icaza decorated the walls. I recognised them because a butcher's promotional calendar that hung in the kitchen at home used Icaza's paintings of charros and horses to remind clients that they sold loin, steaks, ribs, tongue and chicken.

I was admiring them when I heard a voice behind me. "Are you interested in horsemanship?" he asked. I turned around and found myself face to face with Ortiz. "I like Icaza," I replied. "Ah! Icaza, one of the greats," he said. "I've spent years trying to buy more of his work.

They are difficult to get hold of, you have to look hard to find them." With a gesture he invited me to sit down on one of the armchairs in the small lounge. "Clara told me your parents passed away, I am very sorry to hear that. Your father was a very agreeable man. I remember him well." I couldn't tell if he really did remember him or if it was just a crass attempt at public relations.

He sat down in the armchair facing me, at ease. Clara brought him a coffee and a note that Ortiz quickly read and then left on the table between us. He wagged "no" with his finger, and Clara left. I didn't want to waste the ten minutes he'd granted me. Very briefly and without pausing, I told him about Carlos's illegal activities, his murder and the death of my grandmother and parents. I told him I wanted justice; I wanted Zurita, some of his men, Humberto and the Good Boys involved in murdering my brother to be brought to trial, and that I felt my life was in danger. I asked him what his rates were and how likely it was that I could get what I wanted.

Ortiz listened attentively, without interrupting. He ran his hand through his hair. A gold watch glinted on his wrist. "Listen, Juan Guillermo," he said, his tone deliberate, "my rates are very high and the probability of justice being done is very low." "I don't care," I told him. "How much could it cost me?" Ortiz made a mental calculation and then came out with a large figure, which was less than half of what I had in my pockets. "Is that the total cost or the advance?" I asked. "An estimate of my fees and those of my people for taking on the case. There would be . . . let's call them 'unforeseen additional costs'." I assumed he was referring to bribes.

"You always win your cases," I said. He smiled, flattered. "How old are you?" he asked. "Seventeen." He looked me up and down. "I would have guessed twenty-four." He paused and checked his watch. "Look, I'm going to give you some advice. Forget everything and try to rebuild your life." "I can't." I told him about how I'd failed to get my revenge, and how ruthless both the Good Boys and the police were. He took a sip of his coffee and looked at his watch again. I could tell by the look on his face that he was no longer concentrating on what I was saying. Other clients, probably those two men who looked like politicians, must be waiting for him. He was about to stand up. "Wait," I asked him. I took out the stack of notes I had in the right pocket of my jacket and put it on the table between us. Ortiz looked at me in surprise. "Here is fifty per cent of what you quoted, an advance," I said. "Did you steal it?" he asked. "No, it's mine. I inherited it from my parents." He settled back into his chair. "Tell me again about your situation."

He agreed to find out about the case and look over the documents. He believed putting Humberto and several of the Good Boys behind bars was feasible, but that it would be impossible to go after Zurita. Not only was he a very senior officer in the Policía Judicial, he was also a favourite of the president's family. Ortiz knew who he was and seemed certain that things wouldn't end well for him. "He's screwed over a lot of people and he's as corrupt as it gets. But believe me, sooner or later his luck will run out." He generously agreed to charge me only what I'd placed on the table. "That will be enough," he said. I asked him if we needed to sign a contract. "I'm a man of my word," he assured me.

He told me to leave a telephone number where Clara could contact me. He got up to say goodbye and laid a hand on my shoulder. "We will fix this," he said. "Come by tomorrow at five." I asked him if he would sell me the volumes of Richard Burton. "I don't know which ones you mean, where are they?" he said. "In the bookcase in reception." He smiled. "The books downstairs aren't likely to be very good, I bought them by the kilo from a man in La Lagunilla to fill the cabinet. Take whatever you want. Consider it a gift."

Before leaving his office, I managed to glimpse what was written on the note Clara had brought him: "The fat man who arrived with him would like to come in, should I let him?" For some reason, Ortiz hadn't allowed him to come in. He must have been waiting for Avilés to leave so we could speak alone.

I gave Clara Avilés's home phone number. She wrote it down in a notebook. "If something comes up we'll get in touch," she told me. I went down the stairs. Avilés was waiting for me, apprehensive. "They wouldn't let me come in," he said apologetically. "I know," I told him. He seemed irritated that he hadn't been able to accompany me. "You're still a minor," he said sternly, "and you need an adult to advise you." I told him not to worry. "If you come back here again, you're not going in there alone," he said. He picked up a brown paper bag from the table between us. "Here, some nourishment," he said, and passed it to me. Inside was a ham and avocado baguette with four salt sachets, an orange juice and a chocolate bar.

I decided to wait until we'd left the offices. I didn't want to leave the smell of food behind in reception. The pollution from Sergio's snores was more than enough. The receptionist opened the cabinet for me and said that Clara had authorised me to take whatever books I wanted. I took the three by Richard Burton. First editions – a treasure. They were probably worth a lot more than what Ortiz had charged me. A hell of a lot more.

On December 9, 1977, an incident known as "The Punch" changed the lives of two men. There was a basketball match that night between the L.A. Lakers and the Houston Rockets. It was a tense, contentious game. After a rebound off the board was picked up by Kevin Kunnert, Houston's power forward, Rudy Tomjanovich sprinted down to the other end of the court, anticipating a pass so that he could score. The pass never came. Halfway down the court Kunnert was in a tussle with the Lakers' Kermit Washington.

Tomjanovich rushed back to stop the skirmish. Suddenly, he was floored by a punch in the face. The fight stopped. Players from both teams looked down in horror at Tomjanovich. He was lying in a pool of blood, his face shattered. A dazed Tomjanovich thought the scoreboard had fallen on top of him.

He later found out that Washington, who was more than two metres tall, thought he was about to attack. He spun on his axis and punched him with all his weight. The blow was so brutal that Tomjanovich's facial bones were knocked loose from his skull. Apart from the blood, Tomjanovich noticed a bitter taste in his mouth. The force of the blow had caused cerebrospinal fluid to leak from his brain.

Tomjanovich underwent surgery to reconstruct his face and fix the fractures. Washington was suspended for two months, the most severe sanction the sports world had ever heard of back then.

Tomjanovich made a full recovery, and after his career as a player ended, he became an NBA coach, leading the Houston Rockets to the Midwest Division title. Washington fell from grace and, although he

624

continued to play, he never escaped the shadow of that punch he threw. Filled with regret, he said that if he could turn back time he would have simply moved out of Tomjanovich's way.

Turns

I called Pato when I got to Avilés's house. He confirmed the inevitable: they knew who'd beaten Humberto up. Once they'd identified me, Zurita's men had headed for my house, broken the lock on the door and turned the place upside down, searching it without a judge's warrant. They dragged mattresses from the beds, threw drawers on the floor, scattered clothes everywhere, just like when they searched for money and drugs after Carlos's death. Two "undercover" vehicles were watching for me on the street, and the Good Boys were smugly walking around the neighbourhood, awaiting my return, unconcerned that doing so could implicate them in Carlos's murder.

Humberto's beating enraged the police and the Good Boys in equal measure. The hunt had begun. I slept soundly despite the danger. I don't know if it was down to exhaustion, or the sense of calm brought about by a particular passage in Burton's book, in which he describes his decision to enter Harar, knowing that they will probably execute him for it.

I woke up around 10.00 a.m. I opened the curtains. The window overlooked the large garden. For a while, I watched two squirrels chasing one another along the branches of an ash tree. I left my room to find the house empty. In the kitchen I found a plate of papaya cut into little squares, pastries and a glass of cream. Next to it was a note: "For your breakfast, lazy".

I sat down to eat. The telephone rang. I didn't pick it up. My mother taught me never to answer the door or pick up the telephone in a house that wasn't mine. It rang several times until I heard Natalia pick it up. A few seconds later she came into the kitchen.

"Phone for you, young man."

I picked up the phone. "Hello, Juan Guillermo, Clara Méndez speaking, Mr Ortiz's assistant. He wants to see you as soon as possible." I told her it would take me about an hour to get there. She told me to hurry and then hung up. I asked Natalia if she knew where Sergio was and she told me he'd gone out to buy the newspaper at the shop at the corner of the market.

I quickly got dressed and ran out to look for him. I spotted him walking through Plaza San Jacinto. He smiled when he saw me. "What bee flew into your bonnet?" I told him about Clara's urgent phone call. "Nothing in life is urgent," he said. We slowly walked back to the house. He took his time brushing his teeth. I urged him to hurry up. "More haste, less speed," he declared.

Despite him dragging his feet we arrived exactly an hour later. The receptionist sent us directly to Ortiz's office. He was sitting at his desk thumbing through some documents, and waved us in. We sat facing him. "Is this gentleman someone you can trust?" he said, nodding at Avilés. "He's like a father to me," I replied. Avilés turned and looked at me in surprise. There was an undeniable trace of pride in his expression.

Ortiz leaned back in his swivel chair and looked at me. "You're more asshole than angel, aren't you?" he said. I asked him why. Ortiz smiled. "The guy you beat to a pulp is in hospital. You broke both his cheekbones, his nose and his right eye socket. He lost three teeth and his scans show several subdural haematomas. He is also crazy. Though it's hard to tell if that was the result of the beating or if he was like that before." I immediately enlightened him: "He was already crazy." Ortiz smiled again. "Maybe he was, maybe he wasn't. The fact is there's a warrant out for your arrest on charges of grievous bodily harm. However . . ." Ortiz placed another piece of paper in front of me. "I put through a request for defence that prevents them from being able to arrest you, for the moment at least. Since there were no witnesses and the only person who's accused you of anything has lost his mind, I don't think you are likely to have any problems."

Ortiz certainly moved fast. I asked him what would happen to Humberto. "From what I've heard, he's unlikely ever to leave the psychiatric unit. And if he does get out with his mind intact, I'll file a case against him for your brother's murder." He planned to proceed against several of the Good Boys as part of the same lawsuit. In order to do this, he said, he'd need to buy key witnesses' testimonies and he was going to need more money. "Buy?" asked Avilés. "Everyone has a price," replied Ortiz ambiguously. "We'll talk more about that later." He paused, placed his elbows on the desk and leaned towards me. "But that isn't all, Juan Guillermo. This morning, a man named Eduardo Martínez Solares showed up at the Bureau of Investigation accusing you of attempted fraud, threatening behaviour, attempted bribery and impersonation." My blood ran cold, I couldn't think of anything to say. Ortiz handed me another document. "I filed a special injunction to get out of that too." I didn't understand why Eduardo had done what he had. I thought we had parted on good terms.

"Let me explain something," Ortiz said. "There needs to be absolute transparency between a client and his attorney. Without it, we get into trouble. Why didn't you tell me that you were using another attorney to try to get your hands on the money in your brother's accounts? In other words, *chamaco*, who the hell did you think you were fooling?" Avilés intervened. "I should have come along the other night to advise Juan Guillermo. He wasn't sure how much to tell you and how much to hold back." "No dice," Ortiz said. "Your boy waltzes in here like Little Orphan Annie, but actually he's too smart for his own good." Ortiz rocked back in his chair and looked at me again. "Now that there's a shit-ton of money on the cards, my rates have increased by a factor of ten, got it?" I was about to tell him to go fuck himself, but Avilés squeezed my arm, knowing I could easily blow the whole thing with my immature braggadocio. "Got it," Avilés said.

Ortiz considered Martínez Solares a minor problem and assured me that we could recover all the money in my brother's accounts within three days. "I regularly have dinner with the president of the Banking Association," he said superciliously. "I can get him to sort it out in a heartbeat." Solares wanted thirty per cent of any monies recovered – in addition to his fees. When I tried to protest, he cut me off. "I am not asking for your opinion. That's how it's going to play." He warned me that it had better be the last time I withheld information from him.

Through his own stupidity, Eduardo failed to get revenge on Carlos by fucking me over, and also missed out on the deal of a lifetime. He had the chance to earn an obscene amount of money just for helping me negotiate with managers from other banks; now Ortiz would pocket the money. Clara came in and handed him a note. Ortiz read it and turned to her. "Tell him we'll see him in a few minutes." As Clara left the room, I saw Avilés checking out her calves – it was a thing with him.

Ortiz turned to me. "I'll get results. You said it yourself, I always win. Rest assured we'll get justice for your brother and I guarantee I'll get every last centavo from those accounts. But to do that – and it's important you understand this – we need to make a deal with Zurita."

I felt my stomach churn. Zurita was as guilty of Carlos's death as Humberto. "No way, he's the enemy," I said to Ortiz. "Look, kid," said Ortiz, "let me give you a little free advice: there are a lot of twists and turns in life. Someone who was an enemy can become your ally, and vice versa. And right now – and maybe only for now – Zurita is willing to be our ally and we shouldn't pass up the opportunity."

I felt sick. Zurita was a vile human being. A killer hiding behind a police badge. Become his ally? I couldn't bear the shame. Ortiz pointed to a door at the back of his office. "Zurita's waiting back there. If you're willing, we can negotiate."

Here I was trying to steer clear of his officers, and here was Zurita, less than fifteen metres away. And with him, my chance to bury a letter opener in his heart. "I'm not talking to that motherfucker," I said stiffly. Avilés, who, until that point, had kept out of the conversation, intervened. "That depends on what you want to get out of this," he said. "I thought you were on my side," I said accusingly. My words seemed to sting. Avilés turned to Ortiz. "Is there somewhere Juan Guillermo and I could talk in private?"

Clara ushered us into a small private room. As soon as the door was closed, Avilés faced me. "Damn it, I've always been on your side, in case you hadn't noticed." I apologised, but he still seemed irritated. He paced around the office until he calmed down. "You need to understand something: your brother was too clever for his own good, and Zurita was sent to shut him down. But however much of a shitbag Zurita is, he didn't kill Carlos." "He let them kill him," I shot back. "You said it yourself: it was 'them' not him."

Just the thought of sitting in the same room as Zurita made me nauseous. Avilés rubbed his face. He looked beleaguered. "If I were to give you just one piece of advice, it would be: forget all this and get out of here right now. But you won't listen. So you need to decide: either you negotiate with this guy and put the people who killed Carlos in prison, or you go your own sweet way and try to find some other way to get your revenge."

I started to shake uncontrollably. My teeth were chattering. The long years of death, vengeance, guilt and grief had all converged in this one decision. Rather than ask if I was alright, or try to comfort me, Avilés did the intelligent thing: he got up, squeezed my shoulder and went to the door. "Take your time. I'll be waiting outside."

As soon as the door closed, I felt a surge of relief. Alone, I could throw up, punch the wall, cry, moan, shout, swear, or simply think. I pinched the bridge of my nose and squeezed my eyes shut. No image came, only darkness, in shades of red. I could hear the air rushing through my nose. I felt the surge of adrenaline flow through my arteries. My muscles were tense, ready for flight or fight. Flight meant leaving the office without telling Ortiz, picking up the money at Avilés's house, taking the bus to Zaragoza and rebuilding my life with the pieces of me that were left. Fight meant facing Zurita, making a deal with him and using him to destroy the Good Boys. Put them behind bars, exterminate them, bury them. Annihilate the henchmen of that perverse and demented god.

I opened the door. Avilés was waiting for me in the hallway, leaning against the wall. "Let's go see Zurita," I said to him. "You sure?" he asked. I nodded. "I can talk to him, you don't have to come," he said to me. "No, I want to see him," I replied, "I need to see him."

PHILOSOPHIÆ NATURALIS
PRINCIPIA MATHEMATICA
AUCTORE ISAACO NEWTONO

LEX I

Corpus omne perseverare in statu suo quiescendi vel movendi uniformiter in directum, nisi quatenus illud a viribus impressis cogitur statum suum mutare.

Every body perseveres in its state of being at rest or of moving uniformly straight forward except insofar as it is compelled to change its state by forces impressed.

LEX II

Mutationem motus proportionalem esse vi motrici impresæ, & fieri secundum lineam rectam qua vis illa imprimitur.

Change in motion is proportional to the motive force impressed and takes place along the straight line in which that force is impressed.

LEX III

Actioni contrariam semper & æqualem esse reactionem: sive sorporum duorum actiones in se mutuo semper esse æquales & in partes contrarias dirigi.

To every action there is always an equal and opposite reaction: or the forces of two bodies on each other are always equal and are directed in opposite directions.

Newton

My father's path diverted from the one his family had always taken. Working class people populated his family tree: construction workers, low-level bureaucrats, public transport operators, ice cream vendors, farm labourers. People who worked up to fifteen hours straight to ensure a household income that was just about decent. My father grew up in a frugal environment. When he was a child they used to have only two meals a day, except on Sundays, when they'd be allowed three. And during weeks when money was tight they could only afford breakfast: a pastry and a coffee with brown sugar which had to last you until bedtime.

When he turned fifteen my father decided not to repeat the pattern. Education and culture, and not gruelling and perfunctory work, would be his escape route from that poor and monotonous world. He studied hard. He went to school in the mornings and worked as an assistant to a blacksmith in the afternoons. At the end of his working day, sweaty and spattered with metal oxide and shavings, he would take the bus to the university library. He would settle into a corner and read one book after another: biographies, literature, physics, essays, philosophy. He became friendly with the guards and they let him stay until midnight, several hours after it closed. He'd walk home, because there would be no public transport at that late hour.

He was the first person in his family for generations to study for a university degree, although he had to drop out before completing it. He married my mother, a middle-class woman who was also committed to educating herself, despite the fact that my grandparents prevented her from going to university.

When Carlos and I were children, my parents strategically placed books throughout the house. In the bathroom, in corridors, on tables, next to the bed. It didn't matter if the books got dirty, wet or torn, if we underlined things or folded down the corners of the pages. My parents thought of them as wartime essentials, not luxury goods. My brother and I caught the cultural gluttony bug from my parents. Read, read, read.

On one of the nights he spent in the university library as a young man, my father came across Newton. He was blown away by his theories. He often quoted him when he wanted to emphasise a point. He insisted that his three laws of motion were more than an explanation of physics: they helped us to understand human nature and psychology. Life was the interaction between actions and reactions, opposing forces, variations and changes. My father took it upon himself to make sure that Carlos and I read, argued and analysed Newton until we'd learned his mathematical principles off by heart.

As I walked towards Zurita, the second law began to echo in my mind: "Change in motion is proportional to the motive force impressed." My brain was regurgitating Newton from the catacombs of my unconscious just minutes before sitting down opposite one of Carlos's killers.

We went into the meeting room. Zurita was sitting at the head of the table with a beer in front of him. He stood up to receive us. He greeted Ortiz effusively and Avilés politely. Then he offered me his hand. I hesitated to take it, but he kept it outstretched and I eventually shook it. His hand was small and delicate, almost feminine. He smelled of Old Spice. I'd expected a mocking and cynical attitude from him, but to my surprise he was respectful and courteous. "It's a pleasure to see you again," he said. A pleasure to see me, when just a few hours earlier his men had destroyed my house, under orders to arrest me?

Ortiz invited us to sit down next to them, but Avilés grabbed my arm and led me to the other end of the table. "We would prefer to sit over here," he said. Avilés demonstrated sound judgement once again. There were four metres between me and my enemy-future-ally.

The first thing Zurita did was make excuses. "What happened to your brother was never personal, it was just part of the job," he said without a hint of emotion. I recalled Bross's words vividly: "Don't take it personally." Zurita continued: "I appreciate that the situation got out of control and that his death was unnecessary." As he spoke, I couldn't stop looking at his tiny, womanish hands. His impeccable nails. Manicure. Soft skin. The hands of a murderer.

He admitted that the Good Boys had turned into a "bit of a head-ache". The Jalisco authorities suspected that they'd committed several crimes there too and had informed the Mexico City police. Zurita announced that it was time to rethink the relationship with them, now that they had returned to Mexico City. "They have taken things too far." He spoke about them as if they were an amateur football team he no longer wished to train after some disappointing results, not a far-right paramilitary group who killed without a second thought.

I was becoming infuriated by the gentle unhurried way he expressed himself – as though behind this almost feminine manner he could mask the brutal, pitiless cop responsible for dozens of deaths. He was an odious snake. There was no question: I despised him.

Zurita warned me that I'd made a serious mistake in attacking Humberto and chided me for taking justice into my own hands. "Although," he said, "I can understand your motivation." He said that while it was his duty to arrest me for my "misguided actions", he had come to talk to me in the hope that we might come to some agreement that would be "to everyone's benefit". It was clear that this "benefit" involved me offering him a lot of money to destroy Humberto and the Good Boys.

"What kind of an agreement?" Avilés asked. Zurita settled into his chair and took a deep breath, as though to give his words a sense of gravity. "As I said, these young men have crossed the line, and Señor Ortiz has told me that Juan Guillermo is seeking to bring those who 'liquidated' his brother to justice. Perhaps we could kill two birds with one stone and all come out on top, but my men need some motivation."

What a pompous and self-important way to solicit a bribe. "How much motivation do they need?" Sergio asked. Ortiz interrupted. "The *comandante* and I have already talked it over, and we think that a hundred thousand pesos could set the wheels in motion. The officers on the scene that night could testify against Humberto and the others involved. And of course, we could offer the neighbours some incentive for their testimony."

"Change of motion is proportional to the motive force impressed," I said aloud. Ortiz and Zurita turned to me. "Pardon?" said Ortiz. "Newton's second law," I explained. "I just want to know how much force will be exerted." Zurita was still staring blankly at me, confused by my Newtonian reference. "We'll do everything we can," he said. I shook my head. "No, not good enough. If I'm going to pay a hundred thousand pesos, I want a guarantee that the greatest possible force will be used against them." "There are many factors that Comandante Zurita cannot control," said Ortiz. "With all due respect, Señor Ortiz, the *comandante* is well versed in apprehending guilty parties and, when he can't find any, he has ways of making them materialise," I retorted. Zurita let out a long breath. "For an additional thirty thousand we can guarantee everything will go smoothly." I agreed; the wheels were set in motion.

Zurita and Ortiz kept their word. They swiftly filed charges, and, one by one, the Good Boys were taken down. Antonio, Josué, Felipe, Saúl and Martín were arrested in dawn raids. They never expected the police to come for them. Confident that they were protected by the secret deals between Humberto and Zurita, they believed themselves untouchable. They were charged with the assault on Don Abraham and his wife, with the murder of Carlos and a number of other crimes

I knew nothing about. They were also indicted for the murder of Quica. To this were added additional charges including intimidation, actual bodily harm, criminal conspiracy, racketeering and even a breach of the prohibition of religious cults. Following hurried, almost summary trials, they were given harsh sentences: fifteen, twenty, up to thirty years in prison for some, such as Antonio, who was identified as the organisation's lieutenant.

Despite his mental illness and the physical injuries from the beating, Humberto was brought to trial. He was found guilty of first-degree murder and intimidation, and was given the maximum prison sentence: forty years. Church leaders pleaded in his favour, only to be told by government officials that the Young People Committed to Christ were out of control and that it would be in the church's best interest to distance itself from their criminal acts. The church leaders reluctantly conceded, although they hired lawyers to appeal the sentences. Javier Arturo Magaña Pérez, better known as Father Arturo, the principal instigator behind the Good Boys' extremism and violence, was not even rebuked, but was granted immunity from prosecution thanks to the privileges he enjoyed as a high-ranking priest.

I spoke to Ortiz about the possibility of getting El Castor Furioso released from prison. He said he thought it would be difficult but not impossible. He would speak to the judge who had sentenced him (a friend of his) and ask him to revise the case and lessen the sentence, or, better yet, grant him early release. Of course, a few thousand pesos would be necessary to grease the judge's palms and facilitate Diego's exoneration.

It was obvious that Zurita had gone after Humberto and the Good Boys not because he was eager to get justice but because they were no longer useful. Their power had steadily grown and they exercised it with growing cruelty. The alliance with them had proven beneficial to Zurita, and therefore for the political system as a whole. But the recruitment of ever more violent and fanatical members, their capacity for organisation, their increasingly extreme ideology, their brazen murders in Jalisco and Guanajuato, and their return to the capital where they'd told Zurita they intended to continue their work of purifying society of "sinners", rang alarm bells for both the Policía Judicial and the Department of the Interior.

The leftist youth movements, savagely repressed in 1968 and 1971, had spooked the government. At first, they'd allowed and even encouraged the growth of far-right groups to combat and contain "communist and anarchist" youth who posed a threat to political stability. When the force and range of action of these small groups crossed the line, the government resolved to act. The events of the Cristero War suggested that an element of the population was in favour of radical Catholicism and little would be required to spark a new conflagration. Better to douse it now before it was too late. In Newton's words: "To every action there is always an equal and opposite reaction."

When Ortiz had said that this was the moment to become Zurita's ally, he must have known that sooner or later the Good Boys and other ultra-Catholic groups would be broken up. Although, over time, it became clear that the government was far from eliminating their organisational abilities or their power.

Fire

The raids were brutal and lightning-fast. One by one the Good Boys were arrested. They dragged some of them out of their homes in the middle of the night and shoved them into the patrol cars, still in their pyjamas. Indignant, their parents kicked up a fuss. Their children were Good Boys, good students who believed in god, upright, clean, nothing like the immoral and corrupt masses who were holding the country back. "Take away the ungodly, the atheists and the communists, leave the believers alone." There was no let-up. Zurita and his men worked tirelessly to track them down, torture and imprison them.

Getting the money back turned out to be more complicated than Ortiz had thought. The president of the Banking Association may have been a friend of his, but it was optimistic to expect that the bank directors would just let so much money go all at once. Nevertheless, using his arsenal of legalistic machinations and clinically corrupt practices, Ortiz assured me he would recover everything in less than two weeks.

During that time, I slept at Avilés's house. Ortiz had suggested that I stay away from the neighbourhood while they "cleaned up". Chelo came to visit me every day and brought King with her. Although he was much better, he still seemed weak. He found it difficult to walk and slept most of the time. Chelo bathed him, brushed him, paid close attention to his recovery and administered his medicine.

One morning, I walked him around Avilés's garden. He ambled happily around on the grass, but as soon as he smelled Colmillo he ran and hid underneath the Maverick. Trembling, he dragged himself under the axle. It took a long time to get him to come out, and when he finally did, he nuzzled against me, still shaking.

I knew King didn't have much time left and I didn't want to expose him to any more stress. I wanted him to spend his last days feeling comfortable. Chelo's parents wouldn't let him in the house, so he was locked in the tiny laundry room in their backyard at night. According to Chelo, he would whine until they let him out.

I asked Chelo to take him back to my house and leave him there only at night. He could sleep on Carlos's bed, wander around the house as he pleased, piss and shit wherever he wanted. It was just as much his house as mine, and he should feel completely at home there.

Although Ortiz had managed to eliminate every single one of the warrants for my arrest, Chelo and I still wanted to go ahead with our plan to go to Coahuila, for a long stretch at least. We could go to a rural town like Zaragoza or to Jorge Jiménez's huge ranch, where we could feel free and just enjoy being together.

One Sunday morning, very early, Avilés knocked on the door. Chelo had stayed the night and she hurried into the bathroom, naked. I opened the door with a towel wrapped around my waist. Avilés looked upset. "Are you alright?" I asked him. "Your friend Jaibo just called. They set fire to your house," he said. I sat down on the bed. It couldn't be true. There was no way it could be true. "Are you sure?" Avilés put his arm around my shoulders. "Yes, I'm so sorry." In the bathroom, Chelo sensed that something bad had happened. "What's wrong?" she called out. I didn't answer. She repeated the question, shouting this time. I got up, picked up her clothes, went into the bathroom and handed them to her. She looked at me anxiously. "But what's happened?" she asked. "Get dressed. I'll explain when you come out."

I called Jaibo. He told me that the fire had been started at around three in the morning. His brother had heard noises on the street and looked out of the window. He saw four guys in hoods go into my house with cans of petrol. Three minutes later he saw them come out, get into a yellow Rambler with Jalisco number plates and speed away towards Churubusco. A short while later he saw smoke coming out of the windows.

640

The flames soon spread through the house. The furniture and the curtains began to crackle. The windows shattered. The flames reached high above the rooftop. Thick smoke curled into the sky.

Jaibo's brother woke his family up. They tried to put the fire out with buckets of water. Other neighbours came out to help. In desperation, they threw water as close to the fire as they could, the heat singeing their arms and faces. They brought out hoses, they threw sand. But their efforts were in vain and the house burned quickly.

The firefighters arrived half an hour later and were only able to stop the fire spreading to the next-door houses. Mine was completely scorched, it was a mass of rubble and soot that looked close to collapsing.

As soon as Chelo came out of the bathroom and I told her what had happened, she went pale. "King!" she howled, frantically. She'd left him in Carlos's room the day before, with a full bowl of food and a tray of water. Given Jaibo's description of the disaster, it seemed unlikely that he'd survived.

We got into the Maverick and headed to the house. As we got close we were greeted by chaos. Several patrol cars blocked the street. Firefighters were still spraying water from the fire truck over the smouldering ruins. Dozens of curious people were crowded together on the other side of the street. A police officer instructed us to keep driving.

We parked two blocks away and walked to the house. The penetrating smell of smoke hung in the air. The fire truck's pump rumbled noisily. One of the cops recognised me and led us to a patrol car. He picked up his radio. "Unit one calling Zodiac, over." "Zodiac, over," replied Zurita. "The displaced person is here," said the cop. "Displaced", that's just what I needed. The cop passed me the radio and pointed at a button. "Press here when you want to talk. Don't press it until the *comandante* says 'over', O.K.?" Zurita spoke first. "Juan Guillermo. We've stirred up the hornet's nest and things could get even uglier," he said. How much uglier could it get if they had destroyed the only tangible thing I had left? He warned me that the Good Boys had set

641

their sights on me and that the arrests had prompted them to mobilise yet more reinforcements from Los Altos de Jalisco, Guanajuato and Zacatecas. "Very vicious people," he said. He also warned me about probable reprisals against my friends. "But they didn't do anything," I argued. "Just in case, tell them to lock the doors to their roofs, to try not to follow the same route or schedule twice, and, if they can, to carry a weapon. Over and out."

I handed the radio back to the cop. How was I supposed to tell my friends that thanks to me their lives were at risk? When had the world spun so utterly out of control and everything become so absurd? I no longer knew who were my enemies. Those I knew were now in prison, but their nameless replacements were even more volatile and deadly.

The firefighters extinguished the smouldering remains. They trooped out, their hands and faces caked with soot, their waterproofs soaking wet. I walked up to the door. One of the firefighters stopped me. "You can't go in there," he said. The cop explained that I was the owner. The firefighter warned me to be careful, not to step on hot embers and on no account to go up to the second floor since it risked collapsing.

I wanted to go in alone so as not to put Avilés and Chelo through it, but they insisted on accompanying me. We walked through dark puddles of ash and water. The front door, which was made of metal, had twisted in the heat. The furniture in the living room and the dining room was burnt to a crisp. The ceilings were black. There was nothing left of my room. The oven and the kitchen sink had fused into one object. Only the refrigerator was still more or less recognisable.

I was still hopeful that King had taken refuge in the yard. We went out to look for him but he wasn't there. I decided to go up to the top floor. I convinced Chelo to wait for me downstairs with Avilés. We didn't know how much weight the weakened floor could take, or if the pillars would be strong enough to support the staircase.

I walked up slowly. Before each step, I checked for broken glass and embers. I went into Carlos's room. The bed was surrounded by debris. I got closer. King's charred corpse lay in the middle of the ash. I squatted down next to the body. The last member of my family, resting at my feet. I fiercely hoped his death hadn't been painful. I stroked what had once been his head. His collar and the metal tag with his name on it were still intact. I took his collar off and put it in my pocket. I decided not to take the body with me. He should stay here, in what had been his house, in the den that had been my brother's bedroom.

I looked around the room. Everything was burnt. The books had been reduced to a grey dust scattered across the floor, the records had melted. The carpet, the mirrors and the closets were scorched. Nothing had survived in my parents' bedroom either. Their clothes, toothbrushes, hairbrushes, creams, shoes, drawers, desks, gone forever.

I walked downstairs. Chelo asked me about King, and I told her he was dead. She hugged me and burst into tears. Avilés tenderly squeezed the back of my neck. We left the house. The neighbours watched in silence. My three friends stuck close to me in a show of solidarity, and Pato invited me to come and stay with his family. Jaibo, who felt guilty for not having been able to stop the fire, promised to organise raffles and collect donations in order to recover something. Agüitas, for once not in tears, offered to help me rebuild the house. I thanked them and asked them all to come and have breakfast at Avilés's house the next day, because I wanted to talk to them. I didn't want to have to look at the scene of the disaster for another second. I said goodbye to my friends quickly and left without looking back.

During the journey home, no-one said a word. What was there to say? Should we weep and wail? Should they try to comfort me? Exhausted from crying, Chelo had fallen asleep on the back seat. Avilés was playing his cassette of *cardenche* music. In that moment, the keening of the cotton pickers expressed more than we could.

I opened the window. I closed my eyes and let the wind hit my face. I felt profoundly free. Now there was nothing tying me to the sombre boat of my dead. The only objects salvaged from my previous life were the ones in the suitcases I'd taken with me to Avilés's house. Everything else had been destroyed in the fire. The purifying fire that had saved me from the weight of the past. Now the chains were gone. I was free.

Far from destroying me, the Good Boys had given me a means of escape. They had taken the only thing tying me to this city and I was more convinced than ever that I would go off somewhere with Chelo. Somewhere far from that wasteland of ash and death. Far from that small, grotesque god those small, grotesque beings believed in.

We spent the afternoon at Avilés's house. Ortiz called to check that I was alright and promised that those responsible would soon be arrested. "Once we get the money from those accounts you'll have more than enough to repair your house and buy another twenty just like it," he said in an attempt to cheer me up, but it had the opposite effect. Why would I want twenty more houses if the one I really cared about was gone forever? He gave me some good news too. The judge – after a "donation" of ten thousand pesos – had granted El Castor Furioso's release order after dismissing his charges. Justice may be blind, but when it comes to money it has a sharp sense of smell.

Thinking about King overwhelmed me. I couldn't get the image of his charred body out of my mind. I hoped he had lost consciousness and collapsed before the fire reached him. In the end, I accepted his death. It was better to have died in three terrible minutes than to suffer agony for weeks, unable to move or, even worse, having to be "put to sleep". I'd like to imagine that King died bravely, barking at the idiotic pyromaniacs who set fire to my house and that he stubbornly stayed put on the bed in an effort to protect Carlos's room.

We went to bed. Chelo hummed a tune to lull me to sleep, her head resting on my chest. Such a sweet, soothing melody. I drifted off with my arms around her and we lay that way until the sun came up. I woke and kissed her on the mouth. Fast asleep, she didn't move. I got up and drew the curtains. The room was east-facing, and the rays of sunlight reached the bed. I looked at Chelo. Her long, slim, naked body. Over time, the scars on her legs had faded. They were no longer livid red welts, but fine pale lines. Far from finding them unattractive, I thought they gave her character.

She woke up and raised her head. The light hitting her face-on made her eyes look even greener. "Good morning," she said. She kneeled on the mattress and hugged me. "When are we going to the ranch?" she asked. "Soon, very soon," I said.

At 9.00 a.m. my friends arrived for breakfast. Natalia made eggs with machaca and avocado, ham and cheese dobladas and hot chocolate. It was a crisp, sunny day and Avilés put a table out in the garden. My friends were impressed by the size of the house. I was sure none of them had ever been inside a house that big or with such a spacious garden. The entrance hall alone must have been more square metres than the biggest house in our barrio.

I told them about Zurita's warning. My friends weren't worried. They were convinced that the Good Boys wouldn't come back to the neighbourhood for a long time. They knew the cops were searching for them and wouldn't risk wandering around in unknown territory. They thought most of them would already be back in their home towns in Los Altos de Jalisco.

After breakfast, I told them I'd be right back. I returned with three canvas bags and gave them one each. "What is it?" asked Pato, curious. "Open them," I said. They untied the string and peered inside. Agüitas looked at me in bewilderment. "What is this?" he asked. "It's a present," I replied. Jaibo pulled out a stack of notes from the bag. "This is a hell of a lot of money," he said. I smiled. They looked pale, dumbfounded. They were acting as though I'd handed them sacks of rattlesnakes. They looked at them with terror. "A hundred thousand pesos each," I told them. Pato pushed his bag to the middle of the table. "I can't accept this," he said, flustered. Agüitas did the same. "Me neither." Avilés intervened. "Juan Guillermo wants to give this to you." Pato shook his head. "It's too much money, we wouldn't know what to do with it." Chelo made them understand that it was a gesture of love and friendship. "You guys are his brothers."

Eventually they accepted it. Jaibo hugged me, and (obviously) Agüitas cried. Pato, less emotional than the others, slapped me on the side of the head. "Idiot," he said, smiling.

They agreed to go with Avilés to open a bank account to deposit the money. They were worried about being robbed on the way, but Sergio showed them the pistol under his jacket. "I'll look out for you," he said.

Freedom

Ortiz and I waited for hours, sitting on uncomfortable cream-coloured plastic benches. Ortiz, wearing an impeccable suit which he bragged had been tailor-made in England, stood up regularly to "stretch his legs". I found it strange that he had come to the prison with me instead of sending one of his multiple assistants or "junior" partners at the firm. When I asked him why he hadn't found somebody else to handle this, his answer couldn't have been blunter: "Because you are my best client in years."

Eventually, we were called. A guard led us down a long corridor. Diego, wearing civilian clothes, was behind thick bars. The guard called Ortiz. "I need to make sure the acquittal and the release order are correct," he explained before leaving. They opened the gate and he went inside.

Ortiz and El Castor Furioso both went to a window. Ortiz reviewed the documents they handed him line by line. Then he turned to Diego and showed him where to sign. Fifteen minutes later, they opened the gate and the two of them came out. El Castor Furioso pulled me into a hug as soon as he saw me. "Thank you, little brother, thank you."

Ortiz said goodbye outside the prison and got into a white Cadillac that was waiting in front of the entrance. El Castor Furioso stopped to look around him. He pointed at the grey prison building. "I thought I would never leave that place," he said with undisguised happiness. He looked around again and then kissed me on the forehead. "Thank you, thank you, thank you," he said. "I would have lost my mind in there." He looked much thinner, and had lost three teeth in an incident he didn't want to tell me about.

I said I would treat him to some ham hock, his favourite food, in a restaurant on Avenida Ermita. Just like I had done with my friends, I gave him a hundred thousand pesos. I had deposited the money in a bank account in his mother's name the day before. He thanked me, barely able to hold back tears. He and his family had nothing. They were barely surviving on the pension of his father, who had been a petroleum worker and died years ago. The apartment he had bought in the Juarez neighbourhood had turned out to be a disaster. The previous owner had died without leaving a will, causing an endless legal wrangle between cousins. He hadn't been able to rent it out because one of the cousins refused to recognise the bill of sale. Ortiz promised to sort out the formalities for the deeds and make sure it was soon in his name.

El Castor Furioso tucked into the ham hock greedily. It must have been exquisite compared to the miserable portions of bland food they served in the prison. He happily gnawed the meat off the bone, slathering his hands and his lips in grease. When he'd finished, he wiped away the grease with a napkin and asked for the dessert menu. As he was looking it over, I asked him straight out if he, Carlos and the rest of them had killed Quica. Diego put the menu down and looked me straight in the eye. "Who told you that?" he asked. "Humberto," I said. He weighed his words carefully before saying, "And you believed that asshole?" He picked up the menu again and was about to order dessert when I stopped him. "So, is it true or not?" He paused again to think. "Some things are better left alone." The response was disturbing. What had happened that was better left alone? I asked him to tell me the truth, no matter how painful. "Carlos thought that Quica had taken advantage of you," he said. "And what did he do?" I asked, still hoping that he'd say that Carlos had had nothing to do with the killing. "I don't want to talk about it anymore," he said. Try as I might, he refused to say more. I told him that doubts would eat away at the image I'd created of my brother. Diego seemed exasperated. "You need to show a little respect; your brother would have done anything for you." "Like kill somebody?" I challenged. "Yeah, like kill somebody."

Just the possibility that Carlos had killed Quica made me feel physically sick. Pinkish blotches appeared on my chest and arms, I felt short of breath. The world seemed to go by in slow motion. There was once again a seventeen-second time lag. Words arrived too late. Cars moved at a different speed. My life was seventeen seconds off, a gap that led to profound melancholy. "Some things are better left alone." Left where? How?

I persuaded Diego not to go back to his mother's house in Unidad Modelo. The Good Boys might be lying in wait, poised to kill him the first chance they got. I offered him a room in Avilés's house, but he decided to stay in a sordid motel on Calzada de Tlalpan, to be close to the barrio and to his mother.

After dropping him off at the motel I wandered around the area. Although it was early, about a dozen prostitutes stood around waiting for clients to sleep with in nearby hotels. The afternoon light mercilessly exposed every imperfection: the patches of cellulite on their arms, the unshaven legs and armpits, the wrinkled brows, the sagging bellies, the pock marks. The make-up they wore did little to help. They were caked with greasy foundation, thick, clumpy mascara and garish red lipstick. They sidled up as I walked past. Still suffering from the seventeen-second delay, I didn't immediately react. "Are you a retard?" a fat woman asked me. I smiled in response. "Yeah, you're a complete fucking halfwit," she cackled. Several of them started mocking me. "You must be from Chihuahua, 'cos you're a needle-dick runt!" a scrawny girl yelled. I needed to put an end to the seventeen-second gap, to answer fast and catch up with the real world. I whipped round. "No, I'm from Tabasco, and I'm too hot for you, bitch." The others cheered my comeback. "The little blonde guy whipped your ass good, Daisy," one shouted.

As I walked on, the women kept laughing and joking behind me.

I got on the metro at Portales station and headed for Izazaga to pay Simon Bross a visit. I wanted to say goodbye and thank him for everything he'd done for me. I also had a cheque, the money for García Allende's fee.

I got off at Pino Suárez. Crowds of people rushed through the passageways, hurrying from one metro line to another. I was moving against the current, pushing past dozens of people running to catch the next train. An urgent crush of bodies. I emerged onto the street. Along the way, I stopped in a second-hand bookshop to look for a copy of *On Forgiveness* by Rosenthal, to replace the one Bross had given me. The shop assistant climbed a ladder to search the shelves, found a copy, shook it to loosen the dust and handed it to me. It was a pocket-size edition, and it was falling apart. The cover was torn, the pages scrawled with notes and words underlined in ink. The notes in the margins suggested the previous owner had studied Political Science. I decided not to buy it. I thought it would be insulting to give him such a mistreated book. Instead, I bought a leather-bound set of the complete works of Pío Baroja. Bross didn't have Baroja and I felt sure that he would consider *The Quest*, *The Tree of Knowledge* and *Memories of a Man of Action* serious literature.

I sat on a park bench to write a letter to Don Abraham and his wife. It took a long time. I explained what had happened, I told them that the ringleaders behind the attack were in prison and begged for their forgiveness. I told them that one day, when I had the courage, I would apologise face to face.

I got to the factory. The cashier greeted me warmly and led me to Bross's office. As soon as he saw me, Bross got up and pulled me into a hug. I handed him the books by Baroja. "A present," I said. "Thank you! I've heard so much about this man," he said. He flicked through the books before putting them down on his desk. "I'll take these home and start reading them tonight."

I updated him on everything that had happened. He asked me if

On Forgiveness had helped me at all. Embarrassed, I admitted that it had infuriated me, and that I'd destroyed it in a rage. "So, it helped you even more than I thought it would," he said with satisfaction. I took out the cheque and started to write. I asked him how much I owed the lawyer. Bross smiled. "Nothing." I urged him to accept a cheque. García Allende was a professional and his time was valuable. "Nothing," Bross repeated, "and if he comes looking for payment, I'll take care of it."

I tried to insist, but he was adamant. "Ruining books, that I can forgive you, but not friendships," he said, "and if you carry on like this, you'll ruin ours."

I asked him to give the letter to Don Abraham. He took it and put it in his pocket. "When you're able to," he said to me, "we'll go speak to him together. You can be sure that he'll forgive you."

We spoke a little about everything. He promised me that next time he saw me he'd bring me some books by a Colombian writer unknown in Mexico, Hernando Téllez. "You'll love him," he said. We said good-bye. He ruffled my hair affectionately. "A lion's mane," he said. He gave me a hug and I left the factory.

When I got back to the house, Avilés, Chelo and Ortiz were waiting for me in the living room. I was surprised to see the lawyer. "Good evening," I greeted him. "You took your time getting back," Ortiz said with a smile and gestured for me to sit down next to Chelo. She grabbed my hand and squeezed it. She looked pale. Avilés had a faint smile on his face. "What's going on?" I whispered to Chelo. She jerked her chin towards the table in front of us. There was an unopened bottle of wine, four glasses and a folder. Ortiz slid the folder towards me. "Open it." I picked it up and opened it. Inside were various cheques in my name. A fortune. An outrageous and exorbitant fortune.

"You are now extremely rich," Ortiz said as he uncorked the bottle of wine. "Let's celebrate," he said. He started to pour the wine into a glass. "There's nothing to celebrate," I said firmly. Ortiz looked at me. "Why?" he asked. "Seventeen seconds," I replied. Ortiz made no effort to understand what I was saying. He finished pouring the wine and raised his glass. "Well, then, I shall celebrate alone."

Ortiz declared that since he'd recovered so much money he would be happy with just a twelve per cent commission. This was still an enormous amount of money. He asked me when I would turn eighteen. I told him my birthday fell on the Cinco de Mayo. "Very patriotic," said Ortiz. "Ignacio Zaragoza would be proud." Chelo smiled and repeated the name "Zaragoza", clearly amused. Ortiz didn't get the joke. "Zaragoza is a small town in Coahuila where these two are thinking of living," explained Avilés. "And what the hell is in Zaragoza to make you want to go into exile there?" Ortiz asked. "Ranches," answered Chelo.

In twelve days, I would be an adult. Ortiz suggested we wait until then and open a couple of bank accounts in my name that day to deposit the cheques.

Twelve days seemed like a lifetime. I didn't want to stay in Mexico City a minute longer. With the Good Boys more dangerous than ever, it would be risky. Not just for me but for Chelo and Avilés. We would leave for Zaragoza that same afternoon, as soon as we had deposited the cheques.

We spoke to Jorge Jiménez who, in his strong northern accent, generously offered to have us to stay at his house as well as on the ranch. He warned us that there was no electricity and therefore no air conditioning. "It's so hot," he said, "you can fry eggs on the rocks." I didn't care, that was where Chelo and I wanted to be. In the middle of the desert, sweating buckets, surrounded by the smell of cows, manure, ash, mesquite and dust.

Reverberations

Ortiz was right: sooner or later Zurita's luck would run out. And it did. He must have believed himself invincible, because he turned down his superiors' offer of an armed escort. One night he drove home and, taking no precautions, stopped the car and got out to open his garage. Instantly, two hooded figures appeared and shot him at point-blank range: three bullets in the chest and three in the stomach. One of the killers walked over to shoot him in the head. This was a mistake. Despite his injuries, Zurita managed to draw his gun and fire two shots into his neck. The man fell back and lay, spewing blood, while the other made off in a waiting car.

A neighbour called the Red Cross. Zurita was rushed to Xoco Hospital, where he underwent surgery. Two bullets had punctured his left lung, another had fractured his collarbone, and the rest were lodged in his intestines. He came through the operation, and, although his condition was still critical, the doctors gave him a good chance of recovering.

The hit man died on the pavement. Zurita's cousins, who lived on the same block, ripped off his hood and stood guard to make sure no-one covered his face with a sheet. "Let everyone see the murderer's face," they said. He was identified as 21-year-old Alfredo de Jesús Sánchez Alba from Mexico City, registered home address Avenida Oriente 160 #56, Unidad Modelo. Alfredo was Antonio's cousin. Witnesses described the vehicle in which his accomplices fled as a yellow Rambler with Jalisco number plates.

In declaring war on the cops, the Good Boys made a crucial mistake. It was one thing to kill atheists, communists and Jews, but another

653

thing entirely to gun down a high-ranking *comandante*. Besides, the operation was a fiasco: one of them had ended up dead and the getaway car had been quickly identified.

In prison, Antonio, Josué and Felipe were tortured to force them to name those who had ordered and carried out Zurita's shooting. They held out for a while until electric probes were inserted into their rectums. High voltage electrical currents seared their insides, and they ended up confessing. Felipe gave names, addresses, details of finances, logistics, informants, traitors. The organisation turned out to be more than simply a gang of young hotheads. It had grown to be a subversive political group with direct links to the highest echelons in the church and the business world, with the tacit support of right-wing civil servants who resented the president's leftist stance.

Humberto, too, was tortured for information, but it proved futile. He was adrift in his roiling madness, and his responses were a jumble of nonsense. At times, he thought the cop beating him was Jesus Christ. He mistook the electric shock inside his rectum for hell and begged the devil to forgive his mother. Humberto was still physically strong, and, remembering his martial arts training when his torturer was distracted, he crushed the man's trachea with a karate chop. Classified as a dangerous inmate, he was placed in solitary confinement in the psych ward.

The official press release summed up the attempted murder of Zurita as "a cowardly attack by seditious groups intent on destabilising national political institutions". Zurita was described as a "crime-fighting crusader". In a classic move by the authoritarian government, the corrupt Zurita was praised to the heavens and the case was never publicly mentioned again. Absolute discretion. Ortiz told me that several of the Good Boys were arrested and sentenced without trial to long prison stretches in remote cities including Tapachula in Chiapas or Ciudad Delicias in Chihuahua. A number of the ringleaders, especially the most violent, were "disappeared" – political jargon for assassinated.

Antonio was found dead in the prison bathroom one morning, his jugular slit with a shard of glass. The prison authorities recorded the cause of death as a "brawl between inmates" and the case was shelved. Despite pressure from his parents, no police investigation was ever carried out. The government threatened the families of Good Boys who had been imprisoned or disappeared with brutal reprisals if they "made waves". The clergy were warned to end any moral and economic support for "far-right agitators", or face the consequences.

Ortiz agreed with me that, while this war was raging, the best thing to do was leave the city as soon as possible. The Good Boys considered me a high-profile target. Not just because of the attack on Humberto, but because they associated me with the crackdown now unleashed upon them. "Leave now," Ortiz told me. "Don't take any risks."

Ortiz made a deal with the president of the Banking Association to let me open an account with the Banco de Comercio and another with the Banco Nacional de México four days before I turned eighteen. We deposited some of the cheques in each account and another two in my account with the Banco Mercantil de Monterrey. Distrustful of banks, I kept the cash.

We planned our departure for the following day. Instead of travelling to Zaragoza by bus, I would fly to San Antonio, where Jorge Jiménez would pick me up and take me to the ranch. Chelo would catch up with me at the end of term, two months later. She wouldn't tell her parents about the plan until a few days before she left. Being staunch conservatives, they would consider a daughter who ran off to live with a man without getting married a loose woman, or, more bluntly, a whore. Their attitude was ridiculous, given that they knew that Chelo was already spending almost every night with me.

Avilés agreed to come with me to Coahuila. He said that it was a good excuse to take a holiday, since he was exhausted from ten years of performing six days a week. A lie. He was coming with me because he wanted to look out for me.

That afternoon the three of us sat in the garden. Avilés had bought a wood-roasted cabrito, with guacamole and flour tortillas, "to get you accustomed to the food up north". He set the table up underneath an ash tree. It was a fresh and sunny afternoon. Despite the fact that Avilés began to tell terrible jokes which Chelo encouraged with loud peals of laughter, a profound sense of nostalgia seeped into all three of us.

Once we had eaten we were quiet, each of us engrossed in our thoughts. The five o'clock light reached the garden through the branches of the trees, and it seemed as though the afternoon had been passed through an amber filter. Chelo, sitting in front of me, reached out her hand and took mine. Sergio, only half-serious, entwined his fingers with ours. "I now pronounce you man and wife," he said, and smiled. Chelo kissed me on the lips. "Good afternoon, my dear husband."

We took the bones and leftover kid to Colmillo. Lately we had only fed him biscuits, and he must have been missing real food. Food for a wolf, not for a dog. He devoured the leftovers the moment we flung them to him.

The plan was to leave Colmillo at Avilés's house. Natalia would feed him, and Paco, Avilés's assistant, would come twice a week to clean and wash the cage, which could only be done by someone who knew how to handle dangerous animals. Once I was established in Zaragoza and we'd set up a place where Colmillo could live, run and even hunt, Avilés and I would come back for him.

We went to bed at 9 p.m. The flight was at 8 a.m. and we had to get to the airport early. Chelo ran a bath and emptied a jar of bath salts into it. Relaxed by the effects of the salts we dozed in the water until it got cold. Then we got into bed naked. We switched off the light and started to talk about our plans for the future, about our lives on the ranch, and how much we would miss one another for these two months. She held me tight and looked at me in the dark. "Would you ever marry me?" she asked. "That's way cheesier than me asking if you wanted to be my girlfriend," I said. She laughed. "Yes, I'm cheesy," she said. I held her head in my hands. "Yes, I would marry you," I whispered into her ear.

We woke up very early to get ready. Paco was coming by to take us to the airport. We sat down for breakfast. Chelo had put on a white uniform and coat for her class in a hospital. That morning they'd be performing open-heart surgery on someone, and because of her good grades the professor had invited her to come and watch. She wasn't sure whether or not she should go. She didn't feel ready to see a person's heart beating.

She helped me fold my clothes and put them in my suitcases. Sitting on the bed as I packed, I stopped for a moment to look out of the window. Colmillo was pacing from one side of the cage to the other. I felt a sense of unease creep over me. What we'd done to Colmillo and what we were about to do – none of it was fair. I shouldn't take him to the desert in Coahuila just to put him in another cage, no matter how big it was. So that the heat could slowly kill him all over again, far away from his natural habitat. "We have to free him," I said to Chelo. She looked up at me. "What are you talking about?" I pointed to Colmillo in the cage. "Colmillo, we should set him free," I replied. "In Coahuila?" she asked. I shook my head. "No, in Canada."

Avilés thought it was a terrible idea. "He's never lived in a forest, or been in contact with any other wolves. He won't know how to hunt, he won't be able to survive the cold." According to Avilés, freeing him meant condemning him to death. "It's the worst thing you could do to that wolf."

I suggested we take him back to the breeding centre where he was born. Perhaps they could tell us what we should do with him. At least he could be with other wolves, in the place where he should have grown up. He'd be returning to his own climate, own territory, own species.

Avilés didn't think that returning Colmillo to the breeding centre was crazy in theory, but in practice it would be complicated. He explained the legal requirements for transporting an animal to another country, which he knew well from the circus business. A health certificate from a vet was necessary, as well as filling in import forms. In some cases, the authorities imposed a period of quarantine on the animal. "The process takes time and doesn't always work out," he explained. The paradox: we wanted to import back into Canada what it had once exported.

He questioned me about the trip to San Antonio and my plan to live in Zaragoza. In my mind these plans had been cancelled, and I told him there would be plenty of time for them in the future. Colmillo was my priority, I said, we needed to focus on getting him to Canada.

Chelo backed me up and was excited at the idea of coming with me. I tried to convince her to stay and finish the semester. She refused. I suggested we stick to the plan of her joining me later. She stubbornly insisted on coming now. "This changes everything," she said. "I go wherever you go."

Avilés called Jorge Jiménez early to explain our change of plans. Jorge was sorry to hear about our decision, but said we would be welcome at his home or his ranch whenever we decided to visit. Avilés spent the rest of the morning sorting out what we needed for Colmillo's journey, and spoke to the customs officers who dealt with the international travel arrangements for the circus about the best route to the Yukon. They recommended we travel overland, across the United States. They advised us not to transport him in a trailer but in the luggage compartment of a truck, as though he were a German Shepherd, and simply hope he remained calm as we drove through customs. They suggested we bring vaccination records and certificates from two different vets, clearly stating that he was a pet. "At no point tell them that he's a wolf," they said, since that would immediately lead to endless questions. And then there would be no way to avoid quarantine.

According to the customs agents, the most convenient route would be to take him to Dallas by truck and fly to Seattle from there. In Seattle, we could rent a car and cross the border into Canada at Lynden–Aldergrove, where security would be more relaxed than elsewhere.

The next day, two of the vets who cared for the circus animals came to Avilés's house to examine Colmillo. Both of them declared him healthy, but pointed out the scars on his nose and head. Admitting they were the result of bashing him with a chair to control him was not an option. Avilés blamed it on the "dog's active personality". Both vets issued us with a health certificate.

We decided to drive all the way to Canada. We didn't want to complicate the journey for Colmillo any more than necessary. We decided to buy a Suburban for the trip, a large four-wheel drive in which Colmillo could travel comfortably. If at any point along the way we couldn't find a hotel for the night, we could sleep in it. A friend of Avilés's was selling one second hand. I paid for it in cash and, later that morning, we registered the change of ownership.

We decided to leave the next day. Avilés calculated it would take us at least a couple of weeks to reach the Canadian border. "This is insane," he declared. "Another one of your fucking insane ideas."

Etymology of Events (Part Four)

Phrases derived from Latin:

TERRA INCOGNITA: Unknown land.

IN LOCO PARENTIS: In place of a parent.

A POSSE AD ESSE: From the possible to the real.

CAUSA MORTIS: When somebody nearing their death gives a gift to those who survive them. Also: Cause of death.

NUNC SCIO QUID SIT AMOR: Now I know what love means.

FORTES FORTUNA ADIUVAT: Fortune favours the brave.

DE NOVO: Afresh.

ABYSSUS ABYSSUM INVOCAT: The abyss summons the abyss.

GRAVIORA MANENT: Graver dangers await. The worst is yet to come.

RES IPSA LOQUITUR: The thing speaks for itself.

GESTA NON VERBA: Actions, not words.

BELLA HORRIDA BELLA: Wars, horrible wars.

NOSCE TE IPSUM: Know yourself.

QUIS CUSTODIET IPSOS CUSTODES: Who will guard the guardians?

POST FACTUM: After the fact.

CASUS BELLI: An act that leads to war.

ANTEBELLUM: Before the war.

AUT VIAM INVENIAM AUT FACIAM: I shall find a path or forge one.

FORTITUDINE VINCIMUS: By endurance we conquer.

INTER SPEM ET METUM: Between hope and fear.

Suns

I can hear bubbling water. Distant sounds from outside. Darkness. My body sways in the water. I don't have enough air. Thumps against the asbestos. A silent scream. The drowsy onset of death. Hands clutching, grabbing. Oxygen. I need oxygen. I open my eyes. Chelo is asleep by my side. I take a deep breath. My throat feels inflamed. My teeth feel like they're about to fall out. I sit on the edge of the bed, exhausted. My brother dies in the water. My parents in the air. My dog in fire. My grandmother on earth. What is death telling me in my dreams?

Chelo burnt her bridges. She didn't want to go to Canada without telling her parents, because she thought it would be disloyal. She didn't foresee the consequences. Her father flew into a rage. He accused her of leaving university to become the "concubine" of an eighteen-year-old "brat". "You walk with a limp thanks to your whoring around on roof-tops." He didn't let her take any of her belongings. No clothes, no shoes, no suitcase. Nothing. "You can take what you're wearing," her father told her. The tirade went on for hours. Chelo attempted a reconcilia-tion. She assured him that I was the man she planned to spend her life with, that it was a serious relationship. Her father mocked her. "Please, Consuelo, don't talk such nonsense. Just because you happen to be sleeping with this boy doesn't make it a 'serious' relationship. He'll finish with you as soon as his passion dries up." Her father's insults struck a chord. It hurt even more that her mother didn't say a thing to defend her. When her father locked himself in his room, warning that if she left, she could forget about ever setting foot in their house again, her mother said: "You need to listen to your father, this is madness, the

661

two of you are much too young." When she arrived at Avilés's house, Chelo was unsmiling and withdrawn, but she didn't cry. "You're in big trouble," she told me. "Now you'll never be rid of me."

We left early. Avilés was at the wheel, I was in the passenger seat, Chelo sat in the middle of the back and Colmillo was in the rear compartment, chained up and with his muzzle on. At first, he kept turning round and round. He couldn't get comfortable until he found a gap between the suitcases and lay down.

After ten hours on the motorway we reached Saltillo, Avilés's home-town. We left Colmillo in a garden that belonged to one of Avilés's brothers and went to buy Chelo what she needed: a toothbrush, under-wear, trousers, blouses, shoes, jackets. We spent the rest of the day in shops in the town centre. People often stopped to say hello to Avilés. "We went to the same secondary school", "I used to go hunting with him", "That skinny guy's sister was so sexy", "This is my ex-wife's cousin". If he ever decided to go into politics, I'd no doubt that Avilés could easily become the mayor of Saltillo.

Avilés went to see his mother and siblings that night. He was insis-tent that we should come with him, but we thought it best he spend time alone with his family. We didn't want to encroach on his privacy. His mother's health was fragile, and she could barely see or hear anything. Why would she want strangers in her house? Why force her to take off her pyjamas and get dressed just for us? Why oblige his siblings to make small talk? We wanted to let Avilés enjoy his family without worrying about us.

Sergio decided to stay the night at his mother's house. Chelo and I checked into a roadside motel in the outskirts of the city, on the highway towards Piedras Negras. The room was spacious and clean. Several trailers were parked outside the rooms. We could hear a couple laughing and then moaning next door. It turned Chelo on. We made love in silence, listening to our neighbours. The guy must have been pretty good, because the woman screamed with pleasure more than once. Then we listened to them talking. She was worried about getting home so late because she knew her husband would ask endless questions. The man laughed. "Do what I do. Act pissed off as soon as you walk through the door, and if he complains about something, get even angrier."

We heard them leave. Curious, we peered through a crack in the curtain. The guy was tall and tough looking, and the woman was short and fat. They walked towards one of the trailers. He wrapped his arms around her waist and she shoved her hand between his butt cheeks. Pure passion.

The next day was my birthday. Naked, Chelo sang me "Las Mañanitas" and placed a chocolate roll with a candle in it on the bed. As soon as I blew it out she started dancing. According to her, it was very sensual, but I couldn't stop laughing as I watched her shaking her butt in the air.

We picked up Avilés from his mother's house. "Happy birthday," he said and handed me a box with a ribbon tied around it. It was a Norwegian, 21-centimetre hunting knife with a wooden handle and a leather sheath. It was a handmade marvel. He told me it was the knife his father used to hunt with. "My grandfather gave it to him when he was a boy." I tried to give it back to him. It had huge sentimental value. Sergio refused. "You'll need it in the Yukon."

We left for the border. We could see the heat rising from the asphalt in waves. It was almost 42°C. As soon as we opened the window the scalding hot air rushed in. We had to stop several times so that Colmillo could drink water, and I rubbed bags of ice all over his body to cool him down. Colmillo wouldn't let Avilés or Chelo near him. As soon as they came too close, the hair on his back would stand on end. If they stayed put he'd growl until they moved away.

We stopped in Zaragoza along the way so that we could finally meet Jorge Jiménez and his mother, Luz Divina. His house was large, fresh and filled with light. The entrance to the garden boasted a large cage housing cardinals, mockingbirds, canaries and even wild quails. A stream teeming with charales ran through it.

Jorge gave me permission to let Colmillo loose in an empty plot of land next to the house, which the stream also ran through. They used it as a garden, storeroom and workshop. Once free, Colmillo sniffed his surroundings. He must have been discovering so many new smells, totally different from the ones he was used to in the city. He drank from the stream, then jumped into the water to cool down.

Jorge and his mother found out that it was my birthday. They generously organised a barbecue feast and invited all their local friends: Marco Aguirre, collector of antiques and archaeological artefacts, and expert in Mexican history; Gudelio Garza and his son Bernardo, the owners of El Olmo, an enormous ranch bordering La Amistad dam, who were obsessive American football fans; Carlos Hyslov, a successful cattle farmer who sold hundreds of heads of cattle a month to the United States; Humberto Enríquez, a homeopathic doctor who offered free consultations to local ranches and owned the Santa Cruz ranch which the San Rodrigo river ran through; his herdsman Raymundo Agüero, expert in breeding roosters for cock fights; Javier Navarro, owner of a chain of furniture stores across the country; Martín Sanchez, a professional hunting guide and renowned baker whose products were sold in all the nearby towns and cities; Carlos Lozano and his son Aarón, owners of an enormous store in Ciudad Acuña that sold bridalwear and school uniforms, and staunch promoters of regional tourism; and Marco Ramos Frayjo, a legendary hunter, Acuña's chief of police, and a man with a profound knowledge of world literature and poetry. Like Bross, Frayjo could effortlessly discuss any author and any subject. They were all friendly and easy to talk to, interesting people with amusing stories to tell, who made pleasant conversation. All of them kindly offered to have us to stay at their houses or ranches, and we received several invitations to go hunting on their land.

Luz Divina was warm and attentive. She was constantly making sure that we were well taken care of. Avilés only had to mention that he liked goat meat, and she sent someone to buy and prepare some immediately. We felt completely at home, as if we were surrounded by people who'd been our friends all our lives. As Avilés put it: "here with my new childhood friends".

We went for a walk around town. Zaragoza was pleasant. A dozen great-tailed grackles were singing in the trees, and their song broke into ethereal soprano notes that sounded for a moment like falling drops of water. In the main square people were sitting on benches shaded by the large mesquite trees. They bought sorbets and ice-lollies from an ice cream store on the corner to combat the heat. A couple of street dogs waited patiently for them to abandon their leftovers in their cardboard cups, ready to lick them clean.

We walked through the streets towards the edge of town. A river and several crystal-clear streams ran through it. You could clearly see fish swimming and algae swaying in the water. Frogs hopped out from between the reeds, then swam away to hide. A roadrunner emerged from the thicket and ran a few metres before stopping to look back at us. Three herdsmen were driving a herd of goats towards some enclosures on the edge of town, kicking up clouds of dust that took a while to settle.

Towards the end of the afternoon we visited Jorge's ranch. The road cut through the immense desert, and the setting sun cast lengthy shadows across the long straight line. The Sierra de Múzquiz looked blue in the distance. A coyote that had been hit by a car lay dead on the asphalt. We stopped to look at it – it was a beautiful animal. The hot wind had puffed up its tail. Chelo kneeled down next to it and ran her hand along its back. "Such soft fur," she said.

We reached Jorge's ranch, Don Abelardo. It was even more beautiful than I had expected. Horses, cows, pigs and chickens wandered outside the main house. Nearby, the sails of a water windmill turned slowly with a pleasant creak as it pumped water from the ground into the tank.

Jorge encouraged us to come and live on the ranch. They were about to join the electric grid, which would allow them to install air conditioning and a refrigerator. Besides, they already had a gas heater for hot water during the winter.

We left Colmillo in a barn and Jorge showed us around the ranch. We drove along a narrow track. The cattle watched us pass, indifferent. They were clearly dazed by the heat, because they refused to move out of our way. We were forced to drive into them, honking the horn to get them to move. A flock of small yellow butterflies alighted on the manure. Chelo passed her hand over them. They darted between her fingers and fluttered around us before settling on the manure again.

A flock of wild turkeys crossed our path. "Females," Avilés said confidently. Startled, they sought refuge in the saltbushes. At the back of the ranch was a dry river bed. The banks were covered with dense woodland. "That's where the deer and javelinas live," said Jorge, pointing to some mesquite trees. "And the turkeys like to sleep in those branches."

I had no doubt that Zaragoza and the ranch would be good places to live. With Luz Divina and Jorge ready to take us in, and our new friends with their diverse interests and lively conversation, the thought of staying was tempting. But I was committed to taking Colmillo back to Canada, and nothing would stop me from fulfilling the promise I'd made to myself.

We said goodbye to Jorge and continued towards Piedras Negras. We crossed the bridge at 10.00 p.m. that night. An immigration agent questioned us at the checkpoint. He asked for our passports and visas and examined them thoroughly. He asked us where we were going. In perfect English, Avilés told him we were headed for Dallas. The agent asked for Colmillo's papers. Avilés handed him the certificates issued by the vets. "He's a German Shepherd?" the official asked. "Yes," Sergio said confidently.

We had to go to the office to collect the permit for travelling further than twenty-five thousand miles into the country, a legal requirement for any foreigner travelling into the interior of the United States. They asked us again where we were going and examined our documents. An agent from the Department of Agriculture asked us a series of questions about Colmillo. He scrutinised the medical documents and reviewed his list of vaccinations. He asked us why he was wearing a muzzle. Avilés told him he'd been trained as a guard dog. It was lucky that he didn't ask us to get him out of the truck, because it would have taken less than a second for the agent to realise how dishonest our use of the word "trained" was.

They issued us with the permit an hour later. Once we were far from the checkpoint, we celebrated the fact that Colmillo hadn't been put into quarantine.

We kept driving until we reached a motel on the highway between Eagle Pass and Uvalde, Texas at two in the morning. On the way to our rooms we saw dozens of green-blue eyes glowing in the headlights. They were white-tailed deer, grazing in the plant pots. Colmillo caught their scent and started turning around inside the truck, barking and launching himself at the windows. As soon as they sensed him the deer ran away at top speed, alarmed, jumping gracefully over the desert shrubs. Colmillo stared at them intently. At least his hunting instinct wasn't completely lost.

The next morning, I went to see Sean in the low-security prison in Hondo, Texas, where he was locked up. Once again, I walked through halls filled with televisions. The sweaty inmates watched, squatting down on the floor in their cut-off trousers, barefoot and shirtless. The heat clung to the walls and the ceiling. Heat upon heat upon heat.

We met in the dirt-floor yard, and sat at a table in the shade of a huisache tree. A couple of inmates were lifting weights by the fence. I was keen to see Sean by myself. He would never approve of my relationship with Chelo. He agreed with her father – they both thought our love was doomed to failure. Sean saw me as an immature young boy, traumatised by orphanhood, clinging to my adolescent love as though it was my only hope. He saw her as an incorrigible slut with no plans to change.

I told Sean about how the last few weeks had been dizzying: my frustrated vengeance against Humberto and his unbridled madness, Zurita's attempted murder and the war between the cops and the Good Boys which had resulted in prison for many of them, and Antonio's death. "Zurita and Antonio brought this upon themselves," he said seriously, and without a hint of satisfaction.

I told him too about getting back all of Carlos's money, about Diego being freed, about my relationship with Chelo, my friendship with Avilés and the journey to take Colmillo back to Canada. Sean squeezed my arm. "You are my brother and I will always support you in everything you decide," he said. I knew that he was referring to Chelo. He didn't understand why I'd fallen in love with the woman my brother and many others had slept with.

I asked him if he needed money. "No, I'm good for now," he replied with a smile. He'd managed his inheritance wisely, and said his costs were covered for a few years. "We created the business of the century," he said. "Enjoy it – for Carlos."

Sean was hoping to be released in less than a year, and wanted to dedicate himself to farming and living a peaceful life for however long he could stand to stay in one place. "You know me, I've always been a bit of a wanderer," he said. I asked him about Quica's death. Sean looked at me, disconcerted. "What about it?" I told him what Humberto had said and how evasive Diego had been when I asked. "It wasn't your brother, that much I can promise. Yes, he beat him up a couple of times because Carlos was convinced Enrique had forced you to have sex with him. But it never went any further." I resented the fact that Carlos thought I could have fucked or been fucked by a guy. I said as much to Sean. "He was just trying to protect you, that's all."

"Fuck his protection," I growled. Sean smiled. "They're both dead now. What's the point in getting angry?" He was right; there was no going back. The dead can't hear us. "So, who did kill Quica?" I asked. I needed a definitive answer. "I'm pretty sure it was the Good Boys, but the truth is that I don't know. What I do know is that it wasn't Carlos." I left it at that. Quica's death would continue to be a mystery, and the doubts would always weigh heavily on me.

One of the guards came over to tell us that visiting hours were over. He seemed almost embarrassed to interrupt us. "Thanks, Choco," Sean said in Spanish. The chicano went to tell the other visitors it was time to leave.

We said goodbye. Sean gave me a fierce bear hug. I was left impregnated with his smell of musk and incarceration. He walked back towards the corridors packed with televisions, Mexicans, chicanos and black men lying on the floor.

We decided not to travel to the Yukon in a straight line or with a particular itinerary. None of us were in a hurry, and we were excited about crossing the United States from end to end. It turned out to be a much more interesting country than I'd imagined. The landscape was varied: there were the desert plains of Texas, the rolling valleys of Oklahoma, the Mississippi river's strong brown current, the fertile valleys of Kansas, Colorado's enormous mountain ranges, Wyoming's vast prairies, the dense forests and snaking rivers of Montana and Idaho.

We became connoisseurs of roadside motels, and other cheap lodgings along our route. Huge neon signs, many of them with their letters hanging off or missing. Rooms that stank of cigarettes, booze and sex. Of toothpaste, cheap soap and insect repellent. Of food, diapers and weed. Of urine, patchouli and floral-scented deodorant. Threadbare sheets, bedspreads with cigarette burns, patches of humidity on the walls. Blocked toilets. Mice, cockroaches, flies. Yellowish water. Plastic curtains in the showers.

We ate in lots of different types of restaurant. From hamburgers and pizzas to sophisticated game dishes, bison, goose, wild boar, armadillo, raccoon, barbecued ribs, roast beef, fried chicken, apple pie, cake, chocolate pudding, iced tea and Nescafé. Vending machines selling Coca-Cola, Pepsi and Dr Pepper.

Heat, rain, floods, hail, gales. Never-ending meadows. Tornados in the distance. Sunburnt farmers. Mexican labourers silently trudging along the edges of farms. Men on horseback herding cattle. Tractors ploughing the soil. Gigantic threshers winnowing wheat in the setting sun. Cattle grazing behind fences. Boundless cornfields barely visible in the mist. Ramshackle trucks. Soaring metal silos. Old men in bib overalls sitting on porches, with their calloused hands and wrinkled faces.

We heard an old black man sing the blues a cappella outside a bus station. In Oklahoma, we saw a show in which a Native American in traditional dress handled rattlesnakes. We went to a rodeo in Cheyenne, Wyoming, where a woman beat the men in the bull-riding contest. We saw wild horses trotting over the prairies. Fishermen on the banks of winding rivers pulling trout from the waters. Women playing cards and smoking cigars in the shade of an oak tree in Idaho. Boxing matches in barns where ruddy young men would give it their all, without any technique whatsoever. Gospel hymns sung in whitewashed wooden churches.

White-tailed deer, coyotes and rattlesnakes in Texas and Oklahoma. Pheasant, quail and partridge in Kansas. Wapiti and a couple of pumas in Colorado. Mule deer and pronghorns in Wyoming. Moose, marmots, prairie dogs, bears and geese in Montana and Idaho. We didn't see a single wolf on our journey.

Finding somewhere to put Colmillo at night became a logistical problem. We tried a portable kennel, but Colmillo simply smashed down the door. The good news was that the kennel was inside the Chevvy, otherwise he could have run away, and being fierce and always ready to attack, would probably have ended up with a cop putting a bullet in his head. The bad news was that, when he broke out of the kennel, he pissed and shat all over the S.U.V.'s seats.

So we ruled out the kennel, even though it was the most practical option. We stayed in hotels located on the outskirts of towns and cities, choosing back rooms that had windows overlooking the open countryside, far from where people might walk past, and would tie Colmillo to a tree or post with a pair of ropes. We always left his muzzle on as a precaution.

One morning in a motel near Denton, Texas, I was woken by the sound of voices, of doors opening and closing. I peered outside. A run-down Packard had pulled up outside our window. A black family were loading their luggage onto the roof. Standing on a bench, the father was tying a rope around their suitcases, while the mother and their young children passed things to him from their room.

We had left Colmillo tied to a lamp post at the far end of the parking lot. The five-year-old was running towards him excitedly. When I saw Colmillo stand up, I knew he would attack. I grabbed my trousers, quickly pulled them on and ran out, barefoot. His parents saw me sprint past and, seeing their son approaching Colmillo, they started running after me.

Colmillo sized the boy up, and when he came close, the wolf bounded. The boy saw him coming and took two steps back, just enough to be out of Colmillo's reach. The wolf had been only centimetres from knocking him down. If he had the child would have been seriously injured, if not killed.

The little boy fell onto his butt in the paved car park, wailing. When I reached him, I scooped him up and carried him a few metres away from Colmillo, where I set him down and tried to console him. His mother rushed up and started hitting me around the head. "You idiot! You idiot!" Her husband tried to restrain her, but the furious woman would not stop. Chelo came out and tried to intervene. Eventually, the woman calmed down. She picked up the child and carried him away.

They headed back towards their room. They stopped in the doorway where the man said something to his wife. He seemed to be explaining something. The woman nodded, head bowed. The man went into the room and returned with something in his hands. They came over to us. They were carrying a bible. The woman apologised. It had been their fault, she said, we had tied up our "dog" in an isolated, safe place, and they shouldn't have taken their eyes off their son.

They presented us with the bible. The man was a travelling preacher, and delivered sermons to labourers in cotton fields. He held impromptu services in shacks, where workers would listen attentively. He lived on donations and the occasional plumbing job.

They invited us to eat lunch with them. They took us to a "barbecue pit" where the majority of the diners were African-American. I ate the most delicious pork ribs I'd ever tasted in my life. Sweet, juicy, covered in a sauce made of honey, tomato paste and brown sugar.

After lunch, I gave the minister two hundred dollars. The man looked at me in astonishment. Nobody had ever given him that much. In a booming voice, he thanked me in the name of Jesus and said that the money would be put to good use, then immediately got up and paid the whole bill, and distributed the money among the cooks and waiters. He said that he still had forty dollars left, which would keep them going for another two weeks.

The incident with the child made us realise that, even in the most isolated motels, we couldn't leave Colmillo in places someone might stumble on him. Finding a place for him to sleep at night became a task that could take hours. We put him in empty water tanks, train wagons parked in sidings, in barns, derelict houses and livestock pens, in buildings about to be demolished. What at first seemed like a chore eventually became the main part of our day. Looking for the right place to leave Colmillo led us to the most out-of-the-way communities in rural America. We struck deals with local people, were invited into their houses, ate with them, got to know their families.

These detours along country roads led us to encounter churches inside barns, schools in motorhomes, diners in school buses, bars in shipping containers, cottages built from glass bottles. American ingenuity at its best.

On one of those roads in Oklahoma we came across a swimming hole in the middle of a forest. It was actually a deep pond under a limestone waterfall. There were some folding chairs on the stone slabs by the edge of the water. Children ran around, women with babies sat enjoying the sun, teenagers pushed each other into the water, young parents taught their children how to swim – only white people, from farming families.

At first Chelo didn't get into her swimsuit. She was still embarrassed at the thought of people seeing her scars, but seeing Sergio peel off his shirt and the deep scars that covered his back and chest, she stopped caring.

The three of us lay down on the limestone. We all had prominent scars, our stories carved in lines. Avilés was discreet and didn't ask Chelo about the grid that covered her legs. I wouldn't have been able to cope with her telling him about Carlos, about the distracted leap that had led to her plunging into the Prietos' yard. Jealousy still seethed within me at the slightest hint of Chelo's promiscuous past.

I leaned against the rock wall. Chelo sat on my lap and hugged me. Her body moulded around mine. I felt her breath on my cheek. I noticed her warm skin, her perfect temperature. The sun beat down on my face. I could hear the distant shouts of children jumping into the pond. Sergio was sitting on the riverbank, engrossed in thought, his mane of hair hanging down his extremely broad, pale back, his feet dangling in the water.

There was a light breeze. Small waves rippled across the swimming hole. Chelo pulled me to her and kissed my neck. "It's my time of the month," she whispered. For a second, I didn't know what she was talking about. "My period," she explained. She looked me in the eye. "I was a week late, I thought I was pregnant." A child was a remote idea, a nebulous creature. Now the possibility of being parents swirled between us. "And?" I asked, trying to figure out if she was sad or relieved. She hugged me tighter. "One day I want to have lots of children with you, but I know we aren't quite . . ." She stopped before finishing the sentence. A sense of loss floated above us, above the teenagers diving into the river, above the leaves of the trees swaying in the wind, above Avilés's white back as he meditated with his eyes fixed on the current. One of Chelo's four to six hundred opportunities to become a mother was dissolving in her menstrual blood. We knew we couldn't and shouldn't be parents, but the faint brush with our possible son or daughter made us both feel bereft.

We fell silent. We quietly watched the waterfall. The day began to wane. Dappled sunlight streamed through the trees. Bats started flitting over the river. Frogs began to croak. A long way away, a rooster crowed. Some white-tailed deer peered through the undergrowth before continuing along the trails.

That same night we stopped in a town. Chelo spoke to a gynaecologist. She explained that we didn't use condoms, that neither of us liked the feeling of the latex. The doctor asked if we were married. "Yes," Chelo replied without hesitation, prompting the doctor to ask why she wasn't wearing a ring. "Because I don't like wearing it," Chelo said bluntly. The doctor grudgingly wrote her a prescription and we stopped at a drugstore to buy contraceptive pills.

The woman behind the counter seemed reluctant to hand them over. She slid them across surreptitiously, as if they were illegal drugs. As Chelo was paying, the woman leaned closer. "Let god be the one to decide whether or not you have children, not you." Chelo glared at her. "If that's true, then let god be the one to tell me," Chelo said.

674

We decided not to cross at Lynden–Aldergrove but at Porthill instead, on the border between Idaho and British Columbia. It was early on a Sunday and the checkpoint was deserted. There were no other vehicles. Our papers were checked by a young, fair-haired border guard of about my age. His head was shaved. He looked like Bill Cone's younger brother. He carried out a perfunctory check of our car and noticed the foreign number plates. "Where are you from?" he asked. "Mexico," I said. "You've come all this way?" I nodded. "Are you agricultural workers?" he asked. "No," Avilés said, "we're tourists." The border guard noticed Colmillo. "And the wolf?" he asked unhesitatingly, not for a moment thinking that it might be a dog. "He's a pet," Avilés said. "We're taking him back to the breeding centre he came from." The guard looked surprised. "You drove all this way here for that?" We nodded. The official did no more than glance at our passports and then handed them back. He gave us permission to cross the border and then idly walked back to his chair inside the booth.

A few metres down the road we saw a sign with a crude drawing of a moose welcoming us to Canada. In a grocery store in the small village of Creston we bought two tents, sleeping bags, gas lamps, food, basic cooking utensils, cutlery, plates, metal cool boxes and two forty-litre plastic barrels for extra petrol. At the shop owner's suggestion, we bought a can of insect repellent for the mosquitoes. "They're a nightmare," he said. He warned us that bears could smell food from kilometres away. "Make sure you hang any food on a tree far from your tent if you don't want any unwanted visitors." He recommended some Canadian music – country, folk and rock – so we bought a few cassettes.

We travelled further inland listening to Gordon Lightfoot. It seemed as though the day would never end. It was 9.00 p.m. and the sun was still shimmering on the horizon. We had reached a vast and desolate place. There were no roadside motels, no cafés or tractors. Nothing but forests, mountains, grasslands and lakes.

We set up camp on a riverbank. We pitched the tents and lit a fire. The shopkeeper was right, the mosquitoes and black flies were a nightmare. Even with the repellent, they constantly buzzed around us. To keep them at bay we surrounded ourselves with lit torches.

Despite having lived alongside them for so long, Colmillo still didn't appear to feel comfortable around Chelo and Avilés. If they so much as went near him, he snarled. They kept their distance and I kept his muzzle on him as an extra precaution.

That night I took him for a walk attached to his chain. It was the first time he'd seen his natural habitat. He sniffed the moss, the ferns, the scent of other animals that had passed that way. The loons' gurgling sounds attracted his attention as they floated against the current trying to catch fish.

I chained him to the Suburban's fender. Exhausted and relaxed, he lay down next to a large rock. It was as hot as the Texan desert, a heavy, humid heat that was close to 38°C. Avilés was sweating profusely. Huge stains were spreading under his arms.

We had bread and Spam for dinner. Attracted by the smell, the black flies swarmed above us and bit us anywhere we hadn't applied repellent – a tiny spot on the neck, behind our ears, our eyelids, our lips.

Just before sunset, there came a deafening roar of frogs croaking in unison, which grew louder as the sun went down. Then a chorus of cicadas joined in. I had never imagined the northern hemisphere would be so loud. A cacophony as deafening as the one I remembered listening to as a child in Cacahoatán, in the jungles of Chiapas.

We put the food away in the coolers and hung them far from the camp, exactly like the man in the grocery store had told us. We got into the tent. It was so hot it was impossible to sleep. We didn't want to take off all our clothes in case a bear wandered too close and we needed to get away fast. A few mosquitoes managed to get into the tent and were constantly biting us, making our skin come up in welts.

In the middle of the night we heard wolves howling in the distance.

Chelo shook me awake. "Listen." I sat up. Their low, penetrating howls were echoing around the canyon walls. The sound made my skin tingle.

Colmillo began to prowl back and forth. I could hear the chain scrape against the Chevvy's fender. This was probably the first time in his life that he'd heard wolves howl. So different and yet so similar to the howl of city dogs.

Colmillo answered with a series of howls. He was finally communicating with his own species. He could finally hear the pack he'd spent so many nights summoning.

Chelo and I poked our heads out of the windows of the tent. Colmillo looked fired-up. Colmillo answered every distant howl with one of his own. Avilés burst out of his tent, determined to shut him up. Indignant, Chelo went out to confront him. "What are you doing?" Avilés shone his torch at her. "What do you mean, what am I doing? Saving his life. If that wolf pack comes here and finds him tied up, they'll kill him, and then they'll kill us." Avilés ordered me to put Colmillo in the S.U.V., where he would be safe.

I lifted him into the luggage compartment. The howls continued on and off for another hour and then silence fell. Only the croaking of frogs and the hoots of an owl remained.

Victory
Victory c
Victory co
Victory com
Victory come
Victory comes
Victory comes w
Victory comes wh
Victory comes whe
Victory comes when

Victory comes when y
Victory comes when yo
Victory comes when you
Victory comes when you l
Victory comes when you le
Victory comes when you lea
Victory comes when you leas
Victory comes when you least
Victory comes when you least e
Victory comes when you least ex
Victory comes when you least exp
Victory comes when you least expe
Victory comes when you least expec
Victory comes when you least expect i

Forests

The flames reach the bedroom. My father gets out of bed. Stumbles into the blazing furniture. Slips. Falls onto the embers. His legs are charred. My mother rushes to help, but she too is trapped in the fire. I watch as they burn. Flames envelop them. I run to get a bucket of water. I must put it out. I go out into the yard, pick up the bucket and rush back. The bucket gets heavier and heavier. I can't move it anymore. I look to see what's making it so heavy. Juan José is floating inside. He is a smiling, greenish mass of flesh. The bucket slips from my hand and falls. Juan José slithers out. He flails like a fish. Gasps. Drowns. I look up again. My house is being destroyed, flames licking it all over. I can't go inside. The heat holds me back. I see Colmillo. He is watching me intently. He seems to want me to follow him, so I do. We walk through burning tentacles. The smoke is blinding. Colmillo leads me to safety.

I wake up. I'm alone in the tent. It's daytime and the heat feels dense and aqueous. I am sweating. I hear Avilés and Chelo chatting on the riverbank. My jaw is aching again, my teeth are clenched. I wipe the sweat off my face and neck. Several mosquitoes are resting on the roof of the tent, and I squash one of them. Blood explodes on my hand. They've been feeding on us. The blood of the many that courses through my veins is inside their tiny stomachs. Me, the big mosquito.

I should fight my ghosts, I can't allow their presence to paralyse me forever. I need to defeat them. I am thousands of miles away from my ruined house, from the cemetery in which my dead now lie, yet here I am, still carrying them with me. So many deaths weighing on my shoulders. I cannot carry on, knowing that a shadow twin lives with me, that a brother will forever be gasping for air, that my parents are bleeding out in an upturned car, that my dog burned to death. I realise that here and now, in this tent, in the midst of this heat, in this strange land, I need to free myself of them. To let them go. Let them go once and for all.

There were three thousand kilometres between Creston in British Columbia and Mayo in the Yukon, the place that Colmillo's papers said the breeding centre was located. We'd already covered four thousand kilometres from Mexico City to the Canadian border. Such vast distances are impossible to grasp unless you travel by car.

The highways in Canada were lonely. We very rarely passed other vehicles, and, when we did, they were almost always freight trucks or trailers. We often camped by the side of the road. Hardly anyone passed at night.

The majority of the towns had no hotels or inns. Some residents would let us stay in their homes for a small sum, but most of them didn't charge us a cent. They enjoyed hosting outsiders and listening to them talk over dinner about the exotic places they were from. Hardly any of them had ever left their towns, let alone Canada. Their world had a radius of only a few kilometres. To them, Mexico sounded incredibly remote, a country lost within the shapeless mass of nations south of the continent. Brazil, Argentina, Puerto Rico, Honduras, they were all the same to them. They didn't know which of them shared borders, which were islands and which were part of the mainland.

The native people were generous. They shared their food without reservation and let us sleep on their beds while they curled up on on their living room sofas or slept on the floor. They gave us presents when we left, as though our visit had been a great honour. We received sculptures carved out of moose antlers, stone arrowheads, boxes of herbal medicines and furs. We gave them Mexican coins in return, which they cherished as if they were highly precious.

680

They were fascinated by Colmillo. Some found the notion of a wolf as a pet hilarious, even absurd. Others found it insulting. They thought tying up and placing a chain and a muzzle on a mythical animal like a wolf was degrading. Their opinion began to change when they saw me interacting with him, and even more so when they found out that the whole reason for our trip was to free him close to where he had been born. Others commended me for having tamed him. "That means you are wilder than him," an old Tsilhqot'in man said to me.

Avilés was not someone who chose to take the shortest or most direct route to any destination. For him the purpose of travel was to discover, experience, learn. We got lost countless times and the further north we travelled, the more limited the network of roads became. When we took a wrong turn, we had to drive around for several kilometres until we found the right way. So instead of taking a few days, the journey took weeks. Avilés always drove to begin with, but he'd get tired halfway through and then the three of us would take turns behind the wheel. When it was my turn, I feared it might trigger within me a latent suicide wish, making me veer suddenly towards a precipice, just like my father had done. But the longer I drove, the more confident I became that this wouldn't happen.

It rained ceaselessly on our journey across British Columbia. The downpours reduced visibility and flooded roads made it hard to keep going. We had to change the windscreen wipers several times. Pitching tents in the deluge was impossible. The one time we tried to, we ended up knee-deep in mud and the Chevvy got stuck. Pulling it out took us half a day. We ended up drenched and filthy.

If it got dark and we didn't find ourselves near a small town where we could spend the night, we slept in our seats inside the S.U.V. Avilés in the front, Chelo and I curled up in the back, and Colmillo comfortable in the luggage compartment.

The electrical storms were an incredibly beautiful sight. The horizon would light up with dozens of lightning bolts that could be seen from kilometres away. The mountain peaks flashed blue for a thousandth of a second and an instant later thunder would boom through the darkness.

One night a bolt of lightning struck close to where we had parked. The rumble of thunder shook the S.U.V. and the four of us jumped up, afraid. A pine tree was split and the top came crashing down in flames, which were quickly doused by the rain. Although the chances of a lightning bolt electrocuting people inside a vehicle were low, Avilés did not want to tempt fate and we decided to get as far away from the storm as we could.

Ten days later, the rain eased off. The clouds dispersed, leaving the sky clear. We stopped the van and got out to admire the landscape. The mountain ranges stood out against the blue of the sky. The air was pristine. A couple of bald eagles flew over us. Three kilometres north of where we stood was the border with the Yukon.

We stopped in a town that strangely enough had a Spanish name: Ranchería. We stayed in a place called the Ranchería Inn, where there had recently been a fire and several rooms had been burnt out. The coiled entrails of wires and pipes could be seen between the blackened walls. The air was still pervaded by the smell of burning. It was as though fire were following me.

Chelo thought sleeping there would bring back bad memories, but I was so tired that it didn't affect me. We had spent six nights trying and failing to sleep in the Chevvy, between Avilés's snores and Colmillo's terrible farts. I was sick of washing in freezing rivers, and desperate to take a hot shower and sleep stretched out in a bed.

Mr Sampson, the owner, apologised for the state of the inn. During the heavy rainfall, a guest had lit a fire and fallen asleep without placing the screen in front of the fireplace. The crackle of the burning logs had spat a hot ember onto the carpet. The flames had spread quickly, and within minutes the timber walls were ablaze. The guest woke up and ran outside, terrified. By the time the firefighters arrived, the flames had already consumed half the building. They could only save three bedrooms and the dining room.

We were the first guests since the accident. Mr Sampson gave us a fifty per cent discount, charging us only four dollars per room, including breakfast. He also let us put Colmillo in a barn behind the inn.

Chelo and I fell fast asleep after a long shower and didn't wake up until mid-morning. Avilés, usually an early riser, got up two hours later. Esther, Mr Sampson's wife, told us that breakfast was usually served only until 9.00 a.m., but that since we were their only guests, she'd make an exception. At 1.00 p.m. she made us pancakes covered in maple syrup, crispy bacon and fried eggs, with freshly baked bread and coffee. We gorged ourselves so much that we couldn't eat anything else for the rest of the day.

Mr Sampson told us it would take around four hours to get to Whitehorse, the Yukon's capital, from Ranchería. We left that afternoon. The sun gleamed on the surface of the huge lakes we passed on the highway. Skeins of snow geese and specklebelly geese flew across the sky, honking loudly. As we rounded a bend, Avilés noticed something in the distance. I was driving and he asked me to stop. He took out his binoculars and scanned the vegetation along the riverbank. From a dense thicket poked the ruins of what looked like a flooded cabin. "What is it?" Chelo asked. Try as we might, we couldn't figure out what it was. Curious, we took a track towards the river and parked on the edge of a slope. We walked down the steep hill covered with pine trees. Once again, we were attacked mercilessly by flies and mosquitoes.

They were the ruins of a wooden steamboat stuck in the mud. It listed to one side, with part of the prow submerged beneath the water. Avilés tried to figure out how it had run aground, but could find no clues that might solve the mystery.

We climbed aboard. We walked cautiously across the hull's rotten wood, aware that it could collapse under our feet at any moment. We

683

climbed the stairs to the wheelhouse. Some of the navigation equipment and the rudder still looked intact. There was some cargo in the stern, covered in canvas. It was rolls of colourful cloth that had faded having been exposed to the elements for so long. I cut off a piece from an indigo batch and took it with me as a keepsake.

We sat on some rocks and admired the shipwreck. The slapping of the water against the keel was regular and rhythmic. "What do you think happened to them?" asked Chelo. The boat must have been there since the end of the nineteenth century. Its cargo of cloth had never been recovered. Even after seventy, eighty years, it was still there underneath the canvas, slowly rotting away. Had the sailors died? What had caused them to run aground? Maybe they had been attacked by native tribes, or a storm had diverted them towards the bank and they ended up stranded in the mud and the thicket.

Sergio stood up, staring intently at the boat. Then he looked back towards us. "I'm not going back to the circus," he said. "Why?" I asked him. "The truth is that I've been looking for a change of scene for a while now," he said. We couldn't understand it. Sergio had the perfect job: risky, interesting, well paid. He insisted that he was tired of performing the same act night after night, bored with the tours, with sleeping in a caravan, with audiences baying for blood. He was thinking of handing over his lions and tigers to Paco, his assistant, who he felt was ready to be his successor. "He's known them since they were cubs, he's been with me for years. He'll be good at it." It was obvious he'd been thinking about his decision for a while. The trip, he told us, reminded him how much he loved exploring new places, getting to know, discovering. He longed for a different life, he said, and seeing the boat run aground had helped him make up his mind. He didn't want to feel stuck anymore.

Avilés smiled when he noticed our sad faces. The news weighed more heavily on us than it did on him. "Don't worry, maybe I'll change my mind," he said, before walking back towards the S.U.V.

We arrived in Whitehorse on a Friday afternoon. Having travelled through towns and villages with at most three hundred inhabitants, the city, with its fifteen thousand people, seemed huge. We had a delicious dinner in their finest restaurant: Alaskan crab, salmon, caribou steak, and something I never thought I'd eat: Dall-sheep meat.

We checked Colmillo into a boarding kennel that specialised in sled dogs, and checked ourselves into a two-star hotel on a corner of the main street. It felt like the ultimate in luxury. The mattresses were firm, there was endless hot water in the shower and the ceiling fan worked. It didn't smell of cigarettes or sex. You couldn't hear a television blaring next door, and aside from a little noise from the street it was very quiet.

At 7 a.m. the next day we left for Mayo. Another long distance to cover. Forests, lakes, plains, infinite straight-line roads, curves that snaked between mountains. We stopped along the way to watch a grizzly bear with two cubs climbing up the foothills. Even at a distance, the mother was intimidating, a huge mass of ash-grey fur. She must have smelled us, because she stopped to watch us. Half of her torso was visible above the underbrush – standing on two legs, she must have been about two metres tall. "Ursus arctos horribilis," Avilés said, giving us the taxonomic name. How horrifying it must have been for those who named it to see a bear charge at a human being and rip him apart in seconds. The bear watched us for a while and then continued uphill.

It took us six hours to get there. Mayo was just a group of houses along dirt roads. We headed to the address written on Colmillo's documents: Mackenzie Breeding Centre, Duncan Avenue #5, Mayo, Yukon, Canada. I'd imagined a modern building filled with cages teeming with wolves and Alaskan Malamutes, something like the photos in the brochure, but all we found was a single wood cabin at the end of the small village, with a wooden roof and moose antlers above a door that was painted red. There was no sign of any wolves or dogs in the front yard. Only dilapidated farm machinery and a pile of logs.

We knocked on the door. Nobody answered. Perhaps the breeding centre had closed or it wasn't the right address. We went back to the group of houses. We drove around until we saw a woman with indigenous features. We asked her about the breeding centre. In broken English, she told us that we had the correct address.

We went back to the cabin. We peered in through a window. It looked lived in. Flowerpots sat on a shelf. Plates, cutlery and a jug of water had been placed on the table. Jackets hung from hooks and we could see pairs of boots lined up next to the door. Chelo suggested we wait.

We sat in the shade of a pine, Colmillo chained to a neighbouring tree. There was a light breeze and luckily no flies or mosquitoes bothered us. We could hear the faint bubbling of the river that passed through the town. We dozed off lying in the grass. A couple of hours later we heard a vehicle approaching along the road. We sat up and saw a run-down Dodge pickup park in front of the cabin. A man and two women got out. The three of them must have been close to seventy-five. We approached them. "Good afternoon," Avilés greeted them. "Is this the Mackenzie breeding centre?" "It's the office," replied the old man, smiling. One of the trio, an old indigenous woman, looked at Colmillo and said something to the man in a native language. The man pointed to the wolf lying in the shade. "She recognises him. It's one of the cubs we bred," he said. "How does she know?" I asked. "Because he's identical to his father," he replied.

He introduced himself as Chuck Mackenzie. The indigenous woman was called Kenojuac, and the white woman was Rosie. The cabin was where they lived and it was the address on the brochure for mail and administration purposes, since the breeding centre itself was located on a remote ranch which the postal service didn't reach.

They invited us in. The house was cool and tidy. They insisted that we stay for lunch. I wanted to go straight to the breeding centre. Chuck warned us that it was two hours away and it was better not to go hungry. They served us a salad of tomatoes and lettuce they had grown themselves in indoor vegetable beds, and delicious bear meat hamburgers. Who would have thought that Ursus arctos horribilis would taste so delicious?

At three in the afternoon we left for the breeding centre. Chuck agreed to lead us in his pickup, since he wanted to go back that night. Before leaving the town, he stopped for supplies and petrol. "There isn't much food there," he said apologetically.

The grocery store was a shed built from sheet metal. On the shelves were bags of rice and beans, bottles of vegetable oil, salt and tinned goods, most of which came from China and had extravagant contents: "swallows' nests", "quails' eggs in brine", "shark fin soup", "chicken with bamboo". Culinary delicacies from the Far East for a town founded by gold panners and trappers. They also sold fresh fish: salmon, turbot, pike and salted cod fillets. You could select your preferred cut from the entire gutted cow that hung from a hook: flank steak, tenderloin, shank, rib, neck. The butcher would cut it and wrap it in newspaper for you to take away.

We filled both vehicles' tanks with petrol, as well as the forty-litre barrels. Chuck tried to pay his bill, but we didn't let him. "Courtesy of the Mexicans," I told him.

I kept him company in his pickup. The road to the ranch was narrow and winding. Much of it wasn't paved, and we had to negotiate long muddy stretches. Chuck explained that it had been a heavy rainy season and many of the rivers had broken their banks, sweeping away the asphalt.

Chuck told me that the breeding centre was a thriving business run by his nephew Robert and his children. One of the conditions of sale imposed on anyone buying a wolf cub was that they report on the animal's condition every six months, confirming that it was emotionally and physically well and being properly cared for. The centre prided itself on sharing "joint responsibility" with the wolves' owners, and offered veterinary and handling advice by mail. They were proud of the fact that they had kept track of every wolf or wolf-dog they had ever sold, except for one, which they had sent to a man in New York, from whom they never heard again. Three had been reported dead within a month of purchase. Two buyers had demanded replacements and the centre had dispatched new cubs. One buyer had written to inform them that his wolf had died in Laredo, Texas, but had not asked them to replace it. That cub was Colmillo. Chuck told me that he knew it as soon as he saw him. "The pair of wolves that produced him only had two litters. Of the fifteen we sold, we've kept track of fourteen. He was the only one missing."

Colmillo had been one of the first pureblood wolf cubs they'd sold, from the original pair's second litter. They were the breeding centre's Adam and Eve: Nujuaqtutuq and Pajamartuq.

The road took us into increasingly flat landscapes as we left the mountains behind us. We reached a wide plain and Chuck turned down a track. There was a barbed wire fence running all the way along it. "This is where the ranch begins," he said. Scattered herds of cows were grazing on the plain that seemed to go on forever.

We covered about fifteen kilometres. We passed under an arch with a sign that said MACKENZIE PLAINS RANCH and reached a group of houses and a row of cages in which dozens of wolves and Alaskan Malamutes prowled.

We parked in front of a garage. A nineteen-year-old blonde woman came out to greet us. Chuck got out of the pickup, greeted her warmly and then introduced us. "This is Patricia, she is in charge of the breeding centre." Patricia offered me her hand to shake. It felt strong and calloused. "Patricia Mackenzie, nice to meet you." I had to repeat my name three times before she could understand it. Chuck told her that I had brought "the cub that died in Laredo". She looked at him, confused. "Stuffed? A photo?" she asked. "Alive," said Chuck.

Chelo and Avilés arrived a little after us. I introduced them to

Patricia and then let Colmillo out with his muzzle on. "He's identical to Nujuaqtutuq!" she exclaimed. I told Patricia that I wanted to set Colmillo free. Just like Avilés, she thought it was dangerous. "It's very risky to free them after they've lived in captivity their entire lives. Their chances of survival are low, if not non-existent," she said.

She invited us to come and see the wolves and suggested we leave Colmillo behind so that he wouldn't get nervous. I chained him to a post far from the cages. Even so, he seemed agitated. He couldn't see the other wolves from where he was, but he was pacing up and down, disturbed by their smell.

We went to the cages. They were large, each one no smaller than two thousand square metres. Patricia took us to one which housed seven wolves. She opened the gate and told us to go in. We were not to worry: they were docile and used to human contact.

Once inside the cage, Patricia shut the gate. She called them by clapping her hands. The wolves ran towards us and circled us, giving little bounds. There were two males and five females. They didn't seem at all aggressive. We spent some time stroking and playing with them. Patricia reiterated what it said in the brochure: "If wolves socialise with humans as cubs, they become excellent pets."

We went into several cages. The wolves and the Alaskan Malamutes were equally affectionate and obedient. The only ones we weren't allowed to visit were the ones that contained she-wolves suckling their young. I asked if Colmillo's parents were still alive. "Yes," she said, "but we keep them in a special place because they are very old now."

She took us to a huge shed in which two large fans were spinning. The wolves lived behind a gate a metre and a half high. Patricia warned us not to get too close because they were wild, and even in their weakened state they could attack us. Nujuaqtutuq was immense. He stood up when he saw us, and limped to a corner of the cage to lie down. A long scar ran along his leg. Another member of our scarred clan. I asked Patricia if it was true what the brochure said, about this wolf having been caught by a legendary Inuit trapper. "Yes," she said, "but my father is the one who should tell you that story." Pajamartuq never came out of her lair. She was lying down in a wooden kennel, and we could only make out a part of her body.

Chuck said goodbye. He had to get back to Mayo before it got dark. Patricia walked him to his car. We stayed in the shed, watching the big grey wolf. They were right: Colmillo's size, colour and intense gaze were identical to his.

Robert Mackenzie came into the shed accompanied by his three children. I recognised him immediately from the photo in the brochure. He introduced us to his boys: Johnny, Eric and Dan. They'd been marking and dehorning the bull calves and apologised to Chelo for smelling of sweat, smoke, manure and blood. "Patricia told me you want to free your wolf," Robert said. I told him about how Colmillo had suffered, tied up and alone. About how I'd adopted him, how difficult it had been to tame him, and how long he'd spent trapped in the small yard in my house. "I feel it's my duty to free him," I said.

Robert was worried that Colmillo lacked the "social tools" to integrate into a pack. "Wolves are very sophisticated animals," he told me. "They use a complex repertoire of signals to communicate with one another." He added that learning how to hunt required living in a pack, and that unless his instinct was highly developed Colmillo wouldn't survive in the wild. To offer him a better quality of life, he suggested I leave him at the breeding centre, where he would live in a large space. I refused. I had not travelled all the way to the Yukon just to prolong Colmillo's captivity. He would be free. Full stop. "Let's see how he interacts with the other wolves in the breeding centre and then decide," Robert proposed. We agreed that the next morning we'd put him in one of the cages with the other wolves and observe how he reacted.

Robert invited us over for dinner. We gave him the supplies we had bought and he asked if he owed us anything. "Courtesy of the Mexicans," Chelo said, smiling. He offered to let us sleep in the small guest cabin behind the main house, but we told him we didn't want to be any trouble and that we could camp outside on the ranch. He insisted. "You're my guests, we'll take care of you."

We had dinner with Linda, his wife, and his six children: Patricia, Mary, Johnny, Eric, Lisa and Dan. The first three were blonde, the others had brown hair. At Patricia's insistence, Robert told us the story of Amaruq and Nujuaqtutuq. How by chance Robert had found Amaruq lying wounded next to a mountain goat and deduced that both had fallen from the top of one of the highest cliffs; that he'd found Nujuaqtutuq days later inside a tattered tent, tied to a sled, thin, anaemic and wounded; about the funeral odyssey, how Amaruq's mother had freed Nujuaqtutuq, how Robert himself had had to go and rescue him, and how he'd happened across the ranch looking for a vet who could help him. We were transfixed by the story, even more so when we found out that Amaruq was Chuck and Kenojuac's son.

Dinner went on until midnight. Holding nothing back, Robert told us the story of John and his madness and how he'd come to adopt his three children. The children didn't seem at all upset by it; Patricia even corrected a few of the details in Robert's story.

When we went to bed it was nearly 1.00 a.m. The full moon lit up the plain, and we didn't need torches to get back to our cabin. There was a gust of wind and we heard a squeak. We looked up. A rusty rooster was spinning on the roof. We looked out towards the horizon. We could hear the cows mooing in the distance. I asked the others if they would like to stay and live in Canada. "Yes," they both replied. "Perhaps I could become a grizzly bear trainer," Sergio said with a chuckle. Chelo liked the idea of a peaceful life on a ranch. "With goats, piglets and horses," she said. "Absolutely," Avilés chimed in, "so long as we don't freeze to death in the winter."

Magic Words

In the very earliest time,
when both people and animals lived on earth,
a person could become an animal if he wanted to
and an animal could become a human being.
Sometimes they were people
and sometimes animals
and there was no difference.
All spoke the same language.
That was the time when words were like magic.
The human mind had mysterious powers.
A word spoken by chance
might have strange consequences.
It would suddenly come alive
and what people wanted to happen could happen –
all you had to do was say it.
Nobody could explain this:
that's the way it was.

Inuit poem (Anonymous)[1]

1 After Nalugiaq Tutanuak (from *Magic Words: Songs and Stories of the Netsilik Inuits*
by Edward Field)

Life

In the morning, we took Colmillo to the cage with the most wolves, nine females and three males. According to Robert, the best thing to do was get him to face a large pack, the hardest test of all. As we led Colmillo closer to the fence the fur on his back stood on end as he set eyes on other wolves for the first time in his life.

Robert and Patricia went in first. The animals greeted them happily, rubbing their heads against their legs. Robert stood at the edge with a long electric cattle prod, ready to intervene if the pack attacked Colmillo.

Patricia opened the door and told Avilés and Chelo they should stay on the other side of it in case the encounter got out of hand. Colmillo's every muscle tensed, he did not take his eyes off the wolves, who watched him from a distance. I took off his muzzle and let slip the chain. When he realised that he was free, Colmillo slowly padded into the middle of the cage. The alpha male of the pack made for him, ready to attack. Instead of adopting a submissive position, Colmillo bared his teeth and firmly stood his ground. The alpha male stopped a metre away and bared his teeth. The other wolves surrounded them. If the alpha male defeated Colmillo, it was likely the whole pack would attack. He would pay dearly for having intruded into another's territory.

The two males sized each other up. They circled one another, growling and baring their fangs. Suddenly, Colmillo charged and a skirmish began. The other wolves snapped at Colmillo, but he was so focused on defeating his adversary that he did not seem to notice.

It was a fierce fight. Colmillo was bigger and stronger, and eventually dominated the other wolf who fled into a corner of the cage, bleeding from his neck. Colmillo had not finished. He turned and lunged at another male, who promptly lay down and rolled onto his back.

The rest of the pack bounded around Colmillo in a display of respect and submission. Patricia and Robert took the wounded wolf to the infirmary. Colmillo's bites were deep and the wolf needed surgery. Patricia, who had trained as a veterinary nurse, performed the operation. Chelo told her she was studying to become a surgeon and assisted her.

Colmillo had passed the first test relatively easily. Robert attributed this to the genes he'd inherited from Nujuaqtutuq, as well as the conditions of his upbringing, which had led him to develop a very aggressive and dominant personality. He told us that he was the largest wolf cub in his litter. Since buyers weren't given the opportunity to choose their cubs, Mackenzie gave each of the cubs a number and they were assigned to their owners at random. That was how Colmillo had ended up with the Prietos.

The breeding centre had been Chuck's project. When Nujuaqtutuq and Pajamartuq's first litter was born, a few acquaintances in the area asked if they could buy a wolf cub. Wolves – feared and revered in the Yukon – had a reputation among some for being good pets, affectionate and calm, ideal for protecting houses and ranches. They sold five wolf cubs from the first litter in less than a week. The extra money helped Robert and Linda maintain their new family, because the extremely harsh winter had killed off a significant number of cows. They were left with two females, and bought a male from an indigenous local. They began to cross the female wolves with Alaskan Malamute studs, and the business started to prosper.

Nujuaqtutuq and Pajamartuq took a while to have another litter. Pajamartuq was bad-tempered, and because of the injury in his right leg Nujuaqtutuq found it difficult to mount her. Colmillo belonged to the second litter Nujuaqtutuq produced, which ended up being the last, because from that moment on he refused to mate with the other she-wolves. Robert admitted that they'd come close to keeping Colmillo. They'd thought of using him as a stud for his size and bearing, but Lisa, the youngest daughter, became fond of another wolf and they ended up choosing him instead.

We left Colmillo inside the cage for several days. His reign as leader wasn't without its complications. The alpha female and another one of the males were constantly challenging him and there were frequent fights. The pack hadn't accepted him and the females shunned him, but Colmillo prevailed by defeating any wolf that stood up to him until he managed to establish his superiority.

The vanquished alpha male recovered from his wounds and was reintroduced into the pack. It didn't take long for him to confront the wolf who had deposed him. As soon as he entered the cage, he charged straight at Colmillo. Again, jaws snapped and a furious battle took place. Colmillo once again overpowered him, but this time his jaw was split open. The blood flowed profusely. Patricia assessed him and decided no treatment was necessary.

Avilés was surprised. Having had no previous contact with other wolves, or even other dogs, Colmillo had firmly established his position within the pack. "He's exceptionally ferocious," Sergio said. Robert thought it would be a good idea to put him in a cage with another pack to see how he coped. If he adapted well, Avilés joked, "I'll eat my words and we'll let him go."

We moved Colmillo to a cage where there were only seven wolves, three males and four females. It was more difficult this time around. Instead of a one-on-one fight with the alpha male, the whole pack set upon him as a group. At first Colmillo was confused, and received several nasty bites. Robert was about to use the electric prod to save him when Colmillo recovered and focused on just one of the wolves. He went after him mercilessly, ignoring the attacks from the others. He fought until the wolf was forced to flee. This unsettled the rest of the pack, and Colmillo took the opportunity to subdue the alpha female. Colmillo battled with her until she lay down, face up, submissive. Injured but triumphant, Colmillo stood in the middle of the cage, ready to fight any one of them. A young female walked over to sniff him with her head lowered. Then each of the wolves approached to pay his or her respects.

Who knows how the years spent tied to a post in the Prietos' yard had affected Colmillo's psyche. Avilés thought that the abuse and isolation had turned him into a daring and fierce animal. Robert insisted that the way Colmillo fought, the way he dominated other wolves, was unheard of. No wolf raised in captivity had ever behaved in such a way. He ruled out putting him into the cage with the Alaskan Malamutes because he was vicious enough to kill the largest of them.

We left Colmillo with that pack for another week. While he adjusted, we helped out on the farm to stave off boredom. Patricia and Chelo had become friends and between the two of them they fed the dogs and the wolves, separated the pregnant wolves from the rest, kept an eye on them when they were giving birth and cleaned the cages.

Avilés and I helped Robert with the cows. We herded the heifers to new pastures, searched on horseback for those that had got lost in the forest, and separated the bull calves from their mothers before branding and dehorning them.

Robert's sons and daughters went to school in Mayo. They were in different grades, but still studied some subjects together. The school only had two teachers and they weren't able to provide an education for all forty children in the town and surrounding area. Chuck collected them from the ranch on Sundays and Robert went to pick them up on Fridays when they got out of school. Our visit happened to coincide with their summer holiday.

The three boys worked on the ranch in the mornings and then had their afternoons free. They enjoyed hunting, and although there was no forest authority monitoring the area, they respected the closed seasons and restrictions. Since the season wouldn't open for another two months, they kept themselves entertained with plenty of other activities. During the few weeks we were with them we went to see waterfalls, kayaked on fast-flowing rivers, went mountain climbing, and watched grizzly bears catching the salmon swimming upstream. They knew the names of every plant, every animal, every star and constellation. They could predict the weather by analysing cloud formations and wind direction. They were prepared for survival in the harshest of winters. They knew how to set traps for animals using only branches and bark, and could light a fire using a knife, a stone and dead leaves. If they ever cut themselves seriously, they could sew up the wound with fibres they pulled from tree trunks and needles they carved from pieces of wood. They could orient themselves in the dark and in the middle of the heaviest snowfall. They could assess the risk of an avalanche just by looking at the shapes of the sheets of snow. They knew how to react if attacked by a predator. With a bear, play dead and cover your head and neck with both arms; with a mountain lion, shout at it and open your coat to seem bigger, and never turn your back to it; if surrounded by a pack of wolves, climb a tree, rip off a branch and smack it against the trunk to scare them off.

Colmillo adapted to his new pack. Patricia tried to convince me to let him stay and live in the breeding centre. Not only was it the best thing for him, he could become a magnificent stud. He had demonstrated he had excellent genes and would improve the quality of future litters.

It was true, Colmillo seemed calm and happy in his small space. He was the dominant male in the pack, they fed him well, he received the best possible treatment and they closely monitored his health. Avilés and Robert also tried to persuade me not to free him. Why expose him to danger? The chances that he would die in his natural habitat were high. As an incentive to letting them keep him, Robert proposed giving me half of the profits generated from the cubs Colmillo fathered and offered us the cabin for as long as we wanted – months or even years.

They convinced me and I accepted. I told Robert that I wasn't interested in making any money, I just wanted Colmillo to have the best possible quality of life. Chelo was delighted; she was certain I'd made the best decision. We decided to stay for a couple more months. After that we would see. I assured Robert we wouldn't be any kind of bother and that we wouldn't interfere in their day-to-day lives, that we were happy to help them in any way they needed.

That night we had an enormous salmon for dinner. Mary had caught it that morning and they had left it to smoke all day. Avilés raved about how delicious it was, and joked in a whisper that it was nearly as good as the trout from La Marquesa. He said it was a shame they had no good white wine to enjoy with it. Linda said they had four bottles of red wine hidden away for special occasions and that it was certainly worth opening one to celebrate our friendship. Robert uncorked a bottle and poured it into our glasses. "*Salud*," Avilés said. "*Salud*," Robert repeated. Everyone drank, except for the younger kids and me.

Once again, we lingered for a long time over the meal. Wine loosened tongues and stories began to come out. Robert told us about his adventures while researching the pipeline route and a close encounter he'd had with a pair of grizzly bears. Lisa and Mary told us about their excursions into the mountains and the native legends they were taught at school. Eric, Dan and Johnny described the time they were nearly trapped in a forest fire started by a bolt of lightning striking a dry pasture. Avilés talked about his trips to Africa and the year he spent with a Maasi tribe. Chelo spoke about the surgeries she had witnessed, and the frustration of not being able to get hold of the correct medicine to treat children suffering from dysentery in the isolated rural areas where she did her social service. Patricia, emboldened by the wine, talked about her father and how much she and her siblings had missed him the first few months after he left. She told us that they had found his abandoned pickup truck years later in a deserted spot, his body leaning against a pine tree a few metres away. Everyone told a story or an anecdote. I remained silent. I wasn't in the mood to talk about my past, it was still too painful.

We went to bed. A little tipsy, Chelo was more affectionate than usual. She hummed a beautiful tune while we made love. Her orgasm was long and satisfying. She kept kissing me as she came. She put her head on my shoulder and soon fell asleep.

I couldn't sleep, I felt restless. My decision didn't feel right. Colmillo's quality of life would definitely be better at the breeding centre, but the idea of him spending the rest of his life trapped within a wire fence disturbed me. He would only ever meet the wolves from the breeding centre, he couldn't hunt his own food, he wouldn't have the chance to win his place in a wild pack or defeat other predators. I didn't want him to be tamed like the other wolves who ran lovingly over to Patricia. I didn't want him to become the father of cubs who in the best case scenario would be treated like French poodles, or else mistreated like Colmillo had been. I preferred that he be attacked and even killed by other wolves than languish in a dark shed like Nujuaqtutuq, his magnificent father.

I got dressed and left the cabin. It would be hours until sunrise, but the geese were already flying towards the fields in search of food. Their loud honking could be heard from kilometres away. I walked to Colmillo's cage. I shone the torch towards him. Alarmed by the light, the wolves paced nervously from one side of the cage to the other, their yellow eyes glinting in the darkness.

I picked up Colmillo's chain and collar, opened the door of the cage and went inside. Two of the female wolves approached me calmly. They curled about my legs, trying to get me to stroke them, but walked away when I paid them no attention. I called Colmillo. Grudgingly he came over. Once again, he seemed sly, unpredictable. It was ironic

699

that he was the wolf in the cage that I feared. I stroked his head until he settled down. No, I could not leave him there. It would be a crushing defeat; it would mean accepting that fear had prevailed. Colmillo deserved to be free.

I fastened his collar around his neck and attached the chain. I led him out of the cage, put him in the back seat of the Suburban, and we left. I drove along the mud path that ran along the edge of the fence. I stopped where it reached the paved road. I hesitated for a moment, unsure which way to go. I turned right. I was certain that the further north I went the less civilisation I would find, which turned out to be true.

I drove for a hundred kilometres without seeing a single house or car. First, I crossed a sweeping plain, then a small mountain range until I got to a forested valley. As at other points along the road, the asphalt had been washed away by the rain and I had to drive slowly over potholes.

After the sun rose, I spotted an almost hidden path between the pine trees. It was obvious that a large herd of wapiti had passed through there. Their footprints were still clear in the mud. I wondered for a moment whether or not I should keep going. I had travelled a long way, and if the S.U.V. got stuck or broke down there was nobody who could help me. I decided to keep going. Fear would not prevail.

I continued for a few kilometres until the path ended in an impenetrable thicket. I parked and let Colmillo out. I fastened the chain to his collar and we started walking through the forest. Half an hour later, we got to a clearing. The sun shone on the horizon and a towering mountain range rose behind the crystalline waters of a river.

I turned to Colmillo, who was keenly observing his surroundings. I crouched down and stroked him. "Do you like it here?" I asked him. He looked back at me, his face centimetres from mine. I took off his collar. Colmillo stayed still. I stood up and took two steps backwards. He seemed to understand that nothing was holding him back. He looked back at me and then turned towards the immense space that had opened up in front of him. Feeling free, he circled one way and then the other. He sniffed the ground and then trotted to the river. Without pausing, he jumped into the water and crossed to the other side. He came out and shook off the water. He looked back at me one last time and then walked deeper into the forest until I could no longer see him.

I waited to see if he would come back. I sat down on the grass. The snow-capped mountains stood out against the sky. The pine needles trembled in the wind. Dragonflies flew over the river. I could hear the water gently lapping against the rocks.

Two hours later Colmillo still hadn't reappeared, and I was relieved. I don't know what I would have done if he had appeared and walked back towards me, tame and submissive. I was happy he had left that way, without the slightest hesitation. He had gambled on nature and freedom. I had no doubt that he would survive, and die old, wild and powerful. (*Victory comes when you least expect it.*)

I walked to the river, and tossed his collar and chain into a deep pool. I watched as they sank to the river bed. In freeing Colmillo, I realised that I had freed myself. I had fought my ghosts in close combat and I had won. I would always love my dead, but I would not long have to carry them with me.

I went back to the Chevvy, climbed in and started the engine, ready to go back to the ranch and be reunited with Avilés and Chelo, my new family. To be reunited with the future. To be reunited, finally, with life.

THE END

GUILLERMO ARRIAGA is a Mexican author, screenwriter, director and producer. His previous novels have been translated into eighteen languages, and his films include the BAFTA-winning "Amores Perros", the Oscar-nominated "Babel", "21 Grams" and "The Burning Plain". In 2017 he won the Mazatlan Prize for Literature for *The Untameable*, and in 2020 his novel *Salvar el Fuego* won the Alfaguara Prize.

FRANK WYNNE is a translator from French and Spanish. His translations include works by Michel Houellebecq, Arturo Pérez-Reverte and Isabel Allende. He won the *Independent* Foreign Fiction Prize with *Windows on the World* by Frédéric Beigbeder.

JESSIE MENDEZ SAYER is a literary translator, editor and former literary scout.